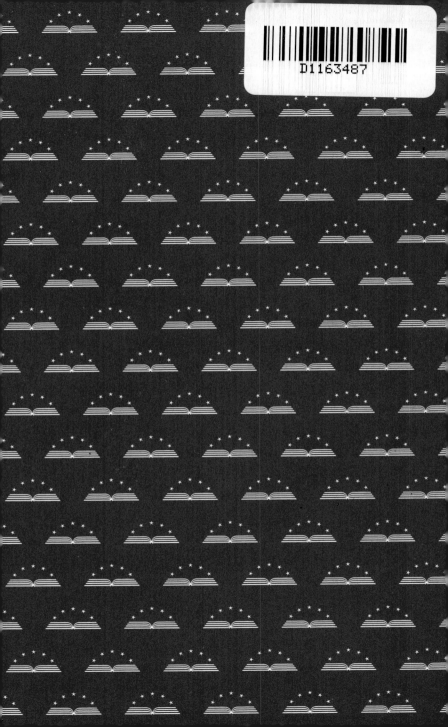

SAUL BELLOW

SAUL BELLOW

NOVELS 1956–1964
Seize the Day
Henderson the Rain King
Herzog

THE LIBRARY OF AMERICA

Manufactured in the United States of America

JAMES WOOD
WROTE THE NOTES FOR THIS VOLUME

Contents

SEIZE THE DAY

Seize the Day

WHEN it came to concealing his troubles, Tommy Wilhelm was not less capable than the next fellow. So at least he thought, and there was a certain amount of evidence to back him up. He had once been an actor—no, not quite, an extra—and he knew what acting should be. Also, he was smoking a cigar, and when a man is smoking a cigar, wearing a hat, he has an advantage; it is harder to find out how he feels. He came from the twenty-third floor down to the lobby on the mezzanine to collect his mail before breakfast, and he believed—he hoped—that he looked passably well: doing all right. It was a matter of sheer hope, because there was not much that he could add to his present effort. On the fourteenth floor he looked for his father to enter the elevator; they often met at this hour, on the way to breakfast. If he worried about his appearance it was mainly for his old father's sake. But there was no stop on the fourteenth, and the elevator sank and sank. Then the smooth door opened and the great dark red uneven carpet that covered the lobby billowed toward Wilhelm's feet. In the foreground the lobby was dark, sleepy. French drapes like sails kept out the sun, but three high, narrow windows were open, and in the blue air Wilhelm saw a pigeon about to light on the great chain that supported the marquee of the movie house directly underneath the lobby. For one moment he heard the wings beating strongly.

Most of the guests at the Hotel Gloriana were past the age of retirement. Along Broadway in the Seventies, Eighties, and Nineties, a great part of New York's vast population of old men and women lives. Unless the weather is too cold or wet they fill the benches about the tiny railed parks and along the subway gratings from Verdi Square to Columbia University, they crowd the shops and cafeterias, the dime stores, the tearooms, the bakeries, the beauty parlors, the reading rooms and club rooms. Among these old people at the Gloriana, Wilhelm felt out of place. He was comparatively young, in his middle forties, large and blond, with big shoulders; his back was heavy and strong, if already a little stooped or thickened. After

3

breakfast the old guests sat down on the green leather armchairs and sofas in the lobby and began to gossip and look into the papers; they had nothing to do but wait out the day. But Wilhelm was used to an active life and liked to go out energetically in the morning. And for several months, because he had no position, he had kept up his morale by rising early; he was shaved and in the lobby by eight o'clock. He bought the paper and some cigars and drank a Coca-Cola or two before he went in to breakfast with his father. After breakfast—out, out, out to attend to business. The getting out had in itself become the chief business. But he had realized that he could not keep this up much longer, and today he was afraid. He was aware that his routine was about to break up and he sensed that a huge trouble long presaged but till now formless was due. Before evening, he'd know.

Nevertheless he followed his daily course and crossed the lobby.

Rubin, the man at the newsstand, had poor eyes. They may not have been actually weak but they were poor in expression, with lacy lids that furled down at the corners. He dressed well. It didn't seem necessary—he was behind the counter most of the time—but he dressed very well. He had on a rich brown suit; the cuffs embarrassed the hairs on his small hands. He wore a Countess Mara painted necktie. As Wilhelm approached, Rubin did not see him; he was looking out dreamily at the Hotel Ansonia, which was visible from his corner, several blocks away. The Ansonia, the neighborhood's great landmark, was built by Stanford White. It looks like a baroque palace from Prague or Munich enlarged a hundred times, with towers, domes, huge swells and bubbles of metal gone green from exposure, iron fretwork and festoons. Black television antennae are densely planted on its round summits. Under the changes of weather it may look like marble or like sea water, black as slate in the fog, white as tufa in sunlight. This morning it looked like the image of itself reflected in deep water, white and cumulous above, with cavernous distortions underneath. Together, the two men gazed at it.

Then Rubin said, "Your dad is in to breakfast already, the old gentleman."

"Oh, yes? Ahead of me today?"

"That's a real knocked-out shirt you got on," said Rubin. "Where's it from, Saks?"

"No, it's a Jack Fagman—Chicago."

Even when his spirits were low, Wilhelm could still wrinkle his forehead in a pleasing way. Some of the slow, silent movements of his face were very attractive. He went back a step, as if to stand away from himself and get a better look at his shirt. His glance was comic, a comment upon his untidiness. He liked to wear good clothes, but once he had put it on each article appeared to go its own way. Wilhelm, laughing, panted a little; his teeth were small; his cheeks when he laughed and puffed grew round, and he looked much younger than his years. In the old days when he was a college freshman and wore a raccoon coat and a beanie on his large blond head his father used to say that, big as he was, he could charm a bird out of a tree. Wilhelm had great charm still.

"I like this dove-gray color," he said in his sociable, good-natured way. "It isn't washable. You have to send it to the cleaner. It never smells as good as washed. But it's a nice shirt. It cost sixteen, eighteen bucks."

This shirt had not been bought by Wilhelm; it was a present from his boss—his former boss, with whom he had had a falling out. But there was no reason why he should tell Rubin the history of it. Although perhaps Rubin knew—Rubin was the kind of man who knew, and knew and knew. Wilhelm also knew many things about Rubin, for that matter, about Rubin's wife and Rubin's business, Rubin's health. None of these could be mentioned, and the great weight of the unspoken left them little to talk about.

"Well, y'lookin' pretty sharp today," Rubin said.

And Wilhelm said gladly, "Am I? Do you really think so?" He could not believe it. He saw his reflection in the glass cupboard full of cigar boxes, among the grand seals and paper damask and the gold-embossed portraits of famous men, García, Edward the Seventh, Cyrus the Great. You had to allow for the darkness and deformations of the glass, but he thought he didn't look too good. A wide wrinkle like a comprehensive bracket sign was written upon his forehead, the point between his brows, and there were patches of brown on his dark blond skin. He began to be half amused at the shadow of his own marveling, troubled, desirous eyes, and his nostrils and his lips. Fair-haired hippopotamus!—that was how he looked to himself. He saw a big round face, a wide, flourishing red mouth, stump teeth. And the hat, too; and the cigar, too. I should have done hard labor all my life, he reflected. Hard honest labor that tires you out and makes you sleep. I'd have worked off my energy and felt better. Instead, I had to distinguish myself—yet.

He had put forth plenty of effort, but that was not the same as working hard, was it? And if as a young man he had got off to a bad start it was due to this very same face. Early in the nineteen-thirties, because of his striking looks, he had been very briefly considered star material, and he had gone to Hollywood. There for seven years, stubbornly, he had tried to become a screen artist. Long before that time his ambition or delusion had ended, but through pride and perhaps also through laziness he had remained in California. At last he turned to other things, but those seven years of persistence and defeat had unfitted him somehow for trades and businesses, and then it was too late to go into one of the professions. He had been slow to mature, and he had lost ground, and so he hadn't been able to get rid of his energy and he was convinced that this energy itself had done him the greatest harm.

"I didn't see you at the gin game last night," said Rubin.

"I had to miss it. How did it go?"

For the last few weeks Wilhelm had played gin almost nightly, but yesterday he had felt that he couldn't afford to lose any more. He had never won. Not once. And while the losses were small they weren't gains, were they? They were losses. He was tired of losing, and tired also of the company, and so he had gone by himself to the movies.

"Oh," said Rubin, "it went okay. Carl made a chump of himself yelling at the guys. This time Doctor Tamkin didn't let him get away with it. He told him the psychological reason why."

"What was the reason?"

Rubin said, "I can't quote him. Who could? You know the way Tamkin talks. Don't ask me. Do you want the *Trib*? Aren't you going to look at the closing quotations?"

"It won't help much to look. I know what they were yester-day at three," said Wilhelm. "But I suppose I better had get the paper." It seemed necessary for him to lift one shoulder in order to put his hand into his jacket pocket. There, among little packets of pills and crushed cigarette butts and strings of cellophane, the red tapes of packages which he sometimes used as dental floss, he recalled that he had dropped some pennies.

"That doesn't sound so good," said Rubin. He meant to be conversationally playful, but his voice had no tone and his eyes, slack and lid-blinded, turned elsewhere. He didn't want to hear. It was all the same to him. Maybe he already knew, being the sort of man who knew and knew.

No, it wasn't good. Wilhelm held three orders of lard in the commodities market. He and Dr. Tamkin had bought this lard together four days ago at 12.96, and the price at once began to fall and was still falling. In the mail this morning there was sure to be a call for additional margin payment. One came every day.

The psychologist, Dr. Tamkin, had got him into this. Tamkin lived at the Gloriana and attended the card game. He had ex-plained to Wilhelm that you could speculate in commodities at one of the uptown branches of a good Wall Street house with-out making the full deposit of margin legally required. It was up to the branch manager. If he knew you—and all the branch managers knew Tamkin—he would allow you to make short-term purchases. You needed only to open a small account.

"The whole secret of this type of speculation," Tamkin had told him, "is in the alertness. You have to act fast—buy it and sell it; sell it and buy in again. But quick! Get to the window and have them wire Chicago at just the right second. Strike and strike again! Then get out the same day. In no time at all you turn over fifteen, twenty thousand dollars' worth of soy beans, coffee, corn, hides, wheat, cotton." Obviously the doctor understood the market well. Otherwise he could not make it sound so simple. "People lose because they are greedy and can't get out when it starts to go up. They gamble, but I do it scientifically. This is not guesswork. You must take a few points and get out. Why, ye gods!" said Dr. Tamkin with his bulging eyes, his bald head, and his drooping lip. "Have you stopped to think how much dough people are making in the market?"

Wilhelm with a quick shift from gloomy attention to the panting laugh which entirely changed his face had said, "Ho, have I ever! What do you think? Who doesn't know it's way beyond nineteen-twenty-eight—twenty-nine and still on the rise? Who hasn't read the Fulbright investigation? There's money everywhere. Everyone is shoveling it in. Money is—is—"

"And can you rest—can you sit still while this is going on?" said Dr. Tamkin. "I confess to you I can't. I think about people, just because they have a few bucks to invest, making fortunes. They have no sense, they have no talent, they just have the extra dough and it makes them more dough. I get so worked up and tormented and restless, so restless! I haven't even been able to practice my profession. With all this money around you don't want to be a fool while everyone else is making. I know guys who make five, ten thousand a week just by fooling around. I know a guy at the Hotel Pierre. There's nothing to him, but he has a whole case of Mumm's champagne at lunch. I know another guy on Central Park South— But what's the use of talking. They make millions. They have smart lawyers who get them out of taxes by a thousand schemes."

"Whereas I got taken," said Wilhelm. "My wife refused to sign a joint return. One fairly good year and I got into the thirty-two-per-cent bracket and was stripped bare. What of all my bad years?"

"It's a businessmen's government," said Dr. Tamkin. "You can be sure that these men making five thousand a week—"

"I don't need that sort of money," Wilhelm had said. "But oh! if I could only work out a little steady income from this. Not much. I don't ask much. But how badly I need—! I'd be so grateful if you'd show me how to work it."

"Sure I will. *I* do it regularly. I'll bring you my receipts if you like. And do you want to know something? I approve of your attitude very much. You want to avoid catching the money fever. This type of activity is filled with hostile feeling and lust. You should see what it does to some of these fellows. They go on the market with murder in their hearts."

"What's that I once heard a guy say?" Wilhelm remarked. "A man is only as good as what he loves."

"That's it—just it," Tamkin said. "You don't have to go

about it their way. There's also a calm and rational, a psychological approach."

Wilhelm's father, old Dr. Adler, lived in an entirely different world from his son, but he had warned him once against Dr. Tamkin. Rather casually—he was a very bland old man—he said, "Wilky, perhaps you listen too much to this Tamkin. He's interesting to talk to. I don't doubt it. I think he's pretty common but he's a persuasive man. However, I don't know how reliable he may be."

It made Wilhelm profoundly bitter that his father should speak to him with such detachment about his welfare. Dr. Adler liked to appear affable. Affable! His own son, his one and only son, could not speak his mind or ease his heart to him. I wouldn't turn to Tamkin, he thought, if I could turn to him. At least Tamkin sympathizes with me and tries to give me a hand, whereas Dad doesn't want to be disturbed.

Old Dr. Adler had retired from practice; he had a considerable fortune and could easily have helped his son. Recently Wilhelm had told him, "Father—it so happens that I'm in a bad way now. I hate to have to say it. You realize that I'd rather have good news to bring you. But it's true. And since it's true, Dad— What else am I supposed to say? It's true."

Another father might have appreciated how difficult this confession was—so much bad luck, weariness, weakness, and failure. Wilhelm had tried to copy the old man's tone and made himself sound gentlemanly, low-voiced, tasteful. He didn't allow his voice to tremble; he made no stupid gesture. But the doctor had no answer. He only nodded. You might have told him that Seattle was near Puget Sound, or that the Giants and Dodgers were playing a night game, so little was he moved from his expression of healthy, handsome, good-humored old age. He behaved toward his son as he had formerly done toward his patients, and it was a great grief to Wilhelm; it was almost too much to bear. Couldn't he see—couldn't he feel? Had he lost his family sense?

Greatly hurt, Wilhelm struggled however to be fair. Old people are bound to change, he said. They have hard things to think about. They must prepare for where they are going. They can't live by the old schedule any longer and all their perspectives change, and other people become alike, kin and acquaintances. Dad is no longer the same person, Wilhelm reflected. He was thirty-two when I was born, and now he's going on eighty. Furthermore, it's time I stopped feeling like a kid toward him, a small son.

The handsome old doctor stood well above the other old people in the hotel. He was idolized by everyone. This was what people said: "That's old Professor Adler, who used to teach internal medicine. He was a diagnostician, one of the best in New York, and had a tremendous practice. Isn't he a wonderful-looking old guy? It's a pleasure to see such a fine old scientist, clean and immaculate. He stands straight and understands every single thing you say. He still has all his buttons. You can discuss any subject with him." The clerks, the elevator operators, the telephone girls and waitresses and chambermaids, the management flattered and pampered him. That was what he wanted. He had always been a vain man. To see how his father loved himself sometimes made Wilhelm madly indignant.

He folded over the *Tribune* with its heavy, black, crashing sensational print and read without recognizing any of the words, for his mind was still on his father's vanity. The doctor had created his own praise. People were primed and did not know it. And what did he need praise for? In a hotel where everyone was busy and contacts were so brief and had such small weight, how could it satisfy him? He could be in people's thoughts here and there for a moment; in and then out. He could never matter much to them. Wilhelm let out a long, hard breath and raised the brows of his round and somewhat circular eyes. He stared beyond the thick borders of the paper.

. . . love that well which thou must leave ere long.

Involuntary memory brought him this line. At first he thought it referred to his father, but then he understood that it was for himself, rather. *He* should love that well. "This thou perceivest, which makes *thy* love more strong." Under Dr. Tamkin's influence Wilhelm had recently begun to remember the poems he used to read. Dr. Tamkin knew, or said he knew, the great English poets and once in a while he mentioned a poem of his own. It was a long time since anyone had spoken to Wilhelm about this sort of thing. He didn't like to think about his college days, but if there was one course that now made sense it was Literature I. The textbook was Lieder and Lovett's *British Poetry and Prose*, a black heavy book with thin pages. Did I read that? he asked himself. Yes, he had read it and there was one accomplishment at least he could recall with pleasure. He had read "Yet once more, O ye laurels." How pure this was to say! It was beautiful.

Sunk though he be beneath the wat'ry floor . . .

Such things had always swayed him, and now the power of such words was far, far greater.

Wilhelm respected the truth, but he could lie and one of the things he lied often about was his education. He said he was an alumnus of Penn State; in fact he had left school before his sophomore year was finished. His sister Catherine had a B. S. degree. Wilhelm's late mother was a graduate of Bryn Mawr. He was the only member of the family who had no education. This was another sore point. His father was ashamed of him.

But he had heard the old man bragging to another old man, saying, "My son is a sales executive. He didn't have the patience to finish school. But he does all right for himself. His income is up in the five figures somewhere."

"What—thirty, forty thousand?" said his stooped old friend.

"Well, he needs at least that much for his style of life. Yes, he needs that."

Despite his troubles, Wilhelm almost laughed. Why, that boasting old hypocrite. He knew the sales executive was no more. For many weeks there had been no executive, no sales, no income. But how we love looking fine in the eyes of the world—how beautiful are the old when they are doing a snow job! It's Dad, thought Wilhelm, who is the salesman. He's selling me. *He* should have gone on the road.

But what of the truth? Ah, the truth was that there were problems, and of these problems his father wanted no part. His father was ashamed of him. The truth, Wilhelm thought, was very awkward. He pressed his lips together, and his tongue went soft; it pained him far at the back, in the cords and throat, and a knot of ill formed in his chest. Dad never was a pal to me when I was young, he reflected. He was at the office or the hospital, or lecturing. He expected me to look out for myself and never gave me much thought. Now he looks down on me. And maybe in some respects he's right.

No wonder Wilhelm delayed the moment when he would have to go into the dining room. He had moved to the end of Rubin's counter. He had opened the *Tribune*; the fresh pages drooped from his hands; the cigar was smoked out and the hat did not defend him. He was wrong to suppose that he was more capable than the next fellow when it came to concealing his troubles. They were clearly written out upon his face. He wasn't even aware of it.

There was the matter of the different names, which, in the hotel, came up frequently. "Are you Doctor Adler's son?" "Yes, but my name is Tommy Wilhelm." And the doctor would say, "My son and I use different monickers. I uphold tradition. He's for the new." The Tommy was Wilhelm's own invention. He adopted it when he went to Hollywood, and dropped the Adler. Hollywood was his own idea, too. He used to pretend that it had all been the doing of a certain talent scout named Maurice Venice. But the scout had never made him a definite offer of a studio connection. He had approached him, but the results of the screen tests had not been good. After the test Wilhelm took the initiative and pressed Maurice Venice until he got him to say, "Well, I suppose you might make it out there." On the strength of this Wilhelm had left college and had gone to California.

Someone had said, and Wilhelm agreed with the saying, that in Los Angeles all the loose objects in the country were collected, as if America had been tilted and everything that wasn't tightly screwed down had slid into Southern California. He himself had been one of these loose objects. Sometimes he told people, "I was too mature for college. I was a big boy, you see. Well, I thought, when do you start to become a man?" After he had driven a painted flivver and had worn a yellow slicker with slogans on it, and played illegal poker, and gone out on Coke dates, he had *had* college. He wanted to try something new and quarreled with his parents about his career. And then a letter came from Maurice Venice.

The story of the scout was long and intricate and there were several versions of it. The truth about it was never told. Wilhelm had lied first boastfully and then out of charity to himself. But his memory was good, he could still separate what he had invented from the actual happenings, and this morning he found it necessary as he stood by Rubin's showcase with his *Tribune* to recall the crazy course of the true events.

I didn't seem even to realize that there was a depression. How could I have been such a jerk as not to prepare for anything and just go on luck and inspiration? With round gray eyes expanded and his large shapely lips closed in severity toward himself he forced open all that had been hidden. Dad I couldn't affect one way or another. Mama was the one who tried to stop me, and we carried on and yelled and pleaded. The more I lied the louder I raised my voice, and charged—like a hippopotamus. Poor Mother! How I disappointed her. Rubin heard Wilhelm give a broken sigh as he stood with the forgotten *Tribune* crushed under his arm.

When Wilhelm was aware that Rubin watched him, loitering and idle, apparently not knowing what to do with himself this morning, he turned to the Coca-Cola machine. He swallowed hard at the Coke bottle and coughed over it, but he ignored his coughing, for he was still thinking, his eyes upcast and his lips closed behind his hand. By a peculiar twist of habit he wore his coat collar turned up always, as though there were a wind. It never lay flat. But on his broad back, stooped with its own weight, its strength warped almost into deformity, the collar of his sports coat appeared anyway to be no wider than a ribbon.

He was listening to the sound of his own voice as he explained, twenty-five years ago in the living room on West End Avenue, "But Mother, if I don't pan out as an actor I can still go back to school."

But she was afraid he was going to destroy himself. She said, "Wilky, Dad could make it easy for you if you wanted to go into medicine." To remember this stifled him.

"I can't bear hospitals. Besides, I might make a mistake and hurt someone or even kill a patient. I couldn't stand that. Besides, I haven't got that sort of brains."

Then his mother had made the mistake of mentioning her nephew Artie, Wilhelm's cousin, who was an honor student at Columbia in math and languages. That dark little gloomy

Artie with his disgusting narrow face, and his moles and self-sniffing ways and his unclean table manners, the boring habit he had of conjugating verbs when you went for a walk with him. "Roumanian is an easy language. You just add a *tl* to everything." He was now a professor, this same Artie with whom Wilhelm had played near the soldiers' and sailors' monument on Riverside Drive. Not that to be a professor was in itself so great. How could anyone bear to know so many languages? And Artie also had to remain Artie, which was a bad deal. But perhaps success had changed him. Now that he had a place in the world perhaps he was better. Did Artie love his languages, and live for them, or was he also, in his heart, cynical? So many people nowadays were. No one seemed satisfied, and Wilhelm was especially horrified by the cynicism of successful people. Cynicism was bread and meat to everyone. And irony, too. Maybe it couldn't be helped. It was probably even necessary. Wilhelm, however, feared it intensely. Whenever at the end of the day he was unusually fatigued he attributed it to cynicism. Too much of the world's business done. Too much falsity. He had various words to express the effect this had on him. Chicken! Unclean! Congestion! he exclaimed in his heart. Rat race! Phony! Murder! Play the Game! Buggers!

At first the letter from the talent scout was nothing but a flattering sort of joke. Wilhelm's picture in the college paper when he was running for class treasurer was seen by Maurice Venice, who wrote to him about a screen test. Wilhelm at once took the train to New York. He found the scout to be huge and oxlike, so stout that his arms seemed caught from beneath in a grip of flesh and fat; it looked as though it must be positively painful. He had little hair. Yet he enjoyed a healthy complexion. His breath was noisy and his voice rather difficult and husky because of the fat in his throat. He had on a double-breasted suit of the type then known as the pillbox; it was chalk-striped, pink on blue; the trousers hugged his ankles.

They met and shook hands and sat down. Together these two big men dwarfed the tiny Broadway office and made the furnishings look like toys. Wilhelm had the color of a Golden Grimes apple when he was well, and then his thick blond hair had been vigorous and his wide shoulders unwarped; he was leaner in the jaws, his eyes fresher and wider; his legs were then still awkward but he was impressively handsome. And he was about to make his first great mistake. Like, he sometimes thought, I was going to pick up a weapon and strike myself a blow with it.

Looming over the desk in the small office darkened by over-built midtown—sheer walls, gray spaces, dry lagoons of tar and pebbles—Maurice Venice proceeded to establish his credentials. He said, "My letter was on the regular stationery, but maybe you want to check on me?"

"Who, *me*?" said Wilhelm. "Why?"

"There's guys who think I'm in a racket and make a charge for the test. I don't ask a cent. I'm no agent. There ain't no commission."

"I never even thought of it," said Wilhelm. Was there perhaps something fishy about this Maurice Venice? He protested too much.

In his husky, fat-weakened voice he finally challenged Wilhelm, "If you're not sure, you can call the distributor and find out who I am, Maurice Venice."

Wilhelm wondered at him. "Why shouldn't I be sure? Of course I am."

"Because I can see the way you size me up, and because this is a dinky office. Like you don't believe me. Go ahead. Call. I won't care if you're cautious. I mean it. There's quite a few people who doubt me at first. They can't really believe that fame and fortune are going to hit 'em."

"But I tell you I do believe you," Wilhelm had said, and bent inward to accommodate the pressure of his warm, panting laugh. It was purely nervous. His neck was ruddy and neatly shaved about the ears—he was fresh from the barbershop; his face anxiously glowed with his desire to make a pleasing impression. It was all wasted on Venice, who was just as concerned about the impression *he* was making.

"If you're surprised, I'll just show you what I mean," Venice had said. "It was about fifteen months ago right in this identical same office when I saw a beautiful thing in the paper. It wasn't even a photo but a drawing, a brassière ad, but I knew right away that this was star material. I called up the paper to ask who the girl was, they gave me the name of the advertising agency; I phoned the agency and they gave me the name of the artist; I got hold of the artist and he gave me the number of the model agency. Finally, finally I got her number and phoned her and said, 'This is Maurice Venice, scout for Kaskaskia Films.' So right away she says, 'Yah, so's your old lady.' Well, when I saw I wasn't getting nowhere with her I said to her, 'Well, miss. I don't blame you. You're a very beautiful thing and must have a dozen admirers after you all the time, boy friends who like to call and pull your leg and give a tease. But as I happen to be a very busy fellow and don't have the time to horse around or argue, I tell you what to do. Here's my number, and here's the number of the Kaskaskia Distributors, Inc. Ask them who am I, Maurice Venice. The scout.' She did it. A little while later she phoned me back, all apologies and excuses, but I didn't want to embarrass her and get off on the wrong foot with an artist. I know better than to do that. So I told her it was a natural precaution, never mind. I wanted to run a screen test right away. Because I seldom am wrong about talent. If I see it, it's there. Get that, please. And do you know who that little girl is today?"

"No," Wilhelm said eagerly. "Who is she?"

Venice said impressively, " 'Nita Christenberry."

Wilhelm sat utterly blank. This was failure. He didn't know the name, and Venice was waiting for his response and would be angry.

And in fact Venice had been offended. He said, "What's the matter with you! Don't you read a magazine? She's a starlet."

"I'm sorry," Wilhelm answered. "I'm at school and don't have time to keep up. If I don't know her, it doesn't mean a thing. She made a big hit, I'll bet."

"You can say that again. Here's a photo of her." He handed Wilhelm some pictures. She was a bathing beauty—short, the usual breasts, hips, and smooth thighs. Yes, quite good, as Wilhelm recalled. She stood on high heels and wore a Spanish comb and mantilla. In her hand was a fan.

He had said, "She looks awfully peppy."

"Isn't she a divine girl? And what personality! Not just another broad in the show business, believe me." He had a surprise for Wilhelm. "I have found happiness with her," he said.

"You have?" said Wilhelm, slow to understand.

"Yes, boy, we're engaged."

Wilhelm saw another photograph, taken on the beach. Venice was dressed in a terry-cloth beach outfit, and he and the girl, cheek to cheek, were looking into the camera. Below, in white ink, was written "Love at Malibu Colony."

"I'm sure you'll be very happy. I wish you—"

"I *know*," said Venice firmly, "I'm going to be happy. When I saw that drawing, the breath of fate breathed on me. I felt it over my entire body.'

"Say, it strikes a bell suddenly," Wilhelm had said. "Aren't you related to Martial Venice the producer?"

Venice was either a nephew of the producer or the son of a first cousin. Decidedly he had not made good. It was easy enough for Wilhelm to see this now. The office was so poor, and Venice bragged so nervously and identified himself so scrupulously—the poor guy. He was the obscure failure of an aggressive and powerful clan. As such he had the greatest sympathy from Wilhelm.

Venice had said, "Now I suppose you want to know where you come in. I seen your school paper, by accident. You take quite a remarkable picture."

"It can't be so much," said Wilhelm, more panting than laughing.

"You don't want to tell me my business," Venice said. "Leave it to me. I studied up on this."

"I never imagined— Well, what kind of roles do you think I'd fit?"

"All this time that we've been talking, I've been watching. Don't think I haven't. You remind me of someone. Let's see who it can be—one of the great old-timers. Is it Milton Sills? No, that's not the one. Conway Tearle, Jack Mulhall? George Bancroft? No, his face was ruggeder. One thing I can tell you, though, a George Raft type you're not—those tough, smooth, black little characters."

"No, I wouldn't seem to be."

"No, you're not that flyweight type, with the fists, from a nightclub, and the glamorous sideburns, doing the tango or the bolero. Not Edward G. Robinson, either—I'm thinking aloud. Or the Cagney fly-in-your-face role, a cabbie, with that mouth and those punches."

"I realize that."

"Not suave like William Powell, or a lyric juvenile like Buddy Rogers. I suppose you don't play the sax? No. But—"

"But what?"

"I have you placed as the type that loses the girl to the George Raft type or the William Powell type. You are steady, faithful, you get stood up. The older women would know better. The mothers are on your side. With what they been through, if it was up to them, they'd take you in a minute. You're very sympathetic, even the young girls feel that. You'd make a good provider. But they go more for the other types. It's as clear as anything."

This was not how Wilhelm saw himself. And as he surveyed the old ground he recognized now that he had been not only confused but hurt. Why, he thought, he cast me even then for a loser.

Wilhelm had said, with half a mind to be defiant, "Is that your opinion?"

It never occurred to Venice that a man might object to stardom in such a role. "Here is your chance," he said. "Now you're just in college. What are you studying?" He snapped his fingers. "Stuff." Wilhelm himself felt this way about it. "You may plug along fifty years before you get anywheres. This way, in one jump, the world knows who you are. You become a name like Roosevelt, Swanson. From east to west, out to China, into South America. This is no bunk. You become a lover to the whole world. The world wants it, needs it. One fellow smiles, a billion people also smile. One fellow cries, the other billion sob with him. Listen, bud—" Venice had pulled himself together to make an effort. On his imagination there was some great weight which he could not discharge. He wanted Wilhelm, too, to feel it. He twisted his large, clean, well-meaning, rather foolish features as though he were their unwilling captive, and said in his choked, fat-obstructed voice, "Listen, everywhere there are people trying hard, miserable, in trouble, downcast, tired, trying and trying. They need a break, right? A break through, a help, luck or sympathy."

"That certainly is the truth," said Wilhelm. He had seized the feeling and he waited for Venice to go on. But Venice had no more to say; he had concluded. He gave Wilhelm several pages of blue hectographed script, stapled together, and told him to prepare for the screen test. "Study your lines in front of a mirror," he said. "Let yourself go. The part should take ahold of you. Don't be afraid to make faces and be emotional. Shoot the works. Because when you start to act you're no more an ordinary person, and those things don't apply to you. You don't behave the same way as the average."

And so Wilhelm had never returned to Penn State. His roommate sent his things to New York for him, and the school authorities had to write to Dr. Adler to find out what had happened.

Still, for three months Wilhelm delayed his trip to California. He wanted to start out with the blessings of his family, but they were never given. He quarreled with his parents and his sister. And then, when he was best aware of the risks and knew a hundred reasons against going and had made himself sick with fear, he left home. This was typical of Wilhelm. After much thought and hesitation and debate he invariably took the course he had rejected innumerable times. Ten such decisions made up the history of his life. He had decided that it would be a bad mistake to go to Hollywood, and then he went. He had made up his mind not to marry his wife, but ran off and got married. He had resolved not to invest money with Tamkin, and then had given him a check.

But Wilhelm had been eager for life to start. College was merely another delay. Venice had approached him and said that the world had named Wilhelm to shine before it. He was to be freed from the anxious and narrow life of the average. Moreover, Venice had claimed that he never made a mistake. His instinct for talent was infallible, he said.

But when Venice saw the results of the screen test he did a quick about-face. In those days Wilhelm had had a speech difficulty. It was not a true stammer, it was a thickness of speech which the sound track exaggerated. The film showed that he had many peculiarities, otherwise unnoticeable. When he shrugged, his hands drew up within his sleeves. The vault of his chest was huge, but he really didn't look strong under the lights. Though he called himself a hippopotamus, he more nearly resembled a bear. His walk was bearlike, quick and rather soft, toes turned inward, as though his shoes were an impediment. About one thing Venice had been right. Wilhelm was photogenic, and his wavy blond hair (now graying) came out well, but after the test Venice refused to encourage him. He tried to get rid of him. He couldn't afford to take a chance on him, he had made too many mistakes already and lived in fear of his powerful relatives.

Wilhelm had told his parents, "Venice says I owe it to myself to go." How ashamed he was now of this lie! He had begged Venice not to give him up. He had said, "Can't you help me out? It would kill me to go back to school now."

Then when he reached the Coast he learned that a recommendation from Maurice Venice was the kiss of death. Venice needed help and charity more than he, Wilhelm, ever had. A few years later when Wilhelm was down on his luck and working as an orderly in a Los Angeles hospital, he saw Venice's picture in the papers. He was under indictment for pandering. Closely following the trial, Wilhelm found out that Venice had indeed been employed by Kaskaskia Films but that he had evidently made use of the connection to organize a ring of call girls. Then what did he want with me? Wilhelm had cried to himself. He was unwilling to believe anything very bad about Venice. Perhaps he was foolish and unlucky, a fall guy, a dupe, a sucker. You didn't give a man fifteen years in prison for that. Wilhelm often thought that he might write him a letter to say how sorry he was. He remembered the breath of fate and Venice's certainty that he would be happy. 'Nita Christenberry was sentenced to three years. Wilhelm recognized her although she had changed her name.

By that time Wilhelm too had taken his new name. In California he became Tommy Wilhelm. Dr. Adler would not accept the change. Today he still called his son Wilky, as he had done for more than forty years. Well, now, Wilhelm was thinking, the paper crowded in disarray under his arm, there's really very little that a man can change at will. He can't change his lungs, or nerves, or constitution or temperament. They're not under his control. When he's young and strong and impulsive and dissatisfied with the way things are he wants to rearrange them to assert his freedom. He can't overthrow the government or be differently born; he only has a little scope and maybe a foreboding, too, that essentially you can't change. Nevertheless, he makes a gesture and becomes Tommy Wilhelm. Wilhelm had always had a great longing to be Tommy. He had never, however, succeeded in feeling like Tommy, and in his soul had always remained Wilky. When he was drunk he reproached himself horribly as Wilky. "You fool, you clunk, you Wilky!" he called himself. He thought that it was a good thing perhaps that he had not become a success as Tommy since that would not have been a genuine success. Wilhelm would have feared that not he but Tommy had brought it off, cheating Wilky of his birthright. Yes, it had been a stupid thing to do, but it was his imperfect judgment at the age of twenty which should be blamed. He had cast off his father's name, and with it his father's opinion of him. It was, he knew it was, his bid for liberty, Adler being in his mind the title of the species, Tommy the freedom of the person. But Wilky was his inescapable self.

In middle age you no longer thought such thoughts about free choice. Then it came over you that from one grandfather you had inherited such and such a head of hair which looked like honey when it whitens or sugars in the jar; from another, broad thick shoulders; an oddity of speech from one uncle, and small teeth from another, and the gray eyes with darkness diffused even into the whites, and a wide-lipped mouth like a statue from Peru. Wandering races have such looks, the bones of one tribe, the skin of another. From his mother he had gotten sensitive feelings, a soft heart, a brooding nature, a tendency to be confused under pressure.

The changed name was a mistake, and he would admit it as freely as you liked. But this mistake couldn't be undone now, so why must his father continually remind him how he had sinned? It was too late. He would have to go back to the pathetic day when the sin was committed. And where was that day? Past and dead. Whose humiliating memories were these? His and not his father's. What had he to think back on that he could call good? Very, very little. You had to forgive. First, to forgive yourself, and then general forgiveness. Didn't he suffer from his mistakes far more than his father could?

"Oh, God," Wilhelm prayed. "Let me out of my trouble. Let me out of my thoughts, and let me do something better with myself. For all the time I have wasted I am very sorry. Let me out of this clutch and into a different life. For I am all balled up. Have mercy."

II

The mail.

The clerk who gave it to him did not care what sort of appearance he made this morning. He only glanced at him from under his brows, upward, as the letters changed hands. Why should the hotel people waste courtesies on him? They had his number. The clerk knew that he was handing him, along with the letters, a bill for his rent. Wilhelm assumed a look that removed him from all such things. But it was bad. To pay the bill he would have to withdraw money from his brokerage account, and the account was being watched because of the drop in lard. According to the *Tribune*'s figures lard was still twenty points below last year's level. There were government price supports. Wilhelm didn't know how these worked but he understood that the farmer was protected and that the SEC kept an eye on the market and therefore he believed that lard would rise again and he wasn't greatly worried as yet. But in the meantime his father might have offered to pick up his hotel tab. Why didn't he? What a selfish old man he was! He saw his son's hardships; he could so easily help him. How little it would mean to him, and how much to Wilhelm! Where was the old man's heart? Maybe, thought Wilhelm, I was sentimental in the past and exaggerated his kindliness—warm family life. It may never have been there.

Not long ago his father had said to him in his usual affable, pleasant way, "Well, Wilky, here we are under the same roof again, after all these years."

Wilhelm was glad for an instant. At last they would talk over old times. But he was also on guard against insinuations. Wasn't his father saying, "Why are you here in a hotel with me and not at home in Brooklyn with your wife and two boys? You're neither a widower nor a bachelor. You have brought me all your confusions. What do you expect me to do with them?"

So Wilhelm studied the remark for a bit, then said, "The roof is twenty-six stories up. But how many years has it been?"

"That's what I was asking you."

"Gosh, Dad, I'm not sure. Wasn't it the year Mother died? What year was that?"

He asked this question with an innocent frown on his

Golden Grimes, dark blond face. *What year was it!* As though he didn't know the year, the month, the day, the very hour of his mother's death.

"Wasn't it nineteen-thirty-one?" said Dr. Adler.

"Oh, was it?" said Wilhelm. And in hiding the sadness and the overwhelming irony of the question he gave a nervous shiver and wagged his head and felt the ends of his collar rapidly.

"Do you know?" his father said. "You must realize, an old fellow's memory becomes unreliable. It was in winter, that I'm sure of. Nineteen-thirty-two?"

Yes, it was age. Don't make an issue of it, Wilhelm advised himself. If you were to ask the old doctor in what year he had interned, he'd tell you correctly. All the same, don't make an issue. Don't quarrel with your own father. Have pity on an old man's failings.

"I believe the year was closer to nineteen-thirty-four, Dad," he said.

But Dr. Adler was thinking, Why the devil can't he stand still when we're talking? He's either hoisting his pants up and down by the pockets or jittering with his feet. A regular mountain of tics, he's getting to be. Wilhelm had a habit of moving his feet back and forth as though, hurrying into a house, he had to clean his shoes first on the doormat.

Then Wilhelm had said, "Yes, that was the beginning of the end, wasn't it, Father?"

Wilhelm often astonished Dr. Adler. Beginning of the end? What could he mean—what was he fishing for? Whose end? The end of family life? The old man was puzzled but he would not give Wilhelm an opening to introduce his complaints. He had learned that it was better not to take up Wilhelm's strange challenges. So he merely agreed pleasantly, for he was a master of social behavior, and said, "It was an awful misfortune for us all."

He thought, What business has he to complain to *me* of his mother's death?

Face to face they had stood, each declaring himself silently after his own way. It was: it was not, the beginning of the end—*some* end.

Unaware of anything odd in his doing it, for he did it all the time, Wilhelm had pinched out the coal of his cigarette and dropped the butt in his pocket, where there were many more. And as he gazed at his father the little finger of his right hand began to twitch and tremble; of that he was unconscious, too.

And yet Wilhelm believed that when he put his mind to it he could have perfect and even distinguished manners, outdoing his father. Despite the slight thickness in his speech—it amounted almost to a stammer when he started the same phrase over several times in his effort to eliminate the thick sound—he could be fluent. Otherwise he would never have made a good salesman. He claimed also that he was a good listener. When he listened he made a tight mouth and rolled his eyes thoughtfully. He would soon tire and begin to utter short, loud, impatient breaths, and he would say, "Oh yes . . . yes . . . yes. I couldn't agree more." When he was forced to differ he would declare, "Well, I'm not sure. I don't really see it that way. I'm of two minds about it." He would never willingly hurt any man's feelings.

But in conversation with his father he was apt to lose control of himself. After any talk with Dr. Adler, Wilhelm generally felt dissatisfied, and his dissatisfaction reached its greatest intensity when they discussed family matters. Ostensibly he had been trying to help the old man to remember a date, but in reality he meant to tell him, "You were set free when Ma died. You wanted to forget her. You'd like to get rid of Catherine, too. Me, too. You're not kidding anyone"—Wilhelm striving to put this across, and the old man not having it. In the end he was left struggling, while his father seemed unmoved.

And then once more Wilhelm had said to himself, "But man! you're not a kid. Even then you weren't a kid!" He looked down over the front of his big, indecently big, spoiled body. He was beginning to lose his shape, his gut was fat, and he looked like a hippopotamus. His younger son called him "a hummuspotamus"; that was little Paul. And here he was still struggling with his old dad, filled with ancient grievances. Instead of saying, "Good-by, youth! Oh, good-by those marvelous, foolish wasted days. What a big clunk I was—I *am*."

Wilhelm was still paying heavily for his mistakes. His wife Margaret would not give him a divorce, and he had to support her and the two children. She would regularly agree to divorce him, and then think things over again and set new and more difficult conditions. No court would have awarded her the amounts he paid. One of today's letters, as he had expected, was from her. For the first time he had sent her a postdated check, and she protested. She also enclosed bills for the boys' educational insurance policies, due next week. Wilhelm's mother-in-law had taken out these policies in Beverly Hills, and since her death two years ago he had to pay the premiums. Why couldn't she have minded her own business! They were his kids, and he took care of them and always would. He had planned to set up a trust fund. But that was on his former expectations. Now he had to rethink the future, because of the money problem. Meanwhile, here were the bills to be paid. When he saw the two sums punched out so neatly on the cards he cursed the company and its IBM equipment. His heart and his head were congested with anger. Everyone was supposed to have money. It was nothing to the company. It published pictures of funerals in the magazines and frightened the suckers, and then punched out little holes, and the customers would lie awake to think out ways to raise the dough. They'd be ashamed not to have it. They couldn't let a great company down, either, and they got the scratch. In the old days a man was put in prison for debt, but there were subtler things now. They made it a shame not to have money and set everybody to work.

Well, and what else had Margaret sent him? He tore the envelope open with his thumb, swearing that he would send any other bills back to her. There was, luckily, nothing more. He put the hole-punched cards in his pocket. Didn't Margaret know that he was nearly at the end of his rope? Of course. Her instinct told her that this was her opportunity, and she was giving him the works.

He went into the dining room, which was under Austro-Hungarian management at the Hotel Gloriana. It was run like a European establishment. The pastries were excellent, especially the strudel. He often had apple strudel and coffee in the afternoon.

As soon as he entered he saw his father's small head in the sunny bay at the farther end, and heard his precise voice. It was with an odd sort of perilous expression that Wilhelm crossed the dining room.

Dr. Adler liked to sit in a corner that looked across Broadway down to the Hudson and New Jersey. On the other side of the street was a supermodern cafeteria with gold and purple mosaic columns. On the second floor a private-eye school, a dental laboratory, a reducing parlor, a veteran's club, and a Hebrew school shared the space. The old man was sprinkling sugar on his strawberries. Small hoops of brilliance were cast by the water glasses on the white tablecloth, despite a faint murkiness in the sunshine. It was early summer, and the long window was turned inward; a moth was on the pane; the putty was broken and the white enamel on the frames was streaming with wrinkles.

"Ha, Wilky," said the old man to his tardy son. "You haven't met our neighbor Mr. Perls, have you? From the fifteenth floor."

"How d'do," Wilhelm said. He did not welcome this stranger; he began at once to find fault with him. Mr. Perls carried a heavy cane with a crutch tip. Dyed hair, a skinny forehead—these were not reasons for bias. Nor was it Mr. Perls's fault that Dr. Adler was using him, not wishing to have breakfast with his son alone. But a gruffer voice within Wilhelm spoke, asking, "Who is this damn frazzle-faced herring with his dyed hair and his fish teeth and this drippy mustache? Another one of Dad's German friends. Where does he collect all these guys? What is the stuff on his teeth? I never saw such pointed crowns. Are they stainless steel, or a kind of silver? How can a human face get into this condition. Uch!" Staring with his widely spaced gray eyes, Wilhelm sat, his broad back stooped under the sports jacket. He clasped his hands on the table with an implication of suppliance. Then he began to relent a little toward Mr. Perls, beginning at the teeth. Each of those crowns represented a tooth ground to the quick, and estimating a man's grief with his teeth as two per cent of the total, and adding to that his flight from Germany and the probable origin of his wincing wrinkles, not to be confused with the wrinkles of his smile, it came to a sizable load.

"Mr. Perls was a hosiery wholesaler," said Dr. Adler.

"Is this the son you told me was in the selling line?" said Mr. Perls.

Dr. Adler replied, "I have only this one son. One daughter. She was a medical technician before she got married—

anesthetist. At one time she had an important position in Mount Sinai."

He couldn't mention his children without boasting. In Wilhelm's opinion, there was little to boast of. Catherine, like Wilhelm, was big and fair-haired. She had married a court reporter who had a pretty hard time of it. She had taken a professional name, too—Philippa. At forty she was still ambitious to become a painter. Wilhelm didn't venture to criticize her work. It didn't do much to him, he said, but then he was no critic. Anyway, he and his sister were generally on the outs and he didn't often see her paintings. She worked very hard, but there were fifty thousand people in New York with paints and brushes, each practically a law unto himself. It was the Tower of Babel in paint. *He* didn't want to go far into this. Things were chaotic all over.

Dr. Adler thought that Wilhelm looked particularly untidy this morning—unrested, too, his eyes red-rimmed from excessive smoking. He was breathing through his mouth and he was evidently much distracted and rolled his red-shot eyes barbarously. As usual, his coat collar was turned up as though he had had to go out in the rain. When he went to business he pulled himself together a little; otherwise he let himself go and looked like hell.

"What's the matter, Wilky, didn't you sleep last night?"

"Not very much."

"You take too many pills of every kind—first stimulants and then depressants, anodynes followed by analeptics, until the poor organism doesn't know what's happened. Then the Luminal won't put people to sleep, and the Pervitin or Benzedrine won't wake them. God knows! These things get to be as serious as poisons, and yet everyone puts all their faith in them."

"No, Dad, it's not the pills. It's that I'm not used to New York any more. For a native, that's very peculiar, isn't it? It was never so noisy at night as now, and every little thing is a strain. Like the alternate parking. You have to run out at eight to move your car. And where can you put it? If you forget for a minute they tow you away. Then some fool puts advertising leaflets under your windshield wiper and you have heart failure a block away because you think you've got a ticket. When you do get stung with a ticket, you can't argue. You haven't got a chance in court and the city wants the revenue."

"But in your line you have to have a car, eh?" said Mr. Perls.

"Lord knows why any lunatic would want one in the city who didn't need it for his livelihood."

Wilhelm's old Pontiac was parked in the street. Formerly, when on an expense account, he had always put it up in a garage. Now he was afraid to move the car from Riverside Drive lest he lose his space, and he used it only on Saturdays when the Dodgers were playing in Ebbets Field and he took his boys to the game. Last Saturday, when the Dodgers were out of town, he had gone out to visit his mother's grave.

Dr. Adler had refused to go along. He couldn't bear his son's driving. Forgetfully, Wilhelm traveled for miles in second gear; he was seldom in the right lane and he neither gave signals nor watched for lights. The upholstery of his Pontiac was filthy with grease and ashes. One cigarette burned in the ashtray, another in his hand, a third on the floor with maps and other waste paper and Coca-Cola bottles. He dreamed at the wheel or argued and gestured, and therefore the old doctor would not ride with him.

Then Wilhelm had come back from the cemetery angry because the stone bench between his mother's and his grandmother's graves had been overturned and broken by vandals. "Those damn teen-age hoodlums get worse and worse," he said. "Why, they must have used a sledge-hammer to break the seat smack in half like that. If I could catch one of them!" He wanted the doctor to pay for a new seat, but his father was cool to the idea. He said he was going to have himself cremated.

Mr. Perls said, "I don't blame you if you get no sleep up where you are." His voice was tuned somewhat sharp, as though he were slightly deaf. "Don't you have Parigi the singing teacher there? God, they have some queer elements in this hotel. On which floor is that Estonian woman with all her cats and dogs? They should have made her leave long ago."

"They've moved her down to twelve," said Dr. Adler.

Wilhelm ordered a large Coca-Cola with his breakfast. Working in secret at the small envelopes in his pocket, he found two pills by touch. Much fingering had worn and weakened the paper. Under cover of a napkin he swallowed a Phenaphen sedative and a Unicap, but the doctor was sharp-eyed and said, "Wilky, what are you taking now?"

"Just my vitamin pills." He put his cigar butt in an ashtray on the table behind him, for his father did not like the odor. Then he drank his Coca-Cola.

"That's what you drink for breakfast, and not orange juice?" said Mr. Perls. He seemed to sense that he would not lose Dr. Adler's favor by taking an ironic tone with his son.

"The caffeine stimulates brain activity," said the old doctor. "It does all kinds of things to the respiratory center."

"It's just a habit of the road, that's all," Wilhelm said. "If you drive around long enough it turns your brains, your stomach, and everything else."

His father explained, "Wilky used to be with the Rojax Corporation. He was their northeastern sales representative for a good many years but recently ended the connection."

"Yes," said Wilhelm, "I was with them from the end of the war." He sipped the Coca-Cola and chewed the ice, glancing at one and the other with his attitude of large, shaky, patient dignity. The waitress set two boiled eggs before him.

"What kind of line does this Rojax company manufacture?" said Mr. Perls.

"Kiddies' furniture. Little chairs, rockers, tables, Jungle-Gyms, slides, swings, seesaws."

Wilhelm let his father do the explaining. Large and stiff-backed, he tried to sit patiently, but his feet were abnormally restless. All right! His father had to impress Mr. Perls? He would go along once more, and play his part. Fine! He would play along and help his father maintain his style. Style was the main consideration. That was just fine!

"I was with the Rojax Corporation for almost ten years," he said. "We parted ways because they wanted me to share my territory. They took a son-in-law into the business—a new fellow. It was his idea."

To himself, Wilhelm said, Now God alone can tell why I have to lay my whole life bare to this blasted herring here. I'm sure nobody else does it. Other people keep their business to themselves. Not me.

He continued, "But the rationalization was that it was too big a territory for one man. I had a monopoly. That wasn't so.

The real reason was that they had gotten to the place where they would have to make me an officer of the corporation. Vice presidency. I was in line for it, but instead this son-in-law got in, and—"

Dr. Adler thought Wilhelm was discussing his grievances much too openly and said, "My son's income was up in the five figures."

As soon as money was mentioned, Mr. Perls's voice grew eagerly sharper. "Yes? What, the thirty-two-per-cent bracket? Higher even, I guess?" He asked for a hint, and he named the figures not idly but with a sort of hugging relish. Uch! How they love money, thought Wilhelm. They adore money! Holy money! Beautiful money! It was getting so that people were feeble-minded about everything except money. While if you didn't have it you were a dummy, a dummy! You had to excuse yourself from the face of the earth. Chicken! that's what it was. The world's business. If only he could find a way out of it.

Such thinking brought on the usual congestion. It would grow into a fit of passion if he allowed it to continue. Therefore he stopped talking and began to eat.

Before he struck the egg with his spoon he dried the moisture with his napkin. Then he battered it (in his father's opinion) more than was necessary. A faint grime was left by his fingers on the white of the egg after he had picked away the shell. Dr. Adler saw it with silent repugnance. What a Wilky he had given to the world! Why, he didn't even wash his hands in the morning. He used an electric razor so that he didn't have to touch water. The doctor couldn't bear Wilky's dirty habits. Only once—and never again, he swore—had he visited his room. Wilhelm, in pajamas and stockings had sat on his bed, drinking gin from a coffee mug and rooting for the Dodgers on television. "That's two and two on you, Duke. Come on—hit it, now." He came down on the mattress—bam! The bed looked kicked to pieces. Then he drank the gin as though it were tea, and urged his team on with his fist. The smell of dirty clothes was outrageous. By the bedside lay a quart bottle and foolish magazines and mystery stories for the hours of insomnia. Wilhelm lived in worse filth than a savage. When the Doctor spoke to him about this he answered, "Well, I have no wife to look after my things." And who—*who!*—had done the leaving? Not Margaret. The Doctor was certain that she wanted him back.

Wilhelm drank his coffee with a trembling hand. In his full face his abused bloodshot gray eyes, moved back and forth. Jerkily he set his cup back and put half the length of a cigarette into his mouth; he seemed to hold it with his teeth, as though it were a cigar.

"I can't let them get away with it," he said. "It's also a question of morale."

His father corrected him. "Don't you mean a moral question, Wilky?"

"I mean that, too. I have to do something to protect myself. I was promised executive standing." Correction before a stranger mortified him, and his dark blond face changed color, more pale, and then more dark. He went on talking to Perls but his eyes spied on his father. "I was the one who opened the territory for them. I could go back for one of their competitors and take away their customers. *My* customers. Morale enters into it because they've tried to take away my confidence."

"Would you offer a different line to the same people?" Mr. Perls wondered.

"Why not? I know what's wrong with the Rojax product."

"Nonsense," said his father. "Just nonsense and kid's talk, Wilky. You're only looking for trouble and embarrassment that way. What would you gain by such a silly feud? You have to think about making a living and meeting your obligations."

Hot and bitter, Wilhelm said with pride, while his feet moved angrily under the table, "I don't have to be told about my obligations. I've been meeting them for years. In more than twenty years I've never had a penny of help from anybody. I preferred to dig a ditch on the WPA but never asked anyone to meet my obligations for me."

"Wilky has had all kinds of experiences," said Dr. Adler.

The old doctor's face had a wholesome reddish and almost translucent color, like a ripe apricot. The wrinkles beside his ears were deep because the skin conformed so tightly to his bones. With all his might, he was a healthy and fine small old man. He wore a white vest of a light check pattern. His hearing-aid doodad was in the pocket. An unusual shirt of red and black stripes covered his chest. He bought his clothes in a college shop farther uptown. Wilhelm thought he had no business to get himself up like a jockey, out of respect for his profession.

"Well," said Mr. Perls. "I can understand how you feel. You want to fight it out. By a certain time of life, to have to start all over again can't be a pleasure, though a good man can always do it. But anyway you want to keep on with a business you know already, and not have to meet a whole lot of new contacts."

Wilhlem again thought, Why does it have to be me and my life that's discussed, and not him and his life? He would never allow it. But I am an idiot. I have no reserve. To me it can be done. I talk. I must ask for it. Everybody wants to have intimate conversations, but the smart fellows don't give out, only the fools. The smart fellows talk intimately about the fools, and examine them all over and give them advice. Why do I allow it? The hint about his age had hurt him. No, you can't admit it's as good as ever, he conceded. Things do give out.

"In the meanwhile," Dr. Adler said, "Wilky is taking it easy and considering various propositions. Isn't that so?"

"More or less," said Wilhelm. He suffered his father to increase Mr. Perls's respect for him. The WPA ditch had brought the family into contempt. He was a little tired. The spirit, the peculiar burden of his existence lay upon him like an accretion, a load, a hump. In any moment of quiet, when sheer fatigue prevented him from struggling, he was apt to feel this mysterious weight, this growth or collection of nameless things which it was the business of his life to carry about. That must be what a man was for. This large, odd, excited, fleshy, blond, abrupt personality named Wilhelm, or Tommy, was here, present, in the present—Dr. Tamkin had been putting into his mind many suggestions about the present moment, the here and now— this Wilky, or Tommy Wilhelm, forty-four years old, father of two sons, at present living in the Hotel Gloriana, was assigned to be the carrier of a load which was his own self, his characteristic self. There was no figure or estimate for the value of this load. But it is probably exaggerated by the subject, T. W. Who is a visionary sort of animal. Who has to believe that he can know why he exists. Though he has never seriously tried to find out why.

Mr. Perls said, "If he wants time to think things over and

have a rest, why doesn't he run down to Florida for a while? Off season it's cheap and quiet. Fairyland. The mangoes are just coming in. I got two acres down there. You'd think you were in India."

Mr. Perls utterly astonished Wilhelm when he spoke of fairyland with a foreign accent. Mangoes—India? What did he mean, India?

"Once upon a time," said Wilhelm, "I did some public-relations work for a big hotel down in Cuba. If I could get them a notice in Leonard Lyons or one of the other columns it might be good for another holiday there, gratis. I haven't had a vacation for a long time, and I could stand a rest after going so hard. You know that's true, Father." He meant that his father knew how deep the crisis was becoming; how badly he was strapped for money; and that he could not rest but would be crushed if he stumbled; and that his obligations would destroy him. He couldn't falter. He thought, The money! When I had it, I flowed money. They bled it away from me. I hemorrhaged money. But now it's almost all gone, and where am I supposed to turn for more?

He said, "As a matter of fact, Father, I am tired as hell."

But Mr. Perls began to smile and said, "I understand from Doctor Tamkin that you're going into some kind of investment with him, partners."

"You know, he's a very ingenious fellow," said Dr. Adler. "I really enjoy hearing him go on. I wonder if he really is a medical doctor."

"Isn't he?" said Perls. "Everybody thinks he is. He talks about his patients. Doesn't he write prescriptions?"

"I don't really know what he does," said Dr. Adler. "He's a cunning man."

"He's a psychologist, I understand," said Wilhelm.

"I don't know what sort of psychologist or psychiatrist he may be," said his father. "He's a little vague. It's growing into a major industry, and a very expensive one. Fellows have to hold down very big jobs in order to pay those fees. Anyway, this Tamkin is clever. He never said he practiced here, but I believe he was a doctor in California. They don't seem to have much legislation out there to cover these things, and I hear a thousand dollars will get you a degree from a Los Angeles correspondence school. He gives the impression of knowing something about chemistry, and things like hypnotism. I wouldn't trust him, though."

"And why wouldn't you?" Wilhelm demanded.

"Because he's probably a liar. Do you believe he invented all the things he claims?"

Mr. Perls was grinning.

"He was written up in *Fortune*," said Wilhelm. "Yes, in *Fortune* magazine. He showed me the article. I've seen his clippings."

"That doesn't make him legitimate," said Dr. Adler. "It might have been another Tamkin. Make no mistake, he's an operator. Perhaps even crazy."

"Crazy, you say?"

Mr. Perls put in, "He could be both sane and crazy. In these days nobody can tell for sure which is which."

"An electrical device for truck drivers to wear in their caps," said Dr. Adler, describing one of Tamkin's proposed inventions. "To wake them with a shock when they begin to be drowsy at the wheel. It's triggered by the change in blood-pressure when they start to doze."

"It doesn't sound like such an impossible thing to me," said Wilhelm.

Mr. Perls said, "To me he described an underwater suit so a man could walk on the bed of the Hudson in case of an atomic attack. He said he could walk to Albany in it."

"Ha, ha, ha, ha, ha!" cried Dr. Adler in his old man's voice. "Tamkin's Folly. You could go on a camping trip under Niagara Falls."

"This is just his kind of fantasy," said Wilhelm. "It doesn't mean a thing. Inventors are supposed to be like that. I get funny ideas myself. Everybody wants to make something. Any American does."

But his father ignored this and said to Perls, "What other inventions did he describe?"

While the frazzle-faced Mr. Penis and his father in the unseemly, monkey-striped shirt were laughing, Wilhelm could not restrain himself and joined in with his own panting laugh. But he was in despair. They were laughing at the man to whom he had given a power of attorney over his last seven hundred dollars to speculate for him in the commodities market. They had bought all that lard. It had to rise today. By ten o'clock, or half-past ten, trading would be active, and he would see.

III

Between white tablecloths and glassware and glancing silverware, through overfull light, the long figure of Mr. Perls went away into the darkness of the lobby. He thrust with his cane, and dragged a large built-up shoe which Wilhelm had not included in his estimate of troubles. Dr. Adler wanted to talk about him. "There's a poor man," he said, "with a bone condition which is gradually breaking him up."

"One of those progressive diseases?" said Wilhelm.

"Very bad. I've learned," the doctor told him, "to keep my sympathy for the real ailments. This Perls is more to be pitied than any man I know."

Wilhelm understood he was being put on notice and did not express his opinion. He ate and ate. He did not hurry but kept putting food on his plate until he had gone through the muffins and his father's strawberries, and then some pieces of bacon that were left; he had several cups of coffee, and when he was finished he sat gigantically in a state of arrest and didn't seem to know what he should do next.

For a while father and son were uncommonly still. Wilhelm's preparations to please Dr. Adler had failed completely, for the old man kept thinking, You'd never guess he had a clean upbringing, and, What a dirty devil this son of mine is. Why can't he try to sweeten his appearance a little? Why does he want to drag himself like this? And he makes himself look so idealistic.

Wilhelm sat, mountainous. He was not really so slovenly as his father found him to be. In some aspects he even had a certain delicacy. His mouth, though broad, had a fine outline, and his brow and his gradually incurved nose, dignity, and in his blond hair there was white but there were also shades of gold and chestnut. When he was with the Rojax Corporation Wilhelm had kept a small apartment in Roxbury, two rooms in a large house with a small porch and garden, and on mornings of leisure, in late spring weather like this, he used to sit expanded in a wicker chair with the sunlight pouring through the weave, and sunlight through the slug-eaten holes of the young hollyhocks and as deeply as the grass allowed into small flowers. This peace (he forgot that that time had had its troubles, too), this peace was gone. It must not have belonged to him, really, for to be here in New York with his old father was more genuinely like his life. He was well aware that he didn't stand a chance of getting sympathy from his father, who said he kept his for real ailments. Moreover, he advised himself repeatedly not to discuss his vexatious problems with him, for his father, with some justice, wanted to be left in peace. Wilhelm also knew that when he began to talk about these things he made himself feel worse, he became congested with them and worked himself into a clutch. Therefore he warned himself, Lay off, pal. It'll only be an aggravation. From a deeper source, however, came other promptings. If he didn't keep his troubles before him he risked losing them altogether, and he knew by experience that this was worse. And furthermore, he could not succeed in excusing his father on the ground of old age. No. No, he could not. I am his son, he thought. He is my father. He is as much father as I am son—old or not. Affirming this, though in complete silence, he sat, and, sitting, he kept his father at the table with him.

"Wilky," said the old man, "have you gone down to the baths here yet?"

"No, Dad, not yet."

"Well, you know the Gloriana has one of the finest pools in New York. Eighty feet, blue tile. It's a beauty."

Wilhelm had seen it. On the way to the gin game you passed the stairway to the pool. He did not care for the odor of the wall-locked and chlorinated water.

"You ought to investigate the Russian and Turkish baths, and the sunlamps and massage. I don't hold with sunlamps. But the massage does a world of good, and there's nothing better than hydrotherapy when you come right down to it. Simple water has a calming effect and would do you more good than all the barbiturates and alcohol in the world."

Wilhelm reflected that this advice was as far as his father's help and sympathy would extend.

"I thought," he said, "that the water cure was for lunatics."

The doctor received this as one of his son's jokes and said with a smile, "Well, it won't turn a sane man into a lunatic. It does a great deal for me. I couldn't live without my massages and steam."

"You're probably right. I ought to try it one of these days. Yesterday, late in the afternoon, my head was about to bust and I just had to have a little air, so I walked around the reservoir, and I sat down for a while in a playground. It rests me to watch the kids play potsy and skiprope."

The doctor said with approval, "Well, now, that's more like the idea."

"It's the end of the lilacs," said Wilhelm. "When they burn it's the beginning of summer. At least, in the city. Around the time of year when the candy stores take down the windows and start to sell sodas on the sidewalk. But even though I was raised here, Dad, I can't take city life any more, and I miss the country. There's too much push here for me. It works me up too much. I take things too hard. I wonder why you never retired to a quieter place."

The doctor opened his small hand on the table in a gesture so old and so typical that Wilhelm felt it like an actual touch upon the foundations of his life. "I am a city boy myself, you must remember," Dr. Adler explained. "But if you find the city so hard on you, you ought to get out."

"I'll do that," said Wilhelm, "as soon as I can make the right connection. Meanwhile—"

His father interrupted, "Meanwhile I suggest you cut down on drugs."

"You exaggerate that, Dad. I don't really— I give myself a little boost against—" He almost pronounced the word "misery" but he kept his resolution not to complain.

The doctor, however, fell into the error of pushing his advice too hard. It was all he had to give his son and he gave it once more. "Water and exercise," he said.

He wants a young, smart, successful son, thought Wilhelm, and he said, "Oh, Father, it's nice of you to give me this medical advice, but steam isn't going to cure what ails me."

The doctor measurably drew back, warned by the sudden weak strain of Wilhelm's voice and all that the droop of his face, the swell of his belly against the restraint of his belt intimated.

"Some new business?" he asked unwillingly.

Wilhelm made a great preliminary summary which involved the whole of his body. He drew and held a long breath, and his color changed and his eyes swam. "New?" he said.

"You make too much of your problems," said the doctor. "They ought not to be turned into a career. Concentrate on real troubles—fatal sickness, accidents." The old man's whole manner said, Wilky, don't start this on me. I have a right to be spared.

Wilhelm himself prayed for restraint; he knew this weakness of his and fought it. He knew, also, his father's character. And he began mildly, "As far as the fatal part of it goes, everyone on this side of the grave is the same distance from death. No, I guess my trouble is not exactly new. I've got to pay premiums on two policies for the boys. Margaret sent them to me. She unloads everything on me. Her mother left her an income. She won't even file a joint tax return. I get stuck. Etcetera. But you've heard the whole story before."

"I certainly have," said the old man. "And I've told you to stop giving her so much money."

Wilhelm worked his lips in silence before he could speak. The congestion was growing. "Oh, but my kids, Father. My kids. I love them. I don't want them to lack anything."

The doctor said with a half-deaf benevolence, "Well, naturally. And she, I'll bet, is the beneficiary of that policy."

"Let her be. I'd sooner die myself before I collected a cent of such money."

"Ah yes." The old man sighed. He did not like the mention of death. "Did I tell you that your sister Catherine—Philippa —is after me again."

"What for?"

"She wants to rent a gallery for an exhibition."

Stiffly fair-minded, Wilhelm said, "Well, of course that's up to you, Father."

The round-headed old man with his fine, feather-white, ferny hair said, "No, Wilky. There's not a thing on those canvases. I don't believe it; it's a case of the emperor's clothes. I may be old enough for my second childhood, but at least the first is well behind me. I was glad enough to buy crayons for her when she was four. But now she's a woman of forty and too old to be encouraged in her delusions. She's no painter."

"I wouldn't go so far as to call her a born artist," said Wilhelm, "but you can't blame her for trying something worth while."

"Let her husband pamper her."

Wilhelm had done his best to be just to his sister, and he had sincerely meant to spare his father, but the old man's tight, benevolent deafness had its usual effect on him. He said, "When it comes to women and money, I'm completely in the dark. What makes Margaret act like this?"

"She's showing you that you can't make it without her," said the doctor. "She aims to bring you back by financial force."

"But if she ruins me, Dad, how can she expect me to come back? No, I have a sense of honor. What you don't see is that she's trying to put an end to me."

His father stared. To him this was absurd. And Wilhelm thought, Once a guy starts to slip, he figures he might as well be a clunk. A real big clunk. He even takes pride in it. But there's nothing to be proud of—hey, boy? Nothing. I don't blame Dad for his attitude. And it's no cause for pride.

"I don't understand that. But if you feel like this why don't you settle with her once and for all?"

"What do you mean, Dad?" said Wilhelm, surprised. "I thought I told you. Do you think I'm not willing to settle? Four years ago when we broke up I gave her everything— goods, furniture, savings. I tried to show good will, but I didn't get anywhere. Why when I wanted Scissors, the dog, because the animal and I were so attached to each other—it was bad enough to leave the kids—she absolutely refused me. Not that she cared a damn about the animal. I don't think you've seen him. He's an Australian sheep dog. They usually have one blank or whitish eye which gives a misleading look, but they're the gentlest dogs and have unusual delicacy about eating or talking. Let me at least have the companionship of this animal. Never." Wilhelm was greatly moved. He wiped his face at all corners with his napkin. Dr. Adler felt that his son was indulging himself too much in his emotions.

"Whenever she can hit me, she hits, and she seems to live for that alone. And she demands more and more, and still more. Two years ago she wanted to go back to college and get another degree. It increased my burden but I thought it would be wiser in the end if she got a better job through it. But still she takes as much from me as before. Next thing she'll want to be a Doctor of Philosophy. She says the women in her family live long, and I'll have to pay and pay for the rest of my life."

The doctor said impatiently, "Well, these are details, not principles. Just details which you can leave out. The dog! You're mixing up all kinds of irrelevant things. Go to a good lawyer."

"But I've already told you, Dad. I got a lawyer, and she got one, too, and both of them talk and send me bills, and I eat my heart out. Oh, Dad, Dad, what a hole I'm in!" said Wilhelm in utter misery. "The lawyers—see?—draw up an agreement, and she says okay on Monday and wants more money on Tuesday. And it begins again."

"I always thought she was a strange kind of woman," said Dr. Adler. He felt that by disliking Margaret from the first and disapproving of the marriage he had done all that he could be expected to do.

"Strange, Father? I'll show you what she's like." Wilhelm took hold of his broad throat with brown-stained fingers and bitten nails and began to choke himself.

"What are you doing?" cried the old man.

"I'm showing you what she does to me."

"Stop that—stop it!" the old man said and tapped the table commandingly.

"Well, Dad, she hates me. I feel that she's strangling me. I can't catch my breath. She just has fixed herself on me to kill me. She can do it at long distance. One of these days I'll be struck down by suffocation or apoplexy because of her. I just can't catch my breath."

"Take your hands off your throat, you foolish man," said his father. "Stop this bunk. Don't expect me to believe in all kinds of voodoo."

"If that's what you want to call it, all right." His face flamed and paled and swelled and his breath was laborious.

"But I'm telling you that from the time I met her I've been a slave. The Emancipation Proclamation was only for colored people. A husband like me is a slave, with an iron collar. The churches go up to Albany and supervise the law. They won't have divorces. The court says, 'You want to be free. Then you have to work twice as hard—twice, at least! Work! you bum.' So then guys kill each other for the buck, and they may be free of a wife who hates them but they are sold to the company. The company knows a guy has got to have his salary, and takes full advantage of him. Don't talk to me about being free. A rich man may be free on an income of a million net. A poor man may be free because nobody cares what he does. But a fellow in my position has to sweat it out until he drops dead."

His father replied to this, "Wilky, it's entirely your own fault. You don't have to allow it."

Stopped in his eloquence, Wilhelm could not speak for a while. Dumb and incompetent, he struggled for breath and frowned with effort into his father's face.

"I don't understand your problems," said the old man. "I never had any like them."

By now Wilhelm had lost his head and he waved his hands and said over and over, "Oh, Dad, don't give me that stuff, don't give me that. Please don't give me that sort of thing."

"It's true," said his father. "I come from a different world. Your mother and I led an entirely different life."

"Oh, how can you compare Mother," Wilhelm said. "Mother was a help to you. Did she harm you ever?"

"There's no need to carry on like an opera, Wilky," said the doctor. "This is only your side of things."

"What? It's the truth," said Wilhelm.

The old man could not be persuaded and shook his round head and drew his vest down over the gilded shirt, and leaned back with a completeness of style that made this look, to anyone out of hearing, like an ordinary conversation between a middle-aged man and his respected father. Wilhelm towered and swayed, big and sloven, with his gray eyes red-shot and his honey-colored hair twisted in flaming shapes upward. Injustice made him angry, made him beg. But he wanted an understanding with his father, and he tried to capitulate to him. He said, "You can't compare Mother and Margaret, and neither can you and I be compared, because you, Dad, were a success. And a success—is a success. I never made a success."

The doctor's old face lost all of its composure and became hard and angry. His small breast rose sharply under the red and black shirt and he said, "Yes. Because of hard work. I was not self-indulgent, not lazy. My old man sold dry goods in Williamsburg. We were nothing, do you understand? I knew I couldn't afford to waste my chances."

"I wouldn't admit for one minute that I was lazy," said Wilhelm. "If anything, I tried too hard. I admit I made many mistakes. Like I thought I shouldn't do things you had done already. Study chemistry. You had done it already. It was in the family."

His father continued, "I didn't run around with fifty women, either. I was not a Hollywood star. I didn't have time to go to Cuba for a vacation. I stayed at home and took care of my children."

Oh, thought Wilhelm, eyes turning upward. Why did I come here in the first place, to live near him? New York is like a gas. The colors are running. My head feels so tight, I don't know what I'm doing. He thinks I want to take away his money or that I envy him. He doesn't see what I want.

"Dad," Wilhelm said aloud, "you're being very unfair. It's true the movies was a false step. But I love my boys. I didn't abandon them. I left Margaret because I had to."

"Why did you have to?"

"Well—" said Wilhelm, struggling to condense his many reasons into a few plain words. "I had to—I had to."

With sudden and surprising bluntness his father said, "Did you have bed-trouble with her? Then you should have stuck it out. Sooner or later everyone has it. Normal people stay with it. It passes. But you wouldn't, so now you pay for your stupid romantic notions. Have I made my view clear?"

It was very clear. Wilhelm seemed to hear it repeated from various sides and inclined his head different ways, and listened and thought. Finally he said, "I guess that's the medical standpoint. You may be right. I just couldn't live with Margaret. I wanted to stick it out, but I was getting very sick. She was one way and I was another. She wouldn't be like me, so I tried to be like her, and I couldn't do it."

"Are you sure she didn't tell *you* to go?" the doctor said.

"I wish she had. I'd be in a better position now. No, it was me. I didn't want to leave, but I couldn't stay. Somebody had to take the initiative. I did. Now I'm the fall guy too."

Pushing aside in advance all the objections that his son would make, the doctor said, "Why did you lose your job with Rojax?"

"I didn't, I've told you."

"You're lying. You wouldn't have ended the connection. You need the money too badly. But you must have got into trouble." The small old man spoke concisely and with great strength. "Since you have to talk and can't let it alone, tell the truth. Was there a scandal—a woman?"

Wilhelm fiercely defended himself. "No, Dad, there wasn't any woman. I told you how it was."

"Maybe it was a man, then," the old man said wickedly.

Shocked, Wilhelm stared at him with burning pallor and dry lips. His skin looked a little yellow. "I don't think you know what you're talking about," he answered after a moment. "You shouldn't let your imagination run so free. Since you've been living here on Broadway you must think you understand life, up to date. You ought to know your own son a little better. Let's drop that, now."

"All right, Wilky, I'll withdraw it. But something must have happened in Roxbury nevertheless. You'll never go back. You're just talking wildly about representing a rival company. You won't. You've done something to spoil your reputation, I think. But you've got girl friends who are expecting you back, isn't that so?"

"I take a lady out now and then while on the road," said Wilhelm. "I'm not a monk."

"No one special? Are you sure you haven't gotten into complications?"

He had tried to unburden himself and instead, Wilhelm thought, he had to undergo an inquisition to prove himself worthy of a sympathetic word. Because his father believed that he did all kinds of gross things.

"There is a woman in Roxbury that I went with. We fell in love and wanted to marry, but she got tired of waiting for my divorce. Margaret figured that. On top of which the girl was a Catholic and I had to go with her to the priest and make an explanation."

Neither did this last confession touch Dr. Adler's sympathies or sway his calm old head or affect the color of his complexion.

"No, no, no, no; all wrong," he said.

Again Wilhelm cautioned himself. Remember his age. He is no longer the same person. He can't bear trouble. I'm so choked up and congested anyway I can't see straight. Will I ever get out of the woods, and recover my balance? You're never the same afterward. Trouble rusts out the system.

"You really *want* a divorce?" said the old man.

"For the price I pay I should be getting something."

"In that case," Dr. Adler said, "it seems to me no normal person would stand for such treatment from a woman."

"Ah, Father, Father!" said Wilhelm. "It's always the same thing with you. Look how you lead me on. You always start out to help me with my problems, and be sympathetic and so forth. It gets my hopes up and I begin to be grateful. But before we're through I'm a hundred times more depressed than before. Why is that? You have no sympathy. You want to shift all the blame on to me. Maybe you're wise to do it." Wilhelm was beginning to lose himself. "All you seem to think about is your death. Well, I'm sorry. But I'm going to die too. And I'm your son. It isn't my fault in the first place. There ought to be a right way to do this, and be fair to each other. But what I want to know is, why do you start up with me if you're not going to help me? What do you want to know about my problems for, Father? So you can lay the whole responsibility on me—so that you won't have to help me? D'you want me to comfort you for having such a son?" Wilhelm had a great knot of wrong tied tight within his chest, and tears approached his eyes but he didn't let them out. He looked shabby enough as it was. His voice was thick and hazy, and he was stammering and could not bring his awful feelings forth.

"You have some purpose of your own," said the doctor, "in acting so unreasonable. What do you want from me? What do you expect?"

"What do I expect?" said Wilhelm. He felt as though he were unable to recover something. Like a ball in the surf, washed beyond reach, his self-control was going out. "I expect *help*!" The words escaped him in a loud, wild, frantic cry and startled the old man, and two or three breakfasters within hearing glanced their way. Wilhelm's hair, the color of whitened honey, rose dense and tall with the expansion of his face, and he said, "When I suffer—you aren't even sorry. That's because you have no affection for me, and you don't want any part of me."

"Why must I like the way you behave? No, I don't like it." said Dr. Adler.

"All right. You want me to change myself. But suppose I could do it—what would I become? What could I? Let's suppose that all my life I have had the wrong ideas about myself and wasn't what I thought I was. And wasn't even careful to take a few precautions, as most people do—like a woodchuck has a few exits to his tunnel. But what shall I do now? More than half my life is over. More than half. And now you tell me I'm not even normal."

The old man too had lost his calm. "You cry about being helped," he said. "When you thought you had to go into the service I sent a check to Margaret every month. As a family man you could have had an exemption. But no! The war couldn't be fought without you and you had to get yourself drafted and be an office-boy in the Pacific theater. Any clerk could have done what you did. You could find nothing better to become than a GI."

Wilhelm was going to reply, and half raised his bearish figure from the chair, his fingers spread and whitened by their grip on the table, but the old man would not let him begin. He said, "I see other elderly people here with children who aren't much good, and they keep backing them and holding them up at a great sacrifice. But I'm not going to make that mistake. It doesn't enter your mind that when I die—a year, two years from now—you'll still be here. I do think of it."

He had intended to say that he had a right to be left in peace. Instead he gave Wilhelm the impression that he meant it was not fair for the better man of the two, and the more useful, the more admired, to leave the world first. Perhaps he meant that, too—a little; but he would not under other circumstances have come out with it so flatly.

"Father," said Wilhelm with an unusual openness of appeal. "Don't you think I know how you feel? I have pity. I want you to live on and on. If you outlive me, that's perfectly okay by me." As his father did not answer this avowal and turned away his glance, Wilhelm suddenly burst out, "No, but you hate me. And if I had money you wouldn't. By God, you have to admit it. The money makes the difference. Then we would be a fine father and son, if I was a credit to you—so you could boast and brag about me all over the hotel. But I'm not the right type of son. I'm too old, I'm too old and too unlucky."

His father said, "I can't give you any money. There would be no end to it if I started. You and your sister would take every last buck from me. I'm still alive, not dead. I am still here. Life isn't over yet. I am as much alive as you or anyone. And I want nobody on my back. Get off! And I give you the same advice, Wilky. Carry nobody on your back."

"Just keep your money," said Wilhelm miserably. "Keep it and enjoy it yourself. That's the ticket!"

IV

Ass! Idiot! Wild boar! Dumb mule! Slave! Lousy, wallowing hippopotamus! Wilhelm called himself as his bending legs carried him from the dining room. His pride! His inflamed feelings! His begging and feebleness! And trading insults with his old father—and spreading confusion over everything. Oh, how poor, contemptible, and ridiculous he was! When he remembered how he had said, with great reproof, "You ought to know your own son"—why, how corny and abominable it was.

He could not get out of the sharply brilliant dining room fast enough. He was horribly worked up; his neck and shoulders, his entire chest ached as though they had been tightly tied with ropes. He smelled the salt odor of tears in his nose.

But at the same time, since there were depths in Wilhelm not unsuspected by himself, he received a suggestion from some remote element in his thoughts that the business of life, the real business—to carry his peculiar burden, to feel shame and impotence, to taste these quelled tears—the only important business, the highest business was being done. Maybe the making of mistakes expressed the very purpose of his life and the essence of his being here. Maybe he was supposed to make them and suffer from them on this earth. And though he had raised himself above Mr. Perls and his father because they adored money, still they were called to act energetically and this was better than to yell and cry, pray and beg, poke and blunder and go by fits and starts and fall upon the thorns of life. And finally sink beneath that watery floor—would that be tough luck, or would it be good riddance?

But he raged once more against his father. Other people with money, while they're still alive, want to see it do some good. Granted, he shouldn't support me. But have I ever asked him to do that? Have I ever asked for dough at all, either for Margaret or for the kids or for myself? It isn't the money, but only the assistance; not even assistance, but just the feeling. But he may be trying to teach me that a grown man should be cured of such feeling. Feeling got me in dutch at Rojax. I had the *feeling* that I belonged to the firm, and my *feelings* were hurt when they put Gerber in over me. Dad thinks I'm too simple. But I'm not so simple as he thinks. What about his feelings? He doesn't forget death for one single second, and that's what makes him like this. And not only is death on his mind but through money he forces me to think about it, too. It gives him power over me. He forces me that way, he himself, and then he's sore. If he was poor, I could care for him and show it. The way I *could* care, too, if I only had a chance. He'd see how much love and respect I had in me. It would make him a different man, too. He'd put his hands on me and give me his blessing.

Someone in a gray straw hat with a wide cocoa-colored band spoke to Wilhelm in the lobby. The light was dusky, splotched with red underfoot; green, the leather furniture; yellow, the indirect lighting.

"Hey, Tommy. Say, there."

"Excuse me," said Wilhelm, trying to reach a house phone. But this was Dr. Tamkin, whom he was just about to call.

"You have a very obsessional look on your face," said Dr. Tamkin.

Wilhlem thought, Here he is, Here he is. If I could only figure this guy out.

"Oh," he said to Tamkin. "Have I got such a look? Well, whatever it is, you name it and I'm sure to have it."

The sight of Dr. Tamkin brought his quarrel with his father to a close. He found himself flowing into another channel.

"What are we doing?" he said. "What's going to happen to lard today?"

"Don't worry yourself about that. All we have to do is hold on to it and it's sure to go up. But what's made you so hot under the collar, Wilhelm?"

"Oh, one of those family situations." This was the moment to take a new look at Tamkin, and he viewed him closely but gained nothing by the new effort. It was conceivable that Tamkin was everything that he claimed to be, and all the gossip false. But was he a scientific man, or not? If he was not, this might be a case for the district attorney's office to investigate. Was he a liar? That was a delicate question. Even a liar might be trustworthy in some ways. Could he trust Tamkin—could he? He feverishly, fruitlessly sought an answer.

But the time for this question was past, and he had to trust him now. After a long struggle to come to a decision, he had given him the money. Practical judgment was in abeyance. He had worn himself out, and the decision was no decision. How had this happened? But how had his Hollywood career begun? It was not because of Maurice Venice, who turned out to be a pimp. It was because Wilhelm himself was ripe for the mistake. His marriage, too, had been like that. Through such decisions somehow his life had taken form. And so, from the moment when he tasted the peculiar flavor of fatality in Dr. Tamkin, he could no longer keep back the money.

Five days ago Tamkin had said, "Meet me tomorrow, and we'll go to the market." Wilhelm, therefore, had had to go. At eleven o'clock they had walked to the brokerage office. On the way, Tamkin broke the news to Wilhelm that though this was an equal partnership he couldn't put up his half of the money just yet; it was tied up for a week or so in one of his patents. Today he would be two hundred dollars short; next week, he'd make it up. But neither of them needed an income from the market, of course. This was only a sporting proposition anyhow, Tamkin said. Wilhelm had to answer, "Of course." It was too late to withdraw. What else could he do? Then came the formal part of the transaction, and it was frightening. The very shade of green of Tamkin's check looked wrong; it was a false, disheartening color. His handwriting was peculiar, even monstrous; the e's were like i's, the t's and l's the same, and the h's like wasps' bellies. He wrote like a fourth-grader. Scientists, however, dealt mostly in symbols; they printed. This was Wilhelm's explanation.

Dr. Tamkin had given him his check for three hundred dollars. Wilhelm, in a blinded and convulsed aberration, pressed and pressed to try to kill the trembling of his hand as he wrote out his check for a thousand. He set his lips tight, crouched with his huge back over the table, and wrote with crumbling, terrified fingers, knowing that if Tamkin's check bounced his own would not be honored either. His sole cleverness was to set the date ahead by one day to give the green check time to clear.

Next he had signed a power of attorney, allowing Tamkin to speculate with his money, and this was an even more frightening document. Tamkin had never said a word about it, but here they were and it had to be done.

After delivering his signatures, the only precaution Wilhelm took was to come back to the manager of the brokerage office and ask him privately, "Uh, about Doctor Tamkin. We were in here a few minutes ago, remember?"

That day had been a weeping, smoky one and Wilhelm had gotten away from Tamkin on the pretext of having to run to the post office. Tamkin had gone to lunch alone, and here was Wilhelm, back again, breathless, his hat dripping, needlessly asking the manager if he remembered.

"Yes, sir, I know," the manager had said. He was a cold, mild, lean German who dressed correctly and around his neck wore a pair of opera glasses with which he read the board. He was an extremely correct person except that he never shaved in the morning, not caring, probably, how he looked to the fumblers and the old people and the operators and the gamblers and the idlers of Broadway uptown. The market closed at three. Maybe, Wilhelm guessed, he had a thick beard and took a lady out to dinner later and wanted to look fresh-shaven.

"Just a question," said Wilhelm. "A few minutes ago I signed a power of attorney so Doctor Tamkin could invest for me. You gave me the blanks."

"Yes, sir, I remember."

"Now this is what I want to know," Wilhelm had said. "I'm no lawyer and I only gave the paper a glance. Does this give

Doctor Tamkin power of attorney over any other assets of
mine—money, or property?"

The rain had dribbled from Wilhelm's deformed, transparent raincoat; the buttons of his shirt, which always seemed
tiny, were partly broken, in pearly quarters of the moon, and
some of the dark, thick golden hairs that grew on his belly
stood out. It was the manager's business to conceal his opinion of him; he was shrewd, gray, correct (although unshaven)
and had little to say except on matters that came to his desk.
He must have recognized in Wilhelm a man who reflected long
and then made the decision he had rejected twenty separate
times. Silvery, cool, level, long-profiled, experienced, indifferent, observant, with unshaven refinement, he scarcely looked
at Wilhelm, who trembled with fearful awkwardness. The manager's face, low-colored, long-nostriled, acted as a unit of perception; his eyes merely did their reduced share. Here was a
man, like Rubin, who knew and knew and knew. He, a foreigner, knew; Wilhelm, in the city of his birth, was ignorant.

The manager had said, "No, sir, it does not give him."

"Only over the funds I deposited with you?"

"Yes, that is right, sir."

"Thank you, that's what I wanted to find out," Wilhelm had
said, grateful.

The answer comforted him. However, the question had no
value. None at all. For Wilhelm had no other assets. He had
given Tamkin his last money. There wasn't enough of it to cover
his obligations anyway, and Wilhelm had reckoned that he
might as well go bankrupt now as next month. "Either broke
or rich," was how he had figured, and that formula had encouraged him to make the gamble. Well, not rich; he did not
expect that, but perhaps Tamkin might really show him how to
earn what he needed in the market. By now, however, he had
forgotten his own reckoning and was aware only that he stood
to lose his seven hundred dollars to the last cent.

Dr. Tamkin took the attitude that they were a pair of gentlemen experimenting with lard and grain futures The money, a
few hundred dollars, meant nothing much to either of them.
He said to Wilhlem, "Watch. You'll get a big kick out of this
and wonder why more people don't go into it. You think the
Wall Street guys are so smart—geniuses? That's because most

of us are psychologically afraid to think about the details. Tell me this. When you're on the road, and you don't understand what goes on under the hood of your car, you'll worry what'll happen if something goes wrong with the engine. Am I wrong?" No, he was right. "Well," said Dr. Tamkin with an expression of quiet triumph about his mouth, almost the suggestion of a jeer. "It's the same psychological principle, Wilhelm. They are rich because you don't understand what goes on. But it's no mystery, and by putting in a little money and applying certain principles of observation, you begin to grasp it. It can't be studied in the abstract. You have to take a specimen risk so that you feel the process, the money-flow, the whole complex. To know how it feels to be a seaweed you have to get in the water. In a very short time we'll take out a hundred-per-cent profit." Thus Wilhelm had had to pretend at the outset that his interest in the market was theoretical.

"Well," said Tamkin when he met him now in the lobby, "what's the problem, what is this family situation? Tell me." He put himself forward as the keen mental scientist. Whenever this happened Wilhelm didn't know what to reply. No matter what he said or did it seemed that Dr. Tamkin saw through him.

"I had some words with my dad."

Dr. Tamkin found nothing extraordinary in this. "It's the eternal same story," he said. "The elemental conflict of parent and child. It won't end, ever. Even with a fine old gentleman like your dad."

"I don't suppose it will. I've never been able to get anywhere with him. He objects to my feelings. He thinks they're sordid. I upset him and he gets mad at me. But maybe all old men are alike."

"Sons, too. Take it from one of them," said Dr. Tamkin. "All the same, you should be proud of such a fine old patriarch of a father. It should give you hope. The longer he lives, the longer your life-expectancy becomes."

Wilhelm answered, brooding, "I guess so. But I think I inherit more from my mother's side, and she died in her fifties."

"A problem arose between a young fellow I'm treating and his dad—I just had a consultation," said Dr. Tamkin as he removed his dark gray hat.

"So early in the morning?" said Wilhelm with suspicion.

"Over the telephone, of course."

What a creature Tamkin was when he took off his hat! The indirect light showed the many complexities of his bald skull, his gull's nose, his rather handsome eyebrows, his vain mustache, his deceiver's brown eyes. His figure was stocky, rigid, short in the neck, so that the large ball of the occiput touched his collar. His bones were peculiarly formed, as though twisted twice where the ordinary human bone was turned only once, and his shoulders rose in two pagoda-like points. At mid-body he was thick. He stood pigeon-toed, a sign perhaps that he was devious or had much to hide. The skin of his hands was aging, and his nails were moonless, concave, clawlike, and they appeared loose. His eyes were as brown as beaver fur and full of strange lines. The two large brown naked balls looked thoughtful—but were they? And honest—but was Dr. Tamkin honest? There was a hypnotic power in his eyes, but this was not always of the same strength, nor was Wilhelm convinced that it was completely natural. He felt that Tamkin tried to make his eyes deliberately conspicuous, with studied art, and that he brought forth his hypnotic effect by an exertion. Occasionally it failed or drooped, and when this happened the sense of his face passed downward to his heavy (possibly foolish?) red underlip.

Wilhelm wanted to talk about the lard holdings, but Dr. Tamkin said, "This father-and-son case of mine would be instructive to you. It's a different psychological type completely than your dad. This man's father thinks that he isn't his son."

"Why not?"

"Because he has found out something about the mother carrying on with a friend of the family for twenty-five years."

"Well, what do you know!" said Wilhelm. His silent thought was, Pure bull. Nothing but bull!

"You must note how interesting the woman is, too. She has two husbands. Whose are the kids? The fellow detected her and she gave a signed confession that two of the four children were not the father's."

"It's amazing," said Wilhelm, but he said it in a rather distant way. He was always hearing such stories from Dr. Tamkin. If you were to believe Tamkin, most of the world was like this.

Everybody in the hotel had a mental disorder, a secret history, a concealed disease. The wife of Rubin at the newsstand was supposed to be kept by Carl, the yelling, loud-mouthed gin-rummy player. The wife of Frank in the barbershop had disappeared with a GI while he was waiting for her to disembark at the French Lines pier. Everyone was like the faces on a playing card, upside down either way. Every public figure had a character-neurosis. Maddest of all were the businessmen, the heartless, flaunting, boisterous business class who ruled this country with their hard manners and their bold lies and their absurd words that nobody could believe. They were crazier than anyone. They spread the plague. Wilhelm, thinking of the Rojax Corporation, was inclined to agree that many businessmen were insane. And he supposed that Tamkin, for all his peculiarities, spoke a kind of truth and did some people a sort of good. It confirmed Wilhelm's suspicions to hear that there was a plague, and he said, "I couldn't agree with you more. They trade on anything, they steal everything, they're cynical right to the bones."

"You have to realize," said Tamkin, speaking of his patient, or his client, "that the mother's confession isn't good. It's a confession of duress. I try to tell the young fellow he shouldn't worry about a phony confession. But what does it help him if I am rational with him?"

"No?" said Wilhelm, intensely nervous. "I think we ought to go over to the market. It'll be opening pretty soon."

"Oh, come on," said Tamkin. "It isn't even nine o'clock, and there isn't much trading the first hour anyway. Things don't get hot in Chicago until half-past ten, and they're an hour behind us, don't forget. Anyway, I say lard will go up, and it will. Take my word. I've made a study of the guilt-aggression cycle which is behind it. I ought to know *something* about that. Straighten your collar."

"But meantime," said Wilhelm, "we have taken a licking this week. Are you sure your insight is at its best? Maybe when it isn't we should lay off and wait."

"Don't you realize," Dr. Tamkin told him, "you can't march in a straight line to the victory? You fluctuate toward it. From Euclid to Newton there was straight lines. The modern age analyzes the wavers. On my own accounts, I took a licking in hides and coffee. But I have confidence. I'm sure I'll out-guess them." He gave Wilhelm a narrow smile, friendly, calming, shrewd, and wizard-like, patronizing, secret, potent. He saw his fears and smiled at them. "It's something," he remarked, "to see how the competition-factor will manifest it-self in different individuals."

"So? Let's go over."

"But I haven't had my breakfast yet."

"I've had mine."

"Come, have a cup of coffee."

"I wouldn't want to meet my dad." Looking through the glass doors, Wilhelm saw that his father had left by the other exit. Wilhelm thought, He didn't want to run into me, either. He said to Dr. Tamkin, "Okay, I'll sit with you, but let's hurry it up because I'd like to get to the market while there's still a place to sit. Everybody and his uncle gets in ahead of you."

"I want to tell you about this boy and his dad. It's highly absorbing. The father was a nudist. Everybody went naked in the house. Maybe the woman found men *with* clothes attrac-tive. Her husband didn't believe in cutting his hair, either. He practiced dentistry. In his office he wore riding pants and a pair of boots, and he wore a green eyeshade."

"Oh, come off it," said Wilhelm.

"This is a true case history."

Without warning, Wilhelm began to laugh. He himself had had no premonition of his change of humor. His face became warm and pleasant, and he forgot his father, his anxieties; he panted bearlike, happily, through his teeth. "This sounds like a horse-dentist. He wouldn't have to put on pants to treat a horse. Now what else are you going to tell me? Did the wife play the mandolin? Does the boy join the cavalry? Oh, Tamkin, you really are a killer-diller."

"Oh, you think I'm trying to amuse you," said Tamkin. "That's because you aren't familiar with my outlook. I deal in facts. Facts always are sensational. I'll say that a second time. Facts *always!* are sensational."

Wilhelm was reluctant to part with his good mood. The doc-tor had little sense of humor. He was looking at him earnestly.

"I'd bet you any amount of money," said Tamkin, "that the facts about you are sensational."

"Oh—ha, ha! You want them? You can sell them to a true confession magazine."

"People forget how sensational the things are that they do. They don't see it on themselves. It blends into the background of their daily life."

Wilhelm smiled. "Are you sure this boy tells you the truth?"

"Yes, because I've known the whole family for years."

"And you do psychological work with your own friends? I didn't know that was allowed."

"Well, I'm a radical in the profession. I have to do good wherever I can."

Wilhelm's face became ponderous again and pale. His whitened gold hair lay heavy on his head, and he clasped uneasy fingers on the table. Sensational, but oddly enough, dull, too. Now how do you figure that out? It blends with the background. Funny but unfunny. True but false. Casual but laborious, Tamkin was. Wilhelm was most suspicious of him when he took his driest tone.

"With me," said Dr. Tanikin, "I am at my most efficient when I don't need the fee. When I only love. Without a financial reward. I remove myself from the social influence. Especially money. The spiritual compensation is what I look for. Bringing people into the here-and-now. The real universe. That's the present moment. The past is no good to us. The future is full of anxiety. Only the present is real—the here-and-now. Seize the day."

"Well," said Wilhelm, his earnestness returning. "I know you are a very unusual man. I like what you say about here-and-now. Are all the people who come to see you personal friends and patients too? Like that tall handsome girl, the one who always wears those beautiful broomstick skirts and belts?"

"She was an epileptic, and a most bad and serious pathology, too. I'm curing her successfully. She hasn't had a seizure in six months, and she used to have one every week."

"And that young cameraman, the one who showed us those movies from the jungles of Brazil, isn't he related to her?"

"Her brother. He's under my care, too. He has some terrible tendencies, which are to be expected when you have an epileptic sibling. I came into their lives when they needed help desperately, and took hold of them. A certain man forty years older than she had her in his control and used to give her fits by suggestion whenever she tried to leave him. If you only knew one per cent of what goes on in the city of New York! You see, I understand what it is when the lonely person begins to feel like an animal. When the night comes and he feels like howling from his window like a wolf. I'm taking complete care of that young fellow and his sister. I have to steady him down or he'll go from Brazil to Australia the next day. The way I keep him in the here-and-now is by teaching him Greek."

This was a complete surprise! "What, do you know Greek?"

"A friend of mine taught me when I was in Cairo. I studied Aristotle with him to keep from being idle."

Wilhelm tried to take in these new claims and examine them. Howling from the window like a wolf when night comes sounded genuine to him. That was something really to think about. But the Greek! He realized that Tamkin was watching to see how he took it. More elements were continually being added. A few days ago Tamkin had hinted that he had once been in the underworld, one of the Detroit Purple Gang. He was once head of a mental clinic in Toledo. He had worked with a Polish inventor on an unsinkable ship. He was a technical consultant in the field of television. In the life of a man of genius, all of these things might happen. But had they happened to Tamkin? Was he a genius? He often said that he had attended some of the Egyptian royal family as a psychiatrist. "But everybody is alike, common or aristocrat," he told Wilhelm. "The aristocrat knows less about life."

An Egyptian princess whom he had treated in California, for horrible disorders he had described to Wilhelm, retained him to come back to the old country with her, and there he had had many of her friends and relatives under his care. They turned over a villa on the Nile to him. "For ethical reasons, I can't tell you many of the details about them," he said—but Wilhelm had already heard all these details, and strange and shocking they were, if true. If true—he could not be free from doubt. For instance, the general who had to wear ladies' silk stockings and stand otherwise naked before the mirror—and all the rest. Listening to the doctor when he was so strangely factual, Wilhelm had to translate his words into his own language, and he could not translate fast enough or find terms to fit what he heard.

"Those Egyptian big shots invested in the market, too, for the heck of it. What did they need extra money for? By association, I almost became a millionaire myself, and if I had played it smart there's no telling what might have happened. I could have been the ambassador." The American? The Egyptian ambassador? "A friend of mine tipped me off on the cotton. I made a heavy purchase of it. I didn't have that kind of money, but everybody there knew me. It never entered their minds that a person of their social circle didn't have dough. The sale was made on the phone. Then, while the cotton shipment was at sea, the price tripled. When the stuff suddenly became so valuable all hell broke loose on the world cotton market, they looked to see who was the owner of this big shipment. Me! They investigated my credit and found out I was a mere doctor, and they canceled. This was illegal. I sued them. But as I didn't have the money to fight them I sold the suit to a Wall Street lawyer for twenty thousand dollars. He fought it and was winning. They settled with him out of court for more than a million. But on the way back from Cairo, flying, there was a crash. All on board died. I have this guilt on my conscience, of being the murderer of that lawyer. Although he was a crook."

Wilhelm thought, I must be a real jerk to sit and listen to such impossible stories. I guess I am a sucker for people who talk about the deeper things of life, even the way he does.

"We scientific men speak of irrational guilt, Wilhelm," said Dr. Tamkin, as if Wilhelm were a pupil in his class. "But in such a situation, because of the money, I wished him harm. I realize it. This isn't the time to describe all the details, but the money made me guilty. *M*oney and *M*urder both begin with *M*. *M*achinery. *M*ischief."

Wilhelm, his mind thinking for him at random, said, "What about *M*ercy? *M*ilk-of-human-kindness?"

"One fact should be clear to you by now. Money-making is aggression. That's the whole thing. The functionalistic explanation is the only one. People come to the market to kill. They say, 'I'm going to make a killing.' It's not accidental. Only they haven't got the genuine courage to kill, and they erect a symbol of it. The money. They make a killing by a fantasy. Now, counting and number is always a sadistic activity. Like hitting. In the Bible, the Jews wouldn't allow you to count them. They knew it was sadistic."

"I don't understand what you mean," said Wilhelm. A strange uneasiness tore at him. The day was growing too warm and his head felt dim. "What makes them want to kill?"

"By and by, you'll get the drift," Dr. Tamkin assured him. His amazing eyes had some of the rich dryness of a brown fur. Innumerable crystalline hairs or spicules of light glittered in their bold surfaces. "You can't understand without first spending years on the study of the ultimates of human and animal behavior, the deep chemical, organismic, and spiritual secrets of life. I am a psychological poet."

"If you're this kind of poet," said Wilhelm, whose fingers in his pocket were feeling in the little envelopes for the Phenaphen capsules, "what are you doing on the market?"

"That's a good question. Maybe I am better at speculation because I don't care. Basically, I don't wish hard enough for money, and therefore I come with a cool head to it."

Wilhelm thought, Oh, sure! That's an answer, is it? I bet that if I took a strong attitude he'd back down on everything. He'd grovel in front of me. The way he looks at me on the sly, to see if I'm being taken in! He swallowed his Phenaphen pill with a long gulp of water. The rims of his eyes grew red as it went down. And then he felt calmer.

"Let me see if I can give you an answer that will satisfy you," said Dr. Tamkin. His flapjacks were set before him. He spread the butter on them, poured on brown maple syrup, quartered them, and began to eat with hard, active, muscular jaws which sometimes gave a creak at the hinges. He pressed the handle of his knife against his chest and said, "In here, the human bosom—mine, yours, everybody's—there isn't just one soul. There's a lot of souls. But there are two main ones, the real soul and a pretender soul. Now! Every man realizes that he has to love something or somebody. He feels that he must go outward. 'If thou canst not love, what art thou?' Are you with me?"

"Yes, Doc, I think so," said Wilhelm listening—a little skeptically but nonetheless hard.

"'What art thou?' Nothing. That's the answer. Nothing. In the heart of hearts—Nothing! So of course you can't stand that and want to be Something, and you try. But instead of being this Something, the man puts it over on everybody instead. You can't be that strict to yourself. You love a *little*. Like you have a dog" (*Scissors!*) "or give some money to a charity drive. Now that isn't love, is it? What is it? Egotism, pure and simple. It's a way to love the pretender soul. Vanity. Only vanity, is what it is. And social control. The interest of the pretender soul is the same as the interest of the social life, the society mechanism. This is the main tragedy of human life. Oh, it is terrible! Terrible! You are not free. Your own betrayer is inside of you and sells you out. You have to obey him like a slave. He makes you work like a horse. And for what? For who?"

"Yes, for what?" The doctor's words caught Wilhelm's heart. "I couldn't agree more," he said. "When do we get free?"

"The purpose is to keep the whole thing going. The true soul is the one that pays the price. It suffers and gets sick, and it realizes that the pretender can't be loved. Because the pretender is a lie. The true soul loves the truth. And when the true soul feels like this, it wants to kill the pretender. The love has turned into hate. Then you become dangerous. A killer. You have to kill the deceiver."

"Does this happen to everybody?"

The doctor answered simply, "Yes, to everybody. Of course, for simplification purposes, I have spoken of the soul; it isn't a scientific term, but it helps you to understand it. Whenever the slayer slays, he wants to slay the soul in him which has gypped and deceived him. Who is his enemy? Him. And his lover? Also. Therefore, all suicide is murder, and all murder is suicide. It's the one and identical phenomenon. Biologically, the pretender soul takes away the energy of the true soul and makes it feeble, like a parasite. It happens unconsciously, unawaringly, in the depths of the organism. Ever take up parasitology?"

"No, it's my dad who's the doctor."

"You should read a book about it."

Wilhelm said, "But this means that the world is full of murderers. So it's not the world. It's a kind of hell."

"Sure," the doctor said. "At least a kind of purgatory. You walk on the bodies. They are all around. I can hear them cry *de profundis* and wring their hands. I hear them, poor human beasts. I can't help hearing. And my eyes are open to it. I have to cry, too. This is the human tragedy-comedy."

Wilhelm tried to capture his vision. And again the doctor looked untrustworthy to him, and he doubted him. "Well," he said, "there are also kind, ordinary, helpful people. They're— out in the country. All over. What kind of morbid stuff do you read, anyway?" The doctor's room was full of books.

"I read the best of literature, science and philosophy," Dr. Tamkin said. Wilhelm had observed that in his room even the TV aerial was set upon a pile of volumes. "Korzybski, Aristotle, Freud, W. H. Sheldon, and all the great poets. You answer me like a layman. You haven't applied your mind strictly to this."

"Very interesting," said Wilhelm. He was aware that he hadn't applied his mind strictly to anything. "You don't have to think I'm a dummy, though. I have ideas, too." A glance at the clock told him that the market would soon open. They could spare a few minutes yet. There were still more things he wanted to hear from Tamkin. He realized that Tamkin spoke faultily, but then scientific men were not always strictly literate. It was the description of the two souls that had awed him. In Tommy he saw the pretender. And even Wilky might not be himself. Might the name of his true soul be the one by which his old grandfather had called him—Velvel? The name of a soul, however, must be only that—soul. What did it look like? Does my soul look like me? Is there a soul that looks like Dad? Like Tamkin? Where does the true soul get its strength? Why does it have to love truth? Wilhelm was tormented, but tried to be oblivious to his torment. Secretly, he prayed the doctor would give him some useful advice and transform his life. "Yes, I understand you," he said. "It isn't lost on me."

"I never said you weren't intelligent, but only you just haven't made a study of it all. As a matter of fact you're a profound personality with very profound creative capacities but also disturbances. I've been concerned with you, and for some time I've been treating you."

"Without my knowing it? I haven't felt you doing anything. What do you mean? I don't think I like being treated without my knowledge. I'm of two minds. What's the matter, don't you think I'm normal?" And he really was divided in mind.

That the doctor cared about him pleased him. This was what he craved, that someone should care about him, wish him well. Kindness, mercy, he wanted. But—and here he retracted his heavy shoulders in his peculiar way, drawing his hands up into his sleeves; his feet moved uneasily under the table—but he was worried, too, and even somewhat indignant. For what right had Tamkin to meddle without being asked? What kind of privileged life did this man lead? He took other people's money and speculated with it. Everybody came under his care. No one could have secrets from him.

The doctor looked at him with his deadly brown, heavy, impenetrable eyes, his naked shining head, his red hanging underlip, and said, "You have lots of guilt in you."

Wilhelm helplessly admitted, as he felt the heat rise to his wide face, "Yes, I think so too. But personally," he added, "I don't feel like a murderer. I always try to lay off. It's the others who get me. You know—make me feel oppressed. And if you don't mind, and it's all the same to you, I would rather know it when you start to treat me. And now, Tamkin, for Christ's sake, they're putting out the lunch menus already. Will you sign the check, and let's go!"

Tamkin did as he asked, and they rose. They were passing the bookkeeper's desk when he took out a substantial bundle of onionskin papers and said, "These are receipts of the transactions. Duplicates. You'd better keep them as the account is in your name and you'll need them for income taxes. And here is a copy of a poem I wrote yesterday."

"I have to leave something at the desk for my father," Wilhelm said, and he put his hotel bill in an envelope with a note. *Dear Dad, Please carry me this month, Yours, W.* He watched the clerk with his sullen pug's profile and his stiff-necked look push the envelope into his father's box.

"May I ask you really why you and your dad had words?" said Dr. Tamkin, who had hung back, waiting.

"It was about my future," said Wilhelm. He hurried down the stairs with swift steps, like a tower in motion, his hands in his trousers pockets. He was ashamed to discuss the matter. "He says there's a reason why I can't go back to my old territory, and there is. I told everybody I was going to be an officer of the corporation. And I was supposed to. It was promised.

But then they welshed because of the son-in-law. I bragged and made myself look big."

"If you was humble enough, you could go back. But it doesn't make much difference. We'll make you a good living on the market."

They came into the sunshine of upper Broadway, not clear but throbbing through the dust and fumes, a false air of gas visible at eye-level as it spurted from the bursting buses. From old habit, Wilhelm turned up the collar of his jacket.

"Just a technical question," Wilhelm said. "What happens if your losses are bigger than your deposit?"

"Don't worry. They have ultra-modern electronic book-keeping machinery, and it won't let you get in debt. It puts you out automatically. But I want you to read this poem. You haven't read it yet."

Light as a locust, a helicopter bringing mail from Newark Airport to La Guardia sprang over the city in a long leap.

The paper Wilhelm unfolded had ruled borders in red ink. He read:

MECHANISM VS FUNCTIONALISM
ISM VS HISM

If thee thyself couldst only see
Thy greatness that is and yet to be,
Thou would feel joy-beauty-what ecstasy.
They are at thy feet, earth-moon-sea, the trinity.

Why-forth then dost thou tarry
And partake thee only of the crust
And skim the earth's surface narry
When all creations art thy just?

Seek ye then that which art not there
In thine own glory let thyself rest.
Witness. Thy power is not bare.
Thou art King. Thou art at thy best.

Look then right before thee.
Open thine eyes and see.
At the foot of Mt. Serenity
Is thy cradle to eternity.

Utterly confused, Wilhelm said to himself explosively, What kind of mishmash, claptrap is this! What does he want from me? Damn him to hell, he might as well hit me on the head, and lay me out, kill me. What does he give me this for? What's the purpose? Is it a deliberate test? Does he want to mix me up? He's already got me mixed up completely. I was never good at riddles. Kiss those seven hundred bucks good-by, and call it one more mistake in a long line of mistakes— Oh, Mama, what a line! He stood near the shining window of a fancy fruit store, holding Tamkin's paper, rather dazed, as though a charge of photographer's flash powder had gone up in his eyes.

But he's waiting for my reaction. I have to say something to him about his poem. It really is no joke. What will I tell him? Who is this King? The poem is written *to* someone. But who? I can't even bring myself to talk. I feel too choked and strangled. With all the books he reads, how come the guy is so illiterate? And why do people just naturally assume that you'll know what they're talking about? No. I don't know, and nobody knows. The planets don't, the stars don't, infinite space doesn't. It doesn't square with Planck's Constant or anything else. So what's the good of it? Where's the need of it? What does he mean here by Mount Serenity? Could it be a figure of speech for Mount Everest? As he says people are all committing suicide, maybe those guys who climbed Everest were only trying to kill themselves, and if we want peace we should stay at the foot of the mountain. In the here-and-now. But it's also here-and-now on the slope, and on the top, where they climbed to seize the day. Surface narry is something he can't mean, I don't believe. I'm about to start foaming at the mouth. "Thy cradle . . ." *Who* is resting in his cradle—in his glory? My thoughts are at an end. I feel the wall. No more. So ——k it all! The money and everything. Take it away! When I have the money they eat me alive, like those piranha fish in the movie about the Brazilian jungle. It was hideous when they ate up that Brahma bull in the river. He turned pale, just like clay, and in five minutes nothing was left except the skeleton still in one piece, floating away. When I haven't got it any more, at least they'll let me alone.

"Well, what do you think of this?" said Dr. Tamkin. He gave a special sort of wise smile, as though Wilhelm must now see what kind of man he was dealing with.

"Nice. Very nice. Have you been writing long?"

"I've been developing this line of thought for years and years. You follow it all the way?"

"I'm trying to figure out who this Thou is."

"Thou? Thou is you."

"Me! Why? This applies to *me*?"

"Why shouldn't it apply to you. You were in my mind when I composed it. Of course, the hero of the poem is sick humanity. If it would open its eyes it would be great."

"Yes, but how do I get into this?"

"The main idea of the poem is *con*struct or *de*struct. There is no ground in between. Mechanism is *de*struct. Money of course is *de*struct. When the last grave is dug, the gravedigger will have to be paid. If you could have confidence in nature you would not have to fear. It would keep you up. Creative is nature. Rapid. Lavish. Inspirational. It shapes leaves. It rolls the waters of the earth. Man is the chief of this. All creations are his just inheritance. You don't know what you've got within you. A person either creates or he destroys. There is no neutrality . . .

"I realized you were no beginner," said Wilhelm with propriety. "I have only one criticism to make. I think 'why-forth' is wrong. You should write 'Wherefore then dost thou . . .' " And he reflected, So? I took a gamble. It'll have to be a miracle, though, to save me. My money will be gone, then it won't be able to destruct me. He can't just take and lose it, though. He's in it, too. I think he's in a bad way himself. He must be. I'm sure because, come to think of it, he sweated blood when he signed that check. But what have I let myself in for? The waters of the earth are going to roll over me.

V

Patiently, in the window of the fruit store, a man with a scoop spread crushed ice between his rows of vegetables. There were also Persian melons, lilacs, tulips with radiant black at the middle. The many street noises came back after a little while from the caves of the sky. Crossing the tide of Broadway traffic, Wilhelm was saying to himself, The reason Tamkin lectures me is that somebody has lectured him, and the reason for the poem is that he wants to give me good advice. Everybody seems to know something. Even fellows like Tamkin. Many people know what to do, but how many can do it?

He believed that he must, that he could and would recover the good things, the happy things, the easy tranquil things of life. He had made mistakes, but he could overlook these. He had been a fool, but that could be forgiven. The time wasted—must be relinquished. What else could one do about it? Things were too complex, but they might be reduced to simplicity again. Recovery was possible. First he had to get out of the city. No, first he had to pull out his money. . . .

From the carnival of the street—pushcarts, accordion and fiddle, shoeshine, begging, the dust going round like a woman on stilts—they entered the narrow crowded theater of the brokerage office. From front to back it was filled with the Broadway crowd. But how was lard doing this morning? From the rear of the hall Wilhelm tried to read the tiny figures. The German manager was looking through his binoculars. Tamkin placed himself on Wilhelm's left and covered his conspicuous bald head. "The guy'll ask me about the margin," he muttered. They passed, however, unobserved. "Look, the lard has held its place," he said.

Tamkin's eyes must be very sharp to read the figures over so many heads and at this distance—another respect in which he was unusual.

The room was always crowded. Everyone talked. Only at the front could you hear the flutter of the wheels within the board. Teletyped news items crossed the illuminated screen above.

"Lard. Now what about rye?" said Tamkin, rising on his toes. Here he was a different man, active and impatient. He parted people who stood in his way. His face turned resolute, and on either side of his mouth odd bulges formed under his mustache. Already he was pointing out to Wilhelm the appearance of a new pattern on the board. "There's something up today," he said.

"Then why'd you take so long with breakfast?" said Wilhelm.

There were no reserved seats in the room, only customary ones. Tamkin always sat in the second row, on the commodities side of the aisle. Some of his acquaintances kept their hats on the chairs for him.

"Thanks. Thanks," said Tamkin, and he told Wilhelm, "I fixed it up yesterday."

"That was a smart thought," said Wilhelm. They sat down.

With folded hands, by the wall, sat an old Chinese business-man in a seersucker coat. Smooth and fat, he wore a white Vandyke. One day Wilhelm had seen him on Riverside Drive pushing two little girls along in a baby carriage—his grand-children. Then there were two women in their fifties, supposed to be sisters, shrewd and able money-makers, according to Tamkin. They had never a word to say to Wilhelm. But they would chat with Tamkin. Tamkin talked to everyone.

Wilhelm sat between Mr. Rowland, who was elderly, and Mr. Rappaport, who was very old. Yesterday Rowland had told him that in the year 1908, when he was a junior at Harvard, his mother had given him twenty shares of steel for his birthday, and then he had started to read the financial news and had never practiced law but instead followed the market for the rest of his life. Now he speculated only in soy beans, of which he had made a specialty. By his conservative method, said Tamkin, he cleared two hundred a week. Small potatoes, but then he was a bachelor, retired, and didn't need money.

"Without dependents," said Tamkin. "He doesn't have the problems that you and I do."

Did Tamkin have dependents? He had everything that it was possible for a man to have—science, Greek, chemistry, poetry, and now dependents too. That beautiful girl with epilepsy, perhaps. He often said that she was a pure, marvelous, spiritual child who had no knowledge of the world. He protected her, and, if he was not lying, adored her. And if you encouraged Tamkin by believing him, or even if you refrained from ques-tioning him, his hints became more daring. Sometimes he said that he paid for her music lessons. Sometimes he seemed to have footed the bill for the brother's camera expedition to Brazil. And he spoke of paying for the support of the orphaned child of a dead sweetheart. These hints, made dully as asides, grew by repetition into sensational claims.

"For myself, I don't need much," said Tamkin. "But a man can't live for himself and I need the money for certain impor-tant things. What do you figure you have to have, to get by?"

"Not less than fifteen grand, after taxes. That's for my wife and the two boys."

"Isn't there anybody else?" said Tamkin with a shrewdness almost cruel. But his look grew more sympathetic as Wilhelm stumbled, not willing to recall another grief.

"Well—there was. But it wasn't a money matter."

"I should hope!" said Tamkin. "If love is love, it's free. Fifteen grand, though, isn't too much for a man of your intelligence to ask out of life. Fools, hard-hearted criminals, and murderers have millions to squander. They burn up the world —oil, coal, wood, metal, and soil, and suck even the air and the sky. They consume, and they give back no benefit. A man like you, humble for life, who wants to feel and live, has trouble— not wanting," said Tamkin in his parenthetical fashion, "to exchange an ounce of soul for a pound of social power—he'll never make it without help in a world like this. But don't you worry." Wilhelm grasped at this assurance. "Just you never mind. We'll go easily beyond your figure."

Dr. Tamkin gave Wilhelm comfort. He often said that he had made as much as a thousand a week in commodities. Wilhelm had examined the receipts, but until this moment it had never occurred to him that there must be debit slips too; he had been shown only the credits.

"But fifteen grand is not an ambitious figure," Tamkin was telling him. "For that you don't have to wear yourself out on the road, dealing with narrow-minded people. A lot of them don't like Jews, either, I suppose?"

"I can't afford to notice. I'm lucky when I have my occupation. Tamkin, do you mean you can save our money?"

"Oh, did I forget to mention what I did before closing yesterday? You see, I closed out one of the lard contracts and bought a hedge of December rye. The rye is up three points already and takes some of the sting out. But lard will go up, too."

"Where? God, yes, you're right," said Wilhelm, eager, and got to his feet to look. New hope freshened his heart. "Why didn't you tell me before?"

And Tamkin, smiling like a benevolent magician, said, "You must learn to have trust. The slump in lard can't last. And just take a look at eggs. Didn't I predict they couldn't go any lower? They're rising and rising. If we had taken eggs we'd be far ahead."

"Then why didn't we take them?"

"We were just about to. I had a buying order in at .24, but the tide turned at .26¼ and we barely missed. Never mind. Lard will go back to last year's levels."

Maybe. But when? Wilhelm could not allow his hopes to grow too strong. However, for a little while he could breathe more easily. Late-morning trading was getting active. The shining numbers whirred on the board, which sounded like a huge cage of artificial birds. Lard fluctuated between two points, but rye slowly climbed.

He closed his strained, greatly earnest eyes briefly and nodded his Buddha's head, too large to suffer such uncertainties. For several moments of peace he was removed to his small yard in Roxbury.

He breathed in the sugar of the pure morning.

He heard the long phrases of the birds.

No enemy wanted his life.

Wilhelm thought, I will get out of here. I don't belong in New York any more. And he sighed like a sleeper.

Tamkin said, "Excuse me," and left his seat. He could not sit still in the room but passed back and forth between the stocks and commodities sections. He knew dozens of people and was continually engaging in discussions. Was he giving advice, gathering information, or giving it, or practicing— whatever mysterious profession he practiced? Hypnotism? Perhaps he could put people in a trance while he talked to them. What a rare, peculiar bird he was, with those pointed shoulders, that bare head, his loose nails, almost claws, and those brown, soft, deadly, heavy eyes.

He spoke of things that mattered, and as very few people did this he could take you by surprise, excite you, move you. Maybe he wished to do good, maybe give himself a lift to a higher level, maybe believe his own prophecies, maybe touch his own heart. Who could tell? He had picked up a lot of strange ideas; Wilhelm could only suspect, he could not say with certainty, that Tamkin hadn't made them his own.

Now Tamkin and he were equal partners, but Tamkin had

put up only three hundred dollars. Suppose he did this not only once but five times; then an investment of fifteen hundred dollars gave him five thousand to speculate with. If he had power of attorney in every case, he could shift the money from one account to another. No, the German probably kept an eye on him. Nevertheless it was possible. Calculations like this made Wilhelm feel ill. Obviously Tamkin was a plunger. But how did he get by? He must be in his fifties. How did he support himself? Five years in Egypt; Hollywood before that; Michigan; Ohio; Chicago. A man of fifty has supported himself for at least thirty years. You could be sure that Tamkin had never worked in a factory or in an office. How did he make it? His taste in clothes was horrible, but he didn't buy cheap things. He wore corduroy or velvet shirts from Clyde's, painted neckties, striped socks. There was a slightly acid or pasty smell about his person; for a doctor, he didn't bathe much. Also, Dr. Tamkin had a good room at the Gloriana and had had it for about a year. But so was Wilhelm himself a guest, with an unpaid bill at present in his father's box. Did the beautiful girl with the skirts and belts pay him? Was he defrauding his so-called patients? So many questions impossible to answer could not be asked about an honest man. Nor perhaps about a sane man. Was Tamkin a lunatic, then? That sick Mr. Perls at breakfast had said that there was no easy way to tell the sane from the mad, and he was right about that in any big city and especially in New York—the end of the world, with its complexity and machinery, bricks and tubes, wires and stones, holes and heights. And was everybody crazy here? What sort of people did you see? Every other man spoke a language entirely his own, which he had figured out by private thinking; he had his own ideas and peculiar ways. If you wanted to talk about a glass of water, you had to start back with God creating the heavens and earth; the apple; Abraham; Moses and Jesus; Rome; the Middle Ages; gunpowder; the Revolution; back to Newton; up to Einstein; then war and Lenin and Hitler. After reviewing this and getting it all straight again you could proceed to talk about a glass of water. "I'm fainting, please get me a little water." You were lucky even then to make yourself understood. And this happened over and over and over with everyone you met. You had to translate and translate, explain and explain, back and forth, and it was the punishment of hell itself not to understand or be understood, not to know the crazy from the sane, the wise from the fools, the young from the old or the sick from the well. The fathers were no fathers and the sons no sons. You had to talk with yourself in the daytime and reason with yourself at night. Who else was there to talk to in a city like New York?

A queer look came over Wilhelm's face with its eyes turned up and his silent mouth with its high upper lip. He went several degrees further—when you are like this, dreaming that everybody is outcast, you realize that this must be one of the small matters. There is a larger body, and from this you cannot be separated. The glass of water fades out. You do not go from simple *a* and simple *b* to the great *x* and *y*, nor does it matter whether you agree about the glass but, far beneath such details, what Tamkin would call the real soul says plain and understandable things to everyone. There sons and fathers are themselves, and a glass of water is only an ornament; it makes a hoop of brightness on the cloth; it is an angel's mouth. There truth for everybody may be found, and confusion is only—only temporary, thought Wilhelm.

The idea of this larger body had been planted in him a few days ago beneath Times Square, when he had gone downtown to pick up tickets for the baseball game on Saturday (a double-header at the Polo Grounds). He was going through an underground corridor, a place he had always hated and hated more than ever now. On the walls between the advertisements were words in chalk: "Sin No More," and "Do Not Eat the Pig," he had particularly noticed. And in the dark tunnel, in the haste, heat, and darkness which disfigure and make freaks and fragments of nose and eyes and teeth, all of a sudden, unsought, a general love for all these imperfect and lurid-looking people burst out in Wilhelm's breast. He loved them. One and all, he passionately loved them. They were his brothers and his sisters. He was imperfect and disfigured himself, but what difference did that make if he was united with them by this blaze of love? And as he walked he began to say, "Oh my brothers—my brothers and my sisters," blessing them all as well as himself.

So what did it matter how many languages there were, or

how hard it was to describe a glass of water? Or matter that a few minutes later he didn't feel anything like a brother toward the man who sold him the tickets?

On that very same afternoon he didn't hold so high an opinion of this same onrush of loving kindness. What did it come to? As they had the capacity and must use it once in a while, people were bound to have such involuntary feelings. It was only another one of those subway things. Like having a hard-on at random. But today, his day of reckoning, he consulted his memory again and thought, I must go back to that. That's the right clue and may do me the most good. Something very big. Truth, like.

The old fellow on the right, Mr. Rappaport, was nearly blind and kept asking Wilhelm, "What's the new figure on November wheat? Give me July soy beans too." When you told him he didn't say thank you. He said, "Okay," instead, or, "Check," and turned away until he needed you again. He was very old, older even than Dr. Adler, and if you believed Tamkin he had once been the Rockefeller of the chicken business and had retired with a large fortune.

Wilhelm had a queer feeling about the chicken industry, that it was sinister. On the road, he frequently passed chicken farms. Those big, rambling, wooden buildings out in the neglected fields; they were like prisons. The lights burned all night in them to cheat the poor hens into laying. Then the slaughter. Pile all the coops of the slaughtered on end, and in one week they'd go higher than Mount Everest or Mount Serenity. The blood filling the Gulf of Mexico. The chicken shit, acid, burning the earth.

How old—old this Mr. Rappaport was! Purple stains were buried in the flesh of his nose, and the cartilage of his ear was twisted like a cabbage heart. Beyond remedy by glasses, his eyes were smoky and faded.

"Read me that soy-bean figure now, boy," he said, and Wilhelm did. He thought perhaps the old man might give him a tip, or some useful advice or information about Tamkin. But no. He only wrote memoranda on a pad, and put the pad in his pocket. He let no one see what he had written. And Wilhelm thought this was the way a man who had grown rich by the murder of millions of animals, little chickens, would act. If there was a life to come he might have to answer for the killing of all those chickens. What if they all were waiting? But if there was a life to come, everybody would have to answer. But if there was a life to come, the chickens themselves would be all right.

Well! What stupid ideas he was having this morning. Phooey!

Finally old Rappaport did address a few remarks to Wilhelm. He asked him whether he had reserved his seat in the synagogue for Yom Kippur.

"No," said Wilhelm.

"Well, you better hurry up if you expect to say *Yiskor* for your parents. I never miss."

And Wilhelm thought, Yes, I suppose I should say a prayer for Mother once in a while. His mother had belonged to the Reform congregation. His father had no religion. At the cemetery Wilhelm had paid a man to say a prayer for her. He was among the tombs and he wanted to be tipped for the *El molai rachamin*. "Thou God of Mercy," Wilhelm thought that meant. *B'gan Aden*—"in Paradise." Singing, they drew it out. *B'gan Ay–den*. The broken bench beside the grave made him wish to do something. Wilhelm often prayed in his own manner. He did not go to the synagogue but he would occasionally perform certain devotions, according to his feelings. Now he reflected, In Dad's eyes I am the wrong kind of Jew. He doesn't like the way I act. Only he is the right kind of Jew. Whatever you are, it always turns out to be the wrong kind.

Mr. Rappaport grumbled and whiffed at his long cigar, and the board, like a swarm of electrical bees, whirred.

"Since you were in the chicken business, I thought you'd speculate in eggs, Mr. Rappaport." Wilhelm, with his warm, panting laugh, sought to charm the old man.

"Oh. Yeah. Loyalty, hey?" said old Rappaport. "I should stick to them. I spent a lot of time amongst chickens. I got to be an expert chicken-sexer. When the chick hatches you have to tell the boys from the girls. It's not easy. You need long, long experience. What do you think, it's a joke? A whole industry depends on it. Yes, now and then I buy a contract eggs. What have you got today?"

Wilhelm said anxiously, "Lard. Rye."

"Buy? Sell?"

"Bought."

"Uh," said the old man. Wilhelm could not determine what he meant by this. But of course you couldn't expect him to make himself any clearer. It was not in the code to give information to anyone. Sick with desire, Wilhelm waited for Mr. Rappaport to make an exception in his case. Just this once! Because it was critical. Silently, by a sort of telepathic concentration, he begged the old man to speak the single word that would save him, give him the merest sign. "Oh, please—please help," he nearly said. If Rappaport would close one eye, or lay his head to one side, or raise his finger and point to a column in the paper or to a figure on his pad. A hint! A hint!

A long perfect ash formed on the end of the cigar, the white ghost of the leaf with all its veins and its fainter pungency. It was ignored, in its beauty, by the old man. For it was beautiful. Wilhelm he ignored as well.

Then Tamkin said to him, "Wilhelm, look at the jump our rye just took."

December rye climbed three points as they tensely watched; the tumblers raced and the machine's lights buzzed.

"A point and a half more, and we can cover the lard losses," said Tamkin. He showed him his calculations on the margin of the *Times.*

"I think you should put in the selling order now. Let's get out with a small loss."

"Get out now? Nothing doing."

"Why not? Why should we wait?"

"Because," said Tamkin with a smiling, almost openly scoffing look, "you've got to keep your nerve when the market starts to go places. Now's when you can make something."

"I'd get out while the getting's good."

"No, you shouldn't lose your head like this. It's obvious to me what the mechanism is, back in the Chicago market. There's a short supply of December rye. Look, it's just gone up another quarter. We should ride it."

"I'm losing my taste for the gamble," said Wilhelm. "You can't feel safe when it goes up so fast. It's liable to come down just as quick."

Dryly, as though he were dealing with a child, Tamkin told him in a tone of tiring patience, "Now listen, Tommy. I have it diagnosed right. If you wish I should sell I can give the sell order. But this is the difference between healthiness and pathology. One is objective, doesn't change his mind every minute, enjoys the risk element. But that's not the neurotic character. The neurotic character—"

"Damn it, Tamkin!" said Wilhelm roughly. "Cut that out. I don't like it. Leave my character out of consideration. Don't pull any more of that stuff on me. I tell you I don't like it."

Tamkin therefore went no further; he backed down. "I meant," he said, softer, "that as a salesman you are basically an artist type. The seller is in the visionary sphere of the business function. And then you're an actor, too."

"No matter what type I am—" An angry and yet weak sweetness rose into Wilhelm's throat. He coughed as though he had the flu. It was twenty years since he had appeared on the screen as an extra. He blew the bagpipes in a film called *Annie Laurie*. Annie had come to warn the young Laird; he would not believe her and called the bagpipers to drown her out. He made fun of her while she wrung her hands. Wilhelm, in a kilt, barelegged, blew and blew and blew and not a sound came out. Of course all the music was recorded. He fell sick with the flu after that and still suffered sometimes from chest weakness.

"Something stuck in your throat?" said Tamkin. "I think maybe you are too disturbed to think clearly. You should try some of my 'here-and-now' mental exercises. It stops you from thinking so much about the future and the past and cuts down confusion."

"Yes, yes, yes, yes," said Wilhelm, his eyes fixed on December rye.

"Nature only knows one thing, and that's the present. Present, present, eternal present, like a big, huge, giant wave— colossal, bright and beautiful, full of life and death, climbing into the sky, standing in the seas. You must go along with the actual, the Here-and-Now, the glory—"

. . . chest weakness, Wilhelm's recollection went on. Margaret nursed him. They had had two rooms of furniture, which was later seized. She sat on the bed and read to him. He made her read for days, and she read stories, poetry, everything in the house. He felt dizzy, stifled when he tried to smoke. They had him wear a flannel vest.

> Come then, Sorrow!
> Sweetest Sorrow!
> Like an own babe I nurse thee on my breast!

Why did he remember that? Why?

"You have to pick out something that's in the actual, immediate present moment," said Tamkin. "And say to yourself here-and-now, here-and-now, here-and-now. 'Where am I?' 'Here.' 'When is it?' 'Now.' Take an object or a person. Anybody. 'Here and now I see a person.' 'Here and now I see a man.' 'Here and now I see a man sitting on a chair.' Take me, for instance. Don't let your mind wander. 'Here and now I see a man in a brown suit. Here and now I see a corduroy shirt.' You have to narrow it down, one item at a time, and not let your imagination shoot ahead. Be in the present. Grasp the hour, the moment, the instant."

Is he trying to hypnotize or con me? Wilhelm wondered. To take my mind off selling? But even if I'm back at seven hundred bucks, then where am I?

As if in prayer, his lids coming down with raised veins, frayed out, on his significant eyes, Tamkin said, " 'Here and now I see a button. Here and now I see the thread that sews the button. Here and now I see the green thread.' " Inch by inch he contemplated himself in order to show Wilhelm how calm it would make him. But Wilhelm was hearing Margaret's voice as she read, somewhat unwillingly,

> Come then, Sorrow!
> .   .   .   .
>
> I thought to leave thee,
> And deceive thee,
> But now of all the world I love thee best.

Then Mr. Rappaport's old hand pressed his thigh, and he said, "What's my wheat? Those damn guys are blocking the way. I can't see."

VI

Rye was still ahead when they went out to lunch, and lard was holding its own.

They ate in the cafeteria with the gilded front. There was the same art inside as outside. The food looked sumptuous. Whole fishes were framed like pictures with carrots, and the salads were like terraced landscapes or like Mexican pyramids; slices of lemon and onion and radishes were like sun and moon and stars; the cream pies were about a foot thick and the cakes swollen as if sleepers had baked them in their dreams.

"What'll you have?" said Tamkin.

"Not much. I ate a big breakfast. I'll find a table. Bring me some yogurt and crackers and a cup of tea. I don't want to spend much time over lunch."

Tamkin said, "You've got to eat."

Finding an empty place at this hour was not easy. The old people idled and gossiped over their coffee. The elderly ladies were rouged and mascaraed and hennaed and used blue hair rinse and eye shadow and wore costume jewelry, and many of them were proud and stared at you with expressions that did not belong to their age. Were there no longer any respectable old ladies who knitted and cooked and looked after their grand-children? Wilhelm's grandmother had dressed him in a sailor suit and danced him on her knee, blew on the porridge for him and said, "Admiral, you must eat." But what was the use of re-membering this so late in the day?

He managed to find a table, and Dr. Tamkin came along with a tray piled with plates and cups. He had Yankee pot roast, purple cabbage, potatoes, a big slice of watermelon, and two cups of coffee. Wilhelm could not even swallow his yogurt. His chest pained him still.

At once Tamkin involved him in a lengthy discussion. Did he do it to stall Wilhelm and prevent him from selling out the rye—or to recover the ground lost when he had made Wil-helm angry by hints about the neurotic character? Or did he have no purpose except to talk?

"I think you worry a lot too much about what your wife and your father will say. Do they matter so much?"

Wilhelm replied, "A person can become tired of looking

himself over and trying to fix himself up. You can spend the entire second half of your life recovering from the mistakes of the first half."

"I believe your dad told me he had some money to leave you."

"He probably does have something."

"A lot?"

"Who can tell," said Wilhelm guardedly.

"You ought to think over what you'll do with it."

"I may be too feeble to do anything by the time I get it. If I get anything."

"A thing like this you ought to plan out carefully. Invest it properly." He began to unfold schemes whereby you bought bonds, and used the bonds as security to buy something else and thereby earned twelve per cent safely on your money. Wilhelm failed to follow the details. Tamkin said, "If he made you a gift now, you wouldn't have to pay the inheritance taxes."

Bitterly, Wilhelm told him, "My father's death blots out all other considerations from his mind. He forces me to think about it, too. Then he hates me because he succeeds. When I get desperate—of course I think about money. But I don't want anything to happen to him. I certainly don't want him to die." Tamkin's brown eyes glittered shrewdly at him. "You don't believe it. Maybe it's not psychological. But on my word of honor. A joke is a joke, but I don't want to joke about stuff like this. When he dies, I'll be robbed, like. I'll have no more father."

"You love your old man?"

Wilhelm grasped at this. "Of course, of course I love him. My father. My mother—" As he said this there was a great pull at the very center of his soul. When a fish strikes the line you feel the live force in your hand. A mysterious being beneath the water, driven by hunger, has taken the hook and rushes away and fights, writhing. Wilhelm never identified what struck within him. It did not reveal itself. It got away.

And Tamkin, the confuser of the imagination, began to tell, or to fabricate, the strange history of *his* father. "He was a great singer," he said. "He left us five kids because he fell in love with an opera soprano. I never held it against him, but admired the way he followed the life-principle. I wanted to do the same. Because of unhappiness, at a certain age, the brain starts to die back." (True, true! thought Wilhelm) "Twenty years later I was doing experiments in Eastman Kodak, Rochester, and I found the old fellow. He had five more children." (False, false!) "He wept; he was ashamed. I had nothing against him. I naturally felt strange."

"My dad is something of a stranger to me, too," said Wilhelm, and he began to muse. Where is the familiar person he used to be? Or I used to be? Catherine—she won't even talk to me any more, my own sister. It may not be so much my trouble that Papa turns his back on as my confusion. It's too much. The ruins of life, and on top of that confusion—chaos and old night. Is it an easier farewell for Dad if we don't part friends? He should maybe do it angrily— "Blast you with my curse!" And why, Wilhelm further asked, should he or anybody else pity me; or why should I be pitied sooner than another fellow? It is my childish mind that thinks people are ready to give it just because you need it.

Then Wilhelm began to think about his own two sons and to wonder how he appeared to them, and what they would think of him. Right now he had an advantage through baseball. When he went to fetch them, to go to Ebbets Field, though, he was not himself. He put on a front but he felt as if he had swallowed a fistful of sand. The strange, familiar house, horribly awkward; the dog, Scissors, rolled over on his back and barked and whined. Wilhelm acted as if there were nothing irregular, but a weary heaviness came over him. On the way to Flatbush he would think up anecdotes about old Pigtown and Charlie Ebbets for the boys and reminiscences of the old stars, but it was very heavy going. They did not know how much he cared for them. No. It hurt him greatly and he blamed Margaret for turning them against him. She wanted to ruin him, while she wore the mask of kindness. Up in Roxbury he had to go and explain to the priest, who was not sympathetic. They don't care about individuals, their rules come first. Olive said she would marry him outside the Church when he was divorced. But Margaret would not let go. Olive's father was a pretty decent old guy, an osteopath, and he understood what it was all about. Finally he said, "See here, I have to advise Olive. She is asking me. I am mostly a freethinker myself, but the girl has to live in this town." And by now Wilhelm and Olive had had a great many troubles and she was beginning to dread his days in Roxbury, she said. He trembled at offending this small, pretty, dark girl whom he adored. When she would get up late on Sunday morning she would wake him almost in tears at being late for Mass. He would try to help her hitch her garters and smooth out her slip and dress and even put on her hat with shaky hands; then he would rush her to church and drive in second gear in his forgetful way, trying to apologize and to calm her. She got out a block from church to avoid gossip. Even so she loved him, and she would have married him if he had obtained the divorce. But Margaret must have sensed this. Margaret would tell him he did not really want a divorce; he was afraid of it. He cried, "Take everything I've got, Margaret. Let me go to Reno. Don't you want to marry again?" No. She went out with other men, but took his money. She lived in order to punish him.

Dr. Tamkin told Wilhelm, "Your dad is jealous of you."

Wilhelm smiled. "Of *me*? That's rich."

"Sure. People are always jealous of a man who leaves his wife."

"Oh," said Wilhelm scornfully. "When it comes to wives he wouldn't have to envy me."

"Yes, and your wife envies you, too. She thinks, He's free and goes with young women. Is she getting old?"

"Not exactly old," said Wilhelm, whom the mention of his wife made sad. Twenty years ago, in a neat blue wool suit, in a soft hat made of the same cloth—he could plainly see her. He stooped his yellow head and looked under the hat at her clear, simple face, her living eyes moving, her straight small nose, her jaw beautifully, painfully clear in its form. It was a cool day, but he smelled the odor of pines in the sun, in the granite canyon. Just south of Santa Barbara, this was.

"She's forty-some years old," he said.

"I was married to a lush," said Tamkin. "A painful alcoholic. I couldn't take her out to dinner because she'd say she was going to the ladies' toilet and disappear into the bar. I'd ask the bartenders they shouldn't serve her. But I loved her deeply. She was the most spiritual woman of my entire experience."

"Where is she now?"

"Drowned," said Tamkin. "At Provincetown, Cape Cod. It must have been a suicide. She was that way—suicidal. I tried everything in my power to cure her. Because," said Tamkin, "my real calling is to be a healer. I get wounded. I suffer from it. I would like to escape from the sicknesses of others, but I can't. I am only on loan to myself, so to speak. I belong to humanity."

Liar! Wilhelm inwardly called him. Nasty lies. He invented a woman and killed her off and then called himself a healer, and made himself so earnest he looked like a bad-natured sheep. He's a puffed-up little bogus and humbug with smelly feet. A doctor! A doctor would wash himself. He believes he's making a terrific impression, and he practically invites you to take off your hat when he talks about himself; and he thinks he has an imagination, but he hasn't, neither is he smart.

Then what am I doing with him here, and why did I give him the seven hundred dollars? thought Wilhelm.

Oh, this was a day of reckoning. It was a day, he thought, on which, willing or not, he would take a good close look at the truth. He breathed hard and his misshapen hat came low upon his congested dark blond face. A rude look. Tamkin was a charlatan, and furthermore he was desperate. And furthermore, Wilhelm had always known this about him. But he appeared to have worked it out at the back of his mind that Tamkin for thirty or forty years had gotten through many a tight place, that he would get through this crisis too and bring him, Wilhelm, to safety also. And Wilhelm realized that he was on Tamkin's back. It made him feel that he had virtually left the ground and was riding upon the other man. He was in the air. It was for Tamkin to take the steps.

The doctor, if he was a doctor, did not look anxious. But then his face did not have much variety. Talking always about spontaneous emotion and open receptors and free impulses, he was about as expressive as a pincushion. When his hypnotic spell failed, his big underlip made him look weak-minded. Fear stared from his eyes, sometimes, so humble as to make you sorry for him. Once or twice Wilhelm had seen that look. Like a dog, he thought. Perhaps he didn't look it now, but he was very nervous. Wilhelm knew, but he could not afford to recognize this too openly. The doctor needed a little room, a little time. He should not be pressed now. So Tamkin went on, telling his tales.

Wilhelm said to himself, I am on his back—his back. I gambled seven hundred bucks, so I must take this ride. I have to go along with him. It's too late. I can't get off.

"You know," Tamkin said, "that blind old man Rappaport—he's pretty close to totally blind—is one of the most interesting personalities around here. If you could only get him to tell his true story. It's fascinating. This is what he told me. You often hear about bigamists with a secret life. But this old man never hid anything from anybody. He's a regular patriarch. Now, I'll tell you what he did. He had two whole families, separate and apart, one in Williamsburg and the other in the Bronx. The two wives knew about each other. The wife in the Bronx was younger; she's close to seventy now. When he got sore at one wife he went to live with the other one. Meanwhile he ran his chicken business in New Jersey. By one wife he had four kids, and by the other six. They're all grown, but they never have met their half-brothers and sisters and don't want to. The whole bunch of them are listed in the telephone book."

"I can't believe it," said Wilhelm.

"He told me this himself. And do you know what else? While he had his eyesight he used to read a lot, but the only books he would read were by Theodore Roosevelt. He had a set in each of the places where he lived, and he brought his kids up on those books."

"Please," said Wilhelm, "don't feed me any more of this stuff, will you? Kindly do not—"

"In telling you this," said Tamkin with one of his hypnotic subtleties, "I do have a motive. I want you to see how some people free themselves from morbid guilt feelings and follow their instincts. Innately, the female knows how to cripple by sickening a man with guilt. It is a very special *de*struct, and she sends her curse to make a fellow impotent. As if she says, 'Unless I allow it, you will never more be a man.' But men like my old dad or Mr. Rappaport answer, 'Woman, what art thou to me?' You can't do that yet. You're a halfway case. You want to follow your instinct, but you're too worried still. For instance, about your kids—"

"Now look here," said Wilhelm, stamping his feet. "One thing! Don't bring up my boys. Just lay off."

"I was only going to say that they are better off than with conflicts in the home."

"I'm deprived of my children." Wilhelm bit his lip. It was too late to turn away. The anguish struck him. "I pay and pay. I never see them. They grow up without me. She makes them like herself. She'll bring them up to be my enemies. Please let's not talk about this."

But Tamkin said, "Why do you let her make you suffer so? It defeats the original object in leaving her. Don't play her game. Now, Wilhelm, I'm trying to do you some good. I want to tell you, don't marry suffering. Some people do. They get married to it, and sleep and eat together, just as husband and wife. If they go with joy they think it's adultery."

When Wilhelm heard this he had, in spite of himself, to admit that there was a great deal in Tamkin's words. Yes, thought Wilhelm, suffering is the only kind of life they are sure they can have, and if they quit suffering they're afraid they'll have nothing. He knows it. This time the faker knows what he's talking about.

Looking at Tamkin he believed he saw all this confessed from his usually barren face. Yes, yes, he too. One hundred false-hoods, but at last one truth. Howling like a wolf from the city window. No one can bear it any more. Everyone is so full of it that at last everybody must proclaim it. It! It!

Then suddenly Wilhelm rose and said, "That's enough of this. Tamkin, let's go back to the market."

"I haven't finished my melon."

"Never mind that. You've had enough to eat. I want to go back."

Dr. Tamkin slid the two checks across the table. "Who paid yesterday? It's your turn, I think."

It was not until they were leaving the cafeteria that Wilhelm remembered definitely that he had paid yesterday too. But it wasn't worth arguing about.

Tamkin kept repeating as they walked down the street that there were many who were dedicated to suffering. But he told Wilhelm, "I'm optimistic in your case, and I have seen a world of maladjustment. There's hope for you. You don't really want to destroy yourself. You're trying hard to keep your feelings open, Wilhelm. I can see it. Seven per cent of this country is committing suicide by alcohol. Another three, maybe, narcotics. Another sixty just fading away into dust by boredom. Twenty more who have sold their souls to the Devil. Then there's a small percentage of those who want to live. That's the only significant thing in the whole world of today. Those are the only two classes of people there are. Some want to live, but the great majority don't." This fantastic Tamkin began to surpass himself. "They don't. Or else, why these wars? I'll tell you more," he said. "The love of the dying amounts to one thing; they want you to die with them. It's because they love you. Make no mistake."

True, true! thought Wilhelm, profoundly moved by these revelations. How does he know these things? How can he be such a jerk, and even perhaps an operator, a swindler, and understand so well what gives? I believe what he says. It simplifies much—everything. People are dropping like flies. I am trying to stay alive and work too hard at it. That's what's turning my brains. This working hard defeats its own end. At what point should I start over? Let me go back a ways and try once more.

Only a few hundred yards separated the cafeteria from the broker's, and within that short space Wilhelm turned again, in measurable degrees, from these wide considerations to the problems of the moment. The closer he approached to the market, the more Wilhelm had to think about money.

They passed the newsreel theater where the ragged shoeshine kids called after them. The same old bearded man with his bandaged beggar face and his tiny ragged feet and the old press clipping on his fiddle case to prove he had once been a concert violinist, pointed his bow at Wilhelm, saying, "You!" Wilhelm went by with worried eyes, bent on crossing Seventy-second Street. In full tumult the great afternoon current raced for Columbus Circle, where the mouth of midtown stood open and the skyscrapers gave back the yellow fire of the sun.

As they approached the polished stone front of the new office building, Dr. Tamkin said, "Well, isn't that old Rappaport by the door? I think he should carry a white cane, but he will never admit there's a single thing the matter with his eyes."

Mr. Rappaport did not stand well; his knees were sunk, while his pelvis only half filled his trousers. His suspenders held them, gaping.

He stopped Wilhelm with an extended hand, having somehow recognized him. In his deep voice he commanded him, "Take me to the cigar store."

"You want me—? Tamkin!" Wilhelm whispered, "You take him."

Tamkin shook his head. "He wants you. Don't refuse the old gentleman." Significantly he said in a lower voice. "This minute is another instance of the 'here-and-now.' You have to live in this very minute, and you don't want to. A man asks you for help. Don't think of the market. It won't run away. Show your respect to the old boy. Go ahead. That may be more valuable."

"Take me," said the old chicken merchant again.

Greatly annoyed, Wilhelm wrinkled his face at Tamkin. He took the old man's big but light elbow at the bone. "Well, let's step on it," he said. "Or wait—I want to have a look at the board first to see how we're doing."

But Tamkin had already started Mr. Rappaport forward. He was walking, and he scolded Wilhelm, saying, "Don't leave me standing in the middle of the sidewalk. I'm afraid to get knocked over."

"Let's get a move on. Come." Wilhelm urged him as Tamkin went into the broker's.

The traffic seemed to come down Broadway out of the sky, where the hot spokes of the sun rolled from the south. Hot, stony odors rose from the subway grating in the street.

"These teen-age hoodlums worry me. I'm ascared of these Puerto Rican kids, and these young characters who take dope," said Mr. Rappaport. "They go around all hopped up."

"Hoodlums?" said Wilhelm. "I went to the cemetery and my mother's stone bench was split. I could have broken somebody's neck for that. Which store do you go to?"

"Across Broadway. That La Magnita sign next door to the Automat."

"What's the matter with this store here on this side?"

"They don't carry my brand, that's what's the matter."

Wilhelm cursed, but checked the words.

"What are you talking?"

"Those damn taxis," said Wilhelm. "They want to run every-body down,"

They entered the cool, odorous shop. Mr. Rappaport put away his large cigars with great care in various pockets while Wilhelm muttered, "Come on, you old creeper. What a poky old character! The whole world waits on him." Rappaport did not offer Wilhelm a cigar, but, holding one up, he asked, "What do you say at the size of these, huh? They're Churchill-type cigars."

He barely crawls along, thought Wilhelm. His pants are dropping off because he hasn't got enough flesh for them to stick to. He's almost blind, and covered with spots, but this old man still makes money in the market. Is loaded with dough, probably. And I bet he doesn't give his children any. Some of them must be in their fifties. This is what keeps middle-aged men as children. He's master over the dough. Think—just think! Who controls everything? Old men of this type. With-out needs. They don't need therefore they have. I need, there-fore I don't have. That would be too easy.

"I'm older even than Churchill," said Rappaport.

Now he wanted to talk! But if you asked him a question in the market, he couldn't be bothered to answer.

"I bet you are," said Wilhelm. "Come, let's get going."

"I was a fighter, too, like Churchill," said the old man. "When we licked Spain I went into the Navy. Yes, I was a gob that time. What did I have to lose? Nothing. After the battle of San Juan Hill, Teddy Roosevelt kicked me off the beach."

"Come, watch the curb," said Wilhelm.

"I was curious and wanted to see what went on. I didn't have no business there, but I took a boat and rowed myself to the beach. Two of our guys was dead, layin' under the Ameri-can flag to keep the flies off. So I says to the guy on duty, there, who was the sentry, 'Let's have a look at these guys. I want to see what went on here,' and he says, 'Naw,' but I talked him into it. So he took off the flag and there were these two tall guys, both gentlemen, lying in their boots. They was very tall. The two of them had long mustaches. They were high-society boys. I think one of them was called Fish, from up the Hudson, a big-shot family. When I looked up, there was

Teddy Roosevelt, with his hat off, and he was looking at these fellows, the only ones who got killed there. Then he says to me, 'What's the Navy want here? Have you got orders?' 'No, sir,' I says to him. 'Well, get the hell off the beach, then.'"

Old Rappaport was very proud of this memory. "Everything he said had such snap, such class. Man! I love that Teddy Roosevelt," he said, "I love him!"

Ah, what people are! He is almost not with us, and his life is nearly gone, but T. R. once yelled at him, so he loves him. I guess it is love, too. Wilhelm smiled. So maybe the rest of Tamkin's story was true, about the ten children and the wives and the telephone directory.

He said, "Come on, come on, Mr. Rappaport," and hurried the old man back by the large hollow elbow; he gripped it through the thin cotton cloth. Re-entering the brokerage office where under the lights the tumblers were speeding with the clack of drumsticks upon wooden blocks, more than ever resembling a Chinese theater, Wilhelm strained his eyes to see the board.

The lard figures were unfamiliar. That amount couldn't be lard! They must have put the figures in the wrong slot. He traced the line back to the margin. It was down to .19, and had dropped twenty points since noon. And what about the contract of rye? It had sunk back to its earlier position, and they had lost their chance to sell.

Old Mr. Rappaport said to Wilhelm, "Read me my wheat figure."

"Oh, leave me alone for a minute," he said, and positively hid his face from the old man behind one hand. He looked for Tamkin, Tamkin's bald head, or Tamkin with his gray straw and the cocoa-colored band. He couldn't see him. Where was he? The seats next to Rowland were taken by strangers. He thrust himself over the one on the aisle, Mr. Rappaport's former place, and pushed at the back of the chair until the new occupant, a red-headed man with a thin, determined face, leaned forward to get out of his way but would not surrender the seat. "Where's Tamkin?" Wilhelm asked Rowland.

"Gee, I don't know. Is anything wrong?"

"You must have seen him. He came in a while back."

"No, but I didn't."

Wilhelm fumbled out a pencil from the top pocket of his coat and began to make calculations. His very fingers were numb, and in his agitation he was afraid he made mistakes with the decimal points and went over the subtraction and multiplication like a schoolboy at an exam. His heart, accustomed to many sorts of crisis, was now in a new panic. And, as he had dreaded, he was wiped out. It was unnecessary to ask the German manager. He could see for himself that the electronic bookkeeping device must have closed him out. The manager probably had known that Tamkin wasn't to be trusted, and on that first day he might have warned him. But you couldn't expect him to interfere.

"You get hit?" said Mr. Rowland.

And Wilhelm, quite coolly, said, "Oh, it could have been worse, I guess." He put the piece of paper into his pocket with its cigarette butts and packets of pills. The lie helped him out—although, for a moment, he was afraid he would cry. But he hardened himself. The hardening effort made a violent, vertical pain go through his chest, like that caused by a pocket of air under the collar bones. To the old chicken millionaire, who by this time had become acquainted with the drop in rye and lard, he also denied that anything serious had happened. "It's just one of those temporary slumps. Nothing to be scared about," he said, and remained in possession of himself. His need to cry, like someone in a crowd, pushed and jostled and abused him from behind, and Wilhelm did not dare turn. He said to himself, I will not cry in front of these people. I'll be damned if I'll break down in front of them like a kid, even though I never expect to see them again. No! No! And yet his unshed tears rose and rose and he looked like a man about to drown. But when they talked to him, he answered very distinctly. He tried to speak proudly.

". . . going away?" he heard Rowland ask.

"What?"

"I thought you might be going away too. Tamkin said he was going to Maine this summer for his vacation."

"Oh, going away?"

Wilhelm broke off and went to look for Tamkin in the men's toilet. Across the corridor was the room where the machinery of the board was housed. It hummed and whirred like mechanical birds, and the tubes glittered in the dark. A couple of businessmen with cigarettes in their fingers were having a conversation in the lavatory. At the top of the closet door sat a gray straw hat with a cocoa-colored band. "Tamkin," said Wilhelm. He tried to identify the feet below the door. "Are you in there, Doctor Tamkin?" he said with stifled anger. "Answer me. It's Wilhelm."

The hat was taken down, the latch lifted, and a stranger came out who looked at him with annoyance.

"You waiting?" said one of the businessmen. He was warning Wilhelm that he was out of turn.

"Me? Not me," said Wilhelm. "I'm looking for a fellow."

Bitterly angry, he said to himself that Tamkin would pay him the two hundred dollars at least, his share of the original deposit. "And before he takes the train to Maine, too. Before he spends a penny on vacation—that liar! We went into this as equal partners."

VII

I was the man beneath; Tamkin was on my back, and I thought I was on his. He made me carry him, too, besides Margaret. Like this they ride on me with hoofs and claws. Tear me to pieces, stamp on me and break my bones.

Once more the hoary old fiddler pointed his bow at Wilhelm as he hurried by. Wilhelm rejected his begging and denied the omen. He dodged heavily through traffic and with his quick, small steps ran up the lower stairway of the Gloriana Hotel with its dark-tinted mirrors, kind to people's defects. From the lobby he phoned Tamkin's room, and when no one answered he took the elevator up. A rouged woman in her fifties with a mink stole led three tiny dogs on a leash, high-strung creatures with prominent black eyes, like dwarf deer, and legs like twigs. This was the eccentric Estonian lady who had been moved with her pets to the twelfth floor.

She identified Wilhelm. "You are Doctor Adler's son," she said.

Formally, he nodded.

"I am a dear friend of your father."

He stood in the corner and would not meet her glance, and

she thought he was snubbing her and made a mental note to speak of it to the doctor.

The linen-wagon stood at Tamkin's door, and the chambermaid's key with its big brass tongue was in the lock.

"Has Doctor Tamkin been here?" he asked her.

"No, I haven't seen him."

Wilhelm came in, however, to look around. He examined the photos on the desk, trying to connect the faces with the strange people in Tamkin's stories. Big, heavy volumes were stacked under the double-pronged TV aerial. *Science and Sanity*, he read, and there were several books of poetry. The *Wall Street Journal* hung in separate sheets from the bed-table under the weight of the silver water jug. A bathrobe with lightning streaks of red and white was laid across the foot of the bed with a pair of expensive batik pajamas. It was a box of a room, but from the windows you saw the river as far uptown as the bridge, as far downtown as Hoboken. What lay between was deep, azure, dirty, complex, crystal, rusty, with the red bones of new apartments rising on the bluffs of New Jersey, and huge liners in their berths, the tugs with matted beards of cordage. Even the brackish tidal river smell rose this high, like the smell of mop water. From every side he heard pianos, and the voices of men and women singing scales and opera, all mixed, and the sounds of pigeons on the ledges.

Again Wilhelm took the phone. "Can you locate Doctor Tamkin in the lobby for me?" he asked. And when the operator reported that she could not, Wilhelm gave the number of his father's room, but Dr. Adler was not in either. "Well, please give me the masseur. I say the massage room. Don't you understand me? The men's health club. Yes, Max Schilper's—how am I supposed to know the name of it?"

There a strange voice said, "Toktor Adler?" It was the old Czech prizefighter with the deformed nose and ears who was attendant down there and gave out soap, sheets, and sandals. He went away. A hollow endless silence followed. Wilhelm flickered the receiver with his nails, whistled into it, but could not summon either the attendant or the operator.

The maid saw him examining the bottles of pills on Tamkin's table and seemed suspicious of him. He was running low on Phenaphen pills and was looking for something else. But he

swallowed one of his own tablets and went out and rang again
for the elevator. He went down to the health club. Through
the steamy windows, when he emerged, he saw the reflection
of the swimming pool swirling green at the bottom of the low-
est stairway. He went through the locker-room curtains. Two
men wrapped in towels were playing Ping-pong. They were
awkward and the ball bounded high. The Negro in the toilet
was shining shoes. He did not know Dr. Adler by name, and
Wilhelm descended to the massage room. On the tables naked
men were lying. It was not a brightly lighted place, and it was
very hot, and under the white faint moons of the ceiling shone
pale skins. Calendar pictures of pretty girls dressed in tiny
fringes were pinned on the wall. On the first table, eyes deeply
shut in heavy silent luxury lay a man with a full square beard
and short legs, stocky and black-haired. He might have been
an orthodox Russian. Wrapped in a sheet, waiting, the man beside him was newly shaved and red from the steambath. He
had a big happy face and was dreaming. And after him was an
athlete, strikingly muscled, powerful and young, with a strong
white curve to his genital and a half-angry smile on his mouth.
Dr. Adler was on the fourth table, and Wilhelm stood over his
father's pale, slight body. His ribs were narrow and small, his
belly round, white, and high. It had its own being, like something separate. His thighs were weak, the muscles of his arms
had fallen, his throat was creased.

The masseur in his undershirt bent and whispered in his ear,
"It's your son," and Dr. Adler opened his eyes into Wilhelm's
face. At once he saw the trouble in it, and by an instantaneous
reflex he removed himself from the danger of contagion, and
he said serenely, "Well, have you taken my advice, Wilky?"

"Oh, Dad," said Wilhelm.

"To take a swim and get a massage?"

"Did you get my note?" said Wilhelm.

"Yes, but I'm afraid you'll have to ask somebody else, because I can't. I had no idea you were so low on funds. How did
you let it happen? Didn't you lay anything aside?"

"Oh, please, Dad," said Wilhelm, almost bringing his hands
together in a clasp.

"I'm sorry," said the doctor. "I really am. But I have set up a rule. I've thought about it, I believe it is a good rule, and I don't want to change it. You haven't acted wisely. What's the matter?"

"Everything. Just everything. What isn't? I did have a little, but I haven't been very smart."

"You took some gamble? You lost it? Was it Tamkin? I told you, Wilky, not to build on that Tamkin. Did you? I suspect—"

"Yes, Dad, I'm afraid I trusted him."

Dr. Adler surrendered his arm to the masseur, who was using wintergreen oil.

"Trusted! And got taken?"

"I'm afraid I kind of—" Wilhelm glanced at the masseur but he was absorbed in his work. He probably did not listen to conversations. "I did. I might as well say it. I should have listened to you."

"Well, I won't remind you how often I warned you. It must be very painful."

"Yes, Father, it is."

"I don't know how many times you have to be burned in order to learn something. The same mistakes, over and over."

"I couldn't agree with you more," said Wilhelm with a face of despair. "You're so right, Father. It's the same mistakes, and I get burned again and again. I can't seem to—I'm stupid, Dad, I just can't breathe. My chest is all up—I feel choked. I just simply can't catch my breath."

He stared at his father's nakedness. Presently he became aware that Dr. Adler was making an effort to keep his temper. He was on the verge of an explosion. Wilhelm hung his face and said, "Nobody likes bad luck, eh Dad?"

"So! It's bad luck, now. A minute ago it was stupidity."

"It is stupidity—it's some of both. It's true that I can't learn. But I—"

"I don't want to listen to the details," said his father. "And I want you to understand that I'm too old to take on new burdens. I'm just too old to do it. And people who will just wait for help—must *wait* for help. They have got to stop waiting."

"It isn't all a question of money—there are other things a father can give to a son." He lifted up his gray eyes and his nostrils grew wide with a look of suffering appeal that stirred his father even more deeply against him.

He warningly said to him, "Look out, Wilky, you're tiring my patience very much."

"I try not to. But one word from you, just a word, would go a long way. I've never asked you for very much. But you are not a kind man, Father. You don't give the little bit I beg you for."

He recognized that his father was now furiously angry. Dr. Adler started to say something, and then raised himself and gathered the sheet over him as he did so. His mouth opened, wide, dark, twisted, and he said to Wilhelm, "You want to make yourself into my cross. But I am not going to pick up a cross. I'll see you dead, Wilky, by Christ, before I let you do that to me."

"Father, listen! Listen!"

"Go away from me now. It's torture for me to look at you, you slob!" cried Dr. Adler.

Wilhelm's blood rose up madly, in anger equal to his father's, but then it sank down and left him helplessly captive to misery. He said stiffly, and with a strange sort of formality, "Okay, Dad. That'll be enough. That's about all we should say." And he stalked out heavily by the door adjacent to the swimming pool and the steam room, and labored up two long flights from the basement. Once more he took the elevator to the lobby on the mezzanine.

He inquired at the desk for Dr. Tamkin.

The clerk said, "No, I haven't seen him. But I think there's something in the box for you."

"Me? Give it here," said Wilhelm and opened a telephone message from his wife. It read, "Please phone Mrs. Wilhelm on return. Urgent."

Whenever he received an urgent message from his wife he was always thrown into a great fear for the children. He ran to the phone booth, spilled out the change from his pockets onto the little curved steel shelf under the telephone, and dialed the Digby number.

"Yes?" said his wife. Scissors barked in the parlor.

"Margaret?"

"Yes, hello." They never exchanged any other greeting. She instantly knew his voice.

"The boys all right?"

"They're out on their bicycles. Why shouldn't they be all right? Scissors, quiet!"

"Your message scared me," he said. "I wish you wouldn't make 'urgent' so common."

"I had something to tell you."

Her familiar unbending voice awakened in him a kind of hungry longing, not for Margaret but for the peace he had once known.

"You sent me a postdated check," she said. "I can't allow that. It's already five days past the first. You dated your check for the twelfth."

"Well, I have no money. I haven't got it. You can't send me to prison for that. I'll be lucky if I can raise it by the twelfth."

She answered, "You better get it, Tommy."

"Yes? What for?" he said. "Tell me. For the sake of what? To tell lies about me to everyone? You—"

She cut him off. "You know what for. I've got the boys to bring up."

Wilhelm in the narrow booth broke into a heavy sweat. He dropped his head and shrugged while with his fingers he arranged nickels, dimes, and quarters in rows. "I'm doing my best," he said. "I've had some bad luck. As a matter of fact, it's been so bad that I don't know where I am. I couldn't tell you what day of the week this is. I can't think straight. I'd better not even try. This has been one of those days, Margaret. May I never live to go through another like it. I mean that with all my heart. So I'm not going to try to do any thinking today. Tomorrow I'm going to see some guys. One is a sales manager. The other is in television. But not to act," he hastily added. "On the business end."

"That's just some more of your talk, Tommy," she said. "You ought to patch things up with Rojax Corporation. They'd take you back. You've got to stop thinking like a youngster."

"What do you mean?"

"Well," she said, measured and unbending, remorselessly unbending, "you still think like a youngster. But you can't do that any more. Every other day you want to make a new start. But in eighteen years you'll be eligible for retirement. Nobody wants to hire a new man of your age."

"I know. But listen, you don't have to sound so hard. I can't get on my knees to them. And really you don't have to sound so hard. I haven't done you so much harm."

"Tommy, I have to chase you and ask you for money that you owe us, and I hate it."

She hated also to be told that her voice was hard.

"I'm making an effort to control myself," she told him.

He could picture her, her graying bangs cut with strict fixity above her pretty, decisive face. She prided herself on being fair-minded. We could not bear, he thought, to know what we do. Even though blood is spilled. Even though the breath of life is taken from someone's nostrils. This is the way of the weak; quiet and fair. And then smash! They smash!

"Rojax take me back? I'd have to crawl back. They don't need me. After so many years I should have got stock in the firm. How can I support the three of you, and live myself, on half the territory? And why should I even try when you won't lift a finger to help? I sent you back to school, didn't I? At that time you said—"

His voice was rising. She did not like that and intercepted him. "You misunderstood me," she said.

"You must realize you're killing me. You can't be as blind as all that. Thou shalt not kill! Don't you remember that?"

She said, "You're just raving now. When you calm down it'll be different. I have great confidence in your earning ability."

"Margaret, you don't grasp the situation. You'll have to get a job."

"Absolutely not. I'm not going to have two young children running loose."

"They're not babies," Wilhelm said. "Tommy is fourteen. Paulie is going to be ten."

"Look," Margaret said in her deliberate manner. "We can't continue this conversation if you're going to yell so, Tommy. They're at a dangerous age. There are teen-aged gangs—the parents working, or the families broken up."

Once again she was reminding him that it was he who had left her. She had the bringing up of the children as her burden, while he must expect to pay the price of his freedom.

Freedom! he thought with consuming bitterness. Ashes in

his mouth, not freedom. Give me my children. For they are mine too.

Can you be the woman I lived with? he started to say. Have you forgotten that we slept so long together? Must you now deal with me like this, and have no mercy?

He would be better off with Margaret again than he was today. This was what she wanted to make him feel, and she drove it home. "Are you in misery?" she was saying. "But you have deserved it." And he could not return to her any more than he could beg Rojax to take him back. If it cost him his life, he could not. Margaret had ruined him with Olive. She hit him and hit him, beat him, battered him, wanted to beat the very life out of him.

"Margaret, I want you please to reconsider about work. You have that degree now. Why did I pay your tuition?"

"Because it seemed practical. But it isn't. Growing boys need parental authority and a home."

He begged her, "Margaret, go easy on me. You ought to. I'm at the end of my rope and feel that I'm suffocating. You don't want to be responsible for a person's destruction. You've got to let up. I feel I'm about to burst." His face had expanded. He struck a blow upon the tin and wood and nails of the wall of the booth. "You've got to let me breathe. If I should keel over, what then? And it's something I can never understand about you. How you can treat someone like this whom you lived with so long. Who gave you the best of himself. Who tried. Who loved you." Merely to pronounce the word "love" made him tremble.

"Ah," she said with a sharp breath. "Now we're coming to it. How did you imagine it was going to be—big shot? Everything made smooth for you? I thought you were leading up to this."

She had not, perhaps, intended to reply as harshly as she did, but she brooded a great deal and now she could not forbear to punish him and make him feel pains like those she had to undergo.

He struck the wall again, this time with his knuckles, and he had scarcely enough air in his lungs to speak in a whisper, because his heart pushed upward with a frightful pressure. He got up and stamped his feet in the narrow enclosure.

"Haven't I always done my best?" he yelled, though his voice sounded weak and thin to his own ears. "Everything comes from me and nothing back again to me. There's no law that'll punish this, but you are committing a crime against me. Before God—and that's no joke. I mean that. Before God! Sooner or later the boys will know it."

In a firm tone, levelly, Margaret said to him, "I won't stand to be howled at. When you can speak normally and have something sensible to say I'll listen. But not to this." She hung up.

Wilhelm tried to tear the apparatus from the wall. He ground his teeth and seized the black box with insane digging fingers and made a stifled cry and pulled. Then he saw an elderly lady staring through the glass door, utterly appalled by him, and he ran from the booth, leaving a large amount of change on the shelf. He hurried down the stairs and into the street.

On Broadway it was still bright afternoon and the gassy air was almost motionless under the leaden spokes of sunlight, and sawdust footprints lay about the doorways of butcher shops and fruit stores. And the great, great crowd, the inexhaustible current of millions of every race and kind pouring out, pressing round, of every age, of every genius, possessors of every human secret, antique and future, in every face the refinement of one particular motive or essence—*I labor, I spend, I strive, I design, I love, I cling, I uphold, I give way, I envy, I long, I scorn, I die, I hide, I want.* Faster, much faster than any man could make the tally. The sidewalks were wider than any causeway; the street itself was immense, and it quaked and gleamed and it seemed to Wilhelm to throb at the last limit of endurance. And although the sunlight appeared like a broad tissue, its actual weight made him feel like a drunkard.

"I'll get a divorce if it's the last thing I do," he swore. "As for Dad— As for Dad— I'll have to sell the car for junk and pay the hotel. I'll have to go on my knees to Olive and say, 'Stand by me a while. Don't let her win. Olive!'" And he thought, I'll try to start again with Olive. In fact, I must. Olive loves me. Olive—

Beside a row of limousines near the curb he thought he saw Dr. Tamkin. Of course he had been mistaken before about the hat with the cocoa-colored band and didn't want to make the same mistake twice. But wasn't that Tamkin who was speaking so earnestly, with pointed shoulders, to someone under the canopy of the funeral parlor? For this was a huge funeral. He looked for the singular face under the dark gray, fashionable hatbrim. There were two open cars filled with flowers, and a policeman tried to keep a path open to pedestrians. Right at the canopy-pole, now wasn't that that damned Tamkin talking away with a solemn face, gesticulating with an open hand?

"Tamkin!" shouted Wilhelm, going forward. But he was pushed to the side by a policeman clutching his nightstick at both end, like a rolling pin. Wilhelm was even farther from Tamkin now, and swore under his breath at the cop who continued to press him back, back, belly and ribs, saying, "Keep it moving there, please," his face red with impatient sweat, his brows like red fur. Wilhelm said to him haughtily, "You shouldn't push people like this."

The policeman, however, was not really to blame. He had been ordered to keep a way clear. Wilhelm was moved forward by the pressure of the crowd.

He cried, "Tamkin!"

But Tamkin was gone. Or rather, it was he himself who was carried from the street into the chapel. The pressure ended inside, where it was dark and cool. The flow of fan-driven air dried his face, which he wiped hard with his handkerchief to stop the slight salt itch. He gave a sigh when he heard the organ notes that stirred and breathed from the pipes and he saw people in the pews. Men in formal clothes and black homburgs strode softly back and forth on the cork floor, up and down the center aisle. The white of the stained glass was like mother-of-pearl, the blue of the Star of David like velvet ribbon.

Well, thought Wilhelm, if that was Tamkin outside I might as well wait for him here where it's cool. Funny, he never mentioned he had a funeral to go to today. But that's just like the guy.

But within a few minutes he had forgotten Tamkin. He stood along the wall with others and looked toward the coffin and the slow line that was moving past it, gazing at the face of the dead. Presently he too was in this line, and slowly, slowly, foot by foot, the beating of his heart anxious, thick, frightening, but somehow also rich, he neared the coffin and paused for his turn, and gazed down. He caught his breath when he looked at the corpse, and his face swelled, his eyes shone hugely with instant tears.

The dead man was gray-haired. He had two large waves of gray hair at the front. But he was not old. His face was long, and he had a bony nose, slightly, delicately twisted. His brows were raised as though he had sunk into the final thought. Now at last he was with it, after the end of all distractions, and when his flesh was no longer flesh. And by this meditative look Wilhelm was so struck that he could not go away. In spite of the tinge of horror, and then the splash of heartsickness that he felt, he could not go. He stepped out of line and remained beside the coffin; his eyes filled silently and through his still tears he studied the man as the line of visitors moved with veiled looks past the satin coffin toward the standing bank of lilies, lilacs, roses. With great stifling sorrow, almost admiration, Wilhelm nodded and nodded. On the surface, the dead man with his formal shirt and his tie and silk lapels and his powdered skin looked so proper; only a little beneath so—black, Wilhelm thought, so fallen in the eyes.

Standing a little apart, Wilhelm began to cry. He cried at first softly and from sentiment, but soon from deeper feeling. He sobbed loudly and his face grew distorted and hot, and the tears stung his skin. A man—another human creature, was what first went through his thoughts, but other and different things were torn from him. What'll I do? I'm stripped and kicked out. . . . Oh, Father, what do I ask of you? What'll I do about the kids—Tommy, Paul? My children. And Olive? My dear? Why, why, why—you must protect me against that devil who wants my life. If you want it, then kill me. Take, take it, take it from me."

Soon he was past words, past reason, coherence. He could not stop. The source of all tears had suddenly sprung open within him, black, deep, and hot, and they were pouring out and convulsed his body, bending his stubborn head, bowing his shoulders, twisting his face, crippling the very hands with which he held the handkerchief. His efforts to collect himself were useless. The great knot of ill and grief in his throat swelled upward and he gave in utterly and held his face and wept. He cried with all his heart.

He, alone of all the people in the chapel, was sobbing. No one knew who he was.

One woman said, "Is that perhaps the cousin from New Orleans they were expecting?"

"It must be somebody real close to carry on so."

"Oh my, oh my! To be mourned like that," said one man and looked at Wilhelm's heavy shaken shoulders, his clutched face and whitened fair hair, with wide, glinting, jealous eyes.

"The man's brother, maybe?"

"Oh, I doubt that very much," said another bystander. "They're not alike at all. Night and day."

The flowers and lights fused ecstatically in Wilhelm's blind, wet eyes; the heavy sea-like music came up to his ears. It poured into him where he had hidden himself in the center of a crowd by the great and happy oblivion of tears. He heard it and sank deeper than sorrow, through torn sobs and cries toward the consummation of his heart's ultimate need.

HENDERSON THE RAIN KING

To my son Gregory

I

WHAT made me take this trip to Africa? There is no quick explanation. Things got worse and worse and worse and pretty soon they were too complicated.

When I think of my condition at the age of fifty-five when I bought the ticket, all is grief. The facts begin to crowd me and soon I get a pressure in the chest. A disorderly rush begins—my parents, my wives, my girls, my children, my farm, my animals, my habits, my money, my music lessons, my drunkenness, my prejudices, my brutality, my teeth, my face, my soul! I have to cry, "No, no, get back, curse you, let me alone!" But how can they let me alone? They belong to me. They are mine. And they pile into me from all sides. It turns into chaos.

However, the world which I thought so mighty an oppressor has removed its wrath from me. But if I am to make sense to you people and explain why I went to Africa I must face up to the facts. I might as well start with the money. I am rich. From my old man I inherited three million dollars after taxes, but I thought myself a bum and had my reasons, the main reason being that I behaved like a bum. But privately when things got very bad I often looked into books to see whether I could find some helpful words, and one day I read, "The forgiveness of sins is perpetual and righteousness first is not required." This impressed me so deeply that I went around saying it to myself. But then I forgot which book it was. It was one of thousands left by my father, who had also written a number of them. And I searched through dozens of volumes but all that turned up was money, for my father had used currency for bookmarks—whatever he happened to have in his pockets— fives, tens, or twenties. Some of the discontinued bills of thirty years ago turned up, the big yellowbacks. For old times' sake I was glad to see them and locking the library door to keep out the children I spent the afternoon on a ladder shaking out books and the money spun to the floor. But I never found that statement about forgiveness.

Next order of business: I am a graduate of an Ivy League university—I see no reason to embarrass my alma mater by naming her. If I hadn't been a Henderson and my father's son, they would have thrown me out. At birth I weighed fourteen pounds, and it was a tough delivery. Then I grew up. Six feet four inches tall. Two hundred and thirty pounds. An enormous head, rugged, with hair like Persian lambs' fur. Suspicious eyes, usually narrowed. Blustering ways. A great nose. I was one of three children and the only survivor. It took all my father's charity to forgive me and I don't think he ever made it altogether. When it came time to marry I tried to please him and chose a girl of our own social class. A remarkable person, handsome, tall, elegant, sinewy, with long arms and golden hair, private, fertile, and quiet. None of her family can quarrel with me if I add that she is a schizophrenic, for she certainly is that. I, too, am considered crazy, and with good reason—moody, rough, tyrannical, and probably mad. To go by the ages of the kids, we were married for about twenty years. There are Edward, Ricey, Alice, and two more—Christ, I've got plenty of children. God bless the whole bunch of them.

In my own way I worked very hard. Violent suffering is labor, and often I was drunk before lunch. Soon after I came back from the war (I was too old for combat duty but nothing could keep me from it; I went down to Washington and pressured people until I was allowed to join the fight), Frances and I were divorced. This happened after V-E Day. Or was it so soon? No, it must have been in 1948. Anyway, she's now in Switzerland and has one of our kids with her. What she wants with a child I can't tell you, but she has one, and that's all right. I wish her well.

I was delighted with the divorce. It offered me a new start in life. I had a new wife already picked out and we were soon married. My second wife is called Lily (maiden name, Simmons). We have twin boys.

Now I feel the disorderly rush—I gave Lily a terrible time, worse than Frances. Frances was withdrawn, which protected her, but Lily caught it. Maybe a change for the better threw me; I was adjusted to a bad life. Whenever Frances didn't like what I was doing, and that was often, she turned away from me. She was like Shelley's moon, wandering companionless. Not so Lily; and I raved at her in public and swore at her in private. I got into brawls in the country saloons near my farm and the troopers locked me up. I offered to take them all on, and they would have worked me over if I hadn't been so prominent in the county. Lily came and bailed me out. Then I had a fight with the vet over one of my pigs, and another with the driver of a snowplow on US 7 when he tried to force me off the road. Then about two years ago I fell off a tractor while drunk and ran myself over and broke my leg. For months I was on crutches, hitting everyone who crossed my path, man or beast, and giving Lily hell. With the bulk of a football player and the color of a gipsy, swearing and crying out and showing my teeth and shaking my head—no wonder people got out of my way. But this wasn't all.

Lily is, for instance, entertaining ladies and I come in with my filthy plaster cast, in sweat socks; I am wearing a red velvet dressing gown which I bought at Sulka's in Paris in a mood of celebration when Frances said she wanted a divorce. In addition I have on a red wool hunting cap. And I wipe my nose and mustache on my fingers and then shake hands with the guests, saying, "I'm Mr. Henderson, how do you do?" And I go to Lily and shake her hand, too, as if she were merely another lady guest, a stranger like the rest. And I say, "How do you do?" I imagine the ladies are telling themselves, "He doesn't know her. In his mind he's still married to the first. Isn't that awful?" This imaginary fidelity thrills them.

But they are all wrong. As Lily knows, it was done on purpose, and when we're alone she cries out to me, "Gene, what's the big idea? What are you trying to do?"

All belted up with the red braid cord, I stand up to her in my velvet bathrobe, sticking out behind, and the foot-shaped cast scraping hard on the floor, and I wag my head and say, "Tchu-tchu-tchu!"

Because when I was brought home from the hospital in this same bloody heavy cast, I heard her saying on the telephone, "It was just another one of his accidents. He has them all the time but oh, he's so strong. He's unkillable." Unkillable! How do you like that! It made me very bitter.

Now maybe Lily said this jokingly. She loves to joke on the telephone. She is a large, lively woman. Her face is sweet, and her character mostly is consistent with it. We've had some pretty good times, too. And, come to think of it, some of the very best occurred during her pregnancy, when it was far advanced. Before we went to sleep, I would rub her belly with baby oil to counteract the stretch marks. Her nipples had turned from pink to glowing brown, and the children moved inside her belly and changed the round shape.

I rubbed lightly and with greatest care lest my big thick fingers do the slightest harm. And then before I put out the light I wiped my fingers on my hair and Lily and I kissed good night, and in the scent of the baby oil we went to sleep.

But later we were at war again, and when I heard her say I was unkillable I put an antagonistic interpretation on it, even though I knew better. No, I treated her like a stranger before the guests because I didn't like to see her behave and carry on like the lady of the house; because I, the sole heir of this famous name and estate, am a bum, and she is not a lady but merely my wife—merely my wife.

As the winters seemed to make me worse, she decided that we should go to a resort hotel on the Gulf, where I could do some fishing. A thoughtful friend had given each of the little twins a slingshot made of plywood, and one of these slingshots I found in my suitcase as I was unpacking, and I took to shooting with it. I gave up fishing and sat on the beach shooting stones at bottles. So that people might say, "Do you see that great big fellow with the enormous nose and the mustache? Well, his great-grandfather was Secretary of State, his great-uncles were ambassadors to England and France, and his father was the famous scholar Willard Henderson who wrote that book on the Albigensians, a friend of William James and Henry Adams." Didn't they say this? You bet they did. There I was at that resort with my sweet-faced anxious second wife who was only a little under six feet herself, and our twin boys. In the dining room I was putting bourbon in my morning coffee from a big flask and on the beach I was smashing bottles. The guests complained to the manager about the broken glass and the manager took it up with Lily; me they weren't willing to confront. An elegant establishment, they accept no Jews, and then they get me, E. H. Henderson. The other kids stopped playing with our twins, while the wives avoided Lily.

Lily tried to reason with me. We were in our suite, and I was in swimming trunks, and she opened the discussion on the slingshot and the broken glass and my attitude toward the other guests. Now Lily is a very intelligent woman. She doesn't scold, but she does moralize; she is very much given to this, and when it happens she turns white and starts to speak under her breath. The reason is not that she is afraid of me, but that it starts some crisis in her own mind.

But as it got her nowhere to discuss it with me she started to cry, and when I saw tears I lost my head and yelled, "I'm going to blow my brains out! I'm shooting myself. I didn't forget to pack the pistol. I've got it on me now."

"Oh, Gene!" she cried, and covered up her face and ran away.

I'll tell you why.

II

BECAUSE her father had committed suicide in that same way, with a pistol.

One of the bonds between Lily and me is that we both suffer with our teeth. She is twenty years my junior but we wear bridges, each of us. Mine are at the sides, hers are in front. She has lost the four upper incisors. It happened while she was still in high school, out playing golf with her father, whom she adored. The poor old guy was a lush and far too drunk to be out on a golf course that day. Without looking or giving warning, he drove from the first tee and on the backswing struck his daughter. It always kills me to think of that cursed hot July golf course, and this drunk from the plumbing supply business, and the girl of fifteen bleeding. Damn these weak drunks! Damn these unsteady men! I can't stand these clowns who go out in public as soon as they get swacked to show how broken-hearted they are. But Lily would never hear a single word against him and wept for him sooner than for herself. She carries his photo in her wallet.

Personally I never knew the old guy. When we met he had already been dead for ten or twelve years. Soon after he died she married a man from Baltimore, of pretty good standing, I have been told—though come to think of it it was Lily herself who told me. However, they could not become adjusted and during the war she got her divorce (I was then fighting in Italy). Anyway, when we met she was at home again, living with her mother. The family is from Danbury, the hatters' capital. It happened that Frances and I went to a party in Danbury one winter night, and Frances was only half willing because she was in correspondence with some intellectual or other over in Europe. Frances is a very deep reader and an intense letter writer and a heavy smoker, and when she got on one of her kicks of philosophy or something I would see very little of her. I'd know she was up in her room smoking Sobranie cigarettes and coughing and making notes, working things out. Well, she was in one of these mental crises when we went to that party, and in the middle of it she recalled something she had to do at once and so she took the car and left, forgetting all about me. That night I had gotten mixed up too, and was the only man there in black tie. Midnight blue. I must have been the first fellow in that part of the state with a blue tuxedo. It felt as though I were wearing a whole acre of this blue cloth, while Lily, to whom I had been introduced about ten minutes before, had on a red and green Christmas-striped dress and we were talking.

When she saw what had happened, Lily offered me a ride, and I said, "Okay." We trod the snow out to her car.

It was a sparkling night and the snow was ringing. She was parked on a hill about three hundred yards long and smooth as iron. As soon as she drove away from the curb the car went into a skid and she lost her head and screamed, "Eugene!" She threw her arms about me. There was no other soul on that hill or on the shoveled walks, nor, so far as I could see, in the entire neighborhood. The car turned completely around. Her bare arms came out of the short fur sleeves and held my head while her large eyes watched through the windshield and the car went over the ice and hoarfrost. It was not even in gear and I reached the key and switched off the ignition. We slid into a snowdrift, but not far, and I took the wheel from her. The moonlight was very keen.

"How did you know my name?" I said, and she said, "Why, everybody knows you are Eugene Henderson."

After we had spoken some more she said to me, "You ought to divorce your wife."

I said to her, "What are you talking about? Is that a thing to say? Besides, I'm old enough to be your father."

We didn't meet again until the summer. This time she was shopping and was wearing a hat and a white piqué dress, with white shoes. It looked like rain and she didn't want to be caught in those clothes (which I noticed were soiled already) and she asked me for a lift. I had been in Danbury buying some lumber for the barn and the station wagon was loaded with it. Lily started to direct me to her house and lost the way in her nervousness; she was very beautiful, but wildly nervous. It was sultry and then it began to rain. She told me to take a right turn and that brought us to a gray cyclone fence around the quarry filled with water—a dead-end street. The air had grown so dark that the mesh of the fence looked white. Lily began to cry out, "Oh, turn around, please! Oh, quick, turn around! I can't remember the streets and I have to go home."

Finally we got there, a small house filled with the odor of closed rooms in hot weather, just as the storm was beginning.

"My mother is playing bridge," said Lily. "I have to phone her and tell her not to come home. There is a phone in my bedroom." So we went up. There was nothing loose or promiscuous about Lily, I assure you. When she took off her clothes she started to speak out in a trembling voice, "I love you! I love you!" And I said to myself as we embraced, "Oh, how can she love you—you—you!" There was a huge knot of thunder, and then a burst of rain on the streets, trees, roofs, screens, and lightning as well. Everything got filled and blinded. But a warm odor like fresh baking arose from her as we lay in her sheets which were darkened by the warm darkness of the storm. From start to finish she had not stopped saying "I love you!" Thus we lay quietly, and the early hours of the evening began without the sun's returning.

Her mother was waiting in the living room. I didn't care too much for that. Lily had phoned her and said, "Don't come home for a while," and therefore her mother had immediately left the bridge party through one of the worst summer storms in many years. No, I didn't like it. Not that the old lady scared me, but I read the signs. Lily had made sure she would be found out. I was the first down the stairs and saw a light beside the chesterfield. And when I got to the foot of the stairs, face to face with her, I said, "Henderson's the name." Her mother was a stout pretty woman, made up for the bridge party in a china-doll face. She wore a hat, and had a patent-leather pocketbook on her stout knees when she sat down. I realized that she was mentally listing accounts against Lily. "In my own house. With a married man." And so on. Indifferent, I sat in the living room, unshaved, my lumber in the station wagon outside. Lily's odor, that baking odor, must have been noticeable about me. And Lily, extremely beautiful, came down the stairs to show her mama what she had accomplished. Acting oblivious, I kept my big boots apart on the carpet and frisked my mustache once in a while. Between them I sensed the important presence of Simmons, Lily's papa, the plumbing supply wholesaler who had committed suicide. In fact he had killed himself in the bedroom adjoining Lily's, the master bedroom. Lily blamed her mother for her father's death. And what was I, the instrument of her anger? "Oh no, pal," I said to myself, "this is not for you. Be no party to this."

It looked as though the mother had decided to behave well. She was going to be big about it and beat Lily at this game. Perhaps it was natural. Anyway, she was highly ladylike to me, but there came a moment when she couldn't check herself, and she said, "I have met your son."

"Oh yes, a slender fellow? Edward? He drives a red M G. You see him around Danbury sometimes."

Presently I left, saying to Lily, "You're a fine-looking big girl, but you oughtn't to have done that to your mother."

The stout old lady was sitting there on the sofa with her hands clasped and her eyes making a continuous line under her brows from tears or vexation.

"Good-by, Eugene," said Lily.

"So long, Miss Simmons," I said.

We didn't part friends exactly.

Nevertheless we soon met again, but in New York City, for Lily had separated from her mother, quitted Danbury, and had a cold-water flat on Hudson Street where the drunks hid from the weather on the staircase. I came, a great weight, a huge shadow on those stairs, with my face full of country color and booze, and yellow pigskin gloves on my hands, and a ceaseless voice in my heart that said, *I want, I want, I want, oh, I want—yes, go on,* I said to myself, *Strike, strike, strike, strike!* And I kept going on the staircase in my thick padded coat, in pigskin gloves and pigskin shoes, a pigskin wallet in my pocket, seething with lust and seething with trouble, and realizing how my gaze glittered up to the top banister where Lily had opened the door and was waiting. Her face was round, white, and full, her eyes clear and narrowed.

"Hell! How can you live in this stinking joint? It stinks here," I said. The building had hall toilets; the chain pulls had turned green and there were panes of plum-colored glass in the doors.

She was a friend of the slum people, the old and the mothers in particular. She said she understood why they had television

sets though on relief, and she let them keep their milk and butter in her refrigerator and filled out their social-security forms
for them. I think she felt she did them good and showed these
immigrants and Italians how nice an American could be. However, she genuinely tried to help them and ran around with her
impulsive looks and said a lot of disconnected things.

The odors of this building clutched at your face, and I was
coming up the stairs and said, "Whew, I am out of condition!"

We went into her apartment on the top floor. It was dirty,
too, but there was light in it at least. We sat down to talk and
Lily said to me, "Are you going to waste the rest of your life?"

With Frances the case was hopeless. Only once after I came
back from the Army did anything of a personal nature take
place between us, and after that it was no soap, so I let her be,
more or less. Except that one morning in the kitchen we had a
conversation that set us apart for good and all. Just a few
words. They went like this:

"And what would you like to do now?"

(I was then losing interest in the farm.)

"I wonder," I said, "if it's too late for me to become a doctor
—if I could enter medical school."

Frances opened her mouth, usually so sober, not to say dismal and straight, and laughed at me; and as she laughed I saw
nothing but her dark open mouth, and not even teeth, which
is certainly strange, for she has teeth, white ones. What had
happened to them?

"Okay, okay, okay," I said.

Thus I realized that Lily was perfectly right about Frances.
Nevertheless the rest did not follow.

"I need to have a child. I can't wait much longer," said Lily.
"In a few years I'll be thirty."

"Am I responsible?" I said. "What's the matter with you?"

"You and I have got to be together," she said.

"Who says so?"

"We'll die if we're not," she said.

A year or so went by, and she failed to convince me. I didn't
believe the thing could be so simple. So she suddenly married
a man from New Jersey, a fellow named Hazard, a broker.
Come to think of it she had spoken of him a few times, but I
thought it was only more of her blackmail. Because she was a

blackmailer. Anyway, she married him. This was her second marriage. Then I took Frances and the two girls and went to Europe, to France, for a year.

Several years of my boyhood were spent in the south of the country, near the town of Albi, where my old man was busy with his research. Fifty years ago I used to taunt a kid across the way, "François, oh François, ta soeur est constipée." My father was a big man, solid and clean. His long underwear was made of Irish linen and his hatboxes were lined with red velvet and he ordered his shoes from England and his gloves from Vitale Milano, Rome. He played pretty well on the violin. My mother used to write poems in the brick cathedral of Albi. She had a favorite story about a lady from Paris who was very affected. They met in a narrow doorway of the church and the lady said, "Voulez-vous que je passasse?" So my mother said, "Passassassez, Madame." She told everyone this joke and for many years would sometimes laugh and say in a whisper, "Passassassez." Gone, those times. Closed, sealed, and gone.

But Frances and I didn't go to Albi with the children. She was attending the Collège de France, where all the philosophers were. Apartments were hard to get but I rented a good one from a Russian prince. De Vogüé mentions his grandfather, who was minister under Nicolas I. He was a tall, gentle creature; his wife was Spanish and his Spanish mother-in-law, Señora Guirlandes, rode him continually. The guy was suffering from her. His wife and kids lived with the old woman while he moved into the maid's room in the attic. About three million bucks, I have. I suppose I might have done something to help him. But at this time my heart was consumed with the demand I have mentioned—*I want, I want!* Poor prince, upstairs! His children were sick, and he said to me that if his condition didn't improve he would throw himself out of the window.

I said, "Don't be nuts, Prince."

Guiltily, I lived in his apartment, slept in his bed, and bathed in his bath twice a day. Instead of helping, those two hot baths only aggravated my melancholy. After Frances laughed at my dream of a medical career I never discussed another thing with her. Around and around the city of Paris I walked every day; all the way to the Gobelin factories and the Père Lachaise Cemetery and St. Cloud I went on foot. The only person who

considered what my life was like was Lily, now Lily Hazard. At
the American Express I received a note from her written on
one of the wedding announcements long after the date of the
marriage. I was bursting with trouble, and as there are a lot of
whores who cruise that neighborhood near the Madeleine, I
looked some of them over, but this terrible repetition within—
I want, I want!—was not stopped by any face I saw. I saw quite
some faces.

"Lily may arrive," I thought. And she did. She cruised the
city in a taxi looking for me and caught up with me near the
Metro Vavin. Big and shining, she cried out to me from
the cab. She opened the antique door and tried to stand on the
runningboard. Yes, she was beautiful—a good face, a clear,
pure face, hot and white. Her neck as she stretched forward
from the door of the cab was big and shapely. Her upper lip
was trembling with joy. But, stirred as she was, she remembered those front teeth and kept them covered. What did I
care then about new porcelain teeth! Blessed be God for the
mercies He continually sends me!

"Lily! How are you, kid? Where did you come from?"

I was terribly pleased. She thought I was a big slob but of
substantial value just the same, and that I should live and not
die (one more year like this one in Paris and something in me
would have rusted forever), and that something good might
even come of me. She loved me.

"What have you done with your husband?" I said.

On the way back to her hotel, down Boulevard Raspail, she
told me, "I thought I should have children. I was getting old."
(Lily was then twenty-seven.) "But on the way to the wedding
I saw it was a mistake. I tried to get out of the car at a stoplight
in my wedding dress, but he caught me and pulled me back.
He punched me in the eye," she said, "and it was a good thing
I had a veil because the eye turned black, and I cried all the
way through the ceremony. Also, my mother is dead."

"What! He gave you a shiner?" I said, furious. "If I ever
come across him again I will break him in pieces. Say, I'm
sorry about your mother."

I kissed her on the eyes, and then we arrived at her hotel on
the Quai Voltaire and were on top of the world, in each other's
arms. A happy week followed; we went everywhere, and Haz-

ard's private detective followed us. Therefore I rented a car and we began a tour of the cathedral towns. And Lily in her marvelous way—always marvelously—began to make me suffer. "You think you can live without me, but you can't," she said, "any more than I can live without you. The sadness just drowns me. Why do you think I left Hazard? Because of the sadness. When he kissed me I felt saddest of all. I felt all alone. And when he—"

"That's enough. Don't tell me," I said.

"It was better when he punched me in the eye. There was some truth in that. Then I didn't feel like drowning."

And I began to drink, harder than ever, and was drunk in every one of the great cathedrals—Amiens, Chartres, Vézelay, and so on. She often had to do the driving. The car was a little one (a Deux Cent Deux décapotable or convertible) and the two of us, of grand size, towered out of the seats, fair and dark, beautiful and drunk. Because of me she had come all the way from America, and I wouldn't let her accomplish her mission. Thus we traveled all the way up to Belgium and back again to the Massif, and if you loved France that would have been fine, but I didn't love it. From start to finish Lily had just this one topic, moralizing: one can't live for this but has to live for that; not evil but good; not death but life; not illusion but reality. Lily does not speak clearly; I guess she was taught in boarding school that a lady speaks softly, and consequently she mumbles, and I am hard of hearing on the right side, and the wind and the tires and the little engine also joined their noise. All the same, from the joyous excitement of her great pure white face I knew she was still at it. With lighted face and joyous eyes she persecuted me. I learned she had many negligent and even dirty habits. She forgot to wash her underthings until, drunk as I was, I ordered her to. This may have been because she was such a moralist and thinker, for when I said, "Wash out your things," she began to argue with me. "The pigs on my farm are cleaner than you are," I told her; and this led to a debate. The earth itself is like that, corrupt. Yes, but it transforms itself. "A single individual can't do the nitrogen cycle all by herself," I said to her; and she said, Yes, but did I know what love *could* do? I yelled at her, "Shut up." It didn't make her angry. She was sorry for me.

The tour continued and I was a double captive—one, of the religion and beauty of the churches which I was not too drunk to see, and two, of Lily, and her glowing and mumbling and her embraces. She said a hundred times if she said it once, "Come back to the States with me. I've come to take you back."

"No," I said finally. "If there was any heart in you at all you wouldn't torture me, Lily. Damn you, don't forget I'm a Purple Heart veteran. I've served my country. I'm over fifty, and I've had my belly full of trouble."

"All the more reason why you should do something now," she said.

Finally I told her at Chartres, "If you don't quit it I'm going to blow my brains out."

This was cruel of me, as I knew what her father had done. Drunk as I was, I could hardly bear the cruelty myself. The old man had shot himself after a family quarrel. He was a charming man, weak, heartbroken, affectionate, and sentimental. He came home full of whisky and would sing old-time songs for Lily and the cook; he told jokes and tap-danced and did corny vaudeville routines in the kitchen, joking with a catch in his throat—a dirty thing to do to your child. Lily told me all about it until her father became so actual to me that I loved and detested the old bastard myself. "Here, you old clog-dancer, you old heart-breaker, you pitiful joker—you cornball!" I said to his ghost. "What do you mean by doing this to your daughter and then leaving her on my hands?" And when I threatened suicide in Chartres cathedral, in the very face of this holy beauty, Lily caught her breath. The light in her face turned fine as pearl. She silently forgave me.

"It's all the same to me whether you forgive me or not," I told her.

We broke up at Vézelay. From the start our visit there was a strange one. The décapotable Deux Cent Deux had a flat when we came down in the morning. It being fine June weather, I had refused to put the car in a garage and in my opinion the management had let out the air. I accused the hotel and stood shouting until the office closed its iron shutter. I changed the tire quickly, using no jack but in my anger heaving up the little car and pushing a rock under the axle. After fighting with the hotel manager (both of us saying, "Pneu, pneu"), my mood was better, and we walked around the cathedral, bought a kilo of strawberries in a paper funnel, and went out on the ramparts to lie in the sun. Yellow dust was dropping from the lime trees, and wild roses grew on the trunks of the apple trees. Pale red, gorged red, fiery, aching, harsh as anger, sweet as drugs. Lily took off her blouse to get the sun on her shoulders. Presently she took off her slip, too, and after a time her brassière, and she lay in my lap. Annoyed, I said to her, "How do you know what I want?" And then more gently, because of the roses on all the tree trunks, piercing and twining and flaming, I said, "Can't you just enjoy this beautiful churchyard?"

"It isn't a churchyard, it's an orchard," she said.

I said, "Your period just began yesterday. So what are you after?"

She said I had never objected before, and that was true. "But I do object now," I said, and we began to quarrel and the quarrel got so fierce I told her she was going back to Paris alone on the next train.

She was silent. I had her, I thought. But no, it only seemed to prove how much I loved her. Her crazy face darkened with the intensity of love and joy.

"You'll never kill me, I'm too rugged!" I cried at her. And then I began to weep from all the unbearable complications in my heart. I cried and sobbed.

"Get in there, you mad bitch," I said, weeping. And I rolled back the roof of the décapotable. It has rods which come out, and then you reef back the canvas.

Under her breath, pale with terror but consumed also with her damned exalted glory, she mumbled as I was sobbing at the wheel about pride and strength and soul and love, and all of that.

I told her, "Curse you, you're nuts!"

"Without you, maybe it's true. Maybe I'm not all there and I don't understand," she said. "But when we're together, *I know.*"

"Hell you know. How come I don't know anything! Stay the hell away from me. You tear me to pieces."

I dumped her foolish suitcase with the unwashed clothes in it on the platform. Still sobbing, I turned around in the station, which was twenty kilometers or so from Vézelay, and I headed for the south of France. I drove to a place on the Vermilion Coast called Banyules. They keep a marine station there, and I had a strange experience in the aquarium. It was twilight. I looked in at an octopus, and the creature seemed also to look at me and press its soft head to the glass, flat, the flesh becoming pale and granular—blanched, speckled. The eyes spoke to me coldly. But even more speaking, even more cold, was the soft head with its speckles, and the Brownian motion in those speckles, a cosmic coldness in which I felt I was dying. The tentacles throbbed and motioned through the glass, the bubbles sped upward, and I thought, "This is my last day. Death is giving me notice."

So much for my suicide threat to Lily.

III

AND now a few words about my reasons for going to Africa. When I came back from the war it was with the thought of becoming a pig farmer, which maybe illustrates what I thought of life in general.

Monte Cassino should never have been bombed; some blame it on the dumbness of the generals. But after that bloody murder, where so many Texans were wiped out, and my outfit also took a shellacking later, there were only Nicky Goldstein and myself left out of the original bunch, and this was odd because we were the two largest men in the outfit and offered the best targets. Later I was wounded too, by a land mine. But at that time, Goldstein and I were lying down under the olive trees—some of those gnarls open out like lace and let the light through—and I asked him what he aimed to do after the war. He said, "Why, me and my brother, if we live and be well, we're going to have a mink ranch in the Catskills." So I said, or my demon said for me, "I'm going to start breeding pigs." And after these words were spoken I knew that if Goldstein had not been a Jew I might have said cattle and not pigs. So then it was too late to retract. So for all I know Goldstein and his brother have a mink business while I have—something else. I took all the handsome old farm buildings, the carriage house with paneled stalls—in the old days a rich man's horses were handled like opera singers—and the fine old barn with the belvedere above the hayloft, a beautiful piece of architecture, and I filled them up with pigs, a pig kingdom, with pig houses on the lawn and in the flower garden. The greenhouse, too—I let them root out the old bulbs. Statues from Florence and Salzburg were turned over. The place stank of swill and pigs and the mashes cooking, and dung. Furious, my neighbors got the health officer after me. I dared him to take me to law. "Hendersons have been on this property over two hundred years," I said to this man, a certain Dr. Bullock.

By my then wife, Frances, no word was said except, "Please keep them off the driveway."

"You'd better not hurt any of them," I said to her. "Those

animals have become a part of me." And I told this Dr. Bullock, "All those civilians and 4Fs have put you up to this. Those twerps. Don't they ever eat pork?"

Have you seen, coming from New Jersey to New York, the gabled pens and runways that look like models of German villages from the Black Forest? Have you smelled them (before the train enters the tunnel to go under the Hudson)? These are pig-fattening stations. Lean and bony after their trip from Iowa and Nebraska, the swine are fed here. Anyway, I was a pig man. And as the prophet Daniel warned King Nebuchadnezzar, "They shall drive thee from among men, and thy dwelling shall be with the beasts of the field." Sows eat their young because they need the phosphorus. Goiter attacks them as it does women. Oh, I made a considerable study of these clever doomed animals. For all pig breeders know how clever they are. The discovery that they were so intelligent gave me a kind of trauma. But if I had not lied to Frances and those animals had actually become a part of me, then it was curious that I lost interest in them.

But I see I haven't got any closer to giving my reasons for going to Africa, and I'd better begin somewhere else.

Shall I start with my father? He was a well-known man. He had a beard and played the violin, and he . . .

No, not that.

Well, then, here: My ancestors stole land from the Indians. They got more from the government and cheated other settlers too, so I became heir to a great estate.

No, that won't do either. What has that got to do with it?

Still, an explanation is necessary, for living proof of something of the highest importance has been presented to me so I am obliged to communicate it. And not the least of the difficulties is that it happened as in a dream.

Well, then, it must have been about eight years after the war ended. I was divorced from Frances and married to Lily, and I felt that something had to be done. I went to Africa with a friend of mine, Charlie Albert. He, too, is a millionaire.

I have always had a soldierly rather than a civilian temperament. When I was in the Army and caught the crabs, I went to get some powder. But when I reported what I had, four medics grabbed me, right at the crossroads, in the open they stripped

me naked and they soaped and lathered me and shaved every
hair from my body, back and front, armpits, pubic hair, mustache, eyebrows, and all. This was right near the waterfront at
Salerno. Trucks filled with troops were passing, and fishermen
and paisanos and kids and girls and women were looking on.
The GIs were cheering and laughing and the paisans laughed,
the whole coast laughed, and even I was laughing as I tried to
kill all four. They ran away and left me bald and shivering,
ugly, naked, prickling between the legs and under the arms,
raging, laughing, and swearing revenge. These are things a
man never forgets and afterward truly values. That beautiful
sky, and the mad itch and the razors; and the Mediterranean,
which is the cradle of mankind; the towering softness of the
air; the sinking softness of the water, where Ulysses got lost,
where he, too, was naked as the sirens sang.

In passing—the crabs found refuge in a crevice; I had dealings afterward with these cunning animals.

The war meant much to me. I was wounded when I stepped
on that land mine and got the Purple Heart, and I was in the
hospital in Naples quite a while. Believe me, I was grateful that
my life was spared. The whole experience gave my heart a large
and real emotion. Which I continually require.

Beside my cellar door last winter I was chopping wood for
the fire—the tree surgeon had left some pine limbs for me—
and a chunk of wood flew up from the block and hit me in the
nose. Owing to the extreme cold I didn't realize what had
happened until I saw the blood on my mackinaw. Lily cried
out, "You broke your nose." No, it wasn't broken. I have a lot
of protective flesh over it but I carried a bruise there for some
time. However as I felt the blow my only thought was *truth*.
Does truth come in blows? That's a military idea if there ever
was one. I tried to say something about it to Lily; she, too, had
felt the force of truth when her second husband, Hazard,
punched her in the eye.

Well, I've always been like this, strong and healthy, rude and
aggressive and something of a bully in boyhood; at college I
wore gold earrings to provoke fights, and while I got an M.A.
to please my father I always behaved like an ignorant man and
a bum. When engaged to Frances I went to Coney Island and
had her name tattooed on my ribs in purple letters. Not that

this cut any ice with her. Already forty-six or forty-seven when I got back from Europe after V-E Day (Thursday, May 8) I went in for pigs, and then I confided to Frances that I was drawn to medicine; and she laughed at me; she remembered how enthusiastic I had been at eighteen over Sir Wilfred Grenfell and afterward over Albert Schweitzer.

What do you do with yourself if you have a temperament like mine? A student of the mind once explained to me that if you inflict your anger on inanimate things, you not only spare the living, as a civilized man ought to do, but you get rid of the bad stuff in you. This seemed to make good sense, and I tried it out. I tried with all my heart, chopping wood, lifting, plowing, laying cement blocks, pouring concrete, and cooking mash for the pigs. On my own place, stripped to the waist like a convict, I broke stones with a sledgehammer. It helped, but not enough. Rude begets rude, and blows, blows; at least in my case; it not only begot but it increased. Wrath increased with wrath. So what do you do with yourself? More than three million bucks. After taxes, after alimony and all expenses I still have one hundred and ten thousand dollars in income absolutely clear. What do I need it for, a soldierly character like me! Taxwise, even the pigs were profitable. I couldn't lose money. But they were killed and they were eaten. They made ham and gloves and gelatin and fertilizer. What did I make? Why, I made a sort of trophy, I suppose. A man like me may become something like a trophy. Washed, clean, and dressed in expensive garments. Under the roof is insulation; on the windows thermopane; on the floors carpeting; and on the carpets furniture, and on the furniture covers, and on the cloth covers plastic covers; and wallpaper and drapes! All is swept and garnished. And who is in the midst of this? Who is sitting there? Man! That's who it is, man!

But there comes a day, there always comes a day of tears and madness.

Now I have already mentioned that there was a disturbance in my heart, a voice that spoke there and said, *I want, I want, I want!* It happened every afternoon, and when I tried to suppress it it got even stronger. It only said one thing, *I want, I want!*

And I would ask, "What do you want?"

But this was all it would ever tell me. It never said a thing except *I want, I want, I want!*

At times I would treat it like an ailing child whom you offer rhymes or candy. I would walk it, I would trot it. I would sing to it or read to it. No use. I would change into overalls and go up on the ladder and spackle cracks in the ceiling; I would chop wood, go out and drive a tractor, work in the barn among the pigs. No, no! Through fights and drunkenness and labor it went right on, in the country, in the city. No purchase, no matter how expensive, would lessen it. Then I would say, "Come on, tell me. What's the complaint, is it Lily herself? Do you want some nasty whore? It has to be some lust?" But this was no better a guess than the others. The demand came louder, *I want, I want, I want, I want, I want!* And I would cry, begging at last, "Oh, tell me then. Tell me what you want!" And finally I'd say, "Okay, then. One of these days, stupid. You wait!"

This was what made me behave as I did. By three o'clock I was in despair. Only toward sunset the voice would let up. And sometimes I thought maybe this was my occupation because it would knock off at five o'clock of itself. America is so big, and everybody is working, making, digging, bulldozing, trucking, loading, and so on, and I guess the sufferers suffer at the same rate. Everybody wanting to pull together. I tried every cure you can think of. Of course, in an age of madness, to expect to be untouched by madness is a form of madness. But the pursuit of sanity can be a form of madness, too.

Among other remedies I took up the violin. One day as I was poking around in a storeroom I found the dusty case and I opened it, and there lay the instrument my father used to play, inside that little sarcophagus, with its narrow scrolled neck and incurved waist and the hair of the bow undone and loose all around it. I tightened the bow screw and scrubbed on the strings. Harsh cries awoke. It was like a feeling creature that had been neglected too long. Then I began to recall my old man. Maybe he would deny it with anger, but we are much alike. He could not settle into a quiet life either. Sometimes he was very hard on Mama; once he made her lie prostrate in her nightgown at the door of his room for two weeks before he would forgive her some silly words, perhaps like Lily's on the telephone when she said I was unkillable. He was a very strong man, too, but as he declined in strength, especially after the death of my brother Dick (which made me the heir), he shut himself away and fiddled more and more. So I began to recall his bent back and the flatness or lameness of his hips, and his beard like a protest that gushed from his very soul—washed white by the trembling weak blood of old age. Powerful once, his whiskers lost their curl and were pushed back on his collarbone by the instrument while he sighted with the left eye along the fingerboard and his big hollow elbow came and went, and the fiddle trembled and cried.

So right then I decided, "I'll try it too." I banged down the cover and shut the clasps and drove straight to New York to a repair shop on 57th Street to have the violin reconditioned. As soon as it was ready I started to take lessons from an old Hungarian fellow named Haponyi who lived near the Barbizon-Plaza.

At this time I was alone in the country, divorced. An old lady, Miss Lenox from across the way, came in and fixed my breakfast and this was my only need at the time. Frances had stayed behind in Europe. And so one day as I was rushing to my lesson on 57th Street with the case under my arm, I met Lily. "Well!" I said. I hadn't seen her in more than a year, not since I put her on that train for Paris, but we were immediately on the old terms of familiarity just as before. Her large, pure face was the same as ever. It would never be steady, but it was beautiful. Only she had dyed her hair. It was now orange, which was not necessary, and it was parted from the middle of her forehead like the two panels of a curtain. It's the curse of these big beauties sometimes that they are short on taste. Also she had done something with mascara to her eyes so that they were no longer of equal length. What are you supposed to do if such a person is "the same as ever"? And what are you supposed to think when this tall woman, nearly six feet, in a kind of green plush suit like the stuff they used to have in Pullman cars and high heels, sways; sturdy as her legs are, great as her knees are, she sways; and in one look she throws away all the principles of behavior observed on 57th Street—as if throwing off the plush suit and hat and blouse and stockings and girdle to the winds and crying, "Gene! My life is misery without you"?

However, the first thing she actually said was, "I am engaged."

"What, again?" I said.

"Well, I could use your advice. We *are* friends. You *are* my friend, you know. I think we're each other's only friends in the world, after all. Are you studying music?"

"Well, if it isn't music then I'm in a gang war," I said. "Because this case holds either a fiddle or a tommy gun." I guess I must have felt embarrassed. Then she began to tell me about the new fiancé, mumbling. "Don't talk like that," I said. "What's the matter with you? Blow your nose. Why do you give me this Ivy League jive? This soft-spoken stuff? It's just done to take advantage of common people and make them bend over so as to hear you. You know I'm a little deaf," I said. "Raise your voice. Don't be such a snob. So tell me, did your fiancé go to Choate or St. Paul's? Your last husband went to President Roosevelt's prep school—whatchumajigger."

Lily now spoke more clearly and said, "My mother is dead."

"Dead?" I said. "Hey, that's terrible. But wait just one minute, didn't you tell me in France that she was dead?"

"Yes," she said.

"Then when did she die?"

"Just two months ago. It wasn't true then."

"Then why did you say it? That's a hell of a way. You can't do that. Are you playing chicken-funeral with your own mother? You were trying to con me."

"Oh, that was very bad of me, Gene. I didn't mean any harm. But this time it is true." And I saw the warm shadows of tears in her eyes. "She is gone now. I had to hire a plane to scatter her ashes over Lake George as she wanted."

"Did you? God, I'm sorry about it," I said.

"I fought her too much," said Lily. "Like that time I brought you home. But *she* was a fighter, and I am one, too. You were right about my fiancé. He did go to Groton."

"Ha, ha, I hit it, didn't I?"

"He's a nice man. He's not what you think. He's very decent and he supports his parents. But when I ask myself whether I could live without him, I guess the answer is yes. But I am learning to get along alone. There's always the universe. A woman doesn't have to marry, and there are perfectly good reasons why people should be lonely."

You know, compassion is useless, too, sometimes I feel. It just lasts long enough to get you in dutch. My heart ached for Lily, and then she tried to con me.

"All right, kid, what are you going to do now?"

"I sold the house in Danbury. I'm living in an apartment. But there was one thing I wanted you to have, and I sent it to you."

"I don't want anything."

"It's a rug," she said. "Hasn't it come yet?"

"Hell, what do I want with your Christly rug! Was it from your room?"

"No."

"You're a liar. It's the rug from your bedroom."

She denied it, and when it arrived at the farm I accepted it from the delivery man; I felt I should. It was creepy-looking and faded, a Baghdad mustard color, the threads surrendering to time and sprigs of blue all over it. It was so ugly I had to laugh. This crummy rug! It tickled me. So I put it on the floor of my violin studio, which was down in the basement. I had poured the concrete there myself but not thick enough, for the damp comes through. Anyway, I thought this rug might improve the acoustics.

All right, then, I'd come into the city for my lessons with that fat Hungarian Haponyi, and I'd see Lily too. We courted for about eighteen months, and then we got married, and then the children were born. As for the violin, I was no Heifetz but I kept at it. Presently the daily voice, *I want, I want,* arose again. Family life with Lily was not all that might have been predicted by an optimist; but I'm sure that she got more than she had bargained for, too. One of the first decisions she made after looking over the whole place as lady of the house was to get her portrait painted and hung with the rest of the family. This portrait business was very important to her and it went on until about six months before I took off for Africa.

So let's look at a typical morning of my married life with Lily. Not inside the house but outside, for inside it is filthy. Let's say it's one of those velvety days of early autumn when the sun is shining on the pines and the air has a spice of cold and stings your lungs with pleasure. I see a large pine tree on my property, and in the green darkness underneath, which somehow the pigs never got into, red tuberous begonias grow, and a broken stone inscription put in by my mother says, "Goe happy rose . . ." That's all it says. There must be more fragments beneath the needles. The sun is like a great roller and flattens the grass. Beneath this grass the earth may be filled with carcasses, yet that detracts nothing from a day like this, for they have become humus and the grass is thriving. When the air moves the brilliant flowers move too in the dark green beneath the trees. They brush against my open spirit because I am in the midst of this in the red velvet dressing gown from the Rue de Rivoli bought on the day that Frances spoke the word divorce. I am there and am looking for trouble. The crimson begonias, and the dark green and the radiant green and the spice that pierces and the sweet gold and the dead transformed, the brushing of the flowers on my undersurface are just misery to me. They make me crazy with misery. To somebody these things may have been given, but that somebody is not me in the red velvet robe. So what am I doing here?

Then Lily comes up with the two kids, our twins, twenty-six months old, tender, in their short pants and neat green jerseys, the dark hair brushed down on their foreheads. And here comes Lily with that pure face of hers going to sit for the portrait. And I am standing on one foot in the red velvet robe, heavy, wearing dirty farm boots, those Wellingtons which I favor when at home because they are so easy to put on and take off.

She starts to get into the station wagon and I say, "Use the convertible. I am going to Danbury later to look for some stuff, and I need this." My face is black and angry. My gums are aching. The joint is in disorder, but she is going and the kids will be playing indoors at the studio while she sits for the portrait. So she puts them in the back seat of the convertible and drives away.

Then I go down to the basement studio and take the fiddle and start warming up on my Sevcik exercises. Ottokar Sevcik invented a technique for the quick and accurate change of position on the violin. The student learns by dragging or sliding his fingers along the strings from first position to third and from third to fifth and from fifth to second, on and on, until the ear and fingers are trained and find the notes with precision. You don't even start with scales, but with phrases, and go up and down the strings, crawling. It is frightful: but Haponyi says it is the only way, this fat Hungarian. He knows about fifty words of English, the main one being "dear." He says, "Dear, take de bow like dis vun, not like dis vun, so. Und so, so, so. Not to kill vid de bow. Make nice. Do not stick. Yo, yo, yo. Seret lek! Nice."

And after all, I am a commando, you know. And with these hands I've pushed around the pigs; I've thrown down boars and pinned them and gelded them. So now these same fingers are courting the music of the violin and gripping its neck and toiling up and down on the Sevcik. The noise is like smashing egg crates. Nevertheless, I thought, if I discipline myself eventually the voice of angels may come out. But anyway I didn't hope to perfect myself as an artist. My main purpose was to reach my father by playing on his violin.

Down in the basement of the house, I worked very hard as I do at everything. I had felt I was pursuing my father's spirit, whispering, "Oh, Father, Pa. Do you recognize the sounds? This is me, Gene, on your violin, trying to reach you." For it so happens that I have never been able to convince myself the dead are utterly dead. I admire rational people and envy their clear heads, but what's the use of kidding? I played in the basement to my father and my mother, and when I learned a few pieces I would whisper, "Ma, this is 'Humoresque' for you." Or, "Pa, listen—'Meditation' from *Thaïs*." I played with dedication, with feeling, with longing, love—played to the point of emotional collapse. Also down there in my studio I sang as I played, "Rispondi! Anima bella" (Mozart). "He was despised and rejected, a man of sorrows and acquainted with grief" (Handel). Clutching the neck of the little instrument as if there were strangulation in my heart, I got cramps in my neck and shoulders.

Over the years I had fixed up the little basement for myself, paneled it with chestnut and put in a dehumidifier. There I keep my little safe and my files and war souvenirs; and there also I have a pistol range. Under foot was now Lily's rug. At her insistence I had got rid of most of the pigs. But she herself was not very cleanly, and for one reason or another we couldn't get anyone from the neighborhood to do the cleaning. Yes, she swept up once in a while, but toward the door and not out of it, so there were mounds of dust in the doorway. Then she went to sit for her portrait, running away from the house altogether while I was playing Sevcik and pieces of opera and oratorio, keeping time with the voice within.

IV

I S IT any wonder I had to go to Africa?

But I have told you there always comes a day of tears and madness.

I had fights, I had trouble with the troopers, I made suicide threats, and then last Xmas my daughter Ricey came home from boarding school. She has some of the family difficulty. To be blunt, I do not want to lose this child in outer space, and I said to Lily, "Keep an eye on her, will you?"

Lily was very pale. She said, "Oh, I want to help her. I will. But I've got to win her confidence."

Leaving the matter to her, I went down the kitchen back stairs to my studio and picked up the violin, which sparkled with rosin dust, and began to practice Sevcik under the fluorescent light of the music stand. I bent down in my robe and frowned, as well I might, at the screaming and grating of those terrible slides. Oh, thou God and judge of life and death! The ends of my fingers were wounded, indented especially by the steel E string, and my collarbone ached and a flaming patch, like the hives, came out on my jowl. But the voice within me continued, *I want, I want!*

But soon there was another voice in the house. Perhaps the music drove Ricey out. Lily and Spohr, the painter, were working hard to get the portrait finished by my birthday. She went away and Ricey, alone, took a trip to Danbury to visit a school chum, but didn't find her way to this girl's house. Instead, as she wandered through the back streets of Danbury she passed a parked car and heard the cries of a newborn infant in the back seat of this old Buick. It was in a shoebox. The day was terribly cold; therefore she brought the foundling back with her and hid it in the clothes closet of her room. On the twenty-first of December, at lunch, I was saying, "Children, this is the winter solstice," and then the infant's cry came out by way of the heating ducts from the register under the buffet. I pulled down the thick, woolly bill of my hunting cap, which, it so happens, I was wearing at the lunch table, and to suppress my surprise I began to talk about something else. For Lily was laughing toward me significantly with the upper lip drawn down over her front teeth, and her white color very warm. Looking at Ricey, I saw that silent happiness had come up into her eyes. At fifteen this girl is something of a beauty, though usually in a listless way. But she was not listless now; she was absorbed in the baby. As I did not know then who the kid was or how it had got into the house, I was startled, thrown, and I said to the twins, "So, there is a little pussy cat upstairs, eh?" They weren't fooled. Try and fool them! Ricey and Lily had baby bottles on the kitchen stove to sterilize. I took note of this caldron full of bottles as I was returning to the basement to practice, but made no comment. All afternoon, by way of the air ducts, I heard the infant squalling, and I went for a walk but couldn't bear the December ruins of my frozen estate and one-time pig kingdom. There were a few prize animals whom I hadn't sold. I wasn't ready to part with them yet.

I had arranged to play "The First Noël" on Xmas Eve, and so I was rehearsing it when Lily came downstairs to talk to me.

"I don't want to hear anything," I said.

"But, Gene," said Lily.

"You're in charge," I shouted, "you are in charge and it's your show."

"Gene, when you suffer you suffer harder than any person I ever saw." She had to smile, and not at my suffering, of course, but at the way I went about suffering. "Nobody expects it. Least of all God," she said.

"As you're in a position to speak for God," I said, "what does He think of your leaving this house every day to go and have your picture painted?"

"Oh, I don't think you need to be ashamed of me," said Lily.

Upstairs was the child, its every breath a cry, but it was no longer the topic. Lily thought I had a prejudice about her social origins, which are German and lace-curtain Irish. But damn it, I had no such prejudice. It was something else that bothered me.

Nobody truly occupies a station in life any more. There are mostly people who feel that they occupy the place that belongs to another by rights. There are displaced persons everywhere.

"For who shall abide the day of His (the rightful one's) coming?"

"And who shall stand when He (the rightful one) appeareth?"

When the rightful one appeareth we shall all stand and file out, glad at heart and greatly relieved, and saying, "Welcome back, Bud. It's all yours. Barns and houses are yours. Autumn beauty is yours. Take it, take it, take it!"

Maybe Lily was fighting along this line and the picture was going to be her proof that she and I were the rightful ones. But there is already a painting of me among the others. They have hard collars and whiskers, while I am at the end of a line in my National Guard uniform and hold a bayonet. And what good has this picture ever done me? So I couldn't be serious about Lily's proposed solution to our problem.

Now listen, I loved my older brother, Dick. He was the sanest of us, with a splendid record in the First World War, a regular lion. But for one moment he resembled me, his kid brother, and that was the end of him. He was on vacation, sitting at the counter of a Greek diner, the Acropolis Diner, near Plattsburg, New York, having a cup of coffee with a buddy and writing a post card home. But his fountain pen was balky, and he cursed it, and said to his friend, "Here. Hold this pen up." The young fellow did it and Dick took out his pistol and shot the pen from his hand. No one was injured. The roar was terrible. Then it was discovered that the bullet which had smashed the pen to bits had also pierced the coffee urn and made a fountain of the urn, which gushed straight across the diner in a hot stream to the window opposite. The Greek phoned for the state troopers, and during the chase Dick smashed his car into an embankment. He and his pal then tried to swim the river, and the pal had the presence of mind to strip his clothes, but Dick had on cavalry boots and they filled up and drowned him. This left my father alone in the world with me, my sister having died in 1901. I was working that summer for Wilbur, a fellow in our neighborhood, cutting up old cars.

But now it is Xmas week. Lily is standing on the basement stairs. Paris and Chartres and Vézelay and 57th Street are far behind us. I have the violin in my hands, and the fatal rug from Danbury under my feet. The red robe is on my back. And the hunting cap? I sometimes think it keeps my head in one piece. The gray wind of December is sweeping down the overhang of the roof and playing bassoons on the loose rain pipes. Notwithstanding this noise I hear the baby cry. And Lily says, "Can you hear it?"

"I can't hear a thing, you know I'm a little deaf," I said, which is true.

"Then how can you hear the violin?"

"Well, I'm standing right next to it, I should be able to hear it," I said. "Stop me if I'm wrong," I said, "but I seem to remember that you told me once I was your only friend in all the world."

"But—" said Lily.

"I can't understand you," I said. "Go away."

At two o'clock there were some callers, and they heard the cries from upstairs but were too well bred to mention them. I'd banked on that. To break up the tension, however, I said, "Would anybody like to visit my pistol range downstairs?" There were no takers and I went below myself and fired a few rounds. The bullets made a tremendous noise among the hot-air ducts. Soon I heard the visitors saying good-by.

Later, when the baby was asleep, Lily talked Ricey into going skating on the pond. I had bought skates for everyone, and Ricey is still young enough to be appealed to in this way. When they were gone, Lily having given me this opportunity, I laid down the fiddle and stole upstairs to Ricey's room. Quietly I opened the closet door and saw the infant sleeping on the chemises and stockings in Ricey's valise, for she had not finished unpacking. It was a colored child, and made a solemn impression on me. The little fists were drawn up on either side of its broad head. About the middle was a fat diaper made of a Turkish towel. And I stooped over it in the red robe and the Wellingtons, my face flaming so that my head itched under the wool cap. Should I close up the valise and take the child to the authorities? As I studied the little baby, this child of sorrow, I felt like the Pharaoh at the sight of little Moses. Then I turned aside and I went and took a walk in the woods. On the pond the cold runners clinked over the ice. It was an early sunset and I thought, "Well, anyway, God bless you, children."

That night in bed I said to Lily, "Well now, I'm ready to talk this thing over."

Lily said, "Oh, Gene, I'm very glad." She gave me a high

mark for this, and told me, "It's good that you are more able to accept reality."

"What?" I said. "I know more about reality than you'll ever know. I am on damned good terms with reality, and don't you forget it."

After a while I began to shout, and Ricey, hearing me carrying on and perhaps seeing me through the door, threatening and shaking my fist, standing on the bed in my jockey shorts, probably became frightened for her baby. On the twenty-seventh of December she ran away with the child. I didn't want the police in on this and phoned Bonzini, a private dick who has done some jobs for me, but before he could get on the case the headmistress called from Ricey's boarding school and said she had arrived and was hiding the infant in the dormitory. "You go up there," I said to Lily.

"Gene, but how can I?"

"How do I know how you can?"

"I can't leave the twins," she said.

"I guess it will interfere with your portrait, eh? Well, I'm just about ready to burn down the house and every picture in it."

"That's not what it is," said Lily, muttering and flushing white. "I have got used to your misunderstanding. I used to want to be understood, but I guess a person must try to live without being understood. Maybe it's a sin to want to be understood."

So it was I who went and the headmistress said that Ricey would have to leave her institution as she had already been on probation for quite a while. She said, "We have the psychological welfare of the other girls to consider."

"What's the matter with you? Those kids can learn noble feelings from my Ricey," I said, "and that's better than psychology." I was pretty drunk that day. "Ricey has an impulsive nature. She is one of those rapturous girls," I said. "Just because she doesn't talk much . . ."

"Where does the child come from?"

"She told my wife she found it in Danbury in a parked car."

"That's not what she says. She claims to be the mother."

"Why, I'm surprised at you," I said. "You ought to know

something about that. She didn't even get her breasts till last year. The girl is a virgin. She is fifty million times more pure than you or I."

I had to withdraw my daughter from the school.

I said to her, "Ricey, we have to give the little boy back. It isn't time yet for you to have your own little boy. His mama wants him back. She has changed her mind, dear." Now I feel I committed an offense against my daughter by parting her from this infant. After it was taken by the authorities from Danbury, Ricey acted very listless. "You know you are not the baby's mama, don't you?" I said. The girl never opened her lips and she made no answer.

As we were on our way to Providence, Rhode Island, where Ricey was going to stay with her aunt, Frances' sister, I said, "Sweetheart, your daddy did what any other daddy would do." Still no answer, and it was vain to try, because the silent happiness of the twenty-first of December was gone from her eyes.

So bound home from Providence alone, I was groaning to myself on the train, and in the club car I took out a deck of cards and played a game of solitaire. A bunch of people waited to sit down but I kept the table to myself, and I was fuddled, but no man in his right mind would have dared to bother me. I was talking aloud and groaning and the cards kept falling on the floor. At Danbury the conductor and another fellow had to help me off the train and I lay on a bench in the station swearing, "There is a curse on this land. There is something bad going on. Something is wrong. There is a curse on this land!"

I had known the stationmaster for a long time; he is a good old guy and kept the cops from taking me away. He phoned Lily to come for me, and she arrived in the station wagon.

But as for the actual day of tears and madness, it came about like this: It is a winter morning and I am fighting with my wife at the breakfast table about our tenants. She has remodeled a building on the property, one of the few I didn't take for the pigs because it was old and out of the way. I told her to go ahead, but then I held back on the dough, and instead of wood, wallboard was put in, with other economies on down the line. She made the place over with a new toilet and had it painted inside and out. But it had no insulation. Came November and the tenants began to feel cool. Well, they were bookish people; they didn't move around enough to keep their body heat up. After several complaints they told Lily they wanted to leave. "Okay, let them," I said. Naturally I wouldn't refund the deposit, but told them to get out.

So the converted building was empty, and the money put into masonite and new toilet and sink and all the rest was lost. The tenants had also left a cat behind. And I was sore and yelling at the breakfast table, hammering with my fist until the coffee pot turned over.

Then all at once Lily, badly scared, paused long and listened, and I listened with her. She said, "Have you seen Miss Lenox in the last fifteen minutes? She was supposed to bring the eggs."

Miss Lenox was the old woman who lived across the road and came in to fix our breakfast. A queer, wacky little spinster, she wore a tam and her cheeks were red and mumpy. She would tickle around in the corners like a mouse and take home empty bottles and cartons and similar junk.

I went into the kitchen and saw this old creature lying dead on the floor. During my rage, her heart had stopped. The eggs were still boiling; they bumped the sides of the pot as eggs will do when the water is seething. I turned off the gas. Dead! Her small, toothless face, to which I laid my knuckles, was growing cold. The soul, like a current of air, like a draft, like a bubble, sucked out of the window. I stared at her. So this is it, the end—farewell? And all this while, these days and weeks, the wintry garden had been speaking to me of this fact and no other; and till this moment I had not understood what this gray and white and brown, the bark, the snow, the twigs, had been telling me. I said nothing to Lily. Not knowing what else to do, I wrote a note DO NOT DISTURB and pinned it to the old lady's skirt, and I went through the frozen winter garden and across the road to her cottage.

In her yard she had an old catalpa tree of which the trunk and lower limbs were painted light blue. She had fixed little mirrors up there, and old bicycle lights which shone in the dark, and in summer she liked to climb up there and sit with her cats, drinking a can of beer. And now one of these cats was looking at me from the tree, and as I passed beneath I denied any blame that the creature's look might have tried to lay upon me. How could I be blamed—because my voice was loud, and my anger was so great?

In the cottage I had to climb from room to room over the boxes and baby buggies and crates she had collected. The buggies went back to the last century, so that mine might have been there too, for she got her rubbish all over the countryside. Bottles, lamps, old butter dishes, and chandeliers were on the floor, shopping bags filled with string and rags, and pronged openers that the dairies used to give away to lift the paper tops from milk bottles; and bushel baskets full of buttons and china door knobs. And on the walls, calendars and pennants and ancient photographs.

And I thought, "Oh, shame, shame! Oh, crying shame! How can we? Why do we allow ourselves? What are we doing? The last little room of dirt is waiting. Without windows. So for God's sake make a move, Henderson, put forth effort. You, too, will die of this pestilence. Death will annihilate you and nothing will remain, and there will be nothing left but junk. Because nothing will have been and so nothing will be left. While something still *is—now!* For the sake of all, get out."

Lily wept over the poor old woman.

"Why did you leave such a note?" she said.

"So nobody should move her until the coroner came," I said. "That's what the law is. I barely felt her myself." I then offered Lily a drink, which she refused, and I filled the water tumbler with bourbon and drank it down. Its only effect was a heartburn. Whisky could not coat the terrible fact. The old lady had fallen under my violence as people keel over during heat waves or while climbing the subway stairs. Lily was aware of this and started to mutter something about it. She was very thoughtful, and became silent, and her pure white color began to darken toward the eyes.

The undertaker in our town has bought the house where I used to take dancing lessons. Forty years ago I used to go there in my patent-leather shoes. When the hearse backed up the drive, I said, "You know, Lily, that trip that Charlie Albert is going to make to Africa? He'll be leaving in a couple of weeks, and I think I'll go along with him and his wife. Let's put the Buick in storage. You won't need two cars."

For once she didn't object to one of my ideas. "Maybe you ought to go," she said.

"I should do something."

So Miss Lenox went to the cemetery, and I went to Idlewild and took a plane.

V

I GUESS I hadn't taken two steps out into the world as a small boy when there was Charlie, a person in several ways like myself. In 1915 we attended dancing school together (in the house out of which Miss Lenox was buried), and such attachments last. In age he is only a year my junior and in wealth he goes me a little better, for when his old mother dies he will have another fortune. It was with Charlie that I took off for Africa, hoping to find a remedy for my situation. I guess it was a mistake to go with him, but I wouldn't have known how to go right straight into Africa by myself. You have to have a specific job to do. The excuse was that Charlie and his wife were going to film the Africans and the animals, for during the war Charlie was a cameraman with Patton's army—he could no more stay at home than I could—and so he learned the trade. Photography is not one of my interests.

Anyway, last year I asked Charlie to come out and photograph some of my pigs. This opportunity to show how good he was at his work pleased him, and he made some first-rate studies. Then we came back from the barn and he said he was engaged. So I told him, "Well, Charlie, I guess you know a lot about whores, but what do you know about girls—anything?"

"Oh," he said, "it's true that I don't know much, but I do know she is unique."

"Yes, I know all about this unique business," I said. (I had heard all about it from Lily but now she was never even at home.)

Nevertheless we went down to the studio to have a drink on his engagement, and he asked me to be his best man. He has almost no friends. We drank and kidded and reminisced about the dancing class, and made tears of nostalgia come to each other's eyes. It was then when we were both melted down that he invited me to come along to Africa where he and his wife would be going for their honeymoon.

I attended the wedding and stood up for him. However, because I forgot to kiss the bride after the ceremony, there developed a coolness on her side and eventually she became my enemy. The expedition that Charlie organized had all new equipment and was modern in every respect. We had a portable generator, a shower, and hot water, and from the beginning I was critical of this. I said, "Charlie, this wasn't the way we fought the war. Hell, we're a couple of old soldiers. What is this?" It wounded me to travel in Africa in this way.

But I had come to this continent to stay. When buying my ticket in New York I went through a silent struggle there at the airlines office (near Battery Park) as to whether or not to get a round-trip ticket. And as a sign of my earnestness, I decided to take it one way. So we flew from Idlewild to Cairo. I went on a bus to visit the Sphinx and the pyramids, and then we flew off again to the interior. Africa reached my feelings right away even in the air, from which it looked like the ancient bed of mankind. And at a height of three miles, sitting above the clouds, I felt like an airborne seed. From the cracks in the earth the rivers pinched back at the sun. They shone out like smelters' puddles, and then they took a crust and were covered over. As for the vegetable kingdom, it hardly existed from the air; it looked to me no more than an inch in height. And I dreamed down at the clouds, and thought that when I was a kid I had dreamed up at them, and having dreamed at the clouds from both sides as no other generation of men has done, one should be able to accept his death very easily. However, we made safe landings every time. Anyway, since I had come to this place under the circumstances described, it was natural to greet it with a certain emotion. Yes, I brought a sizable charge with me and I kept thinking, "Bountiful life! Oh, how bountiful life is." I felt I might have a chance here. To begin with, the heat was just what I craved, much hotter than the Gulf of Mexico, and then the colors themselves did me a world of good. I didn't feel the pressure in the chest, nor hear any voice within. At that time it was silent. Charlie and his wife and I, together with natives and trucks and equipment, were camped near some lake or other. The water here was very soft, with reeds and roots rotted, and there were crabs in the sand. The crocodiles boated around in the lilies, and when they opened their mouths they made me realize how hot a damp creature can be inside. The birds went into their jaws and cleaned their teeth. However, the people in this district were very sad, not lively. On the trees grew a feather-like bloom and the papyrus reeds began to remind me of funeral plumes, and after about three weeks of cooperating with Charlie, helping him with the camera equipment and trying to interest myself in his photographic problems, my discontent returned and one afternoon I heard the familiar old voice within. It began to say, *I want, I want, I want!*

I said to Charlie, "I don't want you to get sore, now, but I don't think this is working out, the three of us together in Africa."

Stolid, he looked me over through his sunglasses. We were beside the water. Was this the kid I used to know in dancing class? How time had changed us both. But we were now, as then, in short pants. His development is broad through the chest. And as I am much the taller, he was looking up, but he was angry, not intimidated. The flesh around his mouth became very lumpy as he deliberated, and then he said, "No? Why not?"

"Well," I said, "I took this chance to get here, Charlie, and I'm very grateful because I've always been a sort of Africa buff, but now I realize that I didn't come to take pictures of it. Sell me one of the jeeps and I'll take off."

"Where do you want to go?"

"All I know is that this isn't the place for me," I said.

"Well, if you want to, shove off. I won't stop you, Gene."

It was all because I had forgotten to kiss his wife after the ceremony, and she couldn't forgive me. What would she want a kiss from me for? Some people don't know when they're well off. I can't say why I didn't kiss her; I was thinking of something else, I guess. But I think she concluded that I was jealous of Charlie, and anyway I was spoiling her African honeymoon.

"So, no hard feelings, eh, Charlie? But it does me no good to travel this way."

"That's okay. I'm not trying to stop you. Just blow."

And that was what I did. I organized a separate expedition that suited my soldierly temperament better. I hired two of Charlie's natives and when we drove away in the jeep I felt better at once. And after a few days, anxious to simplify more and more, I laid off one of the men and had a long conversation with the remaining African, Romilayu. We arrived at an understanding. He said that if I wanted to see some places off the beaten track, he could guide me to them.

"That's it," I said. "Now you've got the idea. I didn't come here to carry on a quarrel with a broad over a kiss."

"Me tek you far, far," he said.

"Oh, man! The farther the better. Why, let's go, let's go," I said. I had found the fellow I wanted, just the right man. We got rid of more baggage and, knowing how attached he was to the jeep, I told him I would give it to him if he would take me far enough. He said the place he was going to guide me to was so remote we could reach it only on foot. "So?" I said. "Let's walk. We'll put the jeep up on blocks, and she's yours when we get back." This pleased him deeply, and when we got to a town called Talusi we left the machine in dead storage in a grass hut. From here we took a plane to Baventai, an old Bellanca, the wings looked ready to drop off, and the pilot was an Arab and flew with bare feet. It was an exceptional flight and ended on a field of hard clay beyond the mountain. Tall Negro cowherds came up to us with their greased curls and their deep lips. I had never seen men who looked so wild and I said to Romilayu, my guide, "This isn't the place you promised to bring me to, is it?"

"Wo, no sah," he said.

We were to travel for another week, afoot, afoot.

Geographically speaking I didn't have the remotest idea where we were, and I didn't care too much. It was not for me to ask, since my object in coming here was to leave certain things behind. Anyway, I had great trust in Romilayu, the old fellow. So for days and days he led me through villages, over mountain trails, and into deserts, far, far out. He himself couldn't have told me much about our destination in his limited English. He said only that we were going to see a tribe he called the Arnewi.

"You know these people?" I asked him.

A long time ago, before he was full grown, Romilayu had visited the Arnewi together with his father or his uncle—he told me many times but I couldn't make out which.

"Anyway, you want to go back to the scenes of your youth," I said. "I get the picture."

I was having a great time out here in the desert among the

stones, and continually congratulated myself on having quit Charlie and his wife and on having kept the right native. To have found a man like Romilayu, who sensed what I was looking for, was a great piece of luck. He was in his late thirties, he told me, but looked much older because of premature wrinkles. His skin did not fit tightly. This happens to many black men of certain breeds and they say it has something to do with the distribution of the fat on the body. He had a bush of dusty hair which he tried sometimes, but vainly, to smooth flat. It was unbrushable and spread out at the sides of his head like a dwarf pine. Old tribal scars were cut into his cheeks and his ears had been mutilated to look like hackles so that the points stuck into his hair. His nose was fine-looking and Abyssinian, not flat. The scars and mutilations showed that he had been born a pagan, but somewhere along the way he had been converted, and now he said his prayers every evening. On his knees, he pressed his purple hands together under his chin, which receded, and with his lips pushed forward and the powerful though short muscles jumping under the skin of his arms, he'd pray. He fetched up deep sounds from his chest, like confiding groans of his soul. This would happen when we stopped to camp at twilight when the swallows were dipping back and forth. Then I would sit on the ground and encourage him; I'd say, "Go on. Tell 'em. And put in a word for me too."

I got clean away from everything, and we came into a region like a floor surrounded by mountains. It was hot, clear, and arid and after several days we saw no human footprints. Nor were there many plants; for that matter there was not much of anything here; it was all simplified and splendid, and I felt I was entering the past—the real past, no history or junk like that. The prehuman past. And I believed that there was something between the stones and me. The mountains were naked, and often snakelike in their forms, without trees, and you could see the clouds being born on the slopes. From this rock came vapor, but it was not like ordinary vapor, it cast a brilliant shadow. Anyway I was in tremendous shape those first long days, hot as they were. At night, after Romilayu had prayed, and we lay on the ground, the face of the air breathed back on us, breath for breath. And then there were the calm stars, turning around and singing, and the birds of the night with heavy bodies, fanning by. I couldn't have asked for anything better. When I laid my ear to the ground I thought I could hear hoofs. It was like lying on the skin of a drum. Those were wild asses maybe, or zebras flying around in herds. And this was how Romilayu traveled, and I lost count of the days. As, probably, the world was glad to lose track of me too for a while.

The rainy season had been very short; the streams were all dry and the bushes would burn if you touched a match to them. At night I would start a fire with my lighter, which was the type in common use in Austria with a long trailing wick. By the dozen they come to about fourteen cents apiece; you can't beat that for a bargain. Well, we were now on a plateau which Romilayu called the Hinchagara—this territory has never been well mapped. As we marched over that hot and (it felt so to me) slightly concave plateau, a kind of olive-colored heat mist, like smoke, formed under the trees, which were short and brittle, like aloes or junipers (but then I'm no botanist) and Romilayu, who came behind me through the strangeness of his shadow, made me think of a long wooden baker's shovel darting into the oven. The place was certainly at baking heat.

Finally one morning we found ourselves in the bed of a good-sized river, the Arnewi, and we walked downstream in it, for it was dry. The mud had turned to clay, and the boulders sat like lumps of gold in the dusty glitter. Then we sighted the Arnewi village and saw the circular roofs which rose to a point. I knew they were just thatch and must be brittle, porous, and light; they seemed like feathers, and yet heavy—like heavy feathers. From these coverings smoke went up into the silent radiance. Also an inanimate glitter came off the ancient thatch. "Romilayu," I said, stopping him, "isn't that a picture? Where are we? How old is this place, anyway?"

Surprised at my question he said, "I no know, sah."

"I have a funny feeling from it. Hell, it looks like the original place. It must be older than the city of Ur." Even the dust had a flavor of great age, I thought, and I said, "I have a hunch this spot is going to be very good for me."

The Arnewi were cattle raisers. We startled some of the skinny animals on the banks, and they started to buck and gallop, and soon we found ourselves amid a band of African kids, naked boys and girls, yelling at the sight of us. Even the tiniest of them, with the big bellies, wrinkled their faces and screeched with the rest, above the bellowing of the cattle, and flocks of birds who had been sitting in trees took off through the withered leaves. Before I saw them it sounded like stones pelting at us and I thought we were under attack. Under the mistaken impression that we were being stoned, I laughed and swore. It amused me that they might be shying rocks at me, and I said, "Jesus, is this the way they meet travelers?" But then I saw the birds beating it through the sky.

Romilayu explained to me that the Arnewi were very sensitive to the condition of their cattle, whom they regarded as their relatives, more or less, and not as domestic animals. No beef was eaten here. And instead of one kid's being sent out with the herd, each cow had two or three child companions; and when the animals were upset, the children ran after them to soothe them. The adults were even more peculiarly attached to their beasts, which it took me some time to understand. But at the time I remember wishing that I had brought some treats for the children. When fighting in Italy I always carried Hershey bars and peanuts from the PX for the bambini. So now, coming down the river bed and approaching the wall of the town, which was made of thorns with some manure and reinforced by mud, we saw some of the kids waiting up for us, the rest having gone on to spread the news of our arrival. "Aren't they something?" I said to Romilayu. "Christ, look at the little pots on them, and those tight curls. Most of them haven't got their second teeth in yet." They jumped up and down, screaming, and I said, "I certainly wish I had a treat for them, but I haven't got anything. How do you think they'd like it if I set fire to a bush with this lighter?" And without waiting for Romilayu's advice I took out the Austrian lighter with the drooping wick, spun the tiny wheel with my thumb, and immediately a bush went flaming, almost invisible in the strong sunlight. It roared; it made a brilliant manifestation; it stretched to its limits and became extinct in the sand. I was left holding the lighter with the wick coming out of my fist like a slender white whisker. The kids were unanimously silent, they only looked, and I looked at them. That's what they call reality's dark dream? Then suddenly everyone scattered again, and the cows galloped. The embers of the bush had fallen by my boots.

"How do you think that went over?" I asked Romilayu. "I meant well." But before we could discuss the matter we were met by a party of naked people. In front of them all was a young woman, a girl not much older, I believe, than my daughter Ricey. As soon as she saw me she burst into loud tears.

I would never have expected this to wound me as it did. It wouldn't have been realistic to go into the world without being prepared for trials, ordeals, and suffering, but the sight of this young woman hit me very hard. Though of course the tears of women always affect me deeply, and not so long before, when Lily had started to cry in our hotel suite on the Gulf, I made my worst threat. But this young woman being a stranger, it's less easy to explain why her weeping loosed such a terrible emotion in me. What I thought immediately was "What have I done?"

"Shall I run back into the desert," I thought, "and stay there until the devil has passed out of me and I am fit to meet human kind again without driving it to despair at the first look? I haven't had enough desert yet. Let me throw away my gun and my helmet and the lighter and all this stuff and maybe I can get rid of my fierceness too and live out there on worms. On locusts. Until all the bad is burned out of me. Oh, the bad! Oh, the wrong, the wrong! What can I do about it? What can I do about all the damage? My character! God help me, I've made a mess of everything, and there's no getting away from the results. One look at me must tell the whole story."

You see, I had begun to convince myself that those few days of lightheartedness, tramping over the Hinchagara plateau with Romilayu, had already made a great change in me. But it seemed that I was still not ready for society. Society is what beats me. Alone I can be pretty good, but let me go among people and there's the devil to pay. Confronted with this weeping girl I was by this time ready to start bawling myself, thinking of Lily and the children and my father and the violin and the foundling and all the sorrows of my life. I felt that my nose was swelling, becoming very red.

Behind the weeping girl other natives were crying along softly. I said to Romilayu, "What the blast is going on?"

"Him shame," said Romilayu, very grave, with that up-standing bush of hair.

Thus this sturdy, virginal-looking girl was crying—simply crying—without gestures; her arms were meekly hanging by her sides and all the facts about her (speaking physically) were shown to the world. The tears fell from her wide cheekbones onto her breasts.

I said, "What's eating this kid? What do you mean, shame? This is very bad, if you ask me, Romilayu. I think we've walked into a bad situation and I don't like the looks of it. Why don't we cut around this town and go back in the desert? I felt a damned sight better out there."

Apparently Romilayu sensed that I was rattled by this delegation shedding tears and he said, "No, no sah. You no be blame."

"Maybe it was a mistake with that bush?"

"No, no, sah. You no mek him cry."

At this I struck myself in the head with my open hand and said, "Why sure! I *would*." (Meaning, "I *would* think first of myself.") "The poor soul is in trouble? Is there something I can do for her? She's coming to me for help. I feel it. Maybe a lion has eaten her family? Are there man-eaters around here? Ask her, Romilayu. Say that I've come to help, and if there are killers in the neighborhood I'll shoot them." I picked up my H and H Magnum with the scope sights and showed it to the crowd. With enormous relief it dawned on me that the crying was not due to any fault of mine, and that something could be done, that I did not have to stand and bear the sight of those tears boiling out. "Everybody! Leave it to me," I said. "Look! Look!" And I started to go through the manual of arms for them, saying, "Hut, hut, hut," as the drill instructors always did.

Everyone, however, went on crying. Only the very little kids with their jack-o'-lantern faces seemed happy at my entertainment. The rest were not done mourning, and covered their faces with their hands while their naked bodies shook.

"Well, Romilayu," I said, "I'm not getting anywhere, and our presence is very hard on them, that's for sure."

"Dem cry for dead cow," he said. And he explained the thing very clearly, that they were mourning for cattle which had died in the drought, and that they took responsibility for the drought upon themselves—the gods were offended, or something like that; a curse was mentioned. Anyway, as we were strangers they were obliged to come forward and confess everything to us, and ask whether we knew the reason for their trouble.

"How should I know—except the drought? A drought is drought," I said, "but my heart goes out to them, because I know what it is to lose a beloved animal." And I began to say, almost to shout, "Okay, okay, okay. All right, ladies—all right, you guys, break it up. That's enough, please. I get it." And this did have some effect on them, as I suppose they heard in the tone of my voice that I felt a certain amount of distress also, and I said to Romilayu, "So ask them what they want me to do. I intend to do something, and I really mean it."

"What you do, sah?"

"Never mind. There must be something that only I can do. I want you to start asking."

So he spoke to them, and the smooth-skinned, humped cattle kept grunting in their gentle bass voices (the African cows do not low like our own). But the weeping died down. And now I began to observe that the coloring of these people was very original and that the dark was more deeply burnt in about the eyes whereas the palms of their hands were the color of freshly washed granite. As if, you know, they had played catch with the light and some of it had come off. These peculiarities of color were altogether new to me. Romilayu had gone aside to speak with someone and left me among the natives, whose sobbing had almost stopped. Just then I deeply felt my physical discrepancies. My face is like some sort of terminal; it's like Grand Central, I mean—the big horse nose and the wide mouth that opens into the nostrils, and eyes like tunnels. So I stood there waiting, surrounded by this black humanity in the aromatic dust, with that inanimate brilliance coming off the thatch of the huts near by.

Then the man with whom Romilayu had been speaking came up and talked to me in English, which astonished me, for I would never have thought that people who spoke English would have been capable of carrying on so emotionally. However, he was not one of those who had carried on. From his

size alone I felt he must be an important person, for he was
built very heavily and had an inch or two on me in stature. But
he was not ponderous, as I am, he was muscular; nor was he
naked like the others, but wore a piece of white cloth tied on
his thighs rather than on his hips proper, and around his belly
was a green silk scarf, and he had a short loose middy type of
blouse, which he wore very free to give his arms lots of play,
which owing to the big muscles they needed. At first he was
rather heavy of expression and I thought he might be looking
for trouble, sizing me up as if I were some kind of human
mushroom, imposing in size but not hard to knock over. I was
very upset, but what upset me was not his expression, which
soon changed for the better; it was, among other things, the
fact that he spoke to me in English. I don't know why I should
have been so surprised—disappointed is the word. It's the great
imperial language of today, taking its turn after Greek and
Latin and so on. The Romans weren't surprised, I don't think,
when some Parthian or Numidian started to speak to them in
Latin; they probably took it for granted. But when this fellow,
built like a champion, in his white drooping cloth and his scarf
and middy, addressed me in English, I was both shaken up and
grieved. Preparing to speak he put his pale, slightly freckled
lips into position, moving them forward, and said, "I am Itelo.
I am here to introduce. Welcome. And how do you do?"

"What? What?" I said, holding my ear.

"Itelo." He bowed.

Quickly, I too bent and bowed in the short pants and corky
white helmet with my overheated face and great nose. My
face can be like the clang of a bell, and because I am hard of
hearing on the right side I have a way of swinging the left into
position, listening in profile and fixing my eyes on some object
to help my concentration. So I did. I waited for him to say
more, sweating boisterously, for I was confounded down to
the ground. I couldn't believe it; I was so sure that I had left
the world. And who could blame me, after that trip across the
mountain floor on which there was no footprint, the stars
flaming like oranges, those multimillion tons of exploding gas
looking so mild and fresh in the dark of the sky; and altogether, that freshness, you know, that like autumn freshness
when you go out of the house in the morning and find the

flowers have waked in the frost with piercing life? When I experienced this in the desert, night and morning, feeling everything to be so simplified, I was quite sure that I had gone clean
out of the world, for, as is common knowledge, the world is
complex. And besides, the antiquity of the place had struck me
so, I was sure I had got into someplace new. And the weeping
delegation; but here was someone who obviously had been
around, as he spoke English, and I had been boasting, "Show
me your enemies and I'll kill them. Where is the man-eater,
lead me to him." And setting bushes on fire, and performing
the manual of arms, and making like a regular clown. I felt extremely ridiculous, and I gave Romilayu a dark, angry look, as
though it were his fault for not having briefed me properly.

But this native, Itelo, did not mean to work me over because
of my behavior on arrival. It never seemed to enter his mind,
even. He took my hand and placed it flat against his breast
saying, "Itelo."

I did likewise, saying, "Henderson." I didn't want to be a
shit about it, you see, but I am not good at suppressing my
feelings. Whole crowds of them, especially the bad ones, wave
to the world from the galleries of my face. I can't prevent them.
"How do you do?" I said. "And say, what's going on around
here—everybody crying to beat the band? My man says it's
because of the cows. This isn't a good time for a visit, eh?
Maybe I should go and come back some other time?"

"No, you be guest," said Itelo, and made me welcome. But
he had observed that I was disappointed and that my offer to
depart was not one hundred per cent gallantry and generosity
and he said, "You thought first footstep? Something new? I am
very sorry. We are discovered."

"If I did expect it," I said, "then it's my own damn fault. I
know the world has been covered. Hell, I'd have to be out of
my mind. I'm no explorer, and anyway that's not what I came
for." So, recalling to mind what I had come for, I started to
look at this fellow more closely to see what he might know
about the greater or deeper facts of life. And first of all I recognized that his heaviness of expression was misleading and
that he was basically a good-humored fellow. Only he was very
dignified. Two large curves starting above his nostrils came

down beside his mouth and gave him the look I had misinterpreted. He had a backed-up posture which emphasized the great strength of his legs and knees, and in the corners of his eyes, which had the same frame of darkness as the others in the tribe, there was a glitter which made me think of gold leaf.

"Well," I said, "I see you have been out in the world anyway. Or is English everybody's second language here?"

"Sir," he said, "oh, no, just only me." Perhaps because of the breadth of his nose he had a tone which was ever so slightly nasal. "Malindi school. I went, and also my late brother. Lot of young fellows sent from all over to Malindi school. After that, Beirut school. I have traveled all over. So I alone speak. And for miles and miles around nobody else, but only Wariri king, Dahfu."

I had completely forgotten to find out, and now I said, "Oh, excuse me, do you happen to be royalty yourself?"

"Queen is my auntie," he said, "Willatale. And you will stay with other auntie, Mtalba. Sir, she lend you her house."

"Oh, that's great," I said. "That's hospitable. And so you're a prince?"

"Oh, yes."

That was better. Owing to his size and appearance I thought from the beginning that he must be distinguished. And then to console me he said that I was the first white visitor here in more than thirty years, so far as he knew. "Well, Your Highness," I said, "you're just as well off not to attract many outsiders. I think you've got a good thing here. I don't know what it is about the place, but I've visited some of the oldest ruins in Europe and they don't feel half as ancient as your village. If it worries you that I'm going to run and broadcast your whereabouts or that I want to take pictures, you can just forget about it. That's not my line at all." For this he thanked me but said there wasn't much of value to attract travelers here. And I'm still not convinced that I didn't penetrate beyond geography. Not that I care too much about geography; it's one of those bossy ideas according to which, if you locate a place, there's nothing more to be said about it.

"Mr. Henderson, sir. Please come in and enter the town," he said.

And I said, "I suppose you want me to meet everyone."

It was gorgeous weather, though far too dry, radiance everywhere, and the very dust of the place aromatic and stimulating. Waiting for us was a company of women, Itelo's wives, naked, and with the dark color worked in deeply around the eyes as if by special action of the sun. The lighter skin of their hands reminded me continually of pink stone. It made both hands and fingers seem larger than ordinary. Later I saw some of these younger women stand by the hour with a piece of string and play cat's cradle, and each pair of players usually had several spectators and they cried, "Awho!" when one of them took over a complicated figure. The women bystanders now laid their wrists together and flapped their hands, which was their form of applause. The men put their fingers in their mouths and whistled, sometimes in chorus. Now that the weeping had ended entirely, I stood laughing under the big soiled helmet, my mouth expanded greatly.

"Well," said Itelo, "we will go to see the queen, my aunt, Willatale, and afterward or maybe the same time the other one, Mtalba." By now a pair of umbrellas had come up, carried by two women. The sun was very rich, and I was sweating, and these two state umbrellas, about eight feet tall and shaped like squash flowers, gave very little shade from such a height. Everybody was extremely good-looking here; some of them would have satisfied the standards of Michelangelo himself. So we went along by twos with considerable ceremony, Itelo leading. I was grinning but pretended that it was a grimace because of the sun. Thus we proceeded toward the queen's compound.

And now I began to understand what the trouble here was all about, the cause of all the tears. Coming to a corral, we saw a fellow with a big clumsy comb of wood standing over a cow—a humped cow like all the rest, but that's not the point; the point is that he was grooming and petting her in a manner I never saw before. With the comb he was doing her forelock, which was thick over the bulge of the horns. He stroked and hugged her, and she was not well; you didn't have to be country bred, as I happen to be, to see at once that something was wrong with this animal. She didn't even give him a knock with her head as a cow in her condition will when she feels affectionate, and the fellow himself was lost in sadness, gloomily combing her. There was an atmosphere of hopelessness around them both. It took a while for me to put all the elements together. You have to understand that these people love their cattle like brothers and sister, like children; they have more than fifty terms just to describe the various shapes of the horns, and Itelo explained to me that there were hundreds of words for the facial expressions of cattle and a whole language of cow behavior. To a limited extent I could appreciate this. I have had great affection for certain pigs myself. But a pig is basically a career animal; he responds very sensitively to human ambitions or drives and therefore doesn't require a separate vocabulary.

The procession had stopped with Itelo and me, and everyone was looking at the fellow and his cow. But seeing how much emotional hardship there was in this sight I started to move on; but the next thing I saw was even sadder. A man of about fifty, white-haired, was kneeling, weeping and shuddering, throwing dust on his head, because his cow was passing away. All watched with grief, while the fellow took her by the horns, which were lyre-shaped, begging her not to leave him. But she was already in the state of indifference and the skin over her eyes wrinkled as if he were only just keeping her awake. At this I myself was swayed; I felt compassion, and I said, "Prince, for Christ's sake, can't anything be done?"

Itelo's large chest lifted under the short, loose middy and he pulled a great sigh as if he did not want to spoil my visit with all this grief and mourning. "I do not think," said Itelo.

Just then the least expected of things happened, which was that I caught a glimpse of water in considerable amounts, and at first I was inclined to interpret this as the glitter of sheet metal coming and going before my eyes keenly. But there is something unmistakable about the closeness of water. I smelled it too and I stopped the prince and said to him, "Check me out on this, will you, Prince? But here is this guy killing himself with lamentation and if I'm not mistaken I actually see some water shining over there to the left. Is that a fact?"

He admitted that it was water.

"And the cows are dying of thirst?" I said. "So there must be something wrong with it? It's polluted? But look," I said, "there must be something you can do with it, strain it or something. You could make big pots—vats. You could boil out the impurities. Hey, maybe it doesn't sound practical, but you'd be surprised, if you mobilized the whole place and everybody pitched in—gung-ho! I know how paralyzing a situation like this can become."

But all the while the prince, though shaking his head up and down as though he agreed, in reality disagreed with me. His heavy arms were folded across his middy blouse, while a tattered shade came down from the squash-flower parasol held aloft by the naked women with their four hands as if they might be carried away by the wind. Only there was no wind. The air was as still as if it were knotted to the zenith and stuck there, parched and blue, a masterpiece of midday beauty.

"Oh . . . thank you," he said, "for good intention."

"But I should mind my own business? You may be right. I don't want to bust into your customs. But it's hard to see all this going on and not even make a suggestion. Can I have a look at your water supply at least?"

With a certain reluctance he said, "Okay. I suppose." And Itelo and I, the two of us almost of a size, left his wives and the other villagers behind and went to see the water. I inspected it, and except for some slime or algae it looked all right, and was certainly copious. A thick wall of dark green stone retained it, half cistern and half dam. I figured that there must be a spring beneath; a dry watercourse coming from the mountain showed what the main source of supply was normally. To prevent evaporation a big roof of thatch was pitched over this cistern, measuring at least fifty by seventy feet. After my long hike I would have been grateful to pull off my clothes and leap into this shady, warm, albeit slightly scummy water to swim and float. I would have liked nothing better than to lie floating under this roof of delicate-looking straw.

"Now, Prince, what's the complaint? Why can't you use this stuff?" I said.

Only the prince had come up with me to this sunken tank; the rest of them stood about twenty yards off, obviously unsettled and in a state of agitation, and I said, "What's eating your people? Is there something in this water?" And I stared in and realized for myself that there was considerable activity just below the surface. Through the webbing of the light I saw first polliwogs with huge heads, at all stages of development, with full tails like giant sperm, and with budding feet. And then great powerful frogs, spotted, swimming by with their neckless thick heads and long white legs, the short forepaws expressive of astonishment. And of all the creatures in the vicinity, bar none, it seemed to me they had it best, and I envied them myself. "So don't tell me! It's the frogs?" I said to Itelo. "They keep you from watering the cattle?"

He shook his head with melancholy. Yes, it was the frogs.

"How did they ever get in here? Where do they come from?"

These questions Itelo couldn't answer. The whole thing was a mystery. All he could tell me was that these creatures, never before seen, had appeared in the cistern about a month ago and prevented the cattle from being watered. This was the curse mentioned before.

"You call this a curse?" I said. "But you've been out in the world. Didn't they ever show you a frog at school—at least a picture of one? These are just harmless."

"Oh, yes, sure," said the prince.

"So you know you don't have to let your animals die because a few of these beasts are in the water."

But about this he could do nothing. He put up his large hands and said, "Mus' be no ahnimal in drink wattah."

"Then why don't you get rid of them?"

"Oh, no, no. Nevah touch ahnimal in drink wattah."

"Oh, come on, Prince, pish-posh," I said. "We could filter them out. We could poison them. There are a hundred things we could do."

He took his lip in his teeth and shut his eyes, meanwhile making loud exhalations to show how impossible my suggestions were. He blew the air through his nostrils and shook his head.

"Prince," I said, "let's you and I talk this over." I grew very intense. "Before long if this keeps up the town is going to be one continuous cow funeral. Rain isn't likely. The season is over. You need water. You've got this reserve of it." I lowered my voice. "Look here, I'm kind of an irrational person myself, but survival is survival."

"Oh, sir," said the prince, "the people is frightened. Nobody have evah see such a ahnimal."

"Well," I said, "the last plague of frogs I ever heard about was in Egypt." This reinforced the feeling of antiquity the place had given me from the very first. Anyway it was due to this curse that the people, led by that maiden, had greeted me with tears by the wall of the town. It was nothing if not extraordinary. So now, when everything fitted together, the tranquil water of the cistern became as black to my eyes as the lake of darkness. There really was a vast number of these creatures woggling and crowding, stroking along with the water slipping over their backs and their mottles, as if they owned the medium. And also they crawled out and thrummed on the wet stone with congested, emotional throats, and blinked with their peculiarly marbled eyes, red and green and white, and I shook my head much more at myself than at them, thinking that a damned fool going out into the world is bound and fated to encounter damned fool phenomena. Nevertheless, I told those creatures, just wait, you little sons of bitches, you'll croak in hell before I'm done.

VI

T HE GNATS were spinning over the sun-warmed cistern, which was green and yellow and dark by turns. I said to Itelo, "You're not allowed to molest these animals, but what if a stranger came along—me for instance—and took them on for you?" I realized that I would never rest until I had dealt with these creatures and lifted the plague.

From his attitude I could tell that under some unwritten law he was not allowed to encourage me in my purpose, but that he and all the rest of the Arnewi would consider me their very greatest benefactor. For Itelo would not answer directly but kept sighing and repeating, "Oh, a very sad time. 'Strodinary bad time." And I then gave him a deep look and said, "Itelo, you leave this to me," and drew in a sharp breath between my teeth, feeling that I had it in me to be the doom of those frogs. You understand, the Arnewi are milk-drinkers exclusively and the cows are their entire livelihood; they never eat meat except ceremonially whenever a cow meets a natural death, and even this they consider a form of cannibalism and they eat in tears. Therefore the death of some of the animals was sheer disaster, and the families of the deceased every day were performing last rites and crying and eating flesh, so it was no wonder they were in this condition. As we turned away I felt as though that cistern of problem water with its algae and its frogs had entered me, occupying a square space in my interior, and sloshing around as I moved.

We went toward my hut (Itelo's and Mtalba's hut), for I wanted to clean up a little before my introduction to the queen, and on the way I read the prince a short lecture. I said, "Do you know why the Jews were defeated by the Romans? Because they wouldn't fight back on Saturday. And that's how it is with your water situation. Should you preserve yourself, or the cows, or preserve the custom? I would say, yourself. Live," I said, "to make another custom. Why should you be ruined by frogs?" The prince listened and said only, "Hm, very interestin'. Is that a fact? 'Strodinary."

We came to the house where Romilayu and I were to stay; it

was within a courtyard and, like all the rest of the houses, round, made of clay, and with a conical roof. All inside seemed very brittle and light and empty. Smoke-browned poles were laid across the ceiling at intervals of about three feet and beyond them the long ribs of the palm leaves resembled whalebone. Here I sat down, and Itelo, who had entered with me and left his followers outside in the sunlight, sat opposite me while Romilayu began to unpack. The heat of the day was now at the peak and the air was perfectly quiet; only in the canes above us, that light amber cone of thatch from which a dry vegetable odor descended, I heard small creatures, beetles and perhaps birds or mice, which stirred and batted and bristled. At this moment I was too tired even for a drink (we carried a few canteens filled with bourbon) and was thinking only of the crisis, and how to destroy the frogs in the cistern. But the prince wanted to talk; and at first I took this for sociability, but presently it appeared that he was leading up to something and I became watchful.

"I go to school in Malindi," he said. "Wondaful, beautiful town." This town of Malindi I later checked into; it was an old dhow port on the east coast famous in the Arab slave trade. Itelo spoke of his wanderings. He and his friend Dahfu, who was now king of the Wariri, had traveled together, taking off from the south. They shipped on the Red Sea in some old tubs and worked on the railroad built by the Turks to the Al Medinah before the Great War. With this I was slightly familiar, for my mother had been wrapped up in the Armenian cause, and from reading about Lawrence of Arabia I had long ago realized how much American education was spread through the Middle East. The Young Turks, and Enver Pasha himself, if I am not mistaken, studied in American schools—though how they got from "The Village Blacksmith" and "sweet Alice and laughing Allegra" to wars and plots and massacres would make an interesting topic. But this Prince Itelo of the obscure cattle tribe on the Hinchagara plateau had attended a mission school in Syria, and so had his Wariri friend. Both had returned to their remote home. "Well," I said, "I guess it was great for you to go and find out what things are like."

The prince was smiling, but his posture had become very tense at the same time; his knees had spread wide apart and he pressed the ground with the thumb and knuckle of one hand. Yet he continued to smile and I realized that we were on the verge of something. We were seated face to face on a pair of low stools within the thatched hut, which gave the effect of a big sewing basket; and everything that had happened to me—the long trek, hearing zebras at night, the sun moving up and down daily like a musical note, the color of Africa, and the cattle and the mourners, and the yellow cistern water and the frogs, had worked so on my mind and feelings that everything was balanced very delicately inside. Not to say precariously.

"Prince," I said, "what's coming off here?"

"When stranger guest comes we allways make acquaintance by wrestle. Invariable."

"That seems like quite a rule," I said, very hesitant. "Well, I wonder, can't you waive it once, or wait a while, as I am completely tuckered out?"

"Oh, no," he said. "New arrival, got to wrestle. Allways."

"I see," I said, "and I reckon you must be the champion here." This was a question I could answer for myself. Naturally, he was the champion, and this was why he had come to meet me and why he had entered the hut. It explained also the excitement of the kids back in the river bed, who knew there would be a wrestling match. "Well, Prince," I said, "I am almost willing to concede without a contest. After all, you have a tremendous build and, as you see, I am an older fellow."

This however he disregarded, and he put his hand to the back of my neck and began to pull me to the ground. Surprised, but still respectful, I said, "Don't, Prince. Don't do that. I think I have the weight advantage on you." As a matter of fact, I didn't know how to take this. Romilayu was standing by but revealed no opinion in answer to the look I shot him. My white helmet, with passport, money, and papers taped into it, fell off and the long-unbarbered karakul hair sprang up at the back of my neck as Itelo tugged me down with him. All the while I was trying—trying, trying, to classify this event. This Itelo was terribly strong, and he got astride me, in his roomy white pants and the short middy, and worked me down on the floor of the hut. But I kept my arms rigid as if they were tied to the sides and let him push and pull me at will. Now I lay on my belly, face in the dust and my legs dragging on the ground.

"Come, come," he kept saying, "you mus' fight me, sir."

"Prince," I said, "with respect, I am fighting."

You couldn't blame him for not believing me, and he climbed over me in the low-hung white pants with his huge legs and bare feet of the same light color as his hands, and dropping onto his side he worked a leg under me as a fulcrum and caught me around the throat. Breathing very hard and saying (closer to my face than I liked), "Fight. Fight, you Henderson. What is the mattah?"

"Your Highness," I said, "I am a kind of commando. I was in the War, and they had a terrific program at Camp Blanding. They taught us to kill, not just wrestle. Consequently, I don't know how to wrestle. But in man-to-man combat I am pretty ugly to tangle with. I know all kinds of stuff, like how to rip open a person's cheek by hooking a finger in his mouth, and how to snap bones and gouge the eyes. Naturally I don't care for that kind of conflict. It so happens I am trying to stay off violence. Why, the last time I just raised my voice it had very bad consequences. You understand," I panted, as the dust had worked up into my nose, "they taught us all this dangerous know-how and I tell you I shrink from it. So let's not fight. We're too high," I said, "on the scale of civilization—we should be giving all our energy to the question of the frogs instead."

As he still continued to pull me by the throat with his arm, I indicated that I wanted to say something really serious. And I told him, "Your Highness, I am really kind of on a quest."

He released me. I think I was not so impulsive or lively—responsive, you see—as he would have liked. I could read all this in his expression as I cleaned the dust from my face with a piece of indigo cloth belonging to the lady of the house. I had pulled it from the rafter. As far as he was concerned, we were now acquainted. Having seen something of the world, at least from Malindi in Africa all the way up into Asia Minor, he must have known what sad sacks were, and as of this moment, to judge by his looks, I belonged in that category. Of course it was true I had been very downcast, what with the voice that said *I want* and all the rest of it. I had come to look upon the phenomena of life as so many medicines which would either cure my condition or aggravate it. But the condition! Oh, my condition! First and last that condition! It made me go around with my hand on my breast like the old picture of Montcalm passing away on the Plains of Abraham. And I'll tell you something, excessive sadness has made me physically heavy, whereas I was once light and fast, for my weight. Until I was forty or so I played tennis, and one season hung up a record of five thousand sets, practically eating and sleeping out of doors. I covered the court like a regular centaur and smashed everything in sight, tearing holes in the clay and wrecking the rackets and bringing down the nets with my volleys. I cite this as proof that I was not always so sad and slow.

"I suppose you are the unbeaten champion here?" I said.

And he said, "That is so. I allways win."

"It doesn't surprise me one single bit."

He answered me carelessly with a glint from the corners of his eyes, for as I had submitted to being rolled in the dust on my face, he thought we had already made acquaintance thoroughly, concluding that I was huge but helpless, formidable in looks, but of one piece like a totem pole, or a kind of human Galápagos turtle. Therefore I saw that to regain his respect I must activate myself, and I decided to wrestle him after all. So I put aside my helmet and stripped off my T-shirt, saying, "Let's give it a try for real, Your Highness." Romilayu was not more pleased by this than he had been by Itelo's challenge, but he was not the type to interfere, and merely looked forward with his Abyssinian nose, his hair making a substantial shadow over it. As for the prince, who had been sitting with a loose, indifferent expression, he livened up and began to laugh when I slipped off the T-shirt. He stood up and crouched, and fenced with his hands, and I did likewise. We revolved around the small hut. Next we began to try grips, and the muscles started into play all over his shoulders. At which I decided that I should make quick use of my weight advantage before my temper could be aroused, for if he punished me, and with those muscles it was very possible, I might lose my head and fall into those commando tricks at that. So I did a very simple thing; I gave him a butt with my belly (on which the name of Frances once tattooed had suffered some expansion) while putting my leg behind him and pushing him in the face, and by this elementary surprise I threw the man over. I was astonished myself that it had worked so easily, though I had hit him pretty brutally with both hands and abdomen, and thought he might be going to the ground only to pull some trick on me; thus I took no chances but followed through with all my bulk, while both my hands covered his face. In this way I shut off sight and breath and gave his head a good bang on the ground, knocking the wind out of him, big as he was. When he slammed to the ground under this assault I threw myself with my knees on his arms and so pinned him.

Thankful that it had not been necessary to call on my murder technique, I let him up at once. I admit the element of surprise (or luck) was overwhelmingly on my side, and that it wasn't a fair test. That he was angry I could see from the change in his color, though the frame of darkness about his eyes showed no change, and he never said a word, but took off his middy and green handkerchief and drew deep breaths which made his belly muscles work inward toward his backbone. We began once more to revolve and several times circled the hut. I concentrated on my footwork, for that's where I am weakest and tend to pull forward like a plow horse with all the power in the neck, chest, belly, and, yes, face. As he now seemed to realize, his best chance was to get me on the mat, where I couldn't use my bulk against him, and as I was stooping toward him, cautious, and with my elbows out crabwise, he ducked under with great speed and caught me beneath the chin, closing in fast behind me and trapping my head. Which he began to squeeze. It wasn't a true headlock but more what your old-timers used to call the chancery grip. He had one arm free and could have used it to bang me across the face, but this didn't seem to be in the rules. Instead he carried me toward the ground and tried to make me fall on my back, but I fell on my front, and very painfully, too, so that I thought I had split myself upward from the navel. Also I got a bad blow on the nose and was afraid the root of it had been parted; I could almost feel the air enter between the separated bones. But somehow I managed to keep a space clear in my brain for counsels of moderation, which was no small achievement in itself. Since that day of zero weather when I was chopping wood and was struck by the flying log and thought, "Truth comes with blows," I had evidently discovered how to take advantage of such experiences, and this was useful to me now, only it took a different form; not "Truth comes with blows" but other words, and these words could not easily have been stranger. They went like this: "I do remember well the hour which burst my spirit's sleep."

Prince Itelo now took a grip high up on my chest with his legs; owing to my girth he could never have closed them about me lower down. As he tightened them, I felt my blood stop and my lips puffed out while my tongue panted and my eyes began to run. But my own hands were at work, and by applying pressure with both thumbs on his thigh near the knee, digging into the muscle (called the adductor, I believe) I was able to bend his leg straight and break his hold. Heaving upward, I snatched at his head; his hair was very short but gave all the grip I needed. Turning him by the hair I caught him at the back and spun him. I had him by the waistband of those loose drawers, my fingers inside, then I lifted him up high. I didn't whirl him at all, as that would have knocked the roof off the place. I threw him on the ground and followed up again, knocking the breath out of him doubly.

I suppose he had been very confident when he saw me, big but old, bulging out and sweating turbulently, heavy and sad. You couldn't blame him for thinking he was the fitter man. And now I almost wish that he had been the winner, for as he was going down, head first, I saw, as you can sometimes glimpse a lone object like a bottle dashing over Niagara Falls, how much bitterness was in his face. He could not believe that a gross old human trunk like myself was taking his championship from him. And when I landed on him for the second time his eyes rolled upward, and this intensity was not caused altogether by the weight I flung upon him.

It certainly did not behoove me to gloat or to act in any way like a proud winner, I can tell you. I felt almost as bad as he did. The whole straw case had almost come down about us when the prince's back struck the floor. Romilayu was standing out of the way against the wall. Though it made my breast ache to win, and my heart winced when I did it, I knelt nevertheless on the prince to make sure he was pinned, for if I had let him up without pinning him squarely he would have been deeply offended.

If the contest had taken place within nature he would have

won, I am willing to bet, but he was not matched against mere bone and muscle. It was a question of spirit, too, for when it comes to struggling I am in a special class. From earliest times I have struggled without rest. But I said, "Your Highness, don't take it so hard." He had covered his face with his hands, the color of washed stone, and didn't even try to rise from the ground. When I tried to comfort him I could think only of things such as Lily would have said. I know damned well that she would have flushed white and looked straight ahead and started to speak under her breath, fairly incoherent. She would have said that any man was only flesh and bone, and that everyone who took pride in his strength would be humbled by and by, and so on. I can tell you by the yard all that Lily would have said, but I myself could only feel for him, dumbly. It wasn't enough that they should be suffering from drought and the plague of frogs, but on top of it all I had to appear from the desert—to manifest myself in the dry bed of the Arnewi River with my Austrian lighter—and come into town and throw him twice in succession. The prince now got on his knees, scooping dust on his head, and then he took my foot in the suede, rubber-soled desert boot and put it on his head. In this position he cried much harder than the maiden and the delegation who had greeted us by the mud-and-thorn wall of the town. But I have to tell you that it wasn't the defeat alone that made him cry like this. He was in the midst of a great and mingled emotional experience. I tried to get my foot off the top of his head, but he held it there persistently, saying, "Oh, Mistah Henderson! Henderson, I know you now. Oh, sir, I know you now."

I couldn't say what I felt, which was: "No, you don't. You never could. Grief has kept me in condition and that's why this body is so tough. Lifting stones and pouring concrete and chopping wood and toiling with the pigs—my strength isn't happy strength. It wasn't a fair match. Take it from me, you are a better man."

Somehow I could never make myself lose any contest, no matter how hard I tried. Even playing checkers with my little children, regardless how I maneuvered to let them win and even while their lips trembled with disappointment (oh, the little kids would be sure to hate me), I would jump all over the board and say rudely, "King me!" though all the while I would be saying to myself, "Oh, you fool, you fool, you fool!"

But I didn't really understand how the prince felt until he rose and wrapped his arms about me and laid his dusty head on my shoulder, saying we were friends now. This hit me where I lived, right in the vital centers, both with suffering and with gratification. I said, "Your Highness, I'm proud. I'm glad." He took my hand, and if this was awkward it was stirring also. I was covered with a strong flush which is the radiance an older fellow may allowably feel after such a victory. But I tried to deprecate the whole thing and said to him, "I have experience on my side. You'll never know how much and what kind."

He answered, "I know you now, sir. I do know you."

VII

THE NEWS of my victory was given out as we left the hut by the dust on Itelo's head and by his manner in walking beside me, so that the people applauded as I came into the sunshine, pulling on my T-shirt and setting the helmet back into place. The women flapped their hands at me from the wrist while opening their mouths to almost the same degree. The men made whistling noises on their fingers, spreading their cheeks wide apart. Far from looking hangdog or grudging, the prince himself participated in the ovation, pointing at me and smiling, and I said to Romilayu, "You know something? This is really a sweet bunch of Africans. I love them."

Queen Willatale and her sister Mtalba were waiting for me under a thatched shed in the queen's courtyard. The queen was seated on a bench made of poles with a red blanket displayed flagwise behind her, and as we came forward, Romilayu with the bag of presents on his back, the old lady opened her lips and smiled at me. To me she was typical of a certain class of elderly lady. You will understand what I mean, perhaps, if I say that the flesh of her arm overlapped the elbow. As far as I am concerned this is the golden seal of character. With not many teeth, she smiled warmly and held out her hand, a relatively small one. Good nature emanated from her; it seemed to puff out on her breath as she sat smiling with many small tremors of benevolence and congratulation and welcome. Itelo indicated that I should give the old woman a hand, and I was astonished when she took it and buried it between her breasts. This is the normal form of greeting here—Itelo had put my hand against his breast—but from a woman I didn't anticipate the same. On top of everything else, I mean the radiant heat and the monumental weight which my hand received, there was the calm pulsation of her heart participating in the introduction. This was as regular as the rotation of the earth, and it was a surprise to me; my mouth came open and my eyes grew fixed as if I were touching the secrets of life; but I couldn't keep my hand there forever and I came to myself and drew it out. Then I returned the courtesy, I held her hand on my chest and said, "Me Henderson. Henderson." The whole court applauded to see how fast I caught on. So I thought, "Hurray for me!" and drew an endless breath into my lungs.

The queen expressed stability in every part of her body. Her head was white and her face broad and solid and she was wrapped in a lion's skin. Had I known then what I know now about lions, this would have told me much about her. Even so, it impressed me. It was the skin of a maned lion, with the wide part not on the front where you would have expected it, but on her back. The tail came down over her shoulder while the paw was drawn up from beneath, and these two ends were tied in a knot over her belly. I can't even begin to tell you how it pleased me. The mane with its plunging hair she wore as a collar, and on this grizzly and probably itching hair she rested her chin. But there was a happy light in her face. And then I observed that she had a defective eye, with a cataract, blueish white. I made the old lady a deep bow, and she began to laugh and her lion-bound belly shook and she wagged her head with its dry white hair at the picture I made bowing in those short pants while I presented my inflamed features, for the blood rushed into my face as I bent.

I expressed regret at the trouble they were having, the drought and the cattle and the frogs, and I said I thought I knew what it was to suffer from a plague and sympathized. I realized that they had to feed on the bread of tears and I hoped I wasn't going to be a bother here. This was translated by Itelo and I think it was well received by the old lady but when I spoke of troubles she smiled right along, as steady as the moonlight at the bottom of a stream. Meanwhile my heart was all stirred and I swore to myself every other minute that I would do something, I would make a contribution here. "I hope I may die," I said to myself, "if I don't drive out, exterminate, and crush those frogs."

I then told Romilayu to start with the presents. And first of all he brought out a plastic raincoat in a plastic envelope. I scowled at him, ashamed to offer this cheap stuff to the old queen, but as a matter of fact I had a perfectly good excuse, which was that I was traveling light. Moreover, I meant to render them a service here that would make the biggest present look silly. But the queen put her hands together at the

wrists and flapped them at me more deliberately than the other
ladies did, and smiled with marvelous constitutional gaiety.
Some of the other women in attendance did the same and those
who were holding infants lifted them up as if to impress the
phenomenal visitor on their memories. The men drew their
mouths wide, whistling on their fingers harmoniously. Years
ago the chauffeur's son, Vince, tried to teach me how to do
this and I held my fingers in my mouth until the skin wrinkled,
but could never bring out those shrieking noises. Therefore I
decided that as my reward for ridding them of the vermin, I
would ask them to teach me to whistle. I thought it would be
thrilling to pipe on my own fingers like that.

I said to Itelo, "Prince, please forgive this shabby present. I
hate like hell to bring a raincoat during a drought. It's like a
mockery, if you know what I mean?"

However, he said the present gave her happiness, and it evidently did. I had stocked up on trinkets and gimmicks through
the back page of the *Times* Sunday sports section and along
Third Avenue, in the hock shops and army-navy stores. To the
prince I gave a compass with small binoculars attached, not
much good even for bird watchers. For the queen's fat sister,
Mtalba, noticing that she smoked, I brought out one of those
Austrian lighters with the long white wick. In some places, especially in the bust, Mtalba was so heavy that her skin had
turned pink from the expansion. Women are bred like that in
parts of Africa where you have to be obese to be considered a
real beauty. She was all gussied up, for at such a weight a
woman can't go without the support of clothes. Her hands
were dyed with henna and her hair stood up stiffly with indigo;
she looked like a very happy and pampered person, the baby of
the family perhaps, and she shone and sparkled with fat and
moisture and her flesh was puckered or flowered like a regular
brocade. At the hips under the flowing gown she was as broad
as a sofa, and she too took my hand and placed it on her breast,
saying, "Mtalba. Mtalba awhonto." I am Mtalba. Mtalba ad-
mires you.

"I admire her, too," I told the prince.

I tried to get him to explain to the queen that the coat
which she had now put on was waterproof, and, as he seemed
unable to find a word for waterproof, I took hold of the sleeve

and licked it. Misinterpreting this she caught and licked me as well. I started to let out a shout.

"No yell, sah," said Romilayu, and made it sound urgent. Whereupon I submitted, and she licked me on the ear and on the bristled cheek and then pressed my head toward her middle.

"All right, now, so what's this?" I said, and Romilayu nodded his bush of hair, saying, "Kay, sah. Okay." In short, this was a special mark of the old lady's favor. Itelo protruded his lips to show that I was expected to kiss her on the belly. To dry my mouth first, I swallowed. The fall I had taken while wrestling had split my underlip. Then I kissed, giving a shiver at the heat I encountered. The knot of the lion's skin was pushed aside by my face, which sank inward. I was aware of the old lady's navel and her internal organs as they made sounds of submergence. I felt as though I were riding in a balloon above the Spice Islands, soaring in hot clouds while exotic odors arose from below. My own whiskers pierced me inward, in the lip. When I drew back from this significant experience (having made contact with a certain power—unmistakable!—which emanated from the woman's middle), Mtalba also reached for my head, wishing to do the same, as indicated by her gentle gestures, but I pretended I didn't understand and said to Itelo, "How come when everybody else is in mourning, your aunts are both so gay?"

He said, "Two women o' Bittahness."

"Bitter? I don't set up to be a judge of bitter and sweet," I said, "but if this isn't a pair of happy sisters, my mind is completely out of order. Why, they're having one hell of a time."

"Oh, happy! Yes, happy—bittah. Most bittah," said Itelo. And he began to explain. A Bittah was a person of real substance. You couldn't be any higher or better. A Bittah was not only a woman but a man at the same time. As the elder Willatale had seniority in Bittahness, too. Some of these people in the courtyard were her husbands and others her wives. She had plenty of both. The wives called her husband, and the children called her both father and mother. She had risen above ordinary human limitations and did whatever she liked because of her proven superiority in all departments. Mtalba was Bittah too and was on her way up. "Both my aunts like you. It is very good for you, Henderson," said Itelo.

"Do they have a good opinion of me, Itelo? Is that a fact?" I said.

"Very good. Primo. Class A. They admire how you look, and also they know you beat me."

"Boy, am I glad my physical strength is good for something," I said, "instead of being a burden, as it mostly has been throughout life. Only, tell me this: can't women of Bittahness do anything about frogs?"

At this he was solemn, and he said no.

Next it was the turn of the queen to ask questions, and first of all she said she was glad I had come. She could not hold still as she spoke, but her head was moved by many small tremors of benevolence, while her breath puffed from her lips and her open hand made passing motions before her face, and then she stopped and smiled, but without parting her mouth, while the live eye opened brightly toward me and the dry white hair rose and fell owing to the supple movement of her forehead.

I had two interpreters, for Romilayu couldn't be left out of things. He had a sense of dignity and position, and was a model of correctness in an African manner as though bred to court life, speaking in a high-pitched drawl and tucking in his chin while he pointed upward ceremoniously with a single finger.

After the queen had welcomed me she wanted to know who I was and where I came from. And as soon as I heard this question a shadow fell on all the pleasure and lightheartedness of the occasion and I began to suffer. I wish I could explain why it oppressed me to tell about myself, but so it was, and I didn't know what to say. Should I tell her that I was a rich man from America? Maybe she didn't even know where America was, as even civilized women are not keen on geography, preferring a world of their own. Lily might tell you a tremendous amount about life's goals, or what a person should or should not expect or do, but I don't believe she could say whether the Nile flows north or south. Thus I was sure that a woman like Willatale didn't ask such a question merely to be answered with the name of a continent. So I stood and considered what I should say, moody, thinking, with my belly hanging forth (scratched under the shirt by the contest with Itelo), my eyes wrinkling almost shut. And my face, I have to repeat, is no common face, but like an unfinished church. I was aware that women were tugging nursing infants from the nipple to hold them up and show them this memorable object. Nature going to extremes in Africa, I think they genuinely appreciated my peculiarities. And so the little kids were crying at the loss of the breast, reminding me of the baby from Danbury brought home by my unfortunate daughter Ricey. This again smote me straight on the spirit, and I had all the old difficulty, thinking of my condition. A crowd of facts came upon me with accompanying pressure in the chest. Who—who was I? A millionaire wanderer and wayfarer. A brutal and violent man driven into the world. A man who fled his own country, settled by his forefathers. A fellow whose heart said, *I want, I want*. Who played the violin in despair, seeking the voice of angels. Who had to burst the spirit's sleep, or else. So what could I tell this old queen in a lion skin and raincoat (for she had buttoned herself up in it)? That I had ruined the original piece of goods issued to me and was traveling to find a remedy? Or that I had read somewhere that the forgiveness of sin was perpetual but with typical carelessness had lost the book? I said to myself, "You must answer the woman, Henderson. She is waiting. But how?" And the process started over again. Once more it was, Who are you? And I had to confess that I didn't know where to begin.

But she saw that I was standing oppressed and, in spite of my capable appearance and rude looks, was dumb, and she changed the subject. By now she understood that the coat was waterproof, so she called over one of the long-necked wives and had her spit on the material and rub in the spittle, then feel inside. She was astonished and told everybody, wetting her finger and laying it against her arm, and again they started to chant, "Awho," and whistle on the fingers and flap their hands, and Willatale embraced me again. A second time my face sank in her belly, that great saffron swelling with the knot of lion skin sinking also, and I felt the power emanating again. I was not mistaken. And one thing I kept thinking as before, which was *the hour that burst the spirit's sleep*. Meanwhile the athletic-looking men continued piping musically, spreading their mouths like satyrs (not that they otherwise suggested satyrs). And the hand-flapping went on, exactly as when ladies are playing catch (they also bend their knees just as the ball comes in). So that at that first sight of the town I felt that living

among such people might change a man for the better. It had
done me some good already, I could tell. And I wanted to do
something for them—my desire for this was something fierce.
"At least," I thought, "if I were a doctor I would operate on
Willatale's eye." Oh, yes, I know what cataract operations are,
and I had no intention of trying. But I felt singularly ashamed
of not being a doctor—or maybe it was shame at coming all
this way and then having so little to contribute. All the ingenuity and development and coordination that it takes to bring
a fellow so quickly and so deep into the African interior! And
then—he is the wrong fellow! Thus I had once again the conviction that I filled a place in existence which should be filled
properly by someone else. And I suppose it was ridiculous that
it should trouble me not to be a doctor, as after all some doctors are pretty puny characters, and not a few I have met are in
a racket, but I was thinking mostly about my childhood idol,
Sir Wilfred Grenfell of Labrador. Forty years ago, when I read
his books on the back porch, I swore I'd be a medical missionary. It's too bad, but suffering is about the only reliable burster
of the spirit's sleep. There is a rumor of long standing that love
also does it. Anyway, I was thinking that a more useful person
might have arrived at this time among the Arnewi, as, for all
the charm of the two women of Bittahness, the crisis was really
acute. And I remembered a conversation with Lily. I asked her,
"Dear, would you say it was too late for me to study medicine?" (Not that she's the ideal woman to answer a practical
question like that.) But she said, "Why, no, darling. It's never
too late. You may live to be a hundred"—a corollary to her belief I was unkillable. So I said to her, "I'd have to live that long
to make it worth while. I'd be starting internship at sixty-three,
when other men are retiring. But also I am not like other men
in this respect because I have nothing to retire from. However,
I can't expect to live five or six lives, Lily. Why, more than half
the people I knew as a young fellow have passed on and here
am I, still planning for the future. And the animals I used to
have, too. I mean a man in his lifetime has six or seven dogs
and then it's time for him to go also. So how can I think about
my textbooks and instruments and enrolling in courses and
studying a cadaver? Where would I find the patience to learn
anatomy now and chemistry and obstetrics?" But at least Lily

didn't laugh at me as Frances had. "If I knew science," I was thinking now, "I could probably think of a simple way to eliminate those frogs."

But anyhow, I felt pretty good, and it was now my turn to receive presents. I got a bolster covered with leopard skin from the sisters, and a basketful of cold baked yams was brought, covered with a piece of straw matting. Mtalba's eyes grew bigger, while her brow rolled up softly and she appeared to suffer about the nose—all signs that she was gone on me. She licked my hand with her small tongue, and I withdrew it and wiped it on my shorts.

But I thought myself very lucky. This was a beautiful, strange, special place, and I was moved by it. I believed the queen could straighten me out if she wanted to; as if, any minute now, she might open her hand and show me the thing, the source, the germ—the cipher. The mystery, you know. I was absolutely convinced she must have it. The earth is a huge ball which nothing holds up in space except its own motion and magnetism, and we conscious things who occupy it believe we have to move too, in our own space. We can't allow ourselves to lie down and not do our share and imitate the greater entity. You see, this is our attitude. But now look at Willatale, the Bittah woman; she had given up such notions, there was no anxious care in her, and she was sustained. Why, nothing bad happened! On the contrary, it all seemed good! Look how happy she was, grinning with her flat nose and gap teeth, the mother-of-pearl eye and the good eye, and look at her white head! It comforted me just to see her, and I felt that I might learn to be sustained too if I followed her example. And altogether I felt my hour of liberation was drawing near when the sleep of the spirit was liable to burst.

There was this happy agitation in me, which made me fix my teeth together. Certain emotions make my teeth itch. Esthetic appreciation especially does it to me. Yes, when I admire beauty I get these tooth pangs, and my gums are on edge. Like that autumn morning when the tuberous flowers were so red, when I was standing in my velvet bathrobe under the green blackness of the pine tree, when the sun was like the coat of a fox, and the animals were barking, when the crows were harsh on that golden decay of the stubble—my gums were hurting sharply then, and now similarly; and with this all my difficult, worried, threatening arrogance appeared to fade from me, and even the hardness of my belly kind of relented and sank down. I said to Prince Itelo, "Look, Your Highness, could you arrange it for me to have a real talk with the queen?"

"You don't talk?" he said, somewhat surprised. "You do talk, Mistah Henderson."

"Oh, a real talk, I mean. Not sociable fiddle-faddle. In earnest," I said. "About the wisdom of life. Because I know she's got it and I wouldn't leave without a sample of it. I'd be crazy to."

"Oh, yes. Very good, very good," he said. "Oh, all right. As you have won me I do not refuse you a difficult interpretation."

"So you know what I mean?" I said. "This is great. This is wonderful. I'll be grateful till my dying day, Prince. You have no idea how this fills my cup." The younger sister of Bittahness, Mtalba, meanwhile was holding my hand, and I said, "What does she want?"

"Oh, she have a strong affection for you. Don' you see she is the most beautiful woman and you the strongest of strong men. You have won her heart."

"Hell with her heart," I said. Then I began to think how to open a discussion with Willatale. What should I concentrate on? Marriage and happiness? Children and family? Duty? Death? The voice that said *I want?* (How could I explain this to her and to Itelo?) I had to find the simplest, most essential points, and all my thinking happens to be complicated. Here is a sample of such thinking, which happens to be precisely what I had on my mind as I stood in that parched courtyard under the mild shade of the thatch; Lily, my after-all dear wife, and she is the irreplaceable woman, wanted us to end each other's solitude. Now she was no longer alone, but I still was, and how did that figure? Next step: help may come either from other human beings or—from a different quarter. And between human beings there are only two alternatives, either brotherhood or crime. And what makes the good such liars? Why, they lie like fish. Evidently they believe there have to be crimes, and lying is the most useful crime, as at least it is on behalf of good. Well, when push comes to shove, I am for the good, all right, but I am very suspicious of them. So, in short, what's the best way to live?

However, I couldn't start at such an advanced point of my thought with the woman of Bittahness. I would have to work my way forward slowly so as to be sure of my ground. Therefore I said to Itelo, "Now please tell the queen for me, friend, that it does wonderful things for me simply to see her. I don't know whether it's her general appearance or the lion skin or what I feel emanating from her—anyway, it puts my soul at rest."

This was transmitted by Itelo and then the queen leaned forward with a tiny falter of her stout body, smiling, and spoke.

"She say she like to see you, too."

"Oh, really." I was beaming. "This is simply great. This is a big moment for me. The skies are opening up. It's a great privilege to be here." Taking away my hand from Mtalba I put my arm around the prince and I shook my head, for I was utterly inspired and my heart was starting to brim over. "You know, you are really a stronger fellow than I am," I said. "I am strong all right, but it's the wrong kind of strength; it's coarse; because I'm desperate. Whereas you really are strong—just strong." The prince was affected by this and started to deny it, but I said, "Look, take it from me. If I tried to explain in detail it would be months and months before you even got a glimmer of what gives. My soul is like a pawn shop. I mean it's filled with unredeemed pleasures, old clarinets, and cameras, and moth-eaten fur. But," I said, "let's not get into a debate over it. I am only trying to tell you how you make me feel out here in this tribe. You're great, Itelo. I love you. I love the old lady, too. In fact you're all pretty damned swell, and I'll get rid of those frogs for you if I have to lay down my life to do it." They all saw that I was moved, and the men began to make the hollow whistle on their fingers and spread their mouths so like satyrs and yet sweetly, softly.

"My aunt says what do you request, sir?"

"Oh, does she? Well, that's wonderful. For a starter ask her what she sees in me since I find it so hard to tell her who I am."

Itelo delivered the question and Willatale furrowed up her

brow in that flexible way peculiar to the Arnewi as a whole, which let the hemisphere of the eye be seen, purely, glistening with human intention; while the other, the white one, though blind, communicated humor as if she were giving me a wink to last me a lifetime. This closed white shutter also signified her inwardness to me. She spoke slowly without removing her gaze, and her fingers moved on her old thigh, shortened by her stoutness, as if taking an impression from Braille. Itelo transmitted her words. "You have, sir, a large personallity. Strong. (I add agreement to her.) Your mind is full of thought. Possess some fundamentall of Bittahness, also." (Good, good!) "You love send . . ." (It took him several seconds to find the word while I was standing, consumed—in this colorful court, on the gold soil, surroundings tinged by crimson, by black; the twigs of the bushes brown and smelling like cinnamon—consumed by desire to hear the judgment of her wisdom on me.)

"Send-sations." I nodded, and Willatale proceeded. "Says . . . you are very sore, oh, sir! Mistah Henderson. You heart is barking." "That's correct," I said, "with all three heads, like Cerberus the watch dog. But why is it barking?" He, however, was listening to her and leaning from the balls of his feet, as if appalled to hear with what kind of fellow he had gone to the mat in the customary ceremony of acquaintance. "Frenezy," he said. "Yes, yes, I'll confirm that," I said. "The woman has a real gift." And I encouraged her. "Tell me, tell me, Queen Willatale! I want the truth. I don't want you to spare me." "Suffah," said Itelo, and Mtalba picked up my hand in sympathy. "Yes, I certainly do." "She say now, Mistah Henderson, that you have a great copacity, indicated by your largeness, and especially your nose." My eyes were big and sad as I touched my face. Beauty certainly vanishes. "I was once a good-looking fellow," I said, "but it certainly is a nose I can smell the whole world with. It comes down to me from the founder of my family. He was a Dutch sausage-maker and became the most unscrupulous capitalist in America."

"You excuse queen. She is fond on you and say she do not wish to make you trouble."

"Because I have enough already. But look, Your Highness, I didn't come to shilly-shally, so don't say anything to inhibit her. I want it straight."

The woman of Bittahness began to speak again, slowly, dwelling on my appearance with her one-eyed dreamy look.

"What does she say—what does she say?"

"She say she wish you tell her, sir, why you come. She know you have to come across mountain and walk a very long time. You not young, Mistah Henderson. You weight maybe a hundred-fifty kilogram; your face have many colors. You are built like a old locomotif. Very strong, yes, I know. Sir, I concede. But so much flesh as a big monument . . ."

I listened, smarting at his words, my eyes wincing into their surrounding wrinkles. And then I sighed and said, "Thank you for your frankness. I know it's peculiar that I came all this way with my guide over the desert. Please tell the queen that I did it for my health." This surprised Itelo, so that he gave a startled laugh. "I know," I said, "superficially I don't look sick. And it sounds monstrous that anybody with my appearance should still care about himself, his health or anything else. But that's how it is. Oh, it's miserable to be human. You get such queer diseases. Just because you're human and for no other reason. Before you know it, as the years go by, you're just like other people you have seen, with all those peculiar human ailments. Just another vehicle for temper and vanity and rashness and all the rest. Who wants it? Who needs it? These things occupy the place where a man's soul should be. But as long as she has started I want her to read me the whole indictment. I can fill her in on a lot of counts, though I don't think I would have to. She seems to know. Lust, rage, and all the rest of it. A regular bargain basement of deformities . . ."

Itelo hesitated, then transmitted as much of this as he could to the queen. She nodded with sympathetic earnestness, slowly opening and closing her hand on the knot of lion skin, and gazing at the roof of the shed—those pipes of amber bamboo and the peaceful, symmetrical palm leaves of the thatch. Her hair floated like a million spider lines, while the fat of her arms hung down over her elbows. "She say," Itelo translated carefully, "world is strange to a child. You not a child, sir?"

"Oh, how wonderful she is," I said. "True, all too true. I have never been at home in life. All my decay has taken place upon a child." I clasped my hands, and staring at the ground I started to reflect with this inspiration. And when it comes to reflection

I am like the third man in a relay race. I can hardly wait to get the baton, but when I do get it I rarely take off in the necessary direction. So what I thought was something like this: The world may be strange to a child, but he does not fear it the way a man fears. He marvels at it. But the grown man mainly dreads it. And why? Because of death. So he arranges to have himself abducted like a child. So what happens will not be his fault. And who is this kidnaper—this gipsy? It is the strangeness of life—a thing that makes death more remote, as in childhood. I was pretty proud of myself, I tell you. And I said to Itelo, "Please say to the old lady for me that most people hate to meet up with a man's trouble. Trouble stinks. So I won't forget your generosity. Now listen—listen," I said to Willatale and Mtalba and Itelo and the members of the court. I started to sing from Handel's *Messiah*: "He was despised and rejected, a man of sorrows and acquainted with grief," and from this I took up another part of the same oratorio, "For who shall abide the day of His coming, and who shall stand when He appeareth?" Thus I sang while Willatale, the woman of Bittahness, queen of the Arnewi, softly shook her head; perhaps admiringly. Mtalba's face gleamed with a similar expression and her forehead began to fold softly upward toward the stiffly standing indigo hair, while the ladies flapped and the men whistled in chorus. "Oh, good show, sir. My friend," Itelo said. Only Romilayu, stocky, muscular, short, and wrinkled, seemed disapproving, but due to his wrinkles he had an ingrained expression of that type, and he may have felt no disapproval at all.

"Grun-tu-molani," the old queen said.

"What's that? What does she say?"

"Say, you want to live. Grun-tu-molani. Man want to live."

"Yes, yes, yes! Molani. Me molani. She sees that? God will reward her, tell her, for saying it to me. I'll reward her myself. I'll annihilate and blast those frogs clear out of that cistern, sky-high, they'll wish they had never come down from the mountains to bother you. Not only I molani for myself, but for everybody. I could not bear how sad things have become in the world and so I set out because of this molani. Grun-tu-molani, old lady—old queen. Grun-tu-molani, everybody!" I raised my helmet to all the family and members of the court.

"Grun-tu-molani. God does not shoot dice with our souls, and therefore grun-tu-molani." They muttered back, smiling at me, "Tu-molani." Mtalba, with her lips shut, but the rest of her face expanded to a remarkable extent with happiness and her little henna-dipped hands with puckered wrists at rest on her hips, was looking into my eyes meltingly.

VIII

Now, I come from a stock that has been damned and derided for more than a hundred years, and when I sat smashing bottles beside the eternal sea it wasn't only my great ancestors, the ambassadors and statesmen, that people were recalling, but the loony ones as well. One got himself mixed up in the Boxer Rebellion, believing he was an Oriental; one was taken for $300,000 by an Italian actress; one was carried away in a balloon while publicizing the suffrage movement. There have been plenty of impulsive or imbecile parties in our family (in French Am-Bay-Seel is a stronger term). A generation ago one of the Henderson cousins got the Corona Italia medal for rescue work during the earthquake at Messina, Sicily. He was tired of rotting from idleness at Rome. He was bored, and would ride his horse inside the Palazzo down from his bedroom and into the salon. After the earthquake he reached Messina by the first train and it is said that he didn't sleep for two entire weeks, but pulled apart hundreds of ruins and rescued countless families. This indicates that a service ideal exists in our family, though sometimes in a setting of mad habit. One of the old Hendersons, although far from being a minister, used to preach to his neighbors, and he would call them by hitting a bell in his yard with a crowbar. They all had to come.

They say that I resemble him. We have the same neck size, twenty-two. I might cite the fact that I held up a mined bridge in Italy and kept it from collapsing until the engineers arrived. But this is in the line of military duty, and a better instance was provided by my behavior in the hospital when I broke my leg. I spent all my time in the children's wards, entertaining and cheering the kids. On my crutches I hopped around the entire place in a hospital gown; I couldn't be bothered to tie the tapes and was open behind, and the old nurses ran after me to cover me, but I wouldn't hold still.

Here we were in the farthest African mountains—damn it, they couldn't be much farther!—and it was a shame that these good people should suffer so from frogs. But it was natural for me to want to relieve them. It so happened that this was something I could probably do, and it was the least that I could undertake under the circumstances. Look what this Queen Willatale had done for me—read my character, revealed the grun-tu-molani to me. I figured that these Arnewi, no exception to the rules, had developed unevenly; they might have the wisdom of life, but when it came to frogs they were helpless. This I already had explained to my own satisfaction. The Jews had Jehovah, but wouldn't defend themselves on the Sabbath. And the Eskimos would perish of hunger with plenty of caribou around because it was forbidden to eat caribou in fish season, or fish in caribou season. Everything depends on the values—the values. And where's reality? I ask you, where is it? I myself, dying of misery and boredom, had happiness, and objective happiness, too, all around me, as abundant as the water in that cistern which cattle were forbidden to drink. And therefore, I thought, this will be one of those mutual-aid deals; where the Arnewi are irrational I'll help them, and where I'm irrational they'll help me.

The moon had already come forward with her long face toward the east and a fleece of clouds behind. It gave me something to gauge the steepness of the mountains by, and I believe they approached the ten-thousand-foot mark. The evening air turned very green and yet the beams of the moon kept their whiteness intact. The thatch became more than ever like feathers, dark, heavy, and plumy. I said to Prince Itelo as we were standing beside one of these iridescent heaps—his company of wives and relatives were still in attendance with the squash-flower parasols—"Prince, I'm going to have a shot at those animals in the cistern. Because I'm sure I can handle them. You aren't involved at all, and don't even have to give an opinion one way or another. I'm doing this on my own responsibility."

"Oh, Mistah Henderson—you 'strodinary man. But sir. Do not be carry away."

"Ha, ha, Prince—pardon me, but this is where you happen to be wrong. If I don't get carried away I never accomplish anything. But that's okay," I said. "Just forget about it."

So then he left us at our hut and Romilayu and I had supper, which consisted mainly of cold yams and hardtack, to which I added a supplement of vitamin pills. On top of this I had a slug of whisky and then I said, "Come on, Romilayu, we'll go over to that cistern and case it by moonlight." I took along a flashlight to use under the thatch, for, as previously noted, a shed was built over it.

These frogs really had it better than anyone else. Here, due to the moisture, grew the only weeds in the village, and this odd variety of mountain frog, mottled green and white, was hopping and splashing, swimming. They say the air is the final home of the soul, but I think that as far as the senses go you probably can't find a sweeter medium than water. So the life of those frogs must have been beautiful, and they fulfilled their ideal, it seemed to me, as they coasted by our feet with those bright wet skins and their white legs and the emotional throats, their eyes like bubbles. While the rest of us, represented by Romilayu and me, were hot and sweaty, burning. In the thatch-intensified shadow of evening my face felt as if it were on fire, as if it were the opening of a volcano. My jaws were all swelled out and I half believed that if I had turned off the flashlight we could have seen those frogs in the cistern by the glare emanating from me.

"They've got it very good, these creatures," I said to Romilayu, "while it lasts." And I swung the big flashlight to and fro over the water in which they were massed. Under other circumstances I might have taken a tolerant or even affectionate attitude toward them. Basically, I had nothing against them.

"What fo' you laugh, sah?"

"Am I laughing? I didn't realize," I said. "These are really great singers. Back in Connecticut we have mostly cheepers, but these have bass voices. Listen," I said, "I can make out all kinds of things. Ta dam-dam-dum. Agnus Dei—Agnus Dei qui tollis peccata mundi, miserere no-ho-bis! It's Mozart. Mozart, I swear! They've got a right to sing miserere, poor little bastards, as the hinge of fate is about to swing back on them."

"Poor little bastards" was what I said, but in actual fact I was gloating—yuck-yuck-yuck! My heart was already fattening in anticipation of their death. We hate death, we fear death, but when you get right down to cases, there's nothing like it. I was sorry for the cows, yes, and on the humane side I was fine. I checked out one hundred per cent. But still I hungered to let fall the ultimate violence on these creatures in the cistern.

At the same time I couldn't help being aware of the discrep-

ancies between us. On the one side these fundamentally harmless little semi-fishes who were not to blame for the fear they
were held in by the Arnewi. On the other side, a millionaire
several times over, six feet four in height, weighing two hundred and thirty pounds, socially prominent, and a combat
officer holding the Purple Heart and other decorations. But I
wasn't responsible for this, was I? However, it remains to be
recorded that I was once more fatally embroiled with animals,
according to the prophecy of Daniel which I had never been
able to shake off—"They shall drive you from among men,
and thy dwelling shall be with the beasts of the field." Not
counting the pigs, to whom I related myself legitimately as a
breeder, there was an involvement with an animal very recently
which weighed heavily on my mind and conscience. On the
eve of my assault on the frogs it was this creature, a cat, I was
thinking of, and I had better tell why.

I have told about the building remodeled by Lily on our
property. She rented it to a mathematics teacher and his wife.
The house had no insulation and the tenants complained and I
evicted them. It was over them and their cat that Lily and I were
having our row when Miss Lenox dropped dead. This cat was
a young male with brown and gray smoky fur.

Twice these tenants came over to the house to discuss the
heating. Pretending to know nothing about it, I followed
the matter with interest, spying on them from upstairs when
they arrived. I listened to their voices in the parlor and knew
Lily was trying to conciliate them. I was lurking in the second-
floor hall in my red bathrobe and the Wellingtons from the
barnyard. Subsequently when Lily tried to discuss it with me I
said to her, "It's your headache. I never wanted strangers
around anyway." I believed that she had brought them on
the place to make friends of them and I was opposed. "What
bothers them? Is it the pigs?" "No," Lily said, "they haven't
said a word against the pigs." "Hah! I have seen their faces
when the mash was cooking," I said, "and I can't understand
why you have to have a second house fixed up when you won't
even take care of the first."

The second and last time they came much more determined
to make their complaint, and I watched from the bedroom,
brushing my hair with a pair of brushes; I saw the smoky tom

cat following them, bounding through the broken stalks of the frozen vegetable garden. Broccoli looks spectacular when the frost hits it. The conference began below, and I couldn't stand it any more and started to stamp my feet on the floor above the parlor. Finally I yelled down the stairs, "Get the hell out of here, and move off my property!"

The tenant said, "We will, but we want our deposit and you ought to foot the moving bill too."

"Good," I said, "you come up and collect the money from me," and I pounded in the stairwell with my Wellingtons and yelled, "Get out!"

And so they did, but the point is they abandoned their cat, and I didn't want a cat going wild on my place. Cats gone wild are bad business, and this was a very powerful animal. I had watched him hunting and playing with a chipmunk. For five years once we had suffered with such a cat who lived in an old woodchuck burrow near the pond. He fought all the barn toms and gave them septic scratches and tore out their eyes. I tried to kill him with poisoned fish and smoke bombs and spent whole days in the woods on my knees near his burrow, waiting to get him. Therefore I said to Lily, "If this animal goes wild like the other one, you'll regret it."

"The people are coming back for him," she said.

"I don't believe it for a minute. They've dumped him. And you don't know what wild cats can be like. Why, I'd rather have a lynx around the place."

We had a hired man named Hannock, and I went to the barn and said to him, "Where's the tom those damned civilians left behind?" It was then late in the fall and he was storing apples, tossing aside windfalls for what pigs there were left. Hannock was very much opposed to the pigs, which had ruined the grass and the garden.

"He's no trouble, Mr. Henderson. He's a good little cat," said Hannock.

"Did they pay you to take care of him?" I said, and he was afraid to say yes and lied to me. In actuality they had given him two bottles of whisky and a case of dried milk (Starlac).

He said, "Naw, they didn't, but I will. He ain't no trouble to me."

"There's going to be no animal abandoned on my property," I said, and I went over the farm calling, "Minnie-Minnie." Finally the cat came into my hands and didn't fight when I lifted him by the scruff and carried him to a room in the attic and locked him in. I sent a registered letter special delivery to the owners and gave them until four o'clock next day to come for him. Otherwise, I threatened, I'd have him put away.

I showed Lily the receipt of the registered letter and told her the cat was in my possession. She tried to prevail on me and even got all dressed at dinner time, with powder on her face. At the table I could feel her tremble and knew she was about to reason with me. "What's the matter? You're not eating," I said, for she normally eats a great deal and I have had restaurant people tell me they never saw a woman who could put away the food like that. Two plank steaks and six bottles of beer are not too much for her when she's in condition. As a matter of fact, I am very proud of Lily's capacity.

"You're not eating, either," was Lily's answer.

"That's because I've got something on my mind. I'm extremely sore," I said. "I'm in a state."

"Baby, don't be like that," she said.

But the emotion, whatever it was, filled me so that my very flesh disagreed with the bones. I felt terrible.

I didn't tell Lily what I was planning to do, but at 3:59 next day, no answer having come from the ex-tenants, I went upstairs to carry out my threat. I carried a shopping bag from Grusan's market and in it was the pistol. There was plenty of light in the small wall-papered attic room. I said to the tom cat, "They've cast you away, kitty." He flattened himself to the wall, arched and bristling. I tried to aim at him from above and finally had to sit on the floor, sighting between the legs of a bridge table which was there. In this small space, I didn't want to fire more than a single shot. From reading about Pancho Villa I had picked up the Mexican method of marksmanship, which is to aim with the forefinger on the barrel and press the trigger with the middle finger, because the forefinger is the most accurate pointer at our disposal. Thus I got the center of his head under my (somewhat twisted) forefinger, and fired, but my will was not truly bent on his death, and I missed. That is the only explanation for missing at a distance of eight feet. I opened the door and he bolted. On the staircase, with her beautiful neck stretched forth and her face white with fear, was Lily. To her a pistol fired in a house meant only one thing—it recalled the death of her father. The shock of the shot was still upon me, the empty shopping bag hung by my side.

"What did you do?" said Lily.

"I tried to do what I said I would. Hell!"

The phone began to ring and I went past her to answer it. It was the tenant's wife, and I said, "What did you wait so long for? Now it's almost too late."

She burst into tears and I myself felt very bad. And I yelled, "Come and take your bloody damned cat away. You city people don't care about animals. Why, you can't just abandon a cat."

The confusing thing is that I always have some real basic motivation, and how I go so wrong, I can never understand.

And so, on the brink of the cistern, the problem of how to eliminate the frogs touched off this other memory. "But this is different," I thought. "Here it is clear, and besides, it will show what I meant by going after that cat." So I hoped, for my heart was wrung by the memory, and I felt tremendous sorrow. It had been a very close thing—almost a deadly sin.

Facing the practical situation, however, I considered various alternatives, like dredging, or poisons, and none of them seemed advisable. I told Romilayu, "The only method that figures is a bomb. One blast will kill all these little buggers, and when they're floating dead on top all we have to do is come and skim them off, and the Arnewi can water their cattle again. It's simple."

When my idea did get across to him at last, he said, "Oh, no, no, sah."

"What, 'No, no, sah!' Don't be a jerk, I'm an old soldier and I know what I'm talking about." But it was no use arguing with him; the idea of an explosion frightened him and I said, "Okay, Romilayu, let's go to our shack then and get some sleep. It's been a big day and we've got lots to do tomorrow."

So we went back to the hut, and he began to say his prayers. Romilayu had begun to get my number; I believe he liked me, but it was dawning on him that I was rash and unlucky and acted without sufficient reflection. So he sank on his knees and his haunches pressed on the muscles of his calves and spread them; his big heels were visible beneath. He pressed his hands together, palm to palm, with the fingers spread wide apart under his chin. Often I would say to him, or mutter, "Put in a good word for me," and I half meant it.

When Romilayu was done praying he lay on his side and tucked one hand between his knees, which were drawn up. The other hand he slipped under his cheek. In this position he always slept. I, too, lay down on my blanket in the dark hut, out of range of the moonbeams. I don't often suffer from insomnia but tonight I had a lot of things on my mind, the prophecy of Daniel, the cat, the frogs, the ancient-looking place, the weeping delegation, the wrestling match with Itelo, and the queen having looked into my heart and telling me of the grun-tu-molani. All this was mixed up in my head and excited me greatly, and I kept thinking of the best way to blow up those frogs. Naturally I know a little something about explosives, and I thought I could take out the two batteries and manufacture a pretty good bomb in my flashlight case by filling it with powder from the shells of my .375 H and H Magnum. They carry quite a charge, believe me, and could be used on an elephant. I had bought the .375 especially for this trip to Africa after reading about it in *Life* or *Look*. A fellow from Michigan who had one went to Alaska as soon as his vacation started; he flew to Alaska and hired a guide to track a Kodiak bear; they found the bear and chased him over cliffs and marshes and shot him at four hundred yards. Myself, I used to have a certain interest in hunting, but as I grew older it seemed a strange way to relate to nature. What I mean is, a man goes into the external world, and all he can do with it is to shoot it? It doesn't make sense. So in October when the season starts and the gun-smoke pours out of the bushes and the animals panic and run back and forth, I go out and pinch the hunters for shooting on my posted property. I take them to the Justice of the Peace and he fines them.

Thus having decided in the hut to take the shells and use them in my bomb, I lay grinning at the surprise those frogs had coming, and also somewhat at myself, because I was anticipating the gratitude of Willatale and Mtalba and Itelo and all the people; and I went so far as to imagine that the queen would elevate me to a position equal to her own. But I would say, "No, no. I didn't leave home to achieve power or glory, and any little favor I do you is free."

With all this going on within me I couldn't sleep, and if I were going to prepare the bomb tomorrow I needed my rest badly. I am something of a crank about sleep, for somehow if I get seven and a quarter hours instead of eight I feel afflicted and drag myself around, although there's nothing really wrong with me. It's just another *idea*. That's how it is with my ideas; they seem to get strong while I weaken.

While I was lying awake I had a visit from Mtalba. Coming in, she shut off the moonlight in the doorway and then sat down near me on the floor, sighing, and took my hand, and talked softly and made me touch her skin, which was certainly wonderfully soft; she had a right to be vain of it. Though I felt it, I acted oblivious and refused to respond, but my bulk lay extended on the blanket and I fixed my gaze on the thatch while I tried to concentrate on putting together the bomb. I unscrewed the top of the flashlight (in thought) and dumped the batteries in the front end; I cut open the shells and let the powder trickle into the flashlight case. But how would I ignite it? The water presented me with a special problem. What would I use for a fuse, and how would I keep it from getting wet? I might take some strands from the wick of my Austrian lighter and soak them for a long time in the fluid. Or else a shoelace; a wax shoelace might be perfect. Such was my line of thought, and all the while Princess Mtalba sat beside me licking me and smooching my fingers. I felt very guilty about that and thought, if she knew what offenses I had committed with those same hands, she might think twice before lifting them to her lips. Now she was on the very finger with which I had aimed the revolver at the cat and a pang shot through it and into my arm and so on through the rest of the nervous system. If she had been able to understand I would have said, "Beautiful lady" (for she was considered a great beauty and I could see why)— "Beautiful lady, I am not the man you think I am. I have incredible things on my conscience and am very fierce in character. Even my pigs were afraid of me."

And yet it isn't always easy to deter women. They do take such types of men upon themselves—drunkards, fools, criminals. Love is what gives them the power to do it, I guess, canceling all those terrible things. I am not dumb and blind, and I have observed a connection between women's love and the great principles of life. If I hadn't picked this up by myself, surely Lily would have pointed it out to me.

Romilayu didn't wake but slept on with one hand slipped under his scarred cheek and the hair swelled out from his head to one side. Glassy rainbows from the moon passed across the doorway, and there were fires outside made with dried dung and thorn branches. The Arnewi were sitting up with their dying cattle. As Mtalba continued to sigh and caress and smooch me and lead my finger-tips over her skin and between her lips, I realized she had come for a purpose, this mountainous woman with the indigo hair, and I lifted my arm and let it fall on Romilayu's face. He opened his eyes then but didn't remove the hand from under his cheek or otherwise change his position.

"Romilayu."

"Whut you want, sah?" said he, still lying there.

"Sit up, sit up. We have a visitor." He was unsurprised by this and he rose. Moonlight came in by way of the wickerwork and the door, the moon growing more clean and pure, as if perfuming the air, not only lighting it. Mtalba sat with her arms at rest upon the slopes of her body. "Find out what is the purpose of this visit," I said.

And so he began to talk to her, and addressed her formally, for he was a great stickler, Romilayu, for correctness, African style, and was on his court manners even in the middle of the night. Then Mtalba started to speak. She had a sweet voice, sometimes rapid and sometimes drawling in her throat. From this conversation the fact came out that she wanted me to buy her, and, realizing that I didn't have the bride price, she had brought it to me tonight. "Got to pay, sah, fo' womans."

"That I know, pal."

"You don' pay, womans no respect himself, sah."

Then I started to say that I was a rich man and could afford any kind of price, but I realized that money had nothing to do with it and I said, "Hah, that's very handsome of her. She is built like Mount Everest but has a lot of delicacy. Tell her I thank her and send her home. What time is it, I wonder. Christ, if I don't get my sleep I'll be in no condition to take on those frogs tomorrow. Don't you see, Romilayu, the thing is up to me alone?"

But he said all the stuff she had brought was lying outside, and she wanted me to see it, and so I rose, highly unwilling, and we went out of the hut. She had come with an escort, and when they saw me in the moonlight with my sun helmet they began to cheer as if I were the groom already—they did it softly as the hour was late. The gifts were lying on a big mat, and they made a large mound—robes, ornaments, drums, paints, and dyes: she gave Romilayu an inventory of the contents and he was transmitting it.

"She's a grand person. A great human being," I said. "Hasn't she got a husband already?" To this there could be no definite answer, as she was a woman of Bittahness and it didn't matter how many times she married. It would do no good, I knew, to tell her that I already had a wife. It hadn't stopped Lily, and it certainly would cut no ice with Mtalba.

To display the greatness of the dowry, Mtalba began to put on some of the robes to the accompaniment of a xylophone made of bones played by one of her party, a fellow with a big knobby ring on his knuckle. He smiled as if he were giving the woman of Bittahness away, and she meantime was showing off the gowns and wrappers, gathering them around her shoulders, and winding them about her hips, which required a separate and broader movement. Sometimes she wore a half-veil across the bridge of her nose, Arab style, which set off her loving eyes and occasionally as she jingled with her hennaed hands she took off, huge but gay, looking back at me over her shoulder with those signs of suffering about her nose and lips which come from love only. She would saunter, she would teeter, depending on the rhythm given by the little xylophone of hollow bones—the feet of a rhinoceros perhaps emptied by the ants. All this was performed by a bluish moonlight, while great white blotches of fire burned at irregular points around the horizon. "I want you to tell her, Romilayu," I said, "that's she's a damned attractive woman and that she certainly has an impressive trousseau."

I'm sure Romilayu translated this into some conventional African compliment.

"However," I added, "I have unfinished business with those

frogs. They and I have a rendezvous tomorrow, and I can't give my full consideration to any important matter until I have settled with them once and for all."

I thought this would send her away but she went on modeling her clothes and dancing, heavy but beautiful—those colossal thighs and hips—and furling her brow at me and sending glances from her eyes. Thus I realized as the night and the dancing wore on that this was enchantment. This was poetry, which I should allow to reach me, to penetrate the practical task of demolishing the frogs in the cistern. And what I had felt when I first laid eyes on the thatched roofs while descending the bed of the river, that they were so ancient, amounted to this same thing—poetry, enchantment. Somehow I am a sucker for beauty and can trust only it, but I keep passing through and out of it again. It never has enough duration. I know it is near because my gums begin to ache; I grow confused, my breast melts, and then bang, the thing is gone. Once more I am on the wrong side of it. However, this tribe of people, the Arnewi, seemed to have it in steady supply. And my idea was that when I had performed my great deed against the frogs, then the Arnewi would take me to their hearts. Already I had won Itelo, and the queen had a lot of affection for me, and Mtalba wanted to marry me, and so what was left was only to prove (and the opportunity was made to order; it couldn't have suited my capacities better) that I was deserving.

And so, Mtalba having touched my hands happily one final time with her tongue, giving me herself and all her goods—after all, it was a fine occasion—I said, "Thank you, and good night, good night all."

They said, "Awho."

"Awho, awho. Grun-tu-molani."

They answered, "Tu-molani."

My heart was expanded with happy emotion and now instead of wanting to sleep I was afraid when they left that if I shut my eyes tonight the feeling of enchantment would disappear. Therefore, when Romilayu after another short prayer—once more on his knees, and hand pressed to hand like a fellow about to dive into eternity—when Romilayu went to sleep, I lay with eyes open, bathed in high feeling.

IX

AND THIS was still with me at daybreak when I got up. It was a fiery dawn, which made the interior of our hut as dark as a root-cellar. I took a baked yam from the basket and stripped it like a banana for my breakfast. Sitting on the ground I ate in the cool air and through the door I could see Romilayu, wrinkled, asleep, lying on his side like an effigy.

I thought, "This is going to be one of my greatest days." For not only was the high feeling of the night still with me, which set a kind of record, but I became convinced (and still am convinced) that things, the object-world itself, gave me a kind of go-ahead sign. This did not come about as I had expected it to with Willatale. I thought that she could open her hand and show me the germ, the true cipher, maybe you recall—if not, I'm telling you again. No, what happened was like nothing previously conceived; it took the form merely of the light at daybreak against the white clay of the wall beside me and had an extraordinary effect, for right away I began to feel the sensation in my gums warning of something lovely, and with it a close or painful feeling in the chest. People allergic to feathers or pollen will know what I'm talking about; they become aware of their presence with the most gradual subtlety. In my case the cause that morning was the color of the wall with the sunrise on it, and when it became deeper I had to put down the baked yam I was chewing and support myself with my hands on the ground, for I felt the world sway under me and I would have reached, if I were on a horse, for the horn of the saddle. Some powerful magnificence not human, in other words, seemed under me. And it was this same mild pink color, like the water of watermelon, that did it. At once I recognized the importance of this, as throughout my life I had known these moments when the dumb begins to speak, when I hear the voices of objects and colors; then the physical universe starts to wrinkle and change and heave and rise and smooth, so it seems that even the dogs have to lean against a tree, shivering. Thus on this white wall with its prickles, like the gooseflesh of matter, was the pink light, and it was similar to flying over the white points of the sea at ten thousand feet as the sun begins to rise. It must have been at least fifty years since I had encountered such a color, and I thought I could remember waking as a tiny boy, alone in a double bed, a black bed, and looking at the ceiling where there was a big oval of plaster in the old style, with pears, fiddles, sheaves of wheat, and angel faces; and outside, a white shutter, twelve feet long and covered with the same pink color.

 Did I say a tiny boy? I suppose I was never tiny, but at age five was like a twelve-year-old, and already a very rough child. In the town in the Adirondacks where we used to stay in summer, in the place where my brother Dick was drowned, there was a water mill, and I used to run in with a stick and pound the flour sacks and escape in the dust with the miller cursing. My old man would carry Dick and me into the mill pond and stand with us under the waterfall, one on each arm. With the beard he looked like a Triton; with his clear muscles and the smiling beard. In the green cold water I could see the long fish lounging a few yards away. Black, with spots of fire; with water embers. Like guys loafing on the pavement. Well then, I tell you, it was evening, and I ran into the mill with my stick and clubbed the floursacks, almost choking with the white powder. The miller started to yell, "You crazy little sonofabitch. I'll break your bones like a chicken." Laughing, I rushed out and into this same pink color, far from the ordinary color of evening. I saw it on the floury side of the mill as the water dropped in the wheel. A clear thin red rose in the sky.

 I never expected to see such a color in Africa, I swear. And I was worried lest it pass before I could get everything I should out of it. So I put my face, my nose, to the surface of this wall. I pressed my nose to it as though it were a precious rose, and knelt there on those old knees, lined and grieved-looking; like carrots; and I inhaled, I snuckered through my nose and caressed the wall with my cheek. My soul was in quite a condition, but not hectically excited; it was a state as mild as the color itself. I said to myself, "*I knew* that this place was of old." Meaning, I had sensed from the first that I might find things here which were of old, which I saw when I was still innocent and have longed for ever since, for all my life—and without which *I could not make it*. My spirit was not sleeping then, I can tell you, but was saying, Oh, ho, ho, ho, ho, ho, ho!

Gradually the light changed, as it was bound to do, but at least I had seen it again, like the fringe of the Nirvana, and I let it go without a struggle, hoping it would come again before another fifty years had passed. As otherwise I would be condemned to die a mere old rioter or dumbsock with three million dollars, a slave to low-grade fear and turbulence.

So now when I turned my thoughts to the relief of the Arnewi, I was a different person, or thought I was. I had passed through something, a vital experience. It was exactly the opposite at Banyules-sur-Mer with the octopus in the tank. That had spoken to me of death and I would never have tackled any big project after seeing that cold head pressed against the glass and growing paler and paler. After the good omen of the light I approached the making of a bomb with confidence, although it presented me with no small amount of problems. It would require all the know-how I had. Especially the fuse, and the whole question of timing. I'd have to wait until the last possible moment before throwing my device into the water. Now, I had followed with great interest the story in the papers of the bomb-scare man in New York, the fellow who had quarreled with the electric company and was bent on revenge. Diagrams of his bombs taken from a locker in Grand Central Station had appeared in the *News* or *Mirror*, and I was so absorbed in them I missed my subway stop (the violin case being between my knees). For I had some pretty accurate ideas about the design of a bomb and always found them of great interest. He had used gas pipes, I believe. I thought then I could have made a better bomb at home but of course I had the advantage on my side of officers' training in the infantry school where there had been a certain amount of guerrilla instruction. However, even a factory-made grenade might have failed in that cistern and the whole thing presented a considerable challenge.

And sitting on the ground with my materials between my legs and my helmet pushed back, I concentrated on the job before me, breaking open the shells and emptying the powder into the flashlight case. I have a positive ability to lose myself in practical tasks. God knows that in the country where I have had so many fights it has become harder and harder for me to find help and I have of necessity turned into my own handyman. I am best at rough carpentry, roofing, and painting, and not so hot as an electrician or plumber. It may not be correct to say that I have an ability to lose myself in practical work; rather what happens is that I become painfully intense, and this is true even when I lay out a game of solitaire. I took out the glass end of the flashlight with the little bulb and fitted it tightly with a circle of wood whittled to shape. Through this I made a hole for the fuse. Now came the tricky part, for the functioning of the apparatus depended on the rate at which the fuse would burn. With this I experimented now and I did not look at Romilayu often, but when I did I saw him shake his head in doubt. To this I tried to pay no attention, but I said at last, "Hell, don't throw gloom. Can't you see that I know what I'm doing?" However, I could see I didn't have his confidence, and so I cursed him in my heart and went on with my lighter, setting fire to lengths of various materials to see how they would burn. But if I could get no support from Romilayu there was at least Mtalba, who returned at an early hour of the morning. She was now wearing a pair of transparent violet trousers and one of those veils over her nose, and she took my hand and pressed it on her breast with great liveliness, as if we had reached an understanding last night. She was full of pep. Serenaded by the rhinoceros-foot xylophone and occasionally a chorus of finger whistles she began to stride—if that is the word (to wade?)—to do her dance, shaking and jolting her rich flesh, her face ornamented with a smile of coquetry and love. She recited to the court what she was doing and what I was doing (Romilayu translating). "The woman of Bittahness who loves the great wrestler, the man who is like two men who have grown together, came to him in the night." "She came to him," said the others. "She brought him the bride price"— here followed an inventory which included about twenty head of cattle who were all named and their genealogy given—"and the bride price was very noble. For she is Bittah and very beautiful. And the bridegroom's face has many colors." "Colors, colors." "And it has hair upon it, the cheeks hang and he is stronger than many bulls. The bride's heart is ready, its doors are standing open. The groom is making a thing." "A thing."

"With fire." "Fire." And sometimes Mtalba kissed her hand in token of my own, and held it out to me, and her face in the lines about the nose exhibited those signs of love-suffering, the pains of love. Meanwhile I was burning a shoelace dipped in lighter fluid, watching closely, my head stooped between my knees, to see how it took the spark. Not bad, I thought. It was promising. A little coal descended. As for Mtalba, time was when I would have felt differently about the love she offered me. It would have seemed much more serious a matter. But, ah! The deep creases have begun to set in beside my ears and once in a while when I raise my head in front of the mirror a white hair appears in my nose, and therefore I told myself it was an imaginary Henderson, a Henderson of her mind she had fallen in love with. Thinking of this, I dropped my lids and nodded my head. But all the while I continued to burn scraps of wick and shoelace and even wisps of paper, and it turned out that a section of shoelace, held for about two minutes in the lighter fluid, served better than any other material. Accordingly I prepared a section of the lace taken from one of my desert boots and threaded it through the hole prepared in the wood block and then I said to Romilayu, "I think she's ready to go."

From stooping over the work I had a dizzy thickness at the back of the head, but it was all right. Owing to the vision of the pink light I was firm of purpose and believed in myself, and I couldn't allow Romilayu to show his doubts and forebodings so openly. I said, "Now, you've got to quit this, Romilayu. I am entitled to your trust, this once. I tell you it is going to work."

"Yes, sah," he said.

"I don't want you to think I'm not capable of doing a good job."

He said again, "Yes, sah."

"There is that poem about the nightingale singing that humankind cannot stand too much reality. But how much unreality can it stand? Do you follow? You understand me?"

"Me unnastand, sah."

"I fired that question right back at the nightingale. So what if reality may be terrible? It's better than what we've got."

"Kay, sah. Okay."

"All right, I let you out of it. It's better than what I've got. But every man feels from his soul that he has got to carry his life to a certain depth. Well, I have to go on because I haven't reached that depth yet. You get it?"

"Yes, sah."

"Hah! Life may think it has got me written off in its records. Henderson: type so and so, with the auk and the platypus and other experiments illustrating such-and-such a principle, and laid aside. But life may find itself surprised, for after all, we are men. I am Man—I myself, singular as it may look. Man. And man has many times tricked life when life thought it had him taped."

"Okay." He shrugged away from me, and offered his thick black hands in resignation.

Speaking so much had worn me out, and I stood clutching the bomb in its aluminum case, ready to carry out the promise I had made to Itelo and his two aunts. The villagers knew this was a big event and were turning out in numbers, chattering or clapping their hands and singing out. Mtalba, who had gone away, came back in a changed costume of red stuff that looked like baize and her indigo-dyed hair freshly buttered, large brass rings in her ears, and a brass collar about her neck. Her people were swirling around in colored rags, and there were cows led on gay halters and tethers; they looked somewhat weak and people came up to give them a kiss and inquire about their health, practically as if they were cousins. Some of the maidens carried pet hens in their arms or perched on their shoulders. The heat was deadening, and the sky steep and barren.

"There is Itelo," I said. I thought that he, too, looked apprehensive. "Neither of these guys has any faith in me," I said to myself, and even though I realized why I didn't especially inspire confidence, my feelings, nevertheless, were stung. "Hi, Prince," I said. He was solemn and he took my hand as they all did here and led it to his chest so that I felt the heat of his body through the white middy, for he was dressed as yesterday in his loose whites with the green silk scarf. "Well, this is the day," I said, "and this is the hour." I showed the aluminum case with its shoelace fuse to his highness and I told Romilayu, "We ought to make arrangements to gather the dead frogs and bury them. We will do the graves-registration detail. Prince, how do your fellow tribesmen feel about these animals in death? Still taboo?"

"Mistah Henderson. Sir. Wattah is . . ." Itelo could not find the words to describe how precious this element was, and he rubbed his fingers with his thumb as if feeling velvet.

"I know. I know just exactly what the situation is. But there's one thing I can tell you, just as I told you yesterday, I love these folks. I have to do something to show my friendship. And I am aware that coming from the great outside it is up to me to take this on myself."

Under the heavy white shell of the pith helmet, the flies were beginning to bite; the cattle brought them along, as cattle will invariably, and so I said, "It is time to start." We set off for the cistern, myself in the lead holding the bomb. I checked to see whether the lighter was in the pocket of my shorts. One shoe dragged, as I had taken out the lace, nevertheless I set a good pace toward the reservoir while I held the bomb above my head like the torch of liberty in New York harbor, saying to myself, "Okay, Henderson. This is it. You'd better deliver on your promise. No horsing around," and so on. You can imagine my feelings!

In the dead of the heat we reached the cistern and I went forward alone into the weeds on the edge. All the rest remained behind, and not even Romilayu came up with me. That was all right, too. In a crisis a man must be prepared to stand alone, and actually standing alone is the kind of thing I'm good at. I was thinking, "By Judas, I should be good, considering how experienced I am in going it by myself." And with the bomb in my left hand and the lighter with the slender white wick in the other—this patriarchal-looking wick—I looked into the water. There in their home medium were the creatures, the polliwogs with fat heads and skinny tails and their budding little scratchers, and the mature animals with eyes like ripe gooseberries, submerged in their slums of ooze. While I myself, Henderson, like a great pine whose roots have crossed and choked one another—but never mind about me now. The figure of their doom, I stood over them and the frogs didn't—of course they couldn't—know what I augured. And meanwhile, all the chemistry of anxious fear, which I know so well and hate so much, was taking place in me—the light wavering before my eyes, the saliva drying, my parts retracting, and the cables of my neck hardening. I heard the chatter of the expectant Arnewi, who held their cattle on ornamented tethers, as a drowning man will hear the bathers on the beach, and I saw Mtalba, who stood between them and me in her red baize like a poppy, the black at the center of the blazing red. Then I blew on the wick of my device, to free it from dust (or for good luck), and spun the wheel of the lighter, and when it responded with a flame, I lit the fuse, formerly my shoelace. It started to burn and first the metal tip dropped off. The spark sank pretty steadily toward the case. There was nothing for me to do but clutch the thing, and fix my eyes upon it; my legs, bare to the heat, were numb. The burning took quite a space of time and even when the point of the spark descended through the hole in the wood, I held on because I couldn't risk quenching it. After this I had to call on intuition plus luck, and as there now was nothing I especially wanted to see in the external world I closed my eyes and waited for the spirit to move me. It was not yet time, and still not time, and I pressed the case and thought I heard the spark as it ate the lace and fussed toward the powder. At the last moment I took a Band-Aid which I had prepared for this moment and fastened it over the hole. Then I lobbed the bomb, giving it an underhand toss. It touched the thatch and turned on itself only once before it fell into the yellow water. The frogs fled from it and the surface closed again; the ripples traveled outward and that was all. But then a new motion began; the water swelled at the middle and I realized that the thing was working. Damned if my soul didn't rise with the water even before it began to spout, following the same motion, and I cried to myself, "Hallelujah! Henderson, you dumb brute, this time you've done it!" Then the water came shooting upward. It might not have been Hiroshima, but it was enough of a gush for me, and it started raining frogs' bodies upward. They leaped for the roof with the blast, and globs of mud and stones and polliwogs struck the thatch. I wouldn't have thought a dozen or so shells from the .375 had such a charge in them, and from the periphery of my intelligence the most irrelevant thoughts, which are fastest and lightest, rushed to the middle as I congratulated myself, the first thought being, "They'd be proud of old Henderson at school." (The infantry school. I didn't get high marks when I was there.) The long legs and white bellies and the thicker shapes of the infant frogs filled the column of water. I myself was spattered with the mud, but I started to yell, "Hey, Itelo—Romilayu! How do you like that? Boom! You wouldn't believe me!"

I had gotten more of a result than I could have known in the first instants, and instead of an answering cry I heard shrieks from the natives, and looking to see what was the matter I found that the dead frogs were pouring out of the cistern together with the water. The explosion had blasted out the retaining wall at the front end. The big stone blocks had fallen and the yellow reservoir was emptying fast. "Oh! Hell!" I grabbed my head, immediately dizzy with the nausea of disaster, seeing the water spill like a regular mill race with the remains of those frogs. "Hurry, hurry!" I started to yell. "Romilayu! Itelo! Oh, Judas priest, what's happening! Give a hand. Help, you guys, help!" I threw myself down against the escaping water and tried to breast it back and lift the stones into place. The frogs charged into me like so many prunes and fell into my pants and into the open shoe, the lace gone. The cattle started to riot, pulling at their tethers and straining toward the water. But it was polluted and nobody would allow them to drink. It was a moment of horror, with the cows of course obeying nature and the natives begging them and weeping, and the whole reservoir going into the ground. The sand got it all. Romilayu waded up beside me and did his best, but these blocks of stone were beyond our strength and because of the cistern's being also a dam we were downstream, or however the hell it was. Anyway, the water was lost—lost! In a matter of minutes I saw (sickening!) the yellow mud of the bottom and the dead frogs settling there. For them death was instantaneous by shock and it was all over. But the natives, the cows leaving under protest, moaning for the water! Soon everyone was gone except for Itelo and Mtalba.

"Oh, God, what's happened?" I said to them. "This is ruination. I have made a disaster." And I pulled up my wet and stained T-shirt and hid my face in it. Thus exposed, I said through the cloth, "Itelo, kill me! All I've got to offer is my life. So take it. Go ahead, I'm waiting."

I listened for his approach but all I could hear, instead of footsteps, were the sounds of heartbreak that escaped from Mtalba. My belly hung forth and I was braced for the blow of the knife.

"Mistah Henderson. Sir! What has happened?"

"Stab me," I said, "don't ask me. Stab, I say. Use my knife if you haven't got your own. It's all the same," I said, "and don't forgive me. I couldn't stand it. I'd rather be dead."

This was nothing but God's own truth, as with the cistern I had blown up everything else, it seemed. And so I held my face in the bagging, sopping shirt with the unbearable complications at heart. I waited for Itelo to cut me open, my naked middle with all its fevers and its suffering prepared for execution. Under me the water of the cistern was turning to hot vapor and the sun was already beginning to corrupt the bodies of the frog dead.

X

I HEARD Mtalba crying, "Aii, yelli, yelli."

"What is she saying?" I asked Romilayu.

"She say, goo'by. Fo' evah."

And Itelo in a trembling voice said to me, "You please, Mistah Henderson, covah down you face."

I asked, "What's the matter? You're not going to take my life?"

"No, no, you won me. You want to die, you got to die you'self. You are a friend."

"Some friend," I said.

I could hear that he was speaking against a great pressure in his throat; the lump in it must have been enormous. "I would have laid down my life to help you," I said. "You saw how long I held that bomb. I wish it had gone off in my hands and blown me to smashes. It's the same old story with me; as soon as I come amongst people I screw something up—I goof. They were right to cry when I showed up. They must have smelled trouble and knew that I would cause a disaster."

Under cover of the shirt, I gave in to my emotions, the emotion of gratitude included. I demanded, "Why for once, just once!, couldn't I get my heart's desire? I have to be doomed always to bungle." And I thought my life-pattern stood revealed, and after such a revelation death might as well ensue as not.

But as Itelo would not stab me, I pulled down the cistern-stained shirt and said, "Okay, Prince, if you don't want my blood on your hands."

"No, no," he said.

And I said, "Then thanks, Itelo. I'll just have to try to carry on from here."

Then Romilayu muttered, "Whut we do, sah?"

"We will leave, Romilayu. It's the best contribution I can make now to the welfare of my friends. Good-by, Prince. Good-by, dear lady, and tell the queen good-by. I hoped to learn the wisdom of life from her but I guess I am just too rash. I am not fit for such companionship. But I love that old

woman. I love all you folks. God bless you all. I'd stay," I said,
"and at least repair your cistern for you . . ."

"Bettah you not, sir," said Itelo.

I took his word for it; after all, he knew the situation best.
And moreover I was too heartbroken to differ with him. Romilayu went back to the hut to collect our stuff while I walked
out of the deserted town. There was not a soul in any of the
lanes, and even the cattle had been pulled indoors so that they
would not have to see me again. I waited by the wall of the town
and when Romilayu showed up we went back into the desert
together. This was how I left in disgrace and humiliation,
having demolished both their water and my hopes. For now
I'd never learn more about the grun-tu-molani.

Naturally Romilayu wanted to go back to Baventai and I
said to him that I knew he had fulfilled his contract. The jeep
was his whenever he wanted it. "However," I asked, "how can
I go back to the States now? Itelo wouldn't kill me. He's a
noble character and friendship means something to him. But I
might as well take this .375 and blow my brains out on the spot
as go home."

"Whut you mean, sah?" said Romilayu, much puzzled.

"I mean, Romilayu, that I went into the world one last time
to accomplish certain purposes, and you saw for yourself what
has happened. So if I quit at this time I'll probably turn into a
zombie. My face will become as white as paraffin, and I'll lie
on my bed until I croak. Which is maybe no more than I deserve. So it's your choice. I can't give any orders now and I
leave it up to you. If you are going to Baventai it will be by
yourself."

"You go alone, sah?" he said, surprised at me.

"If I have to, yes, pal," I said. "For I can't turn back. It's
okay. I have a few rations and four one-thousand-dollar bills in
my hat, and I guess I can find food and water on the way. I can
eat locusts. If you want my gun you can have that too."

"No," said Romilayu, after thinking briefly about it. "You
no go alone, sah."

"You're a pretty regular guy. You're a good man, Romilayu.
I may be nothing but an old failure, having muffed just about
everything I ever put my hand to; I seem to have the Midas
touch in reverse, so my opinion may not be worth having, but

that's what I think. So," I said, "what's ahead of us? Where'll we go?"

"I no know," said Romilayu. "Maybe Wariri?" he said.

"Oh, the Wariri. Prince Itelo went to school with their king—what's his name?"

"Dahfu."

"That's it, Dahfu. Well, then, shall we go in that direction?"

Reluctantly Romilayu said, "Okay, sah." He seemed to have his doubts about his own suggestion.

I picked up more than my share of the burden and said, "Let's go. We may not decide to enter their town. We'll see how we feel about that later. But let's go. I haven't got much hope, but all I know is that at home I'd be a dead man."

Thus we started off toward the Wariri while I was thinking about the burial of Oedipus at Colonus—but he at least brought people luck after he was dead. At that time I might almost have been willing to settle for this.

We traveled eight or ten days more, through country very like the Hinchagara plateau. After the fifth or sixth day the character of the ground changed somewhat. There was more wood on the mountains, although mostly the slopes were still sterile. Mesas and hot granites and towers and acropolises held onto the earth; I mean they gripped it and refused to depart with the clouds which seemed to be trying to absorb them. Or maybe in my melancholy everything looked cocksy-worsy to me. This marching over difficult terrain didn't bother Romilayu, who was as much meant for such travel as a deckhand is meant to be on the water. Cargo or registry or destination makes little difference in the end. With those skinny feet he covered ground and to him this activity was self-explanatory. He was very skillful at finding water and knew where he could stick a straw into the soil and get a drink, and he would pick up gourds and other stuff I would never even have noticed and chew them for moisture and nourishment. At night we sometimes talked. Romilayu was of the opinion that with their cistern empty the Arnewi would probably undertake a trek for water. And remembering the frogs and many things besides I sat beside the fire and glowered at the coals, thinking of my shame and ruin, but a man goes on living and, living, things are either better or worse to a fellow. This will never stop, and all survivors know it. And when you don't die of a trouble somehow you begin to convert it—make use of it, I mean.

Giant spiders we saw, and nets set up like radar stations among the cactuses. There were ants in these parts whose bodies were shaped like diabolos and their nests made large gray humps on the landscape. How ostriches could bear to run so hard in this heat I never succeeded in understanding. I got close enough to one to see how round his eyes were and then he beat the earth with his feet and took off with a hot wind in his feathers, a rusty white foam behind.

Sometimes after Romilayu had prayed at night and lain down I would keep him awake telling him the story of my life, to see whether this strange background, the desert, the ostriches and ants, the night birds, and the roaring of lions occasionally, would take off some of the curse, but I came out still more exotic and fantastic always than any ants, ostriches, mountains. And I said, "What would the Wariri say if they knew who was traveling in their direction?"

"I no know, sah. Dem no so good people like Arnewi."

"Oh they're not, eh? But you won't say anything about the frogs and the cistern, now will you, Romilayu?"

"No, no, sah."

"Thanks, friend," I said. "I don't deserve credit for much, but when all is said and done I had only good intentions. Really and truly it kills me to think how the cattle must be suffering back there without water. No bunk. But then suppose I had satisfied my greatest ambition and become a doctor like Doctor Grenfell or Doctor Schweitzer—or a surgeon? Is there a surgeon anywhere who doesn't lose a patient once in a while? Why, some of those guys must tow a whole fleet of souls behind them."

Romilayu lay on the ground with his hand slipped under his cheek. His straight Abyssinian nose expressed great patience.

"The king of the Wariri, Dahfu, was Itelo's school chum. But you say they aren't good people, the Wariri. What's the matter with them?"

"Dem chillen dahkness."

"Well, Romilayu, you really are a very Christian fellow," I

said. "You mean they are wiser in their generation and all the rest. But as between these people and myself, who do you think has got more to worry about?"

Without changing his position, a glitter of grim humor playing in his big soft eye, he said, "Oh, maybe dem, sah."

As you see, I had changed my mind about by-passing the Wariri, and it was partly because of what Romilayu had told me about them. For I felt I was less likely to do any damage amongst them if they were such tough or worldly savages.

So for nine or ten days we walked, and toward the end of this time the character of the mountains changed greatly. There were domelike white rocks which here and there crumpled into huge heaps, and among these white circles of stone on, I think, the tenth day, we finally encountered a person. It happened while we were climbing, late in the afternoon under a reddening sun. Behind us the high mountains we had emerged from showed their crumbled peaks and prehistoric spines. Ahead shrubs were growing between these rock domes, which were as white as chinaware. Then this Wariri herdsman arose before us in a leather apron, holding a twisted stick, and although he did nothing else he looked dangerous. Something about his figure struck me as Biblical, and in particular he made me think of the man whom Joseph met when he went to look for his brothers, and who directed him along toward Dothan. My belief is that this man in the Bible must have been an angel and certainly knew the brothers were going to throw Joseph into the pit. But he sent him on nevertheless. Our black man not only wore a leather apron but seemed leathery all over, and if he had had wings those would have been of leather, too. His features were pressed deep into his face, which was small, secret, and, even in the direct rays of the red sun, very black. We had a talk with him. I said, "Hello, hello," loudly as if assuming that his hearing was sunk as deeply as his eyes. Romilayu asked him for directions and with his stick the man showed us the way to go. Thus old-time travelers must have been directed. I made him a salute but he didn't appear to think much of it and his leather face answered nothing. So we toiled upward among the rocks along the way he had pointed.

"Far?" I said to Romilayu.

"No, sah. Him say not far."

I now thought we might pass the evening in a town, and after ten days of toilsome wandering I had begun to look forward to a bed and cooked food and some busy sights and even to a thatch over me.

The way grew more and more stony and this made me suspicious. If we were approaching a town we ought by now to have found a path. Instead there were these jumbled white stones that looked as if they had been combed out by an ignorant hand from the elements that make least sense. There must be stupid portions of heaven, too, and these had rolled straight down from it. I am no geologist but the word calcareous seemed to fit them. They were composed of lime and my guess was that they must have originated in a body of water. Now they were ultra-dry but filled with little caves from which cooler air was exhaled—ideal places for a siesta in the heat of noon, provided no snakes came. But the sun was in decline, trumpeting downward. The cave mouths were open and there was this coarse and clumsy gnarled white stone.

We had just turned the corner of a boulder to continue our climb when Romilayu astonished me. He had set his foot up to take a long stride but to my bewilderment he began to slide forward on his hands, and, instead of mounting, lay down on the stones of the slope. When I saw him prostrate, I said, "What the hell is with you? What are you doing? Is this a place to lie down? Get up." But his extended body, pack and all, hugged the slope while his frizzled hair settled motionless among the stones. He didn't answer, and now no answer was necessary, because when I looked up I saw, in front of us and about twenty yards above, a military group. Three tribesmen knelt with guns aimed at us while eight or ten more standing behind them were crowding their rifle barrels together, so that we might have been blown off the hillside; they had the fire power to do it. A dozen guns massed at you is bad business, and therefore I dropped my .375 and raised my hands. Yet I was pleased just the same, due to my military temperament. Also that leathery small man had sent us into an ambush and for some reason this elementary cunning gave me satisfaction, too. There are some things the human soul doesn't need to be tutored in. Ha, ha! You know I was kind of pleased and I imitated Romilayu. Brought to the dust I put my face down among the pebbles and waited, grinning. Romilayu was stretched will-less, in an African manner. Finally one of the men came down, covered by the rest, and without speech but stoically, as soldiers usually do, he took the .375 and ammunition and knives and other weapons, and ordered us to get up. When we did so he frisked us again. The squad above us lowered their guns, which were old weapons, either the Berber type with long barrels and inlaid butts, or old European arms which might have been taken away from General Gordon at Khartoum and distributed all over Africa. Yes, I thought, old Chinese Gordon, poor guy, with his Bible studies. But it was better to die like that than in smelly old England. I have very little affection for the iron age of technology. I feel sympathy for a man like Gordon because he was brave and confused.

To be disarmed in ambush was a joke to me for the first few minutes, but when we were told to pick up our packs and move ahead I began to change my mind. These men were smaller, darker, and shorter than the Arnewi but very tough. They wore gaudy loincloths and marched energetically and after we had gone on for an hour or more I was less merry at heart than before. I began to feel atrocious toward those fellows, and for a small inducement I would have swept them up in my arms, the whole dozen or so of them, and run them over the cliff. It took the recollection of the frogs to restrain me. I suppressed my rash feeling and followed a policy of waiting and patience. Romilayu looked very poorly and I put my arm about him. His face because of the dust of surrender was utterly in wrinkles, and his poodle hair was filled with gray powder and even his mutilated ear was whitened like a cruller.

I spoke to him, but he was so worried he scarcely seemed to hear. I said, "Man, don't be in such a funk, what can they do? Jail us? Deport us? Hold us for ransom? Crucify us?" But my confidence did not reach him. I then told him, "Why don't you ask if they're taking us to the king? He's Itelo's friend. I'm positive he speaks English." In a discouraged voice Romilayu tried to inquire of one of these troopers, but he only said, "Harrrff!" And the muscles of his cheek had that familiar tightness which belongs to the soldier's trade. I identified it right away.

After two or three miles of this quick march upward, scrambling, crawling, and trotting, we came in sight of the town. Unlike the Arnewi village, it had bigger buildings, some of them wooden, and much expanded under the red light of that time of day, which was between sunset and blackness. On one side night had already come in and the evening star had begun to spin and throb. The white stone of the vicinity had a tendency to fall from the domes in round shapes, in bowls or circles, and these bowls were in use in the town for ornamental purposes. Flowers were growing in them in front of the palace, the largest of the red buildings. Before it were several fences of thorn and these rocks, about the size of Pacific man-eating clams, held fierce flowers, of a very red color. As we passed, two sentries screwed themselves into a brace, but we were not marched between them. To my surprise we went by and were taken through the center of town and out among the huts. People left their evening meal to come and have a look, laughing and making high-pitched exclamations. The huts were pretty ordinary, hive-shaped and thatched. There were cattle, and I dimly saw gardens in the last of the light, so I supposed they were better supplied with water here, and on that score they were safe from my help. I didn't take it hard that they laughed at me, but adopted an attitude of humoring them and waved my hand and tipped my helmet. However, I didn't care one bit for this. It annoyed me not to have been given an immediate audience with King Dahfu.

They led us into a yard and ordered us to sit on the ground near the wall of a house somewhat larger than the rest. A white band was painted over the door, indicating an official residence. Here the patrol that had captured us went away, leaving only one fellow to guard us. I could have grabbed his gun and made scrap metal of it in one single twist, but what was the use of that? I let him stand at my back and waited. Five or six hens in this enclosed yard were pecking at an hour when they should have gone to roost, and a few naked kids played a game resembling skip rope and chanted with thick tongues. Unlike the Arnewi children, they didn't come near us. The sky was like terra cotta and then like pink gum, unfamiliar to my nostrils. Then final darkness. The hens and the kids disappeared, and this left us by the feet of the armed fellow, alone.

We waited, and for a violent person waiting is often a bed of troubles. I believed that the man who kept us waiting, the black Wariri magistrate or J.P. or examiner, was just letting us cool our bottoms. Maybe he had taken a look through the rushes of the door while there was still light enough to see my face. This might well have astonished him and so he was reflecting on it, trying to figure out what line to take with me. Or perhaps he was merely curled up in there like an ant to wear out my patience.

And I was certainly affected; I was badly upset. I am probably the worst waiter in the world. I don't know what it is but I am no good at it, it does something to my spirit. Thus I sat, tired and worried, on the ground, and my thoughts were mainly fears. Meanwhile the beautiful night crawled on as a continuum of dark and warmth, drawing the main star with it; and then the moon came along, incomplete and spotted. The unknown examiner was sitting within, and he exulted probably over the indignity of the grand white traveler whose weapons had been taken away and who had to wait without supper.

And now one of those things occurred which life has not been willing to spare me. As I was sitting waiting here on this exotic night I bit into a hard biscuit and I broke one of my bridges. I had worried about that—what would I do in the wilds of Africa if I damaged my dental work? Fear of this has often kept me out of fights and at the time I was wrestling with Itelo and was thrown so heavily on my face I had thought about the effect on my teeth. Back home, unthinkingly eating a caramel in the movies or biting a chicken bone in a restaurant, I don't know how many times I felt a pulling or a grinding and quickly investigated with my tongue, while my heart almost stopped. This time the dreaded thing really happened and I chewed broken teeth together with the hardtack. I felt the jagged shank of the bridge and was furious, disgusted, frightened; damn! I was in despair and there were tears in my eyes.

"Whut so mattah?" said Romilayu.

I took out the lighter and fired it up and I showed him fragments of tooth in my hand, and pulled open my lip, raising the flame so that he could look inside. "I have broken some teeth," I said.

"Oh! Bad! You got lot so pain, sah?"

"No, no pain. Just anguish of spirit," I said. "It couldn't have happened at a worse time." Then I realized that he was horrified to see these molars in the palm of my hand and I blew out the light.

After this I was compelled to recall the history of my dental work.

The first major job was undertaken after the war, in Paris, by Mlle. Montecuccoli. The original bridge was put in by her. You see, there was a girl named Berthe, who was hired to take care of our two daughters, who recommended her. A General Montecuccoli was the last opponent of the great Marshal Turenne. Enemies used to attend each other's funerals in the old days, and Montecuccoli went to Turenne's and beat his breast and sobbed. I appreciated this connection. However, there were many things wrong. Mlle. Montecuccoli had a large bust, and when she forgot herself in the work she pressed down on my face and smothered me, and there were so many drains and dams and blocks of wood in my mouth that I couldn't even holler. Mlle. Montecuccoli with fearfully roused black eyes was meanwhile staring in. She had her office in the Rue du Colisée. There was a stone court, all yellow and gray, with shrunken poubelles, cats tugging garbage out, brooms, pails, and a latrine with slots for your shoes. The elevator was like a sedan chair and went so slowly you could ask the time of day from people on the staircase which wound around it. I had on a tweed suit and pigskin shoes. While waiting in the courtyard before the hut with the official stripe above the door, Romilayu beside me, and the guard standing over us both, I was forced to remember all this. . . . Rising in the elevator. My heart is beating fast, and here is Mlle. Montecuccoli whose fifty-year-old face is heart-shaped, and who has a slender long smile of French, Italian, and Romanian (from her mother) pathos; and the large bust. And I sit down, dreading, and she starts to stifle me as she extracts the nerve from a tooth in order to anchor the bridge. And while fitting the same she puts a stick in my mouth and says, "Grincez! Grincez les dents! Fâchez-vous." And so I grince and fâche for all I'm worth and eat the wood. She grinds her own teeth to show me how.

The mademoiselle thought that on artistic grounds American dentistry was inexcusable and she wanted to give me a new crown in front like the ones she had given Berthe, the children's governess. When Berthe had her appendix out there was nobody but myself to visit her in the hospital. My wife was too busy at the Collège de France. Therefore I went, wearing a derby and carrying gloves. Then this Berthe pretended to be delirious and rolling in the bed with fever. She took my hand and bit it, and thus I knew that the teeth Mlle. Montecuccoli had given her were good and strong. Berthe had broad, shapely nostrils, too, and a pair of kicking legs. I went through a couple of troubled weeks over this same Berthe.

To stick to the subject, however, the bridge Mlle. Montecuccoli gave me was terrible. It felt like a water faucet in my mouth and my tongue was cramped over to one side. Even my throat ached from it, and I went up the little elevator moaning. Yes, she admitted it was a little swollen, but said I'd get used to it soon, and appealed to me to show a soldier's endurance. So I did. But when I got back to New York, everything had to come out.

All this information is essential. The second bridge, the one I had just broken with the hardtack, was made in New York by a certain Doctor Spohr, who was first cousin to Klaus Spohr, the painter who was doing Lily's portrait. While I was in the dentist's chair, Lily was sitting for the artist up in the country. Dentist and violin lessons kept me in the city two days a week and I would arrive in Dr. Spohr's office, panting, with my violin case, after two subways and a few stops at bars along the way, my soul in strife and my heart saying that same old thing. Turning into the street I would sometimes wish that I could seize the whole building in my mouth and bite it in two, as Moby Dick had done to the boats. I tumbled down to the basement of the office where Dr. Spohr had a laboratory and a Puerto Rican technician was making casts and grinding plates on his little wheel.

Reaching behind some smocks to the switch, I turned on the light in the toilet and went in, and after flushing the john made faces at myself and looked into my own eyes saying, "Well?" "And when?" "And wo bist du, soldat?" "Toothless!

Mon capitaine. Your own soul is killing you." And "It's you who makes the world what it is. Reality is *you*."

The receptionist would say, "Been for your violin lesson, Mr. Henderson?"

"Yah."

Waiting for the dentist as I waited now with the fragments of his work in my hand, I'd get to brooding over the children and my past and Lily and my prospects with her. I knew that at this moment with her lighted face, barely able to keep her chin still from intensity of feeling, she was in Spohr's studio. The picture of her was a cause of trouble between me and my eldest son, Edward. The one with the red MG. He is like his mother and thinks himself better than me. Well, he's wrong. Great things are done by Americans but not by the likes of either of us. They are done by people like that man Slocum who builds the great dams. Day and night, thousands of tons of concrete, machinery that moves the earth, lays mountains flat and fills the Punjab Valley with cement grout. That's the type that gets things done. On this my class, Edward's class, the class Lily was so eager to marry into, gets zero. Edward has always gone with the crowd. The most independent thing he ever did was to dress up a chimpanzee in a cowboy suit and drive it around New York in his open car. After the animal caught cold and died, he played the clarinet in a jazz band and lived on Bleecker Street. His income was $20,000 at least, and he was living next door to the Mills Hotel flophouse where the drunks are piled in tiers.

But a father is a father after all, and I had gone as far as California to try to talk to Edward. I found him living in a bathing cabin beside the Pacific in Malibu, so there we were on the sand trying to have a conversation. The water was ghostly, lazy, slow, stupefying, with a vast dull shine. Coppery. A womb of white. Pallor; smoke; vacancy; dull gold; vastness; dimness; fulgor; ghostly flashing. "Edward, where are we?" I said. "We are at the edge of the earth. Why here?" Then I told him, "This looks like a hell of a place to meet. It's got no foundation except smoke. Boy, I must talk to you about things. It's true I'm rough. It may be true I am nuts, but there is a reason for it all. 'The good that I would that I do not.'"

"Well, I don't get it, Dad."

"You should become a doctor. Why don't you go to medical school? Please go to medical school, Edward."

"Why should I?"

"There are lots of good reasons. I happen to know that you worry about your health. You take Queen Bee tablets. Now I *know* that . . ."

"You came all this way to tell me something—is that what it is?"

"You may believe that your father is not a thinking person, only your mother. Well, don't kid yourself, I have made some clear observations. First of all, few people are sane. That may surprise you, Edward, but it really is so. Next, slavery has never really been abolished. More people are enslaved to different things than you can shake a stick at. But it's no use trying to give you a résumé of my thinking. It's true I'm often confused but at the same time I am a fighter. Oh, I am a fighter. I fight very hard."

"What do you fight for, Dad?" said Edward.

"Why," I said, "what do I fight for? Hell, for the truth. Yes, that's it, the truth. Against falsehood. But most of the fighting is against myself."

I understood very well that Edward wanted me to tell him what he should live for and this is what was wrong. This was what caused me pain. For every son expects and every father wishes to provide clear principles. And moreover a man wants to protect his children from the bitterness of things if he can.

A baby seal was weeping on the sand and I was very much absorbed by his situation, imagining that the herd had abandoned him, and I sent Edward to get a can of tunafish at the store while I stood guard against the roving dogs, but one of the beach combers told me that this seal was a beggar, and if I fed him I would encourage him to be a parasite on the beach. Then he whacked him on the behind and without resentment the creature hobbled to the water on his flippers, where the pelican patrols were flying slowly back and forth, and entered the white foam. "Don't you get cold at night, Eddy, on the beach?" I said.

"I don't mind it much."

I felt love for my son and couldn't bear to see him like this.

"Go on and be a doctor, Eddy," I said. "If you don't like blood you can be an internist or if you don't like adults you can be a pediatrician, or if you don't like kids perhaps you can specialize in women. You should have read those books by Doctor Grenfell I used to give you for Christmas. I know damned well you never even opened the packages. For Christ's sake, we should commune with people."

I went back alone to Connecticut, shortly after which the boy returned with a girl from Central America somewhere and said he was going to marry her, an Indian with dark blood, a narrow face, and close-set eyes.

"Dad, I'm in love," he tells me.

"What's the matter? Is she in trouble?"

"No. I tell you I love her."

"Edward, don't give me that," I say. "I can't believe it."

"If it's family background that worries you, then how about Lily?" he says.

"Don't let me hear a single word against your stepmother. Lily is a fine woman. Who is this Indian? I'm going to have her investigated," I say.

"Then I don't understand," he says, "why you don't allow Lily to hang up her portrait with the others. You leave Maria Felucca alone." (If that was her name.) "I love her," he says, with an inflamed face.

I look at this significant son, Edward, with his crew-cut hair, his hipless trunk, his button-down collar and Princeton tie, his white shoes—his practically faceless face. "Gods!" I think. "Can this be the son of my loins? What the hell goes on around here? If I leave him with this girl she will eat him in three bites."

But even then, strangely enough, I felt a shock of love in my heart for this boy. My son! Unrest has made me like this, grief has made me like this. So never mind. Sauve qui peut! Marry a dozen Maria Feluccas, and if it will do any good, let her go and get her picture painted, too.

So Edward went back to New York with his Maria Felucca from Honduras.

I had taken down my own portrait in the National Guard uniform. Neither Lily nor I would hang in the main hall.

Nor was this all I was compelled to remember as Romilayu

and I waited in the Wariri village. For I several times said to Lily, "Every morning you leave to get yourself painted, and you're just as dirty as you ever were. I find kids' diapers under the bed and in the cigar humidor. The sink is full of garbage and grease, and the joint looks as if a poltergeist lived here. You are running from me. I know damned well that you go seventy miles an hour in the Buick with the children in the back seat. Don't look impatient when I bring these subjects up. They may belong to what you consider the lower world, but I have to spend quite a bit of time there."

She looked very white at this and averted her face and smiled as if it would be a long time before I could understand how much good it was doing me to have this portrait painted.

"I know," I said. "The ladies around here gave you the business during the Milk Fund drive. They wouldn't let you on the committee. I know all about it."

But most of all what I recalled with those broken teeth in my hand on this evening in the African mountains was how I had disgraced myself with the painter's wife and dentist's cousin, Mrs. K. Spohr. Before the First World War (she's in her sixties) she was supposed to have been a famous beauty and has never recovered from the collapse of this, but dresses like a young girl with flounces and flowers. She may have been a hot lay once, as she claims, though among great beauties that is rare. But time and nature had blown the whistle on her and she was badly ravaged. However, her sex power was still there and hid in her eyes, like a Sicilian bandit, like a Giuliano. Her hair is red as chili powder and some of this same red is sprinkled on her face in freckles.

One winter afternoon, Clara Spohr and I met in Grand Central Station. I had had my sessions with Spohr the dentist and Haponyi the violin teacher, and I was disgruntled, hastening to the lower level so that my shoes and pants could scarcely keep up with me—hastening through the dark brown down-tilted passage with its lights aswoon and its pavement trampled by billions of shoes, with amoeba figures of chewing gum spread flat. And I saw Clara Spohr coming from the Oyster Bar or being washed forth into this sea, dismasted, clinging to her soul in the shipwreck of her beauty. But she seemed to be sinking. As I passed she flagged me down and took my arm, the one not engaged by my violin, and we went to the club car and started, or continued, to drink. At this same winter hour, Lily was posing for her husband, so she said, "Why don't you get off with me and drive home with your wife?" What she wanted me to say was, "Baby, why go to Connecticut? Let's jump off the train and paint the town red." But the train pulled out and soon we were running along Long Island Sound, with snow, with sunset, and the atmosphere corrupting the shape of the late sun, and the black boats saying, "Foo!" and spilling their smoke on the waves. And Clara was burning and she talked and talked and worked on me with her eyes and her turned-up nose. You could see the old mischief working, the life-craving, which wouldn't quit. She was telling me how she had visited Samoa and Tonga in her youth and had experienced passionate love on the beaches, on the rafts, in the flowers. It was like Churchill's blood, sweat, and tears, swearing to fight on the beaches, and so on. I couldn't help feeling sympathetic, partly. But my attitude is that if people are going to undo themselves before you, you shouldn't do them up again. You should let them retie their own parcels. Toward the last, as we got into the station, she was weeping, this old crook, and I felt terrible. I've told you how I feel when women cry. I was also incensed. We got out in the snow, and I supported her and found a taxi.

When we entered her house, I tried to help her take off her galoshes, but with a cry she lifted me up by the face and began to kiss me. Whereupon, like a fool, instead of pushing her away I kissed back. Yes, I returned the kisses. With the bridgework, new then, in my mouth. It was certainly a peculiar moment. Her shoes had come off with the galoshes. We embraced in the over-heated lamp-lighted entry which was filled with souvenirs of Samoa and of the South Seas, and kissed as if the next moment we were going to be separated by the stroke of death. I have never understood this foolish thing, for I was not passive. I tell you, I kissed back.

Oh, ho! Mr. Henderson. What? Sorrow? Lust? Kissing has-been beauties? Drunk? In tears? Mad as a horsefly on the window pane?

Furthermore Lily and Klaus Spohr saw it all. The studio door was open. Within was a coal fire in the grate.

"Why are you kissing each other like that?" said Lily.

Klaus Spohr never said a word. Whatever Clara saw fit to do was okay by him.

XI

AND NOW I have told you the history of these teeth, which were made of a material called acrylic that's supposed to be unbreakable—fort comme la mort. But my striving wore them out. I have been told (by Lily, by Frances, or by Berthe? I can't remember which) that I grind my jaws in my sleep, and undoubtedly this has had a bad effect. Or maybe I have kissed life too hard and weakened the whole structure. Anyway my whole body was trembling when I spat out those molars, and I thought, "Maybe you've lived too long, Henderson." And I took a drink of bourbon from the canteen, which stung the cut in my tongue. Then I rinsed the fragments in whisky and buttoned them into my pocket on the chance that even out here I might run into someone who would know how to glue them into place.

"Why are they keeping us waiting like this, Romilayu?" I said. Then I lowered my voice, asking, "You don't think they've heard about the frogs, do you?"

"Wo, no, I no t'ink so, sah."

From the direction of the palace we then heard a deep roar, and I said, "Would that be a lion?"

Romilayu replied that he believed it was.

"Yes, I thought so too," I said. "But the animal must be inside the town. Do they keep a lion in the palace?"

He said uncertainly, "Dem mus' be."

The smell of animals was certainly very noticeable in the town.

At last the fellow who was guarding us received a sign in the dark which I didn't see, for he told us to get up and we entered the hut. Inside we were told to sit, and we sat on a pair of low stools. Torchlight was held over us by a couple of women both of whom were shaven. The shape of their heads thus revealed was delicate though large. They parted their large lips and smiled at us and there was some relief for me in those smiles. After we were seated, the women choking their laughter so that the torches wagged and the light was fitful and smoky, in came a man from the back of the house and my relief vanished. It dried right out when he looked at me, and I thought, "He has certainly heard something about me, either about those damned frogs or something else." The clutch of conscience gripped me to the bone. Totally against reason.

Was it a wig he wore? Some sort of official headdress, a hempy-looking business. He took his place on a smooth bench between the torches. On his knees he held a stick or rod of ivory, looking very official; over his wrists were long tufts of leopard skin.

I said to Romilayu, "I don't like the way this man looks at us. He made us wait a long time, and I'm worried. What's your thinking on this?"

"I no know," he said.

I unbuckled the pack and took out a few articles—the usual cigarette lighters and a magnifying glass which I happened to have along. These articles, laid on the ground, were ignored. A huge book was brought forth, a sign of literacy which astonished and worried me. What was it, a guest register or something? Strange guesses leaped up in my mind, completely abandoned to fantasies by now. However, the book turned out to be an atlas, and he opened it toward me with skill in turning large pages, moistening two fingers on his tongue. Romilayu told me, "Him say you show home."

"That's a reasonable request," I said, and got on my knees, and with the lighter and magnifying glass, poring over North America, I found Danbury, Connecticut. Then I showed my passport, the women with those curious tender bald heads meanwhile laughing at my cumbersome kneeling and standing, my fleshiness, and the nervous, fierce, yet appeasing contortions or glowers of my face. This face, which sometimes appears to me to be as big as the entire body of a child, is always undergoing transformations making it as busy, as strange and changeful, as a creature of the tropical sea lying under a reef, now the color of carnations and now the color of a sweet potato, challenging, acting, harkening, pondering, with all the human passions at the point of doubt—I mean the humanity of them lying in doubt. A great variety of expressions was thus hurdling my nose from eye to eye and twisting my brows. I had good cause to hold my temper and try to behave moderately, my record in Africa being not so brilliant thus far.

"Where is the king?" I said. "This gentleman is not the king, is he? I could speak to him. The king knows English. What's all this about? Tell him I want to go straight to his royal highness."

"Wo, no, sah," said Romilayu. "We no tell him. Him police."

"Ha, ha, you're kidding."

But actually the fellow did examine me like a police official, and if you recall my conflict with the state troopers (they came that time to quell me in Kowinsky's tavern near Route 7, and Lily had to bail me out), you may guess how as a man of wealth and an aristocrat, and impatient as I am, I react to police questioning. Especially as an American citizen. In this primitive place. It made my hackles go up. However, I had a great many things lying on my mind and conscience, and I tried to be as politic and cautious as it was in me to be. So I endured this small fellow's interrogation. He was very grim and business-like. We had come from Baventai how long ago? How long had we stayed with the Arnewi and what were we doing? I held my good ear listening for anything resembling the words cistern, water, or frog, though by this time I was aware that I could trust Romilayu, and that he would stand up for me. That's how it is, you bump into people casually by a tropical lake with crocodiles as part of a film-making expedition and you discover the good in them to be almost unlimited. However, Romilayu must have reported the severe drought back there on the Arnewi River, for this man, the examiner, declared positively that the Wariri were going to have a ceremony very soon and make all the rain they needed. "Wak-ta!" he said, and described a downpour by plunging the fingers of both hands downward. A skeptical expression came over my mouth, which I had the presence of mind to conceal. But I was very much handicapped in this interview, as the events of last week had undermined me. I was infinitely undermined.

"Ask him," I said, "why our guns were taken away and when we'll get them back."

The answer was that the Wariri did not permit outsiders to carry arms in their territory. "That's a damned good rule," I said. "I don't blame these guys. They're very smart. It would have been better for all concerned if I had never laid eyes on a firearm. Ask him anyhow to be careful of those scope sights. I doubt whether these characters know much about such high-grade equipment."

The examiner showed a row of unusually mutilated teeth. Was he laughing? Then he spoke, Romilayu translating. What was the purpose of my trip, and why was I traveling like this?

Again that question! Again! It was like the question asked by Tennyson about the flower in the crannied wall. That is, to answer it might involve the history of the universe. I knew no more how to reply than when Willatale had put it to me. What was I going to tell this character? That existence had become odious to me? It was just not the kind of reply to offer under these circumstances. Could I say that the world, the world as a whole, the entire world, had set itself against life and was opposed to it—just down on life, that's all—but that I was alive nevertheless and somehow found it impossible to go along with it? That something in me, my grun-tu-molani, balked and made it impossible to agree? No, I couldn't say that either.

Nor: "You see, Mr. Examiner, everything has become so tremendous and involved, why, we're nothing but instruments of this world's processes."

Nor: "I am this kind of guy, rest is painful to me, and I have to have motion."

Nor: "I'm trying to learn something, before it all gets away from me."

As you can see for yourselves, these are all impossible answers. Having passed them in review, I concluded that the best thing would be to try to snow him a little, so I said that I had heard many marvelous reports about the Wariri. As I couldn't think of any details just then, I was just as glad that he didn't ask me to be specific.

"Could we see the king? I know a friend of his and I am dying to meet him," I said.

My request was ignored.

"Well, at least let me send him a message. I am a friend of his friend Itelo."

To this no reply was made either. The torch-bearing women giggled over Romilayu and me.

We were then conducted to a hut and left alone. They set no guard over us, but neither did they give us anything to eat. There was neither meat nor milk nor fruit nor fire. This was a strange sort of hospitality. We had been held since nightfall and I figured the time now would be half-past ten or eleven. Although what did this velvet night have to do with clocks? You understand me? But my stomach was growling, and the armed fellow, having brought us to our hut, went away and left us. The village was asleep. There were only small stirrings of the kind made by creatures in the night. We were left beside this foul hovel of stale, hairy-seeming old grass, and I am very sensitive about where I sleep, and I wanted supper. My stomach was not so much empty, perhaps, as it was anxious. I touched the shank of the broken bridge with my tongue and resolved that I wouldn't eat dry rations. I rebelled at the thought. So I said to Romilayu, "We'll build a little fire." He did not take to this suggestion but, dark as it was, he saw or sensed what a mood was growing on me and tried to caution me against making any disturbance. But I told him, "Rustle up some kindling, I tell you, and make it snappy."

Therefore he went out timidly to gather some sticks and dry manure. He may have thought I would burn down the town in revenge for the slight. By the fistful, rudely, I pulled out wisps from the thatch, after which I opened the package of de-hydrated chicken noodle soup, mixing it with a little water and a stiffener of bourbon to help me sleep. I poured this in the aluminum cooking kit and Romilayu made a small blaze near the door. On account of the odors we did not dare to venture inside too far. The hut appeared to be a storehouse for odds and ends, worn-out mats and baskets with holes in them, old horns and bones, knives, nets, ropes, and the like. We drank the soup tepid, as it seemed it would never come to a boil, owing to the poverty of the fire. The noodles went down almost unwillingly. After which Romilayu, on his shinbones, said his usual prayers. And my sympathy went out to him, as this did not seem a good place in which we were about to lay our heads. He pressed his collected fingertips close under the chin, groaning from his chest and bending down his credulous head with the mutilated cheeks. He was very worried, and I said, "Tonight you want to make an especially good job, Romilayu." I spoke largely to myself.

But all at once I said, "Ah!" and the entire right side of me grew stiff as if paralyzed, and I could not even bring my lips together. As if the strange medicine of fear had been poured down my nose crookedly and I began to cough and choke. For by a momentary twisting upward of some of the larger chips from the flame I thought I saw a big smooth black body lying behind me within the hut against the wall.

"Romilayu!"

He stopped praying.

"There's somebody in the hut."

"No," he said, "dem nobody here. Jus' me—you."

"I tell you, somebody's in there. Sleeping. Maybe this house belongs to somebody. They should have told us we were going to share it with another party."

Dread and some of the related emotions will often approach me by way of the nose. As when you are given an injection of novocaine and feel the cold liquid inside the membranes and the tiny bones of that region.

"Wait until I find my lighter," I said. And I ground the little wheel of the Austrian lighter with my thumb harshly. There was a flare, and when I advanced into the hut, holding it above me to spread light over the ground, I saw the body of a man. I was then afraid my nose would burst under the pressure of terror. My face and throat and shoulders were all involved in the swelling and trembling that possessed me, and my legs spindled under me, feeling very feeble.

"Is he sleeping?" I said.

"No. Him dead," said Romilayu.

I knew that very well, better than I wished to.

"They have put us in here with a corpse. What can this be about? What are they trying to pull?"

"Wo! Sah, sah!"

I spread my arms before Romilayu, trying to communicate firmness to him and I said, "Man, hold onto yourself."

But I myself experienced a wrinkling inside the belly which made me very weak and faint. Not that the dead are strangers to me. I've seen my share of them and more. Nevertheless it took several moments for me to recover from this swamping by fear, and I thought (under my brows) what could be the meaning of this? Why was I lately being shown corpses—first the old lady on my kitchen floor and only a couple of months later this fellow lying in the dusty litter? He was pressed against the canes and raffia of which this old house was built. I directed Romilayu to turn him over. He wouldn't; he wasn't able to obey and so I handed him the lighter, which was growing hot, and did the job myself. I saw a tall person no longer young but still powerful. Something in his expression suggested that there had been an odor he didn't wish to smell and had averted his head, but the poor guy had to smell it at last. There may be something like that about it; till the moment comes we won't know. But he was scowling and had a wrinkle on his forehead somewhat like a high-water mark or a tidal line to show that life had reached the last flood and then receded. Cause of death not evident.

"He hasn't been gone long," I said, "because the poor sucker isn't hard yet. Examine him, Romilayu. Can you tell anything about him?"

Romilayu could not as the body was naked, and so revealed little. I tried to consult with myself as to what I should do, but I could not make sense, the reason being that I was becoming offended and angry.

"They've done this on purpose, Romilayu," I said. "This is why they made us wait so long and why those broads with the torches were laughing. All the time they were working on this frame-up. If that little crook with the twisted stick was capable of sending us into an ambush, then I don't put it past them to rig up this, either. Boy, they're the children of darkness, all right, just as you said. Maybe this is their idea of a hot practical joke. At daybreak we were supposed to wake up and see that we had spent the night with a corpse. But listen, you go and tell them, Romilayu, that I refuse to sleep in a morgue. I have waked up next to the dead all right, but that was on the battlefield."

"Who I tell?" said Romilayu.

And I started to storm at him, "Go on," I said. "I've given you an order. Go, wake somebody. Judas! This is what I call brass."

Romilayu cried, "Mistah Henderson, sah, whut I do?"

"Do what I tell you," I yelled, and the loathing of the dead I felt and all the rage of a tired man who had broken his bridgework filled me.

And so, unwillingly, Romilayu went out and probably sat

down on a stone somewhere and prayed or wept that he had ever come with me or had been tempted by the jeep, and probably he repented of not having turned back to Baventai alone after the explosion of frogs. Certainly he was too timid to wake anyone with my complaint. And perhaps the thought had come to him, as it now did to me, that we were liable to be accused of a murder. I hurried to the door and leaned out into the thick night, which now smelled malodorous to me, and I said, as loud as I dared, and brokenly, "Come back, Romilayu, where are you? I've changed my mind. Come back, old fellow." For I was thinking that I shouldn't drive him from me, as tomorrow we might have to defend our lives. When he came back we squatted down, the two of us, beside the dead man to deliberate and what I felt was not so much fear now as sadness, a regular drawing pain of sadness. I felt my mouth become very wide with the sorrow of it and the two of us, looking at the body, suffered silently for a while, the dead man in his silence sending a message to me such as, "Here, man, is your being, which you think so terrific." And just as silently I replied, "Oh, be quiet, dead man, for Christ's sake."

Of one thing I presently became convinced, that the presence of this corpse was a challenge which had to be answered, and I said to Romilayu, "They aren't going to put this over on me." I told him what I thought we should do.

"No, sah," he said intensely.

"I have decided."

"No, no, we sleep outside."

"Never," I said. "It will make me look soft. They've unloaded this man on us and the thing for us to do is to give him right back to them."

Romilayu began to moan again, "Wo, wo! Whut we do, sah?"

"We'll do as I said. Now pay attention to me. I tell you I see through the whole thing. They may try to hang this on us. How would you like to stand trial?"

Again I spun the lighter with my thumb, and Romilayu and I saw each other under the small pointed orange flame as I held it up. He suffered from terror of the dead, whereas it was the affront, the challenge, that got me most. It seemed to me absolutely necessary to exert myself, as I was horribly stirred.

And my mind was resolute; I had decided to drag him out of the hut.

"Okay, let's pull him out," I said.

And Romilayu insisted, "No, no. Us go out. I mek you bed on the ground."

"You'll do no such thing. I'm going to take him and stick him right in front of the palace. I can hardly believe that Itelo's friend the king could be involved in any such plot against a visitor."

Romilayu began to moan again, "Wo, no, no, no! Them catch you."

"Well, unloading him in front of the palace probably is too chancy," I conceded. "We'll lay him down somewhere else. But I can't bear not to do anything about it."

"Why you mus'?"

"Because I just must. It's practically constitutional with me. I can never take such things lying down. They just aren't going to do this to us," I said. I was too outraged to be reasoned with. Romilayu put his hands, which, with their shadows, looked like lobsters, to his wrinkled face.

"Wo, dem be trouble."

The provocation of this corpse to me thrust me to the spirit. I was maddened by his presence. The lighter had grown hot again and I blew it out and said to Romilayu, "This body goes, and right now."

I myself, this time, went out to reconnoiter.

Up in the heavens it was like a blue forest—so tranquil! Such a tapestry! The moon itself was yellow, an African moon in its peaceful blue forest, not only beautiful but hungering or craving to become even more beautiful. New ideas as to its beauty were coming back continually from the white heads of the mountain. Again I thought I could hear lions, but as though they were muffled in a cellar. However, everyone seemed asleep. I crept by the sleeping doors and about a hundred yards from the house the lane came to an end and I looked down into a ravine. "Good," I thought. "I'll dump him in here. Then let them blame me for his death." In the far end of the ravine burned a herdsman's fire; otherwise the place was empty. No doubt rats and other scavenging creatures came and went; they always did but I couldn't try to bury the fellow.

It was not for me to worry about what might happen to him in the darkness of this gully.

The moonlight was a big handicap, but a still greater danger came from the dogs. One sniffed me as I was returning to the hut. When I stood still he went away. Dogs are peculiar, though, about the dead. This is a subject which should be studied. Darwin proved that dogs could reason. He had one who watched a parasol float across the lawn and thought about it. But these African village hounds were reminiscent of hyenas. You might reason with an English dog, especially a family pet, but what would I do if these near-wild dogs came running as I carried the corpse to the ravine? How would I deal with them? It came into my head how Dr. Wilfred Grenfell, when he was adrift on an ice floe with his team of huskies, had to butcher some and wrap himself in the skins to save his life. He raised a sort of mast with the frozen legs and paws. This was irrelevant, however. But I thought, what if the dead man's own dog were to appear?

Moreover, it was possible we were being watched. If it was no accident that we had been billeted with this corpse, perhaps the whole tribe was in on the joke; they might even now be spying, holding their mouths and killing themselves with laughter. While Romilayu wept and groaned and I was boiling with indignation.

I sat down at the door of my hut and waited for the blue-white trailing clouds to dim the piecemeal moon, and for the sleep of the villagers, if they were asleep, to deepen.

At last, not because the time was ripe, but because I couldn't bear waiting, I rose and tied a blanket under my chin, a precaution against stains. I had decided to carry the man on my back in case we had to run for it. Romilayu was not strong enough to shoulder the main burden. First I pulled the body away from the wall. Then I took it by the wrists and with a quick turn, bending, hauled it on my back. I was afraid lest the arms begin to exert a grip on my neck from behind. Tears of anger and repugnance began to hang from my eyes. I fought to stifle these feelings back into my chest. And I thought, what if this man should turn out to be a Lazarus? I believe in Lazarus. I believe in the awakening of the dead. I am sure that for some, at least, there is a resurrection. I was never better aware of my belief than when I stooped there with my heavy belly, my face far forward and tears of fear and sorrowful perplexity coming from my eyes.

But this dead man on my back was no Lazarus. He was cold and the skin in my hands was dead. His chin had settled on my shoulder. Determined as only a man can be who is saving his life, I made huge muscles in my jaw and shut my teeth to hold my entrails back, as they seemed to be rising on me. I suspected that if the dead man had been planted on me and the tribe was awake and watching, when I was half way to the ravine they might burst out and yell, "Dead stealer! Ghoul! Give back our dead man!" and they would hit me on the head and lay me out for my sacrilege. Thus I would end—I, Henderson, with all my striving and earnestness.

"You damned fool," I said to Romilayu, who stood off half-concealed. "Pick up this guy's feet, and help me carry. If we see anybody you can just drop them and beat it. I'll run for it alone."

He obeyed me, and, as if dressed in a second man and groaning, my head filled with flashes and thick noises, I went into the lane. And a voice within me rose and said, "Do you love death so much? Then here, have some."

"I do not love it," I said. "Who told you that? That's a mistake."

Near me I then heard the snarl of a dog and I became more dangerous to him than he could possibly be to me. I vowed that if he made trouble I would drop the corpse and tear the animal to pieces with my hands. When he came out bristling and I saw his scruff by moonlight, I made a threatening noise in my throat, and the animal was aghast and shrank from me. Giving a long whine, he beat it. His whining was so unnatural that it should have waked someone, but no, everyone went on sleeping. The huts gaped like open haystacks. Still, however like a heap of hay it may have looked, each was a careful construction, and inside the families of sleepers lay breathing. The air was more than ever like a blue forest, with the moon releasing soft currents of yellow. As I ran, the mountains were all turned over hugely, and the body was shaken, and Romilayu, his head averted, twisted aside, still obeyed me and carried the legs. The ravine was near but the added weight of the corpse sank my feet in the soft soil and the sand poured over my boot tops. I was wearing the type of shoe adopted by the British Infantry in North Africa, and I had improvised myself a new lace with a strip of canvas and it wasn't holding up well. I struggled hard on the short slope that rose to the edge of the ravine, and I said to Romilayu, "Come on. Can't you take just a little more of the weight?" Instead of raising, he pushed, and I stumbled and went down under the burden of the corpse. This was a hard fall and I lay caught in the dusty sand. To my wet eyes the stars appeared elongated, each like a yardstick.

Then Romilayu said hoarsely, "Dem come, dem come."

I got out from under and, when I had freed myself, pushed the body from me into the gully. Something within me begged the dead man for his forgiveness—like, "Oh, you stranger, don't be sore. We have met and parted. I did you no harm. Now go your way and don't hold this against me." Closing my eyes I gave him a heave and he fell on the flat of his back, as it seemed from the thump I heard.

Then on my knees I turned around to see who was coming. Near our hut were several torches and it appeared that someone was looking either for us or for the body. Should we jump into the ravine, too? This would have made fugitives of us, and it was lucky for me that I didn't have the strength to take this leap. I was too bushed, and I suffered pangs in the glands of my mouth. So we remained in the same place until we were discovered by moonlight and a fellow with a gun came running toward us. But his behavior was not hostile, and unless my imagination misled me it was even respectful. He told Romilayu that the examiner wanted to see us again and he did not even look over the edge of the ravine, and no mention of any corpse was made.

We were marched back to the courtyard and without delay were brought before the examiner. Looking about for the two women, I discovered them asleep on some skins at either side of their husband's couch. The messengers he had sent for us entered with their torches.

If they wanted to hang a rap of sacrilege on me, I was guilty all right, having disturbed the rest of their dead. I had some points on my side too, though I had no intention of defending myself. So I waited, one eye almost closed, to hear what this lean fellow in the hemp wig, the examiner, with his leopard-skin cuffs, would say. I was told to sit down and I did so, stooping onto the low stool with my hands on my knees and putting my face forward very attentively.

Now the examiner made no mention of any corpse, but instead asked me a series of curious questions, such as my age and general health and was I a married man and did I have children. To all my answers, translated by poor Romilayu, whose voice showed the strain of terror, the examiner gave deep bows and he frowned, but favorably, and seemed to approve of what he heard. Because he didn't mention the dead man I felt gracious and obliging, if you please, and thought with a certain amount of satisfaction, and maybe even jubilation, that I had passed the ordeal they had set me. It had sickened me, it had wrung me, but in the end my boldness had paid off.

Would I sign my name? For comparison with the passport signature, I supposed. Willingly I dashed the signature down with my liberated and light fingers, saying to myself within, "Ha, ha! Oh, ha, ha, ha, ha, ha, ha! That's okay. You may have my autograph." Where were the ladies? Sleeping with those big contented horizontal mouths and round, shaved, delicate heads. And the torch bearers? Holding up the sizzling lights from which a hairy smoke was departing.

"Well, is everything in order now? I guess it's okay." I was really highly pleased and felt I had accomplished something.

Now the examiner made a curious request. Would I please take off my shirt? At this I balked a little and wanted to know what for. Romilayu couldn't tell me. I was somewhat worried and I said to him in low tones, "Listen, what's all this about?"

"I no know."

"Well, ask the guy."

Romilayu did as I had bid him but only got a repetition of the request.

"Ask him," I said, "if then he'll let us go to sleep peacefully."

As if he understood my terms, the examiner nodded, and I stripped off my T-shirt, which was greatly in need of a wash. The examiner then came up to me and looked me over very closely, which made me feel awkward. I wondered whether I might be asked to wrestle among the Wariri as I had been by Itelo; I thought perhaps I had strayed into a wrestling part of

Africa, where it was the customary mode of introduction. However, this did not seem to be the case.

"Well, Romilayu," I said, "it could be that they want to sell us into slavery. There are reports that they still keep slaves in Saudi Arabia. God! What a slave I'd make. Ha, ha!" I was still in a jesting frame of mind, you see. "Or do they want to put me into a pit and cover me with coals and bake me? The pygmies do that with elephants. It takes about a week's time."

While I was still kidding like this the examiner continued to size me up. I pointed to the name Frances, tattooed at Coney Island so many years ago, and explained that this was the name of my first wife. He did not seem much interested.

I put on my sweaty shirt again and said, "Ask him if we can see the king." This time the examiner was willing to reply. The king, Romilayu translated, wanted to see me tomorrow and to talk to me in my own language.

"That's wonderful," I said. "I have a thing or two to ask him."

Tomorrow, Romilayu repeated, King Dahfu wanted to see me. Yes, yes. In the morning before the day-long ceremonies to end the drought were begun.

"Oh, is that so?" I said. "In that case let's have a little sleep."

So we were allowed at last to rest, not that much of the night remained. All too soon the roosters were screaming and I awoke and grew aware first of foaming red clouds and the huge channel of the approaching sunrise. I then sat up, remembering that the king wished to see us early. Just inside the doorway, against the wall, sitting in very much my own posture, was the dead man. Someone had fetched him back from the ravine.

XII

I SWORE. "This is brain-washing." And I resolved that they would never drive me out of my mind. I had seen dead men before this, plenty of them. In the last year of the war I shared the European continent with about fifteen million of them, though it's always the individual case that's the worst. The corpse was sadly covered with the dust into which I had thrown it, and now that they had fetched him back, my relations with him were no secret, and I decided to sit tight and await the outcome of events. There was nothing more for me to do. Romilayu was still asleep, his hand pressed between his knees, the other under his wrinkled cheek. I saw no reason to wake him. And leaving him in the hut with the dead man, I went into the open air. I was aware of a great peculiarity either in myself or in the day, or in both. I must have been getting the fever from which I was to suffer for a while. It was accompanied by a scratchy sensation in my bosom, a little like eagerness or longing. In the nerves between my ribs this was especially noticeable. It was one of those mixed sensations, comparable to what one feels when smelling the fumes of gasoline. The air was warm and swooning about my face; the colors were all high. Those colors were extraordinary. No doubt my impressions were a consequence of stress and of lack of sleep.

As this was a day of festival the town was already beginning to jump, people were running about, and whether or not they knew whom Romilayu and I had in our hut was never revealed to me. A sweet, spicy smell of native beer burst from the straw walls. The drinking here began apparently at sunrise; there was also a certain amount of what seemed to be drunken noise. I took a cautious walk around and no one paid any particular attention to me, which I interpreted as a good sign. There appeared to be quite a few family quarrels, and some of the older people were particularly abusive and waspish. At which I marveled. A small stone struck me in the helmet, but I assumed it was not aimed at me, for kids were throwing pebbles at one another and tussling, rolling in the dust. A woman ran from her hut and swept them away, screaming and cuffing them.

She did not seem particularly astonished to find herself face to face with me, but turned around and re-entered her house. I peeked in and saw an old fellow lying there on a straw mat. She trod on his back with her bare feet in a kind of massage calculated to straighten out his spinal column, after which she poured liquid fat on him and she skillfully rubbed him, ribs and belly. His forehead wrinkled and his grizzled beard parted. Baring his great old teeth he smiled at me, rolling his eyes toward the doorway where I was standing. "What gives here?" I was thinking, and I went about the small, narrow lanes and looked into the yards and over fences, cautiously, of course, and mindful of the sleeping Romilayu and the dead man sitting against the wall. Several young women were gilding the horns of cattle and painting and ornamenting one another too, putting on ostrich feathers, vulture feathers, and ornaments. Some of the men wore human jaw bones as neckpieces under their chins. The idols and fetishes were being dressed up and whitewashed, receiving sacrifices. An ancient woman with hair in small and rigid braids had dumped yellow meal over one of these figures and was swinging a freshly killed chicken over it. Meanwhile the noise grew in volume, every minute something new added, a rattle, a snare drum, a deeper drum, a horn blast, or a gunshot.

I saw Romilayu come from the door of our hut, and you didn't have to be a fine observer to see what a state he was in. I went toward him and when he caught sight of me above the gathering crowd, probably spotting that white shell on my head, the helmet, before any other portion, he put his hand to his cheek wincingly.

"Yes, yes, yes," I said, "but what can we do? We'll just have to wait. It may not mean a thing. Anyway, the king—what's his name, Itelo's friend, we're supposed to see him this morning. Any minute now he'll send for us and I'll take it up with him. Don't you worry, Romilayu, I'll soon find out what gives. Don't you let on to a thing. Bring our stuff out of the hut and keep an eye on it."

Then with a sort of fast march which was played on the drums, deep drums carried by women of unusual stature, the female soldiers or amazons of the king, Dahfu, there came into the street a company of people carrying large state umbrellas.

Under one of these, a large fuschia-colored business of silk, marched a burly man. One of the other umbrellas had no user and I reckoned, correctly, that it must have been sent for me. "See," I said to Romilayu, "they wouldn't send that luxurious-looking article for a man they were going to frame up. That's a lightning deduction. Just an intuition, but I think we have nothing to worry about, Romilayu."

The drummers marched forward rapidly, the umbrellas twirling and dancing roundly and heavily, keeping time. As these huge fringed and furled silk canopies advanced the Wariri got out of the way. The heavily built man, smiling, had already seen me and extended his burly arms toward me, holding his head and smiling in such a way as to show that he was welcoming me affectionately. He was Horko, who turned out to be the king's uncle. The dress he wore, of scarlet broadcloth, was banded about from his ankles over his chest and up to the armpits. This wrapping was so tight as to make the fat swell upward under his chin and into his shoulders. Two rubies (garnets, maybe?) dragged down the soft flesh of his ears. He had a powerful, low-featured face. As he stepped out of the shade of his state umbrella, the sun flared richly into his eyes and made them seem as much red as black. When he raised his brows the whole of his scalp also moved backward and made a dozen furrows all the way up to the occiput. His hair grew tight and small, peppercorn style, in tiny droplike curls.

Genial, he gave me his hand to shake, in civilized manner, and laughed. He showed a broad, happy-looking, swollen tongue, dyed red as though he had been sucking candy. Adapting my mood to his, I laughed too, corpse or no corpse, and I poked Romilayu in the ribs and said, "See? See? What did I tell you?" Cautious, Romilayu refused to be reassured on such slight evidence. Villagers came about us, laughing with us, although more wildly than Horko, shrugging their shoulders and making pantomimes about me. Many were drunk on pombo, the native beer. The amazons, dressed in sleeveless leather vests, pushed them away. They weren't to get too close to Horko and myself. Corset-like vests were the only garments worn by these large women, who were rather heavy or bunchy in build, and unusually expanded behind.

"Shake, shake," I said to Horko, and he invited me to take

my place under the vacant umbrella. It was a real luxury article, a million-dollar umbrella if I ever saw one.

"The sun's hot," I said, "though it can't be eight o'clock
in the morning. I appreciate the courtesy." I wiped my face,
making looks of friendship, in other words exploiting the situation as much as possible and trying to put the greatest possible distance between us and the corpse.

"Me Horko," he said. "Dahfu uncle."

"Oh, you speak my language," I said, "how lucky for me.
And King Dahfu is your nephew, is he? Hey, what do you know?
And are we going to visit him now? The gentlemen who ques-
tioned us last night said so."

"Me uncle, yes," he said. Then he gave a command to the
amazons, who at once made an about-face which would have
been noisy had they worn boots, and began to pummel out
the same march rhythm on the bass drums. The great umbrellas began again to flash and sway and the light played beautifully on the watered silk as they wheeled. Even the sun seemed
to lie down greedily on them. "Go to palace," said Horko.

"Let's," I said. "Yes, I am eager. We passed it yesterday
coming into town."

Why shouldn't I admit it, I was worried still. Itelo seemed to
think the world and all of his old school friend, Dahfu, and
had spoken of him as though he were one in a million, but on
the basis of my experience thus far with the Wariri I had little
reason to feel comfortable.

I said, above the drums, "Romilayu, where is my man
Romilayu?" I was worried, you see, lest they decide to hold
him in connection with the body. I wanted him by my side. He
was allowed to walk behind me in the procession, carrying all
the gear. Tried in strength and patience, he bent under his
double burden; it was out of the question for me to carry anything. We marched. Considering the size of the umbrellas and
the drums, it was marvelous what speed we made. We flew forward, the drumming amazons before us and behind. And how
different the town was today. Our route was lined with spectators, some of them bending over to spy out my face under the
combined cover of umbrella and helmet. Thousands of hands,
of restless feet, I saw, and faces glaring with heat and curiosity
or intensity or holiday feeling. Chickens and pigs rushed across

the route of the march. Shrill noises, squeals, and monkey shrieks swirled over the pounding of drums.

"This is certainly a contrast," I said, "to yesterday when everything was so quiet. Why was that, Mr. Horko?"

"Yestahday, sad day. All people fast."

"Executions?" I suddenly said. From a scaffold at some distance to the left of the palace I saw, or thought I saw, bodies hanging upside down. Through a peculiarity of the light they were small, like dolls. The atmosphere sometimes will act as a reducing and not only as a magnifying glass. "I certainly hope those are effigies," I said. But my misgiving heart said otherwise. It was no wonder they hadn't made any inquiry about their corpse. What was one corpse to them? They appeared to deal in them wholesale. With this my feverishness increased, plus the scratchiness in my breast, and within my face itself a curious over-ripe sensation developed. Fear. I don't hesitate to admit it. I turned my eyes backward toward Romilayu, but he was lagging under the weight of the equipment and we were separated by a rank of drumming amazons.

So I said to Horko, and was compelled to yell because of the drums, "Seem to be a lot of dead people." We had left the narrow lanes and were in a large thoroughfare approaching the palace.

He shook his big head, smiling with his red-stained tongue, and touched one of his ears, from the lobe of which there dragged a red jewel. He did not hear me.

"Dead people!" I said. And then I told myself, "Don't ask for information with such despair." My face was indeed hot and huge and anxious.

Laughing, he could not admit that he had understood me, not even when I made a pantomime of hanging at the end of a rope. I would have paid four thousand dollars in spot cash for Lily to have been brought here for one single instant, to see how she would square such things with her ideas of goodness. And reality. We had had that terrific argument about reality as a consequence of which Ricey had run away and returned to school with the child from Danbury. I have always argued that Lily neither knows nor likes reality. Me? I love the old bitch just the way she is and I like to think I am always prepared for even the very worst she has to show me. I am a true adorer of life, and if I can't reach as high as the face of it, I plant my kiss somewhere lower down. Those who understand will require no further explanation.

It consoled me for my fears to imagine that Lily would be unable to reply. Though at the present moment I can't for one instant believe that anything would stump her. She'd have an answer all right. But meanwhile we had crossed the parade ground and the sentries had opened the red gate. Here were the hollow stone bowls of yesterday with their hot flowers resembling geraniums, and here was the interior of the palace; it was three stories high with open staircases and galleries, quadrangular and barnlike. At ground level the rooms were doorless, like narrow stalls, open and bare. Here there could be no mistake about it—I heard the roar of a wild beast underneath. No creature but a lion could possibly make such a noise. Otherwise, relative to the streets of the town, the palace was quiet. In the yard were two small huts like doll-houses, each occupied by a horned idol, newly whitewashed this morning. Between these two was a trail of fresh calcimine. A rusty flag which had had too much sun was hung from the turret. It was diagonally divided by a meandering white line.

"Which way to the king?" I said.

But Horko was bound by the rules of etiquette to entertain me and visit with me before my audience with Dahfu. His quarters were on the ground floor. With high ceremony the umbrellas were planted and an old bridge table was brought out by the amazons. It was laid with a cloth of the type that Syrian peddlers used to deal in, red and yellow with fancy Arabic embroideries. Then a silver service was brought, teapot, jelly dishes, covered dishes, and the like. There was hot water, and a drink made of milk mixed with the fresh blood of cattle, which I declined, dates and pineapple, pombo, cold sweet potatoes, and other dishes—mouse paws eaten with a kind of syrup, which I also took a rain-check on. I ate some sweet potatoes and drank the pombo, a powerful beverage which immediately acted on my legs and knees. In my excitement and fever I swallowed several cups of this, since nothing external gave me support, the bridge table being highly rickety; I needed something inside, at least. Half hopefully I thought I was going to be sick. I cannot endure such excitement as I then felt. I did my best to perform the social rigmarole with Horko. He wished me to admire his bridge table, and to oblige him I made him several compliments on it, and said I had one just like it at home. As indeed I do, in the attic. I sat under it when attempting to shoot the cat. I told him it wasn't as nice as his. Ah, it was too bad we couldn't sit as two gentlemen of about the same age, enjoying the fine warm blur of a peaceful morning in Africa. But I was a fugitive and multiple wrong-doer and greatly worried because of the events of the night before. I anticipated that I could clear myself with the king, and several times I thought it was time to rise, and I stirred my large weight and made a start, but the protocol didn't yet allow it. I tried to be patient, cursing the vain waste of fear. Horko, puffing, bent across the frail table, his knuckles like boles, clasping the handle of the silver pot. He poured a hot drink that tasted like steamed hay. Bound by a thousand re-straints, I lifted the cup and sipped with utmost politeness.

At last my reception by Horko was completed and he indi-cated that we should rise. The amazons, in record time, moved away the table and the things, and lined up in formation ready to escort us to the king. Their behinds were pitted like colan-ders. I set my helmet straight and hiked up my short pants and wiped my hands on my T-shirt, for they were damp and I wanted to give the king a dry warm handshake. It means a lot. We started to march toward one of the staircases. Where was Romilayu? I asked Horko. He smiled and said, "Oh, fine. Oh, oh, fine." We were mounting the staircase, and I saw Romilayu below, waiting, dejected, his hands, discouraged, hanging over his knees, and his bent spine sticking out. Poor guy! I thought. I've got to do something for him. Just as soon as this is cleared up I will. I absolutely will. After the catastrophes I've led him into I owe him a real reward.

The outdoor staircase, wide, leisurely, and rambling, took a turn and brought us to the other side of the building. A tree was there and it was shaking and creaking because several men were engaged in a curious task, raising large rocks into the branches with ropes and crude wooden pulleys. They yelled at the ground crew who were pushing these boulders upward and their faces shone with the light of hard work. Horko said to me, and I didn't quite understand how he meant it, that these stones were connected with clouds for the rain they expected to make in the ceremony soon to come. They all seemed very confident that rain would be made today. The examiner last night with his expression, "Wak-ta," had described the downpour with his fingers. But there was nothing in the sky. It was bare of all but the sun itself. There were only, so far, these round boulders in the branches, apparently intended to represent rain clouds.

We came to the third floor, where King Dahfu had his quarters. Horko led me through several wide but low-pitched rooms which seemed to be obscurely supported from beneath; I wouldn't have answered for the beams. There were hangings and curtains. But the windows were narrow, and little could be seen except when a ray of sun would break in here and there and show a rack of spears, a low seat, or the skin of an animal. At the door of the king's apartment, Horko withdrew. I had not expected that and I said, "Hey, where're you going?" But one of the amazons took me by the bare arm and passed me through the door. Before I saw Dahfu himself, I was aware of numbers of women—twenty or thirty was my first estimate— and the density of naked women, their volupté (only a French word would do the job here), pressed upon me from all sides. The heat was great and the predominant odor was feminine. The only thing I could compare it to in temperature and closeness was a hatchery—the low ceiling also is responsible for this association. Seated by the door on a high stool, a stool that resembled an old-fashioned bookkeeper's, was a gray, heavy old woman in the amazon's vest plus a garrison cap of the sort which went out of date with the Italian army at the turn of the century. On behalf of the king she shook my hand.

"How do you do?" I said.

The king! His women cleared a path for me, moving slowly from my way, and I saw him at the opposite end of the room, extended on a green sofa about ten feet in length, crescent-shaped, with heavy upholstery, deeply pocketed and bulging. On this luxurious article he was fully at rest, so that his well-developed athletic body, in knee-length purple drawers of a sort of silk crepe, seemed to float, and about his neck was wrapped a white scarf embroidered in gold. Matching slippers of white satin were on his feet. For all my worry and fever I felt admiration as I sized him up. Like myself, he was a big man, six feet or better by my estimate, and sumptuously at rest. Women attended to his every need. Now and then one wiped his face with a piece of flannel, and another stroked his chest, and one kept his pipe filled and lit and puffed at it for him to keep it going.

I approached or blundered forward. Before I could come too close a hand checked me and a stool was placed for me about five feet from this green sofa. I sat. Between us in a large wooden bowl lay a couple of human skulls, tilted cheek to cheek. Their foreheads shone jointly at me in the yellow way skulls have, and I was confronted by the united eye sockets and nose holes and the double rows of teeth.

The king observed how warily I looked at him and appeared to smile. His lips were large and tumid, the most negroid features of his face, and he said, "Do not feel alarm. These are for employment in the ceremony of this afternoon."

Some voices once heard will never stop resounding in your head, and such a voice I recognized in his from the first words. I leaned forward to get a better look. The king was much amused by my spreading my hands over my chest and belly as if to retain something, and raised himself to examine me. A woman slipped a cushion behind his head, but he knocked it to the floor and lay back again. My thought was, "I haven't run out of luck yet." For I saw that our ambush and capture and interrogation and all the business of billeting us with the dead man, could not have originated with the king. He was not that sort, and although I did not know yet precisely what sort he might be, I was already beginning to rejoice in our meeting.

"Yesterday afternoon, I have receive report of your arrival. I have been so excited. I have scarcely slept last night, thinking about our meeting. . . . Oh, ha, ha. It positively was not good for me," he said.

"That's funny, I didn't get too much sleep myself," I said. "I've had to make do with only a few hours. But I am glad to meet you, King."

"Oh, I am very please. Tremendous. I am sorry over your sleep. But on my own I am please. For me this is a high occasion. Most significant. I welcome you."

"I bring you regards from your friend Itelo," I said.

"Oh, you have encountered with the Arnewi? I see it is your idea to visit some of the remotest places. How is my very dear friend? I miss him. Did you wrestle?"

"We certainly did," I said.

"And who won?"

"We came out about even."

"Well," he said, "you seem a mos' interesting person. Especially in point of physique. Exceptional," he said. "I am not sure I have ever encountered your category. Well, he is very strong. I could not throw him, which gave him very high pleasure. Invariably did."

"I'm beginning to feel my age," I said.

The king said, "Oh, why, nonsense. I think you are like a monument. Believe me, I have never seen a person of your particular endowment."

"I hope you and I do not have to go to the mat, Your Highness," I said.

"Oh, no, no. We have not that custom. It is not local with us. I must request forgiveness from you," he said, "for not arising to a handshake. I ask my generaless, Tatu, to act for me because I am so reluctant to rise. In principle."

"Is that so? Is that so?" I said.

"The less motion I expend, and the more I repose myself, the easier it is for me to attend to my duties. All my duties. Including also the prerogatives of these many wives. You may not think so on first glance, but it is a most complex existence requiring that I husband myself. Sir, tell me frankly—"

"Henderson is the name," I said. Because of the way he lolled, and the way he drew on his pipe, I somehow felt that I was being particularly tested.

"Mr. Henderson. Yes, I should have asked you. I am very sorry for neglecting the civility. But I could hardly contain myself that you were here, sir, a chance for conversation in English. Many things since my return I have felt lacking which I would not have suspected while at school. You are my first civilized visitor."

"Not many people come here?"

"It is by our preference. We have preferred a seclusion, for many generations now, and we are beautifully well hidden in these mountains. You are surprised that I speak English? I assume no. Our friend Itelo must have told you. I adore that man's character. We were steadfastly together through many experiences. It is an intense disappointment to me not to have surprise you more," he said.

"Don't worry, I'm plenty surprised. Prince Itelo told me all about that school that he and you attended in Malindi." As I have emphasized, I was in a peculiar condition, I had an anxious fever, and I was perplexed by the events of last night. But there was something about this man that gave me the conviction that we could approach ultimates together. I went only by his appearance and the tone of his voice, for thus far it seemed to me that there was a touch of frivolousness in his attitude, and that he was trying me out. As for the remoteness of the Wariri, this morning, owing to the peculiarity of my mental condition, the world was not itself; it took on the aspect of an organism, a mental thing, amid whose cells I had been wandering. From mind the impetus came and through mind my course was set, and therefore nothing on earth could really surprise me, utterly.

"Mr. Henderson, I would appreciate if you would return a candid answer to the question I am about to put. None of these women can understand, therefore no hesitancy is required. Do you envy me?"

This was not the moment to tell lies.

"Do you mean would I change places with you? Well, hell, Your Highness—no disrespect intended—you seem to me to be in a very attractive position. But then, I couldn't be at more of a disadvantage," I said. "Almost anyone would win a comparison with me."

His black face had a cocked nose, but it was not lacking in bridge. The reddened darkness of his eyes must have been a family trait, as I had observed it also in his Uncle Horko. But in the king there was a higher quality or degree of light. And now he wanted to know, pursuing the same line of inquiry, "Is it because of all these women?"

"Well, I have known quite a few myself, Your Highness," I said, "though not all at the same time. That seems to be your case. But at present I happen to be very happily married. My wife's a grand person, and we have a very spiritual union. I am not blind to her faults; I sometimes tell her she is the altar of my ego. She is a good woman, but something of a blackmailer. There is such a thing as scolding nature too much. Ha, ha." I have told you I was feeling a little displaced in my mind. And now I said, "Why do I envy you? You are in the bosom of your people. They need you. Look how they stick around and attend to your every need. It's obvious how much they value you."

"While I am in possession of my original youthfulness and strength," he said, "but have you any conception of what will take place when I weaken?"

"What will . . . ?"

"These same ladies, so inordinate of attention, will report me and then the Bunam who is chief priest here, with other priests of the association, will convey me out into the bush and there I will be strangled."

"Oh, no, Christ!" I said.

"Indeed so. I am telling you with utmost faithfulness what a king of us, the Wariri, may look forward to. The priest will attend until a maggot is seen upon my dead person and he will wrap it in a slice of silk and bring it to the people. He will show it in public pronouncing and declaring it to be the king's soul, my soul. Then he will re-enter the bush and, a given time elapsing, he will carry to town a lion's cub, explaining that the maggot has now experienced a conversion into a lion. And after another interval, they will announce to the people the fact that the lion has converted into the next king. This will be my successor."

"Strangled? You? That's ferocious. What sort of an outfit is this?"

"Do you still envy me?" said the king, making the words softly with his large, warm, swollen-seeming mouth.

I hesitated, and he observed, "My deduction from brief observation I give you as follows—that you are probably prone to such a passion."

"What passion? You mean I'm envious?" I said touchily, and forgot myself with the king. Hearing a note of anger, the amazons of the guard who were arrayed behind the wives along the walls of the room, began to stir and grew alert. One syllable from the king quieted them. He then cleared his throat, raising himself upon his sofa, and one of the naked beauties held a salver so that he might spit. Having drawn some to-bacco juice from his pipe, he was displeased and threw the thing away. Another lady retrieved it and cleaned the stem with a rag.

I smiled, but I am certain my smile looked like a grievance. The hairs about my mouth were twisted by it. I was aware, however, that I could not demand an explanation of that re-mark. So I said, "Your Highness, something very irregular happened last night. I don't complain of having fallen into a trap on arrival or my weapons being swiped, but in my hut last night there was a dead body. This is not exactly in the nature of a complaint, as I can handle myself with the dead. Never-theless I thought you ought to know about it."

The king looked really put out over this; there wasn't the least flaw of insincerity in his indignation and he said, "What? I am sure it is a confusion of arrangements. If intentional, I will be very put out. This is a matter I must have looked into."

"I'm obliged to confess, Your Highness, I felt a certain amount of inhospitality and *I* was put out. My man was re-duced to hysterics. And I might as well make a clean breast. Though I didn't want to tamper with your dead, I took it upon myself to remove the body. Only what does it signify?"

"What can it?" he said. "As far as I am aware, nothing."

"Oh, then I am relieved," I said. "My man and I had a very bad hour or two with it. And during the night it was brought back."

"Apologies," said the king. "My most sincere. Genuine. I can see it was horrible and also discommoding."

He didn't ask me for any particulars. He did not say, "Who was it? What was the man like?" Nor did he even seem to care whether it was a man, a woman, or a child. I was so glad to es-cape the anxiety of the thing that at the time I didn't note this peculiar lack of interest.

"There must be quite a number of deaths among you at this time," I said. "On the way over to the palace I could have sworn I saw some fellows hanging."

He did not answer directly, but only said, "We must get you out of the undesirable lodging. So please be my guest in the palace."

"Thank you."

"Your things will be sent for."

"My man, Romilayu, has already brought them, but he hasn't had breakfast."

"Be assured, he will be taken care of."

"And my gun . . ."

"Whenever you have occasion to shoot, it will be in your hands."

"I keep hearing a lion," I said. "Does this have anything to do with the information you gave me about the death of . . ." I did not complete the question.

"What brings you here to us, Mr. Henderson?"

I had an impulse to confide in him—that was how he made me feel, trusting—but as he had steered away the subject from the roaring of the lions, which I clearly heard beneath, I couldn't very well start, just like that, to speak openly and so I said, "I am just a traveler." My position on the three-legged stool suggested that I was crouching there in order to avoid questioning. The situation required an amount of equipoise or calm of mind which I lacked. And I kept wiping or rubbing my nose with my Woolworth bandanna. I tried to figure, "Which of these women might be the queen?" Then, as it might not be polite to stare at the different members of the harem, most of them so soft, supple, and black, I turned my eyes to the floor, aware that the king was watching me. He seemed all ease, and I all limitation. He was extended, floating; I was contracted and cramped. The undersides of my knees were sweating. Yes, he was soaring like a spirit while I sank like a stone, and from my fatigued eyes I could not help looking at him grudgingly (thus becoming actually guilty of the passion he had seen in me), in his colors surrounded by cherishing attention. Suppose there was ultimately such a price to pay? To me it seemed that he was getting full value.

"Do you mind a further inquiry, Mr. Henderson? What kind of traveler are you?"

"Oh . . . that depends. I don't know yet. It remains to be seen. You know," I said, "you have to be very rich to take a trip like this." I might have added, as it entered my mind to do, that some people found satisfaction in *being* (Walt Whitman: "Enough to merely be! Enough to breathe! Joy! Joy! All over joy!"). *Being*. Others were taken up with *becoming*. Being people have all the breaks. Becoming people are very unlucky, always in a tizzy. The Becoming people are always having to make explanations or offer justifications to the Being people. While the Being people provoke these explanations. I sincerely feel that this is something everyone should understand about me. Now Willatale, the queen of the Arnewi, and principal woman of Bittahness, was a Be-er if there ever was one. And at present King Dahfu. And if I had really been capable of the alert consciousness which it required I would have confessed that Becoming was beginning to come out of my ears. Enough! Enough! Time to have Become. Time to Be! Burst the spirit's sleep. Wake up, America! Stump the experts. Instead I told this savage king, "I seem to be kind of a tourist."

"Or a wanderer," he said. "I already am fond of a diffident way which I see you to exhibit."

I tried to make a bow when he said this, but was prevented by a combination of factors, the main one being my crouching position with my belly against my bare knees (incidentally, I badly needed a bath, as sitting in this posture made me aware). "You do me too much credit," I said. "There are a lot of folks at home who have me down for nothing but a bum."

At this stage of our interview I tried to make out, I tried to feel as if with my fingers, the chief characteristics of the situation. Things seemed to be smooth, but how smooth could they really be? According to Itelo, this king, Dahfu, was one hell of a guy. He had gotten a blue-ribbon recommendation. Class A, as Itelo himself would have said. Primo. Actually, I was already greatly taken with him, but it was necessary to remember what I had seen that morning, that I was among savages and that I had been quartered with a corpse and had seen guys hanging upside down by the feet and that the king had made at least one dubious insinuation. Besides, my fever was increasing, and I had to make a special effort to remain alert. From this I developed a great strain at the back of the neck and in my eyes. I was glaring crudely at everything about me, including these women who should have elicited quite another kind of attitude. But my purpose was to see essentials, only essentials, nothing but essentials, and to guard against hallucinations. Things are not what they seem, anyway.

As for the king, his interest in me appeared to increase continually. Half smiling, he scrutinized me with growing closeness. How was I ever to guess the aims and purposes hidden in his heart? God has not given me half as much intuition as I constantly require. As I couldn't trust him, I had to understand him. Understand him? How was I going to understand him? Hell! It would be like extracting an eel from the chowder after it has been cooked to pieces. This planet has billions of passengers on it, and those were preceded by infinite billions and there are vaster billions to come, and none of these, no, not one, can I hope ever to understand. Never! And when I think how much confidence I used to have in understanding— you know?—it's enough to make a man weep. Of course, you may ask, what have numbers got to do with it? And that's right, too. We get too depressed by them, and should be more accepting of multitudes than we are. Being in point of size precisely halfway between the suns and the atoms, living among astronomical conceptions, with every thumb and fingerprint a mystery, we should get used to living with huge numbers. In the history of the world many souls have been, are, and will be, and with a little reflection this is marvelous and not depressing. Many jerks are made gloomy by it, for they think quantity buries them alive. That's just crazy. Numbers are very dangerous, but the main thing about them is that they humble your pride. And that's good. But I used to have great confidence in understanding. Now take a phrase like "Father forgive them; they know not what they do." This may be interpreted as a promise that in time we would be delivered from blindness and understand. On the other hand, it may also mean that with time we will understand our own enormities and crimes, and that sounds to me like a threat.

Thus I was sitting there with my pondering expression. Or maybe it would be more factual and descriptive to say that I was listening to the growling of my mind. Then the king observed, to my surprise, "You do not show too much wear and tear of the journey. I esteem you to be very strong. Oh, vastly. I see at a glance. You tell me you were able to hold your own with Itelo? Perhaps you were practicing mere courtesy. At a snap judgment you do not seem so very courteous. But I will not conceal you are a specimen of development I cannot claim ever to have seen."

First the examiner in the middle of the night, waiving the question of the corpse, had asked me to take off my shirt so he could study my physique, and now the king expressed a similar interest. I could have boasted, "I'm strong enough to run up a hill about a hundred yards with one of your bodies on my back." For I do have a certain pride in my strength (compensatory mechanism). But my feelings had been undergoing a considerable fluctuation. First I was reassured by the person and attitude of the king, and his tone of voice. I had rejoiced. My heart proclaimed a holiday. Then again suspicions supervened, and now the peculiar inquiry about my physique made me sweat anew with anxiety. I remembered, if they were thinking of using me as a sacrifice, that an ideal sacrifice has no blemishes. And so I said that I actually had not been in the best of health and that I felt feverish today.

"You cannot have a fever, as manifestly you are perspiring," said Dahfu.

"That's just another one of my peculiarities," I said. "I can run a high temperature while pouring sweat." He brushed this aside. "And a terrible thing happened to me just last night as I was eating a piece of hardtack," I said. "A real calamity. I broke my bridge." I widened my mouth with my fingers and threw back my head, inviting him to look at the gap. Also I unbuttoned my pocket and showed him the teeth, which I had put there for safekeeping. The king looked into that enormous moat, my mouth. Exactly what his impression was, I can't undertake to relate, but he said, "It does look exceedingly troublesome. Where did this happen?"

"Oh, just before that fellow grilled me," I said. "What do you call him?"

"The Bunam," he said. "Do you find him very dignified? He is top official of all the priests. It is no trouble to conceive how annoyed you were to break the teeth."

"I was fit to be tied," I said. "I could have kicked myself in the head for being so stupid. Of course I can chew on the stumps. But what if the shank should come out? I don't know how familiar you may be with dentistry, Your Highness, but underneath, everything has been ground down to the pulp and if I feel a draft on those stumps, believe me, there's no torment comparable. I have had very bad luck with teeth, as has my wife. Naturally you can't expect teeth to last forever. They wear down. But that's not all. . . ."

"Can there be other things that ail you?" he said. "You do present an appearance of utmost and solid physical organization."

I flushed, and answered, "I have a pretty bad case of hemorrhoids, Your Highness. Moreover I am subject to fainting fits."

Sympathetically he asked, "Not the falling sickness—petit mat or grand mal?"

"No," I said, "what I have defies classification. I've been to the biggest men in New York with this, and they say it isn't epilepsy. But a few years ago I started to have fits of fainting, very unpredictable, without warning. They may come over me while I am reading the paper, or on a stepladder, fixing a window shade. And I have blacked out while playing the violin. Then about a year ago, in the express elevator, going up in the Chrysler Building, it happened to me. It must have been the speed of overcoming gravity that did it. There was a lady in a mink coat next to me. I put my head on her shoulder and she gave a loud scream, and I fell down."

Having been a stoic for so many years I am not skillful in making my ailments sound convincing. Also, from much reading of medical literature I am aware how much mind, just mind itself, we needn't speak of drink or anything like that, lies at the root of my complaints. It was perversity of character that was making me faint. Moreover my heart so often repeated, *I want*, that I felt entitled to a little reprieve, and I found it very restful to pass out once in a while. Nevertheless I began to realize that the king would certainly use me if he could, for, nice as he was, he was also in a certain position with respect to the wives. As he would never make old bones, there was no reason why he should be particularly considerate of me.

I said in a loud voice, "Your Majesty, this has been a wonderful and interesting visit. Who'd ever think! In the middle of Africa! Itelo praised Your Majesty very highly to me. He said you were terrific, and I see you really are. All this couldn't be more memorable, but I don't want to outstay my welcome. I know you are planning to make rain today and probably I will only be in the way. So thanks for the hospitality of the palace, and I wish you all kinds of luck with the ceremony, but I think after lunch my man and I had better blow."

As soon as he saw my intention and while I still spoke, he began to shake his head, and when he did so, the women looked at me with expressions devoid of friendliness, as though I were crossing or exciting the king and costing him strength which might be better employed.

"Oh, no, Mr. Henderson," he said. "It is not even conceivable that we should relinquish you so immediately upon arrival. You have vast social charm, my dear guest. You must believe I should suffer a privation positively gruesome to lose your company. Anyways, I think Fate have intended we should be more intimate. I told you how excited I have been since the announcement of your appearance from the outside world. And so, as the time has come for the ceremonies to begin, I invite you to be my guest."

He put on a generous large-brimmed hat of the same purple color as his drawers, but in velvet. Human teeth, to protect him from the evil eye, were sewed to the crown. He arose from his green sofa but only to lie down again in a hammock. Amazons dressed in their short leather waistcoats were the bearers. Four on either side put their shoulders to the poles, and these shoulders, although they were amazons, were soft. Physical capacity always stirs me, especially in women. I love to watch movies in Times Square of the Olympic Games, in particular those vital Atalantas running and throwing the javelin. I always say, "Look at that! Ladies and gentlemen—look what women can be like!" It appeals to the soldier in me as well as the lover of beauty. I tried to replace those eight amazons with eight women of my acquaintance—Frances, Mlle. Montecuccoli, Berthe, Lily, Clara Spohr, and others—but of them all it was only Lily who had the right stature. I could not think of a matched team. Berthe, though strong, was too broad and Mlle. Montecuccoli had a large bust but lacked the shoulders. These friends, acquaintances, and loved ones could not have carried the king.

At his majesty's request, I walked beside him down the stairs and into the courtyard. He did not lie lazily in his hammock;

his figure had real elegance; it showed his breeding. None of this might have been manifest if I had met him and Itelo during their student days in Beirut. We have all encountered students from Africa, and usually they wear baggy suits and their collars are wrinkled because knotting a tie is foreign to their habits.

In the courtyard the procession was joined by Horko with his umbrellas, amazons, wives, children carrying long sheaves of Indian corn, warriors holding idols and fetishes in their arms which were freshly smeared with ochre and calcimine and were as ugly as human conception could make them. Some were all teeth, and others all nostrils, while several had tools bigger than their bodies. The yard suddenly became very crowded. The sun blasted and blazed. Acetylene does not peel paint more than this sun did the doors of my heart. Foolishly, I told myself that I was feeling faint. (It was owing to my size and strength that this appeared foolish.) And I thought that this was like a summer's day in New York. I had taken the wrong subway and instead of reaching upper Broadway I had gone to Lenox Avenue and 125th Street, struggling up to the sidewalk.

The king said to me, "The Arnewi too have a difficulty of water, Mr. Henderson?"

I thought, "All is lost. The guy has heard about the cistern." But this did not actually appear to be the case. No hint was contained in his manner; he was only looking from the hammock into the windless and cloudless blue.

"Well, I'll tell you, King," I said. "They didn't have much luck in that particular department."

"Oh?" he said thoughtfully. "It is a peculiarity about luck with them, do you know that? A legend exists that we were once the same and one, a single tribe, but separated over the luck question. The word for them in our language is nibai. This may be translated 'unlucky.' Definitely, this is the equivalent in our tongue."

"Is that so? The Wariri feel lucky, eh?"

"Oh yes. In numerous instances. We claim ourselves to be the contrary. The saying is, Wariri ibai. Put in other words, Lucky Wariri."

"You don't say? Well, well. And what's your own opinion of that? Is the saying right?"

"Are we Wariri lucky?" he asked. Unmistakably he was setting me straight, for I had challenged him by the question. I tell you! It was an experience. It was a lesson to me. He pulled his majesty on me so lightly it was hardly noticeable. "We have luck," he said. "Incontrovertibly, it is a fact about the luck. You wouldn't dream how consistent it is."

"So do you think you will have rain today?" I said, grimly grinning.

He answered very mildly, "I have seen rain on days that began like this." And then he added, "I believe I can understand your attitude. It derives from the kindliness of the Arnewi. They have made the impression on you which so commonly they make. Do not forget that Itelo is my special chum and was my sidekick in situations making for great intimacy. Ah, yes, I know the qualities. Generous. Meek. Good. No substitutes should be accepted. On this my agreement is total and complete, Mr. Henderson."

I put my fist to my face and looked at the sky, giving a short laugh and thinking, Christ! What a person to meet at this distance from home. Yes, travel is advisable. And believe me, the world is a mind. Travel is mental travel. I had always suspected this. What we call reality is nothing but pedantry. I need not have had that quarrel with Lily, standing over her in our matrimonial bed and shouting until Ricey took fright and escaped with the child. I proclaimed I was on better terms with the real than she. Yes, yes, yes. The world of facts is real, all right, and not to be altered. The physical is all there, and it belongs to science. But then there is the noumenal department, and there we create and create and create. As we tread our overanxious ways, we think we know what is real. And I was telling the truth to Lily after a fashion. I knew it better, all right, but I knew it because it was mine—filled, flowing, and floating with my own resemblances; as hers was with *her* resemblances. Oh, what a revelation! Truth spoke to me. To *me*, Henderson!

The king's eyes gleamed into mine with such a power of significance that I felt he could, if he wanted to, pass right straight into my soul. He could invest it. I felt this. But because I am

ignorant and untutored in higher things—in higher things I
am a coarse beginner, because of my abused nature—I didn't
know what to expect. However, under the light of King Dahfu's
eyes I comprehended that in bombing the cistern I had not
lost my last chance. No sir. By no means.

Horko, the king's uncle, was still marshaling the procession.
Over the palace walls came howls and sounds surpassing anything I ever heard from mortal throats or lungs. But as soon as
there was a lull the king said to me, "I easily gather, Mr. Traveler, that you have set forth to accomplish a very important
matter."

"Right, Your Majesty. One hundred per cent right," I said,
and bowed. "Otherwise I could have stayed in bed and looked
at a picture atlas or slides of Angkor Wat. I have a box full of
them, in color."

"Deuce. That is what I meant," he said. "And you have left
your heart with our Arnewi friends. We agree, they are excellent. I even have conjectured if it is environment or nature.
Frequently I have inclined to the innate and not the nurture
side. Sometimes I would like to see my friend Itelo. I would
give away a very dear treasure to hear his voice. Unfortunately
I cannot go. My office . . . official capacity. Good impresses
you, eh, Mr. Henderson?"

In the flash of the sun, tiny gold platelets within my eyes
blinding me, I nodded. I said, "Yes, Your Highness. No bunk.
The true good. The honest-to-God good."

"Yes, I know how you feel over it," he said, and spoke with
a weird softness or longing. I could never have believed that I
could take this from anybody, or would ever have to, and least
of all from this person in the royal hammock, with the purple
large-brimmed hat, and the teeth sewed onto it, the huge,
soft, eccentric eyes tinged very slightly with red, and his pink
swelling mouth. "They say," he went on, "that bad can easily
be spectacular, has dash or bravado and impresses the mind
quicker than good. Oh, that is a mistake in my opinion. Perhaps of common good it is true. Many, many nice people. Oh
yes. Their will tells them to perform good, and they do. How
ordinary! Mere arithmetic. 'I have left undone the etceteras I
should have done, and done the etceteras I ought not to have.'
This does not even amount to a life. Oh, how sordid it is to

book-keep. My whole view is opposite or contrary, that good cannot be labor or conflict. When it is high and great, it is too superior. Oh, Mr. Henderson, it is far more spectacular. It is associated with inspiration, and not conflict, for where a man conflicts there he will fall, and if taking the sword also perishes by the sword. A dull will produces a very dull good, of no interest. Where a fellow draws a battle line there he is apt to be found, dead, a testimonial of the great strength of effort, and only effort."

I said eagerly, "Oh King Dahfu—oh, Your Majesty!" He had stirred me so much. By just these few words spoken as he reclined in the hammock. "Do you know the queen over there, that woman of Bittahness, Willatale? She's Itelo's aunt, you know. She was going to instruct me in grun-tu-molani, but one thing and another came up, and—"

But the amazons had put their backs to the poles and the hammock rose and moved forward. And the screams, the excitement! The roars, the deep drum noises, as if the animals were speaking again by means of the skins that had once covered their bodies! It was a great release of sound, like Coney Island or Atlantic City or Times Square on New Year's Eve; at the king's exit from the gate the great cacophony left all the previous noises in my experience far behind.

Shouting, I asked the king, "Where . . . ?"

I bent very close for the reply. ". . . . possess a special . . . a place . . . arena," he said.

I heard no more. The frenzy was so great it was metropolitan. There was such a whirl of men and women and fetishes, and snarls like dog-beating and whines like sickles sharpening, and horns blasting and blazing into the air, that the scale could not be recorded. The bonds of sound were about to be torn to pieces. I tried to protect my good ear by plugging it with my thumb, and even the defective one had more than it could take. At least a thousand villagers must have been in this mob, most of them naked, many painted and gaudy, all using noisemakers and uttering screams. The weather was heavy, sultry, so that my body itched. It was an ugly, dusty heat, and there were times when my face felt as if wrapped up in serge. But I had no time to take note of discomfort, being carried forward beside the king. The procession entered a stadium—I stretch the term—a big enclosure fenced with wood. Within was a quadruple row of benches cut from the white calcareous stone aforementioned. For the king there was a royal box in which I sat, too, under a canopy with floating ribbons, with wives, officials, and other royalty. The amazons in their corset-like vests and large smooth bodies and delicate, shaved, immense heads, round like melons, oval like cantaloupes, long like squashes, were posted all around. Accompanied by his retinue and umbrellas, Horko bowed and salaamed before the king. The family resemblance between these two suggested that they could communicate thoughts merely by looking at each other; sometimes it is like that. The same noses, the same eyes, the same implied message of the race. So, in a silent manner, Horko appeared to me to urge his royal nephew to do something previously discussed. But by the look of him the king wouldn't promise a thing. He was in command here; there could never be any question about that.

Carried aloft by four amazons, one at each leg, came the bridge table. On it was the bowl containing two skulls I had seen a short while ago in the royal apartment. But now they had ribbons tied through the eye sockets, very long and gleaming, of a dark blue color. They were set down before the king, who took note of them with one roll of his eyes and looked no more at them. Meantime this huge Horko, all rolled up so that he stood heel to heel in his crimson sheath, the fat crowded upward to his chin and shoulders, took the liberty of mocking my expression. At least I thought I recognized my own scowl on his face. I didn't mind. I made a short bow to acknowledge that he had taken me off pretty well. And, like the politician he was, he gave me a glad, impudent wave. The colored umbrella wheeled over him and he went back to his box on the king's left and sat down with the examiner who had kept me waiting last night, the character whom Dahfu called the Bunam, and the wrinkled old black-leather fellow who had sent us into the ambush. The one who had arisen out of the white rocks like the man met by Joseph. Who sent Joseph over to Dothan. Then the brothers saw Joseph and said, "Behold, the dreamer cometh." Everybody should study the Bible.

Believe me, I felt like a dreamer, and that's no lie.

"Who is that man all wrinkled like a Greek olive?" I said.

"Beg pardon?" said the king.

"With the Bunam and your uncle."

"Oh, of course. A senior priest. Diviner of a sort."

"Yesterday we met him with a twisted stick," I was saying, when several squads of amazons lined up with muskets and started to aim at the sky. I could not see the .375 anywhere. These large women began to fire salutes, first in honor of the king and the king's late father, Gmilo, and for various others. Then, so the king told me, there was a salute for me.

"For me? You're kidding, Your Highness," I said. But he was not, so I asked him, "Should I stand up?"

"I think it would be widely appreciated," he said.

And I got to my feet, and there were loud shrieks and screams. I thought, "The word has got around how I dealt with that corpse. They know I'm no Milktoast but a person of strength and courage. Plenty of moxie." I was beginning to feel the spirit of the occasion—pervaded by barbaric emotions —the scratchiness in my bosom was greatly aggravated. I had no words to speak, no mortar or bazooka to fire, replying to the guns of the amazons. But I was impelled to make a sound, and therefore I uttered a roar like the great Assyrian bull. You know, to be the center of attention in a crowd always stirs and disturbs me. It had done so when the Arnewi wept and when they gathered near the cistern. Also when shaved in Italy near the stronghold of the ancient Guiscardos that time in Salerno. In a big gathering my father also had a tendency to become excited. He once lifted up the speaker's stand and threw it down into the orchestra pit.

However, I roared. And the acclaim was magnificent. For I was heard. I was seen gripping my chest as I bellowed. The crowd went wild over this, and its yells were, I have to admit it, just like nourishment to me. I reflected, So this is what guys in public life get out of it? Well, well. I no longer wondered that this Dahfu had come back from civilization to be king of his tribe. Hell, who wouldn't be a king, even a small king? It was not a privilege to be missed. (The time of payment to a strong young fellow was remote; the wives couldn't invent enough attentions and expressions of gratitude; he was the darling of their hearts.)

I stood as long as was feasible and luxuriated in this applause, laughing, and I sat down when I had to.

Now, horrified, I saw a grinning face with a mouth like a big open loop and a forehead infinitely wrinkled. It was the sort of vision you might have in a shop window on Fifth Avenue, and, when you turned to see what fantastic apparition New York had thrown up behind you, there would be no one. This face, however, stood its ground and held steady while it grinned at the party in the king's box. Deep bloody cuts were being made meanwhile on the chest that belonged to this face. A green old knife—a cruel clutch. Oh, the man is being slashed and stabbed. Stop, stop! Holy God! Why, this is murder being committed, said I. Through my depths as in a tunnel went a shock like the ones big buildings get from trains which pass beneath.

But the cutting wasn't deep, it was lateral and superficial, and despite the speed of the painted priest who wielded the knife it was done according to plan, and with skill. Ochre was rubbed into the wounds, which must have stung like frenzy, but the fellow grinned and the king said, "This proceeding is about semi-usual, Mr. Henderson. The worry is not necessary. He is thus advanced in his priesthood career and so is very pleased. As to the blood, that is supposed to induce the heavens also to flow, or prime the pumps of the firmament."

"Ha, ha!" I laughed and cried. "Say, King! What's that? Oh, Jesus—come again? The pumps of the firmament? Isn't that the dandiest!"

However, the king had no time for me. At a signal from Horko's box there was an all-out, slam-bang, grand salute of the guns and with it a pounding of the deep liquid bass drums. The king arose. Wild hosannas! Fountains of praise! Faces screaming fiercely with pride and twisted with diverse inspirations. From the basic blackness of the flesh of the tribe there broke or erupted a wave of red color, and the people all arose on the white stone of the grandstands and waved red objects, waved or flaunted. Crimson was the holy-day color of the Wariri. The amazons saluted with purple banners, the king's colors. His purple umbrella was raised, and its taut head swayed.

The king himself was no longer beside me. He had gone down from the box to take a position in the arena. At the other side of the circle, which was no bigger than the infield of a ball park, there arose a tall woman. To the waist she was naked and her head had woolly ringlets. When she came closer I saw that her face was covered with a beautiful design of scars that looked like Braille. Two peaks of this came down beside each ear, and a third descended to the bridge of her nose. As far as the belly she was painted a russet or dull gold color. She was young, for her breasts were small and didn't waver when she walked, as is the case with more adult females, and her arms were long and thin. They manifested the three major bones; I mean the tapered humerus and the radius and ulna. Her face was small and sloping, and when I first saw her from across the field she had no more features than the ball of a flagpole; at a distance she had a face like a gilded apple. She wore a pair of purple trousers, mates to the king's, and was his partner in a game they now began to play. For the first time, I realized that there was a group of shrouded figures in the center of the arena—roughly, let's say, where the pitcher's mound would have been. I figured correctly that these were the gods. Around them and over them the king and this gilded woman began to play a game with the two skulls. Whirling them by the long ribbons, each took a short run and threw them high in the air, above the figures of wood which stood under the tarpaulins—the biggest of these idols about as tall as an old upright Steinway piano. The two skulls flew up high, and then the king and the girl each made the catch. It was very neat. All the noise had died, had gone like the wrinkles of a cloth under the hot iron. A perfectly smooth silence followed the first throws, so you could even hear how hollow the catch sounded. Soon even the whiff the skulls made as they were being whirled around came to my unhandicapped ear. The woman threw her skull. The thick purple and blue ribbons made it look like a flower in the air. I swear before God, it appeared just like a gentian. In midair it passed the skull coming from the hand of the king. Both came streaming down with the blue satin ribbons following, as though they were a couple of ocean polyps. Soon I understood that this wasn't only a game, but a contest, and naturally I rooted for the king. I didn't know but what the penalty for dropping one of those skulls might have been death. Now I myself have become ultra-familiar with death, not only owing to my age, but for a lot of reasons unnecessary to cite at this time. Death and I are just about kissing cousins. But the thought of anything happening to the king was horrible to me. Though his confidence seemed great, and his bounding and his quick turns and his sureness made beautiful watching as he warmed to the game like a fine tennis player or a great rider, and he—well, he was virile to a degree that made all worry superfluous; such a man takes all he does upon himself; nevertheless I trembled and shook for him. I worried for the girl, too. Should either one of them stumble or let the ribbons slip or the skulls collide they might have to pay the ultimate price, like the poor guy I found in my hut. He certainly had not died of natural causes. You can't kid me; I would have made a terrific coroner. But the king and the woman were in top form, from which I judged that he didn't spend all his time on his back, pampered by those dolls of his, for he ran and jumped like a lion, full of power, and he looked magnificent. He hadn't even taken off the purple velvet hat with its adornment of human teeth. And he was equal to the woman, for in my mind she shaped up as the challenger. She behaved like a priestess, seeing to it that he came up to the mark. Because of the gold paint and Braille marks on her face she looked somewhat inhuman. As she sprang, dancing, her breasts were fixed, as if really made of gold, and because of her length and thinness, when she leaped it was something supernatural, like a giant locust.

Then the last pair of throws, and the catch was completed. Each tucked the skull under his arm, like a fencer's mask; each bowed. A tremendous noise followed, and again the crimson flags and rags erupted.

The king was breathing hard as he returned, with that Francis I hat, as Titian might have painted it. He sat down. When he did so, the wives surrounded him with a sheet so that he might not be seen drinking in public. This was taboo. Then they dried his sweat and massaged the muscles of his great legs and his panting belly, loosening the golden drawstring of his purple trousers. I wished to tell him how great he had been. I was dying to say what I felt. Like, "Oh, King, that was royally done. Like a true artist. Goddammit, an artist! King, I love nobility and beautiful behavior." But I couldn't say a thing. I have this brutal reticence of character. Such is the slavery of the times. We are supposed to be cool-mouthed. As I told my son Edward—slavery! And he thought I was a square when I said I loved the truth. Oh, that hurt! Anyway, I often want to say things and they stay in my mind. Therefore they don't actually exist; you can't take credit for them if they never emerge. By mentioning the firmament, the king himself had shown me the way, and I might have told him a lot, right then and there. What? Well, for instance, that chaos doesn't run the whole show. That this is not a sick and hasty ride, helpless, through a dream into oblivion. No, sir! It can be arrested by a thing or two. By art, for instance. The speed is checked, the time is redivided. Measure! That great thought. Mystery! The voices of angels! Why the hell else did I play the fiddle? And why were my bones molten in those great cathedrals of France so that I couldn't stand it and had to booze up and swear at Lily? And I was thinking that if I spoke of this to the king and told him what was in my heart he might become my friend. But the wives were between us with their naked thighs, and their behinds turned toward me, which would have been the height of discourtesy except that they were wild savages. So I had no chance to speak to the king under those inspired conditions. A few minutes later, when I was able again to talk to him, I said, "King, I had a feeling that if either of you missed, the consequences would not be pretty."

Before he answered he moistened his lips, and his chest still moved quickly. "I can explain to you, Mr. Henderson, why the factor of missing is negligible." His teeth shone toward me and the panting made him seem to smile, though there was nothing to smile about. "Some day the ribbons will be tied through here." With two fingers he pointed to his eyes. "My own skull will get the air." He made a gesture of soaring, and said, "Flying."

I said, "Were those the skulls of kings? Relatives of yours?" I didn't have the nerve to ask a direct question about his kinship with those heads. At the thought of making a similar catch, the flesh of my hands pricked and tingled.

But there was no time to go into this. Too much was happening. Now the cattle sacrifices were made, and they were done pretty much without ceremony. A priest with ostrich feathers that sprayed out in every direction threw his arm about the neck of a cow, caught the muzzle, raised her head, and slit her throat as if striking a match on the seat of his pants. She fell to the ground and died. Nobody took much notice.

XIII

A FTER THIS came tribal dances and routines that were strictly like vaudeville. An old woman wrestled with a dwarf, only the dwarf lost his temper and tried to hurt her, and she stopped and scolded. One of the amazons entered the field and picked up the tiny man; with a swinging stride she carried him away under her arm. Cheers and handclapping came from the grandstands. Next there was another performance of an unserious nature. Two guys swung at each other's legs with whips, skipping into the air. Such Roman holiday highjinks were not reassuring to me. I was very nervous. I billowed with nervous feeling and a foreboding of coming abominations. Naturally I couldn't ask Dahfu for a preview. He was breathing deeply and watched with impervious calm.

Finally I said, "In spite of all these operations, the sun is still shining, and there aren't any clouds. I even doubt whether the humidity has increased, though it feels very close."

The king answered me, "Your observation is true, to all appearance. I do not contest you, Mr. Henderson. Nevertheless, I have seen all expectation defied and rain come on days like this. Yes, precisely."

I gave him a squinting, intense look. There was much meaning condensed into this, and I will not try to dilute it for you now. Maybe a certain amount of overweening crept in. But what it mostly expressed was, "Let us not kid each other, Your Royal H. Do you think it's so easy to get what you want from Nature? Ha, ha! I never have got what I asked for." Actually what I said was, "I would almost be willing to make you a bet, King."

I didn't expect the king to take me up so quickly on this. "Oh? Nice. Do you want to propose me a wager, Mr. Henderson?"

I found that my heart was hungry after provocation on this issue. I got involved. Something fierce. And naturally against reason. And I said, "Oh, sure, if you want to bet, I'll bet."

"I agree," said the king, with a smiling look, but stubbornly, too.

263

"Why, King Dahfu, Prince Itelo said you were interested in science."

"Did he tell you," said the guy with evident pleasure, "did he say that I was in attendance at medical school?"

"No!"

"A true fact. I did two years of the course."

"You didn't! You don't know how relevant that is, as a piece of information. But in that case, what sort of a bet are we making? You are just humoring me. You know, Your Highness, my wife Lily subscribes to the *Scientific American*, and so I am in on the rain problem. The technique of seeding the clouds with dry ice hasn't worked out well. Some recent ideas are that, first of all, the rain comes from showers of dust which arrive from outer space. When that dust hits the atmosphere it does something. The other theory which appeals more to me is that the salt spray of the ocean, the sea foam in other words, is one of the main ingredients of rain. Moisture takes and condenses on these crystals carried in the air, as it has to have something to condense on. So, it's a real wowzer, Your Highness. If there were no sea foam, there would be no rain, and if there were no rain there would be no life. How would all the wise guys like that? If the ocean didn't have this peculiar form of beauty the land would be bare." With increasing intimacy, as if confidentially, I laughed and said, "Your Majesty, you have no idea how the whole thing tickles me. Life comes from the cream of the seas. We used to sing a song in school, 'O Marianina. Come O come and turn us into foam.'" I sang for him a little, sotto voce, almost. He liked it; I could tell.

"You do not have a common run of a voice," he said, smiling and gay. I was beginning to feel that the fellow liked me. "And the information is fascinating indeed."

"Ha, I'm glad you see it that way. Boy! That's something, isn't it? But I guess this puts an end to our bet."

"Not of the very least. Just the same, we shall bet."

"Well, King Dahfu, I have opened my big mouth. Allow me to take back what I said about the rain. I am prepared to eat crow. Naturally, as the king you have to back the rain ceremony. So I apologize. So why don't you just say, 'Nuts to you, Henderson,' and forget it?"

"Oh, by no means. No basis for that. We shall bet, and why not?" He spoke with such finality that I had no out to take.

"Okay, Your Highness, have it your way."

"Word of honor. What shall we bet?" he said.

"Anything you want."

"Very good. Whatever I want."

"This is unfair of me. I have to give you good odds," I said. He waved his hand, on which there was a large red jewel. His body had sunk back into the hammock, for he sat and lay by turns. I could see that it pleased him to gamble; he had the character of a betting man. Anyway, my eyes were on this ring of his, a huge garnet set in thick gold and encircled by smaller stones, and he said, "Does the ring appeal?"

"It's pretty nice," I said, meaning that I was reluctant to specify any object.

"What are you betting?"

"I've got cash money on me, but I don't suppose that would interest you. I have a pretty good Rolleiflex in my kit. Not that I've taken any pictures except by accident. I've been too busy out here in Africa. Then there is my gun, an H and H Magnum .375 with telescopic sights."

"I do not foresee how it would be usable if won."

"At home I've got some objects I would be glad to put up," I said. "I've got some beautiful Tamworth pigs left."

"Oh, indeed?"

"I can see you're not interested."

"It would be fitting to bet something personal," he said.

"Oh, yes. The ring is personal. I get it. If I could detach my troubles I'd put them up. They're personal. Ho, ho. Only I wouldn't wish them on my worst enemy. Well, let's see, what do I have that you might use; what have I got that would go with being a king? Carpets? I've got a nice one in my studio. Then there's a velvet dressing gown that might look good on you. There's even a Guarnerius violin. But hey! I've got it— paintings. There's one of me and one of my wife. They're oils."

At this moment I wasn't sure that he heard me, but he said, "You should not assume at all that you have a sure thing."

Then I said, "So? What if I lose?"

"It will be interesting."

This made me begin to worry.

"Well, it is settled. We may match ring against oil portraits. Or let us say that if I win you will remain a guest of mine, a length of time."

"Okay. But how long?"

"Oh, it is too theoretical," he said, looking away. "Let us leave it an open consideration for the moment."

This arrangement made, we both looked upward. The sky was a bald, pale blue and rested on the mountains, windless. I figured that this king must have a lot of delicacy. He wanted to make it up to me for the corpse last night and also to indicate that he would appreciate it if I would visit with him for a while. The discussion ended with the king making a florid African gesture, as if peeling off his gloves or rehearsing the surrender of the ring. I sweated hugely, but my body was not cooled. To try to assuage the heat, I held my mouth open.

Then I said, "Haw, haw! Your Majesty, this is a screwy bet."

At this moment came furious or quarrelsome shouts, and I thought, "Ha, the light part of the ceremony is over." Several men in black plumes, like beggarly bird men—the rusty feathers hung to their shoulders—began to lift the covers from the gods. Disrespectfully, they pulled them away. This irreverence was no accident, if you get what I mean. It was done to raise a laugh, and it did exactly that. These bird or plume characters, encouraged by the laughter, started to perform burlesque antics; they stepped on the feet of the statues, and bowled some of the smaller ones over and made passes at them, mockeries, and so on. The dwarf was set on the knees of one goddess and he rocked the crowd with laughter by puffing his lower lids down and sticking out his tongue, making like a wrinkled lunatic. The family of gods, all quite short in the legs and long in the trunk, was very tolerant about these abuses. Most of them had disproportionate, small faces set on tall necks. All in all, they didn't look like a stern bunch. Just the same they had dignity—mystery; they were after all the gods, and they made the awards of fate. They ruled the air, the mountains, fire, plants, cattle, luck, sickness, clouds, birth, death. Damn it, even the squattest, kicked over onto his belly, ruled over something. The attitude of the tribe seemed to be that it was necessary to come to the gods with their vices on display, as nothing could be concealed from them anyway by ephemeral men. I grasped the idea, but basically I thought it was a big mistake. I wanted to say to the king, "You mean to tell me all this bad blood is necessary?" Also I marveled that such a man should be king over a gang like this. He took it all pretty calmly, however.

By and by they began to move the whole pantheon. Bodily. They started with the smaller gods, whom they handled very roughly and with a lot of wickedness. They let them fall or rolled them around, scolding them as if they were clumsy. Hell! I thought. To me it seemed like a pretty cheap way to behave, although I could see, to be objective about it, plenty of grounds for resentment against the gods. But anyway I didn't care one bit for this. Grumbling, I sat under the shell of my helmet and tried to appear as if it was none of my business.

When this crew of ravens came to the larger statues, they tugged and pulled but couldn't manage, and had to call for help from the crowd. One strong man after another jumped into the arena to pick up an idol, toting it from the original position to, let's say, short center field, while cheers and rooting came from the stands. From the stature and muscular development of the champions who moved the larger idols I gathered that this display of strength was a traditional part of the ceremony. Some approached the bigger gods from behind and clasped arms about their middles, some backed up to them like men unloading flour from the tailgate of a truck and hauled them on their shoulders. One gave a twist to the arms of a figure as I had done to the corpse last night. Seeing my own technique applied, I gave a gasp.

"What is it, Mr. Henderson?" said the king.

"Nothing, nothing, nothing," I said.

The group of gods remaining grew small. The strong men had carted them away, almost all of them. The last of these fellows were superb specimens, and I have a good eye for the points of strong men. During a certain period of my life I took quite an interest in weight-lifting and used to train on the barbells. As everyone knows, the development of the thighs counts heavily. I tried to get my son Edward interested; there might have been no Maria Felucca if I had been able to influence him to build his muscles. Although, when all that is said and done, I have grown this portly front and the other strange distortions that attend all the larger individuals of a species. (Like those mammoth Alaska strawberries.) Oh, my body, my body! Why have we never really got together as friends? I have loaded it with my vices, like a raft, like a barge. Oh, who shall deliver me from the body of this death? Anyway, from these distortions owing to my scale and the work performed by my psyche. And sometimes a voice has counseled me, crazily, "Scorch the earth. Why should a good man die? Let it be some blasted fool who is dumped in the grave." What wickedness! What perversity! Alas, what things go on within a person!

However—I was more and more intensely a spectator—when there were only two gods left, the two biggest (Hummat the mountain god and Mummah the goddess of clouds) there were several strong men who came out and failed. Yes, they flunked. They couldn't stir this Hummat, who had whiskers like a catfish and spines all over his forehead, plus a pair of boulder-like shoulders. After several of them had quit on the job and been hooted and jeered, a fellow came forward wearing a red fez and a kind of jaunty jockstrap of oilcloth. He walked quickly, swinging his open hands, this man who was going to pick up Hummat, and prostrated himself before the god—the first devotional attitude yet shown. Then he went round to the back of the statue and inserted his head under one of its arms. A small taut beard glittered about his round face. He spread his legs, feeling for position with sensitive feet, patting the dust. After this he wiped his hands on his own knees and took hold of Hummat, grasping him by the arm and from beneath in the fork. With huge, set eyes, which became humid from the static effort, he began to lift the great Hummat. From his mouth, distended until the jaws blended with the collar bones, the sinews set in like the thin spokes of a bicycle, and his hip muscles formed large knots at the groin, swelling beside the soiled pants of oilcloth. This was a good man, and I appreciated him. He was my own type. You put a burden in front of him and he clasped it, he threw his chest into it, he lifted, he went to the limit of his strength. "That's the ticket," I said. "Get your back muscles going." As everyone else was cheering, except Dahfu, I got up also and began to yell, "Yay, yaay for you! You got him. You'll do it. You're husky enough. Push—that's it! Now up! Yay, he's doing it. He's going to crack it. Oh, God bless the guy. What a sweetheart! That's a real man—that's the type I love. Go on. Heave-ho. Wow! There he goes. He did it. Ah, thank God!" Then I realized how I had been shouting and I sat down again beside the king, wondering at my own fervor.

The champion tipped Hummat back on his shoulder, and carried the mountain god twenty feet. Among the rest, he set him down on his base. Winded, the man now turned and looked back at Mummah, alone in the middle of the ring. She was even bigger than Hummat. Amid the applause the champion looked her over. And she awaited him. She was very obese, not to say hideous, this female power. They had made her very ponderous, and the strong man facing her seemed already daunted. Not that she forbade you to try. No, in spite of her hideousness she seemed pretty tolerant, even happy-go-lucky like most of the gods. However, she appeared to express confidence in her immovability. The crowd was egging him on, everyone standing; even Horko and his friends in their own box were on foot. His umbrella now threw a shadow of old rose, and in his tight red robe he held out his stout arm and pointed at Mummah with his thumb—that great, wooden, happy Mummah, whose knees gave a little under the weight of her breasts and belly so that she had to spread her fingers on her thighs for support. And, as gross women sometimes do, she had elegant, graceful hands. She awaited the man who would move her.

"You can do her, guy," I too shouted. I asked the king, "What is this fellow's name?"

"The strong man? Oh, that is Turombo."

"What's the matter, doesn't he think he can move her?"

"Evidently he lacks confidence. Every year he can move Hummat, but not Mummah."

"Oh, he must be able to."

"Just the contrary, I fear," said the king, in his curious, singsong, nasal, African English. His large, swelled lips were more red than was the case with others of his tribe. Consequently his mouth was more visible than mouths usually are. "This man, as you see, is powerful, and a good man, as I believe I overheard you to exclaim. But when he has moved

Hummat, he is worn out, and this is annual. Do you see, Hummat has to be moved first, as otherwise he would not permit the clouds passage over the mountains."

Benevolent Mummah, her fat face shone to the sun with splendor. Her tresses of wood were like a stork's nest and broadened upward—a homely, happy, stupid, patient figure, she invited Turombo or any other champion to try his strength.

"You know what it is?" I said to the king. "It's the memory of past defeats—past defeats, you can ask *me* about this problem of past defeats. Brother, I could really tell you. But that's what got him. I just know it."

Turombo, a very short man for his girth and strength, really seemed to be bucking a whole lot of trouble. Those eyes of his, which had grown large and humid with strain when he took a grip on Hummat, now wore a duller light. He was prepared for failure and the motion of his eyes, rolling at us and at the crowd, showed it. This, I want to tell you, I hated to see. Anyway, he tipped his fez to the king with a gesture of dedication that already acknowledged defeat. He had no illusions about Mummah. Nevertheless, he was going to try. He gave his short beard a rub with his knuckles, walking toward her slowly and sizing her up with a view to doing business.

Ambition must have played a very small role in Turombo's life. Whereas in my breast there was a flow—no, that's too limited—there opened up an estuary, a huge bay of hope and ambition. For here was my chance. I knew I could do this. Ye gods! I was shivering and cold. I simply knew that I could lift up Mummah, and I flowed, I burned to go out there and do it. Craving to show what was in me, burning like that bush I had set afire with my Austrian lighter for the Arnewi children. Stronger than Turombo I certainly was. And in the process of proving it, should my heart be ruptured, should the old sack split, okay, then let me die. I didn't care any more. I had longed to do some good to the Arnewi when I arrived and saw their distress. Instead of accomplishing which, I had rashly brought down the full weight of my blind will and ambition upon those frogs. I arrived clothed in light, or thinking so, and I departed draped in shadow and darkness, humiliated, so that perhaps it would have been better to obey my first impulse on arrival, when the young woman burst into tears and I said to myself maybe I should cast away my gun and my fierceness and go into the wilderness until I was fit to meet humankind again. My longing to perform a benefit there, because I was so taken with the Arnewi, and especially old blind-eye Willatale, was sincere and intense, but it was not even a ripple on the desire I felt now in the royal box beside the semi-barbarous king in his trousers and purple velvet hat. So inflamed was my wish to *do* something. For I saw something I could do. Let these Wariri whom so far (with the corpses in the night and all in all) I didn't care for—let them be worse than the sons of Sodom and Gomorrah combined, I still couldn't pass up this opportunity to *do*, and to distinguish myself. To work the right stitch into the design of my destiny before it was too late. So I was glad that Turombo was so meek. I thought he'd better be meek. Even before he had touched Mummah he had implicitly confessed he would never be able to budge her. And that was the way I wanted it. She was mine! And I wanted to say to the king, "I can do it. Let me in there." However, these words found no utterance, for Turombo had already come upon the goddess from behind. He took a lifting stance, crouching, while he folded his thick arms about her belly. Then beside her hip there appeared his face. It was filled with effort, preparation for strain, fear and suffering, as if Mummah, toppling, might crush him beneath her weight. However, she now began to move in his embrace. The stork's nest, her wooden tresses, tipped and swayed like a horizon at sea in rough weather when you stand in the bow of the ship. I put it like that as I felt this motion in my stomach. Turombo heaved from the base like a man trying to uproot an old tree. This was how he labored. But though he shook the old girl he couldn't raise her base from the ground.

The crowd razzed him as he acknowledged at last that this was beyond his strength. He simply couldn't do it. And I rejoiced at the guy's failure. Which is a hell of a thing to admit, but it happens to have been the case. "Good man," I thought to myself. "You are strong but it so happens I am stronger. It's not a personal matter at all. It's only the fates—they willed it.

As in the case of Itelo. This is a job for me. Yield, yield! Cede! Because here comes Henderson! Just let me get my hands on that Mummah, and by God . . . !"

I said to Dahfu, "I'm real sorry he didn't make it. It must be tough on him."

"Oh, it was foregone he could not," said King Dahfu. "I was certain."

Then I began in deepest, grimmest earnest, as only I can be grim, "Your Majesty—" I was excited to the bursting point. I swelled, I was sick, and my blood circulated peculiarly through my body—it was turbid and ecstatic both. It prickled within my face, especially in the nose, as if it might begin to discharge itself there. And as though a crown of gas were burning from my head, so I was tormented. And I said, "Sir, sire, I mean . . . let me! I must."

If the king made any answer I couldn't have heard it just then, because I saw only one face in this hot and dry air, off to my left and deaf to the raging cries made by the crowd against Turombo. A face concentrated exclusively upon me, so that it was detached from all the world. This was the face of the examiner, the guy I had dealt with last night, the man Dahfu called the Bunam. That face! A stare of wrinkled and everlasting human experience was formed on it. I could feel myself how charged those veins of his must be. Ah, holy God! The guy was speaking to me, inexorable. By the furrows of his face and the pressure of his brows and the fullness of his veins he was conveying a message to me. And what he was saying I knew. I heard it. The silent speech of the world to which my most secret soul listened continually now came to me with spectacular clarity. Within—within I heard. Oh, what I heard! The first stern word was *Dummy!* I was greatly shaken by this. And yet there was something there. It was true. And I was obliged, it was my bounden duty to hear. *And nevertheless you are a man. Listen! Harken unto me, you shmohawk! You are blind. The footsteps were accidental and yet the destiny could be no other. So now do not soften, oh no, brother, intensify rather what you are. This is the one and only ticket—intensify. Should you be overcome, you slob, should you lie in your own fat blood senseless, unconscious of nature whose gift you have betrayed, the world will soon take back what the world unsuccessfully sent forth.*

Each peculiarity is only one impulse of a series from the very heart of things—that old heart of things. The purpose will appear at last though maybe not to you. The voice did not sink away. It just stopped. Just like that, it finished what it had to say.

But I understood now why the corpse had been quartered with me. The Bunam was behind it. He sized me up right. He had wanted to see whether I was strong enough to move the idol. And I had met the ordeal. Damn! I had met it at all costs. When I gripped the dead man, his weight had felt to me like the weight of my own limbs fallen asleep and ponderous, but I had fought this revulsion and overcome it, I had lifted up the man. And here was the examiner's grim, exalted, vein-full, knotted, silent face, announcing the results. I had passed. With highest marks. One hundred per cent.

And I said, loudly, "This I must try."

"What is that?" said Dahfu.

"Your Highness," I said, "if it wouldn't be regarded as interference by a foreigner, I think that I could move the statue—the goddess Mummah. I would genuinely like to be of service, as I have certain capacities which ought to be put to definite use. I want to tell you that I didn't make out too well with the Arnewi, where I had a similar feeling. King, I had a great desire to do a disinterested and pure thing—to express my belief in something higher. Instead I landed in a lot of trouble. It's only right that I should make a clean breast."

I was not in control of myself, and thus I wasn't sure how clear my words might be, though my purpose in the comprehensive sense must have been very plain. On the king's face I saw a very mingled look of curiosity and sympathy.

"Do you not rush through the world too hard, Mr. Henderson?"

"Oh, yes, King, I am very restless. But the fact of the matter is I just couldn't continue as I was, where I was. Something had to be done. If I hadn't come to Africa my only other choice would have been to stay in bed. Ideally—"

"Yes, as to the ideal, I have the utmost fascination. What would it have been?"

"Well, King, I can't really say. It's all a puzzle. There is some kind of service motivation which keeps on after me. I have always admired Doctor Wilfred Grenfell. You know I was just

crazy for that man. I would have liked to go on errands of
mercy. Not necessarily with a dog team. But that's just a
detail."

"Oh, I sensed," he said, "I should rather say, I intuited
some such tendency."

"Well, I'd be happy to talk about that afterward," I said.
"Right now I am asking what is the situation? Could I try my
strength against Mummah? I don't know what it is, but I just
have a feeling that I could move her."

He said, "I am obliged to tell you, Mr. Henderson, there
may be consequences."

I should have taken him up on this and asked him what he
meant by that, but I trusted the guy and could not foresee
any really bad consequences. But anyway, that burning, that
craving, that flowing estuary—you see what I mean?—a powerful ambition had me and I was a goner. Moreover, the king
smiled and thus half retracted his warning.

"Do you really have conviction you can do it?" he said.

"All I can say to you, King, is just let me at her. All I want to
do is get my arms around her."

I was in no state to identify the subtleties of the king's attitude. Now he had satisfied the requirements of his conscience,
if any, and caught me, too. No man can do better than that,
hey? But I had got caught up in the thing, and it had regard
only to the unfinished business of years—*I want, I want,* and
Lily, and the grun-tu-molani and the little colored kid brought
home by my daughter from Danbury and the cat I had tried to
destroy and the fate of Miss Lenox and the teeth and the fiddle
and the frogs in the cistern and all the rest of it.

However, the king had not yet given his consent.

In his leopard mantle, walking with tense feet in a narrow-
hipped gait, the Bunam came down from the box where he
had been sitting with Horko. He was followed by the two wives
with their large, shaved, delicate-looking heads and their gay
short teeth. They were bigger than their husband and came
along sauntering behind him and taking it easy.

The examiner, or Bunam, stopped before the king and
bowed. The women, too, bowed. Small signs passed between
them and the king's wives and concubines, or whatever their
classification was, while the examiner addressed Dahfu. He

pointed his index finger upward near his ear like a starter's pistol, bending often and stiffly from the waist. He spoke rapidly but with regularity, and seemed to know his mind very well, and when he had finished he bowed his head again and bent his eyes on me sternly as before, with a world of significance. The veins in his forehead were very heavy.

Dahfu turned to me in his gaudy hammock. In his fingers he still held the ribbons tied to the skull.

"The view of the Bunam is you have been expected. Also you came in time. . . ."

"Your Highness, as to that . . . who can say? If you think the omens are good, I'll go along with you. Listen, Your Highness, I look like a bruiser, and I am gifted in strange ways, mostly physical; but also I am very sensitive. A while back you said something to me about envy and I must admit you kind of hurt my feelings. That's like a poem I once read called, 'Written in Prison.' I can't remember it all, but part of it goes, 'I envy e'en the fly its gleams of joy, in the green woods' and it ends, 'The fly I envy settling in the sun On the green leaf and wish my goal was won.' Now, King, you know as well as I do what goal I'm talking about. Now, Your Highness, I really do not wish to live by any law of decay. Just tell me, how long has the world got to be like this? Why should there be no hope for suffering? It so happens that I believe something can be done, and this is why I rushed out into the world as you have noted. All kinds of motives behind this. There's my wife, Lily, and then there are the children—you must have quite a few of them yourself, so maybe you'll understand how I feel. . . ."

I read sympathy in his face, and I wiped myself with my Woolworth bandanna. My nose, independently, itched within, and seemingly there was nothing I could do for it.

"Truly I regret if I wounded you," he said.

"Well, that's all right. I'm a pretty good judge of men and you are a fine one. And from you I can take it. Besides, truth is truth. Confidentially, I *have* envied flies, too. All the more reason to crash out of prison. Right? If I had the mental constitution to live inside the nutshell and think myself the king of infinite space, that would be just fine. But that's not how I am. King, I am a Becomer. Now you see your situation is different. You are a Be-er. I've just got to stop Becoming. Jesus Christ, when am I going to Be? I have waited a hell of a long time. I suppose I should be more patient, but for God's sake, Your Highness, you've got to understand what it's like with me. So I am asking you. You've got to let me out there. Why it is, I can't say, but I feel called upon to do it, and this may be my main chance." And I spoke to the examiner, who stood in his leopard mantle and cuffs, holding up the bone rod, and said, "Excuse me, sir." I held out a few fingers to him and said, "I will be with you soon." In the heat of my body and fever of mind I couldn't speak with any restraint whatever and I said, "King, I'm going to give you the straight poop about myself, as straight as I can make it. Every man born has to carry his life to a certain depth—or else! Well, King, I'm beginning to see my depth. You wouldn't expect me to back away now, would you?"

He said, "No, Mr. Henderson. In sincerity, I would not."

"Well, this is just one of those moments," I said.

He lay there, having listened with a kind of soft and even musing appreciation. "Well, whatever may come of it, I do grant the permission. As far as I am concerned I do not see why not."

"Thank you, Your Majesty. Thank you."

"Everybody is expectant."

I stood up at once and pulled my shirt over my head and hoisted up my chest broadly and passed my hands over it and over my face, and, with my shorts conforming awkwardly to my trunk, and feeling tall and huge, branded by the sun on the top of my head, I went down into the arena. I kneeled in front of the goddess—one knee. And I sized her up while drying my damp hands with dust and wiping them on my suntan pants. The yells of the Wariri, even the deep drums, came very lightly to my hearing. They occurred on a small, infinitely reduced scale, way out on the circumference of a great circle. The savagery and stridency of these Africans who mauled the gods and strung up the dead by their feet had nothing to do with the emotion of my heart. This was distinct and altogether separate, a thing unto itself. My heart desired only one great object. I had to put my arms about this huge Mummah and raise her up.

As I came closer I saw how huge she was, how over-spilling and formless. She had been oiled, and glittered before my eyes. On her surface walked flies. One of these little sphinxes of the air who sat on her lip was washing himself. How fast a threatened fly departs! The decision is instantaneous and there seems to be no inertia to overcome and there is no super-fluity in the way flies take off. As I began, all the flies fled with a tearing noise into the heat. Never hesitating, I encircled Mummah with my arms. I wasn't going to take no for an answer. I pressed my belly upon her and sank my knees somewhat. She smelled like a living old woman. Indeed, to me she was a living personality, not an idol. We met as challenged and challenger, but also as intimates. And with the close pleasure you experience in a dream or on one of those warm beneficial floating idle days when every desire is satisfied, I laid my cheek against her wooden bosom. I cranked down my knees and said to her, "Up you go, dearest. No use trying to make yourself heavier; if you weighed twice as much I'd lift you anyway." The wood gave to my pressure and benevolent Mummah with her fixed smile yielded to me; I lifted her from the ground and carried her twenty feet to her new place among the other gods. The Wariri jumped up and down in the white stone of their stands, screaming, singing, raving, hugging themselves and one another and praising me.

I stood still. There beside Mummah in her new situation I myself was filled with happiness. I was so gladdened by what I had done that my whole body was filled with soft heat, with soft and sacred light. The sensations of illness I had experienced since morning were all converted into their opposites. These same unhappy feelings were changed into warmth and personal luxury. You know, this kind of thing has happened to me before. I have had a bad headache change into a pain in the gums which is nothing but the signal of approaching beauty. I have known this, then, to pass down from the gums and appear again in my breast as a throb of pleasure. I have also known a stomach complaint to melt from my belly and turn into a delightful heat and go down into the genitals. This is the way I am. And so my fever was transformed into jubilation. My spirit was awake and it welcomed life anew. Damn the whole thing! Life anew! I was still alive and kicking and I had the old grun-tu-molani.

Beaming and laughing to myself, yes, sir, shining with

contentment, I went back to sit beside Dahfu's hammock and wiped my face with a handkerchief, for I was anointed with sweat.

"Mr. Henderson," said the king in his African English voice, "you are indeed a person of extraordinary strength. I could not have more admiration."

"Thanks to you," I said, "for giving me such a wonderful chance. Not just hoisting up the old woman, but to get into my depth. That real depth. I mean that depth where I have always belonged."

I was grateful to him. I was his friend then. In fact, at this moment, I loved the guy.

XIV

AFTER this feat of strength, when the sky began to fill with clouds, I was not so surprised as I might have been. From under my brows I noted their arrival. I was inclined to take it as my due.

"Ah, this shade is just what the doctor ordered," I said to King Dahfu as the first cloud passed across. For the canopy of his box was made only of ribbons, blue and purple, and there were of course the silk umbrellas but these did not really interrupt the brassy glare. However, the large cloud sailing in from eastward not only shaded us, it gave relief from the gaudy color. After my great effort, I sat quiet. My violent feelings seemed to have passed off or to have been transformed. The Wariri, however, were still demonstrating in my honor, flaunting the flags and clattering rattles and ringing hand bells while they climbed over one another with joy. That was all right. I didn't want such special credit for my achievement, especially considering how much I was the gainer personally. So I sat there and sweltered, and I pretended not to notice how the tribe was carrying on.

"But look who's here again," I said. For it was the Bunam. He stood before the box and he had his arms full of leaves and wreaths and grasses and pines. Next to him, proud and smart in her peculiar Italian-style garrison cap, was the stout woman whom Dahfu had had shake my hand when we were introduced, the generaless, as he called her, the leader of all the amazons. Accompanying her were more of these military women in their waistcoats of leather. And the tall woman who had played the skull game with the king appeared in the background, gilded and shining. She was not one of the amazons, no; but she was a personage, very high-ranking, and no great occasion was complete without her. It didn't give me much pleasure to see the Bunam, or examiner, smile, and I wondered whether he had come to express thanks or wanted something further, as the vines and leaves and wreathes and all that fodder led me to expect. Also, the women were strangely equipped. Two of them carried skulls on long rusty iron standards while

others held odd-looking fly whisks which were made of strips
of leather. But then from the way they grasped these instruments I suspected that they were not meant for flies. These
were small whips. Now the drummers joined the group in front
of the royal box and I figured they were about to begin a new
rigmarole and were waiting for the king to give a signal.

"What do they want?" I asked Dahfu, for his look was directed at me rather than at the Bunam and those huge swelled
nude women and the generaless in her antiquated garrison
cap. The rest of them were looking at me, too. They had not
come to the king, but to me. The black-leather angel-fellow,
the man who had risen out of the ground with his crooked
stick and sent Romilayu and me into ambush, was especially
there, standing beside the Bunam. And these people had turned
on me all the darkness, all the expectancy, all the wildness, all
the power, of their eyes. Myself, I had remained stripped, half
naked, cooling off after the labor I had performed and still
panting. And under all this scrutiny of black eyes I began to
worry. The king had tried to warn me that there might be consequences to my tangling with Mummah. But I had not failed.
No, I was brilliant, a success.

"What do they want of me?" I said to Dahfu.

When you got right down to it he was a savage, too. He still
dangled a skull (of perhaps his father) by the long smooth ribbon and wore human teeth sewed to his large-brimmed hat.
Why should I expect any mercy from him when he himself, the
moment he should weaken, would be doomed? I mean, if he
didn't happen to be inspired by good motives, there was no reason to think that he wouldn't let evil happen to an intruding
stranger. No, he might allow all hell to break loose over me.
But under the velvet shade of this softly folded crownlike hat
he parted his high swelled lips and said, "Now, Mr. Henderson. We have news for you. The man who moves Mummah
occupies, in consequence, a position of rain king of the Wariri.
The title of this post is the Sungo. You are now the Sungo, Mr.
Henderson, and that is why they are here."

So I said, vigilant and mistrustful, "Give it to me in plain
English. What does it mean?" And I began to say to myself,
"This is a fine way to repay me for moving their goddess."

"Today you are the Sungo."

"Well that may or may not be okay. Frankly, there's something about it that begins to make me uneasy. These guys look as if they meant business. What business? Now listen, Your Highness, don't sell me down the river. You know what I mean? I thought you liked me."

He moved a little closer to me from his swaying position in the hammock, pushing from the ground with his fingers, and said, "I do like you. Every circumstance thus far have increased my fond feeling. Why do you worry? You are the Sungo for them. They require you to go along."

I don't know why it was, but I couldn't at this moment wholly bring myself to trust the guy. "Just promise me one thing," I said, "if anything bad is going to happen, I would like a chance to send a message to my wife. Just along general lines saying good-by with love, and she has been a good woman to me basically. That's all. And don't hurt Romilayu. He hasn't done anything." I could just hear people back home saying, as at a party for instance, *"That big Henderson finally got his. What, didn't you hear? He went to Africa and disappeared in the interior. He probably bullied some natives and they stabbed him. Good riddance to bad rubbish. They say the estate is worth three million bucks. I guess he knew he was a lunatic and despised people for letting him get away with murder. Well, he was rotten to the heart."* "Rotten to the heart yourselves, you bastards." *"He was full of excess."* "Listen, you guys, my great excess was I wanted to live. Maybe I did treat everything in the world as though it was a medicine—okay! What's the matter with you guys? Don't you understand anything? Don't you believe in regeneration? You think a fellow is just supposed to go down the drain?"

"Oh, Henderson," said the king, "such suspicion. What have made you think harm is imminent for you or your man?"

"Then why are they looking at me like that?"

The Bunam and the leathery-looking herdsman and the barbarous Negro women.

"You do not have a solitary item to fear," said Dahfu. "It is innocuous. No, no," said this strange prince of Africa, "they require your attendance to cleanse ponds and wells. They say you were sent for this purpose. Ha, ha, Mr. Henderson, you indicated earlier it was enviable to be in the bosom of the people. But that is where you now are, too."

"Yes, but I don't know the first thing about it. Anyway, you were born that way."

"Well, do not be ungrateful, Henderson. It is evident you too must have been born for something."

Well, I stood up on that one. This strange, many-figured, calcareous white stone was under my feet. That stone, too, was a world of its own, or more than a single world, world within world, in a dreaming series. I stepped down amid buzzing and cries which sounded like the interval between plays in a base-ball broadcast. The examiner came up from behind and lifted off my helmet, while the stiff and stout old generaless, bending with some trouble, removed my shoes. And after this, useless to resist, she took off my Bermuda shorts. This left me in my jockey underpants, which were notably travel-stained. Nor was that the end, for as the Bunam dressed me in the vines and leaves, the generaless began to strip me of even the last covering of cotton. "No, no," I said, but by that time the underpants were already down around my knees. The worst had happened, and I was naked. The air was my only garment now. I tried to cover up with the leaves. I was dry, I was numb, I was burning, and my mouth worked silently; I tried to shield my nakedness with hands and leaves, but Tatu, the amazon generaless, pulled away my fingers and put one of those many-thonged whips into them. My clothes being taken away, I thought I would give a cry and fall and perish of shame. But I was supported by the hand of the old amazon on my back, and then urged forward. Everybody began to yell, "Sungo, Sungo, Sungolay." Yes, that was me, Henderson, the Sungo. We ran. We left the Bunam and the king behind, and the arena too, and entered the crooked lanes of the town. With feet lacerated by the stones, dazed, running with terror in my bowels, a priest of the rain. No, the king, the rain king. The amazons were crying and chanting in short, loud, bold syllables. The big, bald, sensitive heads and the open mouths and the force and power of those words—these women with the tightly buttoned short leather garments and swelling figures! They ran. And I amidst those naked companions, naked myself, bare fore and aft in the streamers of grass and vine, I was dancing on burnt and cut feet over the hot stones. I had to yell, too. Instructed by the generaless, Tatu, who brought her face near mine with open mouth, shrieking, I too cried, "Ya—na—bu—ni—ho—no—mum—mah!" A few stray men, mostly old, who happened to be in the way were beaten by the women and scrambled for their lives, and I myself hopping naked in the flimsy leaves appeared to strike terror into these stragglers. The skulls on the iron standards were carried along as we ran. They were fixed on sconces. We made a circle of the town way out as far as the gallows. Those were dead men that hung there, each entertaining a crowd of vultures. I passed beneath the swinging heads, having no time to look, for we were running hard now, a hard course; panting and sobbing I was, and saying to myself, Where the hell are we going? We had a destination; it was a big cattle pond; the women drew up here, leaping and chanting, and then about ten of them threw themselves upon me. They picked me up and gave me a heave that landed me in the super-heated sour water in which some longhorned cattle were standing. This water was only about six inches deep; the soft mud was far deeper, and into this I sank. I thought they might mean me to lie there sucked into the bottom of the pond, but now the skull carriers offered me their iron standards, and I latched on to these and was drawn forth. I might almost have preferred to remain there in the mud, so low was my will. Anger was useless. Nor was any humor intended. All was done in the greatest earnestness. I came, dripping stale mud, out of the pond. I hoped at least this would cover my shame, for the flimsy grasses, flying, had left everything open. Not that these big fierce women subjected me to any scrutiny. No, no, they didn't care. But with the whips and skulls and guns I was whirled with them, their rain king, crying in my filth and frenzy, "Ya—na—bu—ni—ho—no—mum—mah!" as before. Yes, here he is, the mover of Mummah, the champion, the Sungo. Here comes Henderson of the U.S.A.—Captain Henderson, Purple Heart, veteran of North Africa, Sicily, Monte Cassino, etc., a giant shadow, a man of flesh and blood, a restless seeker, pitiful and rude, a stubborn old lush with broken bridgework, threatening death and suicide. Oh, you rulers of heaven! Oh, you dooming powers!

Oh, I will black out! I will crash into death, and they will throw me on the dung heap, and the vultures will play house in my paunch. And with all my heart I yelled, "Mercy, have mercy!" And after that I yelled, "No, justice!" And after that I changed my mind and cried, "No, no, truth, truth!" And then, "Thy will be done! Not my will, but Thy will!" This pitiful rude man, this poor stumbling bully, lifting up his call to heaven for truth. Do you hear that?

We were yelling and jumping and whirling through terrified lanes, feet pounding, drums and skulls keeping pace. And meanwhile the sky was filling with hot, gray, long shadows, rain clouds, but to my eyes of an abnormal form, pressed together like organ pipes or like the ocean ammonites of Paleozoic times. With swollen throats the amazons cried and howled, and I, lumbering with them, tried to remember who I was. *Me*. With the slime-plastered leaves drying on my skin. The king of the rain. It came to me that still and all there must be some distinction in this, but of what kind I couldn't say.

Under the thickened rain clouds, a heated, darkened breeze sprang up. It had a smoky odor. This was something oppressive, insinuating, choky, sultry, icky. Desirous, the air was, and it felt tumescent, heavy. It was very heavy. It yearned for discharge, like a living thing. Covered with sweat, the generaless with her arm urged me, rolling great eyes and panting. The mud dried stiffly and made a kind of earth costume for me. Inside it I felt like Vesuvius, all the upper part flame and the blood banging upward like the pitch or magma. The whips were hissing and gave a dry, mean sound, and I wondered what in hell are they doing. After the gust of breeze came deeper darkness, like the pungent heat of the trains when they pass into Grand Central tunnel on a devastated day of August, which is like darkness eternal. At that moment I have always closed my eyes.

But I couldn't close them now. We ran back to the arena, where the tribesmen of the Wariri were waiting. As the rain was still held back, so were their voices from my hearing, by a very thin dam, one of the thinnest. I heard Dahfu saying to me, "After all, Mr. Henderson, you may lose the wager." For we were again in front of his box. He gave an order to Tatu, the generaless, and we all turned and rushed into the arena—I with the rest, spinning around inspired, in spite of my great weight, in spite of the angry cuts on my feet. My heart rioting, my head dazed, and filled with something like the fulgor of that vacant Pacific scene beside which I had walked with Edward. Nothing but white, seething, and the birds arguing over the herrings, with great clouds about. On the many-figured white stones I saw the people standing, leaping, frantic, under the oppression of Mummah's great clouds, those colossal tuberous forms almost breaking. There was a great delirium. They were shrieking, shrieking. And of all these shrieks, my head, the rain king's head, was the hive. All were flying toward me, entering my brain. Above all this I heard the roaring of lions, while the dust was shivering under my feet.

The women about me were dancing, if you want to call it that. They were bounding and screaming and banging their bodies into me. All together we were nearing the gods who stood in their group, with Hummat and Mummah looking over the heads of the rest. And now I wanted to fall on the ground to avoid any share in what seemed to me a terrible thing, for these women, the amazons, were rushing upon the figures of the gods with those short whips of theirs and striking them. "Stop!" I yelled. "Quit it! What's the matter? Are you crazy?" It would have been different, perhaps, if this had been a token whipping and the gods were merely touched with the thick leather straps. But great violence was loosed on these figures, so that the smaller ones rocked as they were beaten while the bigger without any change of face bore it defenseless. Those children of darkness, the tribe, rose and screamed like gulls on stormy water. And then I did fall to the ground. Naked, I threw myself down, roaring, "No, no, no!" But Tatu grasped me by the arm and with an effort raised me to my knees. So that, on my knees, I was pulled forward into this, crawling on the ground. My hand, which had the whip still in it, was lifted once or twice and brought down so that against my will I was made to perform the duty of the rain king. "Oh, I can't do this. You'll never make me," I was saying. "Oh, batter me and kill me. Run a spit up me and bake me over the fire." I tried to hide against the earth and in this posture was struck on the back of the head with a whip and afterward on the face as well, as the women were swinging in all directions now and struck one another as well as me and the gods. Caught up in this madness, I fended off blows from my position on my knees, for it seemed to me that I was fighting for my life, and I yelled. Until a thunder clap was heard.

And then, after a great, neighing, cold blast of wind, the clouds opened and the rain began to fall. Gouts of water like hand grenades burst all about and on me. The face of Mummah, which had been streaked by the whips, was now covered with silver bubbles, and the ground began to foam. The amazons with their wet bodies began to embrace me. I was too stunned to push them off. I have never seen such water. It was like the Dutch flood that swept over Alva's men when the sea walls were opened. In this torrent the people were hidden from me. I looked for Dahfu's box concealed in the storm and I worked my way around the arena, following the white stone with my hand. Then I met Romilayu, who recoiled from me as if I were dangerous to him. His hair was hugely flattened by the storm and his face showed great fear. "Romilayu," I said, "please, man, you've got to help me. Look at the condition I'm in. Find my clothes. Where is the king? Where are they all? Pick up my clothes—my helmet," I said. "I've got to have my helmet."

Naked, I held on to him and bent over, my feet slipping as he led me to the king's box. Four women were holding a cover over Dahfu to keep off the rain and his hammock had been raised. They were carrying him away.

"King, King," I cried.

He drew aside the edge of the cover they had thrown over him. Under it I saw him there in his broad-brimmed hat. I cried out to him, "What has struck us?"

He said simply, "It is rain."

"Rain? What rain? It's the deluge. It feels like the end. . . ."

"Mr. Henderson," he said, "it is a great thing you have performed for us, after which pains we must give you some pleasure, too." And seeing the look on my face he said, "Do you see, Mr. Henderson, the gods know us." And as he was carried from me in his hammock, the eight women supporting the poles, he said, "You have lost the wager."

I was left standing in my coat of earth, like a giant turnip.

XV

THIS is how I became the rain king. I guess it served me right for mixing into matters that were none of my damned business. But the thing had been irresistible, one of those drives which there was no question of fighting. And what had I got myself into? What were the consequences? On the ground floor of the palace, filthy, naked, and bruised, I lay in a little room. The rain was falling, drowning the town, dropping from the roof in heavy fringes, witchlike and gloomy. Shivering, I covered myself with hides and stared with circular eyes, wrapped to the chin in the skins of unknown animals, I kept saying, "Oh, Romilayu, don't be down on me. How was I supposed to know what I was getting myself into?" My upper lip grew long and my nose was distorted; it was aching with the whiplashes and I felt my eyes had grown black and huge. "Oh, I'm in a bad way. I lost the bet and am at the guy's mercy."

But as before Romilayu came through for me. He tried to hearten me a little and said he didn't think that worse was to be expected, and indicated that it was premature for me to feel trapped. He made very good sense. Then he said, "You sleep, sah. T'ink tomorrow."

And I said, "Romilayu, I'm learning more about your good points all the time. You're right, I've got to wait. I'm in a position and don't have a glimmer as to what it is."

Then he, too, prepared for sleep and got down on his shin-bones, clasping his hands with the muscles beginning to jump under his skin and the groans of prayer arising from his chest. I must admit I took some comfort from this.

I said to him, "Pray, pray. Oh, pray, pal, pray like anything. Pray about the situation."

So when he was done he wound himself into the blanket and drew up his knees, slipping his hand under his cheek as usual. But before closing his eyes he said, "Whut fo' you did it, sah?"

"Oh, Romilayu," I said, "if I could explain that I wouldn't be where I am today. Why did I have to blast those holy frogs without looking left or right? I don't know why it is I have such extreme intensity. The whole thing is so peculiar the explanation will have to be peculiar too. Figuring will get me nowhere, it's only illumination that I have to wait for." And thinking of how black things were and how absent any illumination was I sighed and moaned again.

Instead of troubling himself that I hadn't been able to give a satisfactory answer, Romilayu fell asleep, and presently I passed out too while the rain whirled and the lion or lions roared beneath the palace. Mind and body went to rest. It was like a swoon. I had a ten-days' growth of beard on my face. Dreams and visions came to me but I don't need to speak of them; all that is necessary to say is that nature was kind to me and I must have slept twelve hours without stirring, sore in body as I was, with cut feet and a bruised face.

When I awoke the sky was clear and warm, and Romilayu was up and about. Two women, amazons, were in the small room with me. I washed myself and shaved and did my business in a large basin placed in the corner, I assumed, for that purpose. Then the women, whom I had ordered out, came back with some articles of clothing which Romilayu said were the Sungo's, or rain king's, outfit. He insisted that I had better wear them as it might make trouble to refuse. For I was now the Sungo. Therefore I examined these garments. They were green and made of silk, and cut to the same pattern as King Dahfu's—the drawers were, I mean.

"Belong Sungo," said Romilayu. "Now you Sungo."

"Why, these damned pants are transparent," I said, "but I suppose I'd better wear them." I was wearing my stained jockey shorts above-mentioned, and I slipped on the green trousers over them. In spite of my rest I was not in top condition. I still had fever. I suppose it is natural for white men to be ill in Africa. Sir Richard Burton was as close to iron as the flesh can be, and he was taken badly with fever. Speke was even sicker. Mungo Park was sick and staggered around. Dr. Livingstone day in, day out was sick. Hell! Who was I to be immune? One of the amazons, Tamba, who had ugly whiskers growing from her chin, got behind me, lifted my helmet, and combed at my head with a primitive wooden instrument. These women were supposed to render me service.

She said to me, "Joxi, joxi?"

"What does she want? What is this joxi? Breakfast? I have no appetite. I feel too emotional to swallow anything." I drank a little whisky instead from one of the canteens, merely to keep my digestive tract open; I thought it might help my fever as well.

"Dem show you joxi," said Romilayu.

Face downward, Tamba stretched herself on the ground and the other woman, whose name was Bebu, stood upon her back and with her feet she kneaded and massaged her and cracked her vertebrae into place. After she had plied her with those ugly feet—and to judge from the face of Tamba, the process was bliss—they changed positions. Afterward they tried to show me how beneficial it was and how it set them up. Together they tapped their chests with their knuckles.

"Tell them thanks for their good intentions," I said. "It's probably wonderful therapy, but I think I'll pass it by today."

After this Tamba and Bebu lay on the ground and took turns in saluting me formally. Each took my foot and placed it on her head as Itelo had done to acknowledge my supremacy. The women moistened their lips so that the dust should stick to them. When they were done Tatu the generaless came to conduct me to King Dahfu and she went through the identical abasement, with the garrison cap on her head. After this the two women brought me a pineapple on a wooden platter and I forced myself to swallow a slice of it.

Then I went up the stairs with Tatu, who today allowed me to take the lead. Grins, cries, blessings, handclapping, and chanting met me; the older people were especially earnest in speaking to me. I wasn't as yet used to the green costume; it felt both wide and loose about the legs. From the upper gallery I looked out and saw the mountains. The air was exceptionally clear and the mountains were gathered together lap over lap, brown and soft as the coat of a Brahma bull. Also the green looked as fine as fur today. The trees were clear and green, too, and the blossoms underneath were fresh and red in the bowls of white rock. I saw the Bunam's wives pass under us with their short teeth, turning their dainty big shaven heads. I guess I must have caused them to smile in those billowing, swelling, green drawers of the Sungo and the pith helmet and my rubber-soled desert boots.

Indoors, we passed through the anterooms and entered the king's apartment. His big tufted couch was empty, but the wives lay on their cushions and mats gossiping and combing their hair and trimming their fingernails and toes. The atmosphere was very social and talkative. Most of the women lay resting, and their form of relaxation was peculiar; they folded their legs as we might our arms and lay back, perfectly boneless. Amazing. I stared at them. The odor of the room was tropical, like certain parts of the botanical garden, or like charcoal fumes and honey, like hot buckwheat. No one looked at me, they pretended I was nonexistent. To me this appeared kind of impossible, like refusing to see the *Titanic*. Besides, I was the sensation of the place, the white Sungo who had picked up Mummah. But I figured it was improper for me to visit their quarters, and they had no alternative but to ignore me.

We left the apartment by a low door and I found myself then in the king's private chamber. He was sitting on a low backless seat, a square of red leather stretched over a broad frame. A similar seat was brought forward for me, and then Tatu withdrew and sat obscurely near the wall. Once more he and I were face to face. There was no tooth-bordered hat, there were no skulls. He had on the close-fitting trousers and the embroidered slippers. Beside him on the floor was a whole stack of books; he had been reading when I entered, and he folded down the corner of his page, pressed it several times with his knuckle, and put the volume on top of the pile. What sort of reading would interest such a mind? But then what sort of mind was it? I didn't have a clue.

"Oh," he said, "now you have shaved and rested you make a very good appearance."

"I feel like a holy show, that's what I feel like, King. But I understand that you want me to wear this rig, and I wouldn't like to welsh on a bet. I can only say that if you'd let me out I'd be grateful as anything."

"I understand," he said. "I would very much like to do so, but the clothing of the Sungo really is requisite. Except for the helmet."

"I have to be on my guard against sunstroke," I said. "Anyway, I always have some headpiece or other. In Italy during the war I slept in my helmet, too. And it was a metal helmet."

"But surely a headcover indoors is not necessary," he said.

However, I refused to take the hint. I sat before him in my white pith hat.

Of course the king's extreme blackness of color made him fabulously strange to me. He was as black as—as wealth. By contrast his lips were red, and they swelled; and on his head the hair lived (to say that it grew wouldn't be sufficient). Like Horko's, his eyes revealed a red tinge. And even seated on the backless leather chair he was still, as on the sofa or in the hammock, sumptuously at rest.

"King," I said.

From the determination with which I began he understood me and he said, "Mr. Henderson, you are entitled to any explanation within my means to make. You see, the Bunam felt sure you would be strong enough to move our Mummah. I, when I saw what a construction you had, agreed with him. At once."

"Well," I said, "okay, so I'm strong. But how did it all happen? It seems to me that you were sure it would. You bet me."

"That was in a spirit of wager and nothing else," he said. "I knew as little about it as you do."

"Does it always happen like that?"

"Very far from always. Exceedingly seldom."

I looked my canniest, greatly lifting up my brows because I wanted him to see that the phenomenon was not yet explained to my satisfaction. Meanwhile I was trying also to make him out. And there were no airs or ostentations about the man. He was thoughtful in his replies but without making thinker's faces. And when he spoke of himself the facts he told me matched what I had heard from Prince Itelo. At the age of thirteen he had been sent to the town of Lamu and afterward he had gone to Malindi. "All preceding kings for several generations," he said, "have had to be acquainted with the world and have been sent at that same time of life to the school. You show up from nowhere, attend school, then go back. One son in each generation is sent out to Lamu. An uncle goes with him and waits for him there."

"Your Uncle Horko?"

"Yes, it is Horko. He was the link. He waited in Lamu nine years for me. I had moved on with Itelo. I didn't care for that life in the south. The young men at school were spoiled. Kohl on their eyes. Rouge. Chitter-chatter. I wanted more than that."

"Well, you are very serious," I said. "It's obvious. That was how I sized you up from the first."

"After Malindi, Zanzibar. From there Itelo and I shipped as deckhands. Once to India and Java. Then up the Red Sea—Suez. Five years in Syria at denominational school. The treatment was most generous. From my point of view the science instruction was most especially worth while. I was going for an M.D. degree, and would have done it except for the death of my father."

"That's just remarkable," I said. "I'm only trying to put it together with yesterday. With the skulls, and that fellow, the Bunam, and the amazons and the rest of it."

"It is interesting, I do admit. But also it is not up to me, Henderson—Henderson-Sungo—to make the world consistent."

"Maybe you were tempted not to come back?" I asked.

We sat close together, and, as I have noted, his blackness made him fabulously strange to me. Like all people who have a strong gift of life, he gave off almost an extra shadow—I swear. It was a smoky something, a charge. I used to notice it sometimes with Lily and was aware of it particularly that day of the storm in Danbury when she misdirected me to the water-filled quarry and then telephoned her mother from bed. She had it noticeably then. It is something brilliant and yet overcast; it is smoky, bluish, trembling, shining like jewel water. It was similar to what I had felt also arising from Willatale on the occasion of kissing her belly. But this King Dahfu was more strongly supplied with it than any person I ever met.

In answer to my last question he said, "For more reasons than one I could have wished my father to live longer."

As I conceived, the old fellow must have been strangled.

I guess I looked remorseful at having reminded him of his father, for he laughed to put me at ease again, and said, "Do not worry, Mr. Henderson—I must call you Sungo, for you are the Sungo now. Don't worry, I say. It is a subject which could not be avoided. You do not necessarily refresh it. His time came, he died, and I was king. I had to recover the lion."

"What lion are you talking about?" I said.

"Why, I have told you yesterday. Possibly you have forgot—the king's body, the maggot that breeds in it, the king's soul, the lion cub?" I recalled it now. Sure, he had told me this. "Well, then," he said, "this very young animal, set free by the Bunam, the successor king has to capture it within a year or two when it is grown."

"What? You have to hunt it?"

He smiled. "Hunt it? I have another function. To capture it alive and keep it with me."

"So that's the animal I hear below? I could swear I was hearing a lion down there. Jupiter, so that's what it is," I said.

"No, no, no," he said, in that soft way of his. "That is not it, Mr. Henderson-Sungo. You have heard a quite other animal. I have not yet captured Gmilo. Accordingly I am not yet fully confirmed in the rule of king. You find me at a midpoint. To borrow your manner of speaking, I too must complete Becoming."

Despite all the shocks of yesterday I was beginning to comprehend why I felt reassured at first sight of the king. It comforted me to sit with him; it comforted me unusually. His large legs were stretched out as he sat, his back was curved, and his arms were folded on his chest, and on his face there was a brooding but pleasant expression. Through his high-swelled lips a low hum occasionally came. It reminded me of the sound you sometimes hear from a power station when you pass one in New York on a summer night; the doors are open; all the brass and steel is going, lustrous under one little light, and some old character in dungarees and carpet slippers is smoking a pipe with all the greatness of the electricity behind him. Probably I am one of the most spell-prone people who ever lived. Appearances to the contrary, I am highly mediumistic and attuned. "Henderson," I said to myself, and not for the first time, "it's one of those *luth suspendu* deals, *sitôt qu'on le touche il résonne*. And you saw yesterday what savagery can be if you never saw it before, throwing passes with his own father's skull. And now with the lions. Lions! And the man almost a graduate physician. The whole thing is crazy." Thus I reflected. But then I also had to take into account the fact that I have a voice within me repeating, *I want*, raving and demanding, making a chaos, desiring, desiring, and disappointed continually, which drove me forth as beaters drive game. So I had no business to make terms with life, but had to accept such conditions as it would let me have. But at moments I would have been glad to find that my fever alone had originated all that had happened since I left Charlie and his bride and took off on my own expedition—the Arnewi, the frogs, Mtalba, and the corpse and the gallop in vine leaves with those giant women. And now this powerful black personage who soothed me—but was he trustworthy? How about trustworthy? And I, myself, hulking in the green silk pants that went with the office of rain king. I was smarting, harkening, straining my ears, my suspicious eyes. Oh, hell! How shall a man be broken for whom reality has no fixed dwelling! How he shall be broken! So I was sitting in this palace with its raw red walls, and the white rocks amid which the flowers flourished. By the door were amazons, and, more particularly, this fierce old Tatu with big nostrils. She sat dreaming on the floor in her garrison cap.

All the same, as we sat there talking I felt we were men of unusual dimensions. Trustworthiness was a separate issue.

At this time there began a conversation which could never be duplicated anywhere in the world. I hitched up the green pants a little. My head was swayed by the fever but I demanded firmness of myself and I said, speaking steadily, "Your Majesty, I don't intend to back down on the bet. I have certain principles. But I still don't know what this is all about, being dressed up as the rain king."

"It is not merely dress," said Dahfu. "You are the Sungo. It is literal, Mr. Henderson. I could not have made Sungo of you if you had not had the strength to move Mummah."

"Well, that's okay then—but the rest, with the gods? I felt very bad, Your Highness, I don't mind telling you. I could never claim that I led a very good life. I'm sure it's written all over me. . . ." The king nodded. "I've done a hell of a lot of things, too, both as a soldier and a civilian. I'll say it straight out, I don't even deserve to be chronicled on toilet paper. But when I saw them start to beat Mummah and Hummat and all the others, I fell to the ground. It got to be pretty dark out there and I don't know whether you saw that or not."

"I saw you. It is not my idea, Henderson, of how to be."

The king spoke softly. "I have far other ideas. You will see. But shall we speak only to each other?"

"You want to do me a favor, Your Highness, a big favor? The biggest favor possible?"

"Assuredly. Why certainly."

"All right, then, this is it: will you expect the truth from me? That's my only hope. Without it everything else might as well go bust."

He began to smile. "Why, how could I refuse you this? I am glad, Henderson-Sungo, but you must let me make the same request, otherwise it will be worthless if not mutual. But do you have expectation as to the form the truth is to take? Are you prepared if it comes in another shape, unanticipated?"

"Your Majesty, it's a deal. This is a pact between us. Oh, you don't understand how great a favor you're doing me. When I left the Arnewi (and I may as well tell you that I goofed there—maybe you know it) I thought that I had lost my last chance. I was just about to find out about the grun-tu-molani when this terrible thing happened, which was all my fault, and I left under a cloud. Christ, I was humiliated. You see, Your Highness, I keep thinking about the spirit's sleep and when the hell is it ever going to burst. So yesterday, when I became the rain king—oh, what an experience! How will I ever communicate it to Lily (my wife)?"

"I do appreciate this, Mr. Henderson-Sungo. I intentionally wished to keep you with me a while hoping that exchanges of importance would be possible. For I do not find it easy to express myself to my own people. Only Horko has been in the world at all and with him I cannot freely exchange, either. They are against me here. . . ."

This he said almost secretly, and after he spoke his broad lips closed and the room became still. The amazons lay on the floor as if asleep—Tatu in her hat and the other two naked save for the leather jerkin articles they wore. Their black eyes were only just open, but watchful. I could hear the wives behind the thick door of our inner room, stirring there.

"You are right," I said. "It's not just a question of expecting the truth. There's another question, too, of solitude. As if a guy were his own grave. When he comes forth from this burial he doesn't know good from bad. So for instance it has been going through my mind for some time that there is a connection between truth and blows."

"How is that again? You thought what?"

"Well, it's this way. Last winter as I was chopping wood a piece flew up from the block and broke my nose. So the first thing I thought was *truth!*"

"Ah," said the king, and then he began to speak, intimate and low, of a variety of things I had never heard before, and I stared toward him with my eyes grown big. "As things are," he said, "such may appear to be related to the case. I do not believe actually it is so. But I feel there is a law of human nature in which force is concerned. Man is a creature who cannot stand still under blows. Now take the horse—he never needs a revenge. Nor the ox. But man is a creature of revenges. If he is punished he will contrive to get rid of the punishment. When he cannot get rid of punishment, his heart is apt to rot from it. This may be—don't you think so, Mr. Henderson-Sungo? Brother raises a hand against brother and son against father (how terrible!) and the father also against son. And moreover it is a continuity-matter, for if the father did not strike the son, they would not be alike. It is done to perpetuate similarity. Oh, Henderson, man cannot keep still under the blows. If he must, for the time, he will cast down his eyes and think in silence of the ways to clear himself of them. Those primeval blows everybody still feels. The first was supposed to be struck by Cain, but how could that be? In the beginning of time there was a hand raised which struck. So the people are flinching yet. All wish to rid themselves and free themselves and cast the blow upon the others. And this I conceive of as the earthly dominion. But as for the truth content of the force, that is a separate matter."

The room was all shadow, but the heat with its odor of vegetable combustion pervaded the air.

"Wait a minute, now, sire," I said, having frowned and bitten on my lips. "Let me see if I have got you straight. You say the soul will die if it can't make somebody else suffer what it suffers?"

"For a while, I am sorry to say, it then feels peace and joy."

I lifted up my brows, and with difficulty, as the whiplashes all over the unprotected parts of my face were atrocious. I gave him one of my high looks, from one eye, "You are sorry to say, Your Highness? Is this why me and the gods had to be beaten?"

"Well, Henderson, I should have notified you better when you wished to move Mummah. To that extent you are right."

"But you thought I would be the fellow to do the job, and thought so before I laid eyes on them." Then I cut out the reproaches. I said to him, "You want to know something, Your Highness, there are some guys who can return good for evil. Even I understand that. Crazy as I am," I said. I began to tremble in all my length and breadth as I realized on which side of the issue I stood, and had stood all the time.

Curiously, I saw that he agreed with me. He was glad I had said this. "Every brave man will think so," he told me. "He will not want to live by passing on the wrath. A hit B? B hit C?—we have not enough alphabet to cover the condition. A brave man will try to make the evil stop with him. He shall keep the blow. No man shall get it from him, and that is a sublime ambition. So, a fellow throws himself in the sea of blows saying he do not believe it is infinite. In this way many courageous people have died. But an even larger number who had more of impatience than bravery. Who have said, 'Enough of the burden of wrath. I cannot bear my neck should be unfree. I cannot eat more of this mess of fear-pottage.' "

I wish to say at this place that the beauty of King Dahfu's person prevailed with me as much as his words, if not more. His black skin shone as if with the moisture that gathers on plants when they reach their prime. His back was long and muscular. His high-rising lips were a strong red. Human perfections are short-lived, and we love them more than we should, maybe. But I couldn't help it. The thing was involuntary. I felt a pang in my gums, where such things register themselves without my will and then I knew how I was affected by him.

"Yet you are right for the long run, and good exchanged for evil truly is the answer. I also subscribe, but it appears a long way off, for the human specie as a whole. Perhaps I am not the one to make a prediction, Sungo, but I think the noble will have its turn in the world."

I was swayed; I thrilled when I heard this. Christ! I would

have given anything I had to hear another man say this to me. My heart was moved to such an extent that I felt my face stretch until it must have been as long as a city block. I was blazing with fever and mental excitement because of the loftiness of our conversation and I saw things not double or triple merely, but in countless outlines of wavering color, gold, red, green, umber, and so on, all flowing concentrically around each object. Sometimes Dahfu seemed to be three times his size, with the spectrum around him. Larger than life, he loomed over me and spoke with more than one voice. I gripped my legs through the green silk trousers of the Sungo and I am sure I must have been demented at that time. Slightly. I was really sent, and I mean it. The king treated me with classic African dignity, and this is one of the summits of human behavior. I don't know where else people can be so dignified. Here, in the midst of darkness, in a small room in a hidden fold near the equator, in this same town where I had struggled along with the corpse on my back under the moon and the blue forests of heaven. Why, if a spider should get a stroke and suddenly begin to do a treatise on botany or something—a transfigured vermin, do you follow me? This is how I embraced the king's words about nobility's having its turn in the world.

"King Dahfu," I said, "I hope you will consider me your friend. I am deeply affected by what you say. Though I am a little woozy from all the novelty—the strangeness. Nevertheless I feel lucky here. Yesterday I took a beating. Well, all right. Since I am a suffering type of man anyhow, I am glad at least it served a purpose for a change. But let me ask you, when the noble gets its turn—how is that ever going to take place?"

"You would like to know what gives me such a confidence that my prediction will ultimately come?"

"Well, sure," I said, "of course. I am curious as all get-out. I mean what practical approach do you recommend?"

"I do not conceal, Mr. Henderson-Sungo, that I have a conception about it. As a matter of fact I do not wish it to be a secret with me. I am most eager to advance it to you. I am glad you want to consider me as a friend. Without reserve, I am developing a similar attitude toward you. Your coming has made me joyful. About the Sungo trouble I am genuinely very sorry. We could not refrain from making use of you. It was because of the circumstances. You will pardon me." This was practically an order, but I was only too glad to obey it, and I pardoned the guy, all right. I was not too corrupted or beat on the head by life to identify the extraordinary. I saw that he was some kind of genius. Much more than that. I realized that he was a genius of my own mental type.

"Well, sure, Your Highness. No question about that. I wanted you to make use of me yesterday. I said so myself."

"Well, thank you, Mr. Henderson-Sungo. So that is over. Do you know from the flesh standpoint you are something of a figure? You are rather monumental. I am speaking somatically."

At this I became somewhat stiff, as it had a dubious sound, and I said, "Is that so?"

The king exclaimed, "Do not let us go backward on our truth agreement, Mr. Henderson."

At this I got off my high horse. "Oh, no, Your Highness. That stands," I said. "Come what may. That was no bull. I meant every word and I want you to hold me to it."

This pleased him, and he told me, "I observed before, as to truth, a person may be unready to receive except what he has anticipated as true. However, I was referring to your outer man as a formation. It speaks for itself in many ways."

With his eyes he referred to the pile of books beside his seat as though they had a bearing on the matter. I turned my head to read the titles but the room was too obscurely lighted for that.

He said, "You are very fierce-looking."

This is no news to me; nevertheless, from him, this observation hurt me. "Well, what do you want?" I said. "I am the type of guy who couldn't survive without disfigurement. Life has worked me over. It wasn't just the war, either. . . . I got a bad wound, you know. But the shots of life . . ." I gave myself a bang on the breast. "Right here! You know what I mean, King? But naturally I don't want even such a life as mine to be thrown away, the fact that I have sometimes threatened suicide to the contrary notwithstanding. If I can't make an active contribution at least I should illustrate something. Even that I don't know anything about. I don't seem to illustrate a thing."

"Oh, this is erroneous of you. You illustrate volumes," he said. "To me you are a treasure of illustrations. I do not condemn your looks. Only I see the world in your constitution. In my medical study this became the greatest of fascinations to me and independently I have made a thorough study of the types, resulting in an entire classification system, as: The agony. The appetite. The obstinate. The immune elephant. The shrewd pig. The fateful hysterical. The death-accepting. The phallic-proud or hollow genital. The fast asleep. The narcissus intoxicated. The mad laughers. The pedantics. The fighting Lazaruses. Oh, Henderson-Sungo, how many shapes and forms! Numberless!"

"I see. This is quite a subject."

"Oh, yes, indeed. I have devoted years, and observed all the way from Lamu to Istanbul and Athens."

"A big chunk of the world," I said. "So tell me, what do I illustrate most?"

"Why," he said, "everything about you, Henderson-Sungo, cries out, 'Salvation, salvation! What shall I do? What must I do? At once! What will become of me?' And so on. That is bad."

At this moment I could not have concealed how astonished I was even if I had taken a Ph.D. degree in concealment, and I mused, "Yes. This was what Willatale was beginning to tell me, I guess. Grun-tu-molani was just a starter."

"I know that Arnewi expression," said the king. "Yes, I have been there, too, with Itelo. I understand what this grun-tu-molani implies. Indeed I do. And I know the lady also, a great success, a human gem, a triumph of the type—I refer to my system of classification. Granted, grun-tu-molani is much, but it is not alone sufficient. Mr. Henderson, more is required. I can show you something now—something without which you will never understand thoroughly my special aim nor my point of view. Will you come with me?"

"Where to?"

"I cannot say. You must trust me."

"Well, sure. Okay. I guess. . . ."

My consent was all he wanted and he rose, and Tatu, who had been sitting by the wall with the garrison cap over her eyes, got up too.

XVI

F ROM this small room the door opened into a long gallery
screened with thatch. Tatu, the amazon, let us out and
then followed us. The king was already far ahead of me down
this private gallery of his. I tried to keep up with him, and the
necessity of walking faster made me feel how yesterday's cuts
had crippled my feet. So I hobbled and shambled while Tatu in
her sturdy military stride came behind me. She had bolted the
door of the small room from outside so that nobody could follow, and after we had crossed the gallery, which was about fifty
feet long, she lifted another heavy wood bolt from the door at
that end. This must have weighed like iron, for her knees sank,
but the old woman had a powerful build and knew her job.
The king went through, and I saw a staircase descending. It
was wide enough, but dark—black ahead. A corrupt moldering
smell rose from this darkness, which made me choke a little.
But the king went right through into the moldering darkness
and I thought, "What this calls for is a miner's lamp or a cage
of canaries," trying to josh the fears out of my heart. "But
okay," I thought, "if I've got to go, down I go. One, two,
three, and on your way, Captain Henderson." You see, at such
a moment, I would call on my military self. Thus I mastered
my anxious feelings, chiefly by making my legs go, and entered
this darkness. "King?" I said, when I was in. But there was no
answer. My voice had a quaver, I heard it myself, and then I
caught the rapid pounding of steps below. I extended both
arms, but found no rail or wall. However, by the cautious use
of my feet I discovered that the stairs were broad and even. All
light from above was cut off when Tatu slammed the door.
Next moment I heard a heavy bolt bump into place. Now I
had no alternative except to follow downward or to sit down
and wait until the king turned back to me. With which alternative I risked the loss of his respect and all the rest that I had
gained yesterday by overcoming Mummah. Therefore I continued, while I told myself what a rare and probably great man
that king was, how he must be nothing less than a genius, and
how astonishing his personal beauty was, how the hum he

made reminded me of that power station on 16th Street in
New York on a hot night, how we were friends, and bound by
a truth-telling agreement; finally, how he predicted that nobility had a greater future than ever. Of all the elements in the
catalogue, this last had most appeal to me. Thus I groped with
sore feet after him and kept saying to myself, "Have faith,
Henderson, it's about time you had some faith." Presently
there was some light and the end of the staircase came in view.
The width of the stairs was due to the architectural crudeness
of the palace. I was now beneath the building. Daylight came
from a narrow opening above my head; this light was originally yellow but became gray by contact with stones. In the
opening two iron spikes were set to keep even a child from
creeping through. Examining my situation I found a small passage cut from the granite which led downward to another
flight of stairs, which were of stone too. These were narrower
and ran to a great depth, and soon I found them broken, with
grass springing and soil leaking out through the cracks. "King,"
I called, "King, hey, are you down there, Your Highness?"

    But nothing came from below except drafts of warm air that
lifted up the spider webs. "What's the guy's hurry?" I thought,
and my cheeks twitched and I continued to go down. Instead
of cooling, the air appeared warmer, the light filled up the
stony space like a gray and yellow fluid, the surfaces of the wall
acting as a filter, for the atmosphere was distributed as evenly
as water. I came to the bottom, the last few steps being of earth
and the bases of the walls themselves mixed with soil. Which
recalled to me the speckled vision of twilight at Banyules-sur-
Mer in that aquarium, where I saw that creature, the octopus,
pressing its head against the glass. But where I had felt coldness there, here I felt very warm. I proceeded, feeling my apparel—the helmet, of course, but even the green silk pants of
the rain king, which were light and flimsy—as excessive, a drag
on me. By and by the walls became more spacious and
widened into a sort of cave. To the left the tunnel went off into
darkness. This I certainly had no intention of entering. The
other way, there stood a semicircular wall in which there was a
large door barred with wood. It was partly open and on the
edge of this door I saw Dahfu's hand. For about the count of
twenty, this was as much of him as I saw, but it wasn't neces-

sary now to ask myself where he had been leading me. A low ripping sound behind the door was self-explanatory. It was the lion's den. And because the door was ajar I thought it advisable not to budge. I froze where I was, as there was only the king between me and the animal, of which I now began to see glimpses. This beast was not the one he had to capture. I didn't yet understand exactly what his relations with it were, but I did realize that he himself had no hesitation about entering, but had to prepare the animal for me. I was expected to go into the den with him. There was no question about that. And now when I heard that ripping, soft, dangerous sound the creature made, I felt as if I had got astride a rope. Seemingly it passed between my knees. I was under strict orders to myself to have faith, but as a soldier I had to think of my line of retreat, and here I was in a bad way. If I went up the stairs, at the top I would encounter a bolted door. It would do no good to knock or cry. Tatu would never open, and I could see myself chased all the way up and lying there with the animal washing its face in my blood. I expected the liver to go first, as with beasts of prey it is like that, they eat the most nutritious and valuable organ immediately. My other course lay into that dark tunnel, and this I speculated led to another closed door, probably. So I stood in those sad green pants with the stained jockey shorts under them, trying to steel myself. Meanwhile the snarling and ripping rose and fell and I became also aware of the voice of the king; he was talking to the animal, sometimes in Wariri, and sometimes in English, perhaps for my benefit, in order to reassure me. "Easy, easy, sweetheart. Here, here, my dolly." Thus it was a female, and he spoke low and steadily, calming her, and without raising his voice he said to me, "Henderson-Sungo, she now knows you are there. Gradually you must advance closer—little by little."

"Should I, Your Highness?"

He raised his hand toward me from the door, and his fingers moved. I came forward one step and I cannot deny that there lay over my consciousness the shadow of the cat I had attempted to shoot under the bridge table. There was little besides the king's arm that I could see. He kept beckoning and I took extremely small steps in my rubber-soled shoes. The snarls of the animal were now as sharp as thorns to me, and

blind patches as big as silver dollars came and went before my
eyes. Between these opaque interruptions I could see the body
of the animal as it flowed back and forth before the opening—
the calm, murderous face and clear eyes and the heavy feet.
The king reached backward and touched me; he gathered my
arm in his fingers and drew me to his side. He now held me in
his arm. "King, what do you need me here for?" I said in a
whisper. The lioness, in turning, then bumped into me and
when I felt her I gave a sigh.

The king said, "Make no sign," and he began again to speak
to the lioness, saying, "Oh, my sweetheart, dolly girl, this is
Henderson." She rubbed herself against him so that I felt the
stress of her weight through the medium of his body. She
stood well above our hips in height. When he touched her her
whiskered mouth wrinkled so that the root of each hair showed
black. She then moved off, returned behind us, came back
again, and this time began to investigate me. I felt her muzzle
touch upward first at my armpits, and then between my legs,
which naturally made the member there shrink into the shelter
of my paunch. Clasping me and holding me up, the king still
talked softly and calmingly to her while her breath blew out
the green silk of the Sungo trousers. I was gripping the inside
of my cheek with my teeth, including the broken bridgework,
while my eyes shut, slowly, and my face became, as I was highly
aware, one huge mass of acceptance directed toward fate. Suffering. (Here is all that remains of a certain life—take it away!
was implied by my expression.) But the lioness withdrew her
head from my crotch and began once more to walk back and
forth, the king saying to me (my comforter), "Henderson-
Sungo, it is all right. She is going to accept you easily."

"How do you know?" I said, dry in the throat.

"How do I know!" He spoke with a peculiar stress of confidence. "How do *I* know?" He gave a low laugh, saying, "Why
I know her—this is Atti."

"That's swell. It may seem obvious to you," I said, "but
me . . ." My words ended, for she was making her swing
back and I caught a glance from her eyes. They were so great,
so clear, like circles of wrath. Then she passed me, rubbing
against Dahfu's side; her belly swung softly, and she turned
again and plunged her head under his hand, taking a caress

from it. She went again to the far side of the den, this large, stone-walled room which filtered the gray and yellow light. She walked back along the walls, and when she snarled the freckles at the base of her whiskers were velvet and dark. The king, in a delighted, playful voice, nasal, African, and songlike, would call out after her, "Atti, Atti." And he said, "Ain't she the most beautiful?" Then he instructed me, "You will stand still, Mr. Henderson-Sungo."

I said, whispering fiercely, "No, no, don't move," but he didn't heed me. "King, for Christ's sake," I said. He tried to indicate that I should not worry, but was so taken up with his lioness, showing me how happy relations were between them, that in moving from me his step resembled the bounds he had made in the arena yesterday throwing the skulls. Yes, as he had done yesterday he danced and jumped, in his gold-embroidered white slippers, with powerful legs. There was something so proud and, seemingly, lucky about those legs in the neat, close trousers. Even through intensest fear it reached my mind that a man with such legs must be lucky. I wished that he would not push his luck, however, or demonstrate his relationship with her in just that way, since so much confidence may often be the prelude to a crash, or my experience isn't worth a nickel. Still the lioness trotted near him, keeping her head under his fingers. He led her from me to the far side of the den, where a wooden platform or bench was raised against the wall on heavy posts. Here he sat down, taking her head on his knee, scratching and stroking, while she pretended to box at him. She sat on her haunches while her paws struck. I saw the action of her shoulders while he pulled her ears, which were small and round. Not an inch did I stir from the position I was left in, not even to reset my helmet when it sank over my brows with the wrinkling of my forehead that resulted from the intensity of my concentration. No, I stood there half deaf, half blind, with my throat closing and all the sphincters shut. Meanwhile the king had taken one of those easy positions of his, and was resting on his elbow. He had such a relaxed way about him, and every moment of his earthly life the extra shadow of brilliance was with him—the sign of an intenser gift of being. Atti stood with forepaws on the edge of the trestle, licking his breastbone; her tongue rasped and flexed against his skin and he raised one of his legs and laid it playfully over her back. At which I felt so smothered I almost passed out, and I don't know whether the cause of this was fear for his safety or something else. I don't know what— rapture, maybe. Admiration. He stretched himself out at full length on this platform, and lying down isn't worth speaking of except as this king did it. It was a thing of art with him, and maybe he had not been joking when he said he kept strong by lying down, since it really seemed to add to his vitality. The animal with a soft, deep, ripping noise got set on her great, claw-hiding, hind paws and bounded up beside him. On the trestle she walked up and down, now and then glancing at me as if she were guarding him. When she looked at me it was with that round, clear stare out of the vast background of natural severity. There was no direct threat in this, it lacked anything personal; nevertheless it made my hair, though cramped by the helmet, stir all over my head. I continued to entertain the obscure worry that my intended crime against the cat world might somehow be known here. Also I was anxious about the hour that burst the spirit's sleep. I might have misapprehended the nature of it completely. How did I know that it might not be the judgment hour for me?

However, there were no practical alternatives present. I could do nothing but stand. Which I did. Finally the king extended his hand from behind the lioness, who at that time was striding back and forth over him. He pointed to the door, calling, "Please shut it, Mr. Henderson." And he added, "Open door makes her very uneasy."

So I asked him, "Is it okay to move?" My throat sounded badly rusted.

"Very slow," he said, "but do not worry, as she does what I tell her, precisely."

I stole to the door, stepping backward, and when I had reached it in very slow motion I wanted to continue through it and sit down outside to wait. But under no circumstances, come hell or high water, could I afford to weaken my connection with the king. Therefore I leaned against the door and closed it with my weight, sighing inwardly as I sank against it. I was all broken up. I couldn't take crisis after crisis after crisis, like this.

"Now move forward, Henderson-Sungo," he said. "So far it is admirable. Just a little quicker, only not abrupt. You will be better on closer approach. Lion is far-sighted. Her eyes are meant for viewing at a distance. Come closer."

I approached, cursing under my breath, him and his lion both, trembling and watching the tip of her tail as it swiped back and forth as regular as a metronome. In the middle of the floor I had no more support in all of God's world than a stone.

"More, more. Nearer," he said, and gestured with two fingers. "She will get used to you."

"If I don't die of it," I said.

"Oh, no, Henderson, she will have an influence upon you as she has had upon me."

When I was within reach he pulled me to him, meanwhile thrusting away the face of the animal with his left hand. With great difficulty I clambered up beside him. Then I wiped my face. Needlessly, for owing to the fever it was entirely dry. Atti paced to the end of the platform and swung back. The king fended her off from the back of my head which bristled like a sea urchin when she approached. She sniffed at my back. The king was smiling and thought we were getting on famously. I cried a little. Then she went away and the king said, "Do not be so exceedingly troubled, Henderson-Sungo."

"Oh, Your Highness, I can't help myself. It's what I feel. It's not only that I'm scared of her, and I'm scared all right, but it isn't that alone. It's the richness of the mixture. That's what's getting me. The richness of the mixture. And what I can't understand is why, when fear has taken me on and licked me so many times, I still am not able to stand it." And I went on sobbing, but not too loud, as I didn't want to provoke anything.

"Try, better, to appreciate the beauty of this animal," he said. "Do not think I am attempting to submit you to any ordeal for ordeal's sake. Do you think it is a nerve test? Wash your brain? Honor bright, such is not the case. If I were not positive of my control I would not lead you into such a situation. That would truly be scandalous." He had his hand with the garnet ring on the beast's neck, and he said, "If you will remain where you are, I will give you the fullest confidence."

He jumped down from the platform, and the abruptness of

this gave me a bad shock. I felt a burst of terror go off in my chest. The lioness leaped as soon as he did and the two of them together walked to the center of the den. He stopped and gave her an order. She sat. He spoke again and she stretched out on her back, opening her mouth, and then he crouched and pushed his arm into her jaws, bearing down against the wrinkled lips while her tail as she sprawled made a big arc on the stone, sweeping it with utmost power. Withdrawing the arm he made her stand again, and then he crept underneath her and put his legs about her back; his white-slippered feet crossed upon her haunches and his arms about her neck. Face to face she carried him up and down while he talked to her. She snarled, but not at him, seemingly. Together they went clear around the den and back to the platform, where she stood making her soft ripping noise and wrinkling her lips back. He hung on in his purple trousers, looking up at me. Till then I had only thought that I had seen the strangeness of the world. Obviously I had never even begun to see a thing! As he hung from her, smiling upside down into my face, with his high-swelled lips, I realized I had never even had a clue. Brother, this was what you call mastery—genius, that's all. The animal herself was aware of it. On her own animal level it was clear beyond any need of interpretation that she loved the guy. Loved him! With animal love. I loved him too. Who could have helped it?

I said, "That beats anything I ever saw."

He dropped from the animal and pushed her aside with his knee, then vaulted to the platform again. At the same moment Atti also returned and shook the trestle.

"Now is your opinion different, Mr. Henderson?"

"King, it's different. It's as different as can be."

"However, I note," he said, "you still are in fear."

I tried to say I wasn't but my face began to work and I couldn't get those words out. Then I began to cough, with my fist placed, thumb in, before my mouth, and my eyes watered. I finally said, "It's a reflex."

The animal was pacing by and the king irresistibly took me by the wrist and pressed my hand on her flank. Slowly her fur passed under my fingertips and the nails became like five burning tapers. The bones of the hand became incandescent.

After this a frightful shock passed right up the arm into the chest.

"Now you have touched her, and what do you think?"

"What I think?" I tried to get my lower lip under control by means of my teeth. "Oh, Your Majesty, please. Not everything in one day. I am doing my best."

He admitted to me, "It is true I am attempting rapid progress. But I wish to overcome your preliminary difficulties in quick time."

I smelled my fingers, which had taken a peculiar odor from the lioness. "Listen," I said, "I suffer a lot from impatience myself. But I have to say that there is just so much I can take at one time. I still have wounds on my face from yesterday, and I'm afraid she'll smell fresh blood. I understand nobody can control these animals once they scent it."

This marvelous man laughed at me and said, "Oh, Henderson-Sungo, you are exquisite." (*That* I never suspected of myself.) "You are real precious to me, and do you know," he said, "not many persons have touched lions."

"I could have lived without it," was the answer I might have made. But as he thought so highly of lions I kept it to myself, mostly. I merely muttered.

"And how you are afraid! Really! In the highest degree. I am really delighted by it. I have never seen such a fear manifestation. It resembled anxious pleasure to me. Do you know, many strong people love this blended fear and satisfaction the most? I think you must be of that type. In addition, I love when your brows move. They are really ex-traordinary. And your chin gets like a peach stone, and you have a very strangulation color and facial swelling, and your mouth spread very wide. And when you cried! I adored when you began to cry."

I knew that this was not really personal but came from his scientific or medical absorption in these manifestations. "What happens to your labium inferiorum?" he said, still interested in my chin. "How do you get so innumerable puckers in the flesh?" (This was extremely revealing to me.) He was so superior to me and overwhelmed me so with his presence, with the extra shadow or smoky brilliancy that he had, and with his lion-riding, that I let him say everything without challenge. When the king had made several more marveling observations about my nose and my paunch and the lines in my knees, he told me, "Atti and I influence each other. I wish you to become a party to this."

"Me?" I didn't know what he was talking about.

"You must not feel because I make observations of your constitution that I do not appreciate how remarkable you are in other levels."

"Do I understand you to say, Your Highness, that you have plans for me with this animal?"

"Yes, and shall explain them."

"Well, I think we should proceed carefully," I said. "I don't know how much strain my heart can take. As my fainting fits indicate I can't take too much. Moreover, how do you think she would behave if I keeled over?"

Then he said, "Perhaps you have had enough exposure to Atti for the first day." He left the platform again, the animal following. There was a heavy gate raised by a rope that passed over a grooved wheel about eighteen feet above the ground by means of which the king let the lioness out of the den into a separate enclosure. I have never seen any member of the cat species pass through a door except on its own terms, and she was no exception. She needed to loiter in and out while the king hung on to the rope by which the gate was suspended. As she was in exit I wanted to suggest that he should give her a boot in the tail to help her with the decision, since obviously he was her master, but under those conditions I couldn't really presume. At last, in that soft, narrow stride, so easy, so deliberate, so vigilant, she entered the next room. Releasing the hawser, the king let the great panel slide. It hit the stone with a loud noise and he rejoined me on the trestle looking very pleasant. Peaceful. He leaned backward and his lids, large-veined, sank a little and he breathed calmly, resting. Sitting close to him in my barbaric trousers with the jockey shorts visible under them, it seemed to me that something more than the planks beneath sustained him. For after all, I was on them, and I was not similarly sustained. At any rate I sat and waited for him to complete his rest. Once again I brought to mind that old prophecy Daniel made to Nebuchadnezzar. *They shall drive thee from among men, and thy dwelling shall be with the beasts of the field.* The lion odor was still very keen on my fingers. I smelled it repeatedly and there returned to my thoughts the frogs of the Arnewi, the cattle whom they venerated, the tenants' cat I had tried to murder, to say nothing of the pigs I had bred. Sure enough, this prophecy had a peculiar relevance to me, implying perhaps that I was not entirely fit for human companionship.

The king, having completed a short rest, was ready to speak.

"Now, then, Mr. Henderson," he began to say in his exotic and specially accented way.

"Well, King, you were going to explain to me why it was desirable to associate with this lion. So far I haven't got a clue. Oh, am I confused!"

"I am to make the matter clear," he said, "so first of all I shall tell you how and what about the lions. A year ago or more I captured Atti. There is a traditionary way among the Wariri for obtaining a lion if you need him. Beaters go forth and the animal is driven into what we call a hopo, and this is a very large affair embracing several miles out in the bush. The animals are aroused by noises with drums and horns and pursued into the wide end of the hopo and toward the narrow. At that narrow end is the trap, and I myself as king am obliged to make the capture. In this way Atti was obtained. I have to tell you that any lion except my father, Gmilo, is forbidden and illicit. Atti was brought here in a condition of severest disapproval and opposition, causing a great anxiety and partisanship. Especially the Bunam."

"Say, what's the matter with those guys?" I said. "They don't deserve a king like you. With a personality like yours, you could rule a big country."

The king was glad, I think, to hear this from me. "Notwithstanding," he said, "there is considerable trouble with the Bunam and my Uncle Horko and others, to say nothing of the queen mother and some of the wives. For, Mr. Henderson, there is only one tolerable lion, who is the late king. It is conceived the rest are mischief-makers and evildoers. Do you see? The main reason why the late king has to be recaptured by his successor is that he cannot be left out there in company with such evildoers. The witches of the Wariri are said to hold an illicit intercourse with bad lions. Even some children assumed to come of such a union are dangerous. I add if a man can prove his wife has been unfaithful with a lion, he demands an extreme penalty."

"This is very peculiar," I said.

"Summarizing," the king went on, "I am the object of a double criticism. Firstly I have not yet succeeded in obtaining Gmilo, my father-lion. Secondly it is said that because I keep Atti I am up to no good. Before all opposition, however, I am determined to keep her."

"What do they want?" I said. "You should abdicate, like the Duke of Windsor?"

He answered with a soft laugh, then said, in the deeply founded stillness of the room—with the yellow-gray air weighing on us, deepening, darkening slowly—"I have no such intention."

"Well," I said, "if your back is up about it, that I understand perfectly."

"Henderson-Sungo," he said, "I see I must tell you more about this. From a very early age the king will bring his successor here. Thus I used to visit my lion-grandfather. His name was Suffo. Thus from my small childhood I have been on familiar or intimate terms with lions, and the world did not offer me any replacement. And I so missed the lion connection that when Gmilo my father died and I was notified at school of the tragic occurrence, despite my love of the medical course I was not one hundred per cent reluctant. I may go so far as to assert that I was weak from a continuing lack of such a relationship and went home to be replenished. Naturally it would have been the best of fortune to capture Gmilo at once. But as instead I caught Atti, I could not give her up."

I took a fold of my gaudy pants to wipe my face which, due to the fever, was ominously dry. Just then I should have been pouring sweat.

"And still," he said, "Gmilo must be taken. I will capture him."

"I wish you loads of luck."

He then took me by the wrist with a sharp pressure and said, "I would not blame you, Mr. Henderson, for wishing this to be delusion or a hallucination. But for my sake, as you have applied to me for reciprocal truth-telling, I request you to be patient and keep a firm hold."

About a handful of sulfa pills would do me a lot of good, I thought.

"Oh, Mr. Henderson-Sungo," he said, after a long instant of thought, keeping his uncanny pressure on my wrist—there was seldom any abruptness in what he did. "Yes, I easily could understand that—delusion, imagination, dreaming. However, this is not dreaming and sleeping, but waking. Ha, ha! Men of most powerful appetite have always been the ones to doubt reality the most. Those who could not bear that hopes should turn to misery, and loves to hatreds, and deaths and silences, and so on. The mind has a right to its reasonable doubts, and with every short life it awakens and sees and understands what so many other minds of equally short life span have left behind. It is natural to refuse belief that so many small spans should have made so glorious one large thing. That human creatures by pondering should be *correct*. This is what makes a fellow gasp. Yes, Sungo, this same temporary creature is a master of imagination. And right now this very valuable possession appears to make him die and not to live. Why? It is astonishing what a fact that is. Oh, what a distressing picture, Henderson," he said. "To come to the upshot, do not doubt me, Dahfu, Itelo's friend, your friend. For you and I have become united as friends and you must give me your confidence."

"That's okay by me, Your Royal Highness," I said. "That suits me down to the ground. I don't understand you yet, but I am willing to go along on suspended judgment. And don't worry too much about the hallucination possibility. When you come right down to it, there aren't many guys who have stuck with real life through thick and thin, like me. It's my most basic loyalty. From time to time I've lost my head, but I've always made a comeback, and by God, it hasn't been easy, either. But I love the stuff. Grun-tu-molani!"

"Yes," he said, "indeed so. This is an attitude which I endorse. Grun-tu-molani. But in what shape and form? Now, Mr. Henderson, I am convinced you are a man of wide and spacious imagination, and that also you need. . . . You particularly *need*."

"Need is on the right track," I said. "The form it actually takes is, *I want, I want*."

Astonished, he asked me, "Why, what is that?"

"There's something in me that keeps that up," I said. "There have been times when it hardly ever let me alone."

This struck him full-on, so to speak, and he sat perfectly still with his hands mounted on his large thighs, and his face with his high-rising mouth and his wide, open-nostriled, polished nose looking at me.

"And you hear this?"

"I used to hear it practically all the time," I said.

In a low tone he said, "What is it? Demanding birthright? How strange! This is a very impressive manifestation. I have no memory of a previous description of it. Has it ever said what it wants?"

"No," I said, "never. I haven't been able to get it to name names."

"So extraordnary," he said, "and terribly painful, eh? But it will persist until you have replied, I gather. I am touched to hear about it. And whatever it is, how hungry it must be. The resemblance is also to a long prison term. But you say it will not declare which want it wants? Nor give specific directions either to live or to die?"

"Well, I have been threatening suicide a lot, Your Highness. Every once in a while something gets into me and I throw my weight around and threaten my wife with blowing my brains out. No, I could never get it to say what it wants, and so far I have provided only what it does not want."

"Oh, death from what we do not want is the most common of all the causes. Well, this is such a remarkable phenomenon, isn't it, Henderson? How much better I can interpret now why you succeeded with Mummah. Solely on the basis of that imprisoned want."

I cried, "Oh, can you see that now, Your Royal Highness? Really? I'm so grateful, you can't have any idea. Why, I can hardly see straight." And that was a fact. A spirit of love and gratitude was moving and pressing and squeezing unbearably inside me. "You want to know what this experience means to me? Why talk about its being strange or illusion? I know it's no illusion when I can speak straight out and tell you what it has been to hear, *I want, I want,* going on and on. With this to lean on I don't have to worry about hallucinations. I know in my bones that what moves me so is the straight stuff. Before I left home I read in a magazine that there are flowers in the desert (that's the Great American Desert) that bloom maybe once in forty or fifty years. It all depends on the amount of rainfall. Now according to this article, you can take the seeds and put them in a bucket of water, but they won't germinate. No, sir, Your Highness, soaking in water won't do it. It has to be the rain coming through the soil. It has to wash over them for a certain number of days. And then for the first time in fifty or sixty years you see lilies and larkspurs and such. Roses. Wild peaches." I was very much choked up toward the end, and I said hoarsely, "The magazine was the *Scientific American*. I think I told you, Your Highness, my wife subscribes to it. Lily. She has a very lively and curious mi—" Mind was what I wished to say. To speak of Lily also moved me very greatly.

"I understand you, Henderson," he said with gravity. "Well, we have a certain mutual comprehension or entente."

"King, thanks," I said. "All right, we're beginning to get somewhere."

"For a while I request you to reserve the thanks. I have to ask first for your patient confidence. Plus, at the very outset, I request you to believe that I did not leave the world and return to my Wariri with an aim of withdrawal."

I might as well say at this place that he had a hunch about the lions; about the human mind; about the imagination, the intelligence, and the future of the human race. Because, you see, intelligence is free now (he said), and it can start anywhere or go anywhere. And it is possible that he lost his head, and that he was carried away by his ideas. This was because he was no mere dreamer but one of those dreamer-doers, a guy with a program. And when I say that he lost his head, what I mean is not that his judgment abandoned him but that his enthusiasms and visions swept him far out.

XVII

THE KING had said that he welcomed my visit because of the opportunity for conversation it gave him, and that was no lie. We talked and talked and talked, and I can't pretend that I completely understood him. I can only say I suspended judgment, listening carefully and bearing in mind how he had warned me that the truth might come in forms for which I was unprepared.

So I will give you a rough summary of his point of view. He had some kind of conviction about the connection between insides and outsides, especially as applied to human beings. And as he had been a zealous student and great reader he had held down the job of janitor in his school library up there in Syria, and sat after closing hours filling his head with out-of-the-way literature. He would say, for instance, "James, *Psychology*, a very attractive book." He had studied his way through a load of such books. And what he was engrossed by was a belief in the transformation of human material, that you could work either way, either from the rind to the core or from the core to the rind; the flesh influencing the mind, the mind influencing the flesh, back again to the mind, back once more to the flesh. The process as he saw it was utterly dynamic. Thinking of mind and flesh as I knew them, I said, "Are you really and truly sure it's like that, Your Highness?"

Sure? He was better than sure. He was triumphantly sure. He reminded me very much of Lily in his convictions. It exalted them both to believe something and they had a tendency to make curious assertions. Dahfu also liked to talk about his father. He told me, for instance, that his late father Gmilo had been a lion type in every respect except the beard and mane. He was too modest to claim a resemblance to lions himself, but I saw it. I had already seen it when he was in the arena leaping and whirling the skulls by the ribbons and catching them. He started with the elementary observation, which many people had made before him, that mountain people were mountain-like, plains people plainlike, water people water-like, cattle people ("Yes, the Arnewi, your pals, Sungo") cattle-like.

"It is a somewhat Montesquieu idea," he said, and thus he went on with endless illustrations. These were things millions of people had noted in their life experience: horse people had bangs and big teeth, large veins, coarse laughter; dogs and masters came to resemble one another; husbands and wives took on a strong similarity. Crouching forward in those green silk pants, I was thinking, "And pigs . . . ?" But the king was saying, "Nature is a deep imitator. And as man is the prince of organisms he is the master of adaptations. He is the artist of suggestions. He himself is his principal work of art, in the body, working in the flesh. What miracle! What triumph! Also, what a disaster! What tears are to be shed!"

"Yes, if you're right, it's mighty saddening," I said.

"Debris of failure fills the tomb and grave," he said, "the dust eats back its own, yet a vital current is still flowing. There is an evolution. We must think of it."

Briefly, he had a full scientific explanation of the way in which people were shaped. For him it was not enough that there might be disorders of the body that originated in the brain. *Everything* originated there. "Although I do not wish to reduce the stature of our discussion," he said, "yet for the sake of example the pimple on a lady's nose may be her own idea, accomplished by a conversion at the solemn command of her psyche; even more fundamentally the nose itself, though part hereditary, is part also her own idea."

My head felt as light as a wicker basket by now, and I said, "A pimple?"

"I mean it as an index to deep desires flaming outward," he said. "But if you are inclined to blame—no! No blame redounds. We are far from so free as to be masters. But just the same the thing is accomplished from within. Disease is a speech of the psyche. That is a permissible metaphor. We say that flowers have the language of love. Lilies for purity. Roses for passion. Daisies won't tell. Ha! I once read this on a cushion embroidery. But, and I am in earnest, the psyche is a polyglot, for if it converts fear into symptoms it also converts hope. There are cheeks or whole faces of hope, feet of respect, hands of justice, brows of serenity, and so forth." He was pleased by the response he read in my face, which must have been a dilly. "Oh?" he said. "I startle you?" He loved that.

In the course of further conferences I told him, "I admit that this idea of yours really hits me where I live—am I so responsible for my own appearance? I admit I have had one hell of a time over my external man. Physically, I am a puzzle to myself."

He said, "The spirit of the person in a sense is the author of his body. I have never seen a face, a nose, like yours. To me that feature alone, from a conversion point of view, is totally a discovery."

"Why, King," I said, "that's the worst news I ever heard, except death in the family. Why should I be responsible, any more than a tree? If I was a willow you wouldn't say such things to me."

"Oh," he said, "you take upon yourself too much." And he went on to explain, citing all kinds of medical evidence and investigations of the brain. He told me, over and over again, that the cortex not only received impressions from the extremities and the senses but sent back orders and directives. And how this really was, and which ventricles regulated which functions, like temperature or hormones, and so on, I really couldn't keep quite clear. He kept talking about vegetal functions, or some such term, and he lost me every other sentence.

Finally he forced on me a whole load of his literature and I had to take it down to my apartment and promise to study it. These books and journals he had carried back from school with him. "How?" I said. And he explained he had come by way of Malindi and bought a donkey there. He had brought nothing else, no clothes (what did he need them for?) or other belongings except a stethoscope and a blood-pressure apparatus. For he really had been a third-year medical student when recalled to his tribe. "That's where I should have gone right after the war—to med school," I said. "Instead of horsing around. Do you think I would have made a good doctor?" He said Oh?—he didn't see why not. At first he exhibited a degree of reserve. But after I convinced him of my sincerity he really appeared to see a future for me. He implied that although I might be doing my internship when other men were retiring from active life, after all, it wasn't a question of other men but of me, E. H. Henderson. I had picked up Mummah. Let's not forget that. Anyway a steeple might fall on me and flatten me out, but apart from such unforeseeable causes I was built to last ninety years. So eventually the king came to take a serious view of my ambition, and he would generally say with great gravity, "Yes, this is a very admirable perspective." There was another matter which he treated with equal gravity, and it was that of my duties as the rain king. When I tried to make a joke about it he stopped me short and said, "It is proper to remember, Henderson, you are the Sungo."

So then my program, minus one factor: Every morning the two amazons, Tamba and Bebu, waited on me and offered me a joxi, or trample massage. Never failing to be surprised and disappointed at my refusal they took the treatment themselves; they administered it to each other. Every morning also I had an interview with Romilayu and tried to reassure him about my conduct. I believe it worried and perplexed him that I was so intimate, frère et cochon, with the king. But I kept telling him, "Romilayu, you've just got to understand. This is a very special king." But he realized from the state I was in that there was more than talk going on between Dahfu and me, there was also an experiment getting under way which I will defer telling you about.

Before lunch, the amazons held a muster. These women with the short vests or jerkins abased themselves before me in the dust. Each moistened her mouth so that the dirt would cling to it, and took my foot and put it on top of her head. There was much pageantry, heat, pressure, solemnity, drumming, and bugling all over the place. And I still had fever. Small fires of disease and eagerness were alight within me. My nose was exceedingly dry even if I was the king of moisture. I stank of lion, too—how noticeably, I can't say. Anyhow, I appeared in the green bloomers with my helmet and my crepe-soled shoes in front of the amazon band. Then they brought up the state umbrellas with their folds like thick eyelids. Women were squeezing bagpipes under their elbows. Amid all this twiddling and screeching the servants opened the bridge chairs and we all sat down to lunch.

Everybody was there, the Bunam, Horko, the Bunam's assistant. It was just as well that this Bunam didn't require much space. For Horko left him very little. Thin and straight, the Bunam looked at me with that everlasting stare of human experience; it took root twistedly between his eyes. His two wives, with bald heads and gay short teeth, both were very sunny. They looked like a pair of real fun-loving girls. Ever and again, Horko smoothed his robe on his belly or gave a touch to the heavy red stones that pulled his earlobes down. A white woolly ball or dumpling was set before me, like farina only coarser and saltier; at least it would do no further harm to my bridgework. I could certainly die of pain before I reached civilization if the metal parts which were anchored on the little stumps of teeth ground down by Mlle. Montecuccoli and Spohr the dentist were to come loose. I reproached myself, for I have a spare and I should never have started without it. Together with the plaster impressions it was in a box, and that box was in the trunk of my Buick. There was a spring that held the jack to the spare tire, and for safe-keeping I had put the box with the extra bridge in the same place. I could see it. I saw it just as if I were lying in that trunk. It was a gray cardboard box, filled with pink tissue paper and labeled "Buffalo Dental Manufacturing Company." Fearing to lose what remained of the bridgework, I chewed even the salty dumplings with extreme caution. The Bunam with that fanatical fold of deep thought ate like everybody else. He and the black-leather fellow looked very occult; the latter always seemed about to unfold a pair of wings and take off. He too was chewing, and as a matter of fact there was a certain amount of Alice-in-Wonderland jollity in the palace yard. Even a number of kids, all head and middle, like little black pumpernickels, were playing a pebble game in the dust.

When Atti roared under the palace, there was no comment. Just Horko, of all people, gave a wince, but it merged rapidly again into his low-featured smile. He was always so gleaming, his very blood must have been like furniture polish. Like the king he had a rich physical gift, and the same eye tinge, only his eyes bulged. And I thought that during those years he had spent in Lamu, while his nephew was away at school in the north, he must have had himself a ball. He was certainly no church-goer, if I am any judge.

Well, it was the same every day. After the ceremonies of the meal I went, attended by the amazons, to Mummah. She had been brought back to her shrine by six men who had carried her laid across heavy poles. I witnessed this myself. Her room, which she shared with Hummat, was in a separate courtyard of the palace where there were wooden pillars and a stone tank with some disagreeable water. This was our special Sungo's supply. My daily visit to Mummah cheered me up. For one thing, the worst part of the day was over (I shall explain in due time) and for another I developed a strong personal attachment to her, due not only to my success but to some quality in her, either as a work of art or as a divinity. Ugly as she was, with the stork-nest tresses and unreliable legs giving under the mass of her body, I attributed benevolent purposes to her. I would say, "Hi-de-do, old lady. Compliments of the season. How's your old man?" For I took Hummat to be married to her, the clumsy old mountain god that Turombo, the champion in the red fez, had lifted up. It looked like a good marriage, and they stood there contented with each other, near the stone tub of rank water. And while I gave Mummah the time of day, Tamba and Bebu filled a couple of gourds and we went through another passage where a considerable troop of the amazons with umbrella and hammock were waiting. Both of these articles were green, like my pants, the Sungo's own color. I was helped into this hammock and lay at the bottom of it, a bursting weight, looking up at the brilliant heaven made still by the force of afternoon heat, and the taut umbrella wheeling, now clockwise, now the other way, with lazy, sleepy fringes. Seldom did we leave the gate of the palace without a rumble from Atti, below, which always made the perspiring, laboring amazons stiffen. The umbrella bearer might waver then and I would catch a straight blow of the sun, one of those buffets of violent fire which made the blood leap into my brain like the coffee in a percolator.

With this reminder of the experiments the king and I were engaged in, pursuing his special aim, we entered the town with one drum following. People came up to Tamba and Bebu with little cups and got a dole of water. Women especially, as the Sungo was also in charge of fertility; you see, it goes together with moisture. This expedition took place every afternoon to the beat of the idle, almost irregular single deep drum. It made a taut and almost failing sound of puncture which, however, was always approximately in rhythm. Out in the sun walked the women coming from their huts with earthenware cups for their drops of tank water. I lay in the shade and listened to the sleepy drum-summons with my fingers heavily linked upon my belly. When we reached the center of town I climbed out. This was the market place. It was also the magistrate's court. Dressed in a red gown, the judge sat on the top of a dunghill. He was a coarse-featured fellow; I didn't care for his looks. There was always a litigation, and the defendant was tied to a pole and gagged by means of a forked stick which stuck into his palate and pressed down his tongue. The trial would stop for me. The lawyers quit hollering and the crowd yelled, "Sungo! Aki-Sungo" (Great White Sungo). I got out and took a bow. Tamba or Bebu would hand me a perforated gourd like the sprinklers that laundresses used in the old days. No, wait—like the as-pergillum the Catholics use in their churches. I would sprinkle them and people would come to me laughing and bowing and offer their backs to the spray, old toothless fellows with griz-zled hair in the cleft of their posteriors and maidens whose breasts pointed toward the ground, strong fellows with power-ful spines. It didn't escape me altogether that there was some mockery mingled with respect for my strength and my office. Anyway, I always saw to it the prisoner tied to the post got his full share, and added water drops to the perspiration on the poor guy's skin.

Such, roughly, were my rain king's duties, but it was the king's special aim that I have to tell you about, and all the lit-erature that he had given me. This I shunned; after our pre-liminary conversation I guessed that there might be trouble in it. There were the two books, which looked pretty well used up, and there were scientific reprints, coverless, with shabby top pages. I looked through a few of these. The print was close and black, and the only clearings in the text were filled with di-agrams of molecules. Otherwise the words were as thick and heavy as tombstones, and I was very disheartened. It was much like taking the limousine to La Guardia Field and passing those cemeteries in Queens. So heavy. Each of the dead having been mailed away, and those stones like the postage stamps death has licked.

Anyway, it was a hot afternoon and I sat down with the lit-erature to see what I could do with it. I was wearing my costume, those green silk drawers, and the helmet with its nipple on the top, and the shoes with the crepe soles trodden out of shape and curled like sneering lips. So that's how it is. Illness and fever have made me sleepy. The sun is very absolute. The stripes of shadow look solid. The air is dreamy with the heat and the mountains in places are like molasses candy, yellow, brittle, cellular, cavey, scorched. They look as if they might be bad for the teeth. And I have this literature. Dahfu and Horko had loaded it on the donkey when they came over the mountains from the coast. Afterward the beast was butchered and fed to the lioness.

Why should I have to read the stuff? I thought. My resistance to it was great. Firstly I was afraid to find out that the king might be a crank; I felt it was not right, after I had come this long way to pierce the spirit's sleep, and picked up Mummah and become rain king, that Dahfu should turn out to be just another eccentric. Therefore I stalled. I laid out a few games of solitaire. After which I felt extremely sleepy and stared at the sun-fixed colors outside, green as paint, brown as crust.

I am a nervous and emotional reader. I hold a book up to my face and it takes only one good sentence to turn my brain into a volcano; I begin thinking of everything at once and a regular lava of thought pours down my sides. Lily claims I have too much mental energy. According to Frances, on the other hand, I didn't have any brain power at all. All I can truly say is that when I read in one of my father's books, "The forgiveness of sin is perpetual," it was just the same as being hit in the head with a rock. I have told, I think, that my father used currency for bookmarks and I assume I must have pocketed the money in that particular book and then forgot even its title. Maybe I didn't want to hear any more than that about sin. Just as it was, it was perfect, and I might have been afraid the guy would spoil it when he went on. Anyway, I am the inspirational, and not the systematic, type. Besides, if I wasn't going to abide by that one sentence, what good would it do to read the entire book?

No, I haven't ever been calm enough to read, and there was a time when I would have dumped my father's books to the pigs if I'd thought it might do them good. Such a supply of books confused me. When I started to read something about France, I realized I didn't know anything about Rome, which came first, and then Greece, and then Egypt, going backward all the time to the primitive abyss. As a matter of fact, I didn't know enough to read one single book. Eventually I found the only things I could enjoy were things like *The Romance of Surgery, The Triumph over Pain*, or medical biographies—like Osler, Cushing, Semmelweis, and Metchnikoff. And owing to my attachment to Wilfred Grenfell I became interested in Labrador, Newfoundland, the Arctic Circle, and finally the Eskimos. You would have thought that Lily would have gone along with me on the Eskimos, but she didn't, and I was very disappointed. The Eskimos are stripped down to essentials and I thought they would appeal to her because she is such a basic type.

Well, she is, and then again, she is not. She's not naturally truthful. Look at the way she lied about all her fiancés. And I'm not sure that Hazard did punch her in the eye on the way to the wedding. How can I be? She told me her mother was dead while the old woman was still living. She lied too about the carpet, for it *was* the one on which her father shot himself. I am tempted to say that ideas make people untruthful. Yes, they frequently lead them into lies.

Lily is something of a blackmailer, also. You know I dearly love that big broad, and for my own amusement sometimes I like to think of her part by part. I start with a hand or a foot or even a toe and go to all the limbs and joints. It gives me wonderful satisfaction. One breast is smaller than the other, like junior and senior; her pelvic bones are not well covered, she is a little gaunt there. But her body looks gentle and pretty. Moreover her face blushes white, which touches me more than anything else. Nevertheless she is reckless and a spendthrift and doesn't keep the house clean and is a con artist and exploits me. Before we were married, I wrote about twenty letters for her all over the place, to the State Department and a dozen or so missions. *She used me as a character reference.* She was going to Burma or to Brazil, and the implied threat was that I would never see her again. I was on the spot. I couldn't louse her up to all these people. But when we were married and I wanted to spend our honeymoon camping among the

Copper Eskimos, she wouldn't hear of it. Anyway (still on the subject of books) I read Freuchen and Gontran de Poncins and practiced living out of doors in winter. I built an igloo with a knife and during zero weather Lily and I fell out because she wouldn't bring the kids and sleep with me under skins as the Eskimos do. I wanted to try that.

I looked through all the readings Dahfu had given me. I knew they were supposed to have a bearing on lions and yet, page after page, not one single reference to any lion. I felt like groaning, like snoozing, like anything except tackling such hard material on this hot African day when the sky was as blue as grain alcohol is white. The first article, which I picked because the opening paragraph looked easy, was signed Scheminsky, and it was not easy at all. But I fought it until I came across the term Obersteiner's allochiria, and there I broke down. I thought, "Hell! What is it all about! Because I told the king I wanted to be a doctor, he thinks I have medical training. I'd better straighten him out on this." The stuff was just too difficult.

But anyway I gave it the best that was in me. I skipped over Obersteiner's allochiria, and in the end managed to make sense of a paragraph here and there. Most of these articles had to do with the relation between body and brain, and they especially emphasized posture, confusions between right and left, and various exaggerations and deformities of sensation. Thus a fellow with a normal leg might be convinced that he had the leg of an elephant. This was very interesting in itself and a few of the descriptions were absolutely dandy. What I kept thinking was, "I'd better scour, brighten, freshen up the old intelligence, and understand what the man is driving at, for my life may depend on it." It was just my luck to think I had found the conditions of life simplified so I could deal with them—finally!—and then to end up in a ramshackle palace reading these advanced medical publications. I suppose there must be few native princes left who are not educated, and all the poly-technical schools enroll gens de couleur from all over the world, and some of them have made prodigious discoveries already. But I never heard of anyone who was precisely on King Dahfu's track. Of course it was possible that he was in a league all by himself. This suggested again that I might find myself in some really hot water with him, for you can't expect people who are in a class by themselves to be reasonable. Being the only occupant of a certain class, I know this from personal experience.

I was taking a short rest from the article by Scheminsky, playing a game of solitaire and breathing hard as I bent over it, when the king's Uncle Horko, on this particular day of heat, entered my room on the first floor of the palace. Behind him came the Bunam, and with the Bunam there was always his companion or assistant, the black-leather man. These three made way to let a fourth person enter, an elderly woman who had the look of a widow. You can seldom be mistaken about widows. They had fetched her in to see me, and from their way of standing aside it was plain she was the principal visitor. Preparatory to rising, I gave a stagger—space was limited in my room and it was already pretty well occupied by Tamba and Bebu, who were lying down, and Romilayu, who was in the corner. There were eight of us in a room not really big enough to hold me. The bed was fixed and couldn't be moved outside. It was covered with hides and native rags, and the spattered cards over which I had been brooding were laid out in four uneven files—I had pushed aside King Dahfu's literature. And now they brought me this elderly woman in a fringed dress that hung from her shoulders to about the middle of her thighs. They filed in from the burning wilds of the African afternoon and, as I had been fixed with the seeing blindness of a card player on the glossy, dirty reds and blacks, I couldn't focus at first on the woman. But then she came near to me, and I saw that she had a round but not perfectly round face. On one side of it the symmetry was out. At the jaw, this was. Her nose was cocked and she had large lips, while the gentle forward projection of her face made it seem that she was offering it to you. Her mouth was somewhat lacking in teeth but I recognized her at once. "Why," I thought, "it's a relative of Dahfu's. She must be his mother." I saw the relationship in the slope of her face and in the lips and the red tinge of her eyes.

"Yasra. Queen," said Horko. "Dahfu mama."

"Ma'am, it's an honor," I said.

She took my hand and placed it on her head, which was

shaved, of course. All the married women had shaven heads. Her action was facilitated by a difference of almost two feet in our heights. Horko and I stood over all the rest. He was wrapped in his red cloth, and the stones in his ears hung like the two lobes of a rooster when he bent to speak to her.

I took off my helmet, baring the huge welts and bruises on my nose and cheeks, left over from the rain ceremony. My eyes must have been a little crazy with solemnity for they drew the notice of the black-leather man, who appeared to point at them and said something to the Bunam. But I put the old queen's hand on my head respectfully saying, "Lady, Henderson at your service. And I really mean it." Over my shoulder I said to Romilayu, "Tell her that." His tuft of hair was close behind me, and under it his forehead was more than usually wrinkled. I saw the Bunam look at the cards and printed matter on the bed, and I scooped them all behind me, as I didn't want the king's property exposed to his scrutiny. Then I told Romilayu, "Say to the queen that she has a fine son. The king is a friend of mine and I am just as much his friend. Say I am proud to know him."

Meantime I thought, "She's in very bad company, ain't she?" because I knew it was the Bunam's job to take the life of the failing king; Dahfu had told me that. Actually Bunam was her husband's executioner—and now the queen came with him late in the afternoon to pay a social call? It didn't seem right.

At home this would have been the cocktail hour. The great wheels and all the sky-marring frames would be slowing, darkening, and the world, with its connivance and invention and its load of striving and desire to transform, would relax its strain.

The old queen may have sensed my thought, for she was sad and troubled. The Bunam was staring at me, evidently meaning to get at me in some way, while Horko, with his low-hung, fleshy face, looked gloomy at first. The purpose of this visit was twofold—to get me to reveal about the lioness and then also to use any influence I might have with the king. He was in trouble, and very seriously, over Atti.

Horko did most of the talking, mixing up the several languages he had picked up during his stay in Lamu. He used a kind of French as well as English and a little Portuguese. His

blood gleamed through his face with a high polish and his ears
were dragged down by their ornaments almost to his fat
shoulders. He introduced the subject by saying a little about
his residence in Lamu—a very up-to-date town, as he described
it. Automobiles, café and music, many languages spoken. "Tout
le monde très distingué, très chic," he said. I shut off my defective ear with one hand and gave him the full benefit of the
other, nodding, and when he saw that I responded to his
Lamu Afro-French, he began to liven up. You could see that
his heart belonged to that town, and for him the years he had
spent there were probably the greatest. It was his Paris. It gave
me no trouble to imagine that he had promoted himself a
house and servants and girls and spent his days in a café in a
seersucker jacket, with a boutonnière maybe, for he was a promoter. He was displeased with his nephew for having gone
away and left him there eight or nine years. "Go away Lamu
school," he said. "Pas assez bon. Bad, bad, I say. No go away
Lamu. We go. He go. Papa King Gmilo die. Moi aller chercher
Dahfu. One years." He lifted a stout finger to me over the bald
head of Queen Yasra, and from his indignation I took it he
must have been held responsible for Dahfu's disappearance. It
was his duty to bring back the heir.

But he observed that I didn't like the tone he took, and said,
"You friend Dahfu?"

"Damn right I am."

"Oh me, too. Roi neveu. Aime neveu. Sans blague.
Dangerous."

"Come on, what is this all about?" I said.

Seeing me dissatisfied, the Bunam spoke sharply to Horko,
and the queen mother, Yasra, gave a cry, "Sasi ai. Ai, sasi,
Sungo." Looking upward at me she must have seen the under-
side of my chin and the mustache and my open nostrils, but
not my eyes, so that she didn't know how I was receiving her
plea, for that is what it was. She therefore began to kiss my
knuckles over and over again, somewhat as Mtalba had done
the night before my doomed expedition against the frogs.
Once more I was aware of a sensitivity there. These hands have
lost shape a good deal as a result of the abuses they have been
subjected to. There was, for instance, the forefinger with which
I had aimed, in imitation of Pancho Villa, at that cat under the

bridge table. "Oh, lady, don't do that," I said. "Romilayu—
Romilayu—tell her to quit it," I said. "If I had as many fingers
as there are hammers to a piano," I told him, "they'd all be
at her service. What does the old queen want? These guys are
putting the squeeze on her, I can see it."

"Help son, sah," said Romilayu at my back.

"From what?" I said.

"Lion witch, sah. Oh, very bad lion."

"They've frightened the old mother," I said, glowering at
the Bunam and his assistant. "This is the sexton-beetle. Not
happy without corpses or putting people away in the grave. I
can smell it on you. And look at this leather-winged bat, his
sidekick. He could play the Phantom of the Opera. He's got a
face like an ant-eater—a soul-eater. You tell them right here
and now I think the king is a brilliant and noble man. Make it
very strong," I said to Romilayu, "for the old lady's sake."

But I could not change the subject no matter how I praised
the king. They had come to brief me about lions. With one
single exception, lions contained the souls of sorcerers. The
king had captured Atti and brought her home in place of his
father Gmilo, who was still at large. They took this very hard,
and the Bunam was here to warn me that Dahfu was impli-
cating me in his witchcraft. "Oh, pooh," I said to these men.
"I never could be a witch. My character is just the opposite."
Between them Horko and Romilayu made me finally feel the
importance and solemnity—the heaviness—of the situation. I
tried to avoid it, but there it was: they laid it on me like a slab
of stone. People were angry. The lioness was causing mischief.
Certain women who had been her enemies in the previous
incarnation were having miscarriages. Also there was the
drought, which I had ended by picking up Mummah. Consequently I was very popular. (Blushing, I felt a kind of surly rose
color in my face.) "It was nothing," I said. But then Horko
told me how bad it was that I went down into the den. I was
reminded again that Dahfu was not in full possession of the
throne until Gmilo was captured. So the old king was forced
to be out in the bush among bad companions (the other lions,
each and every one a proven evildoer). They claimed that the
lioness was seducing Dahfu, and made him incapable of doing
his duty, and it was she who kept Gmilo away.

I tried to say to them that other people took a far different view of lions. I told them that they couldn't be right to condemn all the lions except one, and there must be a mistake somewhere. Then I appealed to the Bunam, seeing that he was obviously the leader of the anti-lion forces. I thought his wrinkled stare, the stern vein of his forehead, and those complex fields of skin about his eyes must signify (even here, where all Africa was burning like oceans of green oil under the absolute and extended sky) what they would have signified back in New York, namely, deep thought. "Well, I think you should go along with the king. He is an exceptional man and does exceptional things. Sometimes these great men have to go beyond themselves. Like Caesar or Napoleon or Chaka the Zulu. In the king's case, the interest happens to be science. And though I'm no expert I guess he's thinking of mankind as a whole, which is tired of itself and needs a shot in the arm from animal nature. You ought to be glad that he's not a Chaka and won't knock you off. Lucky for you he's not the type." I thought a threat might be worth trying. It seemed, however, to have no effect. The old woman still whispered, holding my fingers, while the Bunam, as Romilayu addressed him, doing his best to translate my words, was drawn up with savage stiffness so that only his eyes moved, and they moved very little, but mainly glittered. And then, when Romilayu was through, the Bunam signaled to his assistant by snapping his fingers, and the black-leather man drew from his rag cloak an object which I mistook at first for a shriveled eggplant. He held it by the stalk and brought it toward my face. A pair of dry dead eyes now looked at me, and teeth from a breathless mouth. From the eyes came a listless and *finished* look. They saw me from beyond. One of the nostrils of this toy was flattened down, the other was expanded and the entire face seemed to bark, this black, dry, child-like or dwarfish mummy which was gripped by the neck. My breath burned like mustard, and that voice of inward communication which I had heard when I picked up the corpse tried to speak but it could not rise above a whisper. I suppose some people are more full of death than others. Evidently I happen to have a great death potential. Anyway, I begin to ask (or perhaps it was more a plea than a question), why is it always near me—why! Why can't I get away from it awhile! Why, why!

"Well, what is this thing?" I said.

This was the head of one of the lion-women—a sorceress. She had gone out and had trysts with lions. She had poisoned people and bewitched them. The Bunam's assistant had caught up with her, and she was tried by ordeal and strangled. But she had come back. These people made no bones about it, but said she was the very same lioness that Dahfu had captured. She was Atti. It was a positive identification.

"Ame de lion," said Horko. "En bas."

"I don't know how you can be so sure," I said. I could not take my eyes from the shriveled head with its finished, listless look. It spoke to me as that creature had done in Banyules at the aquarium after I had put Lily on the train. I thought as I had then, in the dim watery stony room, "This is it! The end!"

XVIII

THAT NIGHT Romilayu's praying was more fervent than ever. His lips stretched far forward and the muscles jumped under his skin while his moaning voice rose from the greatest depths. "That's right, Romilayu," I said, "pray. Pour it on. Pray like anything. Give it everything you've got. Come on, Romilayu, pray, I tell you." He didn't seem to me to be putting enough into it, and I flabbergasted him altogether by getting out of bed in the green silk drawers and kneeling beside him on the floor to join him in prayer. If you want to know something, it wasn't the first time in recent years by any means that I had addressed some words to God. Romilayu looked from under that cloud of poodle hair that hung over his low forehead, then sighed and shuddered, but whether with satisfaction at finding I had some religion in me or with terror at hearing my voice suddenly in his channel, or at the sight I made, I couldn't be expected to know. Oh, I got carried away! That withered head and the sight of poor Queen Yasra had got to my deepest feelings. And I prayed and prayed, "Oh, you . . . Something," I said, "you Something because of whom there is not Nothing. Help me to do Thy will. Take off my stupid sins. Untrammel me. Heavenly Father, open up my dumb heart and for Christ's sake preserve me from unreal things. Oh, Thou who tookest me from pigs, let me not be killed over lions. And forgive my crimes and nonsense and let me return to Lily and the kids." Then silent on my heavy knees and palm pressed to palm I went on praying while my weight bowed me nearly to the broad boards.

I was shaken, you see, because I now understood clearly that I was caught between the king and the Bunam's faction. The king was set upon carrying out his experiment with me. He believed that it was never too late for any man to change, no matter how fully formed. And he took me for an instance, and was determined that I should absorb lion qualities from his lion.

When I asked to see him in the morning after the visit of Yasra, the Bunam, and Horko, I was directed to his private pavilion. It was a garden laid out with some signs of formal design. At the four corners were dwarf orange trees. A flowering vine covered the palace wall like bougainvillaea, and here the king was sitting under one of his unfurled umbrellas. He wore his wide velvet hat with the fringe of human teeth and occupied a cushioned seat, surrounded by wives who kept drying his face with little squares of colored silk. They lit his pipe and handed him drinks, making sure that he was screened by a brocaded cloth whenever he took a sip. Beside one of the orange trees an old fellow was playing a stringed instrument. Very long, only a little shorter than a bass fiddle, rounded at the bottom, it stood on a thick peg and was played with a horse-hair bow. It gave thick rasping notes. The old musician himself was all bone, with knees that bent outward and a long shiny head, tier upon tier of wrinkles. A few white weblike hairs were carried in the air behind him.

"Oh, Henderson-Sungo, good you are here. We shall have entertainments."

"Listen, I've got to talk to you, Your Highness," I said. I kept wiping my face.

"Of course, but we shall have dancing."

"But I've got to tell you something, Your Majesty."

"Yes, of course, but there is dancing first. My ladies are entertaining."

His ladies! I thought, and looked about me at this gathering of naked women. For after he had told me that he would be strangled when he couldn't be of any further service to them, I took kind of a dim view of them. But there were some who looked splendid, the tallest ones moving with a giraffe-like elegance, their small faces ornamented with patterns of scars. Their hips and breasts suited their bodies better than any costume could have done. As for their features, they were broad but not coarse; on the contrary, their nostrils were very thin and fine, and their eyes were soft. They were painted and ornamented and perfumed with a musk that smelled a little like sweet coal oil. Some wore beads like hollow walnuts of gold, looped two or three times about themselves and hanging down as far as their legs. Others had corals and beads and feathers, and the dancers wore colored scarves which waved flimsily from their shoulders as they sprinted with elegant long legs across the court and the basic scratching of the music went on as the old fellow pushed his bow, rasp, rasp, rasp.

"But there is something I have got to say to you."

"Yes, I suspected so, Henderson-Sungo. However, we must watch the dancing. That is Mupi, she is excellent." The instrument sobbed and groaned and croaked as the old fellow polished on it with his barbarous bow. Mupi, trying out the music, swayed two or three times, then raised her leg stiff-kneed, and when her foot returned slowly to the ground it seemed to be searching for something. And then she began to rock and continued groping with alternate feet and closed her eyes. The thin beaten gold shells, like hollow walnuts, rustled on this Mupi's body. She took the king's pipe from his hand and knocked out the coals on her thigh, pressing down with her hand, and while she burned herself her eyes, which were very fluid with the pain, never stopped looking into his.

The king whispered to me, "This is a good girl—very good girl."

"She's certainly gone on you," I said. The dancing continued to the croaking of the two-stringed instrument. "Your Highness, I've got to talk . . ." The fringe of teeth clicked as he turned his head with the soft, large-brimmed hat. In the shade of this hat his face was more vivid than ever, especially his hollow-bridged nose and his high-swelled lips.

"Your Highness."

"Oh, you are very persistent. Very well. As you claim it is so urgent, let us go where we can talk." He stood up and his rising caused a great disturbance among the women. They began to spring back and forth, loping across the little pavilion, crying out, and making a clatter with their ornaments; some wept with disappointment that the king was going and some attacked me with shrill voices for taking Dahfu away while several shrieked, "Sdudu lebah!" Lebah—I had already picked the word up—was Wariri for lion. They were warning him about Atti; they were charging him with desertion. The king with a big gesture waved at them, laughing. He seemed very affectionate and I guess he was saying he cared for them all. I was waiting, standing by, huge, my worried face still stiff from the bruises.

The women were right, for Dahfu did not lead me back to

his apartment again but took me again to the den, below. When I realized where he was going I hurried after him saying, "Wait, wait. Let's talk this thing over. Just one single minute."

"I am sorry, Henderson-Sungo, but we are bound to go to Atti. I will listen to you down there."

"Well, forgive me for saying it, King, but you're very stubborn. In case you don't know it you are in a hell of a position."

"Oh, the divil," he said. "I am aware what they are up to."

"They came and showed me the head of a person they claimed was the same as Atti in a former existence."

The king stopped. Tatu had just let us through the door and was standing holding the heavy bolt in her arms, waiting in the gallery. "That is the well-known fear business. We will withstand it. Old man, sometimes things cannot be so nice in cases like this. Do they harass you? It is because I have shown my fondness about you." He took me by the shoulder.

Owing perhaps to the touch of his hand, I almost broke down on the threshold of the stairs. "Here," I said, "I am ready to do almost anything you say. I've taken a lot from life, but basically it hasn't really scared me, King. I am a soldier. All my people have been soldiers. They protected the peasants, and they went on the crusades and fought the Mohammedans. And I had one ancestor on my mother's side—why General U. S. Grant wouldn't even start an engagement without him. He would say, 'Billy Waters here?' 'Present, sir.' 'Very good. Begin the battle.' Hell's bells, I've got martial blood in me. But Your Highness, you're breaking me down with this lion business. And what about your mother?"

"Oh, divil my mother, Sungo," he said. "Do you think the world is nothing but an egg and we are here to set upon it? First come the phenomena. Utterly above all else. I talk to you about a great discovery and you argue me mothers. I am aware they are working the fear business upon her, as well. My mother has outlived father Gmilo already by half of a decade. Come through the door with me and let Tatu close it. Come, come." I stood. He shouted, "Come, I say!" and I stepped through the doorway. I saw Tatu as she labored to place the great chunk of wood which was the bolt. It fell, the door banged, and we were in darkness. The king was running down the stairs.

Where the light came through the grating in the ceiling, that watery, stone-conditioned yellow light, I caught up with him.

He said, "Why are you blustering at me so with your face? You have a perilous expression."

I said, "King, it's the way I feel. I told you before I am mediumistic. And I feel trouble."

"No doubt, as there is trouble. But I will capture Gmilo and the trouble will entirely cease. No one will dispute or contest me then. There are scouts daily for Gmilo. As a matter of fact reports have come of him. I can assure you of a capture very soon."

I said fervently that I certainly hoped he would catch him and get the thing over with, so we could stop worrying about those two strangling characters, the Bunam and the black-leather man. Then they would stop persecuting his mother. At this second mention of his mother he looked angry. For the first time he subjected me to a long scowl. Then he resumed his way down the stairs. Shaken, I followed him. Well, I reflected, this black king happened to be a genius. Like Pascal at the age of twelve discovering the thirty-second proposition of Euclid all by himself.

But why lions?

Because, Mr. Henderson, I replied to myself, you don't know the meaning of true love if you think it can be deliberately selected. You just love, that's all. A natural force. Irresistible. He fell in love with his lioness at first sight—coup de foudre. I went crashing down the weed-grown part of the stairway engaged in this dialogue with myself. At the same time I held my breath as we approached the den. The cloud of fright about me was even more suffocating than before; it seemed to give actual resistance to my face and made my breathing clumsy. My respiration grew thick. Hearing us the beast began to roar in her inner room. Dahfu looked through the grating and said, "It is all right, we may go in."

"Now? You think she's okay? She sounds disturbed to me. Why don't I wait out here?" I said, "till you find out how the wind blows?"

"No, you must come," said the king. "Don't you understand yet, I am trying to do something for you? A benefit? I can hardly think of a person who may need this more. Really the danger of life is negligible. The animal is tame."

"Tame for you, but she doesn't really know me yet. I'm just as ready to take a reasonable chance as the next guy. But I can't help it, I am afraid of her."

He paused, and during this pause I thought I was going down greatly in his estimation, and nothing could have hurt me more than that. "Oh," he said, and he was particularly thoughtful. Silently he paused and thought. In this moment he looked and sounded, again, larger than life. "I think I recall when we were speaking of blows that there was a lack of the brave." Then he sighed and said, with his earnest mouth which even in the shadow of his hat had a very red color, "Fear is a ruler of mankind. It has the biggest dominion of all. It makes you white as candles. It splits each eye in half. More of fear than of any other thing has been created," he said. "As a molding force it comes second only to Nature itself."

"Then doesn't this apply to you, too?"

He said, with a nod of full agreement, "Oh, certainly. It applies. It applies to everyone. Though nothing may be visible, still it is heard, like radio. It is on almost all the frequencies. And all tremble, and all are wincing, in greater or lesser degree."

"And you think there is a cure?" I said.

"Why, I surely believe there is. Otherwise all the better imagining will have to be surrendered. Anyways, I will not urge you to come in with me and do as I have done. As my father Gmilo did. As Gmilo's father Suffo did. As we all did. No. If it is positively beyond you we may as well exchange good-by and go separate ways."

"Wait a minute now, King, don't be hasty," I said. I was mortified and frightened; nothing could have been more painful than to lose my connection with him. Something had gone off in my breast, my eyes filled, and I said, almost choking, "You wouldn't brush me off like that would you, King? You know how I feel." He realized how hard I was taking it; nevertheless he repeated that perhaps it would be better if I left, for although we were temperamentally suited as friends and he had deep affection for me, too, and was grateful for the opportunity to know me and also for my services to the Wariri in lifting up Mummah, still, unless I understood about lions, no

deepening of the friendship was possible. I simply had to know
what this was about. "Wait a minute, King," I said. "I feel
tremendously close to you and I'm prepared to believe what
you tell me."

"Sungo, thank you," he said. "I also am close to you. It is
very mutual. But I require more deep relationship. I desire to
be understood and communicated to. We have to develop an
underlying similarity which lies within you by connection with
the lion. Otherwise, how shall we maintain the truth agreement we made?"

Moved as anything, I said, "Oh, this is hard, King, to be
threatened with loss of friendship."

The threat was exceedingly painful also to him. Yes, I saw
that he suffered almost as hard as I did. Almost. Because who
can suffer like me? I am to suffering what Gary is to smoke.
One of the world's biggest operations.

"I don't understand it," I said.

He took me up to the door and made me look through the
grating at Atti the lioness, and in that soft, personal tone peculiar to him which went strangely to the center of the subject,
he said, "What a Christian might feel in Saint Sophia's church,
which I visited in Turkey as a student, I absorb from lion.
When she gives her tail a flex, it strikes against my heart. You
ask, what can she do for you? Many things. First she is unavoidable. Test it, and you will find she is unavoidable. And
this is what you need, as you are an avoider. Oh, you have accomplished momentous avoidances. But she will change that.
She will make consciousness to shine. She will burnish you.
She will force the present moment upon you. Second, lions
are experiencers. But not in haste. They experience with deliberate luxury. The poet says, 'The tigers of wrath are wiser than
the horses of instruction.' Let us embrace lions also in the
same view. Moreover, observe Atti. Contemplate her. How
does she stride, how does she saunter, how does she lie or gaze
or rest or breathe? I stress the respiratory part," he said. "She
do not breathe shallow. This freedom of the intercostal muscles and her abdominal flexibility" (her lower belly, which was
disclosed to our view, was sheer white) "gives the vital conti-
nuity between her parts. It brings those brown jewel eyes their
hotness. Then there are more subtle things, as how she leaves

hints, or elicits caresses. But I cannot expect you to see this at first. She has much to teach you."

"Teach? You really mean that she might change me."

"Excellent. Precisely. Change. You fled what you were. You did not believe you had to perish. Once more, and a last time, you tried the world. With a hope of alteration. Oh, do not be surprised by such a recognition," he said, seeing how it moved me to discover that my position was understood. "You have told me much. You are frank. This makes you irresistible, as not many are. You have rudiments of high character. You could be noble. Some parts may be so long-buried as to be classed dead. Is there any resurrectibility in them? This is where the change comes in."

"You think there's a chance for me?" I said.

"Not at all impossible if you follow my directions."

The lioness stroked past the door. I heard her low, soft, continuous snarl.

Dahfu now started to go in. My nether half turned very cold. My knees felt like two rocks in a cold Alpine torrent. My mustache stabbed and stung into my lips, which made me realize that I was frowning and grimacing with terror, and I knew that my eyes must be filling with fatal blackness. As before, he took my hand as we entered and I came into the den saying inwardly, "Help me, God! Oh, help!" The odor was blinding, for here, near the door where the air was trapped, it stank radiantly. From this darkness came the face of the lioness, wrinkling, with her whiskers like the thinnest spindles scratched with a diamond on the surface of a glass. She allowed the king to fondle her, but passed by him to examine me, coming round with those clear circles of inhuman wrath, convex, brown, and pure, rings of black light within them. Between her mouth and nostrils a line divided her lip, like the waist of the hourglass, expanding into the muzzle. She sniffed my feet, working her way to the crotch once more and causing my parts to hide in my belly as best they could. She next put her head into my armpit and purred with such tremendous vibration it made my head buzz like a kettle.

Dahfu whispered, "She likes you. Oh, I am glad. I am enthusiastic. I am so proud of both of you. Are you afraid?"

I was bursting. I could only nod.

"Later you will laugh at yourself with amusement. Now it is normal."

"I can't even bring my hands together to wring them," I said.

"Feel paralysis?" he said.

The lioness went away, making a tour of the den along the walls on the thick pads of her feet.

"Can you see?" he said.

"Barely. I can barely see a single thing."

"Let us begin with the walk."

"Behind bars, I'd like that fine. It would be great."

"You are avoiding again, Henderson-Sungo." His eyes were looking at me from under the softly folded velvet brim. "Change does not lie that way. You must form a new habit."

"Oh, King, what can I do? My openings are screwed up tight, both back and front. They may go to the other extreme in a minute. My mouth is all dried out, my scalp is wrinkling up, I feel thick and heavy at the back of my head. I may be passing out."

I remember that he looked at me with keen curiosity, as if wondering about these symptoms from a medical standpoint. "All the resistances are putting forth their utmost," was his comment. It didn't seem possible that the black of his face could be exceeded, and yet his hair, visible at the borders of his hat, was blacker. "Well," he said, "we shall let them come out. I am firmly confident in you."

I said weakly, "I'm glad you think so. If I'm not torn to pieces. If I'm not left down here half-eaten."

"Take my assurance. No such eventuality is possible. Now, watch the way she walks. Beautiful? You said it! Furthermore this is uninstructed, specie-beauty. I believe when the fear has subsided you will be capable of admiring her beauty. I think that part of the beauty emotion does result from an overcoming of fear. When the fear yields, a beauty is disclosed in its place. This is also said of perfect love if I recollect, and it means that ego-emphasis is removed. Oh, Henderson, watch how she is rhythmical in behavior. Did you do the cat in Anatomy One? Watch how she gives her tail a flex. I feel it as if undergoing it personally. Now let us follow her." He began to lead me around after the lioness. I was bent over, and my legs were thick and drunken. The green silk pants no longer floated but were charged with electricity and clung to the back of my thighs. The king did not stop talking, which I was glad of, since his words were the sole support I had. His reasoning I couldn't follow in detail—I wasn't fit to—but gradually I understood that he wanted me to imitate or dramatize the behavior of lions. What is this going to be, I thought, the Stanislavski method? The Moscow Art Theatre? My mother took a tour of Russia in 1905. On the eve of the Japanese War she saw the Czar's mistress perform in the ballet.

I said to the king, "And how does Obersteiner's allochiria and all that medical stuff you gave me to read come into this?"

He patiently said, "All the pieces fit properly. It will presently be clear. But first by means of the lion try to distinguish the states that are given and the states that are made. Observe that Atti is all lion. Does not take issue with the inherent. Is one hundred per cent within the given."

But I said in a broken voice, "If she doesn't try to be human, why should I try to act the lion? I'll never make it. If I have to copy someone, why can't it be you?"

"Oh, shush these objections, Henderson-Sungo. *I* copied her. Transfer from lion to man is possible, I know by experience." And then he shouted, "Sakta," which was a cue to the lioness to start running. She trotted, and the king began to bound after her, and I ran too, trying to keep close to him. "Sakta, sakta," he was crying, and she picked up speed. Now she was going fast along the opposite wall. In a few minutes she would come up behind me.

I started to call to him, "King, King, wait, let me go in front of you, for Christ's sake."

"Spring upward," he called back to me. But I was clumping and pounding after him trying to pass him, and sobbing. In the mind's eye I saw blood in great drops, bigger than quarters, spring from my skin as she sank her claws into me, for I was convinced that as I was in motion I was fair game and she would claw me as soon as she was within range. Or perhaps she would break my neck. I thought that might be preferable. One stroke, one dizzy moment, the mind fills with night. Ah, God! No stars in that night. There is nothing.

I could not catch up with the king, and therefore I pretended to stumble and threw myself heavily on the ground, off to the side, and gave a crazy cry. The king when he saw me prostrate on my belly held out his hand to Atti to stop her, shouting, "Tana, tana, Atti." She sprang sideward and began to walk toward the wooden shelf. From the dust I watched her. She gathered herself down upon her haunches and lightly reached the shelf on which she liked to lie. She pointed one leg outward and started to wash herself with her tongue. The king squatted beside her and said, "Are you hurt, Mr. Henderson?"

"No, I just got jolted," I said.

Then he began to explain. "I intend to loosen you up, Sungo, because you are so contracted. This is why we were running. The tendency of your conscious is to isolate self. This makes you extremely contracted and self-recoiled, so next I wish—"

"Next?" I said. "What next? I've had it. I'm humbled to the dust already. What else am I supposed to do, King, for heaven's sake? First I was stuck with a dead body, then thrown into the cattle pond, clobbered by the amazons. Okay. For the rain. Even the Sungo pants and all that. Okay! But now this?"

With much forbearance and sympathy he answered, picking up a pleated corner of his velvet headgear, the color of thick wine, "Patient, Sungo," he said. "Those aforementioned things were for us, for the Wariri. Do not think I am ever ingrate. But this latter is for you."

"That's what you keep saying. But how can this lion routine cure what I've got?"

The forward slope of the king's face suggested, as his mother's did, that it was being offered to you. "Oh," he said, "high conduct, high conduct! There will never be anything but misery without high conduct. I knew that you went out from home in America because of a privation of high conduct. You have met your first opportunities of it well, Henderson-Sungo, but you must go on. Take advantage of the studies I have made, which by chance are available to you."

I licked my hand, for I had scratched it in falling, and then I sat up, brooding. He squatted opposite me with his arms about his knees. He looked steadily at me across his large folded arms while he tried to make me meet his gaze.

"What do you want me to do?"

"As I have done. As Gmilo, Suffo, all the forefathers did.

They all acted the lion. Each absorbed lion into himself. If you do as I wish, you too will act the lion."

If this body, if this flesh of mine were only a dream, then there might be some hope of awakening. That was what I thought as I lay there smarting. I lay, so to speak, at the bottom of things. Finally I sighed and started to get up, making one of the greatest efforts I have ever made. At this he said, "Why rise, Sungo, since we have you in a prone position?"

"What do you mean, prone position? Do you want me to crawl?"

"No, naturally not, crawl is for a different order of creature. But be on all the fours. I wish you to assume the posture of a lion." He got on all fours himself, and I had to admit that he looked very much like a lion. Atti, with crossed paws, only occasionally looked at us.

"You see?" he said.

And I answered, "Well, you ought to be able to do it. You were brought up on it. Besides, it's your idea. But I can't." I slumped back on the ground.

"Oh," he said. "Mr. Henderson, Mr. Henderson! Is this the man who spoke of rising from a grave of solitude? Who recited me the poem of the little fly on the green leaf in the setting sun? Who wished to end Becoming? Is this the Henderson who flew half around the world because he had a voice which said *I want*? And now, because his friend Dahfu extends a remedy to him, falls down? You dismiss my relationship?"

"Now, King, that's not true. It's just not true, and you know it. I'd do anything for you."

To prove this, I rose up on my hands and feet and stood there with knees sagging, trying to look straight ahead and as much like a lion as possible.

"Oh, excellent," he said. "I am so glad. I was sure you had sufficient flexibility in you. Settle on your knees now. Oh, that is better, much better." My paunch came forward between my arms. "Your structure is far from ordinary," he said. "But I offer you sincerest congratulations on laying aside the former attitude of fixity. Now, sir, will you assume a little more limberness? You appear cast in one piece. The midriff dominates. Can you move the different portions? Minus yourself of some of your heavy reluctance of attitude. Why so sad and so earthen? Now you are a lion. Mentally, conceive of the environment. The sky, the sun, and creatures of the bush. You are related to all. The very gnats are your cousins. The sky is your thoughts. The leaves are your insurance, and you need no other. There is no interruption all night to the speech of the stars. Are you with me? I say, Mr. Henderson, have you consumed much amounts of alcohol in your life? The face suggests you have, the nose especially. It is nothing personal. Much can be changed. By no means all, but very very much. You can have a new poise, which will be your own poise. It will resemble the voice of Caruso, which I have heard on records, never tired because the function is as natural as to the birds. However," he said, "it is another animal you strongly remind me of. But of which?"

I wasn't going to tell him anything. My vocal cords, anyway, seemed stuck together like strands of overcooked spaghetti.

"Oh, truly! How very big you are," he said. He went on in this vein.

At last I found my voice and asked him, "How long do you want me to hold this?"

"I have been observing," he said. "It is very important that you feel *something* of a lion on your maiden attempt. Let us start with the roaring."

"It won't excite her, you think?"

"No, no. Now look, Mr. Henderson, I wish you to picture that you are a lion. A literal lion."

I moaned.

"No, sir. Please oblige me. A real roar. We must hear your voice. It tends to be rather choked. I told you the tendency of your conscious is to isolate self. So fancy you are with your kill. You are warning away an intruder. You may begin with a growl."

Having come so far with the guy there was no way to back out. Not one single alternative remained. I had to do it. So I began to make a rumble in my throat. I was in despair.

"More, more," he said impatiently. "Atti has taken no notice, therefore it is far from the thing."

I let the sound grow louder.

"And glare as you do so. Roar, roar, roar, Henderson-Sungo. Do not be afraid. Let go of yourself. Snarl greatly. Feel the lion. Lower on the forepaws. Up with hindquarters. Threaten me. Open those magnificent mixed eyes. Oh, give more sound. Better, better," he said, "though still too much pathos. Give more sound. Now, with your hand—your paw—attack! Cuff! Fall back! Once more—strike, strike, strike, strike! Feel it. Be the beast! You will recover humanity later, but for the moment, be it utterly."

And so I was the beast. I gave myself to it, and all my sorrow came out in the roaring. My lungs supplied the air but the note came from my soul. The roaring scalded my throat and hurt the corners of my mouth and presently I filled the den like a bass organ pipe. This was where my heart had sent me, with its clamor. This is where I ended up. Oh, Nebuchadnezzar! How well I understand that prophecy of Daniel. For I had claws, and hair, and some teeth, and I was bursting with hot noise, but when all this had come forth, there was still a remainder. That last thing of all was my human longing.

As for the king, he was in a state of enthusiasm, praising me, rubbing his hands together, looking into my face. "Oh, good, Mr. Henderson. Good, good. You are the sort of man I took you to be," I heard him say when I stopped to draw breath. I might as well go the whole way, I thought, as I was crouching in the dust and the lion's offal, since I had come so far; therefore I gave it everything I had and roared my head off. Whenever I opened my bulging eyes I saw the king in his hat rejoicing by my side, and the lioness on the trestle staring at me, a creature entirely of gold sitting there.

When I could do no more I fell flat on my face. The king thought I might have passed out, and he felt my pulse and patted my cheeks saying, "Come, come, dear fellow." I opened my eyes and he said, "Ah, are you okay? I worried about you. You went from crimson to black starting from the sternum and rising into the face."

"No, I'm all right. How am I doing?"

"Wonderfully, my brother Henderson. Believe me, it will prove beneficial. I will lead Atti away and let you take rest. We have done enough for the first time."

We were sitting on the trestle together and talking after the king had shut Atti in her inner room. He seemed positive that the lion Gmilo was going to turn up very soon. He had been observed in the vicinity. Then he would release the lioness, he told me, and end the controversy with the Bunam. After this he began to talk again about the connection between the body and the brain. He said, "It is all a matter of having a desirable model in the cortex. For the noble self-conception is everything. For as conception is, so the fellow is. Put differently, you are in the flesh as your soul is. And in the manner described a fellow really is the artist of himself. Body and face are secretly painted by the spirit of man, working through the cortex and brain ventricles three and four, which direct the flow of vital energy all over. And this explains what I am so excited about, Henderson-Sungo." For he was highly excited, by now. He was soaring. He was up there with enthusiasm. Trying to keep up with his flight made me dizzy. Also I felt very bitter over some implications of his theory, which I was beginning to understand. For if I was the painter of my own nose and forehead and of such a burly stoop and such arms and fingers, why, it was an out-and-out felony against myself. What had I done! A bungled lump of humanity! Oh, ho, ho, ho, ho! Would death please wash me away and dissolve this giant collection of errors. "It's the pigs," I suddenly realized, "the pigs! Lions for him, pigs for me. I wish I was dead."

"You are pensive, Henderson-Sungo."

I came near holding a grudge against the king at that moment. I should have realized that his brilliance was not a secure gift, but like this ramshackle red palace rested on doubtful underpinnings.

Now he began to give me a new sort of lecture. He said that nature might be a mentality. I wasn't sure quite what he meant by that. He wondered whether even inanimate objects might have a mental existence. He said that Madame Curie had written something about the beta particles issuing like flocks of birds. "Do you remember?" he said. "The great Kepler believed that the whole planet slept and woke and breathed. Was this talking through his hat? In that case the mind of the human may associate with the All-Intelligent to perform certain work. By imagination." And then he began to repeat what a procession of monsters the human imagination had created instead. "I have subsumed them under the types I mentioned," he said, "as the appetite, the agony, the fateful-hysterical, the fighting Lazaruses, the immune elephants, the mad laughers, the hollow genital, and so on. Think of what there could be instead by different imaginations. What gay, brilliant types, what merriment types, what beauties and goodness, what sweet cheeks or noble demeanors. Ah, ah, ah, what we could be! Opportunity calls to rise to summits. You should have been such a summit, Mr. Henderson-Sungo."

"Me?" I said, still dazed by my own roaring. My mental horizon was far from clear, although the clouds on it were not low and dark.

"So you see," said Dahfu, "you came to me speaking of grun-tu-molani. What could be grun-tu-molani upon a background of cows?"

Swine! he might have said to me.

It was vain to curse Nicky Goldstein for this. It was not his fault that he was a Jew, that he had announced he was going to raise minks in the Catskills and that I had told him I was going to raise pigs. Fate is much more complex than that. I must have been committed to pigs long before I laid eyes on Goldstein. Two sows, Hester and Valentina, used to follow me about with freckled bellies and sour, red, rust-gleaming bristles, silky in luster, stiff as pins to the touch. "Don't let them loll in the driveway," said Frances. That was when I warned her, "You'd better not hurt them. Those animals have become a part of me."

Well, had those creatures become a part of me? I hesitated to come clean with Dahfu and to ask him right out bluntly whether he could see their influence. Secretly investigating myself, I felt my cheekbones. They stuck out like the mushrooms that grow from the trunks of trees, those mushrooms which prove to be as white as lard when you break them open. Under my helmet, my fingers crept toward my eyelashes. Pigs' eyelashes occur only on the upper lid. I had some on the lower, but they were sparse and blunt. When a boy I had practiced to become like Houdini and tried to pick up needles from the floor with my eyelashes while hanging upside down from the foot of my bed. He had done it. I never managed to, but that was not because my eyelashes were too short. Oh, I had changed all right. Everybody changes. Change is ordained. Changes must come. But how? The king would say that they were directed by the master-image. And now I felt my jowls, my snout; I did not dare to look down at what had happened to me. Hams. Tripes, a whole caldron full of them. Trunk, a fat cylinder. It seemed to me that I couldn't even breathe without grunting. Brother! I put my hand over my nose and mouth and looked with distressed eyes at the king. But he heard the guttural vibration of the vocal cords and said, "What is the peculiar noise you are making, Henderson-Sungo?"

"What does it sound like, King?"

"I don't know. An animal syllable? Oddly, you look well after your exertion."

"I don't feel so well. I'm not one of your summits. You know that as well as I do."

"You show the work of a powerful and original although blockaded imagination."

"Is that what you see?" I said.

He said, "What I see is greatly mixed. Fantastic elements have fought forth from your body. Excrescences. You are an exceptional amalgam of vehement forces." He sighed and gave a quiet smile; his mood was very quiet just then. He said, "We do not speak in blame terms. So many factors are mediating. Fomenting. Promulgating. Everyone is different. A billion small things unperceived by the object of their influence. True, pure intelligence does best it can, but who can judge? Negative and positive elements strive, and we can only look at them and wonder or weep. You may sometimes see a clear case of angel and vulture in collision. The eye is of heaven, the nose gives a certain flare. But face and body are the book of the soul, open to the reader of science and sympathy." Grunting, I looked at him.

"Sungo," he said, "listen painstakingly, and I will tell you what I have a strong conviction about." I did as he said, for I thought he might tell me something hopeful about myself. "The career of our specie," he said, "is evidence that one imagination after another grows literal. Not dreams. Not mere dreams. I say not mere dreams because they have a way of growing actual. At school in Malindi I read all of Bulfinch. And I say not mere dream. No. Birds flew, harpies flew, angels flew, Daedalus and son flew. And see here, it is no longer dreaming and story, for literally there is flying. You flew here, into Africa. All human accomplishment has this same origin, identically. Imagination is a force of nature. Is this not enough to make a person full of ecstasy? Imagination, imagination, imagination! It converts to actual. It sustains, it alters, it redeems! You see," he said, "I sit here in Africa and devote myself to this in personal fashion, to my best ability, I am convinced. What Homo sapiens imagines, he may slowly convert himself to. Oh, Henderson, how glad I am that you are here! I have longed for somebody to discuss with. A companion mind. You are a godsend to me."

XIX

AROUND the palace was a vegetable and mineral junkyard. The trees were niggardly and grew with gnarls and spikes. Then there were the flowers, which also lay in the Sungo's department. My girls watered them and they thrived in those white hollow stones. The sun made the red blossoms extremely sleek and taut. Daily, I would come up from the den all shaken by my roaring, my throat grated, my head in fever and my eyes like wet soot, weak in the legs, and especially delicate and trembling in the knees. All I needed then was the weight of the sun to make me feel like a convalescent. You know how it is about some people when they convalesce from wasting diseases. They become strangely sensitive; they go around and muse; little sights pierce them, they get sentimental; they see beauty in all the corners. So, watched by all, I would go and bend over those flowers, I would stoop hopelessly with my eyes of damp soot at the bowls of petrified mineral junk filled with soaked humus and sniff the flowers and grunt and sigh with a sort of heavy, beady wretchedness, the Sungo pants sticking to me and the hair on my head, especially at the back, thriving. I was growing black curls, thicker than usual, like a merino sheep, very black, and they were unseating my helmet. Maybe my mind, beginning to change sponsors, so to speak, was stimulating the growth of a different man.

Everybody knew where I was coming from, and I presume had heard me roaring. If I could hear Atti they could hear me. Watched by all, and watched dangerously by enemies, mine and the king's, I lumbered out into the yard and tried to smell the flowers. Not that they had a smell. They had only the color. But that was enough; it fell on my soul, clamoring, while Romilayu always came up behind to offer support, if needed. ("Romilayu, what do you think of these flowers? They are noisy as hell," I said.) At this time, when I must have seemed contaminated and dangerous due to contact with the lion, he did not shrink from me or seek safety in the background. He did not let me down. And since I love loyalty beyond anything else, I tried to show that I excused him from all his obligations to me. "You're a true pal," I said. "You deserve much more than a jeep from me. I want to add something to it." I patted him on the bushy head—my hand seemed very thick; each of my fingers felt like a yam—and then I grunted all the way back to my apartment. There I lay down to rest. I was all roared out. The very marrow was gone from my bones, so that they felt hollow. I lay on my side, heaving and groaning, with that expanded envelope, my belly. Sometimes I imagined that I was from the trotters to the helmet, all six feet four inches of me, the picture of that familiar animal, freckled on the belly, with broken tusks and wide cheekbones. True, inside, my heart ran with human feeling, but externally, in the rind if you like, I showed all the strange abuses and malformations of a lifetime.

To tell the truth, I didn't have full confidence in the king's science. Down there in the den, while I went through the utmost hell, he would idle around, calm, easy and almost languid. He would tell me that the lioness made him feel very peaceful. Sometimes as we lay on the trestle after my exercises, all three of us together, he would say, "It is very restful here. Why, I am floating. You must give yourself a chance. You must try. . . ." But I had almost blacked out, before, and I was not yet prepared to start floating.

Everything was black and amber, down there in the den. The stone walls themselves were yellowish. Then straw. Then dung. The dust was sulphur-colored. The skin of the lioness lightened gradually from the dark of the spine, toward the chest a ground-ginger shade, and on the belly white pepper, and under the haunches she became as white as the Arctic. But her small heels were black. Her eyes also were ringed absolutely with black. At times she had a meat flavor on her breath.

"You must try to make more of a lion of yourself," Dahfu insisted, and that I certainly did. Considering my handicaps, the king declared I was making progress. "Your roaring still is choked. Of course it is natural, as you have such a lot to purge," he would say. That was no lie, as everyone knows. I would have hated to witness my own antics and hear my own voice. Romilayu admitted he had heard me roar, and you couldn't blame the rest of the natives for thinking that I was Dahfu's understudy in the black arts, or whatever they accused him of practicing. But what the king called pathos was actually (I couldn't help myself) a cry which summarized my entire course on this earth, from birth to Africa; and certain words crept into my roars, like "God," "Help," "Lord have mercy," only they came out "Hooolp!" "Moooorcy!" It's funny what words sprang forth. "Au secours," which was "Secooooooooor" and also "De profooooondis," plus snatches from the "Messiah" (He was despised and rejected, a man of sorrows, etcetera). Unbidden, French sometimes comes back to me, the language in which I used to taunt my little friend François about his sister.

So I would roar and the king would sit with his arm about his lioness, as though they were attending an opera performance. She certainly looked very formal in attire. After a dozen or so of these agonizing efforts I would feel dim and dark within the brain and my arms and legs would give out.

Allowing me a short rest, he made me try again and again. Afterward he was very sympathetic. He would say, "I assume now you are feeling better, Mr. Henderson?"

"Yes, better."

"Lighter?"

"Sure, lighter, too, Your Honor."

"More calm?"

Then I would begin to snort. I was all jolted up within. My face was boiling; I was lying in the dust, and I would sit up to look at the two of them.

"How are your emotions?"

"Like a caldron, Your Highness, a regular caldron."

"I see you are laboring with a lifetime accumulation." Then he would say, almost pityingly, "You are still afraid of Atti?"

"Damn right I am. I'd sooner jump out of a plane. I wouldn't be half so scared. I applied for paratroops in the war. Come to think of it, Your Highness, I think I could bail out at fifteen thousand feet in these pants and stand a good chance."

"Your humor is delicious, Sungo."

This man was completely lacking in what we all know as civilized character.

"I am sure that you soon will begin to feel something of what it is to be a lion. I am convinced of your capacity. The old self is resisting?"

"Oh yes, I feel that old self more than ever," I said. "I feel it all the time. It's got a terrific grip on me." I began to cough and grunt, and I was in despair. "As if I were carrying an eight-hundred-pound load—like a Galápagos turtle. On my back."

"Sometimes a condition must worsen before bettering," he said, and he began to tell me of diseases he had known when he was on the wards as a student, and I tried to picture him as a medical student in white coat and white shoes instead of the velvet hat adorned with human teeth and the satin slippers. He held the lioness by the head; her broth-colored eyes watched me; those whiskers, suggesting diamond scratches, seemed so cruel that her own skin shrank from them at the base. She had an angry nature. What can you do with an angry nature?

This was why, when I returned from the den, I felt as I did in the torrid light of the yard, with its stone junk and the red flowers. Horko's bridge table was set up under the umbrella for lunch, but first I went to rest and get my wind back, and I would think, "Well, maybe every guy has his own Africa. Or if he goes to sea, his own ocean." By which I meant that as I was a turbulent individual, I was having a turbulent Africa. This is not to say, however, that I think the world exists for my sake. No, I really believe in reality. That's a known fact.

Each day I grew more aware that everybody knew where I had spent the morning and feared me for it—I had arrived like a dragon; maybe the king had sent for me to help him defy the Bunam and overturn the religion of the whole tribe. And I tried to explain to Romilayu at least that Dahfu and I were not practicing any evil. "Look, Romilayu," I told him, "the king just happens to have a very rich nature. He didn't have to come back and put himself at the mercy of his wives. He did it because he hopes to benefit the whole world. A fellow may do many a crazy thing, and as long as he has no theory about it we forgive him. But if there happens to be a theory behind his actions everybody is down on him. That's how it is with the king. But he isn't hurting me, old fellow. It's true it sounds like it, but don't you believe it. I make that noise of my own free will. If I don't look well, that's because I haven't been feeling well; I have a fever, and the inside of my nose and throat are inflamed. (Rhinitis?) I guess the king would give me something for it if I asked him but I don't feel like telling him."

"I don' blame you, sah."

"Don't get me wrong. The human race needs guys like this

king more than ever. Change must be possible! If not, it's too damn bad."

"Yes, sah."

"Americans are supposed to be dumb but they are willing to go into this. It isn't just me. You have to think about white Protestantism and the Constitution and the Civil War and capitalism and winning the West. All the major tasks and the big conquests were done before my time. That left the biggest problem of all, which was to encounter death. We've just got to do something about it. It isn't just me. Millions of Americans have gone forth since the war to redeem the present and discover the future. I can swear to you, Romilayu, there are guys exactly like me in India and in China and South America and all over the place. Just before I left home I saw an interview in the paper with a piano teacher from Muncie who became a Buddhist monk in Burma. You see, that's what I mean. I am a high-spirited kind of guy. And it's the destiny of my generation of Americans to go out in the world and try to find the wisdom of life. It just is. Why the hell do you think I'm out here, anyway?"

"I don' know, sah."

"I wouldn't agree to the death of my soul."

"Me Methdous, sah."

"I know it, but that would never help me, Romilayu. And please don't try to convert me, I'm in trouble enough as it is."

"I no bothah you."

"I know. You are standing by me in my hour of trial, God bless you for it. I also am standing by King Dahfu until he captures his father, Gmilo. When I get to be a friend, Romilayu, I am a devoted friend. I know what it is to lie buried in yourself. One thing I have learned, though I am a hard man to educate. I tell you, the king has a rich nature. I wish I could learn his secret."

Then Romilayu with the scars shining on his wrinkled face (manifestations of his former savagery) but with soft sympathetic eyes which contained a light that didn't come from the air (it could never have penetrated the shade, like an umbrella pine, that grew across his low forehead), wanted to know what secret I was trying to get from Dahfu.

"Why," I said, "there's something about danger that doesn't perplex the guy. Look at all the things he has to fear, and still look at the way he lies on that sofa. You've never seen that. He has an old green sofa upstairs which must have been brought by the elephants a century ago. And the way he lies on it, Romilayu! And the females wait on him. But on the table near him he has those two skulls used at the rain ceremony, one his father's and the other his grandfather's. Are you married, Romilayu?" I asked him.

"Yes, sah, two time. But now got one wife."

"Why, that's just like me. And I have five children, including twin boys about four years old. My wife is very big."

"Me, six children."

"Do you worry about them? It's a wild continent still, no two ways about that. I am all the time worrying lest my two little kids wander off in the woods. We ought to get a dog—a big dog. But we'll be living in town anyway from now on. I am going to go to school. Romilayu, I am going to send a letter to my wife, and you are going to take it to Baventai and mail it. I promised you baksheesh, old man, and here are the papers for the jeep, made over to you. I wish I could take you back to the States with me, but since you have a family it's not practical." His face expressed very little pleasure at the gift. It wrinkled especially hard, and as I knew him by now I said, "Hell, man, don't be toying with tears all the time. What's to cry over?"

"You in trouble, sah," he said.

"Yes, I know I am. But since I'm a reluctant type of fellow, life has decided to use strong measures on me. I am a shunner, Romilayu, and so this serves me right. What's the matter, old pal, do I look bad?"

"Yes, sah."

"My feelings always did leak into my looks," I said. "That's the type of constitution I have. Is it that woman's head they showed us that worries you?"

"Dem kill you, maybe?" said Romilayu.

"Okay, that Bunam is a bad actor. The guy is a scorpion. But don't forget I am the Sungo. Doesn't Mummah protect me? I think maybe my person is sacred. Besides, with my twenty-two neck they'd have to have two guys to strangle me. Ha, ha! You mustn't worry about me, Romilayu. As soon as this business with the king is completed and I have helped him capture his dad, I'll join you in Baventai."

"Please God, 'e mek quick," said Romilayu.

When I mentioned the Bunam to the king, he laughed at me. "When I possess Gmilo, I am absolute master," he said.

"But that animal is raging and killing out there in the savanna," I said, "and you act as though you had him safe in storage already."

"Lions do not often leave a given locale," he said. "Gmilo is near here. Any day he will be encountered. Go and write the letter to your missis," Dahfu told me, laughing very low on his green sofa amid his black troop of nude women.

"I'm going to write to her today," I said.

So I went down to have lunch with the Bunam and Horko. Horko, the Bunam, and the Bunam's black-leather man were always waiting for me at the bridge table under the umbrella. "Gentlemen . . ." "Asi Sungo," said everyone. I was always aware that these people had heard me roaring and probably could smell the odor of the den on me. But I brazened it out. The Bunam, when he did glance my way, which was rarely, was very somber. I thought, "I may get you first. No man can know that and you'd better not push me hard." The behavior of Horko on the other hand was invariably genial, and he hung out his red tongue and leaned over the little table with his knuckles like tree boles until it swayed with his weight. There was an air of intrigue under the transparent silk of the umbrella, while entertainers skipped for us out in the sun and feet flitted in and out of robes as Horko's people danced to amuse us and the old musician played his pendulum viol and others drummed and blew in the palace junkyard with its petrified brains of white stone and the red flowers growing in the humus.

After lunch came the daily water duty. The laboring women, with deep stress marks on the skin of their shoulders from the poles, carried me out into the lanes of the town where the dust of the ruts was reduced to a powder. The lone drum bumped after me; it seemed to warn people to stay away from this Henderson, the lion-contaminated Sungo. People still came to look at me out of curiosity, but not in their previous numbers, nor did they particularly want to be sprinkled by the crazy rain king. So that when we got to the dunghill at the center of town where the court was situated, I made a point of getting on my feet and sprinkling right and left. This was stoically taken. The magistrate in his crimson gown seemed as if he would have stopped me if he had had the power. However, nothing was done. The prisoner with the forked stick in his mouth leaned his face against the post he was tied to. "I hope you win, pal," I said to him and got back into my hammock.

That afternoon I wrote to Lily as follows:

"Honey, you are probably worried about me, but I suppose you have known all along that I was alive."

Lily claimed she could always tell how I was. She had some kind of privileged love-intuition.

"The flight here was spectacular."

Like hovering all the way inside a jewel.

"We are the first generation to see the clouds from both sides. What a privilege! First people dreamed upward. Now they dream both upward and downward. This is bound to change something, somewhere. For me the entire experience has been similar to a dream. I liked Egypt. Everybody was in basic white rags. From the air the mouth of the Nile looked like raveled rope. In some places the valley was green and it was yellow. The cataracts resembled seltzer. When we landed in Africa itself and Charlie and I put the show on the road, it wasn't exactly what I had hoped in leaving home." *As I discovered a pestilence when I entered the old lady's house and realized that I must put forth effort or go down in shame.* "Charlie did not relax in Africa. I was reading R. F. Burton's *First Footsteps in East Africa* plus Speke's *Journal*, and we didn't see eye to eye about any subject. So we parted company. Burton thought a lot of himself. He was very good with the épée and saber and he spoke everyone's language. I picture him as resembling General Douglas MacArthur in character, very conscious of having a historical role and thinking of classical Rome and Greece. Personally, I had to decide to follow a different course, as by any civilized standard I am done for. However, the geniuses love common life a great deal."

When he got back to England, Speke blew his brains out. This

*biographical detail I spared Lily. By genius I mean somebody like
Plato or Einstein. Light itself was all Einstein needed. What
could be more common?*

"There was a fellow around named Romilayu, and we became friends, though at first he was scared of me. I asked him
to show me uncivilized parts of Africa. There are very few of
these left. There are modern governments springing up and
educated classes. I myself have met such educated African royalty and am the guest right now of a king who is almost an
M.D. Nevertheless, I am off the beaten track, without question, and I have Romilayu (he is a wonderful guy) and Charlie
himself, indirectly, to thank for that. To a certain extent it has
been terrible, and continues to be. A few times I could have
given up my soul as easily as a fish lets out a bubble. You know,
Charlie is not a bad egg, at heart. But I shouldn't have come
along on a honeymoon trip. I was a fifth wheel. She is one of
those Madison Avenue dollies who have their back teeth
pulled to produce a fashionable look (sunken cheeks)."

*But on further recollection I see that the bride could never in
the world forgive me for my behavior at the wedding. I was best
man, and it was a formal occasion, and it wasn't only that I
didn't kiss her, but that I was somehow alone in the cab with her
instead of Charlie on the way down to Gemignano's restaurant
after the ceremony. In my inside pocket, rolled up, was a sheet of
music—Mozart's "Turkish Rondo" for two violins. I was drunk;
how did I get through a violin lesson? At Gemignano's I was very
obnoxious. I said, Is this Parmesan cheese or is it Rinso? I spat it
out on the tablecloth, and after this I blew my nose in my foulard.
Curse my memory for being so complete!*

"Did you send a wedding present for me or not? We must
send a present. Get some steak knives, for God's sake. I want
to tell you that I owe Charlie a lot. Without him I might have
gone to the Arctic instead, among the Eskimos. This experience in Africa has been tremendous. It has been tough, it has
been perilous, it has been something! But I've matured twenty
years in twenty days."

*Lily would not sleep in the igloo with me, but I continued my
polar experiments anyway. I snared a few rabbits. I practiced
spear-throwing. I built a sled, following the descriptions in the*

books. Four or five coats of frozen urine on the runners and they scooted over the snow like steel. I am positive that I could have arrived at the Pole. But I don't think I would have found what I was looking for there. In that case, I would have overwhelmed the world from the North with my trampling. If I couldn't have my soul it would cost the earth a catastrophe.

"Here they don't know what tourists are, and therefore I'm not a tourist. There was a woman who told her friend, 'Last year we went around the world. This year I think we're going somewhere else.' Ha, ha! Sometimes the mountains here seem very porous, yellow and brown, and remind me of those old molasses sponge candies. I have my own room in the palace. This is a very primitive part of the world. Even the rocks look primitive. From time to time I have a smoldering fever. It feels like one of those coal mines that have been sealed because of combustion. Otherwise I seem to have benefited physically here, except that I have a persistent grunt. I wonder if this is new, or did you ever notice it at home?

"How are the twins and Ricey and Edward? I would like to stop in Switzerland on the way home and see little Alice. I may have my teeth looked after, too, while in Geneva. You might tell Dr. Spohr for me that the bridge broke one morning at breakfast. Send me the spare c/o American Embassy, Cairo. It is in the trunk of the convertible under the wire spring that fastens the jack to the spare tire. I put it there for safekeeping.

"I promised Romilayu a bonus if he would take me off the beaten track. We have made two stops. Humankind has to sway itself more intentionally toward beauty. I met a person who is called The Woman of Bittahness. She looked like a fat old lady, merely, but she had tremendous wisdom and when she took a look at me she thought I was a kind of odd ball, but that didn't faze her, and she said a couple of marvelous things. First she told me that the world was strange to me. It is strange to a child. But I am no child. This gave me pleasure and pain, both."

The Kingdom of Heaven is for children of the spirit. But who is this nosy, gross phantom?

"Of course there's strangeness and strangeness. One kind of strangeness may be a gift, and another kind a punishment. I wanted to tell the old lady that everybody understands life except me—how did she account for it? I seem to be a very vain and foolish, rash person. How did I get so lost? And never mind whose fault it is, how do I get back?"

It is very early in life, and I am out in the grass. The sun flames and swells; the heat it emits is its love, too. I have this self-same vividness in my heart. There are dandelions. I try to gather up this green. I put my love-swollen cheek to the yellow of the dandelions. I try to enter into the green.

"Then she told me I had grun-tu-molani, which is a native term hard to explain but on the whole it indicates that you want to live, not die. I wanted her to tell more about it. Her hair was like fleece and her belly smelled like saffron; she had a cataract in one eye. I'm afraid I will never be able to see her again, because I goofed and we had to get out. I can't go into details. But without Prince Itelo's friendship I might have been in serious trouble. I thought I had lost my opportunity to study my life with the aid of a really wise person, and I was very downcast over it. But I love Dahfu, king of the second tribe we came to. I am with him now and have been given an honorary title, King of the Rain, which is merely standard, I guess, like getting the key to the city from Jimmy Walker used to be. A costume goes with it. But I am not in a position to tell you much more, except in general terms. I am participating in an experiment with the king (almost an M.D., I told you) and this is an ordeal, daily." *The animal's face is pure fire to me. Every day, I have to close my eyes.*

"Lily, I probably haven't said this lately, but I have true feeling for you, baby, which sometimes wrings my heart. You can call it love. Although personally I think that word is full of bluff." *Especially for somebody like me, called from nonexistence into existence: what for? What have I got to do with husbands' love or wives' love? I am too peculiar for that kind of stuff.*

"When Napoleon was out at St. Helena, he talked a lot about morals. It was a little late. A lot he cared for them. So I'm not going to discuss love with you. If you think you are in the clear you can go ahead and talk about it. You said you couldn't live for sun, moon, and stars alone. You said your mother was dead when she wasn't, which was certainly very neurotic of you. You got engaged a hundred times and were always out of breath. You conned me. Is this how love acts? All right, then. But I expected you to help me. This king here is one of the most intelligent people in the world, and I have great faith in him, and he tells me I should move from the states that I myself make into the states which are of themselves. Like if I stopped making such a noise all the time I might hear something nice. I might hear a bird. Are the wrens still nesting in the cornices? I saw the straw sticking out and was amazed that they could get inside." *I could never take after the birds. I would crash all the branches. I would have scared the pterodactyl from the skies.*

"I am giving up the violin. I guess I will never reach my object through it," *to raise my spirit from the earth, to leave the body of this death. I was very stubborn. I wanted to raise myself into another world. My life and deeds were a prison.*

"Well, Lily, everything is going to be different from now on. When I get back I am going to study medicine. My age is against it, but that's just too damn bad, I'm going to do it anyway. You can't imagine how keen I am to get into the laboratory. I can still remember the smell of those places. Formaldehyde. I'll be among a bunch of young kids, I realize, doing chemistry and zoology and physiology and physics and math and anatomy. I expect it to be quite an ordeal, especially dissecting the cadaver." *"Once more, Death, you and me."* "However, I have had to have dealings with the dead anyway and haven't made a buck on any of them. I might as well do something in the interests of life, for a change." *What is it, now, this great instrument? Played wrong, why does it suffer so? Right, how can it achieve so much, reaching even God?* "Bones, muscles, glands, organs. Osmosis. I want you to enroll me at Medical Center and give my name as Leo E. Henderson. The reason for that I will tell you when I get home. Aren't you excited? Dearest girl, as a doctor's wife you'll have to be more clean, bathe more often and wash your things. You will have to get used to broken sleep, night calls and all of that. I haven't decided yet where to practice. I guess if I tried it at home I'd scare the neighbors to pieces. If I put my ear against their chests as an M.D., they'd jump out of their skins.

"Therefore, I may apply for missionary work, like Dr. Wilfred Grenfell or Albert Schweitzer. Hey! Axel Munthe—how about him? Naturally China is out, now. They might catch us and brain-wash us. Ha, ha! But we might try India. I do want to get my hands on the sick. I want to cure them. Healers are sacred." *I have been so bad myself I believe there must be a virtue in me, finally.* "Lily, I'm going to quit knocking myself out."

I don't think the struggles of desire can ever be won. Ages of longing and willing, willing and longing, and how have they ended? In a draw, dust and dust.

"If Medical Center won't let me in, apply first to Johns Hopkins and then to every other joint in the book. Another reason why I want to stop in Switzerland is to look into the medical-school situation. I could talk to people there, explain things, and maybe they would let me in.

"So get busy, dear, with those letters, and another thing: sell the pigs. I want you to sell Kenneth the Tamworth boar and Dilly and Minnie. Get rid of them.

"We are funny creatures. We don't see the stars as they are, so why do we love them? They are not small gold objects but endless fire."

Strange? Why shouldn't it be strange? It is strange. It is all strange.

"I haven't been drinking at all, here, except for a few nips taken while writing this letter. At lunch they serve you a native beer called 'pombo' which is pretty good. They ferment the pineapple. Everybody is very animated here. Folks with feathers, folks with ribbons, with scarf decorations, rings, bracelets, beads, shells, gold walnuts. Some of the harem women walk like giraffes. Their faces slope forward. The king's face has very much of a slope. He is very brilliant and opinionated.

"Sometimes I feel as though I had a whole troop of pygmies jumping up and down inside me, yelling and carrying on. Isn't that odd? Other times I am very calm, calmer than I have ever been.

"The king believes that one should have a suitable image of himself. . . ."

I believe that I tried to explain to Lily what Dahfu's ideas were, but Romilayu lost the last few pages of the letter, and I suppose that it's just as well that he did, for when I wrote them

I had had quite a bit to drink. In one I think I said, or maybe I merely thought it, "I had a voice that said, I want! *I* want? I? It should have told me *she* wants, *he* wants, *they* want. And moreover, it's love that makes reality reality. The opposite makes the opposite."

XX

Romilayu and I said good-by in the morning and when he finally set off with the letter to Lily I had a very unwholesome feeling. My very stomach seemed to drop as his wrinkled face looked through the closing gates of the palace. I believe that he expected at the last minute to be called back by his changeable and irrational employer. But I only stood there in the carapace-like helmet and those pants which made me seem as though I had gotten lost from my troop of Zouaves. The gate shut on Romilayu's scarred and seamed gaze, and I felt unreasonably low. But Tamba and Bebu diverted me from my sadness. As usual they saluted me by lying in the dust and putting my foot on their heads, and then Tamba settled herself on her belly so that Bebu might do the joxi with her feet. She trod her back, spine, neck, and buttocks, which seemed to give Tamba heavenly pleasure. She closed her eyes, groaning and basking. I thought I must try this one day; it must be beneficial, it contented these people so; however, this was not the day for it, I was too sad.

The air was warming quickly but there were still arrears of the stinging cold of night; I felt it through the thin green stuff I wore. The mountain, the one named for Hummat, was yellow; the clouds were white and had great weight. They lay at about the height of Hummat's throat and shoulders, like a collar. Indoors, I sat and waited for the morning to increase in warmth, hands folded, mentally preparing for my daily exposure to Atti while I earnestly tried to reason: I must change. I must not live on the past, it will ruin me. The dead are my boarders, eating me out of house and home. The hogs were my defiance. I was telling the world that it was a pig. I must begin to think how to live. I must break Lily from blackmail and set love on a true course. Because after all Lily and I were very lucky. But then what could an animal do for me? In the last analysis? Really? A beast of prey? Even supposing that an animal enjoys a natural blessing? We had our share of this creature-blessing until infancy ended. But now aren't we required to complete something else—project number two—the second blessing? I couldn't tell such things to the king, he was so stuck on lions. I have never seen a person so gone on any creatures. And I couldn't refuse to do what he wanted owing to the way I felt about him. Yes, in some ways the fellow was remarkably like a lion, but that didn't prove lions had made him so. This was more of Lamarck. In college we had laughed Lamarck right out of the classroom. I remembered what the teacher said, that this was a bourgeois idea of the autonomy of the individual mind. All sons of rich men, we were, or almost all, and yet we laughed at the bourgeois ideas until we almost split a gut. Well, I reflected, wrinkling my brow to the limit, missing Romilayu keenly, this is the payoff of a lifetime of action without thought. If I had to shoot at that cat, if I had to blow up frogs, if I had to pick up Mummah without realizing what I was getting myself into, it was not out of line to crouch on all fours and roar and act the lion. I might have been learning about the grun-tu-molani instead, under Willatale. But I will never regret my feeling toward this man—Dahfu, I mean; I would have done a great deal more to keep his friendship.

So I was brooding in my palace room when Tatu came in, wearing the ancient Italian garrison cap. Thinking this was the daily summons to join the king in the den, I heavily got up, but she began to tell me by word and gesture that I should stay where I was and wait for the king. He was coming.

"What's up?" I said. However, nobody could explain, and I tidied myself a little in anticipation of the king's visit; I had let myself grow filthy and bearded, as it was scarcely suitable to get all cleaned up in order to stand on all fours, roaring and tearing the earth. Today, however, I went to Mummah's cistern and washed my face, my neck, and my ears and let the sun dry me on the threshold of my apartment. It soon did. Meanwhile I regretted that I had sent Romilayu away so soon, for this morning brought to mind more things that I should have told Lily. That wasn't all I had to say, I thought. I love her. By God! I goofed again. But I didn't have much time to spend on regret, for Tatu was coming toward me across the rough yard of the palace, gesturing with both arms and saying, "Dahfu. Dahfu ala-mele." I rose and she led me through the passages of the ground floor to the king's outdoor court. Already he was in his hammock, under the purple shadow of his giant silk umbrella. He held his velvet hat in his fist and beckoned with it, and when he saw me above him his swelled lips opened. He fitted the hat over his raised knee and said, smiling, "I suppose you gather what day it is."

"I figure—"

"Yes, it is the day. Lion day for me."

"This is it, eh?"

"Bait has been eaten by a young male. He fit the description of Gmilo."

"Well, it must be great," I said, "to think you are going to be reunited with a dear parent. I only wish such a thing could happen to me."

"Well, Henderson," he said (this morning he took an exceptional pleasure in my company and conversation), "do you believe in immortality?"

"There's many a soul that would tell you it could never stay another round with life," I said.

"Do you really say so? But you know more of the world than I do. However, Henderson, my good friend, this is a high occasion for me."

"Is there a good chance that it is your dad, the late king? I wish I had known. I wouldn't have sent Romilayu away. He left this morning. Your Highness. Could we send a runner after him?"

The king paid no attention to this, and I figured his excitement was running too high to allow him to consider my practical arrangements. What was Romilayu to him on a day like this?

"You will share the hopo with me," he said, and, although I didn't know what this meant, I of course agreed. My own umbrella approached, this hollow or sheath of green with transverse fibers in the silk transparency which helped to convince me that it was no vision but an object, for why should a vision bother to have such transverse lines? Eh? The pole was held by big female hands. Bearers brought my hammock.

"Do we go after the lion in a hammock?" I said.

"When we reach the bush we will continue on our feet," he said.

So I got into the hammock of the Sungo with one of those heavy utterances of mine, sinking into it. It looked to me as if the two of us were going out barehanded to capture the animal—this lion, that had eaten the old bull, and was sleeping deeply somewhere in the standing grass.

Shaven-headed women flitted near us, shrill and nervous, and a gaudy crowd had collected, just as on the day of the rain ceremony—drummers, men in paint, shells, and feathers, and buglers who blew some practice blasts. The bugles were about a foot long and had big mouths of green oxide metal. They made a devil of a blast, like the taunt of fear, those instruments. So with the bugles and drums and rattles and noisemakers of the beaters' party gathered around us, we were carried through the gates of the palace. The arms of the amazons shook with the strain of lifting me. Various people came and looked at me as we were going into the town; they gazed down into the hammock. Among them were the Bunam and Horko, the latter expecting me, I felt, to say something to him. However, I didn't say a word.

I looked back at them with my huge red face. The beard had begun to grow out like a broom and the fever, which had gone up again, affected my eyes and ears. A tremor in the cheeks occasionally surprised me; I could do nothing about this, and I reckoned that under the influence of lions the nerves of my jaws and nose and chin were undergoing an unsettling change. The Bunam had come in order to communicate with me or warn me; I could see that. I wanted to demand my H and H Magnum with the scope sights from him but of course I didn't have the words for "give" and "gun." The women struggled with my weight and the hammock bulged out greatly at the bottom and nearly touched the ground. The poles were almost too much for their shoulders as they carried the brutal white rain king with his swarthy, reddened face and dirty helmet and gaudy pants and big, hairy shins. The people whooped and clapped and leaped up and down in their rags and hides, flaunting pieces of dyed hair as pennants, women with babies that swung at their long spongy breasts and fellows with teeth broken or missing. As far as I could tell they were not enthusiastic for the king; they demanded that he bring home Gmilo, the right lion, and get rid of the sorceress, Atti. Without a sign he passed among them in his hammock. I knew his face was bathed by the shadow of the purple umbrella, and he was wearing his large velvet hat, as attached to it as I was to the helmet. Hat, hair, and face were in close union under the tinged light of the silk arch, and he lay and rested with that same sumptuous ease which I had admired from the beginning. Above him, as above me, strange hands clasped the ornamented pole of the umbrella. The sun now shone with power and covered the mountains and the stones close at hand with shimmering layers. Near to the ground it was about to materialize into gold leaf. The huts were holes of darkness and the thatch had a sick, broken radiance over it.

Until we got to the town limits I kept saying to myself, "Reality! Oh, reality! Damn you anyhow, reality!"

In the bush the women set me down and I stepped from the hammock onto the blazing ground. This was the hard-packed white, solar-looking rock. The king, too, was standing. He looked back at the crowd, which had remained near the wall of the town. With the game-beaters was the Bunam, and, following very closely, a white creature, a man completely dyed or calcimined. Under the coat of chalk I recognized him. It was the Bunam's man, the executioner. I identified him by the folds of his narrow face in this white metamorphosis.

"What's the idea of this?" I asked, going up to Dahfu over the packed stone and the stubble of weeds.

"No idea," the king said.

"Is he always like this at a lion hunt?"

"No. Different days, different colors, according to the reading of the omens. White is not the best omen."

"What are they trying to pull off here? They're giving you a bad send-off."

The king behaved as though he could not be bothered. Any human lion would have done as he did. Nevertheless he was irritated if not pierced by this. I made a very heavy half turn to stare at this ill-omened figure that had come to injure the king's self-confidence on the eve of this event, reunion with the soul of his father. "This whitewash is serious?" I said to the king.

Widely separated, his eyes had two separate looks; as I spoke to him they mingled again into one. "They intend it so."

"Sire," I said, "you want me to do something?"

"What thing?"

"You name it. On a day like this to be interfered with is dangerous, isn't it? It ought to be dangerous for them, too."

"Oh? No. What?" he said. "They are living in the old universe. Why not? That is part of my bargain with them, isn't it?" Something of the gold tinge of the stones came into his smile, brilliantly. "Why, this is my great day, Mr. Henderson. I can afford all the omens. After I have captured Gmilo they can say nothing more."

"Sticks and stones will break my bones but this is idle superstition, and so forth. Well, Your Highness, if that's the way you take it, fine, okay." I looked into the rising heat, which borrowed color from the stones and plants. I had expected the king to speak harshly to the Bunam and his follower who was painted with the color of bad omen, but he only made one remark to them. His face appeared very full under that velvet hat with the large brim and the crown full of soft variations. The umbrellas had stayed behind. The women, the king's wives, stood at the low wall of the town at assorted heights; they watched and cried certain (I suppose farewell) things. The stones paled more and more with the force of the heat. The women sent strange cries of love and encouragement or warning or good-by. They waved, they sang, and they signed with the two umbrellas, which went up and down. The beaters, silent, had not stopped for us but went away with the bugles, spears, drums, and rattles, in a solid body. There were sixty or seventy of them, and they started from us in a mass but gradually dispersed toward the bush. Antlike they began to spread into the golden weeds and boulders of the slope. These boulders, as noted before, were like gross objects combed down from above by an ignorant force.

The departure of the beaters left the Bunam, the Bunam's wizard, the king, and myself, the Sungo, plus three attendants with spears standing about thirty yards from the town.

"What did you tell them?" I asked the king.

"I have said to the Bunam I would accomplish my purpose notwithstanding."

"You should give them each a kick in the tail," I said, scowling at the two guys.

"Come, Henderson, my friend," Dahfu said, and we began to walk. The three men with spears fell in behind us.

"What are these fellows for?"

"To help maneuver in the hopo," he said. "You will see when we come to the small end of the place. That is better than explanation."

As we went down into the high grass of the bush he raised his sloping face with the smooth low-bridged nose and scented the air. I breathed it in, too. Dry and fine, it had an odor like fermented sugar. I began to be aware of the tremble of insects as they played their instruments underneath the stems, down at the very base of the heat.

The king began to go quickly, not so much walking as bounding, and as we followed, the spearmen and I, it occurred to me that the grass was high enough to conceal almost any animal except an elephant and that I didn't have so much as a diaper pin to defend myself with.

"King," I said. "Hisst. Wait a minute." I couldn't raise my voice here; I sensed that this was not the time to make a noise. He probably didn't like this, for he wouldn't stop, but I kept on calling in low tones and finally he waited for me. Greatly worked up, I stared into his eyes at close range, fought a few moments for air, and then said, "Not even a weapon? Just like this? Are you supposed to catch this animal by the tail?"

He decided to be patient with me. I could see the decision being taken. This I would swear to. "The animal, and I hope it is Gmilo, is probably within the area of the hopo. See here, Henderson, I must not be armed. What if I were to wound Gmilo?" He spoke of this possibility with horror. I had failed before (what was the matter with me?) to observe how profoundly excited he was. I had not seen through his cordiality.

"What if?"

"My life would be required as for any harm to a living king."

"And what about me—I'm not supposed to defend myself either?"

He did not answer for a moment. Then he said, "You are with me."

There was nothing I could say after that. I decided that I would do the best I could with my helmet, which would be to strike the animal on the muzzle and confuse it. I grumbled that he would have been better off in Syria or Lebanon as a mere student, and, although I spoke unclearly, he understood me and said, "Oh, no, Henderson-Sungo. I am lucky and you know it." In his close-fitting breeches, he set off again. My trousers hampered me as I rushed over the ground behind him. As for the three men with spears, they gave me very little confidence. Any minute I expected the lion to burst on me like an eruption of fire, to knock me down and tear me into flames of blood. The king mounted on a boulder and drew me up with him. He said, "We are near the north wall of the hopo." He pointed it out. It was built of ragged thorns and dead growths of all sorts, heaped and piled to a thickness of two or three feet. Coarse, croaky-looking flowers grew there; they were red and orange and at the center they were blotted with black, and it gave me a sore throat just to look at them. This hopo was a giant funnel or triangle. At the base it was open, while at the apex or spout was the trap. Only one of the two sides was built by human hands. The other was a natural formation of rock, the bank of an old river, probably, which rose to the height of a cliff. Beside the high wall of brush and thorn was a path which the king's feet found under the spiky yellow grass. We continued toward the small end of the hopo over fallen ribs of branches and twists of vine. From the hips, which were small, his figure broadened or loomed greatly toward the shoulders. He walked with powerful legs and small buttocks.

"You certainly are on fire to come to grips with this animal," I said.

Sometimes I think that pleasure comes only from having your own way, and I couldn't help feeling that this was assimilated by the king from the lions. To have your will, that's what pleasure is, in spite of all the thought that has been done. And he was dragging me along with the power of his personal greatness, because he was so brilliant and had a strong gift of life, manifested in the smoky, bluish trembling of his extra shadow. Because he was bound to have his way. And therefore I lumbered after him without a weapon for protection unless you counted the helmet, unless I could pull down these green pants and bag the animal in them—they might almost have been roomy enough for that.

Then he stopped and turned to me, and said, "You were equally on fire when it came to lifting up the Mummah."

"That's correct, Your Highness," I said. "But did I know what I was doing? No, I didn't."

"But I do."

"Well, okay, King," I said. "It's not for me to question it. I'll do whatever you say. But you told me that the Bunam and the other fellow in the white pigment were from the old universe and I assumed you were out of it."

"No, no. Do you know how to replace the whole thing? It cannot be done. Even if, on supreme moments, there is no old and is no new, but only an essence which can smile at our arrangement—smile even at being human. That is so full of itself," he said. "Nevertheless a play of life has to be allowed. Arrangements must be made." Here his mind was somewhat beyond me, so I didn't interfere with him, and he said, "To Gmilo, the lion Suffo was his father. To me, grandfather. Gmilo, my father. As, if I am going to be the king of the Wariri, it has to be. Otherwise, how am I the king?"

"Okay, I get you," I said. "King," I told him, and I spoke so earnestly it might almost have sounded like a series of threats, "you see these hands? This is your second pair of hands. You see this trunk?" I put my hand on my chest. "It is your reservoir, like. Your Highness, in case anything is going to happen, I want you to understand how I feel." My heart was very much aroused. I began to suffer in the face. In recognition of the fellow's nobleness, I fought to spare him the grossness of my emotions. This was in the shade of the hopo wall, under the embroidery of stiff thorns. The narrow track along the hopo was black and golden, as when grass burns in broad daylight and the heat is visible.

"Thank you, Mr. Henderson. I have understood how you feel." After a quiet hesitation, he said, "Should I guess? Death is on your mind?"

"It's on my mind, all right."

"Oh yes, very much. You are exceptionally given to it."

"Over the years, I've gotten involved with it a lot."

"Exceptionally. Exceptionally," he said as if he were discussing one of my problems with me. "Sometimes I think it is helpful to think of burial in a relation to the earth's crust.

What is the radius? Four thousand five hundred miles more or less, to the core of the earth. No, graves are not deep but insignificant, a mere few feet from the surface and not far from fearing and desiring. More or less the same fear, more or less the same desire for thousands of generations. Child, father, father, child doing the same. Fear the same. Desire the same. Upon the crust, beneath the crust, again and again and again. Well, Henderson, what are the generations for, please explain to me? Only to repeat fear and desire without a change? This cannot be what the thing is for, over and over and over. Any good man will try to break the cycle. There is no issue from that cycle for a man who do not take things into his hands."

"Oh, King, wait a minute. Once out of the light, it's enough. Does it have to be four thousand five hundred miles to be the grave? How can you talk like that?" But I understood him all the same. All you hear from guys is desire, desire, desire, knocking its way out of the breast, and fear, striking and striking. Enough already! Time for a word of truth. Time for something notable to be heard. Otherwise, accelerating like a stone, you fall from life to death. Exactly like a stone, straight into deafness, and till the last repeating *I want I want I want*, then striking the earth and entering it forever! As a matter of fact, I thought, out in the African sun from which the hooked wall of thorn temporarily cooled me: It's a pleasure when harsh objects like thorns do something for you. Under the black barbs that the bushes had crocheted above us, I thought it out and agreed: the grave was relatively shallow. You couldn't go many miles inside before you found the molten part of the earth. Mainly nickel, I think—nickel, cobalt, pitchblende, or what they call the magma. Almost as it was torn from the sun.

"Let us go," he said. I followed him more willingly after that short talk. He could convince me of almost anything. For his sake I accepted the discipline of being like a lion. Yes, I thought, I believed I could change; I was willing to overcome my old self; yes, to do that a man had to adopt some new standard; he must even force himself into a part; maybe he must deceive himself a while, until it begins to take; his own hand paints again on that much-painted veil. I would never make a lion, I knew that; but I might pick up a small gain here and there in the attempt.

I can't be sure that I have reported accurately all the things the king said. I may have spoiled some of them a little so that I could assimilate them.

Anyway, I followed him empty-handed toward the end of the hopo. Probably the lion had already wakened, for the beaters, about three miles away, had begun to make their noise. It sounded very distant, far out in the golden stripes of the bush. An air-blue, sleepy heat wavered in front of us, and while I squinted against the sprays and flashes of sunlight I saw a sudden elevation in the hopo wall. It was a thatched shelter which sat on a platform, twenty-five or thirty feet in the air. A ladder of vines hung down, and the king took hold of it eagerly, this crude, slack-looking thing. He began to climb it sailor fashion, from the side, pulling himself powerfully and steadily up to the platform. From the dry grass and brown fibers of the doorway he said, "Take hold, Mr. Henderson." He had crouched to hold out the ladder to me and I saw his head, on which was the pleated, tooth-sewn hat, only slightly above his powerful knees. Illness, strangeness, and danger combined and ganged up on me. Instead of an answer, a sob came out of me. It must have been laid down early in my life, for it was stupendous and rose from me like a great sea bubble from the Atlantic floor.

"What is the matter, Mr. Henderson?" Dahfu said.

"God knows."

"Is something wrong with you?"

I kept my head lowered as I shook it. The roaring I had done, I believe, had loosened my whole structure and liberated some things which belonged at the bottom. And this was no time to trouble the king, on his great day of joy.

"I'm coming, Your Highness," I said.

"Take a moment's breath if you need it."

He walked about on the platform under the elevated hut, then came back to the edge again. He looked down from that fragile dome of straw. "Now?" he said.

"Will it bear our weight, up there?"

"Come on, come on, Henderson," he said.

I took hold of the ladder and began climbing, placing both feet on each rung. The spearmen had stood and waited until I (the Sungo) joined the king. Now they passed under the ladder and took up a position around the corner of the hopo.

Here, at the end, the construction was primitive but seemed thorough. A barred gate would be dropped to trap the lion after the other game had been driven through, and the men would prod the animal into position with their spears so that the king could effect the capture.

On the fragile ladder, which wavered under my weight, I reached the platform and sat down on the floor of poles lashed together. It was like a heat-borne raft. I began to size up the situation. The whole setup was no deeper than a thimble when compared to the volume offered by a full-grown lion.

"This is it?" I said to the king after I had studied the layout.

"As you see it," he said.

Now on the platform stood this shell of straw, and from the opening on the interior side of the hopo I saw suspended a woven cage weighted with rocks at the bottom. It was bell-shaped and made of semi-rigid vines which were, however, as tough as cables. A vine rope passed through a pulley suspended from a pole which was attached at one end to the roof-tree of the hut and at the other was fixed into the side of the cliff, a width of ten or twelve feet. Below it ran another pole from the floor of the hut; it too was set in the rock at the other end. On this pole or catwalk, no wider than my wrist, if that wide, the king would balance himself with the rope and the bell-shaped net, and when the lion was driven in Dahfu would center the net and let it drop. Releasing his rope, he was supposed to capture the lion.

"This . . . ?"

"What do you think?" he said.

I couldn't bring myself to say much about it, but, hard as I fought my feelings, I couldn't submerge them—not on this particular day. I was visibly struggling with them.

He said, "I captured Atti here."

"Yes, with this same rig?"

"And Gmilo captured Suffo."

I said, "Take the advice of a . . . I know that I'm not much . . . But I think the world of you, Your Highness. Don't . . ."

"Why, what is the matter with your chin, Mr. Henderson? It is moving up and down."

I brought my upper teeth down on my lip. By and by I said,

"Your Highness, excuse it. I'd rather cut my throat than demoralize you on a day like this. But does the thing have to be done from up here?"

"It must."

"Can't there be an innovation? I'd do anything, drug the animal . . . give him a Mickey . . ."

"Thank you, Henderson," he said. I think his gentleness with me was more than I deserved. He didn't remind me in so many words that he was king of the Wariri. I soon reminded myself of this fact. He allowed me to be present—his companion. I must not interfere.

"Oh, Your Majesty," I said.

"Yes, Henderson, I know. You are a man of many qualities. I have observed," he said.

"I thought maybe I fitted into one of your bad types," I said.

At this he laughed somewhat. He was sitting cross-legged at the opening of the hut that faced the hopo and the cliff, and he began to enumerate, half musingly, "The agony, the appetite, the immune, the hollow, and all of that. No, I promise you, Henderson, that I have never classified you with a bad group. You are a compound. Maybe a large amount of agony. Maybe a small touch of the Lazarus. But I cannot fully subsume you. No rubric will fully hold you. Maybe because we are friends. One sees much more in a friend. Rubrics will not do with friends."

"I had a little too much business with a certain type of creature for my own good," I said. "If I had it to do over again, it would be different."

We sat on the shaky platform under the gold straw belfry of thatch. The light was finely grated on the floor. We crouched, waiting under the fibers and straw. The odor of plants came up on the air-blue heat in gusts, and because of my fever I had a feeling that I had found, in midair, a changing point between matter and light. I was watching it being carried from within and thought I saw crying and writhing outside. Not able to stand this sense of things, I got up and stepped on the pole the king was supposed to balance on.

"What are you doing?"

I was trying it out for him. I said, "I am checking on the Bunam."

"You must not stand there, Henderson."

My weight was bowing the wood, but there was no crackling, it was a very hard wood and I was satisfied by the test. I lifted myself back to the platform and we sat together, or crouched, outside the grass wall of the shelter on a narrow projection of the floor, almost within reach of the weighted trap which hung waiting. Opposite us was the cliff of gritty rock, and, following the line of it beyond the end of the hopo, over the heads of the waiting spearmen, I saw a sort of small stone building deep in the ravine. I hadn't noticed it before because in this ravine, or gorge, there was a small forest of cactuses which produced a red bud, or berry, or flower, and this partly blocked it from view.

"Does somebody live there, below?"

"No."

"Is it abandoned? Used? In our part of the country, where farming has gone to hell, you come across old houses everywhere. But that's a crazy place for a residence," I said.

The rope by which the cage or net was slung had been tied to the doorpost, and the king's head was resting against the knot. "It is not for living," he told me without glancing toward the building.

A tomb? I thought. Whose tomb?

"I think they are driving rapidly. Ah! Do you think you can see them? It is getting loud." He stood, and I did too, and shaded my eyes from the glare while I strained my forehead.

"No, I don't see."

"I neither, Henderson. This is the most hard part. I have waited all my life, and we are within the last hour."

"Well, Your Highness," I said, "for you it should be easy. You have known these animals all your life. You are bred for this; you are a pro. If there's anything I love to see, it's a guy who's good at his work. Whether it's a rigger or steeplejack or window-washer or any person who has strong nerves and a skilled body . . . You had me worried when you started that skull dance, but after a minute of it I would have backed you to my last dime." And I took out my wallet, which I kept taped to the inside of the helmet, and to make these moments easier for him, within the rising blare of the horns and the constant running of the drums (while we sat as if marooned in the illuminated air), I said, "Your Highness, did I ever show you these pictures of my wife and children?" I started to look for them in the bulky wallet. I had my passport there, and four one-thousand-dollar bills, taking no chances on traveler's checks in Africa. "Here's my wife. We spent a lot of money on a portrait and had difficulties all through. I begged her not to hang it and almost had a nervous breakdown over it. But this photograph of her is a beauty." In it Lily wore a low-necked dress of polka dots. She looked very amused. It was toward me that she was smiling, for I was at the camera. She was saying affectionately that I was a fool; I probably had been clowning around. Owing to the smile her cheeks were high and full; in the picture you couldn't tell how pure and pale her color was. The king took it from me, and I have to hand it to him that at a moment like this he could contemplate Lily's picture.

"She is a serious person," he said.

"Do you think she looks like a doctor's wife?"

"I think she looks like any serious person's wife."

"But I guess she wouldn't agree about your species idea, Your Highness, because she decided that I was the only fellow in the world she could marry. One God, one husband, I guess. Well, here are the kids. . . ."

Without comment he looked at Ricey and Edward, little Alice in Switzerland, the twins. "They are not identical, Your Majesty, but they both cut their first tooth on the same day." The next flap of celluloid held a snapshot of myself; I was in the red robe and hunting cap with the violin under my chin and an expression on my face which I had never noticed before. Quickly I turned to my Purple Heart citation.

"Oh? That is so? You are Captain Henderson?"

"I didn't keep the commission. Maybe you'd like to see my scars, Your Highness. The thing happened with a land mine. I didn't get the worst of it. I was thrown about twenty feet. Now here in the thigh you can't see it so well, because it's sunken and the hair has grown over and hidden it. The belly wound was the bad one. My insides started to fall out. I held in my guts and walked bent over to the dressing station."

"You are very pleased about your trouble, Henderson?"

He would always say such things to me and introduce an unforeseen perspective. I have forgotten some of them, but he once asked my opinion about Descartes. "Do you agree with the fellow's proposition that the animal is a soulless machine?" Or, "Do you think that Jesus Christ is still a source of human types, Henderson, as a model-force? I have often thought about my physical types, as the agony, the appetite, and the rest, to be possibly degenerate forms of great originals, as Socrates, Alexander, Moses, Isaiah, Jesus. . . ." This, and the like, was his unforeseen way of conversation.

He observed that I was peculiar about trouble and suffering. And, yes, I knew what he was saying as we sat on those poles beside the lavish bristle of the thatch, this grotesque, dry, hairy, piercing vegetable skeleton. As he waited to achieve his heart's desire, he was telling me that suffering was the closest thing to worship that I knew anything about. Believe me, I knew my man, and strange as he was I understood him. I *was* monstrously proud of my suffering. I thought there was nobody in the world that could suffer quite like me.

But we could not speak quietly to each other any more, for the noise was too near. The sounds of cicadas had been going up in vertical spirals, like columns of thinnest shining wire. Now we would hear none of the minor sounds at all. The spearmen behind the hopo lifted up the barred gate to let through the creatures whom the beaters had flushed. For the grasses of the bush were beginning to quiver, as water will when a fish-filled net approaches the surface.

"Look there," said Dahfu. He pointed to the cliff side of the hopo, where deer with twisted horns were running; whether they were gazelles or elands I couldn't say. A buck was in the lead. He had tall, twisted horns like smoked glass, and he leaped in terror with blasting breath and huge eyes. On one knee, Dahfu was watching the grass for signs, sighting across his forearm so that his nose was almost covered. The small animals were making currents in the grass. Flocks of birds went straight up, like masses of notes; they flew toward the cliffs and down into the ravine. The deer clattered beneath us. I looked below. Those were planks at the bottom. I hadn't noticed that. They were raised six or eight inches from the ground, and the king said, "Yes. After the capture, Henderson, wheels are put under so the animal can be transported." He stooped low to call instructions to the spearmen. When he bent, I wanted to hold on to him, but I had never touched his person. I wasn't sure it would be right.

After the buck and the three does, which squeezed through the narrow opening of the hopo with heart-bursting terror, came a crowd of small beasts; they rushed the opening like immigrants. More cautious, a hyena showed up, and, unlike the other creatures who didn't know we were there, this creature shot a look up at us on the platform and gave its shallow, batlike snarl. I looked for something to throw at it. But there was nothing with us on the platform to throw and I spat down instead.

"Lion is there—lion, lion!" The king stood, pointing, and about a hundred yards away, I saw a slow stirring in the grass, not the throbbing of the smaller animals but a circular, heavy disturbance which a powerful body made.

"Do you think that would be Gmilo? Hey, hey, hey—is he here? You can take him, King. I know you can." I had risen on the narrow stand of floor projecting from beneath the grass wall, and I was thrusting and cranking my arm up and down as I spoke.

"Henderson—do not," he said.

Nevertheless I took a step in his direction, and then he cried out at me; his face was angry. So I squatted down and shut my mouth. My blood was full of fever, as if it flowed open to the glare of the sun.

The king then set foot on the slender pole and took two turns of the cage rope around his arm and began to release the knot against which he had rested his head during our wait. The cage, with its big irregular meshes of vine and the hooflike stone weights, swung from the more rigid part at the bottom. Except for the rocks the thing had almost no substance; it was as near to being air as a Portuguese man-of-war is to being water. The king had thrown off his hat; it would have got in his way; and about his tight-grown hair, which rose barely an eighth of an inch above his scalp, the blue of the atmosphere seemed to condense, as when you light a few sticks in the woods and about these black sticks the blue begins to wrinkle.

The sunlight deformed my face with strain, for I was exposed to it as I hung over the end of the hopo like a gargoyle.
The light was hard enough then to leave bruises. And still, in
spite of the blasts of the beaters, the cicadas were drilling away,
sending up those spirals of theirs. On the cliff side of the hopo
the rock was showing its character. It muttered it would let
nothing through. All things must wait for it. The small blossoms of the cactus in the ravine, if they were blossoms and not
berries, foamed red, and the spines pierced me. Things seemed
to speak to me. I inquired in silence about the safety of the
king who had a crazy idea that he must capture lions. But I got
no reply. This was not the purpose of their speech. They only
declared themselves, each according to its law, declaring what
it was; nothing at all referred to the king. So I crouched there,
sick with heat and dread. My feeling about him had crowded
aside everything else within me, which put some pressure on
the neighboring organs.

With banging and with horn blasts and whooping and
screams, the beaters came on, the ones at the rear leaping up
from the grass, which was shoulder high, and blowing de-
praved notes on those horns of green and russet metal. Shots
were fired in the air, maybe with my own scope-sight H and H
Magnum. And at the front the spears were stitching and jab-
bing in disorder.

"Did you see that, Mr. Henderson—a mane?" Dahfu leaned
forward on the pole, holding the rope, and the rock weights
banged together over his head. I couldn't bear to see him balanced there on a mere kite stick, with that fringe of stones
clattering and wheeling inches above him on the circular contraption. Any one of them might have stunned him.

"King, I can't stand this. Be careful, for Christ's sake. This is
no machine to horse around with." It was enough, I told myself, that this noble man had to risk his life on that primitive invention; he didn't have to make the thing more dangerous
than it was. However, there may have been no safe way to do
it. And then he did look very practiced as he balanced on the
narrow shaft. The rock weights circled with spasmodic power
at the king's pull. This intricate clumsy rig clattered around
and around like a merry-go-round, and the netted shadow
wheeled on the ground.

For the count of about twenty heartbeats I only partly knew where I was or what was happening. Mainly I kept a fixed watch on the king, ready to hurl myself down if he should fall. Then, at the very doors of consciousness, there was a snarl and I looked down from this straw perch—I was on my knees—into the big, angry, hair-framed face of the lion. It was all wrinkled, contracted; within those wrinkles was the darkness of murder. The lips were drawn away from the gums, and the breath of the animal came over me, hot as oblivion, raw as blood. I started to speak aloud. I said, "Oh my God, whatever You think of me, let me not fall under this butcher shop. Take care of the king. Show him Thy mercy." And to this, as a rider, the thought added itself that this was all mankind needed, to be conditioned into the image of a ferocious animal like the one below. I then tried to tell myself because of the clearness of those enraged eyes that only visions ever got to be so hyperactual. But it was no vision. The snarling of this animal was indeed the voice of death. And I thought how I had boasted to my dear Lily how I loved reality. "I love it more than you do," I had said. But oh, unreality! Unreality, unreality! That has been my scheme for a troubled but eternal life. But now I was blasted away from this practice by the throat of the lion. His voice was like a blow at the back of my head.

The barred door had dropped. Small creatures were still escaping through the gaps in streaks of fur, springing and writhing, frantically coiling. The lion rushed under us and threw his weight against these bars. Was he Gmilo? I had been told that Gmilo's ears had been marked as a cub, before he was released by the Bunam. But of course you had to catch the animal before you could look at his ears. This might well be Gmilo. Behind the barrier the men prodded him with the spears while he fought at the shafts and tried to catch them in his jaws. They were too deft for him. In the front rank forty or fifty spear points feinted and worked toward him, while from the back there flew stones, at which the animal shook his huge face with the yellow corded hair which made his forequarters so huge. His small belly was fringed, and also his forelegs, like a plainsman's buckskins. Compared with this creature Atti was no bigger than a lynx.

Balancing on the pole in his slippers, Dahfu released one turn of the rope from his upper arm; the net bucked, and the motion and the clacking of the stones caught the lion's eye. The beaters screamed up at Dahfu, "Yenitu lebah!" Ignoring them, he held fast to the line and turned around the rim of the net, which was now level with his eyes. Stone battered stone as the contraption spun around; the lion rose on his hind legs and threw a blow at these weights. Foremost among the beaters was the white-painted Bunam's man, who darted in and knocked the animal on the cheek with a spear butt. From top to bottom this fellow was clad in his dirty white, like kid leather, his hair covered with the chalky paste. I now felt the weight of the lion against the posts that held up the platform. They were no thicker than stilts and when he hit them they vibrated. I thought the structure was going to crash, and I clutched the floor, for I expected that I might be carried down like a water tower when a freight train jumps the tracks and crashes it to splinters, with a ton of water gushing in the air. Under Dahfu's feet the pole swayed, but he rode out the shock with rope and net.

"King, for God's sake!" I wanted to cry. "What have we got into?"

Again a thick flock of stones flew forward. Some struck the hopo wall but others found the animal and drove him under the circling weights of that cursed net of vines. God curse all vines and creepers! The king began to sway out as he pushed and maneuvered this bell of knots and stones.

I was freed for one moment from my dumbness. My voice returned and I said to him, "King, take it easy. Mind what you're doing." Then a globe arose in my throat, about the size of a darning egg.

That I could see was almost the only proof I had that life continued. For a time all else was cut off.

The lion, getting up on his back legs, struck again at the dipping net. It was now within reach and he caught his claws in the vines. Before he could pull free the king let fall the trap. The rope streaked down from the pulley, the weights rumbled on the boards like a troop of horses, and the cone fell on the lion's head. I was lying on my belly, with my arm stretched out toward the king, but he came to the edge of the platform un-helped by me and cried, "What do you think! Henderson, what do you think!"

The beaters screamed. The lion should have been carried to the ground by the weight of the stones, but he was still standing nearly upright. He was caught on the head, and his forepaws spread out the vines and he fell, fighting. His hind-quarters were not caught in the net. The air seemed to grow dark in the pit of the hopo from his roaring. I lay with my hand still extended to the king, but he didn't take it. He was looking downward at the netted face of the lion, the maned belly and armpits, which brought back to me the road north of Salerno and myself being held by the medics and shaved from head to foot for crabs.

"Does it look like Gmilo? Your Highness, what's your guess?" I said. I didn't understand the situation one bit.

"Oh, it is wrong," the king said.

"What's wrong?"

He was startled by a realization of something I had so far missed. I was stunned by the roars and screams of the capture, and watched the terrible labor of the legs, and the claws black and yellow which issued like thorns from the great pads of the lion's feet.

"You've got him. What the hell. What now?"

But now I understood what was the matter, for nobody could approach the animal to examine his ears; he was able to turn beneath the net, and, his hindquarters being free, you couldn't get near him.

"Rope his legs, somebody," I yelled.

The Bunam was below and signaled upward with his ivory stick. The king pushed off from the edge of the platform and took hold of the rope which had been stopped in the pulley by a knot. The overhead pole was bucking and dancing as he got hold of the frayed tail of the rope. He hauled at it, and the pul-ley started to scream. The lion was incompletely caught, and the king was going to try to work the net over the animal's hindquarters.

I called to him, "King, think it over once. You can't do it. He weighs half a ton, and he's got a solid grip on the net." I didn't realize that only the king could remedy the situation and no one could come between him and the lion, as the lion might be the late King Gmilo. Thus it was entirely up to the king to complete the capture. The pummeling of the drums and the bugling and stone-throwing had stopped, and from the crowd there was only a shout now and then heard when the lion was not roaring. Individual voices were commenting to the king on the situation, which was a bad one.

I stood up saying, "King, I'll go down and look at his ear, just tell me what to look for. Hold it, King, hold." But I doubt whether he heard me. His legs were wide apart in the center of the pole, which bowed deeply and swung and swayed under the energetic movement of his legs, and the rope and pulley and the block made cries as if resined, and the stone weights clattered on the planks. The lion fought on his back and the whole construction swayed. Again I thought the entire hopo tower would collapse and I gripped the straw behind me. Then I saw some smoke or dust above the king and realized that this came from the fastenings of hide that held the block of the pully to the wood. The king's weight and the pull of the lion had been too much for these fastenings. One had torn, that was the puff I saw. And now the other went.

"King Dahfu!" I yelled out.

He was falling. Block and pulley smashed down on the stone before the fleeing beaters. The king had fallen onto the lion. I saw the convulsion of the animal's hindquarters. The claws tore. Instantly there came blood, before the king could throw himself over. I now hung from the edge of the platform by my fingers, hung and then fell, shouting as I went. I wish this had been the eternal pit. The king had rolled himself from the lion. I pulled him farther away. Through the torn clothing his blood sprang out.

"Oh, King! My friend!" I covered up my face.

The king said, "Wo, Sungo." The surfaces of his eyes were strange. They had thickened.

I took off my green trousers to tie up the wound. These were all I had to hand, and they did no good but were instantly soaked.

"Help him! Help!" I said to the crowd.

"I did not make it, Henderson," the king said to me.

"Why, King, what are you talking about? We'll carry you

back to the palace. We'll put some sulfa powder into this and stitch you up. You'll tell me what to do, Your Majesty, being the doctor of us two."

"No, no, they will never take me back. Is it Gmilo?"

I ran and caught the rope and pulley and threw the wooden block like a bolo at the still thrusting legs; I wound the rope around them a dozen times, almost tearing the skin from them and yelling, "You devil! Curse you, you son of a bitch!" He raged back through the net. The Bunam then came and looked at the ears. He reached back and called authoritatively for something. His man in the dirty white paint handed him a musket and he put the muzzle against the lion's temple. When he fired the explosion tore part of the creature's head away.

"It was not Gmilo," the king said.

He was glad his blood would not be on his father's head.

"Henderson," he said, "you will see no harm comes to Atti."

"Hell, Your Highness, you're still king, you'll take care of her yourself." I began to cry.

"No, no, Henderson," he said. "I cannot be . . . among the wives. I would have to be killed." He was moved over these women. Some of them he must have loved. His belly through the torn clothing looked like a grate of fire and some of the beaters were already giving death shrieks. The Bunam stood apart, he kept away from us.

"Bend close," said Dahfu.

I squatted near his head and turned my good ear toward him, the tears meanwhile running between my fingers, and I said, "Oh, King, King, I am a bad-luck type. I am a jinx, and death hangs around me. The world has sent you just the wrong fellow. I am contagious, like Typhoid Mary. Without me you would have been okay. You are the noblest guy I ever met."

"It's the other way around. The shoe is on the other foot. . . . The first night you were here," he explained as a fellow will under the creeping numbness, "that body was the former, the Sungo before you. Because he could not lift Mummah . . ." His hand was bloody; he put thumb and forefinger weakly to his throat.

"They strangled him? My God! And what about that big fellow Turombo, who couldn't pick her up? Ah, he didn't want to become the Sungo, it's too dangerous. It was wished on me. I was the fall guy. I was had."

"Sungo also is my successor," he said, touching my hand.

"I take your place? What are you talking about, Your Highness!"

Eyes closing, he nodded slowly. "No child of age, makes the Sungo king."

"Your Highness," I said, and raised my weeping voice, "what have you pulled on me? I should have been told what I was getting into. Was this a thing to do to a friend?"

Without reopening his eyes, but smiling in his increasing weakness the king said, "It was done to me. . . ."

Then I said, "Your Majesty, move over and I'll die beside you. Or else be me and live; I never knew what to do with life anyway, and I'll die instead." I began to rub and beat my face with my knuckles, crouching in the dust between the dead lion and the dying king. "The spirit's sleep burst too late for me. I waited too long, and I ruined myself with pigs. I'm a broken man. And I'll never make out with the wives. How can I? I'll follow you soon. These guys will kill me. King! King!"

But the king had little life left in him now, and we soon parted. He was picked up by the beaters, the end of the hopo was opened and we started to go down the ravine among the cactuses toward that stone building I had first seen from the platform at the top of the wall. On the way he died of the hemorrhage.

This small house built of flat slabs had two wooden doors of the stockade type which opened into two chambers. His body was laid down in one of these. Into the other they put me. I scarcely knew what was happening anyway, and I let them lead me in and bolt the door.

XXI

A T ONE TIME, much earlier in this life of mine, suffering had a certain spice. Later on it started to lose this spice; it became merely dirty, and, as I told my son Edward in California, I couldn't bear it any more. Damn! I was tired of being such a monster of grief. But now, with the king's death, it was no longer a topic and it had no spice at all. It was only terrible. Weeping and mourning I was put into the stone room by the old Bunam and his white-dyed assistant. Though the words came out broken, I repeated the one thing, "It's wasted on dummies." (Life is.) "They give it to dummies and fools." (We are where other men ought to be.) So they led me inside, crying my head off. I was too bereaved to ask any questions. By and by a person rising from the floor startled me. "Who the hell is that?" I asked. Two open, wrinkled hands were raised to caution me. "Who are you?" I said again, and then I recognized a head of hair shaped like an umbrella pine and big dusty feet as deformed as vegetable growths.

"Romilayu!"

"Me here too, sah."

They hadn't let him get off with the letter to Lily, but picked him up just as he was leaving town. So even before the hunt began they had decided that they didn't want my whereabouts to be known to the world.

"Romilayu, the king is dead," I said.

He tried to comfort me.

"That marvelous guy. Dead!"

"Fine gen'a'man, sah."

"He thought he could change me. But I met him too late in life, Romilayu. I was too gross. Too far gone."

All I had left in the way of clothing was shoes and helmet, T-shirt and the jockey shorts, and I sat on the floor, where I bent over double and cried without limit. Romilayu at first could not help me.

But maybe time was invented so that misery might have an end. So that it shouldn't last forever? There may be something in this. And bliss, just the opposite, is eternal? That is no time in bliss. All the clocks were thrown out of heaven.

I never took another death so hard. As I had tried to stop his bleeding, there was blood all over me and soon it was dry. I tried to rub it off. Well, I thought, maybe this is a sign that I should continue his existence? How? To the best of my ability. But what ability have I got? I can't name three things in my whole life that I did right. So I broke my heart over this, too.

Thus the day passed and the night passed, too, and in the morning I felt light, dry and hollow. As if I were drifting, like an old vat. All the moisture was on the outside. Inside, I was hollow, dark, and dry; I was sober and empty. And the sky was pink. I saw it through the bars of the door. The Bunam's black-leather man, still in his coat of white, was our custodian, and brought us baked yams and other fruit. Two amazons, but not Tamba and Bebu, were his staff, and everyone treated me with peculiar deference. During the day I said to Romilayu, "Dahfu said that when he died I should be king."

"Dem call you Yassi, sah."

"Does that mean king?" That was what it meant. "Some king," I said, musing. "It's goofy." Romilayu made no comment whatever. "I would have to be husband to all those wives."

"You no like dat, sah?"

"Are you crazy, man?" I said. "How could I even think of taking over that bunch of females? I have all the wife I need. Lily is just a marvelous woman. Anyway, the king's death has hurt me too much. I am stricken, can't you see, Romilayu? I am stricken down and I can't function at all. This has broken me."

"You no look so too-bad, sah."

"Oh, you want to make me feel better. But you should see my heart, Romilayu. I have a punchy heart. It's had more beating than it can take. They've kicked it around far too much. Don't let this big carcass of mine fool you. I am far too sensitive. Anyway, Romilayu, it's true I shouldn't have bet against the rain on that day. It didn't look like good will on my part. But the king, God bless the guy, let me walk into a trap. I wasn't really stronger than that man Turombo. He could have lifted up Mummah. He just didn't want to become the Sungo. He faked himself out of it. It's too dangerous a position. This the king did to me."

"But him dange'ah too," said Romilayu.

"Yes, and so he was. Why should I ask to have it better than he? You're right, old fellow. Thanks for setting me straight." I thought a while, then asked him, as a man of proven good sense, "Don't you think I'd scare those girls?" I grimaced to illustrate my meaning somewhat. "My face is half the length of another person's body."

"I don't t'ink so, sah."

"Isn't it?" I touched it. "Well, I won't stay, anyhow. Though I will never have another chance to become a king, I guess." And thinking deeply about the great man, just dead, just settled for good and all into nothing, into dark night, I felt he had picked me to step into his place. It was up to me, if I wanted to turn my back on home, where I had been nothing. He believed that I was royal material, and that I might make good use of a chance to start life anew. And so I sent my thanks to him, through the stone wall. But I said to Romilayu, "No, I'd break my heart here trying to fill his position. Besides, I have to go home. And anyway, I am no stud. No use kidding, I am fifty-six, or going on it. I'd shake in my boots that the wives might turn me in. And I'd have to live under the shadow of the Bunam and Horko and those people, and never be able to face old Queen Yasra, the king's mother. I made her a promise. Oh, Romilayu, as if I had ability to promise anything on. Let's get out of here. I feel like a lousy impostor. The only decent thing about me is that I have loved certain people in my life. Oh, the poor guy is dead. Oh, ho, ho, ho, ho! It kills me. It could be time we were blown off this earth. If only we didn't have hearts we wouldn't know how sad it was. But we carry around these hearts, these spotty damn mangoes in our breasts, which give us away. And it isn't only that I'm scared of all those wives, but there'll be nobody to talk to any more. I've gotten to that age where I need human voices and intelligence. That's all that's left. Kindness and love." I fell into mourning again, for this was how I had gone on without intermission since being shut in the tomb, and I kept it up a while longer, as I recall. Then suddenly I said to Romilayu, "Pal, the king's death was no accident."

"Whut you mean, sah?"

"It was no accident. It was a scheme, I begin to be convinced of it. Now they can say he was punished for keeping Atti, having her under the palace. You know they wouldn't hesitate to murder the guy. They thought I'd be more pliable than the king. Would you put this past these guys?"

"No sah."

"You bet, no sah. If I ever get my hands on any of these characters I'll crush them like old beer cans." I ground my hands together to show what I would do, and bared my teeth and growled. Perhaps I had learned from lions after all, and not the grace and power of movement that Dahfu had got out of his rearing among them, but the more cruel aspect of the lion, according to my shorter and shallower experience. When you get right down to it, a fellow can't predict what he will pick up in the form of influence. I think that Romilayu was somewhat upset by this jump from mourning to retribution, but he seemed to realize that I wasn't myself, altogether; he was ready to make allowances for me, being really a very generous and understanding type, and quite a Christian fellow. I said, "We must think of crashing out of here. Let's case the joint. Actually, where are we? And what can we do? And what have we got?"

"We got knife, sah," said Romilayu, and he showed it to me. It was his hunting knife, and he had slipped it into his hair when the Bunam's men came after him on the outskirts of the town.

"Oh, good man," I said, and took the knife from him in a stabbing position.

"Dig, bettah," he said.

"Yes, that makes sense. You're right. I'd like to get hold of the Bunam," I said, "but that would be a luxury. Revenge is a luxury. I've got to be canny. Hold me back, Romilayu. It's up to you to restrain me. You see I'm beside myself, don't you? What's next door?" We began to go over the wall, and after a minute examination we found a chink high up between the slabs of stone and we began to dig at it, taking turns with the knife. Sometimes I held Romilayu up in my arms, and some-times I let him stand on my back while I was on all fours. For him to stand on my shoulders was impracticable, as the ceiling was too low.

"Yes, somebody tampered with the block and pulley at the hopo," I kept saying.

"Maybe, sah."

"There can't be any maybes about it. And why did the Bunam grab you? Because it was a plot against Dahfu and me. Of course, the king let me in for a lot of trouble, too, by allowing me to move Mummah. That he did."

Romilayu dug, revolving the knife blade in the mortar, and he scraped and scooped out the scrapings with his forefinger. The dust fell over me.

"But the king lived under threat of death himself, and what he lived with I could live with. He was my friend."

"You friend, sah?"

"Well, love may be like this, too, old fellow," I explained. "I suppose my dad wished, I *know* he wished, that I had gotten drowned instead of my brother Dick, up there near Plattsburg. Did this mean he didn't love me? Not at all. I, too, being a son, it tormented the old guy to wish it. Yes, if it had been me instead, he would have wept almost as much. He loved both his sons. But Dick should have lived. He was wild only that one time, Dick was; he may have been smoking a reefer. It was too much of a price to pay for one single reefer. Oh, I don't blame the old guy. Except it's life; and have we got any business to chide it?"

"Yes, sah," he said. He was keenly digging, and I knew he didn't follow me.

"How can you chide it? It has a right to our respect. It does its stuff, that's all. I told that man next door I had a voice that said, *I want*. What did it want?"

"Yes, sah" (scooping more mortar over me).

"It wanted reality. How much unreality could it stand?"

He dug and dug. I was on all fours, and my words were spoken toward the floor. "We're supposed to think that nobil-ity is unreal. But that's just it. The illusion is on the other foot. They make us think we crave more and more illusions. Why, I don't crave illusions at all. They say, Think big. Well, that's boloney of course, another business slogan. But greatness! That's another thing altogether. Oh, greatness! Oh, God! Romilayu, I don't mean inflated, swollen, false greatness. I don't mean pride or throwing your weight around. But the universe itself being put into us, it calls out for scope. The eternal is bonded onto us. It calls out for its share. This is why guys can't bear to be so cheap. And I had to do something about it. Maybe I should have stayed at home. Maybe I should have learned to kiss the earth." (I did so now.) "But I thought I was going to explode, back there. Oh, Romilayu, I wish I could have opened my heart entirely to that poor guy. I'm all torn up over his death. I've never had it so bad.

"But I will show those schemers, if I ever get the chance," I said.

Quietly, Romilayu chipped and dug, then he put his eye to the hole and said, low, "I see, sah."

"What do you see?"

He was silent and dismounted. I stood, rubbing the grit from my back, and put my eye to the hole. There I saw the figure of the dead king. He was wrapped in a shroud of leather, and his features were invisible, for the flap was down over his face. At the hips and feet the body was tied with thongs. The Bunam's assistant was the death-watcher and sat on a stool by the door, sleeping. It was very hot in both these rooms. Beside him were two baskets of cold baked yams. And to the handle of one of these baskets there was tethered a lion cub, still spotted as very young cubs are. I judged it was two or three weeks old. The fellow's sleep was heavy, though he sat on a backless stool. His arms were slack and pressed between his chest and thighs, the hands with their gorged veins nearly dropped to the ground. With hatred in my heart I said to myself, "You wait, you crook. I'll get around to you." Due to the peculiarities of the light, he appeared as white as satin; only his nostrils and the furrows of his cheeks were black. "I'll fix your wagon," I promised him in silence.

"Well, Romilayu," I said. "This time let's use our heads. We won't do as we did the first night here with the body of the other fellow, the Sungo before me. Let us plot. First, I am in line for the throne. They wouldn't want to hurt me, as I'd be a figurehead in the tribe and they would run the show to please themselves. They've got the lion cub, who is my dead friend, so they are moving along pretty fast and we have to move fast, too. Boy, we've got to move even faster."

"Whut you do, sah?" he said, growing worried at my tone.

"Bust out, naturally. Do you think we can make it back to Baventai as we are?"

He couldn't or wouldn't say what he thought of this, and I asked, "It looks bad, eh?"

"You sick," said Romilayu.

"Hah. I can make it if you can. You know how I am when I get going. Are you kidding? I could walk across Siberia on my hands. And anyway, pal, there's no choice. Absolutely the best in me comes out at times like this. It's the Valley Forge element in me. It'll be tough, all right. We'll pack along those yams. That ought to help. You won't stay behind, will you?"

"Wo, no, sah. Dem kill me."

"Then just resign yourself," I said. "I don't think those amazons sit up all night. This is the twentieth century, and they can't make a king of me if I don't let them. Nobody can call me chicken on account of that harem. But, Romilayu, I think it would be smart to act as if I wanted the position. They wouldn't want any harm to come to me. It would put them in a hell of a fix to hurt me. Besides, they must figure that we'd never be fools enough to go through two or three hundred miles of no man's land without food or a gun."

Seeing me in this mood, Romilayu was frightened. "We have to stick together," I said to him, however. "If they should strangle me after a few weeks—and it's likely; I'm in no condition to boast or make big promises—what would happen to you? They'd kill you, too, to protect their secret. And how much grun-tu-molani do you have? You want to live, kid?"

He had no time to answer then, as Horko came to pay us a visit. He smiled, but his behavior was somewhat more formal than before. He called me Yassi and showed his fat red tongue, which he might have done to cool himself after his long walk through the heat of the bush; however, I thought it signified respect.

"How do you do, Mr. Horko?"

Greatly satisfied, he bowed from the waist while he kept his forefinger above his head. The upper part of him was always much crowded by the tight sheath, his court dress of red, and he was congested in the face. The red jewels in his ears dragged them down, and as he grinned I looked at him, but not openly, with hatred. As there was nothing I could do, however, I converted all this hatred into wiliness, and when he said, "You now king. Roi Henderson. Yassi Henderson," I answered, "Yes, Horko. Very sorry about Dahfu, aren't we?"

"Oh, very sorry. Dommage," he said, for he loved to use the phrases he had picked up in Lamu.

Humankind is still fooling around with hypocrisy, I thought. They don't realize that it's too late even for that.

"No more Sungo. You Yassi."

"Yes, indeed," I said. I instructed Romilayu, "Tell the gentleman I am glad to be Yassi, and it's a great honor. When do we start?"

We had to wait, said Romilayu, interpreting, until the worm came from the king's mouth. And then the worm would become a tiny lion, and this cub, the little lion, would become the Yassi.

"If pigs were in this, I'd become an emperor, not just a bush-league king," I said, and took a bitter relish in my own remark. I wished Dahfu had been alive to hear it. "But tell Mr. Horko" (he inclined his thick face, smiling, while the ear-stones dropped again like sinkers; I could have twisted his head and pulled it off with great satisfaction) "it's a terrific honor. Though the late king was a bigger and better man than I am, I will do the best job I can. I think we have a great future. I ran away from home in the first place because I didn't have enough to do in my own country, and this is the type of opportunity I have hoped for." This was how I spoke, and I glowered, but made the glowers seem sincere. "How long do we have to stay in this death house?"

"Him say just three, fo' days, sah."

"Okay?" said Horko. "Not long. You marry toutes les leddy." He started to throw his fingers to show by tens how many there were. Sixty-seven.

"Don't worry about a thing," I said to him.

And when he had left, with ceremony, showing that he felt I was indeed in the bag, I said to Romilayu, "We're going out of here tonight."

Romilayu looked up at me in silence, his upper lip growing very long with despair.

"Tonight," I repeated. "We have the moon. Last night it was bright enough to read the telephone directory by. Have we been in this town a full month?"

"Yes, sah—Whut we do?"

"You'll start yelling in the night. You'll say I've been bitten by a snake, or something. That leather fellow will come with the two amazons to see what's wrong. If he doesn't open the door we'll have to try another scheme. But suppose the door *is* opened. Then take this stone—you understand?—and jam it in by the hinge so the door won't close. That's all we need. Now where's your knife?"

"Me keep knife, sah."

"I don't need it. Yes, you keep the knife. All right, do you follow me? You'll holler that the Sungo Yassi, or whatever I am to these murderers, is bitten by a snake. My leg is swelling fast. And you must stand by the door ready to jam it." I showed him exactly what I wanted done.

So when night began, I sat plotting, concentrating my ideas and trying to protect their clarity from my fever, which increased every afternoon and rose far into the night. I had to fight against delirium, as my condition was aggravated by the suffocation of the tomb and the hours of vigil I spent at the chink in the wall straining one eye at a time toward the dead figure of the king. Sometimes I imagined that I could see some of the features under the flap of the cowl. But this was more mental . . . mental deceit; dream. My head was out of order, as I realized even then. I was most aware of it at night, under the influence of fever, when mountains and idols and cattle and lions, and gross black women, the amazons, and the face of the king and the thatch of the hopo visited my mind, coming and going unannounced. However, I held tight and waited for moonrise, the time I had chosen to go into action. Romilayu didn't sleep. From the corner where he lay propped his gaze was never interrupted. I could find him by his eyes, which were always there.

"You no change you min', sah?" he once or twice asked.

"No, no. No change."

And when I judged the time was right, I took a deep, stiff

breath, so that my sternum gave a crack. My ribs were sore. "Go!" I said to Romilayu. The fellow next door was certainly sleeping, for I had heard no stir since nightfall. I picked Romilayu up in my arms and held him to the chink we had dug out. Clutching him, I could feel the tremors that ran through his body, and he began to yell and stammer. I added some groans as if from the background, and then the Bunam's man woke up. I heard his feet. Then he must have stood listening as Romilayu repeated in his quaver, "Yassi k'muti!" K'muti I had heard from the beaters as they carried Dahfu toward the tomb. K'muti—he is dying. It must have been the last word to reach his ears. "Wunnutu zazai k'muti. Yassi k'muti." It's not a hard language; I was picking it up fast.

Then the door of the king's tomb opened and the Bunam's man began to shout.

"Oh," said Romilayu to me, "him call two sojer leddy, sah."

I set him on his feet and lay down on the floor. "The stone is ready," I said. "Go to the door and do your stuff. If we don't get out we haven't got a month to live."

I saw torchlight through the door, which meant that the amazons had come on the double, and it is the most curious thing of all that it was the murder in my heart which calmed me most. It gave me confidence. It was like a balm to me that if I got my hands on the Bunam's narrow-faced man I would be the death of him. "Him at least I will do in," I kept thinking. So, fully calculating, I made cries of fear and weakness—and I gloated at these sounds of weakness, for I really did feel that my strength was low just then but that it would come back to me as soon as I touched the Bunam's man. A strip of board was removed from the door. By the lifted flare the Bunam's man saw me writhing, clutching my leg. The bolt was dropped, and one of the amazons began to open the door. "The stone," I cried as if in pain, and I saw by the flare that Romilayu had pushed the stone oblong below the hinge exactly as I told him, although the point of a spear held by the amazon was right under his chin. He retreated toward me. This I saw under the great, lapping, torn smoky tissue of the fire. The amazon yelled when I pulled her off her feet. The spear point scraped the wall, and I prayed it hadn't touched Romilayu. I struck the woman's head against the stones. Under the circumstances I couldn't afford to make any allowance for her femininity. The fire had been dashed out and the door swiftly closed, but it stuck on the stone just enough to let me get my fingers on the edge. Both the other amazon and the Bunam's man pulled against me, but I tore the thing open. I worked in silence. I was now covered by the night air, which did me good immediately. First I hit the second amazon only with the edge of my hand, a commando trick. It was enough. It lamed her, and she fell to the ground. All this was still in silence, for they made no more noise than I did. Then I went after the man, who was escaping to the other side of the mausoleum. Three strides and I caught him by the hair. I lifted him straight up at arm's length so that he could see my face by the almost risen moon. I snarled. All the skin of his face was drawn upward by the force of my clutch, so that his eyes slanted. As I took him by the throat and began to choke him, Romilayu ran up to me yelling, "No, no, sah."

"I'm going to strangle him."

"No kill him, sah."

"Don't interfere," I yelled, and shook the Bunam's man up and down by the hair. "*He* is the killer. That man inside is dead because of him." But I had stopped choking the Bunam's wizard. I swung his whitened body by the head. No sound came forth.

"You no kill him," said Romilayu earnestly, "Bunam no chase us."

"There's murder in my heart, Romilayu," I said.

"You be my friend, sah?"

"I'll break some of his bones, then. I'll make a deal with you," I said. "You have a right to make a claim on me. Yes, you're my friend. But what about Dahfu? Wasn't he my friend, too? All right, I won't break bones. I'll beat him."

But I didn't beat him, either. I flung the man into the room we had been locked in, and the two amazons with him. Romilayu took away their spears, and we bolted the door. We then went into the other chamber. The moon had now risen and every object was visible. Romilayu picked up the basket of yams, while I walked over to the king.

"Now we go, sah?"

I looked under the cowl. The face was swelled and lumpy,

very much distorted. Owing to the effects of the heat, despite the love I felt for him I was obliged to turn away. "Good-by, King," I said. I left him.

But then I had an impulse as we were going. The tethered cub was spitting at us and I picked him up.

"Whut you do?"

"This animal is coming with us," I said.

XXII

ROMILAYU started to protest, but I held the creature to me, hearing its tiny snarl and pricked in the chest by its claws. "The king would want me to take it along," I said. "Look, he's got to survive in some form. Can't you see?" The moonlit horizon was extremely clear. It had the effect of making me feel logical. Light was released over us from the summits of the mountains. Thirty miles of terrain opened before us, the path of our flight. I suppose that Romilayu could have pointed out to me that this animal was the child of my enemy who had deprived me of Dahfu. "Well, so look," I said, "I didn't kill that guy. So if I spared him . . . Romilayu, let's not stand here and gab. I can't leave the animal behind and I won't. Look," I said, "I can carry it in my helmet. I don't need it at night." As a matter of fact the night breeze was doing my fever good.

Romilayu gave in to me, and we started our flight, leaping through the shadows of the moon up the side of the ravine. We put the hopo between ourselves and the town, and headed into the mountains, on a straight course for Baventai. I ran behind with the cub, and all that night we did double time, so that by sunrise we had about twenty miles behind us.

Without Romilayu I couldn't have lasted two of the ten days that it took to reach Baventai. He knew where the water was and which roots and insects we could eat. After the yams gave out, as they did on the fourth day, we had to forage for grubs and worms. "You could be a survival instructor for the Air Force," I told him. "You'd be a jewel to them," I also said to him. "So at last I'm living on locusts, like Saint John. 'The voice of one that crieth in the wilderness.'" But we had this lion, which had to be fed and cared for. I doubt whether any such handicap was ever seen before. I had to mince grubs and worms with the knife in my palm and make a paste, and I fed the little creature by hand. During the day, when I had to have the helmet, I carried the cub under my arm, and sometimes I led him on the leash. He slept in the helmet, too, with my wallet and passport, teething on the leather and in the end devouring most of it. I then carried my documents and the four one-thousand-dollar bills inside my jockey shorts.

From gaunt cheeks, my whiskers grew in various colors, and during most of the trek I was demented and raving. I would sit and play with the cub, whom I named Dahfu, while Romilayu foraged. I was too simple in the head to help him. Nevertheless, in many essential matters my mind was very clear and even fine or delicate. As I ate the cocoons and the larvae and ants, crouching in the jockey shorts with the lion lying under me for shade, I spoke oracles and sang—yes, I remembered many songs from nursery and school, like "Fais do-do," "Pierrot," "Malbrouck s'en va-t'en guerre," "Nut Brown Maiden," and "The Spanish Guitar," while I fondled the animal, which had made a wonderful adjustment to me. He rolled between my feet and scratched my legs. Although on a diet of worms and grubs he could not have been very healthy. I feared and Romilayu hoped that the animal would die. But we were lucky. We had the spears and Romilayu killed a few birds. I am pretty sure we killed a bird of prey that had got too near and that we feasted on it.

And on the tenth day (as Romilayu told me afterward, for I had lost count) we came to Baventai, sitting parched on its rocks, but not so parched as we were. The walls were white as eggs, and the brown Arabs in their clothes and muffles watched us arise from the sterile road, myself greeting everyone with two fingers for victory, like Churchill, and giving a cracked, crying, black-throated laugh of survival, holding out the cub Dahfu by the scruff to all those head-swathed and silent men, and the women who revealed only eyes, and the black herdsmen with sunny fat melting from their hair. "Get the band. Get the music," I was saying to them all.

Pretty soon I folded, but I made Romilayu promise to look out for the little animal. "This is Dahfu to me," I said. "Don't let anything happen, please, Romilayu. It would ruin me now. I can't threaten you, old fellow," I said. "I'm too weak, and I can only beg."

Romilayu said I shouldn't worry. At least he told me, "Wo-kay, sah."

"I can beg," I said to him. "I'm not what I thought I was.

"One thing, Romilayu . . ." I was in a native house and lying on a bed while he, squatting beside me, took the animal from my arms. "Is it promised? Between the beginning and the end, is it promised?"

"Whut promise, sah?"

"Well, I mean something *clear*. Isn't it promised? Romilayu, I suppose I mean the reason—*the* reason. It may be postponed until the last breath. But there is justice. I believe there is justice, and that much is promised. Though I am not what I thought."

Romilayu was about to console me, but I said to him, "You don't have to give me consolation. Because the sleep is burst, and I've come to myself. It wasn't the singing of boys that did it," I said. "What I'd like to know is why this has to be fought by everybody, for there is nothing that's struggled against so hard as coming-to. We grow these sores instead. Burning sores, fertile sores." I held the lion on my breast, the child of our murderous enemy. Because of my weakness and fatigue, I was reduced to grimacing at Romilayu. "Don't let me down, old pal," was what I tried to say.

Then I let him take the animal from me and I slept for a while and had dreams, or I didn't sleep but lay on the cot in somebody's house, and those were not dreams but hallucinations. One thing however I kept saying to myself and telling Romilayu, and this was that I had to get back to Lily and the children; I would never feel right until I saw them, and especially Lily herself. I developed a bad case of homesickness. For I said, What's the universe? Big. And what are we? Little. I therefore might as well be at home where my wife loves me. And even if she only seemed to love me, that too was better than nothing. Either way, I had tender feelings toward her. I remembered her in a variety of ways; some of her sayings came back to me, like one should live for this and not for that; not evil but good, not death but life, and all the rest of her theories. But I suppose it made no difference what she said, I wouldn't be kept from loving her even by her preaching. Frequently Romilayu came up to me, and in the worst of my delirium his black face seemed to me like shatter-proof glass to which everything had been done that glass can endure.

"Oh, you can't get away from rhythm, Romilayu," I recall saying many times to him. "You just can't get away from it. The left hand shakes with the right hand, the inhale follows the exhale, the systole talks back to the diastole, the hands play patty-cake, and the feet dance with each other. And the seasons. And the stars, and all of that. And the tides, and all that junk. You've got to live at peace with it, because if it's going to worry you, you'll lose. You can't win against it. It keeps on and on and on. Hell, we'll never get away from rhythm, Romilayu. I wish my dead days would quit bothering me and leave me alone. The bad stuff keeps coming back, and it's the worst rhythm there is. The repetition of a man's bad self, that's the worst suffering that's ever been known. But you can't get away from regularity. But the king said I should change. I shouldn't be an agony type. Or a Lazarus type. The grass should be my cousins. Hey, Romilayu, not even Death knows how many dead there are. He could never run a census. But these dead should go. They *make* us think of them. That is their immortality. In us. But my back is breaking. I'm loaded down. It isn't fair—what about the grun-tu-molani?"

He showed me the little creature. It had survived all the hardships and was thriving like anything.

So after several weeks in Baventai, beginning to recover, I said to my guide, "Well, kid, I suppose I'd better get moving while the cub is still small. I can't wait till he grows into a lion, can I? It will be a job to get him back to the States even if he's half grown."

"No, no. You too sick, sah."

And I said, "Yes, the flesh is not in such hot shape. But I will beat this rap. It's merely some disease. Otherwise, I'm well."

Romilayu was much opposed but I made him take me in the end to Baktale. There I bought a pair of pants and the missionary let me have some sulfa until my dysentery was under control. That took a few days. After this I slept in the back of the jeep with the lion cub under a khaki blanket, while Romilayu drove us to Harar, Ethiopia. That took six days. And in Harar I made Romilayu a few hundred dollars' worth of presents. I filled the jeep with all sorts of stuff.

"I was going to stop over in Switzerland and visit my little daughter Alice," I said. "My youngest girl. But I guess I don't look well, and there's no use frightening the kid. I'd better do it another time. Besides, there's the cub."

"You tek him home?"

"Where I go he goes," I said. "And Romilayu, you and I will get together again one day. The world is not so loose any more. You can locate a man, provided he stays alive. You have my address. Write to me. Don't take it so hard. Next time we meet I may be wearing a white coat. You'll be proud of me. I'll treat you for nothing."

"Oh, you too weak to go, sah," said Romilayu. "I 'fraid to leave you go."

I took it every bit as hard as he did.

"Listen to me, Romilayu, I'm unkillable. Nature has tried everything. It has thrown the book at me. And here I am."

He saw, however, that I was feeble. You could have tied me up with a ribbon of haze.

And after we had said good-by, finally, for good, I realized that he still dogged my steps and kept an eye on me from a distance as I went around Harar with the cub. My legs quaked, my beard was like the purple sage, and I was sightseeing in front of old King Menelik's palace, accompanied by the lion, while bushy Romilayu, fear and anxiety in his face, watched from around the corner to make sure I didn't collapse. For his own good I paid no attention to him. When I boarded the plane he still was observing me. It was the Khartoum flight and the lion was in a wicker basket. The jeep was beside the airstrip and Romilayu was in it, praying at the wheel. He held together his hands like giant crayfish and I knew he was doing his utmost to obtain safety and well-being for me. I cried, "Romilayu!" and stood up. Several of the passengers seemed to think I was about to overturn the small plane. "That black fellow saved my life," I said to them.

However, we were now in the air, flying over the shadows of the heat. I then sat down and brought out the lion, holding him in my lap.

In Khartoum I had a hassle with the consular people about arrangements. There was quite a squawk about the lion. They said there were people who were in the business of selling zoo animals in the States, and they told me if I didn't go about it in the right way the lion would have to be in quarantine. I said I was willing to go to a vet and get some shots, but I told them, "I'm in a hurry to get home. I've been sick and I can't stand any delay." The guys said they could see for themselves that I had been through quite a bit. They tried to pump me about my trip, and asked how I had lost all my stuff. "It's none of your lousy business," I said. "My passport is okay, isn't it? And I've got dough. My great-grandfather was head of your crummy outfit, and he was no cold-storage, Ivy League, button-down, broken-hipped civilian like you. All you fellows are just the same. You think U.S. citizens are dummies and morons. Listen, all I want from you is to expedite— Yes, I saw a few things in the interior. Yes, I did. I have had a look into some of the fundamentals, but don't expect me to tickle your idle curiosity. I wouldn't talk even to the ambassador, if he asked me."

They didn't like this. I had the staggers in their office. The lion was on the fellows' desk and knocked down their stapler and nipped them through the clothes. They got rid of me the fastest way they could, and I flew into Cairo that same evening. There I called Lily on the transatlantic phone. "It's me, baby," I cried. "I'm coming home Sunday." I knew she must be pale and going paler, purer and purer in the face as she always did under great excitement, and that her lips must have moved five or six times before she could get out a word. "Baby, I'm coming home," I said. "Speak clearly, don't mumble now." "Gene!" I heard, and after that the waves of half the world, the air, the water, the earth's vascular system, came in between. "Honey, I aim to do better, can you hear? I've had it now." Of what she said I could make out no more than two or three words. Space with its weird cries came between. I knew she was speaking about love; her voice thrilled, and I guessed she was moralizing and calling me back. "For a big broad you sound very tiny," I kept saying. She could hear me all right. "Sunday, Idlewild. Bring Donovan," I said. This Donovan is an old lawyer who was a trustee of my father's estate. He must be eighty now. I thought I might need his legal help on account of the lion.

This was Wednesday. On Thursday we flew to Athens. I thought I should see the Acropolis. So I hired a car and a guide, but I was too ill and in too much confusion to take in very much of it. The lion was with us, on a leash, and except for the suntans I had bought in Baktale I was dressed as in Africa, same helmet, same rubber shoes. My beard had grown out considerably; on one side it gushed out half white but with many streaks of blond, red, black, and purple. The embassy people had suggested a shave to make identification easier from the passport. But I did not take their advice. As far as the Acropolis went, I saw something on the heights, which was yellow, bonelike, rose-colored. I realized it must be very beautiful. But I couldn't get out of the automobile, and the guide didn't even suggest it. Altogether he said very little, almost nothing; however, his eyes showed what he thought. "There are reasons for it all," I said to him.

On Friday I got to Rome. I bought a corduroy outfit, burgundy colored, and an alpine hat with Bersagliere feathers, plus a shirt and underpants. Except to buy this stuff I didn't leave my room. I wasn't eager to make a show of myself on the Via Veneto walking the cub on a leash.

On Saturday we flew again by way of Paris and London, which was the only arrangement I could make. To see either place again I had no curiosity. Or any other place, for that matter. For me the best part of the flight was over water. I couldn't seem to get enough of it, as if I had been dehydrated —the water, combing along, endless, the Atlantic, deep. But the depth made me happy. I sat by the window, in the clouds. The sea was thickened by the late, awful, air-blind, sea-blanched sun. We were carried over the calm swarm of the water, the lead-sealed but expanding water, the heart of the water.

Other passengers were reading. Personally, I can't see that. How can you sit in a plane and be so indifferent? Of course, they weren't coming from mid-Africa like me; they weren't discontinuous with civilization. They arose from Paris and London into the skies with their books. But I, Henderson, with my glowering face, with corduroy and Bersagliere feathers— the helmet was inside the wicker basket with the cub, as I figured he needed a familiar object to calm him on this novel, exciting trip—I couldn't get enough of the water, and of these upside-down sierras of the clouds. Like courts of eternal heaven. (Only they aren't eternal, that's the whole thing; they are seen once and never seen again, being figures and not abiding realities; Dahfu will never be seen again, and presently I will never be seen again; but every one is given the components to see: the water, the sun, the air, the earth.)

The stewardess offered me a magazine to calm me down, seeing how overwrought I was. She was aware that I had the lion cub Dahfu in the baggage compartment, as I had ordered chops and milk for him, and there was a certain inconvenience about my going back and forth constantly and prowling around the rear of the plane. She was an understanding girl, and finally I told her what it was all about, that the lion cub was important to me, and that I was bringing him home to my wife and children. "It's a souvenir of a very dear friend," I said. It was also an enigmatic form of that friend, I might have tried to explain to this girl. She was from Rockford, Illinois. Every twenty years or so the earth renews itself in young maidens. You know what I mean? Her cheeks had the perfect form that belongs to the young; her hair was kinky gold. Her teeth were white and posted on every approach. She was all sweet corn and milk. Blessings on her hips. Blessings on her thighs. Blessings on her soft little fingers which were somewhat covered by the cuffs of her uniform. Blessings on that rough gold. A wonderful little thing; her attitude was that of a pal or playmate, as is common with Midwestern young women. I said, "You make me think of my wife. I haven't seen her in months."

"Oh? How many months?" she said.

That I couldn't tell her, for I didn't know the date. "Is it about September?" I asked.

Astonished, she said, "Honestly, don't you know? It'll be Thanksgiving next week."

"So late! I missed out on enrollment. I'll have to wait until next semester. You see, I got sick in Africa and had a delirium and lost count of time. When you go in deep you run that risk, you know that, don't you, kid?"

She was amused that I called her kid.

"Do you go to school?"

"Instead of coming to ourselves," I said, "we grow all kinds of deformities and enormities. At least something can be done for those. You know? While we wait for the day?"

"Which day, Mr. Henderson?" she said, laughing at me.

"Haven't you ever heard the song?" I said. "Listen, and I'll sing you a little of it." We were back at the rear of the plane where I was feeding the animal Dahfu. I sang, "And who shall abide the day of His coming (the day of His coming)? And who shall stand when He appeareth (when He appeareth)?"

"That is Handel?" she said. "That's from Rockford College."

"Correct," I said. "You are a sensible young woman. Now I have a son, Edward, whose wits were swamped by all that cool jazz. . . . I slept through my youth," I went on as I was feeding the lion his cooked meat. "I slept and slept like our first-class passenger." Note: I must explain that we were on one of those strato-cruisers with a regular stateroom, and I had noticed the stewardess going in there with steak and champagne. The fellow never came out. She told me he was a famous diplomat. "I guess he just has to sleep, it's costing so much," I commented. "If he has insomnia it'll be a terrible let-down to a man in his position. You know why I'm impatient to see my wife, miss? I'm eager to know how it will be now that the sleep is burst. And the children, too. I love them very much—I think."

"Why do you say think?"

"Yes, I think. We'll have to see. You know we're a very funny family for picking up companions. My son Edward had a chimpanzee who was dressed in a cowboy suit. Then in California he and I nearly took a little seal into our lives. Then my daughter brought home a baby. Of course we had to take it away from her. I hope she will consider this lion as a replacement. I hope I can persuade her."

"There's a little kid on the plane," said the stewardess. "He'd probably adore the lion cub. He looks pretty sad."

And I said, "Who is it?"

"Well, his parents were Americans. There's a letter around his neck that tells the story. This kid doesn't speak English at all. Only Persian."

"Go on," I said to her.

"The father worked for oil people in Persia. The kid was raised by Persian servants. Now he's an orphan and going to live with grandparents in Carson City, Nevada. At Idlewild I'm supposed to turn him over to somebody."

"Poor little bastard," I said. "Why don't you bring him, and we'll show him the lion."

So she fetched the boy. He was very white and wore short pants with strap garters and a little dark green sweater. He was a blackhaired boy, like my own. This kid went to my heart. You know how it is when your heart drops. Like a fall-bruised apple in the cold morning of autumn. "Come here, little boy," I said, and reached for the child's hand. "It's a bad business," I told the stewardess, "to ship a little kid around the world alone." I took the cub Dahfu and gave it to him. "I don't think he knows what it is—he probably imagines it's a kitty."

"But he likes it."

As a matter of fact the animal did lighten the boy's melancholy, and so we let them play. And when we went back to our seats I kept him with me and tried to show him pictures in the magazine. I gave him his dinner, and at night he fell asleep in my lap, and I had to ask the girl to keep her eye on the lion for me—I couldn't move now. She said he was asleep, too.

And during this leg of the flight, my memory did me a great favor. Yes, I was granted certain recollections and they have made a sizable difference to me. And after all, it's not all to the bad to have had a long life. Something of benefit can be found in the past. First I was thinking, Take potatoes. They actually belong to the deadly nightshade family. Next I thought, Actually, pigs don't have a monopoly on grunting, either.

This reflection made me remember that after my brother Dick's death I went away from home, being already a big boy of about sixteen, with a mustache, a college freshman. The reason why I left was that I couldn't bear to see the old man mourn. We have a beautiful house, a regular work of art. The foundations are of stone and three feet thick; the ceilings are eighteen feet. The windows are twelve, and start at the floor, so that the light fills everything through that kind of marred old-fashioned glass. There's a peace that even I haven't been able to destroy, in those old rooms. Only one thing is wrong: the joint isn't modern. It's not like the rest of life at all, and therefore it's misleading. And as far as I was concerned, Dick could have had it. But the old man, gushing white beard from all his face, he made me feel our family line had ended with Dick up in the Adirondacks, when he shot at the pen and plugged the Greek's coffee urn. Dick also was a curly-headed man with broad shoulders, like the rest of us. He was drowned in the wild mountains, and now my dad looked at me and despaired.

An old man, disappointed, of failing strength, may try to reinvigorate himself by means of anger. Now I understand it. But I couldn't see it at sixteen, when we had a falling out. I was working that summer wrecking old cars, cutting them up for junk with the torch. I was lord and master of the wrecked cars, at a place about three miles from home. It did me good to work in this wrecking yard. That summer I did nothing but dismantle cars. I was grease and rust all over and scalded and dazzled with the cutting torch, and I made mountains of fenders and axles and car innards. On the day of Dick's funeral, I went to work, too. And in the evening, when I washed my-self in the back of the house under the garden hose, I was gasping as the chill water rushed over my head, and the old man came out on the back porch, in the dark green of the vines. By the side was a neglected orchard which later I cut down. The water blurted over me. It was cold as outer space. Fiercely, the old man started to yell at me. The hose bubbled on my head while inside I was hotter than the cutting torch that I took to all those old death cars from the highway. My father in his grief swore at me. I knew he meant it because he put aside his customary elegance of words. He cursed, I guess, be-cause I didn't comfort him.

So I went away. I hitchhiked to Niagara Falls. I reached Nia-gara and stood looking in. I was entranced by the crash of the water. Water can be very healing. I went on the *Maid of the Mists*, the old one, since burned, and through the Cave of the Winds, and the rest of it. And then I went on up to Ontario and picked up a job in an amusement park. This was most of all what I recalled on the plane, with the head of the American-Persian child on my lap, the North Atlantic leading its black life beneath us as the four propellers were fanning us home-ward.

It was Ontario, then, though I don't remember which part

of the province. The park was a fairground, too, and Hanson, the guy in charge, slept me in the stables. There the rats jumped back and forth over my legs at night, and fed on oats, and the watering of the horses began at daybreak, in the blue light that occurs at the end of darkness in the high latitudes. The Negroes came to the horses at this blue time of the night, when the damp was heavy.

I worked with Smolak. I almost had forgotten this animal, Smolak, an old brown bear whose trainer (also Smolak; he had been named for him) had beat it with the rest of the troupe and left him on Hanson's hands. There was no need of a trainer. Smolak was too old and his master had dusted him off. This ditched old creature was almost green with time and down to his last teeth, like the pits of dates. For this shabby animal Hanson had thought up a use. He had been trained to ride a bike, but now he was too old. Now he could feed from a dish with a rabbit; after which, in a cap and bib, he drank from a baby bottle while he stood on his hind legs. But there was one more thing, and this was where I came in. There was a month yet to the end of the season, and every day of this month Smolak and I rode on a roller coaster together before large crowds. This poor broken ruined creature and I, alone, took the high rides twice a day. And while we climbed and dipped and swooped and swerved and rose again higher than the Ferris wheels and fell, we held on to each other. By a common bond of despair we embraced, cheek to cheek, as all support seemed to leave us and we started down the perpendicular drop. I was pressed into his long-suffering, age-worn, tragic, and discolored coat as he grunted and cried to me. At times the animal would wet himself. But he was apparently aware I was his friend and he did not claw me. I took a pistol with blanks in case of an assault; it never was needed. I said to Hanson, as I recall, "We're two of a kind. Smolak was cast off and I am an Ishmael, too." As I lay in the stable, I would think about Dick's death and about my father. But most of the time I lived not with horses but with Smolak, and this poor creature and I were very close. So before pigs ever came on my horizon, I received a deep impression from a bear. So if corporeal things are an image of the spiritual and visible objects are renderings of invisible ones, and if Smolak and I were outcasts together, two humorists before the crowd, but brothers in our souls—I enbeared by him, and he probably humanized by me—I didn't come to the pigs as a tabula rasa. It only stands to reason. Something deep already was inscribed on me. In the end, I wonder if Dahfu would have found this out for himself.

Once more. Whatever gains I ever made were always due to love and nothing else. And as Smolak (mossy like a forest elm) and I rode together, and as he cried out at the top, beginning the bottomless rush over those skimpy yellow supports, and up once more against eternity's blue (oh, the stuff that has been done within this envelope of color, this subtle bag of life-giving gases!) while the Canadian hicks were rejoicing underneath with red faces, all the nubble-fingered rubes, we hugged each other, the bear and I, with something greater than terror and flew in those gilded cars. I shut my eyes in his wretched, time-abused fur. He held me in his arms and gave me comfort. And the great thing is that he didn't blame me. He had seen too much of life, and somewhere in his huge head he had worked it out that for creatures there is nothing that ever runs unmingled.

Lily will have to sit up with me if it takes all night, I was thinking, while I tell her all about this.

As for this kid resting against me, bound for Nevada with nothing but a Persian vocabulary—why, he was still trailing his cloud of glory. God knows, I dragged mine on as long as I could till it got dingy, mere tatters of gray fog. However, I always knew what it was.

"Well, look at you two," said the hostess, meaning that the kid also was awake. Two smoothly gray eyes moved at me, greatly expanded into the whites—new to life altogether. They had that new luster. With it they had ancient power, too. You could never convince me that *this was for the first time.*

"We are going to land for a while," said the young woman.

"The hell you say. Have we crept up on New York so soon? I told my wife to meet me in the afternoon."

"No, it's Newfoundland, for fuel," she said. "It's getting on toward daylight. You can see that, can't you?"

"Oh, I'm dying to breathe some of this cold stuff we've been flying through," I said. "After so many months in the Torrid Zone. You get what I mean?"

"I guess you'll have an opportunity," said the girl.

"Well, let me have a blanket for this child. I'll give him a breath of fresh air, too."

We started to slope and to go in, at which time there was a piercing red from the side of the sun into the clouds near the sea's surface. It was only a flash, and next gray light returned, and cliffs in an ice armor met with the green movement of the water, and we entered the lower air, which lay white and dry under the gray of the sky.

"I'm going to take a walk. Will you come with me?" I said to the kid. He answered me in Persian. "Well, it's okay," I said. I held out the blanket, and he stood on the seat and entered it. Wrapping him, I took him in my arms. The stewardess was going in to that invisible first-class passenger with coffee.

"All set? Why, where's your coat?" she asked me.

"That lion is all the baggage that I have," I said. "But that's all right. I'm country bred. I'm rugged."

So we were let out, this kid and I, and I carried him down from the ship and over the frozen ground of almost eternal winter, drawing breaths so deep they shook me, pure happiness, while the cold smote me from all sides through the stiff Italian corduroy with its broad wales, and the hairs of my beard turned spiky as the moisture of my breath froze instantly. Slipping, I ran over the ice in those same suede shoes. The socks were rotting within and crumbled, as I had never got around to changing them. I told the kid, "Inhale. Your face is too white from your orphan's troubles. Breathe in this air, kid, and get a little color." I held him close to my chest. He didn't seem to be afraid that I would fall with him. While to me he was like medicine applied, and the air, too; it also was a remedy. Plus the happiness that I expected at Idlewild from meeting Lily. And the lion? He was in it, too. Laps and laps I galloped around the shining and riveted body of the plane, behind the fuel trucks. Dark faces were looking from within. The great, beautiful propellers were still, all four of them. I guess I felt it was my turn now to move, and so went running—leaping, leaping, pounding, and tingling over the pure white lining of the gray Arctic silence.

HERZOG

To Pat Covici, *a great editor and,*
better yet, a generous friend,
this book is affectionately dedicated

IF I am out of my mind, it's all right with me, thought Moses Herzog.

Some people thought he was cracked and for a time he himself had doubted that he was all there. But now, though he still behaved oddly, he felt confident, cheerful, clairvoyant, and strong. He had fallen under a spell and was writing letters to everyone under the sun. He was so stirred by these letters that from the end of June he moved from place to place with a valise full of papers. He had carried this valise from New York to Martha's Vineyard, but returned from the Vineyard immediately; two days later he flew to Chicago, and from Chicago he went to a village in western Massachusetts. Hidden in the country, he wrote endlessly, fanatically, to the newspapers, to people in public life, to friends and relatives and at last to the dead, his own obscure dead, and finally the famous dead.

It was the peak of summer in the Berkshires. Herzog was alone in the big old house. Normally particular about food, he now ate Silvercup bread from the paper package, beans from the can, and American cheese. Now and then he picked raspberries in the overgrown garden, lifting up the thorny canes with absentminded caution. As for sleep, he slept on a mattress without sheets—it was his abandoned marriage bed—or in the hammock, covered by his coat. Tall bearded grass and locust and maple seedlings surrounded him in the yard. When he opened his eyes in the night, the stars were near like spiritual bodies. Fires, of course; gases—minerals, heat, atoms, but eloquent at five in the morning to a man lying in a hammock, wrapped in his overcoat.

When some new thought gripped his heart he went to the kitchen, his headquarters, to write it down. The white paint was scaling from the brick walls and Herzog sometimes wiped mouse droppings from the table with his sleeve, calmly wondering why field mice should have such a passion for wax and paraffin. They made holes in paraffin-sealed preserves; they gnawed birthday candles down to the wicks. A rat chewed into a package of bread, leaving the shape of its body in the layers of slices. Herzog ate the other half of the loaf spread with jam. He could share with rats too.

All the while, one corner of his mind remained open to the external world. He heard the crows in the morning. Their harsh call was delicious. He heard the thrushes at dusk. At night there was a barn owl. When he walked in the garden, excited by a mental letter, he saw roses winding about the rain spout; or mulberries—birds gorging in the mulberry tree. The days were hot, the evenings flushed and dusty. He looked keenly at everything but he felt half blind.

His friend, his former friend, Valentine, and his wife, his ex-wife Madeleine, had spread the rumor that his sanity had collapsed. Was it true?

He was taking a turn around the empty house and saw the shadow of his face in a gray, webby window. He looked weirdly tranquil. A radiant line went from mid-forehead over his straight nose and full, silent lips.

Late in spring Herzog had been overcome by the need to explain, to have it out, to justify, to put in perspective, to clarify, to make amends.

At that time he had been giving adult-education lectures in a New York night school. He was clear enough in April but by the end of May he began to ramble. It became apparent to his students that they would never learn much about The Roots of Romanticism but that they would see and hear odd things. One after another, the academic formalities dropped away. Professor Herzog had the unconscious frankness of a man deeply preoccupied. And toward the end of the term there were long pauses in his lectures. He would stop, muttering "Excuse me," reaching inside his coat for his pen. The table creaking, he wrote on scraps of paper with a great pressure of eagerness in his hand; he was absorbed, his eyes darkly circled. His white face showed everything—everything. He was reasoning, arguing, he was suffering, he had thought of a brilliant alternative—he was wide-open, he was narrow; his eyes, his mouth made everything silently clear—longing, bigotry, bitter anger. One could see it all. The class waited three minutes, five minutes, utterly silent.

At first there was no pattern to the notes he made. They

were fragments—nonsense syllables, exclamations, twisted proverbs and quotations or, in the Yiddish of his long-dead mother, *Trepverter*—retorts that came too late, when you were already on your way down the stairs.

He wrote, for instance, *Death—die—live again—die again — live.*

No person, no death.

And, *On the knees of your soul? Might as well be useful. Scrub the floor.*

Next, *Answer a fool according to his folly lest he be wise in his own conceit.*

Answer not a fool according to his folly, lest thou be like unto him.

Choose one.

He noted also, *I see by Walter Winchell that J. S. Bach put on black gloves to compose a requiem mass.*

Herzog scarcely knew what to think of this scrawling. He yielded to the excitement that inspired it and suspected at times that it might be a symptom of disintegration. That did not frighten him. Lying on the sofa of the kitchenette apartment he had rented on 17th Street, he sometimes imagined he was an industry that manufactured personal history, and saw himself from birth to death. He conceded on a piece of paper, *I cannot justify.*

Considering his entire life, he realized that he had mismanaged everything—everything. His life was, as the phrase goes, ruined. But since it had not been much to begin with, there was not much to grieve about. Thinking, on the malodorous sofa, of the centuries, the nineteenth, the sixteenth, the eighteenth, he turned up, from the last, a saying that he liked:

Grief, Sir, is a species of idleness.

He went on taking stock, lying face down on the sofa. Was he a clever man or an idiot? Well, he could not at this time claim to be clever. He might once have had the makings of a clever character, but he had chosen to be dreamy instead, and the sharpies cleaned him out. What more? He was losing his hair. He read the ads of the Thomas Scalp Specialists, with the exaggerated skepticism of a man whose craving to believe was deep, desperate. Scalp Experts! So . . . he was a formerly handsome man. His face revealed what a beating he had taken.

But he had asked to be beaten too, and had lent his attackers strength. That brought him to consider his character. What sort of character was it? Well, in the modern vocabulary, it was narcissistic; it was masochistic; it was anachronistic. His clinical picture was depressive—not the severest type; not a manic depressive. There were worse cripples around. If you believed, as everyone nowadays apparently did, that man was the sick animal, then was he even spectacularly sick, exceptionally blind, extraordinarily degraded? No. Was he intelligent? His intellect would have been more effective if be had had an aggressive paranoid character, eager for power. He was jealous but not exceptionally competitive, not a true paranoiac. And what about his learning?—He was obliged to admit, now, that he was not much of a professor, either. Oh, he was earnest, he had a certain large, immature sincerity, but he might never succeed in becoming systematic. He had made a brilliant start in his Ph.D. thesis—*The State of Nature in 17th and 18th Century English and French Political Philosophy.* He had to his credit also several articles and a book, *Romanticism and Christianity.* But the rest of his ambitious projects had dried up, one after another. On the strength of his early successes he had never had difficulty in finding jobs and obtaining research grants. The Narragansett Corporation had paid him fifteen thousand dollars over a number of years to continue his studies in Romanticism. The results lay in the closet, in an old valise—eight hundred pages of chaotic argument which had never found its focus. It was painful to think of it.

On the floor beside him were pieces of paper, and he occasionally leaned down to write.

He now set down, *Not that long disease, my life, but that long convalescence, my life. The liberal-bourgeois revision, the illusion of improvement, the poison of hope.*

He thought awhile of Mithridates, whose system learned to thrive on poison. He cheated his assassins, who made the mistake of using small doses, and was pickled, not destroyed.

Tutto fa brodo.

Resuming his self-examination, he admitted that he had been a bad husband—twice. Daisy, his first wife, he had treated miserably. Madeleine, his second, had tried to do *him* in. To his son and his daughter he was a loving but bad father. To his own parents he had been an ungrateful child. To his country, an indifferent citizen. To his brothers and his sister, affectionate but remote. With his friends, an egotist. With love, lazy. With brightness, dull. With power, passive. With his own soul, evasive.

Satisfied with his own severity, positively enjoying the hardness and factual rigor of his judgment, he lay on his sofa, his arms rising behind him, his legs extended without aim.

But how charming we remain, notwithstanding.

Papa, poor man, could charm birds from the trees, crocodiles from mud. Madeleine, too, had great charm, and beauty of person also, and a brilliant mind. Valentine Gersbach, her lover, was a charming man, too, though in a heavier, brutal style. He had a thick chin, flaming copper hair that literally gushed from his head (no Thomas Scalp Specialists for him), and he walked on a wooden leg, gracefully bending and straightening like a gondolier. Herzog himself had no small amount of charm. But his sexual powers had been damaged by Madeleine. And without the ability to attract women, how was he to recover? It was in this respect that he felt most like a convalescent.

The paltriness of these sexual struggles.

With Madeleine, several years ago, Herzog had made a fresh start in life. He had won her away from the Church—when they met, she had just been converted. With twenty thousand dollars inherited from his charming father, to please his new wife, he quit an academic position which was perfectly respectable and bought a big old house in Ludeyville, Massachusetts. In the peaceful Berkshires where he had friends (the Valentine Gersbachs) it should be easy to write his second volume on the social ideas of the Romantics.

Herzog did not leave academic life because he was doing badly. On the contrary, his reputation was good. His thesis had been influential and was translated into French and German. His early book, not much noticed when it was published, was now on many reading lists, and the younger generation of historians accepted it as a model of the new sort of history, "history that interests *us*"—personal, *engagée*—and looks at the past with an intense need for contemporary relevance. As long as Moses was married to Daisy, he had led the perfectly ordinary life of an assistant professor, respected and stable. His first work showed by objective research what Christianity was to Romanticism. In the second he was becoming tougher, more assertive, more ambitious. There was a great deal of ruggedness actually, in his character. He had a strong will and a talent for polemics, a taste for the philosophy of history. In marrying Madeleine and resigning from the university (because she thought he should), digging in at Ludeyville, he showed a taste and talent also for danger and extremism, for heterodoxy, for ordeals, a fatal attraction to the "City of Destruction." What he planned was a history which really took into account the revolutions and mass convulsions of the twentieth century, accepting, with de Tocqueville, the universal and durable development of the equality of conditions, the progress of democracy.

But he couldn't deceive himself about this work. He was beginning seriously to distrust it. His ambitions received a sharp check. Hegel was giving him a great deal of trouble. Ten years earlier he had been certain he understood his ideas on consensus and civility, but something had gone wrong. He was distressed, impatient, angry. At the same time, he and his wife were behaving very peculiarly. She was dissatisfied. At first, she hadn't wanted him to be an ordinary professor, but she changed her mind after a year in the country. Madeleine considered herself too young, too intelligent, too vital, too sociable to be buried in the remote Berkshires. She decided to finish her graduate studies in Slavonic languages. Herzog wrote to Chicago about jobs. He had to find a position for Valentine Gersbach, too. Valentine was a radio announcer, a disk-jockey in Pittsfield. You couldn't leave people like Valentine and Phoebe stuck in this mournful countryside, alone, Madeleine said. Chicago was chosen because Herzog had grown up there, and was well-connected. So he taught courses in the Downtown College and Gersbach became educational director of an FM station in the Loop. The house near Ludeyville was closed up—twenty thousand dollars' worth of house, with books and English bone china and new appliances abandoned to the spiders, the moles, and the field mice—Papa's hard-earned money!

The Herzogs moved to the Midwest. But after about a year of this new Chicago life, Madeleine decided that she and

Moses couldn't make it after all—she wanted a divorce. He had to give it, what could he do? And the divorce was painful. He was in love with Madeleine; he couldn't bear to leave his little daughter. But Madeleine refused to be married to him, and people's wishes have to be respected. Slavery is dead.

The strain of the second divorce was too much for Herzog. He felt he was going to pieces—breaking up—and Dr. Edvig, the Chicago psychiatrist who treated both Herzogs, agreed that perhaps it was best for Moses to leave town. He came to an understanding with the dean of the Downtown College that he might come back when he was feeling better, and on money borrowed from his brother Shura he went to Europe. Not everyone threatened with a crackup can manage to go to Europe for relief. Most people have to keep on working; they report daily, they still ride the subway. Or else they drink, they go to the movies and sit there suffering. Herzog ought to have been grateful. Unless you are utterly exploded, there is always something to be grateful for. In fact, he was grateful.

He was not exactly idle in Europe, either. He made a cultural tour for the Narragansett Corporation, lecturing in Copenhagen, Warsaw, Cracow, Berlin, Belgrade, Istanbul, and Jerusalem. But in March when he came to Chicago again his condition was worse than it had been in November. He told his dean that it would probably be better for him to stay in New York. He did not see Madeleine during his visit. His behavior was so strange and to her mind so menacing, that she warned him through Gersbach not to come near the house on Harper Avenue. The police had a picture of him and would arrest him if he was seen in the block.

It was now becoming clear to Herzog, himself incapable of making plans, how well Madeleine had prepared to get rid of him. Six weeks before sending him away, she had had him lease a house near the Midway at two hundred dollars a month. When they moved in, he built shelves, cleared the garden, and repaired the garage door; he put up the storm windows. Only a week before she demanded a divorce, she had his things cleaned and pressed, but on the day he left the house, she flung them all into a carton which she then dumped down the cellar stairs. She needed more closet space. And other things happened, sad, comical, or cruel, depending on one's point of view.

Until the very last day, the tone of Herzog's relations with Madeleine was quite serious—that is, ideas, personalities, issues were respected and discussed. When she broke the news to him, for instance, she expressed herself with dignity, in that lovely, masterful style of hers. She had thought it over from every angle, she said, and she had to accept defeat. They could not make the grade together. She was prepared to shoulder some of the blame. Of course, Herzog was not entirely unprepared for this. But he had really thought matters were improving.

All this happened on a bright, keen fall day. He had been in the back yard putting in the storm windows. The first frost had already caught the tomatoes. The grass was dense and soft, with the peculiar beauty it gains when the cold days come and the gossamers lie on it in the morning; the dew is thick and lasting. The tomato vines had blackened and the red globes had burst.

He had seen Madeleine at the back window upstairs, putting June down for her nap, and later he heard the bath being run. Now she was calling from the kitchen door. A gust from the lake made the framed glass tremble in Herzog's arms. He propped it carefully against the porch and took off his canvas gloves but not his beret, as though he sensed that he would immediately go on a trip.

Madeleine hated her father violently, but it was not irrelevant that the old man was a famous impresario—sometimes called the American Stanislavsky. She had prepared the event with a certain theatrical genius of her own. She wore black stockings, high heels, a lavender dress with Indian brocade from Central America. She had on her opal earrings, her bracelets, and she was perfumed; her hair was combed with a new, clean part and her large eyelids shone with a bluish cosmetic. Her eyes were blue but the depth of the color was curiously affected by the variable tinge of the whites. Her nose, which descended in a straight elegant line from her brows, worked slightly when she was peculiarly stirred. To Herzog even this tic was precious. There was a flavor of subjugation in his love for Madeleine. Since she was domineering, and since he loved her, he had to accept the flavor that was given. In this confrontation in the untidy parlor, two kinds of egotism were present, and Herzog from his sofa in New York now contem-

plated them—hers in triumph (she had prepared a great moment, she was about to do what she longed most to do, strike
a blow) and his egotism in abeyance, all converted into passivity. What he was about to suffer, he deserved; he had sinned
long and hard; he had earned it. This was it.

In the window on glass shelves there stood an ornamental
collection of small glass bottles, Venetian and Swedish. They
came with the house. The sun now caught them. They were
pierced with the light. Herzog saw the waves, the threads of
color, the spectral intersecting bars, and especially a great blot
of flaming white on the center of the wall above Madeleine.
She was saying, "We can't live together any more."

Her speech continued for several minutes. Her sentences
were well formed. This speech had been rehearsed and it
seemed also that he had been waiting for the performance to
begin.

Theirs was not a marriage that could last. Madeleine had
never loved him. She was telling him that. "It's painful to have
to say I never loved you. I never will love you, either," she said.
"So there's no point in going on."

Herzog said, "I do love you, Madeleine."

Step by step, Madeleine rose in distinction, in brilliance, in
insight. Her color grew very rich, and her brows, and that
Byzantine nose of hers, rose, moved; her blue eyes gained by
the flush that kept deepening, rising from her chest and her
throat. She was in an ecstasy of consciousness. It occurred to
Herzog that she had beaten him so badly, her pride was so
fully satisfied, that there was an overflow of strength into her
intelligence. He realized that he was witnessing one of the very
greatest moments of her life.

"You should hold on to that feeling," she said. "I believe it's
true. You do love me. But I think you also understand what a
humiliation it is to me to admit defeat in this marriage. I've
put all I had into it. I'm crushed by this."

Crushed? She had never looked more glorious. There was an
element of theater in those looks, but much more of passion.

And Herzog, a solid figure of a man, if pale and suffering,
lying on his sofa in the lengthening evening of a New York
spring, in the background the trembling energy of the city,
a sense and flavor of river water, a stripe of beautifying and

dramatic filth contributed by New Jersey to the sunset, Herzog in the coop of his privacy and still strong in body (his health was really a sort of miracle; he had done his best to be sick) pictured what might have happened if instead of listening so intensely and thoughtfully he had hit Madeleine in the face. What if he had knocked her down, clutched her hair, dragged her screaming and fighting around the room, flogged her until her buttocks bled. What if he had! He should have torn her clothes, ripped off her necklace, brought his fists down on her head. He rejected this mental violence, sighing. He was afraid he was really given in secret to this sort of brutality. But suppose even that he had told *her* to leave the house. After all, it was *his* house. If she couldn't live with him, why didn't she leave? The scandal? There was no need to be driven away by a little scandal. It would have been painful, grotesque, but a scandal was after all a sort of service to the community. Only it had never entered Herzog's mind, in that parlor of flashing bottles, to stand his ground. He still thought perhaps that he could win by the appeal of passivity, of personality, win on the ground of being, after all, Moses—Moses Elkanah Herzog—a good man, and Madeleine's particular benefactor. He had done everything for her—everything!

"Have you discussed this decision with Doctor Edvig?" he said. "What does he think?"

"What difference could his opinion make to me? He can't tell me what to do. He can only help me understand. . . . I went to a lawyer," she said.

"Which lawyer?"

"Well, Sandor Himmelstein. Because he is a buddy of yours. He says you can stay with him until you make your new arrangements."

The conversation was over, and Herzog returned to the storm windows in the shadow and green damp of the back yard—to his obscure system of idiosyncrasies. A person of irregular tendencies, he practiced the art of circling among random facts to swoop down on the essentials. He often expected to take the essentials by surprise, by an amusing stratagem. But nothing of the sort happened as he maneuvered the rattling glass, standing among the frost-scorched drooping tomato vines tied to their stakes with strips of rag. The plant scent was strong. He continued with the windows because he couldn't allow himself to feel crippled. He dreaded the depths of feeling he would eventually have to face, when he could no longer call upon his eccentricities for relief.

In his posture of collapse on the sofa, arms abandoned over his head and legs stretched away, lying with no more style than a chimpanzee, his eyes with greater than normal radiance watched his own work in the garden with detachment, as if he were looking through the front end of a telescope at a tiny clear image.

That suffering joker.

Two points therefore: He knew his scribbling, his letter-writing, was ridiculous. It was involuntary. His eccentricities had him in their power.

There is someone inside me. I am in his grip. When I speak of him I feel him in my head, pounding for order. He will ruin me.

It has been reported, he wrote, *that several teams of Russian Cosmonauts have been lost; disintegrated, we must assume. One was heard calling "SOS—world SOS." Soviet confirmation has been withheld.*

Dear Mama, As to why I haven't visited your grave in so long . . .

Dear Wanda, Dear Zinka, Dear Libbie, Dear Ramona, Dear Sono, I need help in the worst way. I am afraid of falling apart. Dear Edvig, the fact is that madness also has been denied me. I don't know why I should write to you at all. Dear Mr. President, Internal Revenue regulations will turn us into a nation of bookkeepers. The life of every citizen is becoming a business. This, it seems to me, is one of the worst interpretations of the meaning of human life history has ever seen. Man's life is not a business.

And how shall I sign this? thought Moses. Indignant citizen? Indignation is so wearing that one should reserve it for the main injustice.

Dear Daisy, he wrote to his first wife, *I know it's my turn to visit Marco in camp on Parents' Day but this year I'm afraid my presence might disturb him. I have been writing to him, and keeping up with his activities. It is unfortunately true, however, that he blames me for the breakup with Madeleine and feels I have deserted also his little half-sister. He is too young to under-stand the difference between the two divorces.* Here Herzog asked himself whether it would be appropriate to discuss the matter further with Daisy and, picturing to himself her handsome and angry face as she read his as yet unwritten letter, he decided against this. He continued, *I think it would be best for Marco not to see me. I have been sick—under the doctor's care.* He noted with distaste his own trick of appealing for sympathy. A personality had its own ways. A mind might observe them without approval. Herzog did not care for his own personality, and at the moment there was apparently nothing he could do about its impulses. *Rebuilding my health and strength gradually*—as a person of sound positive principles, modern and liberal, news of his progress (if true) should please her. As the victim of those impulses she must be looking in the paper for his obituary.

The strength of Herzog's constitution worked obstinately against his hypochondria. Early in June, when the general revival of life troubles many people, the new roses, even in shop windows, reminding them of their own failures, of sterility and death, Herzog went to have a medical checkup. He paid a visit to an elderly refugee, Dr. Emmerich, on the West Side, facing Central Park. A frowzy doorman with an odor of old age about him, wearing a cap from a Balkan campaign half a century gone, let him into the crumbling vault of the lobby. Herzog undressed in the examining room—a troubled, dire green; the dark walls seemed swollen with the disease of old buildings in New York. He was not a big man but he was sturdily built, his muscles developed by the hard work he had done in the country. He was vain of his muscles, the breadth and strength of his hands, the smoothness of his skin, but he saw through this too, and he feared being caught in the part of the aging, conceited handsome man. Old fool, he called himself, glancing away from the small mirror, the graying hair, the wrinkles of amusement and bitterness. Through the slats of the blind he looked instead at the brown rocks of the park, speckled with mica, and at the optimistic leaping green of June. It would tire soon, as leaves broadened and New York deposited its soot on the summer. It was, however, especially beautiful now, vivid in all particulars—the twigs, the small darts and subtly swelling shapes of green. Beauty is not a human invention. Dr.

Emmerich, stooped but energetic, examined him, sounded his chest and back, flashed the light in his eyes, took his blood, felt his prostate gland, wired him for the electrocardiograph.

"Well, you are a healthy man—not twenty-one, but strong."

Herzog heard this with satisfaction, of course, but still he was faintly unhappy about it. He had been hoping for some definite sickness which would send him to a hospital for a while. He would not have to look after himself. His brothers, who had given up on him, more or less, would rally to him then and his sister Helen might come to take care of him. The family would meet his expenses and pay for Marco and June. That was out, now. Apart from the little infection he had caught in Poland, his health was sound, and even that infection, now cured, had been nonspecific. It might have been due to his mental state, to depression and fatigue, not to Wanda. For one horrible day he had thought it was gonorrhea. He must write to Wanda, he thought as he pulled his shirttails forward, buttoned his sleeves. *Chère Wanda*, he began, *Bonnes nouvelles. T'en seras contente.* It was another of his shady love affairs in French. For what other reason had he ground away at his Frazer and Squair in high school, and read Rousseau and de Maistre in college? His achievements were not only scholarly but sexual. And were those achievements? It was his pride that must be satisfied. His flesh got what was left over.

"Then what is the matter with you?" said Dr. Emmerich. An old man, hair grizzled like his own, face narrow and witty, looked up into his eyes. Herzog believed he understood his message. The doctor was telling him that in this decaying office he examined the truly weak, the desperately sick, stricken women, dying men. Then what did Herzog want with him? "You seem very excited," Emmerich said.

"Yes, that's it. I am excited."

"Do you want Miltown? Snakeroot? Do you have insomnia?"

"Not seriously," said Herzog. "My thoughts are shooting out all over the place."

"Do you want me to recommend a psychiatrist?"

"No, I've had all the psychiatry I can use."

"Then what about a holiday? Take a young lady to the country, the seashore. Do you still have the place in Massachusetts?"

"If I want to reopen it."

"Does your friend still live up there? The radio announcer. What is the name of the big fellow with red hair, with the wooden leg?"

"Valentine Gersbach is his name. No, he moved to Chicago when I—when we did."

"He's a very amusing man."

"Yes. Very."

"I heard of your divorce—who told me? I am sorry about it."

Looking for happiness—ought to be prepared for bad results.

Emmerich put on his Ben Franklin eyeglasses and wrote a few words on the file card. "The child is with Madeleine in Chicago, I suppose," said the doctor.

"Yes—"

Herzog tried to get Emmerich to reveal his opinion of Madeleine. She had been his patient, too. But Emmerich would say nothing. Of course not; a doctor must not discuss his patients. Still, an opinion might be construed out of the glances he gave Moses.

"She's a violent, hysterical woman," he told Emmerich. He saw from the old man's lips that he was about to answer; but then Emmerich decided to say nothing, and Moses, who had an odd habit of completing people's sentences for them, made a mental note about his own perplexing personality.

A strange heart. I myself can't account for it.

He now saw that he had come to Emmerich to accuse Madeleine, or simply to talk about her with someone who knew her and could take a realistic view of her.

"But you must have other women," said Emmerich. "Isn't there somebody? Do you have to eat dinner alone tonight?"

Herzog had Ramona. She was a lovely woman, but with her too there were problems, of course—there were bound to be problems. Ramona was a businesswoman, she owned a flower shop on Lexington Avenue. She was not young—probably in her thirties; she wouldn't tell Moses her exact age—but she was extremely attractive, slightly foreign, well-educated. When she inherited the business she was getting her M.A. at Columbia in art history. In fact, she was enrolled in Herzog's evening course. In principle, he opposed affairs with students, even with students like Ramona Donsell, who were obviously made for them.

Doing all the things a wild man does, he noted, *while remaining all the while an earnest person. In frightful earnest.*

Of course it was just this earnestness that attracted Ramona. Ideas excited her. She loved to talk. She was an excellent cook, too, and knew how to prepare shrimp Arnaud, which she served with Pouilly Fuissé. Herzog had supper with her several nights a week. In the cab passing from the drab lecture hall to Ramona's large West Side apartment, she had said she wanted him to feel how her heart was beating. He reached for her wrist, to take her pulse, but she said, "We are not young children, Professor," and put his hand elsewhere.

Within a few days Ramona was saying that this was no ordinary affair. She recognized, she said, that Moses was in a peculiar state, but there was something about him so dear, so loving, so healthy, and basically so steady—as if, having survived so many horrors, he had been purged of neurotic nonsense—that perhaps it had been simply a question of the right woman, all along. Her interest in him quickly became serious, and he consequently began to worry about her, to brood. He said to her a few days after his visit to Emmerich that the doctor had advised him to take a holiday. Ramona then said, "Of course you need a holiday. Why don't you go to Montauk? I have a house there, and I could come out weekends. Perhaps we could stay together all of July."

"I didn't know you owned a house," said Herzog.

"It was up for sale a few years ago, and it was really too big for me, alone, but I had just divorced Harold, and I needed a diversion."

She showed him colored slides of the cottage. With his eye to the viewer, he said, "It's very pretty. All those flowers." But he felt heavy-hearted—dreadful.

"One can have a marvelous time there. And you really ought to get some cheerful summer clothes. Why do you wear such drab things? You still have a youthful figure."

"I lost weight last winter, in Poland and Italy."

"Nonsense—why talk like that! You know you're a good-looking man. And you even take pride in being one. In

Argentina they'd call you *macho*—masculine. You like to come on meek and tame, and cover up the devil that's in you. Why put that little devil down? Why not make friends with him— well, why not?"

Instead of answering, he wrote mentally, *Dear Ramona— Very dear Ramona. I like you very much—dear to me, a true friend. It might even go farther. But why is it that I, a lecturer, can't bear to be lectured? I think your wisdom gets me. Because you have the complete wisdom. Perhaps to excess. I do not like to refuse correction. I have a lot to be corrected about. Almost everything. And I know good luck when I see it.* . . . This was the literal truth, every word of it. He did like Ramona.

She came from Buenos Aires. Her background was international—Spanish, French, Russian, Polish, and Jewish. She had gone to school in Switzerland and still spoke with a slight accent, full of charm. She was short but had a full, substantial figure, a good round seat, firm breasts (all these things mattered to Herzog; he might think himself a moralist but the shape of a woman's breasts mattered greatly). Ramona was unsure of her chin but had confidence in her lovely throat, and so she held her head fairly high. She walked with quick efficiency, rapping her heels in energetic Castilian style. Herzog was intoxicated by this clatter. She entered a room provocatively, swaggering slightly, one hand touching her thigh, as though she carried a knife in her garter belt. It seemed to be the fashion in Madrid, and it delighted Ramona to come on playfully in the role of a tough Spanish broad—*una navaja en la liga*; she taught him the expression. He thought often of that imaginary knife when he watched her in her underthings, which were extravagant and black, a strapless contrivance called the Merry Widow that drew in the waist and trailed red ribbons below. Her thighs were short, but deep and white. The skin darkened where it was compressed by the elastic garment. And silky tags hung down, and garter buckles. Her eyes were brown, sensitive and shrewd, erotic and calculating. She knew what she was up to. The warm odor, the downy arms, the fine bust and excellent white teeth and slightly bowed legs—they all worked. Moses, suffering, suffered in style. His luck never entirely deserted him. Perhaps he was luckier than he knew. Ramona tried to tell him so. "That bitch did you a favor," she said. "You'll be far better off."

Moses! he wrote, *winning as he weeps, weeping as he wins. Evidently can't believe in victories.*

Hitch your agony to a star.

But at the silent moment at which he faced Ramona he wrote, incapable of replying except by mental letter, *You are a great comfort to me. We are dealing with elements more or less stable, more or less controllable, more or less mad. It's true. I have a wild spirit in me though I look meek and mild. You think that sexual pleasure is all this spirit wants, and since we are giving him that sexual pleasure, then why shouldn't everything be well?*

Then he realized suddenly that Ramona had made herself into a sort of sexual professional (or priestess). He was used to dealing with vile amateurs lately. *I didn't know that I could make out with a true sack artist.*

But is that the secret goal of my vague pilgrimage? Do I see myself to be after long blundering an unrecognized son of Sodom and Dionysus—an Orphic type? (Ramona enjoyed speaking of Orphic types.) A petit-bourgeois Dionysian?

He noted: *Foo to all those categories!*

"Perhaps I will buy some summer clothes," he answered Ramona.

I do like fine apparel, he went on. *I used to rub my patent-leather shoes with butter, in early childhood. I overheard my Russian mother calling me "Krasavitz." And when I became a gloomy young student, with a soft handsome face, wasting my time in arrogant looks, I thought a great deal about trousers and shirts. It was only later, as an academic, that I became dowdy. I bought a gaudy vest in the Burlington Arcade last winter, and a pair of Swiss boots of the type I see now the Village fairies have adopted. Heartsore? Yes,* he further wrote, *and dressed-up, too. But my vanity will no longer give me much mileage and to tell you the truth I'm not even greatly impressed with my own tortured heart. It begins to seem another waste of time.*

Soberly deliberating, Herzog decided it would be better not to accept Ramona's offer. She was thirty-seven or thirty-eight years of age, he shrewdly reckoned, and this meant that she was looking for a husband. This, in itself, was not wicked, or even funny. Simple and general human conditions prevailed among the most seemingly sophisticated. Ramona had not learned those erotic monkeyshines in a manual, but in adventure, in confusion, and at times probably with a sinking heart, in brutal and often alien embraces. So now she must yearn for stability. She wanted to give her heart once and for all, and level with a good man, become Herzog's wife and quit being an easy lay. She often had a sober look. Her eyes touched him deeply.

Never idle, his mind's eye saw Montauk—white beaches, flashing light, glossy breakers, horseshoe crabs perishing in their armor, sea robins and blowfish. Herzog longed to lie down in his bathing trunks, and warm his troubled belly on the sand. But how could he? To accept too many favors from Ramona was dangerous. He might have to pay with his freedom. Of course he didn't need that freedom now; he needed a rest. Still, after resting, he might want his freedom again. He wasn't sure of that, either. But it was a possibility.

A holiday will give me more strength to bring to my neurotic life.

Still, Herzog considered, he did look terrible, caved-in; he was losing more hair, and this rapid deterioration he considered to be a surrender to Madeleine and Gersbach, her lover, and to all his enemies. He had more enemies and hatreds than anyone could easily guess from his thoughtful expression.

The night-school term was coming to an end, and Herzog convinced himself that his wisest move was to get away from Ramona too. He decided to go to the Vineyard, but, thinking it a bad thing to be entirely alone, he sent a night letter to a woman in Vineyard Haven, an old friend (they had once considered having an affair but this had never materialized and they were instead tenderly considerate of each other). In the wire he explained the situation and his friend Libbie Vane (Libbie Vane-Erikson-Sissler; she had just married for the third time and the house in the Haven belonged to her husband, an industrial chemist) telephoned him promptly, and very emotionally and sincerely invited him to come and stay as long as he liked.

"Rent me a room near the beach," Herzog requested.

"Come and stay with us."

"No, no. I can't do that. Why, you've just gotten married."

"Oh, Moses—please, don't be so romantic. Sissler and I have been living together three years."

"Still, it is a honeymoon, isn't it?"

"Oh, stop this nonsense. I'll be hurt if you don't stay here. We have six bedrooms. You come right out, I've heard what a rough time you've been having."

In the end—it was inevitable—he accepted. He felt, however, that he was acting badly. By wiring, he had practically forced her to invite him. He had helped Libbie greatly about ten years before, and he would have been more pleased with himself if he had not made her pay off. He knew better than to ask for help. He was making a bore of himself—doing the weak thing, the corrupt thing.

But at least, he thought, I don't have to make matters worse. I won't bore Libbie with my troubles, or spend the week crying on her bosom. I'll take them out to dinner, her and her new husband. You have to fight for your life. That's the chief condition on which you hold it. Then why be halfhearted? Ramona is right. Get some light clothes. You can borrow more dough from brother Shura—he likes that, and he knows you'll repay. That's living by the approbative principle—you pay your debts.

Therefore, he went shopping for clothes. He examined the ads in *The New Yorker* and *Esquire*. These now showed older men with lined faces as well as young executives and athletes. Then, after shaving more closely than usual and brushing his hair (could he bear to see himself in the brilliant triple mirrors of a clothing store?), he took the bus uptown. Starting at 59th Street, he worked his way down Madison Avenue into the forties and back toward the Plaza on Fifth. Then the gray clouds opened before the piercing sun. The windows glittered and Herzog looked into them, shamefaced and excited. The new styles seemed to him reckless and gaudy—madras coats, shorts with melting bursts of Kandinsky colors, in which middle-aged or paunchy old men would be ludicrous. Better puritan restraint than the exhibition of pitiful puckered knees and varicose veins, pelican bellies and the indecency of haggard faces under sporty caps. Undoubtedly Valentine Gersbach, who had beat him out with Madeleine, surmounting the handicap of a wooden leg, could wear those handsome brilliant candy stripes. Valentine was a dandy. He had a thick face and heavy jaws; Moses thought he somewhat resembled Putzi Hanfstaengl,

Hitler's own pianist. But Gersbach had a pair of extraordinary eyes for a red-haired man, brown, deep, hot eyes, full of life. The lashes, too, were vital, ruddy-dark, long and childlike. And that hair was bearishly thick. Valentine, furthermore, was exquisitely confident of his appearance. You could see it. He knew he was a terribly handsome man. He expected women— all women—to be mad about him. And many were, weren't they? Including the second Mrs. Herzog.

"Wear that? Me?" said Herzog to the salesman in a Fifth Avenue shop. But he bought a coat of crimson and white stripes. Then he said over his shoulder to the salesman that in the Old Country his family had worn black gabardines down to the ground.

From a youthful case of acne, the salesman had a rough skin. His face was red as a carnation, and he had a meat-flavored breath, a dog's breath. He was a trifle rude to Moses, for when he asked his waist size and Moses answered, "Thirty-four" the salesman said, "Don't boast." That had slipped out, and Moses was too gentlemanly to hold it against him. His heart worked somewhat with the painful satisfaction of restraint. Eyes lowered, he trod the gray carpet to the fitting room, and there, disrobing and working the new pants up over his shoes, he wrote the fellow a note. *Dear Mack. Dealing with poor jerks every day. Male pride. Effrontery. Conceit. Yourself obliged to be agreeable and winsome. Hard job if you happen to be a grudging, angry fellow. The candor of people in New York! Bless you, you are not nice. But in a false situation, as we all are. Must manage some civility. A true situation might well prove unendurable to us all. From civility I now have some pain in my belly. As for gabardines, I realize there are plenty of beards and gabardines just around the corner, in the diamond district. O Lord!* he concluded, *forgive all these trespasses. Lead me not into Penn Station.*

Dressed in Italian pants, furled at the bottom, and a blazer with slender lapels, red and white, he avoided full exposure in the triple, lighted mirror. His body seemed unaffected by his troubles, survived all blasts. It was his face that was devastated, especially about the eyes, so that it made him pale to see himself.

Preoccupied, the salesman among silent clothes racks did

not hear Herzog's footfalls. He was brooding. Slow business. Another small recession. Only Moses was spending today. Money he intended to borrow from his money-making brother. Shura was not tight-fisted. Nor was brother Willie, for that matter. But Moses found it easier to take it from Shura, also something of a sinner, than from Willie, who was more respectable.

"The back fit all right?" Herzog turned.

"Like tailor-made," the salesman said.

He couldn't have cared less. It was perfectly plain. I can't get his interest, Herzog recognized. Then I'll do without, and screw him, too. I'll decide for myself. It's my move. Thus strengthened, he stepped between the mirrors, looking only at the coat. It was satisfactory.

"Wrap it up," he said. "I'll take the pants, too, but I want them today. Now."

"Can't do it. The tailor's busy."

"Today, or it's no dice," said Herzog. "I have to leave town." Two can play this hard-nosed game.

"I'll see if I can get a rush on it," the salesman said.

He went, and Herzog undid the chased buttons. They had used the head of some Roman emperor to adorn the jacket of a pleasure-seeker, he noted. Alone, he put his tongue out at himself and then withdrew from the triple mirror. He remembered how much pleasure it gave Madeleine to try on clothes in shops and how much heart and pride there was in her when she looked at herself, touching, adjusting, her face glowing but severe, too, with the great blue eyes, the vivid bangs, the medallion profile. The satisfaction she took in herself was positively plural—imperial. And she had told Moses during one of their crises that she had had a new look at herself nude before the bathroom mirror. "Still young," she said, taking inventory, "young, beautiful, full of life. Why should I waste it all on you."

Why, God forbid! Herzog looked for something to write a note with, having left paper and pencil in the dressing room. He jotted on the back of the salesman's pad, *A bitch in time breeds contempt.*

Looking through piles of beachwear, now silently laughing at himself as if his heart were swimming upward, Herzog bought a pair of trunks for the Vineyard, and then a rack of

old-fashioned straw hats caught his attention and he decided
to have one of those too.

And was he getting all these things, he asked, because old
Emmerich had prescribed a rest? Or was he preparing for new
shenanigans—did he anticipate another entanglement at the
Vineyard? With whom? How should he know with whom?
Women were plentiful everywhere.

At home, he tried on his purchases. The bathing trunks
were a little tight. But the oval straw hat pleased him, floating
on the hair which still grew thickly at the sides. In it he looked
like his father's cousin Elias Herzog, the flour salesman who
had covered the northern Indiana territory for General Mills
back in the twenties. Elias with his earnest Americanized clean-
shaven face ate hard-boiled eggs and drank prohibition beer—
home-brewed Polish piva. He gave the eggs a neat rap on the
rail of the porch and peeled them scrupulously. He wore colorful sleeve garters and a skimmer like this one, set on this same
head of hair shared also by *his* father, Rabbi Sandor-Alexander
Herzog, who wore a beautiful beard as well, a radiant, broad-
strung beard that hid the outline of his chin and also the velvet collar of his frock coat. Herzog's mother had had a
weakness for Jews with handsome beards. In her family, too,
all the elders had beards that were thick and rich, full of religion. She wanted Moses to become a rabbi and he seemed to
himself gruesomely unlike a rabbi now in the trunks and straw
hat, his face charged with heavy sadness, foolish utter longing
of which a religious life might have purged him. That mouth!
—heavy with desire and irreconcilable anger, the straight nose
sometimes grim, the dark eyes! And his figure!—the long veins
winding in the arms and filling in the hanging hands, an ancient system of greater antiquity than the Jews themselves. The
flat-topped hat, a crust of straw, had a red and white band,
matching the coat. He removed the tissue paper from the
sleeves and put it on, swelling out the stripes. Bare-legged, he
looked like a Hindu.

Consider the lilies of the field, he remembered, *they toil not,
neither do they spin, yet Solomon in all his glory was not arrayed . . .*

He had been eight years old, in the children's ward of the
Royal Victoria Hospital, Montreal, when he learned those

words. A Christian lady came once a week and had him read aloud from the Bible. He read, *Give and it shall be given unto you: good measure, pressed down and shaken together and running over shall men give unto your bosom.*

From the hospital roof hung icicles like the teeth of fish, clear drops burning at their tips. Beside his bed, the goyische lady sat in her long skirts and button shoes. The hatpin projected from the back of her head like a trolley rod. A paste odor came from her clothing. And then she had him read, *Suffer the little children to come unto me.* She seemed to him a good woman. Her face, however, was strained and grim.

"Where do you live, little boy?"

"On Napoleon Street."

Where the Jews live.

"What does your father do?"

My father is a bootlegger. He has a still in Point-St. Charles. The spotters are after him. He has no money.

Only of course Moses would never have told her any of this. Even at five he would have known better. His mother had instructed him. "You must never say."

There was a certain wisdom in it, he thought, as if by staggering he could recover his balance, or by admitting a bit of madness come to his senses. And he enjoyed a joke on himself. Now, for instance, he had packed the summer clothes he couldn't afford and was making his getaway from Ramona. He knew how things would turn out if he went to Montauk with her. She would lead him like a tame bear in Easthampton, from cocktail party to cocktail party. He could imagine that— Ramona laughing, talking, her shoulders bare in one of her peasant blouses (they were marvelous, feminine shoulders, he had to admit that), her hair in black curls, her face, her mouth painted; he could smell the perfume. In the depths of a man's being there was something that responded with a quack to such perfume. Quack! A sexual reflex that had nothing to do with age or subtlety, wisdom, experience, history, *Wissenschaft, Bildung, Wahrheit.* In sickness or health there came the old quack-quack at the fragrance of perfumed, feminine skin. Yes, Ramona would lead him in his new pants and striped jacket, sipping a martini . . . Martinis were poison to Herzog and he couldn't bear small talk. And so he would suck in his belly and stand on aching feet—he, the captive professor, she the mature, successful, laughing, sexual woman. Quack, quack!

His bag was packed, and he locked the windows and pulled the shades. He knew the apartment would smell mustier than ever when he came back from his bachelor holiday. Two marriages, two children, and he was setting off for a week of *carefree* rest. It was painful to his instincts, his Jewish family feelings, that his children should be growing up without him. But what could he do about that? To the sea! To the sea!— What sea? It was the bay—between East Chop and West Chop it wasn't sea; the water was quiet.

He went out, fighting his sadness over this solitary life. His chest expanded, and he caught his breath. "For Christ's sake, don't cry, you idiot! Live or die, but don't poison everything."

Why this door should need a police lock he didn't know. Crime was on the increase, but he had nothing worth stealing. Only some excited kid might think he had, and lie in wait, hopped-up, to hit him on the head. Herzog led the metal foot of the lock into its slot in the floor and turned the key. He then checked to be sure he hadn't forgotten his glasses. No, they were in his breast pocket. He had his pens, notebook, checkbook, a piece of kitchen towel he had torn off for his handkerchief, and the plastic container of Furadantin tablets. The tablets were for the infection he had caught in Poland. He was cured of it now, but he took an occasional pill just to be on the safe side. That was a frightening moment in Cracow, in the hotel room, when the symptom appeared. He thought, The clap—at last! After all these years. At my time of life! His heart sank.

He went to a British doctor, who scolded him sharply. "What have you been up to? Are you married?"

"No."

"Well, it isn't a clap. Pull up your trousers. You'll want a shot of penicillin, I suppose. All Americans do. Well, I shan't give it. Take this sulfa. No booze, mind you. Drink tea."

They are unforgiving about sexual offenses. The fellow was angry, biting, a snotty Limey doctor. And I so vulnerable, heavy with guilt.

I should have known that a woman like Wanda would not

infect me with gonorrhea. She is *sincere*, loyal, devout toward the body, the flesh. She has the religion of civilized people, which is pleasure, creative and polymorphous pleasure. Her skin is subtle, white, silken, animate.

Dear Wanda, wrote Herzog. But she knew no English and he changed to French. *Chère Princesse, Je me souviens assez souvent . . . Je pense à la Marszalkowska, au brouillard.* Every third-, fourth-, tenth-rate man of the world knew how to woo a woman in French, and so did Herzog. Though he was not the type. The feelings he wanted to express were genuine. She had been extremely kind to him when he was ill, troubled, and what made her kindness even more significant was the radiant, buxom Polish beauty of the woman. She had weighty golden-reddish hair and a slightly tilted nose but with very fine lines, the tip amazingly delicate and shapely for such a fleshy person. Her color was white, but a healthy, strong white. She was dressed, like most women in Warsaw, in black stockings and long slender Italian shoes, but her fur coat was worn to the hide.

In my grief did I know what I was doing? noted Herzog on a separate page, as he waited for the elevator. *Providence,* he added, *takes care of the faithful. I sensed that I would meet such a person. I have had terrific luck.* "Luck" was many times underscored.

Herzog had seen her husband. He was a poor, reproachful-looking man, with heart disease. The sole fault Herzog had found with Wanda was that she insisted he meet Zygmunt. Moses had not yet grasped what this meant. Wanda rejected the suggestion of a divorce. She was perfectly satisfied with her marriage. She said it was all any marriage could be.

Ici tout est gâché.

Une dizaine de jours à Varsovie—pas longtemps. If you could call those foggy winter intervals days. The sun was shut up in a cold bottle. The soul shut up inside me. Enormous felt curtains kept the drafts out of the hotel lobby. The wooden tables were stained, warped, tea-scalded.

Her skin was white and remained white through every change of emotion. Her greenish eyes seemed let into her Polish face (nature, the seamstress). A full, soft-bosomed woman, she was too heavy for the stylish tapering Italian shoes she wore. Standing without the heels, in her black hose, her figure was very solid indeed. He missed her. When he took her hand, she said, "Ah, ne toushay pas. C'est dangeray." But she didn't mean it at all. (How he doted on his memories! What a funny sensual bird he was! Queer for recollections, perhaps? But why use harsh words. He was what he was.)

Still, he had been continually aware of drab Poland, in all directions freezing, drab, and ruddy gray, the stones still smelling of war-time murders. He thought he scented blood. He went many times to visit the ruins of the ghetto. Wanda was his guide.

He shook his head. But what could *he* do? He pressed the elevator button again, this time with the corner of his Gladstone bag. He heard the sound of smooth motion in the shaft—greased tracks, power, efficient black machinery.

Guéri de cette petite maladie. He ought not to have mentioned it to Wanda, for she was simply shocked and hurt. *Pas grave du tout,* he wrote. He had made her cry.

The elevator stopped and he ended, *J'embrasse ces petites mains, amie.*

How do you say blond little cushioned knuckles in French?

IN THE CAB through hot streets where brick and brownstone buildings were crowded, Herzog held the strap and his large eyes were fixed on the sights of New York. The square shapes were vivid, not inert, they gave him a sense of fateful motion, almost of intimacy. Somehow he felt himself part of it all—in the rooms, in the stores, cellars—and at the same time he sensed the danger of these multiple excitements. But he'd be all right. He was overstimulated. He had to calm down these overstrained galloping nerves, put out this murky fire inside. He yearned for the Atlantic—the sand, the brine flavor, the therapy of cold water. He knew he would think better, clearer thoughts after bathing in the sea. His mother had believed in the good effects of bathing. But she had died so young. *He* could not allow himself to die yet. The children needed him. His duty was to live. To be sane, and to live, and to look after the kids. This was why be was running from the city now, overheated, eyes smarting. He was getting away from all burdens, practical questions, away also from Ramona. There were times when you wanted to creep into hiding, like an animal. Although he didn't know what lay ahead except the confining train which would impose rest on him (you can't run in a train) through Connecticut, Rhode Island, and Massachusetts, as far as Woods Hole, his reasoning was sound. Seashores are good for madmen—provided they're not too mad. He was all ready. The glad rags were in the bag under his feet, and the straw hat with the red and white band? It was on his head.

But all at once, the seat of the cab heating in the sun, he was aware that his angry spirit had stolen forward again, and that he was about to write letters. *Dear Smithers,* he began. *The other day at lunch*—those bureaucratic lunches which are a horror to me; my hindquarters become paralyzed, my blood fills up with adrenalin; my heart! I try to look right and proper but my face turns dead with boredom, my fantasy spills soup and gravy on everybody, and I want to scream out or faint away—*we were asked to suggest topics for new lecture courses and I said what about a series on marriage. I might as well have said "Currants"*

or *"Gooseberries."* Smithers is extremely happy with his lot.
Birth is very chancy. Who knows what may happen? But his lot
was to be Smithers and that was tremendous luck. He looks
like Thomas E. Dewey. The same gap between the front teeth,
the neat mustache. *Look, Smithers, I do have a good idea for a
new course. You organization men have to depend on the likes of
me. The people who come to evening classes are only ostensibly
after culture. Their great need, their hunger, is for good sense,
clarity, truth—even an atom of it. People are dying—it is no
metaphor—for lack of something real to carry home when day is
done. See how willing they are to accept the wildest nonsense.*
O Smithers, my whiskered brother! what a responsibility we
bear, in this fat country of ours! Think what America could
mean to the world. Then see what it is. What a breed it might
have produced. But look at us—at you, at me. Read the paper,
if you can bear to.

But the cab had passed 30th Street and there was a cigar
store on the corner which Herzog had entered a year ago to
buy a carton of Virginia Rounds for his mother-in-law, Tennie,
who lived a block away. He remembered going into the phone
booth to tell her he was coming up. It was dark in there, and
the patterned tin lining was worn black in places. *Dear Tennie,
Perhaps we'll have a talk when I get back from the seashore. The
message you sent through Lawyer Simkin that you didn't understand why I no longer came to see you is, to say the least, hard to
figure. I know your life has been tough. You have no husband.*
Tennie and Pontritter were divorced. The old impresario lived
on 57th Street, where he ran a school for actors, and Tennie
had her own two rooms on 31st, which looked like a stage set
and were filled with mementos of her ex-husband's triumphs.
All the posters were dominated by his name,

PONTRITTER
DIRECTS EUGENE O'NEILL, CHEKHOV

Though no longer man and wife, they had a relationship still.
Pontritter took Tennie riding in his Thunderbird. They attended openings, went to dinner together. She was a slender
woman of fifty-five, somewhat taller than Pon. But he was burly,
masterful, there was a certain peevish power and intelligence in
his dark face. He liked Spanish costumes, and when Herzog

last saw him he was wearing white duck trousers of bull-fighter's cut and alpargatas. Powerful, isolated threads of coarse white grew from his tanned scalp. Madeleine had inherited his eyes.

No husband. No daughter, Herzog wrote. But he began again, *Dear Tennie, I went to see Simkin about a certain matter, and he said to me, "Your mother-in-law's feelings are hurt."*

Simkin, sitting in his office, occupied a grand Sykes chair, beneath enormous rows of law books. A man is born to be orphaned, and to leave orphans after him, but a chair like that chair, if he can afford it, is a great comfort. Simkin was not so much sitting as lying in this seat. With his large thick back and small thighs, his head shaggy and aggressive and his hands folded small and timid on his belly, he spoke to Herzog in a diffident, almost meek tone. He called him "Professor" but not mockingly. Though Simkin was a clever lawyer, very rich, he respected Herzog. He had a weakness for confused high-minded people, for people with moral impulses like Moses. Hopeless! Very likely he looked at Moses and saw a grieving childish man, trying to keep his dignity. He noted the book on Herzog's knee, for Herzog typically carried a book to read on the subway or in the bus. What was it that day, Simmel on religion? Teilhard de Chardin? Whitehead? It's been years since I was really able to concentrate. Anyway, there was Simkin, short but also burly, eyes wreathed with twisting hairs, looking at him. In conversation his voice was very small, meek, almost faint, but when he answered his secretary's signal and switched on the intercom, it suddenly expanded. He said loudly and sternly, "Yah?"

"Mr. Dienstag on the phone."

"Who? That schmuck? I'm waiting for that affidavit. Tell him plaintiff will kick his ass if he can't produce it. He better get it this afternoon, that ludicrous shmegeggy!" Amplified, his tones were oceanic. Then he switched off, and said with resumed meekness to Moses, "Vei, vei! I get so tired of these divorces. What a situation! It gets more corrupt. Ten years ago I thought I could still keep up with it all. I felt I was worldly enough for it—realistic, cynical. But I was wrong. It's too much. This shnook of a chiropodist—what a hellcat *he* married. First she said she didn't want children, then she did, didn't, did. Finally, she threw her diaphragm in his face. Went to the bank. Took thirty grand of joint money from the vault. Said he tried to push her in front of a car. Fought with his mother about a ring, furs, a chicken, God knows. And then the husband found letters to her from another fellow." Simkin rubbed his cunning, imposing head with small hands. Then he showed his small regular teeth, iron-hard, as though about to smile, but this was a reflective preliminary. He gave a compassionate sigh. "You know, Professor, Tennie's hurt by your silence."

"I suppose so. But I can't bring myself to go there yet."

"Sweet woman. And what a family of hellers! I'm just passing the message on, because she asked me."

"Yes."

"Very decent, Tennie . . ."

"I know. She knitted me a scarf. It took a year. I got it in the mail about a month ago. I should acknowledge it."

"Yes, why don't you. She's no enemy."

Simkin liked him; Herzog didn't doubt that. But as a practical realist a man like Simkin had to perform exercises, and a certain amount of malice kept him in condition. A fellow like Moses Herzog, a little soft-headed or impractical but ambitious mentally, somewhat arrogant, too, a pampered futile fellow whose wife had just been taken away from him under very funny circumstances (far funnier than the case of the chiropodist which made Simkin bring his little hands together with a small cry of mock horror)—this Moses was irresistible to a man like Simkin who loved to pity and to poke fun at the same time. He was a Reality-Instructor. Many such. I bring them out. Himmelstein is another, but cruel. It's the cruelty that gets me, not the realism. Of course Simkin knew all about Madeleine's affair with Valentine Gersbach, and what he didn't know his friends Pontritter and Tennie would tell him.

Tennie had led a bohemian life for thirty-five years, following her husband as if she had married a grocer not a theatrical genius, and she remained a kindly, elder-sister sort of woman, with long legs. But the legs went bad, and her dyed hair turned stiff and quill-like. She wore butterfly-shaped eyeglasses, and "abstract" jewelry.

What if I did come to see you? asked Herzog. *Then I'd sit in your parlor being nice, while bursting with the wrongs your daughter did me. The same wrongs you have accepted from Pont-ritter, and forgiven him.* She prepares the old man's income-tax returns for him. Keeps all his records, washes his socks. Last time, I saw his socks drying on the radiator in her bathroom. And she had been telling me how happy she was now that she was divorced—free to go her own way and develop her own personality. *I'm sorry for you, Tennie.*

But that beautiful masterful daughter of yours came to your apartment with Valentine, didn't she, and sent you with your little granddaughter to the zoo while they made love in your bed. He with the gushing red hair, and she with the blue eyes, beneath. What am I supposed to do now—come and sit and talk about plays and restaurants? Tennie would tell him about that Greek place on Tenth Avenue. She already had told him half a dozen times. "A friend" (Pontritter himself, of course) "took me to dinner at the Marathon. It was really so different. You know, the Greek people cook ground meat and rice in grape leaves, with very interesting spices. Anybody who feels like it can dance solo. The Greek people are very uninhibited. You should see those fat men take off their shoes and dance in front of the whole crowd." Tennie spoke with a girlish sweetness and affection to him, obscurely fond of him. Her teeth were like the awkward second teeth of a seven-year-old child.

Oh, yes, thought Herzog. Her condition is worse than mine. Divorced at fifty-five, still showing off her legs, unaware they now are gaunt. And diabetic. And the menopause. And abused by her daughter. If in self-defense, Tennie has a bit of wickedness, hypocrisy, and cunning of her own, how can you blame her? Of course she gave us, or lent—it was sometimes a loan and sometimes a wedding present—that hand-wrought Mexican silver cutlery, and she wants it back. That's why she sent word through Simkin about her hurt feelings. She doesn't want to lose her silver. It's not exactly cynical, either. She wants to be friends, and she wants the silver too. It's her treasure. *It's in the vault, in Pittsfield. Too heavy to lug to Chicago. I'll return it, of course. By and by.* I never could hang on to valuables—silver, gold. With me, money is not a medium. I am money's medium. It passes through me—taxes, insurance, mortgage, child support, rent, legal fees. All this dignified blundering costs plenty. If I married Ramona, it would be easier, perhaps.

The cab was held up by trucks in the garment district. The electric machines thundered in the lofts and the whole street quivered. It sounded as though cloth were being torn, not sewn. The street was plunged, drowned in these waves of thunder. Through it a Negro pushed a wagon of ladies' coats. He had a beautiful beard and blew a gilt toy trumpet. You couldn't hear him.

Then the traffic opened and the cab rattled in low gear and jerked into second. "For Christ sake, let's make time," the driver said. They made a sweeping turn into Park Avenue and Herzog clutched the broken window handle. It wouldn't open. But if it opened dust would pour in. They were demolishing and raising buildings. The Avenue was filled with concrete-mixing trucks, smells of wet sand and powdery gray cement. Crashing, stamping pile-driving below, and, higher, structural steel, interminably and hungrily going up into the cooler, more delicate blue. Orange beams hung from the cranes like straws. But down in the street where the buses were spurting the poisonous exhaust of cheap fuel, and the cars were crammed together, it was stifling, grinding, the racket of machinery and the desperately purposeful crowds—horrible! He had to get out to the seashore where he could breathe. He ought to have booked a flight. But he had had enough of planes last winter, especially on the Polish airline. The machines were old. He took off from Warsaw airport in the front seat of a two-engine LOT plane, bracing his feet on the bulkhead before him and holding his hat. There were no seat belts. The wings were dented, the cowls scorched. There were mail pouches and crates sliding behind. They flew through angry spinning snow clouds over white Polish forests, fields, pits, factories, rivers dogging their banks, in, out, in, and a terrain of white and brown diagrams.

Anyway, a holiday should begin with a train ride, as it had when he was a kid in Montreal. The whole family took the streetcar to the Grand Trunk Station with a basket (frail, splintering wood) of pears, overripe, a bargain bought by Jonah Herzog at the Rachel Street Market, the fruit spotty, ready for wasps, just about to decay, but marvelously fragrant. And inside the train on the worn green bristle of the seats, Father Herzog sat peeling the fruit with his Russian pearl-handled knife. He peeled and twirled and cut with European efficiency. Meanwhile, the locomotive cried and the iron-studded cars began to move. Sun and girders divided the soot geometrically. By the factory walls the grimy weeds grew. A smell of malt came from the breweries.

The train crossed the St. Lawrence. Moses pressed the pedal and through the stained funnel of the toilet he saw the river frothing. Then he stood at the window. The water shone and curved on great slabs of rock, spinning into foam at the Lachine Rapids, where it sucked and rumbled. On the other shore was Caughnawaga, where the Indians lived in shacks raised on stilts. Then came the burnt summer fields. The windows were open. The echo of the train came back from the straw like a voice through a beard. The engine sowed cinders and soot over the fiery flowers and the hairy knobs of weed.

But that was forty years behind him. Now the train was ribbed for speed, a segmented tube of brilliant steel. There were no pears, no Willie, no Shura, no Helen, no Mother. Leaving the cab, he thought how his mother would moisten her handkerchief at her mouth and rub his face clean. He had no business to recall this, he knew, and turned toward Grand Central in his straw hat. He was of the mature generation now, and life was his to do something with, if he could. But he had not forgotten the odor of his mother's saliva on the handkerchief that summer morning in the squat hollow Canadian station, the black iron and the sublime brass. All children have cheeks and all mothers spittle to wipe them tenderly. These things either matter or they do not matter. It depends upon the universe, what it is. These acute memories are probably symptoms of disorder. To him, perpetual thought of death was a sin. Drive your cart and your plow over the bones of the dead.

In the crowds of Grand Central Station, Herzog in spite of all his efforts to do what was best could not remain rational. He felt it all slipping away from him in the subterranean roar of engines, voices, and feet and in the galleries with lights like drops of fat in yellow broth and the strong suffocating fragrance of underground New York. His collar grew wet and the sweat ran from his armpits down his ribs as he bought the ticket, and then he picked up a copy of the *Times*, and was about to get a bar of Cadbury's Caramello, but he denied himself that, thinking of the money he had spent on new clothes which would not fit if he ate carbohydrates. It would give the victory to the other side to let himself grow fat, jowly, sullen, with broad hips and a belly, and breathing hard. Ramona wouldn't like it either, and what Ramona liked mattered considerably. He seriously considered marrying her, notwithstanding that he seemed, just now, to be buying a ticket to escape from her. But this was in her best interests, too, if he was so confused—both visionary and muddy as he felt now, feverish, damaged, angry, quarrelsome, and shaky. He was going to phone her shop, but in his change there was only one nickel left, no dimes. He would have to break a bill, and he didn't want candy or gum. Then he thought of wiring her and saw that he would seem weak if he sent a telegram.

On the sultry platform of Grand Central he opened the bulky *Times* with its cut shreds at the edges, having set the valise on his feet. The hushed electric trucks were rushing by with mail bags, and he stared at the news with a peculiar effort. It was a hostile broth of black print *MoonraceberlinKhrushchwarncommitteegalacticXrayPhouma*. He saw twenty paces away the white soft face and independent look of a woman in a shining black straw hat which held her head in depth and eyes that even in the signal-dotted obscurity reached him with a force she could never be aware of. Those eyes might be blue, perhaps green, even gray—he would never know. But they were bitch eyes, that was certain. They expressed a sort of female arrogance which had an immediate sexual power over him; he experienced it again that very moment—a round face, the clear gaze of pale bitch eyes, a pair of proud legs.

I must write to Aunt Zelda, he suddenly decided. They mustn't think they can get away with it—make such a fool of me, put me on. He folded the thick paper and hurried into the train. The bitch-eyed girl was on the other track, and good riddance. He went into a New Haven car, and the russet door closed behind him on pneumatic hinges, stiff and hissing. The air inside was chill, air-conditioned. He was the first passenger and had his choice of seats.

He sat in a cramped position, pressing the valise to his chest, his traveling-desk, and writing rapidly in the spiral notebook.

*Dear Zelda, Of course you have to be loyal to your niece. I am just
on outsider. You and Herman said I was one of the family. If I
was patsy enough to be affected (at my age) by this sort of "heartfelt" family garbage, why I deserve what I got. I was flattered by
Herman's affection, because of his former underworld acquaintances. I was overcome with happy pride at being found "regular." It meant my muddled intellectual life, as a poor soldier of
culture, hadn't ruined my human sympathies. What if I had
written a book on the Romantics? A politician in the Cook County
Democratic organization who knew the Syndicate, the Juice men,
the Policy kings, Cosa Nostra, and all the hoods, still found me
good company,* heimisch, *and took me along to the races, the
hockey games.* But Herman is even more marginal to the Syndicate than poor Herzog to the practical world and both are at
home in a pleasant heimisch environment and love the Russian
bath and tea and smoked fish and herrings afterward. With
restless women conspiring at home.

*As long as I was Mady's good husband, I was a delightful per-
son. Suddenly, because Madeleine decided that she wanted out—
suddenly, I was a mad dog. The police were warned about me
and there was talk of committing me to an institution. I know
that my friend and Mady's lawyer, Sandor Himmelstein, called
Dr. Edvig to ask whether I was crazy enough to be put in Man-
teno or Elgin. You took Madeleine's word as to my mental condition and so did others.*

*But you knew what she was up to—knew why she left Ludeyville
for Chicago, why I had to find a job there for Valentine Gersbach,
knew that I went house-hunting for the Gersbachs and arranged
the private school for little Ephraim Gersbach. It must be very
deep and primitive, the feeling people—women—have against a
deceived husband, and I know now that you helped your niece by
having Herman take me away to the hockey game.*

Herzog was not angry at Herman—he didn't believe he was
part of the conspiracy. *The Blackhawks against the Maple-Leafs.*
Uncle Herman, mild, decent, clever, neat, in black loafers and
beltless slacks, his high fedora standing up at the front like a
fire helmet, his shirt with a tiny gargoyle on the breast pocket.
In the rink the players mixed like hornets—swift, padded, yellow, black, red, rushing, slashing, whirling over the ice. Above
the rink the tobacco smoke lay like a cloud of flash powder,

explosive. Over the p.a. system the management begged the spectators not to throw pennies to catch the blades of the skates. Herzog with circled eyes tried to relax in Herman's company. He even won a bet and took him to Fritzel's for cheesecake. All the big names of Chicago were there. And what must Uncle Herman have been thinking? Suppose that he also knew that Madeleine and Gersbach were together? In spite of the air-conditioned chill of the New Haven car, Herzog felt the sweat break out on his face.

Last March when I came back from Europe, a case of nerves, and arrived in Chicago to see what could be done, if anything, to restore a little order, I was really in a goofy state. Partly it may have been the weather, and the time changes. It was spring in Italy. Palm trees in Turkey. In Galilee, the red anemones among stones. But in Chicago I ran into a blizzard in March. I was met by Gersbach, still my dearest friend as recently as that, looking at me with compassion. He wore a storm coat, black galoshes, a Kelly-green scarf, and had Junie in his arms. He hugged me. June kissed me on the face. We went to the waiting room and I unpacked the toys and little dresses I had bought, and a Florentine wallet for Valentine and Polish amber beads for Phoebe Gersbach. As it was past Junie's bedtime and the snowfall was getting heavy, Gersbach took me to the Surf Motel. He said he couldn't book me at the Windermere, closer to the house, a ten-minute walk. By morning a ten-inch snow had fallen. The lake was heaving and lit by white snow to a near horizon of storming gray. I phoned Madeleine but she hung up on me; Gersbach, but he was out of his office; Dr. Edvig, but he couldn't give me an appointment till next day. His own family, his sister, his stepmother, Herzog avoided. He went to see Aunt Zelda.

There were no cabs that day. He rode the buses, freezing when he changed in his covert-cloth coat and thin-soled loafers. The Umschands lived in a new suburb, to hell and gone, beyond Palos Park, on the fringe of the Forest Preserves. The blizzard had stopped by the time he got there, but the wind was cutting, and lumps of snow fell from twigs. Frost sealed the shop windows. At the package store, Herzog, not much of a drinker, picked up a bottle of Guckenheimer's 86 proof. It was early in the day, but his blood was cold. Thus he spoke to Aunt Zelda with a whisky breath.

"I'll heat the coffee up. You must be solid ice," she said.

In the suburban kitchen of enamel and copper, the white molded female forms bulged from all sides. The refrigerator, as if it had a heart, and the range with gentian flames under the pot. Zelda had made up her face and wore gold slacks and plastic-heeled slippers—transparent. They sat down. Looking through the glass-topped table, Herzog could see that her hands were pressed between her knees. When he began to talk, she lowered her eyes. She had a blond complexion, but her eyelids were darker, warmer, more brown, discolored but with a thick blue line drawn on each by a cosmetic pencil. Her downcast look, Moses at first took as agreement or sympathy; but he realized how wrong he was when he observed her nose. It was full of mistrust. By the way it moved he realized that she rejected everything he was saying. But he knew he was immoderate—worse than that, temporarily deranged. He tried to get a grip on himself. Half buttoned, red-eyed, unshaved, he looked disgraceful. Indecent. He was telling Zelda his side of the case. "I know she's turned you against me—poisoned your mind, Zelda."

"No, she respects you. She fell out of love with you, that's all. Women fall out of love."

"Love? Madeleine loved me? You know that's just middle-class bunk."

"She was crazy about you. I know she adored you once, Moses."

"No, no! Don't work on me like that. You know it isn't true. She's sick. She's a diseased woman—I took care of her."

"I'll admit you did," said Zelda. "What's true is true. But what disease . . ."

"Ah!" said Herzog harshly. "So you love the truth!"

He saw Madeleine's influence in this; she was forever talking about the truth. She could not bear lying. Nothing could throw Madeleine into a rage so quickly as a lie. And now she had Zelda on the same standard—Zelda, with dyed hair as dry as excelsior and the purplish lines on her lids, these caterpillar forms—Oh! thought Herzog in the train, the things women apply to their own flesh. And we must go along, must look, listen, heed, breathe in. And now Zelda, her face a little lined, her soft, powerful nostrils dilated with suspicion, and fascinated at his state (there was reality in Herzog now, not seen when he was affable), was giving him the business about truth.

"Haven't I always leveled with you?" she said. "I am not just another surburban hausfrau."

"You mean because Herman says he knows Luigi Boscolla, the hoodlum?"

"Don't pretend you can't understand me. . . ."

Herzog did not want to offend her. It suddenly was plain what made her talk like this. Madeleine had convinced Zelda that she too was exceptional. Everyone close to Madeleine, everyone drawn into the drama of her life became exceptional, deeply gifted, brilliant. It had happened also to him. By his dismissal from Madeleine's life, sent back into the darkness, he became again a spectator. But he saw Aunt Zelda was inspired by a new sense of herself. Herzog envied her even this closeness to Madeleine.

"Well, I know you aren't like the other wives out here. . . ."

Your kitchen is different, your Italian lamps, your carpets, your French provincial furniture, your Westinghouse, your mink, your country club, your cerebral palsy canisters are all different.

I am sure you were sincere. Not insincere. True insincerity is hard to find.

"Madeleine and I have always been more like sisters," said Zelda. "I'd love her no matter how she acted. But I'm glad to say she's been terrific, a serious person."

"Junk!"

"Just as serious as you are."

"Returning a husband like a cake dish or a bath towel to Field's."

"It didn't work out. You have your faults too. I'm sure you won't deny that."

"How could I?"

"Overbearing, gloomy. You brood a lot."

"That's true enough."

"Very demanding. Have to have your own way. She says you wore her out, asking for help, support."

"It's all correct. And more. I'm hasty, irascible, spoiled. And what else?"

"You've been reckless about women."

"Since Madeleine threw me out, maybe. Trying to get back my self-respect."

"No, while you still were married." Zelda's mouth tightened.

Herzog felt himself redden. A thick, hot, sick pressure filled his chest. His heart felt ill and his forehead instantly wet.

He muttered, "She made it tough for me, too. Sexually."

"Well, being older . . . But that's bygones," said Zelda. "Your big mistake was to bury yourself in the country so you could finish that project of yours—that study of whatchamajig You never did wind it up, did you?"

"No," Herzog said.

"Then what was *that* all about."

Herzog tried to explain what it was about—that his study was supposed to have ended with a new angle on the modern condition, showing how life could be lived by renewing universal connections; overturning the last of the Romantic errors about the uniqueness of the Self; revising the old Western, Faustian ideology; investigating the social meaning of Nothingness. And more. But he checked himself, for she did not understand, and this offended her, especially as she believed she was no common hausfrau. She said, "It sounds very grand. Of course it must be important. But that's not the point. You were a fool to bury yourself and her, a young woman, in the Berkshires, with nobody to talk to."

"Except Valentine Gersbach, and Phoebe."

"That's right. That was bad. Especially winters. You should have had more sense. That house made a prisoner of her. It must have been just dreary, washing and cooking, and to have to hush the baby, or you'd raise hell, she said. You couldn't think when June was crying, and you'd rush from your room hollering."

"Yes, I was stupid—a blockhead. But that was one of the problems I was working on, you see, that people can be free now but the freedom doesn't have any content. It's like a

howling emptiness. Madeleine shared my interests, I thought
—she's a studious person."

"She says you were a dictator, a regular tyrant. You bullied
her."

I do seem to be a broken-down monarch of some kind, he
was thinking, like my old man, the princely immigrant and in-
effectual bootlegger. And life was very bad in Ludeyville—terrible, I admit. But then didn't we buy the house because she
wanted to, and move out when she wanted to? And didn't I
make all the arrangements, even for the Gersbachs—so we
could all leave the Berkshires together?

"What else did she complain of?" said Herzog.

Zelda considered him for a moment as though to see
whether he was strong enough to take it, and said, "You were
selfish."

Ah, that! He understood. The ejaculatio praecox! His look
became stormy, his heart began to pound, and he said, "There
was some trouble for a while. But not in the last two years.
And hardly ever with other women." These were humiliating
explanations. Zelda did not have to believe them, and that
made him the pleader, and put him at a frightful disadvantage.
He couldn't invite her upstairs for a demonstration, or produce affidavits from Wanda or Zinka. (Recalling, in the still
standing train, the thwarted and angry eagerness of these attempted explanations, he had to laugh. Nothing but a wan
smile passed over his face.) What crooks they were—Madeleine, Zelda . . . others. Some women didn't care how badly
they damaged you. A girl, in Zelda's view, had a right to expect
from her husband nightly erotic gratification, safety, money,
insurance, furs, jewelry, cleaning women, drapes, dresses,
hats, night clubs, country clubs, automobiles, theater!

"No man can satisfy a woman who doesn't want him," said
Herzog.

"Well, isn't that your answer?"

Moses started to speak but he felt that he was going to make
another foolish outcry. His face paled again and he kept his
mouth shut. He was in terrible pain. It was so bad that he was
far past claiming credit for his power to suffer as he had at
times done. He sat silent, and heard the clothes dryer below
whirling.

"Moses," said Zelda, "I want to make sure of one thing."
"What—"

"*Our* relationship." He was no longer looking at her darkened, painted lids but into her eyes, bright and brown. Her nostrils tensed softly. She showed him her sympathetic face. "We still are friends," she said.

"Well . . ." said Moses. "I'm fond of Herman. Of you."

"I *am* your friend. And I'm a truthful person."

He saw himself in the train window, hearing his own words clearly. "I think you're on the level."

"You believe me, don't you."

"I want to, naturally."

"You should. I've got your interests at heart, too. I keep an eye on little June."

"I'm grateful for that."

"But Madeleine is a good mother. And you don't have to worry. She doesn't run around with men. They phone her all the time, chasing after her. Well—she is a beauty, and a very rare type, too, because she is so brilliant. Down there in Hyde Park—as soon as everybody knew about the divorce, you'd be surprised who all started to call her."

"Good friends of mine, you mean."

"If she was just a fly-by-night, she could have her choice of men. But you know how serious she is. Anyhow, people like Moses Herzog don't grow on bushes, either. With your brains and charm, you won't be easy to replace. Anyhow, she's always at home. She's rethinking everything—her whole life. And there is nobody else. You know you can believe me."

Of course if you considered me dangerous it was your duty to lie. And I know I looked bad, my face swelled up, eyes red and wild. *Female deceit, though, is a deep subject. Thrills of guile. Sexual complicity, conspiracy. Getting in on it. I watched you bully Herman to get a second car, and I know how you can bitch! You thought I might kill Mady and Valentine. But when I found out, why didn't I go to the pawnshop and buy a gun? Simpler yet, my father left a revolver in his desk. It's still there. But I'm no criminal, don't have it in me; frightful to myself, instead. Anyway, Zelda, I see you had tremendous pleasure, double excitement, lying from an overflowing heart.*

All at once the train left the platform and entered the tunnel.

Temporarily in darkness, Herzog held his pen. Smoothly the trickling walls passed. In dusty niches bulbs burned. Without religion. Then came a long incline and the train rose from underground and rode in sudden light on the embankment above the slums, upper Park Avenue. In the east Nineties an open hydrant gushed and kids in clinging drawers leaped screaming. Now came Spanish Harlem, heavy, dark, and hot, and Queens far off to the right, a thick document of brick, veiled in atmospheric dirt.

Herzog wrote, *Will never understand what women want. What do they want? They eat green salad and drink human blood.*

Over Long Island Sound the air grew clearer. It gradually became very pure. The water was level and easy, soft blue, the grass brilliant, spattered with wildflowers—plenty of myrtle among these rocks, and wild strawberries blossoming.

I now know the whole funny, nasty, perverted truth about Madeleine. Much to think about. He now had ended.

But at the same high rate of speed, Herzog streaked off on another course, writing to an old friend in Chicago, Lucas Asphalter, a zoologist at the university. *What's gotten into you? I often read "human-interest" paragraphs but I never expect them to be about my friends. You can imagine how it shook me to see your name in the* Post. *Have you gone crazy? I know you adored that monkey of yours, and I'm sorry he's dead. But you should have known better than to try to revive him by mouth-to-mouth respiration. Especially as Rocco died of TB and must have been jumping with bugs.* Asphalter was queerly attached to his animals. Herzog suspected that he tended to humanize them. That macaque monkey of his, Rocco, was not an amusing creature, but obstinate and cranky, with a poor color, like a glum old Jewish uncle. But of course if he was slowly dying of consumption, he couldn't have looked very optimistic. Asphalter, so cheerful himself and indifferent to practical interests, something of a marginal academic type, without his Ph.D., taught comparative anatomy. With thick crepe-soled shoes, he wore a stained smock; he was bereaved of hair, of his youth, too, poor Luke. The sudden loss of his hair had left him with only one lock at the front, and made his handsome eyes, his arched brows prominent, his nostrils darker, hairier. I hope he hasn't swallowed Rocco's bacilli. There's a new, deadlier strain at large, they say, and tuberculosis is coming back. Asphalter was a bachelor at forty-five. His father had owned a flophouse on Madison Street. In his youth, Moses had been there often, visiting. And although for an interval of ten or fifteen years he and Asphalter had not been close friends, they had found, suddenly, a great deal in common. In fact it had been from Asphalter that Herzog learned what Madeleine was up to, and the part Gersbach had been playing in his life.

"Hate to tell you this, Mose," said Asphalter, in his office, "but you're mixed up with some awful nuts."

This was two days after the March blizzard. You wouldn't have known it had been raging winter that same week. The casement window was open on the Quadrangle. All the grimy cottonwoods had sprung to life, released red catkins from their sheaths. These dangled everywhere, perfuming the gray courtyard with its shut-in light. Rocco with sick eyes sat on his own straw chair, his look lusterless, his coat the color of stewed onions.

"I can't stand to see you knock yourself out," Asphalter said. "I'd better tell you—we have a lab assistant here who sits with your little girl, and she's been telling me about your wife."

"What about her?"

"And Valentine Gersbach. He's always there, on Harper Avenue."

"Sure. I know. He's the only reliable person on the scene. I trust him. He's been an awfully good friend."

"Yes, I know—I know, I know," said Asphalter. His pale round face was freckled, and his eyes large, fluid, dark, and, for Moses's sake, bitter in their dreaminess. "I certainly know. Valentine's quite an addition to the social life of Hyde Park, what's left of it. How did we ever get along without him. He's so genial—he's so noisy, with those Scotch and Japanese imitations, and that gravel voice. He drowns all conversation out. Full of life! Oh, yes, he's full of it! And because you brought him here, everybody thinks he's your special pal. He says so himself. Only . . ."

"Only what?"

Tense and quiet, Asphalter asked, "Don't you know?" He became very pale.

"What should I know?"

"I took it for granted because your intelligence is so high—way off the continuum—that you knew something or suspected."

Something frightful was about to descend on him. Herzog nerved himself for it.

"Madeleine, you mean? I understand, of course, that by and by, because she's still a young woman, she must . . . she will."

"No, no," said Asphalter. "Not by and by." He blurted it out. "All the while."

"Who!" said Herzog. All his blood rose, and just as quickly and massively left his brain. "You mean Gersbach?"

"That's right." Asphalter now had no control whatever over the nerves of his face; it had gone soft with the pain he felt. His mouth looked chapped, with black lines.

Herzog began to shout, "You can't talk like that! You can't say that!" He stared at Lucas, outraged. A dim, sick, faint feeling came over him. His body seemed to shrink, abruptly drained, hollow, numbed. He almost lost consciousness.

"Open your collar," said Asphalter. "My God, you aren't fainting, are you?" He began to force Herzog's head down. "Between the knees," he said.

"Let up," said Moses, but his head was hot and damp and he sat doubled over while Asphalter gave him first aid.

All the while, the large brown monkey, with arms folded over his chest, and red, dry eyes, was looking on, silently disseminating his grimness. Death, thought Herzog. The real thing. The animal was dying.

"You better?" Asphalter said.

"Just open a window. These zoology buildings stink."

"The window is open. Here, drink some water." He handed Moses a paper cup. "Take one of these. Take this first, and then the green and white. Prozine. I can't get the cotton out of the bottle. My hands are shaking."

Herzog refused the pills. "Luke . . . Is this really true, about Madeleine and Gersbach?" he said.

Intensely nervous, pale, warm, looking at him with his dark

eyes, his mottled face, Asphalter said, "Christ! you don't think I'd invent such a thing. I probably haven't been tactful. I thought you must have had a pretty good idea. . . . But it's absolutely true." Asphalter in his soiled lab coat put it to him with a complicated helpless gesture—I lay it all before you, was what it said. His breathing was labored. "You didn't know *anything*?"

"No."

"But doesn't it make sense? Doesn't it add up now?"

Herzog rested his weight on the desk, knitting his fingers tightly. He stared at the dangling catkins, reddish and violet. Not to burst, not to die—to stay alive, was all he could hope for. "Who told you?" be said.

"Geraldine."

"Who?"

"Gerry—Geraldine Portnoy. I thought you knew her. Mady's sitter. She's down in the anatomy lab."

"What . . ."

"Human anatomy, in the Med School, around the corner. I go out with her. In fact, you know her, she was in one of your classes. Do you want to talk to her?"

"No," said Herzog violently.

"Well, she's written you a letter. She gave it to me and said she'd leave it up to me, whether I should hand it over or not."

"I can't read it now."

"Take it," said Asphalter. "You may want to read it later."

Herzog stuffed the envelope into his pocket.

He was wondering, as he sat in the plush seat of the train, holding his valise desk, and leaving New York State at seventy m.p.h., why he hadn't cried in Asphalter's office. He could burst into tears easily enough, and he was not inhibited with Asphalter, they were such old friends, so similar in their lives— their backgrounds, their habits, temperaments. But when Asphalter raised the lid, revealed the truth, something bad was released in his office overlooking the Quadrangle; like an odor, hot and raw; or a queer human fact, almost palpable. Tears were not relevant. The cause was too perverse, altogether too odd for all concerned. And then, too, Gersbach was a frequent weeper of distinguished emotional power. The hot tear was often in his magnanimous ruddy-brown eye. Only a few days earlier, when Herzog landed at O'Hare and hugged his little daughter, Gersbach had been there, a powerful, burly figure with tears of compassion in his eyes. So evidently, thought Moses, he's fucked up weeping for me, too. At moments I dislike having a face, a nose, lips, because he has them.

Yes, the shadow of death was on Rocco, then.

"Damn unpleasant," said Asphalter. He smoked a bit and put out his cigarette. The tray was filled with long butts—he used up two or three packs a day. "Let's have some drinks. Let's all have dinner tonight. I'm taking Geraldine to the Beachcomber, near-north. You can size her up for yourself."

Now Herzog had to consider some strange facts about Asphalter. It's possible that I influenced him, my emotionalism transmitted itself to him. He had taken that brooding, hairy Rocco into his heart. How else could you account for such agitation—lifting Rocco in his arms and forcing his lips open, breathing mouth to mouth. I suspect Luke may be in a very bad way. I must try to think about him as he is—strangeness and all.

You'd better take the tuberculin test. I had no idea that you . . . Herzog broke off. A dining-car steward rang the chimes for lunch, but Herzog had no time to eat. He was about to begin another letter.

Dear Professor Byzhkovski, I thank you for your courtesy in Warsaw. Owing to the state of my health, our meeting must have been unsatisfactory to you. I sat in his apartment making paper hats and boats out of the *Trybuna Ludu* while he tried to get a conversation going. The professor—that tall powerful man in a sandy-tweed shooting costume of knickers and Norfolk jacket—must have been astonished. I'm convinced he has a kind nature. His blue eyes are the good sort. A fat but shapely face, thoughtful and manly. I kept folding the paper hats—I must have been thinking of the children. Mme. Byzhkovski asked me did I want jam in my tea, bending over hospitably. The furniture was richly polished, old, of a vanished Central European epoch—but then this present epoch is vanishing, too, and perhaps faster than all the others. *I hope you will forgive me. I have now had an opportunity to read your study of the American Occupation of West Germany. Many of the facts are disagreeable.* But I was never consulted by President Truman, nor by Mr. McCloy. *I must confess I haven't examined the German question as closely as I should. None of the governments are truthful, in my opinion. There is also an East German question not even touched upon in your monograph.*

I wandered in Hamburg into the red-light district. That is, I was told that I should see it. Some of the whores, in black lace underthings, wore German military boots and rapped at you with riding crops on the windowpanes. Broads with red complexions, calling and grinning. A cold, joyless day.

Dear Sir, wrote Herzog. *You have been very patient with the Bowery bums who enter your church, pass out drunk, defecate in the pews, break bottles on the gravestones, and commit more nuisances. I would suggest that as you can see Wall Street from your church door you might prepare a pamphlet to explain that the Bowery gives additional significance to it. Skid Row is the contrasting institution, therefore necessary. Remind them of Lazarus and Dives. Because of Lazarus, Dives gets an extra kick, a bonus, from his luxuries.* No, I don't believe Dives is having such a hot time, either. And if he wants to free himself, the doom of Skid Row awaits him. If there were a beautiful poverty, a moral poverty in America, that would be subversive. Therefore it has to be ugly. Therefore the bums are working for Wall Street—confessors of the name. But the Reverend Beasley, where does he get his dough?

We have thought too little on this.

He then wrote, *Credit Department, Marshall Field & Co. I am no longer responsible for the debts of Madeleine P. Herzog. As of March 10, we ceased to be husband and wife. So don't send me any more bills—I was knocked over by the last—more than four hundred dollars. For purchases made after the separation. Of course I should have written sooner—to what is called the credit nerve-center—*Is there such a thing? Where can you find it?—*but I temporarily lost my bearings.*

Dear Professor Hoyle, I don't think I understand just how the Gold-Pore Theory works. How the heavier metals—iron, nickel—get to the center of the earth, I think I see. But what about the concentration of lighter metals? Also, in your explanation of the formation of smaller planets, including our tragic earth, *you speak of adhesive materials that bind the agglomerates of precipitated matter. . . .*

The wheels of the cars stormed underneath. Woods and pastures ran up and receded, the rails of sidings sheathed in rust, the dipping racing wires, and on the right the blue of the Sound, deeper, stronger than before. Then the enameled shells of the commuters' cars, and the heaped bodies of junk cars, the shapes of old New England mills with narrow, austere windows; villages, convents; tugboats moving in the swelling fabric-like water; and then plantations of pine, the needles on the ground of a life-giving russet color. So, thought Herzog, acknowledging that his imagination of the universe was elementary, the novae bursting and the worlds coming into being, the invisible magnetic spokes by means of which bodies kept one another in orbit. Astronomers made it all sound as though the gases were shaken up inside a flask. Then after many billions of years, light-years, this childlike but far from innocent creature, a straw hat on his head, and a heart in his breast, part pure, part wicked, who would try to form his own shaky picture of this magnificent web.

Dear Dr. Bhave, he began again, I *read of your work in the* Observer *and at the time thought I'd like to join your movement. I've always wanted very much to lead a moral, useful, and active life. I never knew where to begin. One can't become Utopian. It only makes it harder to discover where your duty really lies. Persuading the owners of large estates to give up some land to impoverished peasants, however* . . . These dark men going on foot through India. In his vision Herzog saw their shining eyes, and the light of spirit within them. You must start with injustices that are obvious to everybody, not with big historical perspectives. *Recently, I saw* Pather Panchali. *I assume you know it, since the subject is rural India. Two things affected me greatly—the old crone scooping the mush with her fingers and later going into the weeds to die; and the death of the young girl in the rains.* Herzog, almost alone in the Fifth Avenue Playhouse, cried with the child's mother when the hysterical death music started. Some musician with a native brass horn, imitating sobs, playing a death noise. It was raining also in New York, as in rural India. His heart was aching. He too had a daughter, and his mother too had been a poor woman. He had slept on sheets made of flour sacks. The best type for the purpose was Ceresota.

What he had vaguely in mind was to offer his house and property in Ludeyville to the Bhave movement. But what could Bhave do with it? Send Hindus to the Berkshires? It wouldn't be fair to them. Anyway, there was a mortgage. A gift should be made in what they call "fee simple," and for that I'd have to raise another eight thousand bucks, and the Internal Revenue wouldn't give me a deduction on it. Foreign charities probably don't count. Bhave would be doing him a favor. That house was one of his biggest mistakes. It was bought in a dream of happiness, an old ruin of a place but with enormous possibilities—great old trees, formal gardens he could restore in his spare time. The place had been deserted for years. Duck hunters and lovers would break in and use it; and when Herzog posted the property the lovers and the hunters played jokes on him. Someone came in the night and left a used sanitary napkin in a covered dish on his desk, where be kept bundles of notes for his Romantic studies. That was his reception by the natives. A momentary light of self-humor passed over his face as the train flashed through meadows and sunny pines. Suppose I accepted the challenge. I could be Moses, the old Jew-man of Ludeyville, with a white beard, cutting the grass under the washline with my antique reel-mower. Eating woodchucks.

He wrote to his cousin Asher, in Beersheba, *I mentioned an old photograph of your father in his Czarist uniform. I have asked my sister Helen to look for it.* Asher had served in the Red Army and was wounded. He was now an electro-welder, a moody-looking man with strong teeth. He went with Moses to visit the Dead Sea. It was sultry. They sat down in the mouth of a salt mine to cool off. Asher said, "Don't you have a picture of my father?"

Dear Mr. President, I listened to your recent optimistic message on the radio and thought that in respect to taxes there was little to justify your optimism. The new legislation is highly discriminatory and many believe it will only aggravate unemployment problems by accelerating automation. This means that more adolescent gangs will dominate the underpoliced streets of big cities. Stresses of overpopulation, the race question . . .

Dear Doktor Professor Heidegger, I should like to know what you mean by the expression "the fall into the quotidian." When did this fall occur? Where were we standing when it happened?

Mr. Emmett Strawforth, U.S. Public Health Service, he wrote. *Dear Emmett, I saw you on television making a damn fool of yourself. Since we were undergraduates together (M. E. Herzog '38) I feel free to tell you what I think of your philosophy.*

Herzog crossed this out and readdressed his letter to the *New York Times. Again a government scientist, Dr. Emmett Strawforth, has come forward with the Philosophy of Risk in the controversy over fallout, to which has now been added the problem of chemical pesticides, contamination of ground water, etc. I am as deeply concerned with the social and ethical reasoning of scientists as I am with those other forms of poisoning. Dr. Strawforth on Rachel Carson, Dr. Teller on the genetic effects of radioactivity. Recently Dr. Teller argued that the new fashion of tight pants, by raising body temperatures, could affect the gonads more than fallout. People greatly respected in their generation often turn out to be dangerous lunatics. Take Field Marshal Haig. He drowned hundreds of thousands of men in the mudholes of Flanders. Lloyd George was obliged to sanction this because Haig was such an important and respected leader. Such people simply have to be allowed to do their stuff. How paradoxical it is that a man who uses heroin may get a 20-year sentence for what he does to himself. . . .* They'll see what I mean.

Dr. Strawforth says we must adopt his Philosophy of Risk with regard to radioactivity. Since Hiroshima (and Mr. Truman calls people Bleeding Hearts when they question his Hiroshima decision) life in civilized countries (because they survive through a balance of terror) stands upon a foundation of risk. So argues Dr. Strawforth. But then he compares human life to Risk Capital in business. What an idea! Big business takes no chances, as the recent stockpiling investigation showed. I should like to call your attention to one of de Tocqueville's prophecies. He believed modern democracies would produce less crime, more private vice. Perhaps he should have said less private crime, more collective crime. Much of this collective or organizational crime has the object precisely of reducing risk. Now I know it's no cinch to manage the affairs of this planet with its population exceeding 2 billion. The number itself is something of a miracle and throws our practical ideas into obsolescence. Few intellectuals have grasped the social principles behind this quantitative transformation.

Ours is a bourgeois civilization. I am not using this term in its

Marxian sense. Chicken! *In the vocabularies of modern art and religion it is bourgeois to consider that the universe was made for our safe use and to give us comfort, ease, and support. Light travels at a quarter of a million miles per second so that we can see to comb our hair or to read in the paper that ham hocks are cheaper than yesterday. De Tocqueville considered the impulse toward well-being as one of the strongest impulses of a democratic society. He can't be blamed for underestimating the destructive powers generated by this same impulse.* You must be out of your mind to write to the *Times* like this! There are millions of bitter Voltairean types whose souls are filled with angry satire and who keep looking for the keenest, most poisonous word. You could send in a poem instead, you nitwit. Why should you be more right out of sheer distraction than they are out of organization? You ride in their trains, don't you? Distraction didn't build the railroad. Go on, write a poem, and kill 'em with bitterness. They print little poems as fillers on the editorial page. But he continued his letter, nevertheless. *Nietzsche, Whitehead, and John Dewey wrote on the question of Risk. . . . Dewey tells us that mankind distrusts its own nature and tries to find stability beyond or above, in religion or philosophy. To him the past often means the erroneous.* But Moses checked himself. Come to the point. But what was the point? The point was that there were people who could destroy mankind and that they were foolish and arrogant, crazy, and must be begged not to do it. Let the enemies of life step down. Let each man now examine his heart. Without a great change of heart, I would not trust myself in a position of authority. Do I love mankind? Enough to spare it, if I should be in a position to blow it to hell? Now let us all dress in our shrouds and walk on Washington and Moscow. Let us lie down, men, women, and children, and cry, "Let life continue—we may not deserve it, but let it continue."

In every community there is a class of people profoundly dangerous to the rest. I don't mean the criminals. For them we have punitive sanctions. I mean the leaders. Invariably the most dangerous people seek the power. While in the parlors of indignation the right-thinking citizen brings his heart to a boil.

Mr. Editor, we are bound to be the slaves of those who have power to destroy us. I am not speaking of Strawforth any more. I

knew him at school. We played ping-pong at the Reynolds Club.
He had a white buttocky face with a few moles, and fat curling
thumbs that put a cheating spin on the ball. Clickety-clack over
the green table. I don't believe his I.Q. was so terribly high,
though maybe it was, but he worked hard at his math and
chemistry. While I was fiddling in the fields. Like the grasshoppers in Junie's favorite song.

> Grasshoppers three a-fiddling went.
> Hey-ho, never be still.
> They paid no money towards their rent
> But all day long with elbows bent
> They fiddled a song called Rillabyrillaby
> They fiddled a song called Rillabyrill.

Delighted, Moses began to grin. His face wrinkled tenderly
at the thought of his children. How well kids understand what
love is! Marco was entering an age of silence and restraint with
his father, but Junie was exactly as Marco had been. She stood
on her father's lap to comb his hair. His thighs were trodden
by her feet. He embraced her small bones with fatherly hunger
while her breath on his face stirred his deepest feelings.

He had been wheeling the child's stroller on the Midway,
saluting students and faculty with a touch to the brim of his
green velours hat, a mossier green than the slopes and hollow
lawns. Under the tucks of her velvet bonnet, the little girl had
very much her Papa's looks, so he thought. He smiled at her
with large creases, dark eyes, while reciting nursery rhymes:

> "There was an old woman
> Who flew in a basket
> Seventeen times as high as the moon."

"More," the child said.

> "And where she was going
> Nobody could tell you
> For under her arm she carried a broom."

"More, more."

The warm lake wind drove Moses westward, past the gray
gothic buildings. He had had the child at least, while mother
and lover were undressing in a bedroom somewhere. And if,

even in that embrace of lust and treason, they had life and nature on their side, he would quietly step aside. Yes, he would bow out.

The conductor (one of an ancient vanishing breed, this gray-faced conductor) took the ticket from Herzog's hatband. As he punched it, he seemed about to say something. Perhaps the straw hat carried him back to old times. But Herzog was finishing his letter. *Even if Strawforth were a philosopher-king, should we give him the power to tamper with the genetic foundations of life, pollute the atmosphere and the waters of the earth? I know it is cranky to be indignant. But . . .*

The conductor left a punched cardboard slip under the metal of the seat number and went away, leaving Moses still writing on his valise. He might have gone to the club car, of course, where there were tables, but there he'd have to buy drinks, talk to people. Besides, he had one of his most essential letters to write, to Dr. Edvig, the psychiatrist in Chicago.

So, Edvig, Herzog wrote, *you turn out to be a crook too! How pathetic!* But this was no way to begin. He started over. *My dear Edvig, I have news for you.* Ah, yes, much better this way. A provoking thing about Edvig was that he behaved as if he were the one with all the news—this calm Protestant Nordic Anglo-Celtic Edvig with his grizzled little beard, clever, waving, mounting hair, and glasses, round, clean, and glittering. *Admittedly, I came to you in a bad way. Madeleine made psychiatric treatment a condition of our staying together. If you remember, she said I was in a dangerous mental state. I was allowed to choose my own psychiatrist. Naturally I picked one who had written on Barth, Tillich, Brunner, etc. Especially since Madeleine, though Jewish, had had a Christian phase as a Catholic convert and I hoped you might help me to understand her. Instead, you went for her yourself. You did, it's undeniable, the more you learned from me that she was beautiful, had a brilliant mind, by no means sane, and was religious, to boot.* And she and Gersbach managed and planned every step I took. They figured a headshrinker could help to ease me out—a sick man, exceptionally neurotic, perhaps even hopeless. Anyway the cure would keep me busy, absorbed in my own case. Four afternoons a week they knew where I was, on the couch, and so were safe in bed. *I was near the point of breakdown, the day I came to see you—wet weather, trickling snow, the overheated bus.* The snow certainly made my heart no cooler. The street plastered with yellow leaves. That elderly person in her green plush hat, unturbulent green, and like a deadly bag in soft folds on her head. But it was not such a bad day at that. Edvig said I was not off my rocker. Simply a reactive-depressive.

"But Madeleine says I'm insane. That I . . ." Eager and trembling, his sore spirit distorted his face, swelled his throat, painfully. But he was encouraged by the kindness of Edvig's bearded smile. He then did his best to draw Edvig out, but all he would tell him that day was that depressives tended to form frantic dependencies and to become hysterical when cut off, when threatened with loss. "And of course," he added, "from what you tell me, you haven't been guiltless. And she sounds like an angry person to begin with. When did she lapse from the Church?"

"I'm not sure. I thought she was through long ago. But last Ash Wednesday she had the soot on her forehead. I said 'Madeleine, I thought you stopped being a Catholic. But what do I see between your eyes, ashes?' But she said, 'I don't know what you're talking about.' She tried to pass it off as one of my delusions, or something. But it was no delusion. It was a spot. I swear it was at least half a spot. But her attitude seems to be, a Jew like me, what would I know about this stuff."

Herzog could see that Edvig was fascinated by every word about Madeleine. Nodding, he raised his head, his chin rose at every sentence, he touched his neat beard, his lenses glittered, he smiled. "You feel she's a Christian?"

"She feels I'm a Pharisee. She says so."

"Ah?" Edvig sharply commented.

"Ah, what?" Moses said. "You agree with her?"

"How can I? I scarcely know you. But what do you think of the question?"

"Do you think that any Christian in the twentieth century has the right to speak of Jewish Pharisees? From a Jewish standpoint, you know, this hasn't been one of your best periods."

"But do you think your wife has a Christian outlook?"

"I think she has some home-brewed otherworldly point of

view." Herzog sat straighter in his chair, and pronounced his words with slight portentousness, perhaps. "I don't agree with Nietzsche that Jesus made the whole world sick, infected it with his slave morality. But Nietzsche himself had a Christian view of history, seeing the present moment always as some crisis, some fall from classical greatness, some corruption or evil to be saved from. I call that Christian. And Madeleine has it, all right. To some extent many of us do. Think we have to recover from some poison, need saving, ransoming. Madeleine wants a savior, and for her I'm no savior."

This was the kind of thing Edvig apparently expected from Moses. Shrugging and smiling, he took it all as analytic material and seemed very pleased. He was a fair, mild man; his shoulders had a certain slender squareness. Old-fashioned, with pink nearly colorless frames, his glasses made him drably, humbly, thoughtful and medical.

By degrees, and I don't quite know how it happened, Madeleine became the principal figure in the analysis, and dominated it as she dominated me. And came to dominate you. I began to notice how impatient you were to meet her. Because of the unusual facts of the case you said you had to interview her. By and by you were deep in discussions of religion with her. And finally, you were treating her, too. You said you could see why she had fascinated me. And I said, "I told you she was extraordinary. She's brilliant, the bitch, a terror!" So you knew, at least, if I was stoned out of my skull (as they say), it was by no ordinary woman. As for Mady, she enriched her record by conning you. It all added to her depth. And because she was getting her Ph.D. in Russian religious history (I guess), your sessions with her, at twenty-five bucks a throw, were for several months a course of lectures on Eastern Christianity. After this, she began to develop strange symptoms.

First, she accused Moses of hiring a private detective to spy on her. She began this accusation with the slightly British diction he had learned to recognize as a sure sign of trouble. "I should have thought," she said, "you'd have been far too clever to engage such an obvious type."

"Engage," said Herzog. "Whom have I engaged?"

"I mean that horrible man—that stinking, fat man in the

sports coat." Madeleine, absolutely sure of herself, flashed him one of her terrible looks. "I defy you to deny this. And it's simply beneath contempt."

Seeing how pale she had become, he cautioned himself to be careful and above all not to mention the British manner. "But, Mady, this is simply a mistake."

"It is no mistake. I never dreamed you might be capable of this."

"But I don't know what you're talking about."

Her voice began to rise and tremble. She said fiercely, "You sonofabitch! Don't give me this soft treatment. I know all your fucking tricks." Then she shrieked, "This must stop! I will not have a dick tailing me!" Staring, those marvelous eyes grew red.

"But why would I have you followed, Mady? I don't understand. What could I find out?"

"Now that man dogged my steps around F-Field's, all afternoon." She often stammered when she was enraged. "I waited in the l-l-ladies' room half an hour, and when I came out he was still there. Then in the I.C. tunnel . . . when I was buying f-f-flowers."

"Maybe it was only some fellow trying to pick you up. It's got nothing to do with me."

"That was a dick!" She clenched her fists. Her lips were frighteningly thin, and her whole body trembled. "He was sitting on the screen porch next door this afternoon when I got home."

Moses, pale, said, "You point him out, Mady. I'll go right up to him. . . . Just show the man to me."

Edvig termed this a paranoid episode, and Herzog said, "Really?" He took this in for a moment and then exclaimed, with a burst of feeling, looking at the doctor with large eyes, "Do you really think this was a delusion? Do you mean to tell me she's disturbed? Insane?"

Edvig said, conservatively, measuring his words, "One incident like this doesn't indicate insanity. I meant precisely what I said, a paranoid episode."

"But it's she who's sick, sicker than I am."

Ah, poor girl! It was a clinical matter. She was really unwell. Toward the sick, Moses was always especially compassionate.

He assured Edvig, "If she really is as you say, I'll have to watch my step. I must try to take care of her."

Charity, as if it didn't have enough trouble in this day and age, will always be suspected of morbidity—sado-masochism, perversity of some sort. All higher or moral tendencies lie under suspicion of being rackets. Things we simply honor with old words, but betray or deny in our very nerves. At any rate, Edvig did not congratulate Moses on his pledge to look after Madeleine.

"What I must do," said Edvig, "is inform her of this tendency."

But it did not seem to disturb Madeleine to be warned professionally against paranoid delusions. She said it wasn't exactly news to her that she was abnormal. In fact, she took the whole thing calmly. "Anyway, it'll never be boring," was what she said to Herzog.

The trouble was not over yet. For a week or two, Field's delivery truck was bringing jewelry, cigarette boxes, coats and dresses, lamps, carpets, almost daily. Madeleine could not recall making these purchases. In ten days she ran up a twelve-hundred-dollar bill. All these articles were choice, very beautiful—there was some satisfaction in that. She did things in style, even when unbalanced. As he sent them back, Moses felt very tender toward her. Edvig predicted that she would never lapse into a true psychosis, but would have such spells for the rest of her life. It was melancholy for Moses, but perhaps his sighs expressed some satisfaction too. It was possible.

The deliveries presently stopped. Madeleine turned back to her graduate studies. But one night, in the disorderly bedroom, when they were both naked, and Herzog, lifting the sheet, made a sharp remark about the old books underneath (big, dusty volumes of an ancient Russian encyclopedia), it was too much for her. She began to scream at him, and threw herself on the bed, tearing off blankets and sheets, slamming books on the floor, then attacking the pillows with her nails, giving a wild, choked scream. There was a plastic cover on the mattress, and this she clutched and twisted, still cursing him shrilly, inarticulate, an odd white grime in the corners of her mouth.

Herzog picked up the overturned lamp. "Madeleine—don't you think you ought to take something . . . for this?"

Stupidly, he reached out a hand to soothe her, and at once she straightened and hit him in the face, too clumsily to hurt him. She jumped at him with her fists, not pummeling womanlike, but swinging like a street fighter with her knuckles. Herzog turned and took these blows on his back. It was necessary. She was sick.

Maybe it's just as well that I didn't hit her. I might have won back her love. But I can tell you that my meekness during these crises infuriated her, as if I was trying to beat her at the religious game. I know you discussed agapé with her, and similar high ideas, but the least sign of the same in me put her in a frenzy. She thought I was a faker. For in her paranoid mind I was disintegrated into my primitive elements. This is why I suggest her attitude might have changed if I had belted her. Paranoia is perhaps the normal state of mind in savages. And if my soul, out of season, out of place, experienced these higher emotions, I could get no credit for them anyway. Not from you, with your attitudes toward good intentions. I've read your stuff about the psychological realism of Calvin. I hope you don't mind my saying that it reveals a lousy, cringing, grudging conception of human nature. This is how I see your Protestant Freudianism.

Edvig sat calmly through Herzog's description of the assault in the bedroom, smiling a bit. Then he said, "Why do you suppose it happened?"

"Something about the books, maybe. Interference with her studies. If I say the house is dirty, it stinks, she thinks I'm criticizing her mind and forcing her back into housework. Disrespectful of her rights as a person . . ."

Edvig's emotional responses were unsatisfactory. When he needed a feeling reaction, Herzog had to get it from Valentine Gersbach. Accordingly, he took his troubles to him. But first, ringing Gersbach's doorbell, he had to face the coldness (he couldn't understand it) of Phoebe Gersbach, who answered. She was looking very gaunt, dry, pale, strained. Of course— the Connecticut landscape raced, rose, contracted, opened its depths, and the Atlantic water shone—of course, Phoebe knew her husband was sleeping with Madeleine. And Phoebe had only one business in life, one aim, to keep her husband and protect her child. Answering the bell, she opened the door on foolish, feeling, suffering Herzog. He had come to see his friend.

Phoebe was not strong; her energy was limited; she must have been past the point of irony. And as for pity, what would she have pitied him for? Not adultery—that was too common to be taken seriously by either of them. Anyway, to her, having Madeleine's body could never seem a big deal. She might have pitied Herzog's stupid eggheadedness, his clumsy way of putting his troubles into high-minded categories; or simply his suffering. But she probably had only enough feeling for the conduct of her own life, and no more. Moses was sure that she blamed him for aggravating Valentine's ambitions—Gersbach the public figure, Gersbach the poet, the television-intellectual, lecturing at the Hadassah on Martin Buber. Herzog himself had introduced him to cultural Chicago.

"Val's in his room," she said. "Excuse me, I've got to get the kid ready for Temple."

Gersbach was putting up bookshelves. Deliberate, heavy, slow-moving, he measured the wood, the wall, and jotted figures on the plaster. He handled the level masterfully, looked over the toggle bolts. With his thick, ruddy-dark, judicious face and his broad chest and his artificial leg which made him stand tilted, he concentrated on the choice of a bit for the electric drill as he listened to Herzog's account of Madeleine's strange assault.

"We were getting into bed."

"Well?" He made an effort to be patient.

"Both naked."

"Did you try anything?" said Gersbach. A severe note entered his voice.

"Me? No. She's built a wall of Russian books around herself. Vladimir of Kiev, Tikhon Zadonsky. In my bed! It's not enough they persecuted my ancestors! She ransacks the library. Stuff from the bottom of the stacks nobody has taken out in fifty years. The sheets are full of crumbs of yellow paper."

"Have you been complaining again?"

"Maybe I have, a little. Eggshells, chop bones, tin cans under the table, under the sofa. . . . It's bad for June."

"There's your mistake! Right there—she can't bear that

nagging, put-upon tone. If you expect me to help straighten this out, I've got to tell you. You and she—it's no secret from anybody—are the two people I love most. So I must warn you, *chaver*, get off the lousy details. Just knock off all chicken shit, and be absolutely level and serious."

"I know," said Herzog, "she's going through a long crisis—finding herself. And I know I have a bad tone, sometimes. I've gone over this ground with Edvig. But Sunday night . . ."

"Are you sure you didn't make a pass?"

"No. It so happens we had intercourse the night before."

Gersbach seemed extremely angry. He gazed at Moses with burning ruddy-dark eyes and said, "I didn't ask you that. My question was only about Sunday night. You've got to learn what the score is, God damn it! If you don't level with me, I can't do a frigging thing for you."

"Why shouldn't I level with you?" Moses was astonished by this vehemence, by Gersbach's fierce, glowing look.

"You don't. You're damn evasive."

Moses considered the charge under Gersbach's intense red-brown gaze. He had the eyes of a prophet, a *Shofat*, yes, a judge in Israel, a king. A mysterious person, Valentine Gersbach. "We had intercourse the night before. But as soon as it was done she turned on the light, picked up one of those dusty Russian folios, put it on her chest, and started to read away. As I was leaving her body, she was reaching for the book. Not a kiss. Not a last touch. Only her nose, twitching."

Valentine gave a faint smile. "Maybe you should sleep separately."

"I could move into the kid's room, I suppose. But June is restless as it is. She wanders around at night in her Denton sleepers. I wake up and find her by my bed. Often wet. She's feeling the strain."

"Now knock it off, about the kid. Don't use her in this."

Herzog bowed his head. He felt threatened by tears. Gersbach sighed and walked along his wall slowly, bending and straightening like a gondolier. "I explained to you last week . . ." he said.

"You'd better tell me once more. I'm in a state," said Herzog.

"Now you listen to me. We'll go over the ground again."

Grief greatly damaged—it positively wounded—Herzog's handsome face. Anyone he had ever injured by his conceit might now feel revenged to see how ravaged he looked. The change was almost ludicrous. And the lectures Gersbach read him—those were so spirited, so vehement, gross, they were ludicrous, too, a parody of the intellectual's desire for higher meaning, depth, quality. Moses sat by the window in raw sunlight, listening. The drapery with gilt-grooved rods lay on the table with planks and books. "One thing you can be sure, *bruder*," said Valentine. "I have no ax to grind. In this thing, I just have no prejudice." Valentine loved to use Yiddish expressions, to misuse them, rather. Herzog's Yiddish background was genteel. He heard with instinctive snobbery Valentine's butcher's, teamster's, commoner's accent, and he put himself down for it—My God! those ancient family prejudices, absurdities from a lost world. "Let's cut out all the *shtick*," said Gersbach. "Let's say you're a crumb. Let's say even you're a criminal. There's nothing—nothing!—you could do to shake my friendship. That's no shit, and you know it! I can take what you've done to me."

Moses, astonished again, said, "What have I done to you?"

"Hell with that. *Hob es in drerd.* I know Mady is a bitch. And maybe you think I never wanted to kick Phoebe in the ass. That *klippa*! But that's the female nature." He shook his abundant hair into place. It had fiery-dark depths. At the back it was brutally barbered. "You've taken care of her for some time, okay, I know. But if she's got a disgusting father and a *kvetsch* of a mother, what else should a man do? And expect nothing in return."

"Well, of course. But I spent twenty grand in about a year. Everything I inherited. Now we've got this rotten hole on Lake Park with the I.C. trains passing all night. The pipes stink. The house is all trash and garbage and Russian books and the kid's unwashed clothes. And there I am, returning Coke bottles and vacuuming, burning paper and picking up veal bones."

"The bitch is testing you. You're an important professor, invited to conferences, with an international correspondence. She wants you to admit her importance. You're a *ferimmter mensch*."

Moses, to save his soul, could not let this pass. He said quietly, *"Berimmter."*

"Fe—be, who cares. Maybe it's not so much your reputation as your egotism. You could be a real *mensch.* You've got it in you. But you're effing it up with all this egotistical shit. It's a big deal—such a valuable person dying for love. Grief. It's a lot of bull!"

Dealing with Valentine was like dealing with a king. He had a thick grip. He might have held a scepter. He *was* a king, an emotional king, and the depth of his heart was his kingdom. He appropriated all the emotions about him, as if by divine or spiritual right. He could do more with them, and therefore he simply took them over. He was a big man, too big for anything but the truth. (Again, the truth!) Herzog had a weakness for grandeur, and even bogus grandeur (was it ever entirely bogus?).

They went out to clear their heads in the fresh winter air. Gersbach in his great storm coat, belted, bareheaded, exhaling vapor, kicking through the snow with the all-battering leg. Moses held down the brim of his dead-green velours hat. His eyes couldn't bear the glitter.

Valentine spoke as a man who had risen from terrible defeat, the survivor of sufferings few could comprehend. His father had died of sclerosis. He'd get it, too, and expected to die of it. He spoke of death majestically—there was no other word for it—his eyes amazingly spirited, large, rich, keen, or, thought Herzog, like the broth of his soul, hot and shining.

"Why when I lost my leg," said Gersbach. "Seven years old, in Saratoga Springs, running after the balloon man; he blew his little *fifel.* When I took that short cut through the freight yards, crawling under cars. Lucky the brakeman found me as soon as the wheel took off my leg. Wrapped me in his coat and rushed me to the hospital. When I came to, my nose was bleeding. Alone in the room." Moses listened, white, the frost did not change his color. "I leaned over," Gersbach went on, as if relating a miracle. "A drop of blood fell on the floor, and as it splashed I saw a little mouse under the bed who seemed to be staring at the splash. It backed away, it moved its tail and whiskers. And the room was just full of bright sunlight. . . ." (There are storms on the sun itself, but here all is peaceful and temperate, thought Moses.) "It was a little world, underneath the bed. Then I realized that my leg was gone."

Valentine would have denied that the tears in his eyes were for himself. No: curse *that*, he'd have said. Not for him. They were for that little kid. There were stories about himself, too, that Moses had told a hundred times, so he couldn't complain of Gersbach's repetitiveness. Each man has his own batch of poems. But Gersbach almost always cried, and it was strange, because his long curling coppery lashes stuck together; he was tender but he looked rough, his face broad and rugged, heavy-bristled, and his chin positively brutal. And Moses recognized that under his own rules the man who had suffered more was more special, and he conceded willingly that Gersbach had suffered harder, that his agony under the wheels of the boxcar must have been far deeper than anything Moses had ever suffered. Gersbach's tormented face was stony white, pierced by the radiant bristles of his red beard. His lower lip had almost disappeared beneath the upper. His great, his hot sorrow! Molten sorrow!

Dr. Edvig, Herzog wrote, *Your opinion, repeated many times, is that Madeleine has a deeply religious nature. At the time of her conversion, before we were married, I went to church with her more than once. I clearly remember . . . In New York . . .*

At her insistence. One morning when Herzog brought her to the church door in a cab she said he had to come in. He must. She said no relationship between them was possible if he didn't respect her faith. "But I don't know anything about churches," said Moses.

She got out of the cab and went up the stairs quickly, expecting that he would follow. He paid the driver and caught up with her. She pushed the swinging door open with her shoulder. She put her hand in the font and crossed herself, as if she'd been doing it all her life. She'd learned that in the movies, probably. But the look of terrible eagerness and twisted perplexity and appeal on her face—where did that come from? Madeleine in her gray suit with the squirrel collar, her large hat, hurried forward on high heels. He followed slowly, holding his salt-and-pepper topcoat at the neck as he took off his hat. Madeleine's body seemed gathered upward in the breast and shoulders, and her face was red with excitement. Her hair was pulled back severely under the hat but escaped in wisps to form sidelocks. The church was a new building—small, cold, dark, the varnish shining hard on the oak pews, and blots of flame standing motionless near the altar. Madeleine genuflected in the aisle. Only it was more than genuflection. She sank, she cast herself down, she wanted to spread herself on the floor and press her heart to the boards—he recognized that. Shading his face on both sides, like a horse in blinders, he sat in the pew. What was he doing here? He was a husband, a father. He was married, he was a Jew. Why was he in church?

The bells tinged. The priest, quick and arid, rattled off the Latin. In the responses, Madeleine's high clear voice led the rest. She crossed herself. She genuflected in the aisle. And then they were in the street again and her face had recovered its normal color. She smiled and said, "Let's go to a nice place for breakfast."

Moses told the cabbie to go to the Plaza.

"But I'm not dressed for it," she said.

"In that case I'll take you to Steinberg's Dairy, which I prefer anyway."

But Madeleine was putting on lipstick, and fluffing out her blouse, and checking her hat. How lovely she could be! Her face was gay and round, pink, the blue of her eyes was clear. Very different from the terrifying menstrual ice of her rages, the look of the murderess. The doorman ran down from his rococo shelter in front of the Plaza. The wind was blowing hard. She swept into the lobby. Palms and pink-toned carpets, gilding, footmen . . .

I don't quite understand what you mean by "religious." A religious woman may find she doesn't love her lover or her husband. But what if she should hate him? What if she should wish continually for his death? What if she should wish it most fervently when they were making love? What if in the act of love he should see that wish shining in her blue eyes like a maiden's prayer? Now, I am not simple-minded, Dr. Edvig. I often wish I were. It hardly does much good to have a complex mind without actually being a philosopher. I don't expect a religious woman to be lovable, a saintly pussycat. But I would like to know how you decided that she is deeply religious.

Somehow I got into a religious competition. You and Madeleine and Valentine Gersbach all talking religion to me—so I tried it out. To see how it would feel to act with humility. As though such idiotic passivity or masochistic crawling or cowardice were humility, or obedience, not terrible decadence. Loathsome! O, patient Griselda Herzog! I put up the storm windows as an act of love, and left my child well provided, paying the rent and the fuel and the phone and insurance, and packing my valise. As soon as I was gone, Madeleine, your saint, sent my picture to the cops. If I ever set foot on the porch again to see my daughter, she was going to call the squad car. She had a warrant ready. The kid was brought to me, and taken home, by Valentine Gersbach, who also gave me advice and consolation, religion. He brought me books (by Martin Buber). He commanded me to study them. I sat reading I and Thou, Between God and Man, The Prophetic Faith *in a nervous fever. Then we discussed them.*

I'm sure you know the views of Buber. It is wrong to turn a man (a subject) into a thing (an object). By means of spiritual dialogue, the I-It relationship becomes an I-Thou relationship. God comes and goes in man's soul. And men come and go in each other's souls. Sometimes they come and go in each other's beds, too. You have dialogue with a man. You have intercourse with his wife. You hold the poor fellow's hand. You look into his eyes. You give him consolation. All the while, you rearrange his life. You even make out his budget for years to come. You deprive him of his daughter. And somehow it is all mysteriously translated into religious depth. And finally your suffering is greater than his, too, because you are the greater sinner. And so you've got him, coming and going. You told me my hostile suspicions of Gersbach were unfounded, even, you hinted, paranoid. Did you know he was Madeleine's lover? Did she tell you? No, or you wouldn't have said that. She had good reason to fear being followed by a private investigator. There was nothing at all neurotic about it. Madeleine, your patient, told you what she liked. You knew nothing. You know nothing. She snowed you completely. And you fell in love with her yourself, didn't you? Just as she planned. She wanted you to help her dump me. She would have done it in any case. She found you, however, a useful instrument. As for me, I was your patient. . . .

DEAR *Governor Stevenson,* Herzog wrote, gripping his seat in the hurtling train, *Just a word with you, friend. I supported you in 1952. Like many others I thought this country might be ready for its great age in the world and intelligence at last assert itself in public affairs—a little more of Emerson's* American Scholar, *the intellectuals coming into their own. But the instinct of the people was to reject mentality and its images, ideas, perhaps mistrusting them as foreign. It preferred to put its trust in visible goods. So things go on as before with those who think a great deal and effect nothing, and those who think nothing evidently doing it all. You might as well be working for them, I suppose. I am sure the Coriolanus bit was painful, kissing the asses of the voters, especially in cold states like New Hampshire. Perhaps you did contribute something useful in the last decade, showing up the old-fashioned self-intensity of the "humanist," the look of the "intelligent man" grieving at the loss of his private life, sacrificed to public service. Bah! The general won because he expressed low-grade universal potato love.*

Well, Herzog, what do you want? An angel from the skies? This train would run him over.

Dear Ramona, you mustn't think because I've taken a powder, briefly, that I don't care for you. I do! I feel you close about me, much of the time. And last week, at that party, when I saw you across the room in your hat with flowers, your hair crowded down close to your bright cheeks, I had a glimpse of what it might be like to love you.

He exclaimed mentally, Marry me! Be my wife! End my troubles!—and was staggered by his rashness, his weakness, and by the characteristic nature of such an outburst, for he saw how very neurotic and typical it was. We must be what we are. That is necessity. And what are we? Well, here he was trying to hold on to Ramona as he ran from her. And thinking that he was binding her, he bound himself, and the culmination of this clever goofiness might be to entrap himself. Self-development, self-realization, happiness—these were the titles under which these lunacies occurred. Ah, poor fellow!—and Herzog momentarily joined the objective world in looking down on himself. He too could smile at Herzog and despise him. But there still remained the fact. *I* am Herzog. I have to *be* that man. There is no one else to do it. After smiling, he must return to his own Self and see the thing through. But there was a brainstorm for you—the third Mrs. Herzog! This was what infantile fixations did to you, early traumata, which a man could not molt and leave empty on the bushes like a cicada. No true individual has existed yet, able to live, able to die. Only diseased, tragic, or dismal and ludicrous fools who sometimes hoped to achieve some ideal by fiat, by their great desire for it. But usually by bullying all mankind into believing them.

From many points of view, Ramona truly was a desirable wife. She was understanding. Educated. Well situated in New York. Money. And sexually, a natural masterpiece. What breasts! Lovely ample shoulders. The belly deep. Legs brief and a little bowed but for that very reason especially attractive. It was all there. Only he was not through with love and hate elsewhere. Herzog had unfinished business.

Dear Zinka, I dreamed about you last week. In my dream we were taking a walk in Ljubljana, and I had to get my ticket for Trieste. I was sorry to leave. But it was better for you that I should. It was snowing. Actually, it did snow, not only in the dream. Even when I got to Venice. This year I covered half the world, and saw people in such numbers—it seems to me I saw everybody but the dead. Whom perhaps I was looking for. *Dear Mr. Nehru, I think I have a most important thing to tell you. Dear Mr. King, The Negroes of Alabama filled me with admiration. White America is in danger of being depoliticalized. Let us hope this example by Negroes will penetrate the hypnotic trance of the majority. The political question in modern democracies is one of the reality of public questions. Should all of these become matters of fantasy the old political order is ended. I for one wish to go on record recognizing the moral dignity of your group. Not the Powells, who want to be as corrupt as white demagogues, nor the Muslims building on hate.*

Dear Commissioner Wilson—I sat next to you at the Narcotics Conference last year—Herzog, a stocky fellow, dark eyes, scar on his neck, grizzled, in an Ivy League suit (selected by his wife), a bad cut (far too youthful for my figure). *I wonder if you will allow me to make a few observations on your police force? It's not the fault of any single person that civil order can't be maintained in a community. But I am concerned. I have a small daughter who lives near Jackson Park, and you know as well as I do the parks are not properly policed. Gangs of hoodlums make it worth your life to go in. Dear Mr. Alderman, Must the Army have its Nike missile site on the Point? Perfectly futile, I believe, obsolete, and taking up space. Plenty of other sites in the city. Why not move this useless junk to some blighted area?*

Quickly, quickly, more! The train rushed over the landscape. It swooped past New Haven. It ran with all its might toward Rhode Island. Herzog, now barely looking through the tinted, immovable, sealed window felt his eager, flying spirit streaming out, speaking, piercing, making clear judgments, uttering final explanations, necessary words only. He was in a whirling ecstasy. He felt at the same time that his judgments exposed the boundless, baseless bossiness and willfulness, the nagging embedded in his mental constitution.

Dear Moses E. Herzog, Since when have you taken such an interest in social questions, in the external world? Until lately, you led a life of innocent sloth. But suddenly a Faustian spirit of discontent and universal reform descends on you. Scolding. Invective.

Dear Sirs, The Information Service was kind enough to send a package from Belgrade containing articles of winter wear. I did not want to take my long-johns to Italy, the paradise of exiles, *and regretted it. It was snowing when I got to Venice. I couldn't get into the vaporetto with my valise.*

Dear Mr. Udall, A petroleum engineer I met recently in a Northwest jet told me our domestic oil reserves were almost used up and that plans had been completed for blasting the polar caps with hydrogen bombs to get at the oil beneath. What about that?

Shapiro!

Herzog had a lot to explain to Shapiro, and he was certainly waiting for his explanations. Shapiro was not good-humored although his face wore a good-humored look. His nose was sharp and angry and his lips appeared to be smiling away their anger. His cheeks were white and plump, and his thin hair was combed straight back, glistening in the Rudolph Valentino or

Ricardo Cortez style of the twenties. He had a dumpy figure, but wore natty clothes.

Still, Shapiro was in the right this time. *Shapiro, I should have written sooner to tell you . . . to apologize . . . to make amends. . . .* But I have a splendid excuse—trouble, sickness, disorder, afflictions. *You've written a fine monograph. I hope I made that clear in my review. My memory abandoned me complete in one place, and I was all wrong about Joachim da Floris.* You and Joachim must both forgive me. I was in a terrible state. Having agreed to review Shapiro's study before the trouble broke, Herzog couldn't get out of it. He dragged the heavy volume with him all over Europe in his valise. It caused much pain in his side; he feared a hernia from it, and also ran up considerable overweight charges. Herzog kept reading away at it for the sake of the discipline, and under a growing burden of guilt. Abed in Belgrade, at the Metropol, with bottles of cherry juice, the trolley cars whizzing past in the frozen night. *Finally, in Venice, I sat down and wrote my review.*

My excuse for the botch I made now follows:

I assume, since he's at Madison, Wisconsin, *you've heard that I blew up in Chicago last October. We left the house in Ludeyville some time ago. Madeleine wanted to finish her degree in Slavonic languages. She had about ten courses in linguistics to take, and she got interested also in Sanskrit. Perhaps you can guess how she would work at things—her interests, passions. Do you remember that when you came to see us in the country two years ago, we discussed Chicago?* Whether it would be safe to live in that slum.

Shapiro in his stylish pin-striped suit, pointed shoes, as if dressed for dinner, sat on Herzog's lawn. He has the profile of a thin man. His nose is sharp but his throat sags and his cheeks hang a little toward the lips. Shapiro is very courtly. And he was impressed with Madeleine. He thought her so beautiful, so intelligent. Well, she is. The conversation was spirited. Shapiro had come to see Moses ostensibly to get "advice"—actually to ask a favor—but he was enjoying Madeleine's company. She excited him and he was laughing as he drank his quinine water. The day was hot but he didn't loosen his conservative necktie. His sharp black shoes glistened; and he has fat feet, with bulging insteps. On the grass, mowed by himself, Moses sat in torn wash pants. Stirred by Madeleine, Shapiro was particularly lively, almost shrieking when he laughed, and his laughter becoming more frequent, wilder, uncaused. His manner at the same time grew more formal, measured, judicious. He spoke in long sentences, Proustian he may have thought—actually Germanic, and filled with incredible bombast. "On balance, I should not venture to assay the merit of the tendency without more mature consideration," he was saying. Poor Shapiro! What a brute he was! That snarling, wild laugh of his, and the white froth forming on his lips as he attacked everyone. Madeleine was greatly stirred by him too, and on her high manners. They found each other exceedingly stimulating.

She came from the house with the bottles and glasses on the tray—cheese, liver paste, crackers, ice, herring. She had on blue trousers and a yellow Chinese blouse, the coolie hat I bought her on Fifth Avenue. She said she was subject to sunstroke. Stepping quickly, she advanced from the shadow of the house into the sparkling grass, the cat leaping from her path, the bottles and glasses clinking. She hastened because she didn't want to miss any of the conversation. As she bent to set things out on the lawn table, Shapiro couldn't keep his eyes from the shape of her behind in the tight cotton-knit fabric.

Madeleine, "stuck away in the woods," was avid for scholarly conversation. Shapiro knew the literature of every field— he read *all* the publications; he had accounts with book dealers all over the world. When he found that Madeleine was not only a beauty but was preparing for her doctoral examination in Slavonic languages, he said, "How delightful!" And it was he himself who knew, betraying the knowledge by affectation, that for a Russian Jew from Chicago's West Side that "How delightful!" was inappropriate. A German Jew from Kenwood might have gotten away with it—old money, in the dry-goods business since 1880. But Shapiro's father had had no money, and peddled rotten apples from South Water Street in a wagon. There was more of the truth of life in those spotted, spoiled apples, and in old Shapiro, who smelled of the horse and of produce, than in all of these learned references.

Madeleine and the dignified visitor were talking about the

Russian Church, Tikhon Zadonsky, Dostoevski, and Herzen. Shapiro made a great production of learned references, correctly pronouncing all foreign words whether in French, German, Serbian, Italian, Hungarian, Turkish, or Danish, snapping them out and laughing—that hearty, sucking, snarling, undirected laugh, teeth moist, head worked back onto his shoulders. Ha! The thorns crackled. ("Like the cracking of thorns under a pot is the laughter of fools.") The cicadas in great numbers were singing. That year, they came out of the ground.

Under such stimulation, Mady's face did strange things. The tip of her nose moved, and her brows, which needed no help from cosmetics, rose with nervous eagerness, repeatedly, as if she were trying to clear her eyesight. Dr. Edvig said this was a diagnostic trait of paranoia. Beneath the huge trees, surrounded by the Berkshire slopes, with not another house in sight to spoil the view, the grass was fresh and dense, the slender, fine grass of June. The red-eyed cicadas, squat forms vividly colored, were wet after molting, sopping, immobile; but drying, they crept, hopped, tumbled, flew, and in the high trees kept up a continuous chain of song, shrilling.

Culture—ideas—had taken the place of the Church in Mady's heart (a strange organ that must be!). Herzog sat thinking his own thoughts on the grass in Ludeyville, his wash pants torn, feet bare, but his face that of an educated Jewish gentleman with fine lips, dark eyes. He watched his wife, on whom he doted (with a troubled, angry heart, another oddity among hearts) as she revealed the wealth of her mind to Shapiro.

"My Russian is not what it could be," said Shapiro.

"But how much you know about my subject," Madeleine said. She was very happy. The blood glowed in her face, and her blue eyes were warm and brilliant.

They opened a new subject—the Revolution of 1848. Shapiro had sweated through his starched collar. Only a dollar-crazed Croatian steelworker would have bought such a striped shirt. And what were his views of Bakunin, Kropotkin? Did he know Comfort's work? He did. Did he know Poggioli? Yes. He didn't feel that Poggioli had done full justice to certain important figures—Rozanov, for instance. Though Rozanov was cracked on certain questions, like the Jewish ritual bath, still he was a great figure, and his erotic mysticism was highly original—highly. Leave it to those Russians. What hadn't they done for Western Civilization, all the while repudiating the West and ridiculing it! Madeleine, Herzog thought, became almost dangerously excited. He could tell, when her voice grew reedy, when her throat sounded positively like a clarinet, that she was bursting with ideas and feelings. And if Moses did not join in, if he sat there, in her own words, like a clunk, bored, resentful, he proved he didn't respect her intelligence. Now Gersbach always boomed along in conversation. He was so emphatic in style, so impressive in his glances, looked so clever that you forgot to inquire whether he was making sense.

The lawn was on an elevation with a view of fields and woods. Formed like a large teardrop of green, it had a gray elm at its small point, and the bark of the huge tree, dying of dutch blight, was purplish gray. Scant leaves for such a vast growth. An oriole's nest, in the shape of a gray heart, hung from twigs. God's veil over things makes them all riddles. If they were not all so particular, detailed, and very rich I might have more rest from them. But I am a prisoner of perception, a compulsory witness. They are too exciting. Meantime I dwell in yon house of dull boards. Herzog was worried about that elm. Must he cut it down? He hated to do it. Meanwhile the cicadas all vibrated a coil in their bellies, a horny posterior band in a special chamber. Those billions of red eyes from the enclosing woods looked out, stared down, and the steep waves of sound drowned the summer afternoon. Herzog had seldom heard anything so beautiful as this massed continual harshness.

Shapiro mentioned Soloviëv—the younger one. Did he really have a vision, in the British Museum, of all places? It so happened that Madeleine had made a study of the younger Soloviëv, and this was her opportunity. She had enough confidence now in Shapiro to speak freely—it would be appreciated, genuinely. She gave a brief lecture on the career and thought of this dead Russian. Her offended look passed over Moses. She complained that he never really listened to her. *He* wanted to shine all the time. But that wasn't it. He had heard her lecture on this subject many times, and far into the night. He didn't dare say he was sleepy. Anyway, it had to be *quid pro quo*, given these conditions—buried in the remote Berkshires—

for he had to discuss knotty points of Rousseau and Hegel with her. He relied completely on her intellectual judgments. Before Soloviëv, she had talked of no one but Joseph de Maistre. And before de Maistre—Herzog made up the list— the French Revolution, Eleanor of Aquitaine, Schliemann's excavations at Troy, extrasensory perception, then tarot cards, then Christian Science, before that, Mirabeau; or was it mystery novels (Josephine Tey), or science fiction (Isaac Asimov)? The intensity was always high. If she had one constant interest it was murder mysteries. Three or four a day, she'd read.

Black and hot under the green, the soil gave off its dampness. Herzog felt it in his bare feet.

From Soloviëv, Mady naturally turned to Berdyaev, and while speaking of *Slavery and Freedom*—the concept of *Sobornost*— she opened the jar of pickled herring. Saliva spurted to Shapiro's lips. Quickly, he pressed his folded handkerchief to the corners of his mouth. Herzog remembered him as a greedy eater. In the cubicle they had shared at school, he used to chew his pumpernickel-and-onion sandwiches with an open mouth. Now at the smell of spice and vinegar Shapiro's eyes flooded, though he managed to keep his portly, good-humored, sharp-nosed, refined look as he pressed the handkerchief to his shaven jowls. His plump hairless hand—his quivering fingers. "No, no," he said, "thank you very much, Mrs. Herzog. Delightful! But I have a stomach condition." Condition! He had ulcers. Vanity kept him from saying it; the psychosomatic implications were unflattering. Later that afternoon, he vomited in the wash basin. He must have eaten squid, thought Herzog, who had to do the cleaning up. Why didn't he use the toilet bowl—too stout to bend?

But that was in the aftermath of his visit. Before that, Moses recalled, there was a visit from the Gersbachs, Valentine and Phoebe. They stopped their little car under the catalpa tree— then in flower, though last year's pods still hung from the twigs. Out came Valentine, in his swaying stride, and Phoebe, pale at every season of the year, calling after him in her complaining voice, "Val—Va-al." She was returning a casserole she had borrowed, one of Madeleine's great iron pots, red as lobster shell—Descoware, made in Belgium. These visits often gave Herzog a depressed feeling he couldn't account for.

Madeleine sent him for more folding chairs. Perhaps it was the rotted honey fragrance of the white catalpa bells that got him. Faintly lined with pink within, heavy with pollen dust, they dropped on the gravel. Too beautiful! Little Ephraim Gersbach was making a pile of bells. Moses was glad to go for the chairs, into the musty disorder of the house, down to the stony deaf security of the cellar. He took his time about the chairs.

When he returned, they were speaking of Chicago. Gersbach, standing with his hands in his hip pockets, his face just shaved and his plumelike hair revealing heavy copper depths, was saying that his advice was to get the hell out of this backwater. Nothing interesting had happened here since the Battle of Saratoga, over the hills, for Christ's sake. Phoebe, looking tired and pale, smoked her cigarette, faintly smiling, and hoping, probably, to be let alone. Among assertive, learned, or eloquent people, she seemed to feel her dowdiness and insufficiency. Actually she was far from stupid. She had fine eyes, a bosom, good legs. If only she didn't make herself look like the head nurse, letting her dimples lengthen into disciplinary creases.

"Chicago, by all means!" said Shapiro. "That's the school for graduate studies. A little woman like Mrs. Herzog is just what the old place needs, too."

Fill your big mouth with herring, Shapiro! Herzog thought, and mind your own fucking business. Madeleine gave her husband a rapid sidelong look. She was flattered, happy. She wanted him to be reminded, if he had forgotten, how high a value other people set upon her.

Anyway, Shapiro, I was in no mood for Joachim da Floris and the hidden destiny of Man. Nothing seemed especially hidden—it was all painfully clear. Listen, you said long ago, already pompous as a young student, that someday we would "join issue," meaning there were important differences between us even then. I think it must have started in that seminar on Proudhon and the long arguments we had, back and forth with old Larson, about the decay of the religious foundations of civilization. Are all the traditions used up, the beliefs done for, the consciousness of the masses not yet ready for the next development? Is this the full crisis of dissolution? Has the filthy moment come when moral feeling dies, conscience disintegrates, and respect for liberty, law,

*public decency, all the rest, collapses in cowardice, decadence,
blood? Old Proudhon's visions of darkness and evil can't be passed
over. But we mustn't forget how quickly the visions of genius become the canned goods of the intellectuals. The canned sauerkraut
of Spengler's "Prussian Socialism," the commonplaces of the
Wasteland outlook, the cheap mental stimulants of Alienation,
the cant and rant of pipsqueaks about Inauthenticity and For-
lornness. I can't accept this foolish dreariness. We are talking
about the whole life of mankind. The subject is too great, too deep
for such weakness, cowardice—too deep, too great, Shapiro. It torments me to insanity that you should be so misled. A merely aesthetic critique of modern history! After the wars and mass
killings! You are too intelligent for this. You inherited rich blood.
Your father peddled apples.*

*I don't pretend that my position, on the other hand, is easy. We
are survivors in this age, so theories of progress ill become us, because we are intimately acquainted with the costs. To realize that
you are a survivor is a shock. At the realization of such election,
you feel like bursting into tears. As the dead go their way, you
want to call to them, but they depart in a black cloud of faces,
souls. They flow out in smoke from the extermination chimneys,
and leave you in the clear light of historical success—the technical
success of the West. Then you know with a crash of the blood that
mankind is making it—making it in glory though deafened by
the explosions of blood. Unified by the horrible wars, instructed in
our brutal stupidity by revolutions, by engineered famines directed by "ideologists" (heirs of Marx and Hegel and trained in
the cunning of reason), perhaps we, modern humankind (can it
be!), have done the nearly impossible, namely, learned something.
You know that the decline and doom of civilization refuses to follow the model of antiquity. The old empires are shattered but those
same one-time powers are richer than ever. I don't say that the
prosperity of Germany is altogether agreeable to contemplate. But
there it is, less than twenty years after the demonic nihilism of
Hitler destroyed it. And France? England? No, the analogy of the
decline and fall of the classical world will not hold for us. Something else is happening, and that something lies closer to the vision of Comte—the results of rationally organized labor—than to
that of Spengler. Of all the evils of standardization in the old bourgeois Europe of Spengler, perhaps the worst was the standardized*

pedantry of the Spenglers themselves—this coarse truculence born in the Gymnasium, *in cultural drill administered by an old-fashioned bureaucracy.*

I intended in the country to write another chapter in the history of Romanticism as the form taken by plebeian envy and ambition in modern Europe. Emergent plebeian classes fought for food, power, sexual privileges, of course. But they fought also to inherit the aristocratic dignity of the old regimes, which in the modern age might have claimed the right to speak of decline. In the sphere of culture the newly risen educated classes caused confusion between aesthetic and moral judgments. They began with anger over the industrial defilement of landscapes (Ruskin's British "Vales of Tempe") and ended by losing sight of the old-fashioned moral characteristics of the Ruskins. Reaching at last the point of denying the humanity of the industrialized, "banalized" masses. It was easy for the Wastelanders to be assimilated to totalitarianism. Here the responsibility of artists remains to be assessed. To have assumed, for instance, that the deterioration of language and its debasement was tantamount to dehumanization led straight to cultural fascism.

I planned also to consider the whole question of models, of imitatio, *in the history of civilization. After long study of the* ancien régime *I was ready to risk a theory concerning the effects of the high traditions of the court, the politics, the theater of Louis XIV on French (and therefore European) personality. Circumstances of bourgeois privacy in the modern age deprived individuals of scope for Grand Passions, and it is here that one of the most fascinating but least amiable tendencies of the Romantics develops. (One of the results of this sort of personal drama is that, to the colonial world, Western Civilization dramatized itself as Aristocratic.) I had a chapter in progress, when you visited, called "The American Gentleman," a short history of social climbing. And there was I, myself, in Ludeyville, as Squire Herzog. The Graf Pototsky of the Berkshires. It was quite a funny twist of events, Shapiro. While you and Madeleine were tossing your heads, coquetting, bragging, showing off your clean sharp teeth—the learned badinage—I was trying to take stock of my position. I understood that Madeleine's ambition was to take my place in the learned world. To overcome me. She was reaching her final elevation, as queen of the intellectuals, the castiron bluestocking.*

And your friend Herzog writhing under this sharp elegant heel.

Ah, Shapiro, the victor of Waterloo drew apart to shed bitter tears for the dead (slain under his orders). Not so my ex-Missis. She does not live between two contradictory Testaments. She is stronger than Wellington. She wants to live in the delirious professions, *as Valéry calls them—trades in which the main instrument is your opinion of yourself and the raw material is your reputation or standing.*

As for your book, there is too much imaginary history in it. Much of it is simply utopian fiction. I will never change my mind about that. Nevertheless, I thought your idea about milleniarianism and paranoia very good. Madeleine, by the way, lured me out of the learned world, got in herself, slammed the door, and is still in there, gossiping about me.

It was not terribly original, this idea of Shapiro's, but he did a good clear job. *In my review I tried to suggest that clinical psychologists might write fascinating histories. Put professionals out of business. Megalomania for the Pharaohs and Caesars. Melancholia in the Middle Ages. Schizophrenia in the eighteenth century. And then this Bulgarian, Banowitch, seeing all power struggles in terms of paranoid mentality*—a curious, creepy mind, that one, convinced that madness always rules the world. The Dictator must have living crowds and also a crowd of corpses. The vision of mankind as a lot of cannibals, running in packs, gibbering, bewailing its own murders, pressing out the living world as dead excrement. Do not deceive yourself, dear Moses Elkanah, with childish jingles and Mother Goose. Hearts quaking with cheap and feeble charity or oozing potato love have not written history. Shapiro's snarling teeth, his salivating greed, the dagger of an ulcer in his belly give him true insights, too. Fountains of human blood that squirted from fresh graves! Limitless massacre! I never understood it!

I took a list of the traits of paranoia from a psychiatrist recently—I asked him to jot them down for me. It might aid my understanding, I thought. He did this willingly. I put the scribbled paper in my wallet and studied it like the plagues of Egypt. Just like "DOM, SFARDEYA, KINNIM" in the Haggadah. It read "Pride, Anger, Excessive 'Rationality,' Homosexual Inclinations, Competitiveness, Mistrust of Emotion, Inability to Bear Criticism, Hostile Projections, Delusions." It's all there—all! I've thought about Mady in every category, and though the portrait isn't yet complete I know I can't abandon a tiny child to her. Mady is no Daisy. Daisy is a strict, moody woman, but dependable. Marco has come through all right.

Abandoning the letter to Shapiro—it raised too many painful thoughts, and this was precisely the sort of thing he must avoid if he was not to lose the benefit of a holiday—he turned to his brother Alexander. *Dear Shura,* he wrote, *I think I owe you 1500 bucks. How about making it a round 2000. I need it. In the process of pulling myself together.* Shura was a generous brother. The Herzogs had their characteristic family problems, but stinginess was not one of their traits. Moses knew that the rich man would push a button and say to his secretary, "Send a check to screw-loose Moses Herzog." His handsome stout white-haired brother in his priceless suit, vicuña coat, Italian hat, his million-dollar shave and rosy manicured fingers with big rings, looking out of his limousine with princely hauteur. Shura knew everyone, paid off everyone, and despised everyone. Toward Moses his contempt was softened by family feeling. Shura was your true disciple of Thomas Hobbes. Universal concerns were idiocy. Ask nothing better than to prosper in the belly of Leviathan and set a hedonistic example to the community. It amused Shura that his brother Moses should be so fond of him. Moses loved his relatives quite openly and even helplessly. His brother Willie, his sister Helen, even the cousins. It was childish of him; he knew that. He could only sigh at himself, that he should be so undeveloped on that significant side of his nature. He sometimes tried to think, in his own vocabulary, whether this might be his archaic aspect, prehistoric. Tribal, you know. Associated with ancestor worship and totemism.

Also, as I have been having legal troubles, I wonder whether you could recommend a lawyer. Perhaps one of Shura's own legal staff who would not charge Moses for his services.

He now composed a letter in his head to Sandor Himmelstein, the Chicago lawyer who had looked after him last autumn, after Madeleine put him out of the house. *Sandor! Last time we were in touch, I wrote from Turkey. Of all places!* And yet that suited Sandor, in a way; it was Arabian Nights country and Sandor himself might have come out of a bazaar, for all that he had his office on the fourteenth floor of the Burnham Building, up the street from City Hall. Herzog had met him in the steam bath at Postl's Health Club, at Randolph and Wells. He was a short man, misshapen from the loss of part of his chest. In Normandy, he always said. He had probably been a sort of large dwarf when he enlisted. It must have been possible to get a commission in the Judge Advocate's branch though a dwarf. It made Herzog uneasy, perhaps, that he had been discharged from the Navy owing to his asthma and never saw action. Whereas this dwarf and hunchback was disabled by a mine near the beachhead. The wound had made a hunchback of him. Anyway, that was Sandor, with a proud, sharp, handsome face, pale mouth and sallow skin, grand nose, thin gray hair. *In Turkey I was in sad condition.* Partly, again, the weather. Spring was struggling to come in, but the winds changed. The sky closed over the white mosques. It snowed. The trousered, mannish Turkish women veiled their stern faces. I never expected to see them striding so powerfully. Coal had been dumped in the street, but the laborers had not appeared to shovel it, so the furnace was out. Herzog drank plum brandy and tea in the café, and chafed his hands and worked his toes inside his shoes to keep the blood going. He was worried about his circulation at that time. To see the early flowers covered by snow increased his gloom.

I sent you this belated bread-and-butter note, to thank you and Bea for taking me under your roof. Acquaintances, not old friends. I'm sure I was a terrible house guest. Sick and angry—broken by this lousy grief. Taking pills for my insomnia but still unable to sleep, going about drugged, and the whisky gave me tachycardia. I should have been in a padded cell. *Gratitude! I was deeply grateful.* But the politic gratitude of weakness, of the sufferer, furious underneath. Sandor took me over. I was inept. He moved me into his house, far south, ten blocks from the Illinois Central. Mady had kept the car, claiming she needed it for Junie, to take her to the zoo and the like.

Sandor said, "You won't mind sleeping next to the booze, I guess," for the cot was unfolded beside the bar. The room was full of Carmel Himmelstein's high-school crowd. "Get out!"

Sandor cried shrilly at the adolescents. "Can't see through the goddamn cigarette smoke! Look at these Coke bottles filled with butts." He turned on the air-conditioner, and Moses, still red with the cold of the day, but with white circles under his eyes, held his valise, the same valise that now lay in his lap. Sandor cleared the glasses from several shelves. "Unpack, kid," he said. "Put your stuff here. We eat in twenty minutes. Good chow. Sauerbraten. Bea's specialty."

Obedient, Moses set out his things—toothbrush, razor, Desenex powder, sleeping pills, his socks, Shapiro's monograph, and an old pocket edition of Blake's poems. The slip of paper on which Dr. Edvig had listed the traits of paranoia was his bookmark.

After dinner, that first night in the Himmelsteins' living room, Herzog began reluctantly to understand that in accepting Sandor's hospitality he had made still another characteristic mistake.

"You'll get over this. That's all right. You'll make it," said Sandor. "I'll put my dough on you. You're my boy."

And Beatrice, with her black hair and her pretty pink mouth which needed no rouge, said, "Moses, we know how you must feel."

"The bitches come and the bitches go," said Sandor. "My whole practice, almost, is these bitches. You should know what they carry on, and what happens in this city of Chicago." He shook his heavy head and his lips came together with the pressure of disgust. "If she wants to go, fuck her! Let her go! You'll be okay. So you were a sucker! Big deal! Every man is a sucker for some type of broad. I always got clobbered by the blue-eyed kind, myself. But I had the sense to fall in love with this beautiful pair of brown eyes. Isn't she great?"

"She certainly is." It had to be said. And it was actually not too difficult. Moses had not lived forty-odd years without learning to get through these moments. Among narrow puritans, this is lying; but with civilized people only civility.

"I'll never know what she saw in a wreck like me. Anyway, Moses, you just stay with us for a while. At a time like this, you shouldn't be without friends. Sure, I know you have family of your own in this town. I see your brothers at Fritzl's. I talked to your middle brother just the other day."

"Willie."

"He's a fine fellow—very active in Jewish life, too," said Sandor. "Not like that *macher*, Alexander. Always some scandal about him. Now he's connected with the Juice racket, and next with Jimmy Hoffa, and then he's in with the Dirksen bunch. Well, okay, your brothers are big shots. But they'd make you eat your heart out. Here nobody'll ask any questions."

"With us you can just let yourself go," said Beatrice.

"Well, I don't understand this thing at all," said Moses. "Mady and I had our ups and downs from the start. But things were improving. Last spring we discussed the marriage and whether we were getting along well enough to continue—a practical question came up: whether I should tie myself up with a lease. She said that as soon as she finished her thesis we'd have a second child. . . ."

"I'll tell you," said Sandor. "It's your own frigging fault, too, if you want my opinion."

"Mine? What do you mean?"

"Because you're a highbrow and married a highbrow broad. Somewhere in every intellectual is a dumb prick. You guys can't answer your own questions—still, I see hope for you, Mose."

"What hope?"

"You're not like those other university phonies. You're a *mensch*. What good are those effing eggheads! It takes an ignorant bastard like me to fight liberal causes. Those silk-stocking Yale squares may have a picture of Learned Hand in the office, but when it comes to getting mixed up in Trumbull Park, or fighting those yellowbellies in Deerfield or standing up for a man like Tompkins—" Sandor was proud of his record in the case of Tompkins, a Negro in the postal service whom he had defended.

"Well, I suppose they were out to get Tompkins because he was a Negro," said Herzog. "But unfortunately, he was a drunk. You told me that yourself. And there was a question as to his competence."

"Don't go around repeating that," said Sandor. "It'll be used the wrong way. You going to blab what I told you confidentially? It was a question of justice. Aren't there any white drunks on civil service? Not much!"

"Sandor—Beatrice. I feel terrible. Another divorce—out again, at my time of life. I can't take it. I don't know . . . it feels like death."

"Shush, what are you talking!" said Sandor. "It's pitiful because of the kid, but you'll get over it."

At that time, when you thought, and I agreed, that I shouldn't be alone, perhaps I really should have been alone, Herzog wrote.

"Look, I'll handle the whole thing for you," Sandor assured him. "You'll come out of all this dreck smelling like a roast. Leave it to me, will you? Don't you trust me? You think I'm not leveling with you?"

I ought to have taken a room at the Quadrangle Club.

"You can't be left to yourself," said Sandor. "You're not the type. A human being! A *mensch*! Your heart has been shat on. And you have about as much practical sense as my ten-year-old, Sheldon, you poor bastard."

"I'm going to shake this off. I'm not going to be a victim. I hate the victim bit," said Moses.

Himmelstein sat in his wing chair, his feet tucked under his short belly. His eyes were moist, the color of freshly sliced cucumber, with fine lashes. He chewed a cigar. His ugly nails were polished. He had his manicure at the Palmer House. "A strong-minded bitch," he said. "Terrifically attractive. Loves to make up her mind. Once decided, decided forever. What a will power. It's a type."

"Still, she must have loved you once, Moses," said Bea. She spoke very, very slowly—that was her manner. Her dark brown eyes were set within strong orbital bones. Her lips were pink and vivid. Moses did not want to meet her gaze; he would have to hold it long and earnestly and nothing would come of it. He knew he had her sympathy but that she could never approve of him.

"I don't think she loved me," said Moses.

"I'm sure she did."

It was the middle-class female solidarity, defending a nice girl from charges of calculation and viciousness. Nice girls marry for love. But should they fall out of love, they must be free to love another. No decent husband will oppose the heart. This is orthodox. Not utterly bad. But a new orthodoxy. Anyway, thought Moses, he was in no position to quarrel with Beatrice. He was in her house, taking comfort from her.

"You don't know Madeleine," he said. "When I met her, she needed a lot of help. The sort only a husband can provide . . ."

I know how long—endless—people's stories are when they have grievances. And how tedious for everyone.

"I happen to think she's a nice person," said Bea. "At first she looked stuck-up and acted suspicious, but when I got to know her she turned out to be friendly and very nice. Basically, she must be a good person."

"Shit! People are nice, most of them. You've got to give 'em a chance," said Sandor, sallow and handsome

"Mady planned it all out," said Herzog. "Why couldn't she break off before I signed the lease?"

"Because she has to keep a roof over the kid's head," said Sandor. "What do you expect?"

"What *I expect?*" Herzog stood up, struggling for words. His face was white, his eyes dilated, fixed. He stared at Sandor, who was seated like a sultan, the small heels gathered under his bulging belly. Then he became aware that Beatrice with her pretty, lusterless look was warning him not to anger Sandor. His blood pressure was liable to shoot up dangerously when he was crossed.

Herzog wrote, *I was thankful for your friendship. I was in a state, though. One of those states in which one makes great, impossible demands. In anger people become dictatorial. Hard to take.* I was trapped there. Sleeping next to the bar. My heart went out to poor Tompkins. No wonder he hit the bottle when Sandor took him over.

"You're not going to fight for the kid's custody, are you?" Sandor said to Herzog.

"Suppose I do?"

"Well," said Sandor, "speaking as a lawyer, I can see you with a jury. They'll look at Madeleine, blooming and lovely, then you, haggard and gray-haired, and bam there goes your custody suit. That's the jury system. Dumber than cave men, those bastards—I know this isn't easy for you to hear, but I better say it. Guys at our time of life must face facts."

"Facts!" said Herzog, faint, groping, outraged.

"I know," said Sandor. "I'm ten years older. But after forty it's all the same. If you can get it up once a week, you should be grateful."

Beatrice tried to restrain Sandor, but he said, "Shut up." He then turned to Moses again, shaking his head so that it gradually sank toward his disfigured breast, and his shoulder blades jutted behind, coracoid through the white-on-white shirt. "What the fuck does *he* know what it is to face facts. All he wants is everybody should love him. If not, he's going to scream and holler. All right! After D-Day, I lay smashed up in that effing limey hospital—a cripple. Why, Christ! I had to walk out under my own power. And what about his pal Valentine Gersbach? *There's* a man for you! That gimpy red-head knows what real suffering is. But he lives it up—three men with six legs couldn't get around like that effing peg-leg. It's okay, Bea—Moses can take it. Otherwise, he'd be just another Professor Jerk. I wouldn't even bother with the sonofabitch."

Herzog was incoherent with anger. "What do you mean? Should I die because of my hair? What *about* the child?"

"Now, don't stand there rubbing your hands like a god-damn fool—Christ, I hate a fool," Sandor shouted. His green eyes were violently clear, his lips were continually tensing. He must have been convinced that he was cutting the dead weight of deception from Herzog's soul, and his long white fingers, thumbs and forefingers worked nervously.

"What! Die? Hair? What the hell are you babbling! I only said they'd give the kid to a young mother."

"Madeleine put you up to that. She planted this, too. To keep me from suing."

"She *nothing*! I'm trying to tell you for your own good. This time, she calls the shots. She wins, and you lose. Maybe she wants somebody else."

"Does she? Did she tell you that?"

"She told me nothing. I said *maybe*. Now calm down. Pour him a drink, Bea. Out of his own bottle. He doesn't like Scotch."

Beatrice went to fetch Herzog's own bottle of Gucken-heimer's 86 proof.

"Now," said Sandor, "stop this baloney. Don't be a clown, man." His look changed, and he let some kindness flow toward Herzog. "Well, when you suffer, you really suffer. You're a real, genuine old Jewish type that digs the emotions. I'll give you that. I understand it. I grew up on Sangamon Street, remember, when a Jew was still a Jew. I know about suffering—we're on the same identical network."

Herzog the passenger noted, *For the life of me, I couldn't understand. I often thought I was going to have apoplexy, to burst. The more comfort you gave me, the closer I came to death's door. But what was I doing? Why was I in your house?*

It must have been funny how I grieved. Looking from my room at the leafless weeds in back. Brown, delicate frames of ragweed. Milkweed with the discharged pods gaping. Or else gazing at the dark gray face of the television.

On Sunday morning, early, Sandor called Herzog into the living room. "Man," he said, "I found one hell of an insurance policy for you."

Moses, tying his robe about him as he came from his bed by the bar, didn't understand.

"What?"

"We can get you a terrific policy to cover the kid."

"What's this about?"

"I told you last week but you must've been thinking of other things. If you get sick, have an accident, lose an eye, even if you go nuts, Junie will be protected."

"But I'm going to Europe, and I have travel insurance."

"That's if you die. But here, even if you have a mental breakdown and have to go to an institution the kid still gets her monthly support."

"Who says I'm breaking down?"

"Listen, you think I'm doing this for myself? I'm in the middle here," said Sandor, stamping a bare foot on the thick pile of the carpet.

Sunday, with gray fog from the lake and the ore boats lowing like waterborne cattle. You could hear the emptiness of the hulls. Herzog would have given anything to be a deckhand bound for Duluth.

"Either you want my legal advice or you don't," said Sandor. "I want to do the best for all of you. True?"

"Well, here I am to prove it. You've taken me into your house."

"Okay, so let's talk sense. With Madeleine you're not going to have trouble. She gets no alimony. She'll be married soon. I took her to lunch at Fritzel's, and guys who haven't given Sandor H. the time of day for years came running with a hard-on, tripping over themselves. That includes the rabbi of my temple. She's some dish."

"You're a lunatic. And I know what she is."

"What do you mean—she's less of a whore than most. We're all whores in this world, and don't you forget it. I know damn well *I'm* a whore. And you're an outstanding shnook, I realize. At least the eggheads tell me so. But I bet you a suit of clothes you're a whore, too."

"Do you know what a mass man is, Himmelstein?"

Sandor scowled. "How's that?"

"A mass man. A man of the crowd. The soul of the mob. Cutting everybody down to size."

"What soul of the mob! Don't get highfalutin. I'm talking facts, not shit."

"And you think a fact is what's nasty."

"Facts *are* nasty."

"You think they're true because they're nasty."

"And you—it's all too much for you. Who told you you were such a prince? Your mother did her own wash; you took boarders; your old man was a two-bit moonshiner. I know you Herzogs and your *Yiches*. Don't give me that hoity-toity. I'm a Kike myself and got my diploma in a stinking night school. Okay? Now let's both knock off this crap, dreamy boy."

Herzog, subdued, much shaken, had no answer. What had he come here for? Help? A forum for his anger? Indignation for his injustices? But it was Sandor's forum, not his. This fierce dwarf with protruding teeth and deep lines in his face. His lopsided breast protruded from his green pajama top. But this was Sandor's bad, angry state, thought Herzog. He could be attractive, too, generous, convivial, even witty. The lava of that heart may have pushed those ribs out of shape, and the force of that hellish tongue made his teeth protrude. Very well, Moshe Herzog—if you must be pitiable, sue for aid and succor, you will put yourself always, inevitably, in the hands of these angry spirits. Blasting you with their "truth." This is what your masochism means, *mein zisse n'shamele.* The good are attracted by men's perceptions and think not for themselves. You must cleanse the gates of vision by self-knowledge, by experience. Besides which, opposition is true friendship. So they tell me.

"You want to take care of your own kid, don't you?" said Sandor.

"Sure I do. But you told me the other day that I might as well forget about her, that she'd grow up a stranger to me."

"That's right. She won't even know you next time you see her."

Sandor was thinking of his own kids, those hamsters; not my daughter, made of finer clay. *She* won't forget me. "I don't believe it," said Herzog.

"As the lawyer, I have a social obligation to the child. I've got to protect her."

"*You?* I'm her father."

"You may crack up. Or else die."

"Mady is just as liable to die. Why don't we write the insurance on her?"

"She'd never let you. That's not part of the woman's deal. It's the man's deal."

"Not this man's. Madeleine swings her weight like a male. She made all these decisions to take the kid and throw me in the street. She thinks she can be both mother and father. I'll pay the premiums on *her* life."

Sandor suddenly began to yell. "I don't give a shit about her. I don't give a shit about you. I'm looking after that child."

"What makes you so sure I'll die first?"

"And is this the woman you love?" Sandor said in a lower tone. Apparently, he had remembered his dangerously high blood pressure. An elaborate effort occurred which involved his pale eyes, and his lips, and which pitted his chin. He said more evenly, "I'd take that policy myself if I could pass the physical. It would give me pleasure to croak and leave my Bea a rich widow. I'd like that."

"Then she could go to Miami, and dye her hair."

"That's right. While I turn green like an old penny, in my box, and she screws around. I don't grudge her."

"All right, Sandor—" said Herzog. He wanted to end this talk. "Just now I don't feel like making arrangements for my death."

"What's so great about your effing death?" Sandor cried. His figure straightened. He stood very close to Herzog, who was somewhat frightened by his shrillness and stared down, wide-eyed, at the face of his host. It was strong-cut and coarsely handsome. The small mustache bristled, a fierce green, milky poison rose to his eyes; his mouth twisted. "I'm getting out of this case!" Himmelstein began to scream.

"What's the matter with you!" Herzog said. "Where's Beatrice! Beatrice!"

But Mrs. Himmelstein only shut her bedroom door.

"She'll go to a shyster firm!"

"For God's sake, stop screaming."

"They'll kill you."

"Sandor, quit this."

"Put you over a barrel. Tear your hide off."

Herzog held his ears. "I can't stand it."

"Tie your guts in knots. Sonofabitch. They'll put a meter on your nose, and charge you for breathing. You'll be locked up back and front. Then you'll think about death. You'll pray for it. A coffin will look better to you than a sports car."

"But I didn't leave Madeleine."

"I've done this to guys myself."

"What harm did I do her."

"The court doesn't care. You signed papers—did you read them?"

"No, I took your word."

"They'll throw the book at you in court. She's the mother—the female. She's got the tits. They'll crush you."

"But I'm not guilty of anything."

"She hates you."

Sandor no longer screamed. He had resumed his normal loudness. "Jesus! You don't know anything," he said. "You an educated man? Thank God my old pa didn't have the dough to send me to the U. of C. I worked in the Davis Store and went to John Marshall. Education? It's a laugh! You don't know what goes on."

Moses was shaken. He began to reconsider. "All right—" he said.

"What's all right?"

"I'll take a policy on my life."

"Not as a favor to me!"

"Not as a favor . . ."

"It's a big bite—four hundred and eighteen bucks."

"I'll find the money."

Sandor said, "All right, my boy. Finally you make some sense. Now what about some breakfast—I'll cook porridge." In his green paisley pajamas he set off for the kitchen on his long, slipperless feet. Following in the corridor, Herzog heard a cry from Sandor at the kitchen sink. "Look at this crap! Not a pot—not a dish—there isn't a spoon that's clean. It stinks of garbage. It's just a sewer here!" The old dog, obese and bald, escaped in fear, claws rapping on the tiles—clickclick, click-click. "Spendthrift bitches!" he shouted at the women of his house. "Frigging lice! All they're good for is to wag their asses at the dress shops and play gidgy in the bushes. Then they come home, and gorge cake and leave plates smeared with chocolate in the sink. That's what gives them the pimples."

"Easy, Sandor."

"Do I ask for much? The old veteran cripple runs up and down City Hall, from courtroom to courtroom—out to Twenty-sixth and California. For them! Do they care if I have to suck up to all kinds of pricks to get a little business?" Sandor began to rake out the sink. He threw eggshells and orange rinds into the corner beside the garbage pail—coffee grounds. He worked himself into a rage and began to smash dishes and glassware. His long fingers, like those of a hunchback, gripped the plates soiled with icing. Without losing beauty of gesture—amazing!—he shattered them on the wall. He knocked over the dish drainer and the soap powder, and then he wept with anger. And also at himself, that he should have such emotions. His open mouth and jutting teeth! The long hairs streamed from his disfigured breast.

"Moses—they're killing me! Killing their father!"

The daughters lay listening in their rooms. Young Sheldon was in Jackson Park with his scout troup. Beatrice did not appear.

"We don't have to have porridge," said Herzog.

"No, I'll wash a pot." He was still shedding tears. Under the torrential tap his manicured fingers scrubbed the aluminum with steel wool.

When he grew calmer, he said, "You know, Moses, I've been to a psychiatrist about these effing dishes. They cost me twenty bucks an hour. Moses, what am I going to do with my kids. Sheldon's going to be all right. Tessie's maybe not so bad. But Carmel! I don't know how to handle her. I'm afraid the boys are getting into her pants already. Prof, while you're here, I don't ask anything from you" (in return for bed and board, he meant) "but I'd appreciate it if you'd take an interest in her mental development. This is her chance to know an intellectual —a famous person—an authority. Will you talk to her?"

"About what?"

"Books—ideas. Take her for a walk. Discuss with her. Please, Moses, I'm begging you!"

"Well, of course I'll talk to her."

"I asked the rabbi—but what good are these reform rabbis? I know I'm a vulgar bastard, The Terrible-Tempered Mr. Bang. I work for these kids. . . ."

He squeezes the poor. Buys credit paper from merchants who sell fancy goods on installments to prostitutes on the South Side. And it's all very well for me to surrender my daughter, but his little hamsters have to have elevating discourses.

"If Carmel was a little older, I'd say, marry her."

Moses, pale and startled, said, "She's a very attractive girl. Far too young, of course."

Sandor put his long arm about Herzog's waist and drew him close. "Don't be such a rolling stone, Prof. Start leading a normal life. Where the hell haven't you been—Canada, Chicago, Paris, New York, Massachusetts. Your brothers have done okay right here, in this town. Of course, what's good enough for Alexander and Willie isn't good enough for a *macher* like you. Moses E. Herzog—he has no money in the bank, but you can look up his name in the library."

"I hoped that Madeleine and I would settle down."

"Out in the sticks? Don't be nuts. With that chick? Are you kidding? Come back to the home town. You're a West Side Jew. I used to see you as a kid in the Jewish People's Institute. Slow down. Stop knocking yourself out. I love you better than my own effing family. You never pulled that phony Harvard stuff on me. Stick with the folks—with good hearts. With love. Jesus! What d'ye say?" He drew away his big handsome sallow head a little distance, to look into Herzog's eyes, and Herzog felt the circuit of affection enclosing them again. Himmelstein's face with its long yellow grooves was joyful. "Can you sell that dump in the Berkshires?"

"I might."

"Hell, it's settled then. Take a loss if you have to. They've ruined Hyde Park, but you don't want to live with those longhair shmoes anyhow. Rent in my neighborhood."

Though he was tired out, and suffering at heart like a fool, Herzog listened like a child to a tale.

"Get yourself a housekeeper closer to your own age. And a good lay, too. What's wrong with that? Or we'll find you a gorgeous brownskin housekeeper. No more Japs for you."

"What do you mean?"

"You know what I mean. Or maybe what you need is a girl who survived the concentration camps, and would be grateful for a good home. And you and I will lead the life. We'll go to the Russian bath on North Avenue. They hit me at Omaha Beach, but screw 'em all, I'm still going. We'll live it up. We'll find an orthodox shul—enough of this Temple junk. You and me—we'll track down a good *chazan*. . . ." Forming his lips so that the almost invisible mustache thinly appeared, Sandor began to sing, "*Mi pnei chatoenu golino m'artzenu.*" And for our sins we were exiled from our land. "You and me, a pair of old-time Jews." He held Moses with his dew-green eyes. "You're my boy. My innocent kind-hearted boy."

He gave Moses a kiss. Moses felt the potato love. Amorphous, swelling, hungry, indiscriminate, cowardly potato love.

"Oh, you sucker," Moses cried to himself in the train. "Sucker!"

I left you money for an emergency. You turned it all over to Madeleine to buy clothes. Were you her lawyer, or mine?

I might have understood, from the way he spoke of his female clients and assaulted all the men. But my God! how did I get into all of that? Why did I become involved with him at all? I must have wanted such absurd things to happen to me. I was so far gone in foolishness that even they, those Himmelsteins, knew more than I. And showed me the facts of life, and taught me the truth.

Revenged with hate on my own proud inanities.

In the mild end of the afternoon, later, at the waterside in Woods Hole, waiting for the ferry, he looked through the green darkness at the net of bright reflections on the bottom. He loved to think about the power of the sun, about light, about the ocean. The purity of the air moved him. There was no stain in the water, where schools of minnows swam. Herzog sighed and said to himself, "Praise God—praise God." His breathing had become freer. His heart was greatly stirred by the open horizon; the deep colors; the faint iodine pungency of the Atlantic rising from weeds and mollusks; the white, fine, heavy sand; but principally by the green transparency as he looked down to the stony bottom webbed with golden lines. Never still. If his soul could cast a reflection so brilliant, and so intensely sweet, he might beg God to make such use of him. But that would be too simple. But that would be too childish. The actual sphere is not clear like this, but turbulent, angry. A vast human action is going on. Death watches. So if you have some happiness, conceal it. And when your heart is full, keep your mouth shut also.

He had moments of sanity, but he couldn't maintain the balance for very long. The ferry came, he boarded it, pulling his hat tight in the sea wind, slightly shamefaced because he enjoyed this typical moment of a holiday. The cars were loaded in a cloud of blowing sand and marl while Herzog looked down from the upper deck. During the crossing he rested his feet on his up-ended valise, taking the sun, watching the boats through half-lidded eyes.

In Vineyard Haven he caught a cab at the dock. It turned right on the main street parallel to the harbor, lined with big trees—water, sails on the right, and the road passing under leaves filled with sun. Big gilt letters shone on red store fronts.

The shopping center was as bright as a stage set. The taxi went slowly, as if the old engine had a heart condition. It passed the public library, and pillared driveways, great lyre-shaped elm trees and sycamores with patches of white bark—he noted the sycamores. These trees held an important place in his life. The green of evening was settling in, and the blue of the water, when your eyes turned from the shadows of the grass, seemed paler and paler. The cab turned right again, toward the shore, and Herzog got out, missing half of the driver's directions as he paid. "Down the stairs—up again. I get it. Okay." He saw Libbie waiting on the porch in a bright dress, and waved to her. She blew him a kiss.

At once he knew that he had made a mistake. Vineyard Haven was not the place for him. It was lovely, and Libbie was charming, one of the most charming women in the world. But I should never have come. It just isn't right, he thought. He appeared to be looking for the wooden treads on the slope, hesitating, a strong-looking man, holding his valise in a double grip like a player about to throw a forward pass. His hands were broad, heavily veined; not the hands of a man whose occupation was mental, but of a born bricklayer or housepainter. The breeze swelled out his light clothes and then fitted them tightly to his body. And what a look he had—such a face! Just then his state of being was so curious that he was compelled, himself, to see it—eager, grieving, fantastic, dangerous, crazed and, to the point of death, "comical." It was enough to make a man pray to God to remove this great, bone-breaking burden of selfhood and self-development, give himself, a failure, back to the species for a primitive cure. But this was becoming the up-to-date and almost conventional way of looking at any single life. In this view the body itself, with its two arms and vertical length, was compared to the Cross, on which you knew the agony of consciousness and separate being. For that matter, he had been taking this primitive cure, administered by Madeleine, Sandor, et cetera; so that his recent misfortunes might be seen as a collective project, himself participating, to destroy his vanity and his pretensions to a personal life so that he might disintegrate and suffer and hate, like so many others, not on anything so distinguished as a cross, but down in the mire of post-Renaissance, post-humanistic, post-Cartesian dissolution, next door to the Void. Everybody was in the act. "History" gave everyone a free ride. The very Himmelsteins, who had never even read a book of metaphysics, were touting the Void as if it were so much salable real estate. This little demon was impregnated with modern ideas, and one in particular excited his terrible little heart: you must sacrifice your poor, squawking, niggardly individuality—which may be nothing anyway (from an analytic viewpoint) but a persistent infantile megalomania, or (from a Marxian point of view) a stinking little bourgeois property—to historical necessity. And to truth. And truth is true only as it brings down more disgrace and dreariness upon human beings, so that if it shows anything except evil it is illusion, and not truth. But of course he, Herzog, predictably bucking such trends, had characteristically, obstinately, defiantly, blindly but without sufficient courage or intelligence tried to be a *marvelous* Herzog, a Herzog who, perhaps clumsily, tried to live out marvelous qualities vaguely comprehended. Granted he had gone too far, beyond his talents and his powers, but this was the cruel difficulty of a man who had strong impulses, even faith, but lacked clear ideas. What if he failed? Did that really mean that there was no faithfulness, no generosity, no sacred quality? Should he have been a plain, unambitious Herzog? No. And Madeleine would never have married such a type. What she had been looking for, high and low, was precisely an ambitious Herzog. In order to trip him, bring him low, knock him sprawling and kick out his brains with a murderous bitch foot. Oh, what a confusion he had made—what a waste of intelligence and feeling! When he thought of the endless anxious tedium of courtship and marriage with all that he had invested in arrangements— merely in practical measures, in trains and planes and hotels and department stores, and banks where he had banked, in hospitals, in doctors and drugs, in debts; and, for himself, the nights of rigid insomnia, the yellow boring afternoons, the trials by sexual combat, and all the horrible egomania of it, he wondered that he had survived at all. He wondered, even, why he should have wanted to survive. Others in his generation wore themselves out, died of strokes, of cancer, willed their own deaths, conceivably. But he, despite all blunders, fuckyknuckles that he was, he must be cunning, tough. He survived.

And for what? What was he hanging around for? To follow this career of *personal relationships* until his strength at last gave out? Only to be a smashing success in the private realm, a king of hearts? Amorous Herzog, seeking love, and embracing his Wandas, Zinkas, and Ramonas, one after another? But this is a female pursuit. This hugging and heartbreak is for women. The occupation of a man is in duty, in use, in civility, in politics in the Aristotelian sense. Now then, why am I arriving here, in Vineyard Haven, on a *holiday* no less! Heartbroken, and gussied up, with my Italian pants and my fountain pens, and my grief—to bother and pester poor Libbie, and exploit her affections, forcing her to pay off because I was so kind and decent when *her* last husband, Erikson, went off his rocker and tried to stab her and take the gas himself? At which time, yes, I was very helpful. But if she hadn't been so very beautiful, sexual, and obviously attracted to me, would I have been such a willing friend and helper? And it's not much to be pleased with that I bother her now, a bride of a few months, with my troubles. Have I come to collect the quid pro quo? Turn around, Moshe-Hanan, and catch the next ferry back. All you needed was a train ride. It has turned the trick.

Libbie came down the path to greet him, and gave him a kiss. She was dressed for the evening in an orange or poppy-colored cocktail dress. It took Moses an extra moment to determine whether the fragrance he smelled came from the nearby bed of peonies or from her neck and shoulders. She was unaffectedly happy to see him. By fair means or not, he had made a friend of her.

"How are you!"

"I'm not going to stay," said Herzog. "It's not right."

"What are you talking about? You've been traveling for hours. Come inside and meet Arnold. Sit down and have a drink. You *are* funny."

She laughed at him, and he was obliged to laugh with her. Sissler came out on the porch, a man in his fifties, untidy and sleepy but cheerful, and began to make welcoming sounds in his deep voice. He had on a pair of large pink slacks with a rubberized waistband.

"He says he's already on his way back, Arnold. I told you he was funny."

"You traveled all this way to tell us? Come in—come in. I was going to light a fire. It gets colder in an hour and people are coming to dinner. What about a drink? Scotch or bourbon? Maybe you'd like a swim instead?" Sissler gave him a broad, amiable, wrinkled, black-eyed smile. These eyes were small and there were spaces between his teeth; he was bald, his back hair was thick and projected like one of those large tree mushrooms that grow on the mossy side of a trunk. Libbie had married a comfortable, wise old dog, the kind who always turned out to have large reserves of understanding and humanity. In the brighter light of the seaward side of the house she looked extremely well, happy, her face tanned and smooth. On her mouth she wore poppy-colored lipstick, and gold-mesh jewelry on her arm, a heavy gold chain on her neck. She had aged a little—she must be thirty-eight or thirty-nine, was his guess, but her dark, close-set eyes, which gave her a fluid and merged gaze (she had a delicate, lovely nose), were clearer than he had ever seen them. She was in the time of life when the later action of heredity begins, the blemishes of ancestors appear—a spot, or the deepening of wrinkles, at first increasing a woman's beauty. Death, the artist, very slow, putting in his first touches. Now to Sissler it couldn't matter less. He had already accepted this, would rumble on in his Russian accent, and be the same forthright businessman to the day of his death. When that moment came, because of his bunchy back hair, he would have to die lying on his side.

Ideas that depopulate the world.

But as Herzog accepted a drink, and heard himself in a clear voice saying thanks, and saw how he sat down in a chintz-covered chair, his psychological reading suggested that it might not be Sissler whose deathbed he saw in this vision, but some other person who had a wife. Maybe it was even himself who was dying in fantasy. He had had a wife—two wives—and been the object of such death-flavored fantasies himself. Now: the first requirement of stability in a human being was that the said human being should really desire to exist. This is what Spinoza says. It is necessary for happiness (*felicitas*). He can't behave well (*bene agere*), or live well (*bene vivere*), if he himself doesn't want to live. But if it's also natural, as psychology says, to kill mentally (one thought-murder a day keeps the psychiatrist away), then the desire to exist is not steady enough to support a good life. Do I want to exist, or want to die? But at this social moment he couldn't expect to answer such questions, and he swallowed freezing bourbon from the clinking glass instead. The whisky went down, burning pleasurably in his chest like a tangled string of fire. Below he saw the pockmarked beach, and flaming sunset on the water. The ferry was returning. As the sun went down, its wide hull suddenly filled with electric lights. In the calm sky a helicopter steered toward Hyannis Port, where the Kennedys lived. Big doings there, once. The power of nations. What do we know about it? Moses felt a sharp pang at the thought of the late President. (I wonder what I would say to a President in actual conversation.) He smiled a little as he remembered his mother boasting to Aunt Zipporah about him. "What a little tongue it has. Moshele could talk to the President." But at that time the President was Harding. Or was it Coolidge? Meantime the conversation was going on. Sissler was trying to make Moses feel at home—I must seem obviously shook up—and Libbie looked concerned.

"Ah, don't worry about me," said Moses. "I'm just a little excited by things." He laughed. Libbie and Sissler exchanged a look, but grew easier. "This is a fine house you have. Is it rented?"

"I own it," said Sissler.

"Is that so. Wonderful place. Summer only, isn't it? You could winterize it easily."

"It would cost fifteen grand, or more," said Sissler.

"That much? I suppose labor and materials are higher on this island."

"I could do the work myself, sure," said Sissler. "But we come here to rest. I understand you're a property owner, too."

"Ludeyville, Mass," said Herzog.

"Where is that?"

"Berkshires. Near the Connecticut corner of the state."

"Must be a beautiful spot of country."

"Oh, it's beautiful all right. Too remote, though. Far from everything."

"What about another drink?"

Perhaps Sissler thought the liquor would calm him.

"Moses probably wants to clean up after his trip," said Libbie.

"I'll show him his room."

Sissler carried Herzog's valise up.

"This is a fine old staircase," said Moses. "Couldn't duplicate it today for thousands. They put a lot of work into it, for a summer house."

"Sixty years ago they still had craftsmen," said Sissler. "Take a look at the doors—bird's-eye maple. Here's where you are. I think you got everything here—towels, soap. Some neighbors are coming this evening. One single lady. A singer. Miss Elisa Thurnwald. Divorced."

The room was wide and comfortable, and had a view of the bay. The bluish beacons of the two points, East and West Chop, were lighted.

"This is a fine spot," said Herzog.

"Unpack. Make yourself at home. Don't be in any hurry to go. I know you were a good friend to Libbie when she was up against it. She told me how you protected her from that blow-top, Erikson. He even tried to stab the poor kid. She didn't have anybody but you to turn to."

"As a matter of fact, Erikson had nobody else to turn to, either."

"What's the diff?" Sissler said, with his rugged face a little averted but only so that his small shrewd eyes might see Herzog from the angle required for the fullest consideration "You stood up for her. To me that's everything. Not just because I love the kid, either, but because there's so many creeps in circulation. You got trouble, I can see that. Jumping out of your skin. You got a soul—haven't you, Moses." He shook his head, smoking his cigarette with two stained fingers pressed to his mouth, his voice rumbling. "Can't dump the sonofabitch, can we? Terrible handicap, a soul."

Moses answered in a low voice. "I'm not even sure I've got the thing still."

"I would say yes. Well . . ." He turned his wrist to catch the last of the light on his gold watch. "You got time to rest up a little."

He left, and Moses lay on the bed a while—a good mattress,

a clean comforter. He lay for a quarter of an hour without thinking, lips parted, legs and arms extended, breathing quietly as he gazed at the figures of the wallpaper until they were hidden in darkness. When he stood up it was not to wash and dress but to write a farewell note on the maple desk. There was stationery in the drawer.

Have to go back. Not able to stand kindness at this time. Feelings, heart, everything in strange condition. Unfinished business. Bless you both. And much happiness. Toward end of summer, perhaps, if you will give me a rain check. Gratefully, Moses.

He stole from the house. The Sisslers were in the kitchen. Sissler was making a clatter with the ice trays. Moses rapidly descended and was out of the screen door with frantic swiftness, softly. He passed through the bushes into the neighboring lot. Up the path, and back to the ferry slip. He took a cab to the airport. All he could get at this hour was a Boston flight. He took it and caught a plane for Idlewild at Boston airport. At eleven P.M. he was lying in his own bed, drinking warm milk and eating a peanut-butter sandwich. It had cost him a pretty penny, all of this travel.

He kept Geraldine Portnoy's letter always on his bed table, and he picked it up now and reread it before he fell asleep. He tried to remember how he had felt when he had first read it, in Chicago, after some delay.

Dear Mr. Herzog, I am Geraldine Portnoy, Lucas Asphalter's friend. You may remember. . . . May remember? Moses had read faster (the script was feminine—progressive-school printing turned cursive and the i's dotted with curious little open circles), trying to swallow the whole letter at once, turning the pages to see whether the gist of the thing was underscored anywhere. *Actually I took your course in Romantics as Social Philosophers. We differed about Rousseau and Karl Marx. I have come around to your view, that Marx expressed metaphysical hopes for the future of mankind. I took what he said about materialism far too literally.* My view! It's common, and why does she want to make me dangle like this—why doesn't she get on with it? He had tried again to find the point, but all those circular open dots fell on his vision like snow and masked the message. *You probably never noticed me, but I liked you, and as* *a friend of Lucas Asphalter—he just adores you, he says you are just a feast of the most human qualities—I have of course heard a lot about you, growing up in Lucas' old neighborhood, and how you played basketball in the Boys' Brotherhood of the Republic, in the good old Chicago days on Division Street. An uncle of mine by marriage was one of the coaches—Jules Hankin.* I think I do recall Hankin. He wore a blue cardigan, and parted his hair in the middle. *I don't want you to get me wrong. I don't want to meddle in your affairs. And I am not an enemy of Madeleine's. I sympathize with her, too. She is so vivacious, intelligent, and such a charmer, and has been so warm and frank with me. For quite a while, I admired her and as a younger woman was very pleased by her confidences.* Herzog flushed. Her confidences would include his sexual disgrace. *And as a former student, I was of course intrigued to hear of your private life, but was also surprised by her freedom and willingness to talk, and soon saw she wanted to win me over, for some reason. Lucas warned me to look out for something dikey, but then any intense feeling between members of the same sex is often, and unjustly, under suspicion. My scientific background has taught me to make more cautious generalizations, and resist this creeping psychoanalysis of ordinary conduct. But she did want to win me to her side, although far too subtle to pour it on, as they say. She told me that you had very fine human and intellectual qualities, though neurotic and with an intolerable temper which often frightened her. However, she added, you could be great, and after two bad, loveless marriages perhaps you would devote yourself to the work you were meant to do. Emotional relationships you were not really good at. It was soon obvious that she would never have given herself to a man who lacked distinction of intelligence or feeling. Madeleine said that for the first time in her life she knew clearly what she was doing. Until now it was all confusion and there were even gaps of time she couldn't account for. In marrying you, she was in this mixup and might have remained so but for a certain break. It is extremely exciting to talk with her, she gives a sense of a significant encounter—with life—a beautiful, brilliant person with a fate of her own. Her experiences are rich, or pregnant. . . .* What is this? Herzog had thought. Is she going to tell me that Madeleine is going to have a child? Gersbach's child! No! How wonderful—what luck for me. If she has a kid out of wedlock,*

I can petition for Junie's custody. Eagerly, he had devoured the rest of the page, turned over. No, Madeleine was not pregnant. She'd be far too clever to let that happen. She owed her survival to intelligence. It was part of her sickness to be shrewd. She was not pregnant, then. *I was not merely a graduate student who helped with the child, but a confidante. Your little girl is greatly attached to me, and I find her a most extraordinary child. Exceptional, really. I love Junie with more than the usual affection, oh far more, than one has for the children one meets in this way. I understand the Italians are supposed to be the most child-oriented culture in the West (judge by the figure of the Christ child in Italian painting), but obviously Americans have their own craze about child psychology. Everything is done for children, ostensibly. To be fair, I think Madeleine is not bad with little June, basically. She tends to be authoritarian. Mr. Gersbach, who has an ambiguous position in this household, is very amusing to the child, on the whole. She calls him Uncle Val, and I often see him giving her a piggyback, or tossing her in the air.* Here Herzog had set his teeth, angry, scenting danger. *But I have to report one disagreeable thing, and I talked this over with Lucas. This is that, coming to Harper Avenue the other night, I heard the child crying. She was inside Gersbach's car, and couldn't get out, and the poor little thing was shaking and weeping. I thought she had shut herself in while playing, but it was after dark, and I didn't understand why she would be outside, alone, at bedtime.* Herzog's heart had pounded with dangerous thick beats at these words. *I had to calm her, and then I found out that her Mama and Uncle Val were having a quarrel inside, and Uncle Val had taken her by the hand and led her out to the car, and told her to play a while. He shut her up and went back in the house.* I can see him mount the stairs while Junie screams in fright. I'll kill him for that—so help me, if I don't! He reread the concluding lines. *Luke says you have a right to know such things. He was going to phone but I felt it would be upsetting and harmful to hear this over the phone. A letter gives one a chance to consider—think matters over, and reach a more balanced view. I don't think Madeleine is a bad mother, actually.*

He was at his letter-writing again in the morning. The little desk at the window was black, rivaling the blackness of his fire escape, those rails dipped in asphalt, a heavy cosmetic coat of black, rails equidistant but appearing according to the rules of perspective. He had letters to write. He was busy, busy, in pursuit of objects he was only now, and dimly, beginning to understand. His first message today, begun half-consciously as he was waking up, was to Monsignor Hilton, the priest who had brought Madeleine into the Church. Sipping his black coffee, Herzog in his cotton paisley robe narrowed his eyes and cleared his throat, already aware of the anger, the pervasive indignation he felt. The Monsignor should know what effect he had on the people he tampered with. *I am the husband, or ex-husband, of a young woman whom you converted, Madeleine Pontritter, the daughter of the well-known impresario. Perhaps you remember, she took instruction from you some years ago and was baptized by you. A recent Radcliffe graduate, and very beautiful. . . .* Was Madeleine really such a great beauty, or did the loss of her make him exaggerate—did it make his suffering more notable? Did it console him that a beautiful woman had dumped him? But she had done it for that loud, flamboyant, ass-clutching brute Gersbach. Nothing can be done about the sexual preferences of women. That's ancient wisdom. Nor of men. Quite objectively, however, she was a beauty. So was Daisy, in her time. I myself was once handsome, but spoiled my looks with conceit . . . *Her complexion healthy and pink, fine dark hair gathered in a bun behind and a fringe on her forehead, a slender neck, heavy blue eyes and a Byzantine nose which came straight down from the brow. The bangs concealed a forehead of considerable intellectual power, the will of a demon,* or else outright mental disorder. *She had a great sense of style. As soon as she began to take instruction she bought crosses and medals and rosaries, and suitable clothes. But then, she was just a girl, really, just out of college. Still, I believe she understood many things better than I. And I want you to know, Monsignor, that I am not writing with the purpose of ex-*

posing Madeleine, or attacking you. I simply believe you may be
interested to find out what may happen, or actually does happen,
when people want to save themselves from . . . I suppose the
word is nihilism.

Now then, what does happen? What actually did happen?
Herzog tried to understand, staring at the brick walls to which
he had fled again from the Vineyard. I had that room in
Philadelphia—that one-year job—and I was commuting to
New York three or four times a week on the Pennsylvania
train, to visit Marco. Daisy swore there would be no divorce.
And, for a time, I was shacked up with Sono Oguki, but she
didn't answer my purpose. Not *serious* enough. I wasn't getting much work done. Routine classes in Philadelphia. They
were bored with me, and I with them. Papa got wind of my
dissolute life, and was angry. Daisy wrote him all about it, but
it was none of Papa's business. What actually happened? I gave
up the shelter of an orderly, purposeful, lawful existence because it bored me, and I felt it was simply a slacker's life. Sono
wanted me to move in with her. But I thought that would
make me a squaw man. So I took my papers and books, and
my Remington office machine with the black hood, and my
records and oboe and music down to Philadelphia.

Dragging back and forth on the train, wearing himself
out—the best sacrifice he could offer. He went to visit his little
boy, and faced the anger of his ex-wife. Daisy would try to be
stolid. It did great harm to her looks. She met Moses at the top
of the stairs, her arms crossed, turning herself into a square figure with green eyes and chopped hair, waiting to say he must
bring Marco home within two hours. He had a horror of these
meetings. Of course she always knew exactly what he was doing, whom he was seeing, and now and then would say,
"How's Japan?" or "How's the Pope?" It was not funny. She
had good qualities, but a sense of humor was not among
them.

Moses prepared for his outings with Marco. The time passed
heavily otherwise. On the train he memorized facts about the
Civil War—dates, names, battles—so that while Marco was
eating his hamburger at the Zoo Cafeteria, where they always
went, they could talk. "Now it's time to tell you about Beauregard," he said. "This part is very exciting." But Herzog

could only try to fix his mind on General Beauregard or on Island Number 10 or Andersonville. He was thinking how to deal with Sono Oguki, whom he was deserting for Madeleine—it felt like a desertion. The woman was waiting for him to call; he knew that. And he was often tempted, when Madeleine was too busy with the Church and refused to see him, to drop in and have a talk, nothing more, with Sono. This confusion was ugly, and he despised himself for creating it. Was this all the work a man could find to do?

Losing self-respect! Lacking clear ideas!

He could see that Marco sympathized with his confused father. He played the game with Moses, asking more questions about the Civil War simply because it was all that he had to offer. The child would not reject his well-meant gift. There was love in that, thought Herzog, wrapped in his paisley cotton, his coffee turning cold. These children and I love one another. But what can I give them? Marco would look at him with clear eyes, his pale child's face, the Herzog face, freckled, his hair crew-cut, by his own choice, and somewhat alien. He had his Grandmother Herzog's mouth. "Well, okay, kid, I've got to go back to Philadelphia now," said Herzog. He felt, on the contrary, nothing necessary about this return to Philadelphia. Philadelphia was entirely a mistake. What need *was* there to ride that train? Was it necessary, for instance, to see Elizabeth and Trenton? Were they waiting for him to look at them? Was his single cot in Philadelphia expecting him? "It's just about train time, Marco." He pulled out his pocket watch, a gift twenty years ago from his father. "Take care on the subway. And around the neighborhood, too. Don't go down into Morningside Park. There are gangs down there."

He repressed the impulse to dial Sono Oguki's number from a sidewalk booth and got on the subway instead, which carried him to Penn Station. In his long brown coat, tight in the shoulders and misshapen by the books stuffed into the pockets, he walked the underground tunnel of shops—flowers, cutlery, whisky, doughnuts and grilled sausages, the waxy chill of the orangeade. Laboriously he climbed into the light-filled vault of the station, the great windows dustily dividing the autumn sun—the stoop-shouldered sun of the garment district. The mirror of the gum machine revealed to Herzog how pale he was, unhealthy—wisps from his coat and wool scarf, his hat and brows, twisting and flaming outward in the overfull light and exposing the sphere of his face, the face of a man who was keeping up a front. Herzog smiled at this earlier avatar of his life, at Herzog the victim, Herzog the would-be lover, Herzog the man on whom the world depended for certain intellectual work, to change history, to influence the development of civilization. Several boxes of stale paper under his bed in Philadelphia were going to produce this very significant result.

So, by the expanding iron gate with its crimson plaque, lettered in gold, Herzog holding his unpunched ticket marched down to the train. His shoelaces were dragging. Ghosts of an old physical pride were still about him. On the lower level the cars, smoky red, were waiting. Was he coming or going? At times he didn't know.

The books in his pockets were Pratt's short history of the Civil War and several volumes of Kierkegaard. Although he had given up tobacco, Herzog was still drawn to the smoker. He liked the fumes. Sitting in a dirty plush seat he took out a book and read *For dying means that it is all over, but dying the death means to experience death,* trying to think what this might signify. If . . . Yes . . . No . . . on the other hand, if existence is nausea then faith is an uncertain relief. Or else— be demolished by suffering and you will feel the power of God as he restores you. Fine reading for a depressive! Herzog, at his desk, smiled. He let his head fall into his hands, almost silently laughing. But on the train he was laboriously studying, totally serious. All who live are in despair.(?) And that is the sickness *unto* death.(?) It is that a man refuses to be what he is.(?)

He closed the book as the train reached the junk heaps of New Jersey. His head was hot. He found coolness by pressing the large Stevenson button on his lapel to his cheek. The smoke in the car was sweet, rotten, rich. He sucked it deep into his lungs—a stirring foulness; he raptly breathed in the swampiness of old pipes. The wheels were speeding with a sharp racket, biting the rails. The cold fall sun flamed over the New Jersey mills. Volcanic shapes of slag, rushes, dumps, refineries, ghostly torches, and presently the fields and woods. The short oaks bristled like metal. The fields turned blue. Each radio spire was like a needle's eye with a drop of blood in it. The dull bricks of Elizabeth fell behind. At dusk Trenton approached like the heart of a coal fire. Herzog read the municipal sign— TRENTON MAKES, THE WORLD TAKES!

At nightfall, in a cold electric glitter, came Philadelphia.

Poor fellow, his health was not good.

Herzog was grinning as he thought of the pills he had taken, and the milk he had drunk in the night. By his bed in Philadelphia there often stood a dozen bottles. He sipped milk to calm his stomach.

Living amid great ideas and concepts, insufficiently relevant to the present, day-by-day, American conditions. You see, Monsignor, if you stand on television in the ancient albs and surplices of the Roman church there are at least enough Irishmen, Poles, Croatians watching in saloons to understand you, lifting elegant arms to heaven and glancing your eyes like a silent movie star—Richard Barthelmess or Conway Tearle; the R.C. working class takes great pride in him. *But I, a learned specialist in intellectual history, handicapped by emotional confusion . . . Resisting the argument that scientific thought has put into disorder all considerations based on value . . . Convinced that the extent of universal space does not destroy human value, that the realm of facts and that of values are not eternally separated. And the peculiar idea entered my (Jewish) mind that we'd see about this! My life would prove a different point altogether. Very tired of the modern form of historicism which sees in this civilization the defeat of the best hopes of Western religion and thought, what Heidegger calls the second Fall of Man into the quotidian or ordinary. No philosopher knows what the ordinary is, has not fallen into it deeply enough. The question of ordinary human experience is the principal question of these modern centuries, as Montaigne and Pascal, otherwise in disagreement, both clearly saw.—The strength of a man's virtue or spiritual capacity measured by his ordinary life.*

One way or another the no doubt mad idea entered my mind that my own actions had historic importance, and this (fantasy?) made it appear that people who harmed me were interfering with an important experiment.

Herzog tragically sipping milk in Philadelphia, a frail hopeful lunatic, tipping the carton to quiet his stomach and drown his unquiet mind, courting sleep. He was thinking of Marco,

Daisy, Sono Oguki, Madeleine, the Pontritters, and now and
then of the difference between ancient and modern tragedy
according to Hegel, the inner experience of the heart and the
deepening of individual character in the modern age. His own
individual character cut off at times both from facts and from
values. But modern character is inconstant, divided, vacillat-
ing, lacking the stone-like certitude of archaic man, also deprived of the firm ideas of the seventeenth century, clear,
hard theorems.

Moses wanted to do what he could to improve the human
condition, at last taking a sleeping pill, to preserve himself. In
the best interests of everyone. But when he met his Philadelphia class in the morning, he could hardly see his lecture notes.
His eyes were swollen and his head asleep, but his anxious
heart beat faster than ever.

*Madeleine's father, a powerful personality, first-rate intelli-
gence, many of the peculiar and grotesque vanities of theatrical
New York in him, however, told me I might do her a great deal of
good.* He said, "Well, it's about time she quit hanging around
with queers. She's like a lot of bluestocking college girls—all
her friends are homosexuals. She's got more faggots at her feet
than Joan of Arc. It's a good sign that she's interested in you."
But the old man also thought him a poor fish. That psychological fact was not concealed. He had come to see Pontritter
in his studio—Madeleine had said, "My father insists on
having a talk with you. I wish you'd stop in." He found Pontritter dancing the samba or the cha-cha (Herzog didn't know
one from the other) with his own instructress, a middle-aged
Filipino woman who had once belonged to a well-known tango
team (Ramon and Adelina). Adelina had put on weight in the
middle, but her long legs were thin. Her makeup didn't much
lighten her dark face. Pontritter, this immense figure of a man
with single white fibers growing from his tanned scalp (he
used a sun lamp all winter) was making tiny steps in his canvas,
rope-soled slippers. His seat-fallen trousers moved from side to
side as he swayed his wide hips. His blue eyes were severe. The
music played, sucking and knocking, tiny, rapping, scraping
steel-band rhythms. When it stopped, Pontritter said with
somewhat distant interest, "You Moses Herzog?"

"That's right."

"In love with my daughter?"

"Yes."

"It isn't doing much for your health, I see."

"I haven't been too well, Mr. Pontritter."

"Everyone calls me Fitz. This is Adelina. Adelina—Moses. He's laying my daughter. I thought I'd never live to see the day. Well, congratulations . . . Hope Sleeping Beauty will wake up."

"'*Allo, guapo,*" said Adelina. There was nothing personal in this greeting. Adelina's eyes were concentrated on the lighting of her cigarette. She took a match from Pontritter's hand. Herzog remembered thinking how purely external that match game was, under the studio skylight. Artificial heat or none at all.

Later in the day, he had a talk with Tennie Pontritter, too. As Tennie spoke of her daughter, tears quickly came to her eyes. She had a smooth, long-suffering countenance, slightly tearful even when she smiled, and most mournful when you met her by chance, as Moses did on Broadway, and saw her face—she was above the average height—coming toward him, large, smooth, kindly, with permanent creases of suffering beside her mouth. She invited him to sit with her in Verdi Square, the tattered grass plot railed in and always surrounded by a seated throng of dying old men and women, and by begging cripples, lesbians swaggering like truck drivers and fragile Negro homosexuals with dyed hair and earrings.

"I don't have much influence with my daughter," said Tennie. "I love her dearly, of course. It hasn't been easy. I had to stand by Fitz. He was blacklisted for years. I couldn't be disloyal. After all, he is a great artist. . . ."

"I believe it. . . ." Herzog muttered. She had waited for him to accept this.

"He's a giant," said Tennie. She had learned to say such things with utter conviction. Only a Jewish woman of a good, culture-respecting background—her father had been a tailor and a member of the Arbeiter-Ring, a Yiddishist—could sacrifice her life to a great artist as she had done. "In a mass society!" she said. She looked at him still with the same sisterly gentleness and appeal. "A money society!" He wondered at this. Madeleine had told him, very bitter toward her parents, that the old man needed fifty thousand a year, and that he got it, too, the old Svengali, out of women and stage-struck suckers. "So Mady thinks I let her down. She doesn't understand—hates her father. I can tell you this, Moses, I think people must trust you instinctively. I see that Mady does, and she's *not* a trusting girl. So I think she must be in love with you."

"*I* am, with her," said Moses, emotionally.

"You must love her—I think you do. . . . Things are so complicated."

"That I'm older—married? Is that what you mean?"

"You won't hurt her, will you? No matter what she thinks, I am her mother. I have a mother's heart, whatever she says." She began crying, softly. "Oh, Mr. Herzog . . . I'm always between the two of them. I know we haven't been conventional parents. She feels I just turned her out into the world. And there's nothing *I* can do. It's up to you. You'll have to give the child the only thing that can help her." Tennie took off her elaborate glasses, now making no effort to disguise her weeping. Her face, her nose reddened, and her eyes, shaped to make what seemed to Moses a crooked appeal, darkened blindly with tears. There was a measure of hypocrisy and calculation in Tennie's method, but behind this, again, was real feeling for her daughter and her husband; and behind this real feeling there was something still more meaningful and somber. Herzog was all too well aware of the layers upon layers of reality—loathsomeness, arrogance deceit, and then—God help us all!—truth, as well. He understood he was being manipulated by Madeleine's worried mother. Thirty years the bohemian wife, the platitudes of that ideology threadbare, cynically exploited by old Pontritter, Tennie remained faithful, chained in the dull silver "abstract" jewelry that she wore.

But it would never happen to her daughter, if she could help it. And Madeleine was just as determined that it should not. And this was where Moses came in, on the bench in Verdi Square. His face was shaven, his shirt was clean, his nails clean, his legs, somewhat heavy in the thighs, were crossed, and he listened to Tennie very thoughtfully—for a man whose mind had stopped working. It was too full of his grand projects to think anything clearly. Of course he understood that Tennie was setting him up, and that he was a sucker for just the sort of appeal she made. He had a weakness for good deeds, and she flattered this weakness, asking him to save this headstrong deluded child of hers. Patience, loving-kindness, and virility would accomplish this. But Tennie flattered him even more subtly. She was telling Moses that he could bring stability into the life of this neurotic girl and cure her by his steadiness. Among this crowd of the aged, dying, and crippled, Tennie making her appeal to Moses for his help, stirred his impure sympathies intensely. Repulsively. His heart felt sick. "I adore Madeleine, Tennie," he said. "You don't have to worry. I'll do everything possible."

An eager, hasty, self-intense, and comical person.

Madeleine had an apartment in an old building, and Herzog stayed with her when he was in town. They slept together on the studio sofa with the morocco cover. Moses pressed her body all night with fervor, exaltation. She was not so fervent, but then she was a recent convert. Besides, one lover is always more moved than the other. Sometimes she had tears of anger and misery in her eyes and complained of her sinfulness. Still, she wanted it, too.

At seven in the morning, seeming to anticipate the alarm clock by a split second, she stiffened, and when it rang she was already exclaiming with suffocated anger, "Damn!" and striding to the bathroom.

The fixtures were old-fashioned in this place. These had been luxury apartments in the 1890s. The broad-mouthed faucets ran a shattering stream of cold water. She dropped her pajama top so that she was bare to the waist, and washed herself with a cloth, purifying herself with angry vigor, her blue-eyed face growing red, her breasts pink. Silent, barefooted, wearing his trench coat as a robe, Herzog came in and sat on the edge of the tub, watching.

The tiles were a faded cherry color, and the toothbrush rack, the fixtures, were ornate, old nickel. The water stormed from the faucet, and Herzog watched as Madeleine transformed herself into an older woman. She had a job at Fordham, and the first requirement, to her mind, was to look sober and mature, long in the Church. His open curiosity, the fact that he familiarly shared the bathroom with her, his nakedness under the trench coat, his pallid morning face in this setting of disgraced Victorian luxury—it all vexed her. She did not look at him while making her preparations. Over her brassière and slip she put a high-necked sweater, and to protect the shoulders of the sweater she wore a plastic cape. It kept the makeup from crumbling on the wool. Now she began to apply her cosmetics —the bottles and powders filled the shelves above the toilet. Whatever she did, it was with unhesitating speed and efficiency, headlong, but with the confidence of an expert. Engravers, pastry cooks, acrobats on the trapeze worked in this manner. He thought she was too reckless at it—going too fast, about to have a spill, but that never happened. First she spread a layer of cream on her cheeks, rubbing it into her straight nose, her childish chin and soft throat. It was gray, pearly bluish stuff. That was the base. She fanned it with a towel. Over this she laid the makeup. She worked with cotton swabs, under the hairline, about the eyes, up the cheeks and on the throat. Despite the soft rings of feminine flesh, there was already something discernibly dictatorial about that extended throat. She would not let Herzog caress her face downward—it was bad for the muscles. Seated, watching, on the edge of the luxurious tub, he put on his pants, tucked in his shirt. She took no notice of him; she was trying in some way to be rid of him as her daytime life began.

    She put on a pale powder with her puff, still at the same tilting speed, as if desperate. Then she turned swiftly to examine the work—right profile, left profile—bracing at the mirror, holding her hands as if to support her bust but not actually touching it. She was satisfied with the powder. She put touches of Vaseline on her lids. She dyed the lashes with a tiny coil. Moses participated in all this, intensely, silently. Still without pauses or hesitations, she put a touch of black in the outer corner of each eye, and redrew the line of her brows to make it level and earnest. Then she picked up a pair of large tailor's shears and put them to her bangs. She seemed to have no need to measure; her image was fixed in her will. She cut as if discharging a gun, and Herzog felt an impulse of alarm, shortcircuited. Her decisiveness fascinated him, and in such fascination he discovered his own childishness He, an able-bodied person seated on the edge of the pompous old tub, the enamel

wreathed with hairlike twistings like cooked rhubarb, absorbed
in this transformation of Madeleine's face. She primed her lips
with waxy stuff, then painted them a drab red, adding more
years to her age. This waxen mouth just about did it. She
moistened a finger on her tongue, and brushed a few last
touches on. That was it. She looked with level-browed gravity
in the mirror and seemed satisfied. Yes, this was just right. She
put on a long heavy tweed skirt, which hid her legs. High heels
tilted her ankles slightly. And now the hat. It was gray, with a
low crown, wide-brimmed. When she drew it over her sleek
head she became a woman of forty—some white, hysterical,
genuflecting hypochondriac of the church aisles. The wide
brim over her anxious forehead, her childish intensity, her fear,
her religious will—the pity of the whole thing! While he, the
worn, unshaven, sinful Jew, endangering her redemption—his
heart ached. But she barely gave him a glance. She had put on
the jacket with the squirrel collar and was reaching under to
adjust the shoulder pads. That hat! It was made like coil bas-
ketry of one long gray tape, about half an inch wide, like the
hat worn by the Christian lady who had read the Bible with
him in the hospital ward in Montreal. "The wind bloweth
where it listeth, and thou hearest the sound thereof. . . ."
There was even a hatpin. The job was finished. Her face was
smooth and middle-aged. Only the eyeballs hadn't been
touched, and the tears seemed about to spring from them. She
looked angry—furious. She wanted him there at night. She
would even, half with rancor, take his hand and put it on her
breast as they were falling asleep. But in the morning she would
have liked him to disappear. And he was not used to this; he
was used to being a favorite. But he was dealing with a new female generation, that was what he told himself. To her he was
a fatherly, graying, patient seducer (he could not believe it!).
But the parts had been distributed. She had her white convert's face and Herzog couldn't refuse to play opposite.

"You should have some breakfast," he said.

"No. It'll make me late."

The pastes had dried on her skin. She put on a big pectoral
cross. She had been a Catholic for only three months, and
already because of Herzog she couldn't be confessed, not by
Monsignor, anyway.

Conversion was a theatrical event for Madeleine. Theater— the art of upstarts, opportunists, would-be aristocrats. Monsignor himself was an actor. One role, but a fat one. *Obviously she had religious feeling, but the glamour and the social climbing were more important. You are famous for converting celebrities, and she went to you.* Nothing but the best for our Mady. *The Jewish interpretation of the high-minded Christian lady or gentleman is a curious chapter in the history of social theater.* The Dignities continually replenished from below. Where would any distinguished person come from, if not the masses? With the devotion and fire of transcendent resentment. *I don't deny that it did much for me as well. It reflected very favorably on me to be involved in such an issue.*

"You'll get sick going to work on an empty stomach. Have breakfast with me and I'll pay your cab fare out to Fordham."

Decisively, but awkwardly, she left the bathroom, her stride hampered by the long ugly skirt. She wanted to fly, but with the cartwheel hat, the tweeds, the religious medals, the large pectoral cross, her heavy heart, getting off the ground was not easy.

He trailed her through the mirror-paneled room, past framed prints of Flemish altarpieces, gilt, green, and red. The door-knobs and locks were immobilized by many coats of paint. Madeleine tugged, impatiently. Herzog coming up behind her jerked open the white front door. They went down a corridor where bags of garbage were put out on the once luxurious carpet, and down in the decayed elevator, out of the trapped air of the black shaft into the porphyry façade of the moldy lobby, into the crowded street.

"Aren't you coming? What are you doing?" said Madeleine.

Perhaps he was not yet fully awake. Herzog was loitering for a moment near the fish store, arrested by the odor. A thin muscular Negro was pitching buckets of ground ice into the deep window. The fish were packed together, backs arched as if they were swimming in the crushed, smoking ice, bloody bronze, slimy black-green, gray-gold—the lobsters were crowded to the glass, feelers bent. The morning was warm, gray, damp, fresh, smelling of the river. Pausing on the metal doors of the sidewalk elevator, Moses received the raised pattern of the steel through his thin shoe soles; like Braille. But he did not interpret a message. The fish were arrested, lifelike, in the white, frothing, ground ice. The street was overcast, warm and gray, intimate, unclean, flavored by the polluted river, the sexually stirring brackish tidal odor.

"I can't wait for you, Moses," said Madeleine, peremptory, over her shoulder.

They went into the restaurant and sat at the yellow formica table.

"What were you dawdling for?"

"Well, my mother came from the Baltic provinces. She loved fish."

But Madeleine was not to be interested in Mother Herzog, twenty years dead, however mother-bound this nostalgic gentleman's soul might be. Moses, thinking, ruled against himself. He was a fatherly person to Madeleine—he couldn't expect her to consider *his* mother. She was one of the *dead* dead, without effect on the new generation.

On the yellow-plated table was a red flower. The sharp dots of the blossom in a metal holder, or choker, sunk to the neck. Curious to know whether it was plastic too, Herzog touched it. Finding it real, he quickly drew back his fingers. Madeleine was watching.

"You *know* I'm in a hurry," she said.

She was fond of English muffins. He ordered them. She called after the waitress, "Tear mine. Please don't slice them." She tilted her chin to Moses, then, and said, "Moses, is my makeup on all right—on my neck?"

"With your complexion, you don't need any of this."

"But is it ragged?"

"No. Am I going to see you later?"

"I'm not sure. I've been invited for cocktails out at Fordham—for one of the missionaries."

"But afterwards—I can catch a late train to Philly."

"I promised Mother. . . . She's having trouble again with the old man."

"I thought it was all settled—divorce."

"She's such a slave!" said Madeleine. "She can't let go, and neither will he. It's to his advantage. She still goes to that rotten acting school after hours and keeps his books. He's the

great thing in her life—another Stanislavsky. She sacrificed herself and if he's not a great genius what was it all for! Therefore
he *is* a great genius. . . ."

"I've heard people say what a brilliant director he was."

"He has *something*," said Madeleine. "Almost a female kind
of insight. And he drugs people—it's evil the way he does it.
Tennie says he spends about fifty thousand a year just on himself alone. He uses all his genius to burn that money."

"It sounds to me as though she's keeping his books for your
sake—trying to save what she can for you."

"He'll leave nothing but lawsuits and debts. . . ." She set
her teeth in the toasted muffin—they were girlish, short. But
then, she did not eat. She put the muffin down, and her eyes
filled in their strange manner.

"What's wrong? Eat."

She pushed away the plate, however. "I've asked you not to
phone me, up at Fordham. It upsets me. I have to keep the two
things separate."

"I'm sorry. I won't."

"I've been beside myself. I'm ashamed to go to Monsignor
for confession."

"Won't another priest do?"

She put down her cup with a sharp crack of clumsy restaurant china. A pale lipstick mark was on the rim. "The last priest
bawled hell out of me about you. He asked how long *had* I
been in the Church? Why *was* I baptized if I was going to act
like this within a few months!" The great eyes of the middle-
aged woman she had made herself up to be accused him. Across
her white face were the straight brows she had given herself.
He thought he could see the true outline beneath.

"God! I'm sorry," said Moses. He looked contrite. "I don't
want to make trouble." This was certainly untrue. On the contrary, he was bent on making trouble. He thought difficulty
was the whole object. She wanted Moses and the Monsignor
to struggle over her. It heightened the sexual excitement. He
fought her apostasy in the sack. And certainly the Monsignor
made female converts with his burning eyes.

"I feel miserable—miserable," she said. "It'll be Ash
Wednesday soon, and I can't take Communion till I confess."

"That's awkward. . . ." Moses really did sympathize with her, but he wouldn't offer to bow out.

"And what about marriage? How can we marry?"

"Things can be worked out—the Church is a wise old institution."

"At the office they talk about Joe DiMaggio, when he wanted to marry Marilyn Monroe. And the Tyrone Power case—one of his last marriages was performed by a prince of the Church. The other day there was another thing in Leonard Lyons about Catholic divorces." Madeleine read all the gossip columnists. Her bookmarks in St. Augustine and in her missal were clippings from the *Post* and *Mirror*.

"Favorable?" asked Moses, doubling his muffin over and pressing it—it was buttered too thickly.

Madeleine's large, violet eyes seemed swollen. Her thoughts were strained with these difficulties, many times analyzed. "I have an appointment with an Italian priest in the Society for the Propagation of the Faith. He's a canon-law expert. I phoned him yesterday."

In the Church twelve weeks, she already knew everything.

"It would be easier if Daisy would divorce me," said Herzog.

"She's *got* to give you a divorce." Madeleine's voice rose sharply. Herzog found himself looking at the face which had been prepared for the Jesuits, uptown. But something had happened—some string had tightened and twisted in her breast, and her figure grew rigid. Her fingertips whitened as she pressed the edge of the table and glared at him, her lips thinning and the color darkening under the tubercular pallor of her makeup. "What makes you think I intend to have a life-long affair with you? I want some action."

"But Mady—you know how I feel. . . ."

"Feel? Don't give me that line of platitudes about feelings. I don't believe in it. I believe in God—sin—death—so don't pull any sentimental crap on me."

"No—now listen." He put on his fedora, as if he hoped to derive some authority from it.

"I want to be married," she said. "This other stuff is just balls! My mother had to live a bohemian life. She worked, while Pontritter carried on. He bribed me with nickels when I saw him with one of his broads. You know how I learned my ABC's? From Lenin's *State and Revolution*. Those people are insane!"

Probably so, Herzog mentally agreed. But now Madeleine wants white Christmases and Easter bunnies and to live perhaps in one of those streets of brick, semi-detached parochial houses in the dull wilderness of Queens borough, fussing over Communion dresses, with a steady Irish husband who sweeps up the crumbs at the biscuit factory.

"Maybe I have become a fanatic about conventional things," said Madeleine. "But I won't have it any other way. You and I have got to marry in the Church, otherwise I quit. Our children will be baptized and brought up in the Church." Moses gave a dumb half-nod. Compared with her he felt static, without temperament. The powdered fragrance of her face stirred him (my gratitude for art, was his present reflection, any sort of art).

"My childhood was a grotesque nightmare," she went on. "I was bullied, assaulted, ab-ab-ab . . ." she stammered.

"Abused?"

She nodded. She had told him this before. He could not bring this sexual secret of hers to light.

"It was a grown man," she said. "He paid me to keep it quiet."

"Who was he?"

Her eyes were sullenly full and her pretty mouth desperately vengeful but silent.

"It happens to many, many people," he said. "Can't base a whole life on that. It doesn't mean that much."

"What—a whole year of amnesia not mean much? My fourteenth year is blacked out."

She couldn't accept this broad-minded consolation from Herzog. Perhaps it seemed to her a kind of indifference. "My parents damn near destroyed me. All right—it doesn't matter now," she said. "I believe in my Savior, Jesus Christ. I'm not afraid of d-death now, Moses. Pon said we all died and rotted in the grave. Saying that to a girl of six or seven. He ought to be punished for it. But now I'm willing to go on living, and to bring children into the world, provided that I have something to tell them when they ask me about death and the grave. But don't expect me to go along in the ordinary loose way— without rules. No! It'll be these rules or nothing."

Moses watched her as though he were submerged, through the vitreous distortion of deep water.

"Do you hear me?"

"Oh, yes," he said, "Yes. I do."

"I've got to go now. Father Francis is never a minute late." She picked up her handbag and hurried away, her cheeks shaken by the abruptness of her steps. She wore very high heels.

Rushing into the subway on one of those mornings, she caught a heel in the hem of her skirt and fell, injuring her back. She limped up to the street and took a taxi to the office but Father Francis sent her to the doctor, who taped her heavily and told her to go home. There she found Moses, still half dressed, having a thoughtful cup of coffee (he was thinking continually, but nothing clear resulted).

"Help me!" Madeleine said.

"What happened?"

"I fell in the subway. I'm hurt." Her voice was piercing.

"You'd better lie down," he said. He unpinned her hat, and carefully unbuttoned her jacket and sweater, took off her skirt and slip. The clear, pink color of her body was disclosed below the makeup line at the base of her neck. He took off the pectoral cross.

"Get me pajamas." She was shivering. The broad tapes had a strongly medicated smell. He led her to the bed and lay down with her to warm and comfort her, just as she wanted him to. There was a March snow, that grimy day. He did not go back to Philadelphia.

"I punished myself for my sins," Madeleine repeated.

I thought it might interest you to learn the true history of one of your converts, Monsignor. Ecclesiastical dolls—gold-threaded petticoats, whining organ pipes. The actual world, to say nothing of the infinite universe, demanded a sterner, a real masculine character.

Like whose? thought Herzog. Mine, for instance? And, instead of concluding this letter to Monsignor, he wrote out, for his own use, one of June's favorite nursery rhymes.

> *I love little pussy, her coat is so warm*
> *And if I don't hurt her, she'll do me no harm.*
> *I'll sit by the fire and give her some food,*
> *And pussy will love me because I am good.*

That's more like it, he thought. Yes. You must aim the imagination also at yourself, point-blank.

But when all was said and done, Madeleine didn't marry in the Church, nor did she baptize her daughter. Catholicism went the way of zithers and tarot cards, bread-baking and Russian civilization. And life in the country.

With Madeleine, Herzog had made his second attempt to live in the country. For a big-city Jew he was peculiarly devoted to country life. He had forced Daisy to endure a freezing winter in eastern Connecticut while he was writing *Romanticism and Christianity*, in a cottage where the pipes had to be thawed with candles and freezing blasts penetrated the clapboard walls while Herzog brooded over his Rousseau or practiced on the oboe. The instrument had been left to him at the death of Aleck Hirshbein, his roommate at Chicago, and Herzog with his odd sense of piety (much heavy love in Herzog; grief did not pass quickly, with him) taught himself to play the instrument and, come to think of it, the sad music must have oppressed Daisy even more than the months of cold fog. Perhaps Marco's character had been affected by the experience, too; at times he showed a streak of melancholy.

But with Madeleine it was going to be altogether different. She dropped from the Church and after a struggle with Daisy and her lawyers and his own, and under pressure from Tennie and Madeleine, Moses was divorced and remarried. The wedding supper was cooked by Phoebe Gersbach. Herzog, at his desk, gazing at great scrolls of cloud (the sky unusually clear for New York), remembered the Yorkshire pudding and the home-made cake. Phoebe baked incomparable banana cakes, light, moist, white icing. A doll bride and groom. And Gersbach, boisterous, yucking it up, poured whisky, wine, pounded the table, danced, stumping, with the bride. He wore one of his favorite loose sports shirts, which opened on his big chest and slipped away from his shoulders softly. Male decolleté. There were no other guests.

The house in Ludeyville was bought when Madeleine became pregnant. It seemed the ideal place to work out the problems Herzog had become involved with in *The Phenomenology of Mind*—the importance of the "law of the heart" in Western traditions, the origins of moral sentimentalism and related matters, on which he had distinctly different ideas. He was going—he smiled secretly now, admitting it—to wrap the subject up, to pull the carpet from under all other scholars, show them what was what, stun them, expose their triviality once and for all. It was not simple vanity, but a sense of responsibility that was the underlying motive. That he would say for himself. He was a *bien pensant* type. He took seriously Heinrich Heine's belief that the words of Rousseau had turned into the bloody machine of Robespierre, that Kant and Fichte were deadlier than armies. He had a small foundation grant, and his twenty-thousand-dollar legacy from Father Herzog went into the country place.

He turned into its caretaker. Twenty thousand and more would have gone down the drain if he hadn't thrown himself into the work—Papa's savings, representing forty years of misery in America. I don't understand how it was possible, thought Herzog. I was in a fever when I wrote the check. I didn't even look.

But after the papers were signed he inspected the house as if for the first time. It was unpainted, gloomy, with rotting Victorian ornaments. Nothing on the ground floor but a huge hole like a shell crater. The plaster was coming down—moldy, thready, sickening stuff hung from the laths. The old fashioned knob-and-tube wiring was dangerous. Bricks were dropping from the foundations. The windows leaked.

Herzog learned masonry, glazing, plumbing. He sat up nights studying the *Do-It-Yourself Encyclopedia*, and with hysterical passion he painted, patched, tarred gutters, plastered holes. Two coats of paint counted for nothing on old, open-grained wood. In the bathroom the nails hadn't been set and their heads worked through the vinyl tiles, which came loose like playing cards. The gas radiator was suffocating. The electric heater blew fuses. The tub was a relic; it rested on four

metal talons, toylike. You had to crouch in it and sponge yourself. Still, Madeleine had come back from Sloane's Bath Shop
with luxurious fixtures, scallop-shell silver soap dishes and bars
of Ecusson soap, thick Turkish towels. Herzog worked in the
rusty slime of the toilet tank, trying to get the cock and ball to
work. At night he heard the trickle that was exhausting the
well.

A year of work saved the house from collapse.

In the cellar was another lavatory with thick walls like a
bunker. In summer the crickets liked it best, and so did Herzog. Here he loitered over a ten-cent bargain Dryden and
Pope. Through a chink he saw the fiery morning of high summer, the wicked spiny green of vines, and the tight, shapely
heads of wild roses, the huge elm in front, dying on him, the
oriole's nest, gray and heart-shaped. He read, "I am His Highness' dog at Kew." But Herzog had a touch of arthritis in the
neck. The stony cell became too damp. He removed the top of
the tank with a grating noise and pulled the rubber fitting to
release the water. The parts were rusty, stiff.

> . . . His Highness' dog at Kew,
> Pray tell me, Sir, whose dog are you?

Mornings he tried to reserve for brainwork. He corre-
sponded with the Widener Library to try to get the *Abhand-
lungen der Königlich Sächsischen Gesellschaft der Wissenschaft.*
His desk was covered with unpaid bills, unanswered letters. To
raise money, he took on hackwork. University presses sent manuscripts for his professional judgment. They lay in bundles,
unopened. The sun grew hot, the soil was damp and black,
and Herzog looked with despair on the thriving luxuriant life
of the plants. He had all this paper to get through, and no
help. The house was waiting—huge, hollow, urgent. QUOS
VULT PERDERE DEMENTAT, he lettered in dust. The gods were
working on him, but they hadn't demented him enough yet.

In commenting on monographs, Moses' very hand rebelled.
Five minutes at a letter and he got writer's cramp. His look
turned wooden. He was running out of excuses. *I regret the
delay. A bad case of poison ivy has kept me from my desk.* Elbows
on his papers, Moses stared at half-painted walls, discolored
ceilings, filthy windows. Something had come over him. He

used to be able to keep going, but now he worked at about two per cent of efficiency, handled every piece of paper five or ten times and misplaced everything. It was too much! He was going under.

He picked up the oboe. In his dark study, vines clutching the bulging screen, Herzog played Handel and Purcell—jigs, bourrées, contredanses, his face puffed out, fingers fleet on the keys, the music hopping and tumbling, absent-minded and sad. Below, the washing machine ran, two steps clockwise, one step counter. The kitchen was foul enough to breed rats. Egg yolks dried on the plates, coffee turned green in the cups—toast, cereal, maggots breeding in marrow bones, fruit flies, house flies, dollar bills, postage stamps and trading stamps soaking on the formica counter.

Madeleine, to get away from his music, slammed the screen door, slammed the car door. The motor roared. The Studebaker had a split in the muffler. She started down the slope. Unless you remembered to bear right the tailpipe would scrape on the rocks. Herzog played softer as he waited for the sound. That muffler would come off one of these days, but he had stopped mentioning it to her. He had too many subjects of this sort. They made her angry. Through a cover of honeysuckle that bent the screen inward he watched for her to reappear on the second curve of the slope. Pregnancy had thickened her features but she was still beautiful. Such beauty makes men breeders, studs and servants. As she drove, her nose worked involuntarily under the sight-obscuring fringe of her hair (all part of the process of steering). Her fingers, some elegant, some nail-bitten, gripped the agate steering wheel. He declared it was unsafe for a pregnant woman to drive. He thought she must at least get a driver's license. She said if a state trooper stopped her, she could sweet-talk him.

When she was gone, he dried the oboe, looked over the reeds, shut the frowzy plush case. He wore fieldglasses about his neck. Once in a while he tried to examine a bird. Usually it was gone before he could get it in focus. Abandoned, he sat at his desk, a flush door on wrought-iron legs. Philodendrons grew from the base of his lamp, twining about the iron. With a rubber band he shot wads of paper at the horseflies on the paint-streaked windows. He was not a skillful painter. He tried a spray gun at first, attaching it to the rear of the vacuum cleaner, a very efficient blower. Muffled in rags to protect the lungs, Moses sprayed ceilings, but the gun speckled the windows and banisters and he went back to the brush. Dragging the ladder and buckets and rags and thinners, scraping with his putty knife, he patched and painted, reaching left, right, above, this stretch, beyond, way out, to the corner, to the molding, his taut hand trying to achieve a straight line, laying paint on in big strokes or in an agony of finesse. Spattered and streaming sweat when the frenzy wore off, he went into the garden. Stripped naked, he fell in the hammock.

Meanwhile, Madeleine toured the antique shops with Phoebe Gersbach, or brought home loads of groceries from the Pittsfield supermarkets. Moses was continually after her about money. Beginning his reproaches, he tried to keep his voice low. It was always something trivial that set him off—a bounced check, a chicken that had rotted in the icebox, a new shirt torn up for rags. Gradually his feelings became very fierce.

"When are you going to stop bringing home this junk, Madeleine—these busted commodes, these spinning wheels."

"We have to furnish the place. I can't stand these empty rooms."

"Where's all the dough going? I'm working myself sick." He felt black with rage inside.

"I pay the bills—what do you think I do with it?"

"You said you had to learn to handle money. No one ever trusted you. Well, you're being trusted now and the checks are bouncing. The dress shop just phoned—Milly Crozier. Five hundred bucks on a maternity outfit. Who's going to be born—Louis Quatorze?"

"Yes, I know, your darling mother wore flour sacks."

"You don't need a Park Avenue obstetrician. Phoebe Gersbach used the Pittsfield hospital. How can I get you to New York from here? It's three and a half hours."

"We'll go ten days before."

"What about all this work?"

"You can carry your Hegel to the city. You haven't cracked a book in months anyway. The whole thing is a neurotic mess. These bushels of notes. It's grotesque how disorganized you are. You're no better than any other kind of addict—sick with abstractions. Curse Hegel, anyway, and this crappy old house. It needs four servants, and you want me to do all the work."

Herzog made himself dull by repeating what was right. He was maddening, too. He realized it. He appeared to know how everything ought to go, down to the smallest detail (under the category of "Free Concrete Mind," misapprehension of a universal by the developing consciousness—reality opposing the "law of the heart," alien necessity gruesomely crushing individuality, *und-soweiter*). Oh, Herzog granted that he was in the wrong. But all he asked, it seemed to him, was a bit of co-operation in his effort, benefiting everyone, to work toward a meaningful life. Hegel was curiously significant but also utterly cockeyed. Of course. That was the whole point. Simpler and without such elaborate metaphysical rigmarole was Spinoza's Prop. XXXVII; man's desire to have others rejoice in the good in which he rejoices, not to make others live according to his way of thinking—*ex ipsius ingenio*.

Herzog, mulling over these ideas as he all alone painted his walls in Ludeyville, building Versailles as well as Jerusalem in the green hot Berkshire summers. Time and again he was brought down from the ladder to the telephone. Madeleine's checks were bouncing.

"Jesus Christ!" he cried out. "Not again, Mady!"

She was ready for him in a bottle-green maternity blouse and knee-length stockings. She was becoming very stout. The doctor had warned her not to eat candy. On the sly, she greedily devoured enormous Hershey bars, the thirty-cent size.

"Can't you add! There's not a damn reason in the world for these checks to come back." Moses glared at her.

"Oh—here we go with this same petty stuff."

"It's not petty. It's damn serious. . . ."

"I suppose you'll start on my upbringing now—my lousy, free-loading bohemian family, all chiselers. And you gave me your good name. I know this routine backwards."

"Do I repeat myself? Well, so do you, Madeleine, with these checks."

"Spending your dead father's money. Dear Daddy! That's what you choke on. Well, he was *your* father. I don't ask you to share *my* horrible father. So don't try to force your old man down my throat."

"We've got to have a little order in these surroundings."

Madeleine said quickly, firmly, and accurately, "You'll never get the surroundings *you* want. Those are in the twelfth century somewhere. Always crying for the old home and the kitchen table with the oilcloth on it and your Latin book. Okay—let's hear your sad old story. Tell me about your poor mother. And your father. And your boarder, the drunkard. And the old synagogue, and the bootlegging, and your Aunt Zipporah . . . Oh, what balls!"

"As if you didn't have a past of your own."

"Oh, balls! So now we're going to hear how you SAVED me. Let's hear it again. What a frightened puppy I was. How I wasn't strong enough to face life. But you gave me LOVE, from your big heart, and rescued me from the priests. Yes, cured me of menstrual cramps by servicing me so good. You SAVED me. You SACRIFICED your freedom. I took you away from Daisy and your son, and your Japanese screw. Your important time and money and attention." Her wild blue glare was so intense that her eyes seemed twisted.

"Madeleine!"

"Oh—shit!"

"Just think a minute."

"Think? What do you know about thinking?"

"Maybe I married you to improve my mind!" said Herzog. "I'm learning."

"Well, I'll teach you, don't worry!" said the beautiful, pregnant Madeleine between her teeth.

Herzog noted, from a favorite source—*Opposition is true friendship. His house, his child, yea, all that a man hath will he give for wisdom.*

The husband—a beautiful soul—the exceptional wife, the angelic child and the perfect friends all dwelt in the Berkshires together. The learned professor sat at his studies. . . . Oh, he had really been asking for it. Because he insisted on being the ingénu whose earnestness made his own heart flutter—*zisse n'shamele*, a sweet little soul, Tennie had called Moses. At forty; to earn such a banal reputation! His forehead grew wet. Such stupidity deserved harsher punishment—a sickness, a jail sentence. Again, he was only being "lucky" (Ramona, food and wine, invitations to the seashore). Still, extreme self-abuse was not really interesting to him, either. It was not the most relevant thing. *Not* to be a fool might not be worth the difficult alternatives. Anyway, who was that non-fool? Was it the power-lover, who bent the public to his will—the scientific intellectual who administered a budget of billions? Clear eyes, a hard head, a penetrating political intelligence—the organizational realist? Now wouldn't it be nice to be one? But Herzog worked under different orders—doing, he trusted, the work of the future. The revolutions of the twentieth century, the liberation of the masses by production, created private life but gave nothing to fill it with. This was where such as he came in. The progress of civilization—indeed, the survival of civilization—depended on the successes of Moses E. Herzog. And in treating him as she did, Madeleine injured a great project. This was, in the eyes of Moses E. Herzog, what was so grotesque and deplorable about the experience of Moses E. Herzog.

A very special sort of lunatic expects to inculcate his principles. Sandor Himmelstein, Valentine Gersbach, Madeleine P. Herzog, Moses himself. *Reality instructors. They want to teach you—to punish you with—the lessons of the Real.*

Moses, a collector of pictures, had kept a photograph of Madeleine, aged twelve, in riding habit. She was posed with the horse, about to mount, a stocky long-haired girl with fat wrists and desperate dark shadows under her eyes, premature signs of suffering and of a craving for revenge. In jodhpurs, boots, and bowler she had the hauteur of the female child who knows it won't be long before she is nubile and has the power to hurt. This is mental politics. The strength to do evil is sovereignty. She knew more at twelve than I did at forty.

Now Daisy had been a very different sort of person—cooler, more regular, a conventional Jewish woman. Herzog had photographs of her, too, in his foot locker under the bed, but there was no need to examine pictures, he could evoke her face at will—slant green eyes, large ones, kinky, golden but lusterless hair, a clear skin. Her manner was shy but also rather stubborn. Without difficulty, Herzog saw her as she had appeared on a summer morning beneath the El on 51st Street, Chicago, a college student with grimy texts—Park and Burgess, Ogburn and Nimkoff. Her dress was simple, thin-striped green-and-white seersucker, square at the neck. Beneath its laundered purity, she had small white shoes, bare legs, and her hair was held at the top by a barrette. The red streetcar came from the slums to the west. It clanged, swayed, wallowed, its trolley shedding thick green sparks, tatters of paper flying in its wake. Moses had stood behind her on the carbolic-reeking platform when she gave her transfer slip to the conductor. From her bare neck and shoulders he inhaled the fragrance of summer apples. Daisy was a country girl, a Buckeye who grew up near Zanesvile. She was childishly systematic about things. It sometimes amused Moses to recall that she had a file card, clumsily printed out, to cover every situation. Her awkward form of organization had had a certain charm. When they were married she put his pocket money in an envelope, in a green metal file bought for budgeting. Daily reminders, bills, concert tickets were pinned by thumbtacks to the bulletin board. Calendars were marked well in advance. Stability, symmetry, order, containment were Daisy's strength.

Dear Daisy, I have a few things to say to you. By my irregularity and turbulence of spirit I brought out the very worst in Daisy. *I* caused the seams of her stockings to be so straight, and the buttons to be buttoned symmetrically. *I* was behind those rigid curtains and underneath the square carpets. Roast breast of veal every Sunday with bread stuffing like clay was due to *my* disorders, my huge involvement—huge but evidently formless—in the history of thought. She took Moses' word for it that he was seriously occupied. Of course a wife's duty was to stand by this puzzling and often disagreeable Herzog. She did so with heavy neutrality, recording her objections each time—once but not more. The rest was silence—such heavy silence as he felt in Connecticut when he was finishing *Romanticism and Christianity.*

The chapter on "Romantics and Enthusiasts" nearly did him in—it almost ended them both. (The Enthusiastic reaction against the scientific mode of suspending belief, intolerable to the expressive needs of certain temperaments.) Here Daisy picked up and left him alone in Connecticut. She had to go back to Ohio. Her father was dying. Moses read the literature of Enthusiasm in his cottage, by the small nickel-trimmed kitchen stove. Wrapped in a blanket like an Indian, he listened to the radio—debated the pros and cons of Enthusiasm with himself.

It was a winter of rocklike ice. The pond like a slab of halite—green, white, resonant ice, bitterly ringing underfoot. The trickling mill dam froze in twisting pillars. The elms, giant harp shapes, made cracking noises. Herzog, responsible to civilization in his icy outpost, lying in bed in an aviator's helmet when the stoves were out, fitted together Bacon and Locke from one side and Methodism and William Blake from the other. His nearest neighbor was a clergyman, Mr. Idwal. Idwal's automobile, a Model A Ford, was running when Herzog's Whippet had frozen solid. They drove to the market together. Mrs. Idwal made graham-cracker pies filled with chocolate gelatin, and left them, neighborly, on Moses' table. He returned from his solitary walks on the pond, in the woods, and found pies in big Pyrex plates on which he warmed his numb cheeks and fingertips. In the morning, eating gelatin pie for breakfast, he saw Idwal, ruddy and small, with steel spectacles, in his bedroom swinging Indian clubs, doing knee-bends in his long underwear. His wife sat in her parlor, hands folded, the spidery design of lace curtains thrown on her face by sunlight. Moses was invited to play his oboe, accompanying Mrs. Idwal, who played a melodeon, on Sunday evenings while the farm families sang hymns. And were they farmers? No, they were the country poor—odd-job people. The little parlor was hot, the air bad, the hymns pierced with Jewish melancholy by Moses and his reeds.

His relations with the Reverend and Mrs. Idwal were excellent until the minister started to give him testimonials by orthodox rabbis who had embraced the Christian faith. The photos of these rabbis in fur hats, bearded, were put down with the pies. The large eyes of those men and especially their lips thrust out from foaming beards began to seem crazy to Moses, and he thought it time to get away from the snowbound cottage. He was afraid for his own sanity, living like this, especially after the death of Daisy's father. Moses thought he saw him, met him in the woods, and when he opened doors he encountered his father-in-law, vivid and characteristic, waiting by a table or sitting in the bathroom.

Herzog made a mistake in rejecting Idwal's rabbis. The

clergyman was keener than ever to convert him and dropped in every afternoon for theological discussions until Daisy returned. Sad, clear-eyed, mostly mute, resistant. But a wife. And the child! The thaws began—ideal for making snowmen. Moses and Marco lined the drive with them. Little anthracite eyes glittered even by starlight. In spring the blackness of night was filled with shrilling cheepers. Herzog's heart began to warm toward the country. The blood-colored sunsets of winter and solitude were behind him. They didn't seem so bad now that he had survived them.

Survival! he noted. *Till we figure out what's what. Till the chance comes to exert a positive influence.* (Personal responsibility for history, a trait of Western culture, rooted in the Testaments, Old and New, the idea of the continual improvement of human life on this earth. What else explained Herzog's ridiculous intensity?) *Lord, I ran to fight in Thy holy cause, but kept tripping, never reached the scene of the struggle.*

He saw through this as well. If nothing else, he was too rich in diseases to be satisfied with such a description. From the middle height of New York, looking down, seeing lunchtime crowds like ants upon smoked glass, Herzog, wrapped in his wrinkled robe and sipping cold coffee, set apart from daily labor for greater achievements, but at present without confidence in his calling, tried now and again to get back to work. *Dear Dr. Mossbach, I am sorry you are not satisfied with my treatment of T. E. Hulme and his definition of Romanticism as "spilt religion." There is something to be said for his view. He wanted things to be clear, dry, spare, pure, cool, and hard. With this I think we can all sympathize. I too am repelled by the "dampness," as he called it, and the swarming of Romantic feelings. I see what a villain Rousseau was, and how degenerate (I do not complain that he was ungentlemanly; it ill becomes me). But I do not see what we can answer when he says "Je sens mon cœur et je connais les hommes." Bottled religion, on conservative principles—does that intend to deprive the heart of such powers— do you think? Hulme's followers made sterility their truth, confessing their impotence. This was their passion.*

Still fighting it out, Herzog was fairly deadly in polemics. His polite formulas often carried much spleen. His docile ways, his modest conduct—he didn't deceive himself. The certainty of being right, a flow of power, rose in his bowels and burned in his legs. Queer, the luxurious victories of anger! There was passionate satire in Herzog. Still he knew that the demolition of error was not *it*. He began to have a new horror of winning, of the victories of untrammeled autonomy. *Man has a nature, but what is it? Those who have confidently described it, Hobbes, Freud, et cetera, by telling us what we are "intrinsically," are not our greatest benefactors. This is true also for Rousseau. I sympathize with Hulme's attack on the introduction by the Romantics of Perfection into human things, but do not like his narrow repressiveness, either. Modern science, least bothered with the definition of human nature, knowing only the activity of investigation, achieves its profoundest results through anonymity, recognizing only the brilliant functioning of intellect. Such truth as it finds may be nothing to live by, but perhaps a moratorium on definitions of human nature is now best.*

Herzog abandoned this theme with characteristic abruptness.

Dear Nachman, he wrote. *I know it was you I saw on 8th St. last Monday. Running away from me.* Herzog's face darkened. *It was you. My friend nearly forty years ago—playmates on Napoleon Street. The Montreal slums.* In a beatnik cap, on the razzle-dazzle street of lion-bearded homosexuals wearing green eye paint, there, suddenly, was Herzog's childhood playmate. A heavy nose, hair white, thick unclean glasses. The stooped poet took one look at Moses and ran away. On gaunt legs, under urgent pressure, he fled to the other side of the street. He turned up his collar and stared into the window of the cheese shop. *Nachman! Did you think I'd ask for the money you owe me? I wrote that off, long ago. It meant very little to me, in Paris after the War. I had it then.*

Nachman had come to Europe to write poetry. He was living in the Arab slum on Rue St. Jacques. Herzog was installed in comfort on the Rue Marbeuf. Wrinkled and dirty, Nachman, his nose red from weeping, his creased face the face of a dying man, appeared at Herzog's door one morning.

"What's happened!"

"Moses, they've taken my wife away—my little Laura."

"Wait a minute—what's up?" Herzog was perhaps a little cold, then, repelled by such excesses.

"Her father. The old man from the floor-covering business. Spirited her away. The old Sorcerer. She'll die without me. The child can't bear life without me. And I can't live without her. I've got to get back to New York."

"Come in. Come in. We can't talk in this lousy hallway."

Nachman entered the little drawing room. It was a furnished apartment in the style of the twenties—spitefully correct. Nachman seemed hesitant to sit down, in his gutter-stained pants. "I've been to all the lines already. There's space on the *Hollandia* tomorrow. Lend me dough or I'm ruined. You're my only friend in Paris."

Honestly, I thought you'd be better off in America.

Nachman and Laura had been wandering up and down Europe, sleeping in ditches in the Rimbaud country, reading Van Gogh's letters aloud to each other—Rilke's poems. Laura was not too strong in the head, either. She was thin, soft-faced, the corners of her pale mouth turned down. She caught the flu in Belgium.

"I'll pay you every penny." Nachman wrung his hands. His fingers had grown knobby—rheumatic. His face was coarse— slack from illness, suffering, and absurdity.

I felt it would be cheaper in the long run to send you back to New York. In Paris I was stuck with you. You see, I don't pretend that I was altruistic. Perhaps, thought Herzog, the sight of *me* frightened *him.* Have I changed even more than he has? Was Nachman horrified to see Moses? *But we did play in the street together. I learned the* aleph-beth *from your father, Reb Shika.*

Nachman's family lived in the yellow tenement just opposite. Five years old, Moses crossed Napoleon Street. Up the wooden staircase with slanted, warped treads. Cats shrank into corners or bolted softly upstairs. Their dry turds crumbled in the darkness with a spicy odor. Reb Shika had a yellow color, Mongolian, a tiny handsome man. He wore a black satin skull-cap, a mustache like Lenin's. His narrow chest was clad in a winter undershirt—Penman's woollens. The Bible lay open on the coarse table cover. Moses clearly saw the Hebrew characters—DMAI OCHICHO—the blood of thy brother. Yes, that was it. God speaking to Cain. Thy brother's blood cries out to me from the earth.

At eight, Moses and Nachman shared a bench in the cellar of the synagogue. The pages of the Pentateuch smelled of mildew, the boys' sweaters were damp. The rabbi, short-bearded, his soft big nose violently pitted with black, scolding them. "You, Rozavitch, you slacker. What does it say here about Potiphar's wife, *V'tispesayu b'vigdi . . .*"

"And she took hold of . . ."

"Of what? *Beged.*"

"*Beged.* A coat."

"A garment, you little thief. *Mamzer!* I'm sorry for your father. Some heir he's got! Some *Kaddish!* Ham and pork you'll be eating, before his body is in the grave. And you, Herzog, with those behemoth eyes—*V'yaizov bigdo b'yodo.*"

"And he left it in her hands."

"Left what?"

"*Bigdo*, the garment."

"You watch your step, Herzog, Moses. Your mother thinks you'll be a great *lamden*—a rabbi. But I know you, how lazy you are. Mothers' hearts are broken by *mamzeirim* like you! Eh! Do I know you, Herzog? Through and through."

The only refuge was the W.C., where the disinfectant camphor balls dwindled in the green trough of the urinal, and old men came down from the shul with webby eyes nearly blind, sighing, grumbling snatches of liturgy as they waited for the water to come. Urine-rusted brass, scaly green. In an open stall, pants dropped to his feet, sat Nachman playing the harmonica. "It's a Long, Long Way to Tipperary." "Love Sends a Little Gift of Roses." The peak of his cap was warped. You heard the saliva in the cells of the tin instrument as he sucked and blew. The bowler-hatted elders washed their hands, gave their beards a finger-combing. Moses observed them.

Almost certainly, Nachman ran away from the power of his old friend's memory. Herzog persecuted everyone with it. It was like a terrible engine.

Last time we met—how many years ago was that?—I went with you to visit Laura. Laura was then in an insane asylum. Herzog and Nachman had transferred at six or seven corners. It was a thousand bus stops out on Long Island. In the hospital the women in green cotton dresses wandered in the corridors on soft shoes, murmuring. Laura had bandaged wrists. It was her third suicide attempt that Moses knew of. She sat in a corner, holding her breasts in her arms, wanting to talk of French literature only. Her face was moony, lips however moving quickly. Moses had to agree with what he understood nothing of—the shape of Valéry's images.

Then he and Nachman left, toward sunset. They crossed the cement yard after an autumn rainfall. From the building, a crowd of ghosts in green uniforms watched the visitors depart. Laura, at the grill, raised her taped wrist, a wan hand. Goodby. Her long thin mouth silently said, Good-by, good-by. The straight hair fell beside her cheeks—a stiff childish figure with female swellings. Nachman was hoarsely saying, "My innocent darling. My bride. They've put her away, the grim ones, the *machers*—our masters. Imprisoned her. As if to love me proved she was mad. But I shall be strong enough to protect our love," said gaunt, furrowed Nachman. His cheeks were sunken. Under the eyes his skin was yellow.

"Why does she keep trying to kill herself?" said Moses.

"The persecution of her family. What do you think? The bourgeois world of Westchester! Wedding announcements, linens, charge accounts, that was what her mother and father expected of her. But this is a pure soul that understands only pure things. She is a stranger here. The family only wants to part us. In New York we were wanderers too. When I came back—thanks to you, and I'll repay you, I'll work!—we didn't have money to rent a room. How could I take a job? Who would look after her? So friends gave us shelter. Food. A cot to lie down. To make love."

Herzog was very curious, but he merely said, "Oh?"

"I wouldn't tell anyone but you, old friend. We had to take care. In our ecstasies we had to warn each other to be more moderate. It was like a holy act—we mustn't make the gods jealous. . . ." Nachman spoke in a throbbing, droning voice. "Good-by, my blessed spirit—my dear one. Good-by." He blew kisses at the window with painful sweetness.

On the way to the bus, he went on lecturing in his unreal way, fervent and dull. "So back of it all is bourgeois America. This is a crude world of finery and excrement. A proud, lazy civilization that worships its own boorishness. You and I were brought up in the old poverty. I don't know how American you've become since the old days in Canada—you've lived here a long time. But I will never worship the fat gods. Not I. I'm no Marxist, you know. I keep my heart with William Blake and Rilke. But a man like Laura's father! You understand! Las Vegas, Miami Beach. They wanted Laura to catch a husband at the Fountainblue, a husband with money. At the edge of doom, beside the last grave of mankind, they will still be counting their paper. Praying over their balance sheets. . . ." Nachman went on with boring persistent power. He had lost teeth, and his jaw was smaller, his gray cheeks were bristly. Herzog could still see him as he had been at six. In fact he could not dismiss his vision of the two Nachmans, side by side. And it was the child with his fresh face, the smiling gap in his front teeth, the buttoned blouse and the short pants that was real, not this gaunt apparition of crazy lecturing Nachman. "Perhaps," he was saying, "people wish life to end. They have polluted it. Courage, honor, frankness, friendship, duty, all made filthy. Sullied. So that we loathe the daily bread that prolongs useless existence. There was a time when men were born, lived, and died. But do you call these men? We are only creatures. Death himself must be tired of us. I can see Death coming before God to say 'What shall I do? There is no more grandeur in being Death. Release me, God, from this meanness.'"

"It isn't as bad as you make out, Nachman," Moses remembered answering. "Most people are unpoetical, and you consider this a betrayal."

"Well, childhood friend, you have learned to accept a mixed condition of life. But I have had visions of judgment. I see mainly the obstinacy of cripples. We do not love ourselves, but persist in stubbornness. Each man is stubbornly, stubbornly himself. Above all himself, to the end of time. Each of these creatures has some secret quality, and for this quality he is prepared to do anything. He will turn the universe upside down, but he will not deliver his quality to anyone else. Sooner let the world turn to drifting powder. This is what my poems are about. You don't think highly of my New Psalms. You're blind, old friend."

"Maybe."

"But a good man, Moses. Rooted in yourself. But a good heart. Like your mother. A gentle spirit. You got it from her. I was hungry and she fed me. She washed my hands and sat me at the table. That I remember. She was the only one who was kind to my Uncle Ravitch, the drunkard. I sometimes say a prayer for her."

Yiskor elohim es nishmas Imi . . . the soul of my mother.

"She's been dead a long time."

"And I pray for you, Moses."

The bus on giant tires advanced through sunset-colored puddles over leaves, ailanthus twigs. Its route was interminable, through the low, brick, suburban, populous vastness.

But fifteen years later, on 8th Street, Nachman ran away. He looked old, derelict, stooped, crooked as he sprinted to the cheese shop. Where is his wife? He must have beat it to avoid explanations. His mad sense of decency told him to shun such an encounter. Or has he forgotten everything? Or would he be glad to forget it? But I, with *my* memory—all the dead and the mad are in my custody, and I am the nemesis of the would-be forgotten. I bind others to my feelings, and oppress them.

Was Ravitch actually your uncle, or only a landtsman? I was never certain.

Ravitch boarded with the Herzogs on Napoleon Street. Like a tragic actor of the Yiddish stage, with a straight drunken nose and a bowler pressing on the veins of his forehead, Ravitch, in an apron, worked at the fruit store near Rachel Street in 1922. There at the market in zero weather he was sweeping a mixed powder of sawdust and snow. The window was covered with large ferns of frost, and against it pressed the piled blood-oranges and russet apples. And that was melancholy Ravitch, red with drink and cold. The project of his life was to send for his family, a wife and two children who were still in Russia. He'd have to find them first, for they were lost during the Revolution. Now and then he soberly cleaned himself up and went to the Hebrew Immigrants' Aid Society to make an inquiry. But nothing ever happened. He drank his pay—a *shicker*. No one judged himself more harshly. When he came out of the saloon he stood wavering in the street, directing traffic, falling among horses and trucks in the slush. The police were tired of throwing him in the drunk tank. They brought him home, to Herzog's hallway, and pushed him in. Ravitch, late at night, sang on the freezing stairs in a sobbing voice.

> "*Alein, alein, alein, alein*
> *Elend vie a shtein*
> *Mit die tzen finger—alein*"

Jonah Herzog got out of bed and turned on the light in the kitchen, listening. He wore a Russian sleeping suit of linen with a pleated front, the last of his gentleman's wardrobe from Petersburg. The stove was out, and Moses, in the same bed with Willie and Shura, sat up, the three of them, under the lumpy wads of the quilt, looking at their father. He stood under the bulb, which had a spike at the end like a German helmet. The large loose twist of tungsten filament blazed. Annoyed and pitying, Father Herzog, with his round head and brown mustache, looked upward. The straight groove between his eyes came and went. He nodded and mused.

> "Alone, alone, alone, alone
> Solitary as a stone
> With my ten fingers—alone"

Mother Herzog spoke from her room, "Yonah—help him in."

"All right," said Father Herzog, but he waited.

"Yonah . . . It's a pity."

"Pity on us, too," said Father Herzog. "Damn it. You sleep, you're free from misery awhile, and he wakes you up. A Jewish drunkard! He can't even do *that* right. Why can't he be *freilich* and cheerful when he drinks, eh? No, he has to cry and tear your heartstrings. Well, curse him." Half laughing, Father Herzog cursed the heartstrings, too. "It's enough that I have to rent a room to a miserable *shicker*."

> "*Al tastir ponecho mimeni*
> I'm broke without a penny.
> Do not hide Thy countenance from us
> Vich nobody can deny."

Ravitch, tuneless and persistent, cried in the black, frozen staircase.

"O'Brien
Lo mir trinken a glesele vi-ine
Al tastir ponecho mimeni
I'm broke without a penny
Vich nobody can deny."

Father Herzog, silent and wry, laughed under his breath. "Yonah—I beg you. *Genug schon.*"
"Oh, give him time. Why should I *schlepp* out my guts."
"He'll wake the whole street."
"He'll be covered with vomit, his pants filled."
But he went. He pitied Ravitch, too, though Ravitch was one of the symbols of his changed condition. In Petersburg there were servants. In Russia, Father Herzog had been a gentleman. With forged papers of the First Guild. But many gentlemen lived on forged papers.

The children still gazed into the empty kitchen. The black cookstove against the wall, extinct; the double gas ring connected by rubber pipe to the meter. A Japanese reed mat protected the wall from cooking stains.

It amused the boys to hear how their father coaxed drunken Ravitch to get on his feet. It was family theater. "*Nu, landtsman?* Can you walk? It's freezing. Now, get your crooked feet on the step—*schneller, schneller.*" He laughed with his bare breath. "Well, I think we'll leave your *dreckische* pants out here. Phew!" The boys pressed together in the cold, smiling.

Papa supported him through the kitchen—Ravitch in his filthy drawers, the red face, dropped hands, the bowler, the drunken grief of his closed eyes.

As for my late unlucky father, J. Herzog, he was not a big man, one of the small-boned Herzogs, finely made, round-headed, keen, nervous, handsome. In his frequent bursts of temper he slapped his sons swiftly with both hands. He did everything quickly, neatly, with skillful Eastern European flourishes: combing his hair, buttoning his shirt, stropping his bone-handled razors, sharpening pencils on the ball of his thumb, holding a loaf of bread to his breast and slicing toward himself, tying parcels with tight little knots, jotting like an artist in his account book. There each canceled page was covered with a carefully drawn X. The 1s and 7s carried bars and streamers.

They were like pennants in the wind of failure. First Father Herzog failed in Petersburg, where he went through two dowries in one year. He had been importing onions from Egypt. Under Pobedonostsev the police caught up with him for illegal residence. He was convicted and sentenced. The account of the trial was published in a Russian journal printed on thick green paper. Father Herzog sometimes unfolded it and read aloud to the entire family, translating the proceedings against Ilyona Isakovitch Gerzog. He never served his sentence. He got away. Because he was nervy, hasty, obstinate, rebellious. He came to Canada, where his sister Zipporah Yaffe was living.

In 1913 he bought a piece of land near Valleyfield, Quebec, and failed as a farmer. Then he came into town and failed as a baker; failed in the dry-goods business; failed as a jobber; failed as a sack manufacturer in the War, when no one else failed. He failed as a junk dealer. Then he became a marriage broker and failed—too short-tempered and blunt. And now he was failing as a bootlegger, on the run from the provincial Liquor Commission. Making a bit of a living.

In haste and defiantly, with a clear tense face, walking with mingled desperation and high style, a little awkwardly dropping his weight on one heel as he went, his coat, once lined with fox, turned dry and bald, the red hide cracking. This coat sweeping open as he walked, or marched his one-man Jewish march, he was saturated with the odor of the Caporals he smoked as he covered Montreal in his swing—Papineau, Mile-End, Verdun, Lachine, Point St. Charles. He looked for business opportunities—bankruptcies, job lots, mergers, fire sales, produce—to rescue him from illegality. He could calculate percentages mentally at high speed, but he lacked the cheating imagination of a successful businessman. And so he kept a little still in Mile-End, where goats fed in the empty lots. He traveled on the tramcar. He sold a bottle here and there and waited for his main chance. American rum-runners would buy the stuff from you at the border, any amount, spot cash, if you could get it there. Meanwhile he smoked cigarettes on the cold platforms of streetcars. The Revenue was trying to catch him. Spotters were after him. On the roads to the border were hijackers. On Napoleon Street he had five mouths to feed.

Willie and Moses were sickly. Helen studied the piano. Shura
was fat, greedy, disobedient, a plotting boy. The rent, back
rent, notes due, doctors' bills to pay, and he had no English,
no friends, no influence, no trade, no assets but his still—no
help in all the world. His sister Zipporah in St. Anne was rich,
very rich, which only made matters worse.

Grandfather Herzog was still alive, then. With the instinct of
a Herzog for the grand thing, he took refuge in the Winter
Palace in 1918 (the Bolsheviks allowed it for a while). The old
man wrote long letters in Hebrew. He had lost his precious
books in the upheaval. Study was impossible now. In the Winter Palace you had to walk up and down all day to find a *min-
yan*. Of course there was hunger, too. Later, he predicted that
the Revolution would fail and tried to acquire Czarist currency, to become a millionaire under the restored Romanoffs.
The Herzogs received packets of worthless rubles, and Willie
and Moses played with great sums. You held the glorious bills
to the light and you saw Peter the Great and Catherine in the
watermarked rainbow paper. Grandfather Herzog was in his
eighties but still strong. His mind was powerful and his
Hebrew calligraphy elegant. The letters were read aloud in
Montreal by Father Herzog—accounts of cold, lice, famine,
epidemics, the dead. The old man wrote, "Shall I ever see the
faces of my children? And who will bury me?" Father Herzog
approached the next phrase two or three times, but could not
find his full voice. Only a whisper came out. The tears were in
his eyes and he suddenly put his hand over his mustached
mouth and hurried from the room. Mother Herzog, large-
eyed, sat with the children in the primitive kitchen which the
sun never entered. It was like a cave with the ancient black
stove, the iron sink, the green cupboards, the gas ring.

Mother Herzog had a way of meeting the present with a
partly averted face. She encountered it on the left but sometimes seemed to avoid it on the right. On this withdrawn side
she often had a dreaming look, melancholy, and seemed to be
seeing the Old World—her father the famous *misnagid*, her
tragic mother, her brothers living and dead, her sister, and her
linens and servants in Petersburg, the dacha in Finland (all
founded on Egyptian onions). Now she was cook, washer-
woman, seamstress on Napoleon Street in the slum. Her hair

turned gray, and she lost her teeth, her very fingernails wrinkled. Her hands smelled of the sink.

Herzog was thinking, however, how she found the strength to spoil her children. She certainly spoiled me. Once, at nightfall, she was pulling me on the sled, over crusty ice, the tiny glitter of snow, perhaps four o'clock of a short day in January. Near the grocery we met an old baba in a shawl who said, "Why are you pulling him, daughter!" Mama, dark under the eyes. Her slender cold face. She was breathing hard. She wore the torn seal coat and a red pointed wool cap and thin button boots. Clusters of dry fish hung in the shop, a rancid sugar smell, cheese, soap—a terrible dust of nutrition came from the open door. The bell on a coil of wire was bobbing, ringing. "Daughter, don't sacrifice your strength to children," said the shawled crone in the freezing dusk of the street. I wouldn't get off the sled. I pretended not to understand. One of life's hardest jobs, to make a quick understanding slow. I think I succeeded, thought Herzog.

Mama's brother Mikhail died of typhus in Moscow. I took the letter from the postman and brought it upstairs—the long latch-string ran through loops under the banister. It was washday. The copper boiler steamed the window. She was rinsing and wringing in a tub. When she read the news she gave a cry and fainted. Her lips turned white. Her arm lay in the water, sleeve and all. We two were alone in the house. I was terrified when she lay like that, legs spread, her long hair undone, lids brown, mouth bloodless, death-like. But then she got up and went to lie down. She wept all day. But in the morning she cooked the oatmeal nevertheless. We were up early.

My ancient times. Remoter than Egypt. No dawn, the foggy winters. In darkness, the bulb was lit. The stove was cold. Papa shook the grates, and raised an ashen dust. The grates grumbled and squealed. The puny shovel clinked underneath. The Caporals gave Papa a bad cough. The chimneys in their helmets sucked in the wind. Then the milkman came in his sleigh. The snow was spoiled and rotten with manure and litter, dead rats, dogs. The milkman in his sheepskin gave the bell a twist. It was brass, like the winding-key of a clock. Helen pulled the latch and went down with a pitcher for the milk. And then Ravitch, hung-over, came from his room, in his heavy sweater, suspenders over the wool to keep it tighter to the body, the bowler on his head, red in the face, his look guilty. He waited to be asked to sit.

The morning light could not free itself from gloom and frost. Up and down the street, the brick-recessed windows were dark, filled with darkness, and schoolgirls by twos in their black skirts marched toward the convent. And wagons, sledges, drays, the horses shuddering, the air drowned in leaden green, the dung-stained ice, trails of ashes. Moses and his brothers put on their caps and prayed together,

> *"Ma tovu ohaleha Yaakov. . . ."*
> "How goodly are thy tents, O Israel."

Napoleon Street, rotten, toylike, crazy and filthy, riddled, flogged with harsh weather—the bootlegger's boys reciting ancient prayers. To this Moses' heart was attached with great power. Here was a wider range of human feelings than he had ever again been able to find. The children of the race, by a never-failing miracle, opened their eyes on one strange world after another, age after age, and uttered the same prayer in each, eagerly loving what they found. What was wrong with Napoleon Street? thought Herzog. All he ever wanted was there. His mother did the wash, and mourned. His father was desperate and frightened, but obstinately fighting. His brother Shura with staring disingenuous eyes was plotting to master the world, to become a millionaire. His brother Willie struggled with asthmatic fits. Trying to breathe he gripped the table and rose on his toes like a cock about to crow. His sister Helen had long white gloves which she washed in thick suds. She wore them to her lessons at the conservatory, carrying a leather music roll. Her diploma hung in a frame. *Mlle. Hélène Herzog . . . avec distinction.* His soft prim sister who played the piano.

On a summer night she sat playing and the clear notes went through the window into the street. The square-shouldered piano had a velveteen runner, mossy green as though the lid of the piano were a slab of stone. From the runner hung a ball fringe, like hickory nuts. Moses stood behind Helen, staring at the swirling pages of Haydn and Mozart, wanting to whine like a dog. Oh, the music! thought Herzog. He fought the insidious blight of nostalgia in New York—softening, heart-rotting emotions, black spots, sweet for one moment but leaving a dangerous acid residue. Helen played. She wore a middy and a pleated skirt, and her pointed shoes cramped down on the pedals, a proper, vain girl. She frowned while she played—her father's crease appeared between her eyes. Frowning as though she performed a dangerous action. The music rang into the street.

Aunt Zipporah was critical of this music business. Helen was not a genuine musician. She played to move the family. Perhaps to attract a husband. What Aunt Zipporah opposed was Mama's ambition for her children, because she wanted them to be lawyers, gentlemen, rabbis, or performers. All branches of the family had the caste madness of *yichus*. No life so barren and subordinate that it didn't have imaginary dignities, honors to come, freedom to advance.

Zipporah wanted to hold Mama back, Moses concluded, and she blamed Papa's failure in America on these white gloves and piano lessons. Zipporah had a strong character. She was witty, grudging, at war with everyone. Her face was flushed and thin, her nose shapely but narrow and grim. She had a critical, damaging, nasal voice. Her hips were large and she walked with wide heavy steps. A braid of thick glossy hair hung down her back.

Now Uncle Yaffe, Zipporah's husband, was quiet-spoken, humorously reserved. He was a small man but strong. His shoulders were wide, and he wore a black beard like King George V. It grew tight and curly on his brown face. The bridge of his nose was dented. His teeth were broad, and one was capped with gold. Moses had smelled the tart flavor of his uncle's breath as they played checkers. Over the board, Uncle Yaffe's broad head with short black twisted hair, a bit bald, was slightly unsteady. He had a mild nervous tremor. Uncle Yaffe, from the past, seemed to find out his nephew at this very instant of time and to look at him with the brown eyes of an intelligent, feeling, satirical animal. His glance glittered shrewdly, and he smiled with twisted satisfaction at the errors of young Moses. Affectionately giving me the business.

In Yaffe's junkyard in St. Anne the ragged cliffs of scrap metal bled rust into the puddles. There was sometimes a line of scavengers at the gate. Kids, greenhorns, old Irishwomen, or Ukrainians and redmen from the Caughnawaga reservation, came with pushcarts and little wagons, bringing bottles, rags, old plumbing or electrical fixtures, hardware, paper, tires, bones to sell. The old man, in his brown cardigan, stooped, and his strong trembling hands sorted out what he had bought. Without straightening his back he could pitch pieces of scrap where they belonged—iron here, zinc there, copper left, lead right, and Babbitt metal by the shed. He and his sons made money during the War. Aunt Zipporah bought real estate. She collected rents. Moses knew that she carried a bankroll in her bosom. He had seen it.

"Well, *you* lost nothing by coming to America," Papa said to her.

Her first reply was to stare sharply and warningly at him. Then she said, "It's no secret how we started out. By labor. Yaffe took a pick and shovel on the CPR until we saved up a little capital. But you! No, you were born in a silk shirt." With a glance at Mama, she went on, "You got used to putting on style, in Petersburg, with servants and coachmen. I can still see you getting off the train from Halifax, all dressed up among the greeners. *Gott meiner!* Ostrich feathers, taffeta skirts! *Greenhorns mit strauss federn!* Now forget the feathers, the gloves. Now—"

"That seems like a thousand years ago," said Mama. "I have forgotten all about servants. I am the servant. *Die dienst bin ich.*"

"Everyone must work. Not suffer your whole life long from a fall. Why must your children go to the conservatory, the Baron de Hirsch school, and all those special frills? Let them go to work, like mine."

"She doesn't want the children to be common," said Papa.

"My sons are not common. They know a page of *Gemara*, too. And don't forget we come from the greatest Hasidic rabbis. Reb Zusya! Herschele Dubrovner! Just remember."

"No one is saying . . ." said Mama.

To haunt the past like this—to love the dead! Moses warned himself not to yield so greatly to this temptation, this peculiar weakness of his character. He was a depressive. Depressives cannot surrender childhood—not even the pains of childhood.

He understood the hygiene of the matter. But somehow his heart had come open at this chapter of his life and he didn't have the strength to shut it. So it was again a winter day in St. Anne, in 1923—Aunt Zipporah's kitchen. Zipporah wore a crimson crepe de Chine wrapper. Discernible underneath were voluminous yellow bloomers and a man's undershirt. She sat beside the kitchen oven, her face flushing. Her nasal voice often rose to a barbed little cry of irony, of false dismay, of terrible humor.

Then she remembered that Mama's brother Mikhail was dead, and she said, "Well—about your brother—what was the matter?"

"We don't know," said Papa. "Who can imagine what a black year they're making back home." (It was always *in der heim*, Herzog reminded himself.) "A mob broke into his house. Cut open everything, looking for *valuta*. Afterwards, he caught typhus, or God knows what."

Mama's hand was over her eyes, as though she were shading them. She said nothing.

"I remember what a fine man he was," said Uncle Yaffe. "May he have a *lichtigen Gan-Eden*."

Aunt Zipporah, who believed in the power of curses, said, "Curse those Bolsheviks. They want to make the world *horav*. May their hands and feet wither. But where are Mikhail's wife and children?"

"No one knows. The letter came from a cousin—Shperling, who saw Mikhail in the hospital. He barely recognized him."

Zipporah said a few more pious things, and then in a more normal manner she added, "Well, he was an active fellow. Had plenty of money, in his time. Who knows what a fortune he brought back from South Africa."

"He shared with us," said Mama. "My brother had an open hand."

"It came easily," said Zipporah. "It's not as if he had to work hard for it."

"How do you know?" said Father Herzog. "Don't let your tongue run away with you, my sister."

But Zipporah couldn't be restrained now. "He made money out of those miserable black Kaffirs! Who knows how! So you had a dacha in Shevalovo. Yaffe was away in the service, in the

Kavkaz. I had a sick child to nurse. And you, Yonah, were running around Petersburg spending two dowries. Yes! You lost the first ten thousand rubles in a month. He gave you another ten. I can't say what else he was doing, with Tartars, gypsies, whores, eating horsemeat, and God only knows what abominations went on."

"What kind of malice is in you?" said Father Herzog, angry.

"I have nothing against Mikhail. He never harmed me," Zipporah said. "But he was a brother who gave, so I am a sister who doesn't give."

"No one said it," Father Herzog said. "But if the shoe fits, you can wear it."

Engrossed, unmoving in his chair, Herzog listened to the dead at their dead quarrels.

"What do you expect?" said Zipporah. "With four children, if I started to give, and indulged your bad habits, it would be endless. It's not my fault you're a pauper here."

"I am a pauper in America, that's true. Look at me. I haven't got a copper to bless my naked skin. I couldn't pay for my own shroud."

"Blame your own weak nature," said Zipporah. "*Az du host a schwachen natur, wer is dir schuldig?* You can't stand alone. You leaned on Sarah's brother, and now you want to lean on me. Yaffe served in the Kavkaz. *A finsternish!* It was too cold for dogs to howl. Alone, he came to America and sent for me. But you—you want *alle sieben glicken.* You travel in style, with ostrich feathers. You're an *edel-mensch.* Get your hands dirty? Not you."

"It's true. I didn't shovel manure *in der heim.* That happened in the land of Columbus. But I did it. I learned to harness a horse. At three o'clock in the morning, twenty below in the stable."

Zipporah waved this aside. "And now, with your still? You had to escape from the Czar's police. And now the Revenue? And you have to have a partner, a *goniff.*"

"Voplonsky is an honest man."

"Who—that *German*?" Voplonsky was a Polish blacksmith. She called him a German because of his pointed military mustaches and the German cut of his overcoat. It hung to the ground. "What have you in common with a blacksmith? You, a descendant of Herschel Dubrovner! And he, a Polisher *schmid* with red whiskers! A rat! A rat with pointed red whiskers and long crooked teeth and reeking of scorched hoof! Bah! Your partner. Wait and see what he does to you."

"I'm not so easy to take in."

"No? Didn't Lazansky swindle you? He gave it to you in the real Turkish style. And didn't he beat your bones also?"

That was Lazansky, in the bakery, a giant teamster from the Ukraine. A huge ignorant man, an *amhoretz* who didn't know enough Hebrew to bless his bread, he sat on his narrow green delivery wagon, ponderous, growling "Garrap" to his little nag and flicking with the whip. His gross voice rolled like a bowling ball. The horse trotted along the bank of the Lachine Canal. The wagon was lettered

LAZANSKY—PATISSERIES DE CHOIX

Father Herzog said, "Yes, it's true he beat me."

He had come to borrow money from Zipporah and Yaffe. He did not want to be drawn into a quarrel. She had certainly guessed the purpose of this visit and was trying to make him angry so that she might refuse him more easily.

"Ai!" said Zipporah. A brilliantly shrewd woman, her many gifts were cramped in this little Canadian village. "You think you can make a fortune out of swindlers, thieves, and gangsters. You? You're a gentle creature. I don't know why you didn't stay in the Yeshivah. You wanted to be a gilded little gentleman. I know these hooligans and *razboiniks*. They don't have skins, teeth, fingers like you but hides, fangs, claws. You can never keep up with these teamsters and butchers. Can you shoot a man?"

Father Herzog was silent.

"If, God forbid, you had to shoot . . ." cried Zipporah. "Could you even hit someone on the head? Come! Think it over. Answer me, *gazlan*. Could you give a blow on the head?"

Here Mother Herzog seemed to agree.

"I'm no weakling," said Father Herzog, with his energetic face and brown mustache. But of course, thought Herzog, all of Papa's violence went into the drama of his life, into family strife, and sentiment.

"They'll take what they like from you, those *leite*," said Zipporah. "Now, isn't it time you used your head? You do have one—*klug bist du*. Make a legitimate living. Let your Helen and your Shura go to work. Sell the piano. Cut expenses."

"Why shouldn't the children study if they have intelligence, talent," said Mother Herzog.

"If they're smart, all the better for my brother," said Zipporah. "It's too hard for him—wearing himself out for spoiled princes and princesses."

She had Papa on her side, then. His craving for help was deep, bottomless.

"Not that I don't love the children," said Zipporah. "Come here, little Moses, and sit on your old *tante*'s knee. What a dear little *yingele*." Moses on the bloomers of his aunt's lap— her red hands held him at the belly. She smiled with harsh affection and kissed his neck. "Born in my arms, this child." Then she looked at brother Shura, who stood beside his mother. He had thick, blocky legs and his face was freckled. "And you?" said Zipporah to him.

"What's wrong?" said Shura, frightened and offended.

"Not too young to bring in a dollar."

Papa glared at Shura.

"Don't I help?" said Shura. "Deliver bottles? Paste labels?"

Papa had forged labels. He would say cheerfully, "Well, children, what shall it be—White Horse? Johnnie Walker?" Then we'd all call out our favorites. The paste pot was on the table.

In secret, Mother Herrog touched Shura's hand when Zipporah turned her eyes on him. Moses saw. Breathless Willie was scampering outside with his cousins, building a snow fort, squeaking and throwing snowballs. The sun came lower and lower. Ribbons of red from the horizon wound over the ridges of glazed snow. In the blue shadow of the fence, the goats were feeding. They belonged to the seltzer man next door. Zipporah's chickens were about to roost. Visiting us in Montreal, she sometimes brought a fresh egg. One egg. One of the children might be sick. A fresh egg had a world of power. Nervous and critical, with awkward feet and heavy hips, she mounted the stairs on Napoleon Street, a stormy woman, a daughter of Fate. Quickly and nervously she kissed her fingertips and touched the mezuzah. Entering, she inspected Mama's housekeeping. "Is everybody well?" she said. "I brought the children an egg." She opened her big bag and took out the present, wrapped in a piece of Yiddish newspaper (*Der Kanader Adler*).

A visit from Tante Zipporah was like a military inspection. Afterwards, Mama laughed and often ended by crying, "Why is she my enemy! What does she want? I have no strength to fight her." The antagonism, as Mama felt it, was mystical—a matter of souls. Mama's mind was archaic, filled with old legends, with angels and demons.

Of course Zipporah, that realist, was right to refuse Father Herzog. He wanted to run bootleg whisky to the border, and get into the big time. He and Voplonsky borrowed from moneylenders, and loaded a truck with cases. But they never reached Rouses Point. They were hijacked, beaten up, and left in a ditch. Father Herzog took the worse beating because he resisted. The hijackers tore his clothes, knocked out one of his teeth, and trampled him.

He and Voplonsky the blacksmith returned to Montreal on foot. He stopped at Voplonsky's shop to clean up, but there was not much he could do about his swollen bloody eye. He had a gap in his teeth. His coat was torn and his shirt and undergarment were blood-stained.

That was how he entered the dark kitchen on Napoleon Street. We were all there. It was gloomy March, and anyway the light seldom reached that room. It was like a cavern. We were like cave dwellers. "Sarah!" he said. "Children!" He showed his cut face. He spread his arms so we could see his tatters, and the white of his body under them. Then he turned his pockets inside out—empty. As he did this, he began to cry, and the children standing about him all cried. It was more than I could bear that anyone should lay violent hands on him—a father, a sacred being, a king. Yes, he was a king to us. My heart was suffocated by this horror. I thought I would die of it. Whom did I ever love as I loved them?

Then Father Herzog told his story.

"They were waiting for us. The road was blocked. They dragged as from the truck. They took everything."

"Why did you fight?" said Mother Herzog.

"Everything we had . . . all I borrowed!"

"They might have killed you."

"They had handkerchiefs over their faces. I thought I recognized . . ."

Mama was incredulous. "*Landtsleit?* Impossible. No Jews could do this to a Jew."

"No?" cried Papa. "Why not! Who says not! Why shouldn't they!"

"Not Jews! Never!" Mama said. "Never. Never! They couldn't have the heart. Never!"

"Children—don't cry. And poor Voplonsky—he could barely creep into bed."

"Yonah," said Mama, "you must give up this whole thing."

"How will we live? We have to live."

He began to tell the story of his life, from childhood to this day. He wept as he told it. Put out at four years old to study, away from home. Eaten by lice. Half starved in the Yeshivah as a boy. He shaved, became a modern European. He worked in Kremenchug for his aunt as a young man. He had a fool's paradise in Petersburg for ten years, on forged papers. Then he sat in prison with common criminals. Escaped to America. Starved. Cleaned stables. Begged. Lived in fear. A *baal-chov*—always a debtor. Shadowed by the police. Taking in drunken boarders. His wife a servant. And this was what he brought home to his children. This was what he could show them—his rags, his bruises.

Herzog, wrapped in his cheap paisley robe, brooded with clouded eyes. Under his bare feet was a small strip of carpet. His elbows rested on the fragile desk and his head hung down. He had written only a few lines to Nachman.

I suppose, he was thinking, that we heard this tale of the Herzogs ten times a year. Sometimes Mama told it, sometimes he. So we had a great schooling in grief. I still know these cries of the soul. They lie in the breast, and in the throat. The mouth wants to open wide and let them out. But all these are antiquities—yes, Jewish antiquities originating in the Bible, in a Biblical sense of personal experience and destiny. What happened during the War abolished Father Herzog's claim to exceptional suffering. We are on a more brutal standard now, a new terminal standard, indifferent to persons. Part of the program of destruction into which the human spirit has poured itself with energy, even with joy. These personal histories, old tales from old times that may not be worth remembering. I remember. I must. But who else—to whom can this matter? So many millions—multitudes—go down in terrible pain. And, at that, moral suffering is denied, these days. Personalities are good only for comic relief. But I am still a slave to Papa's pain. The way Father Herzog spoke of himself! That could make one laugh. His *I* had such dignity.

"You must give it up," Mama cried. "You must!"

"What should I do, then! Work for the burial society? Like a man of seventy? Only fit to sit at deathbeds? *I*? Wash corpses? *I*? Or should I go to the cemetery and wheedle mourners for a nickel? To say *El malai rachamim. I*? Let the earth open and swallow me up!"

"Come, Yonah," said Mama in her earnest persuasive way. "I'll put a compress on your eye. Come, lie down."

"How can I?"

"No, you must."

"How will the children eat?"

"Come—you must lie down awhile. Take off that shirt."

She sat by the bed, silent. He lay in the gray room, on the iron bedstead, covered with the worn red Russian blanket—his handsome forehead, his level nose, the brown mustache. As he had from that dark corridor, Moses now contemplated those two figures.

Nachman, he began again to write, but stopped. How was he to reach Nachman with a letter? He would do better to advertise in the *Village Voice*. But, then, to whom would he send the other letters he was drafting?

He concluded that Nachman's wife was dead. Yes, that must be it. That slender, thin-legged girl with the dark brows that rose high and recurved again beside her eyes, and the wide mouth which curved down at the corners—she had committed suicide, and Nachman ran away because (who could blame him) he would have had to tell Moses all about it. Poor thing, poor thing—she too must be in the cemetery.

THE TELEPHONE RANG—five, eight, ten peals. Herzog looked at his watch. The time astonished him—nearly six o'clock. Where had the day gone? The phone went on ringing, drilling away at him. He didn't want to pick it up. But there were two children, after all—he *was* a father, and he must answer. He reached for the instrument, therefore, and heard Ramona—the cheerful voice of Ramona calling him to a life of pleasure on the thrilling wires of New York. And not simple pleasure but metaphysical, transcendent pleasure—pleasure which answered the riddle of human existence. That was Ramona—no mere sensualist, but a theoretician, almost a priestess, in her Spanish costumes adapted to American needs, and her flowers, her really beautiful teeth, her red cheeks, and her thick, kinky, exciting black hair.

"Hello—Moses? What number is this?"

"This is the Armenian Relief."

"Oh, Moses! It's you!"

"I'm the only man you know old enough to remember the Armenian Relief."

"Last time you said it was the City Morgue. You must be feeling more cheerful. This is Ramona. . . ."

"Of course." Who else has the voice that lifts so light from height to height with foreign charm. "The Spanish lady."

"*La navaja en la liga.*"

"Why, Ramona, I never felt less threatened by knives."

"You sound positively high."

"I haven't spoken to a soul all day."

"I meant to call you, but the shop was very busy. Where were you yesterday?"

"Yesterday? Where *was* I—let me see. . . ."

"I thought you took a powder."

"Me? How could that be?"

"You mean, you wouldn't run out on me?"

Run out on fragrant, sexual, high-minded Ramona? Never in a million years. Ramona had passed through the hell of profligacy and attained the seriousness of pleasure. For when will we civilized beings become really serious? said Kierkegaard. Only when we have known hell through and through. Without this, hedonism and frivolity will diffuse hell through all our days. Ramona, however, does not believe in any sin but the sin against the body, for her the true and only temple of the spirit.

"But you did leave town yesterday," said Ramona.

"How do you know—are you having me tailed by a private eye?"

"Miss Schwartz saw you in Grand Central with a valise in your hand."

"Who? That little Miss Schwartz, in your shop?"

"That's right."

"Well, what do you know . . ." Herzog would not discuss it further.

Ramona said, "Perhaps some lovely woman scared you on the train, and you turned back to your Ramona."

"Oh . . ." said Herzog.

Her theme was her power to make him happy. Thinking of Ramona with her intoxicating eyes and robust breasts, her short but gentle legs, her Carmen airs, thievishly seductive, her skill in the sack (defeating invisible rivals), he felt she did not exaggerate. The facts supported her claim.

"Well, were you running away?" she said.

"Why should I? You're a marvelous woman, Ramona."

"In that case you're being very odd, Moses."

"Well, I suppose I am one of the odder beasts."

"But I know better than to be proud and demanding. Life has taught me to be humble."

Moses shut his eyes and raised his brows. Here we go.

"Perhaps you feel a natural superiority because of your education."

"Education! But I don't know anything. . . ."

"Your accomplishments. You're in *Who's Who*. I'm only a merchant—a petit-bourgeois type."

"You don't really believe this, Ramona."

"Then why do you keep aloof, and make me chase you? I realize you want to play the field. After great disappointments, I've done it myself, for ego-reinforcement."

"A high-minded intellectual ninny, square . . ."

"Who?"

"Myself, I mean."

She went on. "But as one recovers self-confidence, one learns the simple strength of simple desires."

Please, Ramona, Moses wanted to say—you're lovely, fragrant, sexual, good to touch—everything. But these lectures! For the love of God, Ramona, shut it up. But she went on. Herzog looked up at the ceiling. The spiders had the moldings under intensive cultivation, like the banks of the Rhine. Instead of grapes, encapsulated bugs hung in clusters.

I brought all this on myself by telling Ramona the story of my life—how I rose from humble origins to complete disaster. But a man who has made so many mistakes can't afford to ignore the corrections of his friends. Friends like Sandor, that humped rat. Or like Valentine, the moral megalomaniac and prophet in Israel. To all such, one is well advised to listen. Scolding is better than nothing. At least it's company.

Ramona paused, and Herzog said, "It's true—I have a lot to learn."

But I am diligent. I work at it and show steady improvement. I expect to be in great shape on my deathbed. The good die young, but I have been spared to build myself up so that I may end my life as good as gold. The senior dead will be proud of me. . . . I will join the Y.M.C.A. of the immortals. Only, in this very hour, I may be missing eternity.

"Are you listening?" said Ramona.

"Of course."

"What did I just say."

"That I have to trust my instincts more."

"I said I wanted you to come to dinner."

"Oh."

"If only I were a bitch! Then you'd hang on every word."

"But I was going to ask you . . . to come to an Italian restaurant." He was clumsily inventing. At times he was cruelly absentminded.

"I've shopped already," said Ramona.

"But how, if that snooping Miss Schwartz with the blue spectacles saw me running away in Grand Central . . . ?"

"Did I expect you? I figured you had to go to New Haven

for the day—to the Yale library, or some such place. . . .
Please come. Join me for dinner. I'll have to eat alone if you
don't."

"Why, where's your aunt?"

Ramona had her father's elderly sister living with her.

"She's gone to visit the cousins in Hartford."

"Ah—I see." He thought that old Aunt Tamara must be
well used to taking these trips on short notice.

"My aunt understands such things," said Ramona. "Besides,
she likes you so much."

And she thinks I'm a fine new prospect. Besides, one must
make sacrifices for a husbandless niece who has a troubled love
life. Just before meeting Herzog, Ramona had broken off with
an assistant television producer named George Hoberly who
was hard hit, in a pitiable state—close to hysteria. As Ramona
explained it, old Aunt Tamara was Hoberly's great sympathizer
—advised him, consoled him as well as an old woman could.
At the same time, she was almost as excited about Herzog as
Ramona herself. Meditating on Aunt Tamara, Moses thought
he now could better understand Aunt Zelda. The female passion for secrecy and double games. For we must eat our fruit
from the wily serpent's jaws.

Still, Herzog observed that Ramona had genuine family
feeling, and of this he approved. She seemed really fond of her
aunt. Tamara was the daughter of a Polish Czarist official
something-or-other (what harm could there be in making him
a general?). Ramona said about her, "She is very *jeune fille
Russe*"—an excellent description. Aunt Tamara was docile,
girlish, sensitive, impulsive. Whenever she spoke of Papá and
Mamá and her teachers and the Conservatoire her dry breast
filled, and the collarbones stood out tightly. She seemed still to
be trying to decide whether to have a concert career against
her Papá's wishes. Herzog, listening with serious looks, could
not establish whether she had given a recital at the Salle Gaveau
or wanted to give a recital. Old women from Eastern Europe
with dyed hair and senseless cameo brooches had easy access
to his affections.

"Well, then, are you coming or not?" said Ramona. "Why
are you so hard to pin down?"

"I shouldn't go out—I have a lot to do—letters to write."

"What letters! You're such a mystery man. What are these important letters? Business? Perhaps you should discuss it with me, if it is business. Or a lawyer, if you don't trust me. But you have to eat, anyway. Or perhaps you don't eat when you're alone."

"Of course I do."

"Well, then?"

"Okay," said Herzog. "Expect me soon. I'll bring a bottle of wine."

"No, no! Don't do that. I've got some on ice."

He put down the phone. She was emphatic about the wine. Perhaps he had given the impression that he was a little stingy. Or else he had awakened a feeling of protectiveness in her, an effect he often produced. He wondered at times whether he didn't belong to a class of people secretly convinced they had an arrangement with fate; in return for docility or ingenuous good will they were to be shielded from the worst brutalities of life. Herzog's mouth formed a soft but twisted smile as he considered whether he really had inwardly decided years ago to set up a deal—a psychic offer—meekness in exchange for preferential treatment. Such a bargain was feminine, or, extended to trees, animals, childlike. None of these self-judgments had any terror for him; no percentage now in quarreling with what one was. There was the thing—the composite, the mystical achievement of natural forces and his own spirit. He opened the paisley Hong Kong robe and looked at his naked body. He was no child. And the house in Ludeyville, a disaster in every other way, had kept him fit. Wrestling with that old ruin in an effort to recover his legacy made his arms muscular. Extended the lease of narcissism a little while. Gave him strength to carry a heavy-buttocked woman to the bed. Oh, yes—still in fleeting moments the young and glossy stud—such as he really had never been. There were more faithful worshipers of Eros than Moses Elkanah Herzog.

But why was Ramona so firm about wine? Maybe she was afraid he'd turn up with California sauterne. Or, no, she believed in the aphrodisiac power of her own brand. That might be it. Or else he harped more on the subject of money than he knew. A last possibility was that she wanted to surround him with luxuries.

Glancing at his watch, Herzog, with an appearance of efficiency or purpose, failed, anyway, to fix the time in his mind. What he did observe, stooping to the window to get an angle over roofs and walls, was that the sky was reddening. He was astonished that a whole day had been spent scrawling a few letters. And what ridiculous, angry letters! The spite and frenzy in them! Zelda! Sandor! Why write to them at all? And the Monsignor! Between the lines of Herzog's letter the Monsignor would only see a mad, reasoning face, just as Moses saw the brick of those walls between these rods caked in asphalt black. Endless repetition threatens sanity.

Suppose that I am absolutely right and the Monsignor, for instance, absolutely wrong. If I am right, the problem of the world's coherence, and all responsibility for it, becomes mine. How will it make out when Moses E. Herzog has his way? No, why should I take that on myself? The Church has universal understanding. This I consider a harmful, Prussian delusion. Readiness to answer all questions is the infallible sign of stupidity. Did Valentine Gersbach ever admit ignorance of any matter? He was a regular Goethe. He finished all your sentences, rephrased all your thoughts, explained everything.

. . . *I want you to know, Monsignor, that I am not writing with the purpose of exposing Madeleine, or to attack you.* Herzog tore up the letter. Untrue! He despised the Monsignor, wanted to murder Madeleine. Yes, he was capable of killing her. And yet, while filled with horrible rage, he was able also to shave and dress, to be the citizen on the town for an evening of pleasure, groomed, scented, and his face sweetened for kisses. He did not flinch from these criminal fantasies. It's the certainty of punishment that stops me, Herzog thought.

Time to clean up. He turned from the desk and the deepening light of the afternoon and dropping the robe entered the bathroom and turned on the water in the basin. He drank, in the obscurity of the cool tiled room. New York has the sweetest water in the world, for a metropolis. Then he began to soap his face. He could look forward to a good dinner. Ramona knew how to cook, and how to set a table. There would be candles, linen napkins, flowers. Perhaps the flowers were being rushed from the shop now, in evening traffic. On the windowsill of Ramona's dining room pigeons roosted. You heard wings flapping in the airshaft. As for the menu, on a summer evening like this she'd probably prepare vichyssoise, then shrimp Arnaud—New Orleans style. White asparagus. A cool dessert. Rum-flavored ice cream with raisins? Brie and cold-water biscuits? He was judging by previous dinners. Coffee. Brandy. And, all the time, Egyptian music on the phonograph in the adjoining room—Mohammad al Bakkar playing "Port Said" with zithers, drums, and tambourines. In that room was a Chinese rug, the light of the green lamp deep and quiet. Here also she had fresh flowers. If I had to work all day in a flower shop, I wouldn't want to be pursued by the smell of flowers at night. On the coffee table she had art books and international magazines. Paris, Rio, Rome, all were represented. Invariably, also, the latest presents from Ramona's admirers were displayed. Herzog always read the little cards. For what other reason did she leave them? George Hoberly for whom she was cooking shrimp Arnaud last spring still sent her gloves, books, theater tickets, opera glasses. You could trace his love-crazed wanderings up and down New York by the labels. Ramona said he didn't know what he was doing. Herzog was sorry for him.

The bluish-green carpet, the Moorish knickknacks and arabesques, the wide comfortable sofa-bed, the Tiffany lamp with glass like plumage, the deep armchairs by the windows, the downtown view of Broadway and Columbus Circle. And after dinner, when they were settling down here with coffee and brandy, Ramona would ask whether he wouldn't like to take off his shoes. Why not? A free foot on a summer night eases the heart. And by and by, going by precedents, she'd ask why he was so abstracted—was he thinking of his children? Then he'd say . . . he was shaving now, scarcely glancing in the mirror, finding the stubble with his fingertips . . . he'd say that he was no longer so worried about Marco. The boy had a firm character. He was one of the more stable breed of Herzogs. Ramona then would give him level-headed advice about his little daughter. Moses would say how could he abandon her to those psychopaths? Could she doubt that they were psychopaths? Did she want to look again at the letter from Geraldine—the frightful letter that told what they were doing? And there would follow another discussion of Madeleine,

Zelda, Valentine Gersbach, Sandor Himmelstein, the Monsignor, Dr. Edvig, Phoebe Gersbach. Against his will, like an addict struggling to kick the habit, he would tell again how he was swindled, conned, manipulated, his savings taken, driven into debt, his trust betrayed by wife, friend, physician. If ever Herzog knew the loathsomeness of a *particular* existence, knew that the *whole* was required to redeem every separate spirit, it was then, in his terrible passion, which he tried, impossibly, to share, telling his story. Then, in the midst of it, the realization would come over him that he had no right to tell, to inflict it, that his craving for confirmation, for help, for justification, was useless. Worse, it was unclean. (For some reason the French word suited him better, and he said "*Immonde!*" and again, more loudly, "*C'est immonde!*") However, Ramona would tenderly sympathize with him. No doubt she genuinely pitied him, though the injured are, for primitive reasons, unattractive and even ludicrous. In a spiritually confused age, however, a man who could feel as he did might claim a certain distinction. He was beginning to see that his particular brand of short-sightedness, lack of realism, and apparent ingenuousness conferred a high status on him. For Ramona it evidently surrounded him with glamour. And provided that he remain *macho* she would listen with glistening eyes, with more sympathy, and more, and more. She transformed his miseries into sexual excitements and, to give credit where it was due, turned his grief in a useful direction. Cannot agree with Hobbes that where there is no overawing power men have no pleasure (*voluptas*) in keeping company but instead (*molestia*) a great deal of grief. There is always an overawing power, namely, one's terror. To set aside these theoretical considerations, however, when he was done, having drunk four or five glasses of Armagnac from the Venetian decanter, far above the Puerto Rican disorders of the street, it would be Ramona's turn. You treat me right, I treat you right.

He continued shaving, like a blind man, by touch and by sound, the sound of bristle and blade.

Ramona was highly experienced at entertaining gentlemen. The shrimp, wine, flowers, lights, perfumes, the rituals of undressing, the Egyptian music whining and clanging, bespoke practice, and he regretted that she'd had to live this way, but it flattered him, also. Ramona was astonished that any woman should find fault with Moses. He told her that he was often a flat failure with Madeleine. It might be the release of his angry feeling against Mady that improved his performance. At this Ramona looked severe.

"I don't know—it might be *me*—have you considered that?" she said. "Poor Moses—unless you're having a bad time with a woman you can't believe you're being serious."

Moses rinsed his face with pleasant witch hazel, a brimming handful, and blew upon his cheeks from the corners of his mouth. He tuned in Polish dance music on the small transistor radio on the glass shelf over the sink, and powdered his feet. Then he gave in for a while to the impulse to dance and leap on the soiled tiles, some of which came free from the grout and had to be kicked under the tub. It was one of his oddities in solitude to break out in song and dance, to do queer things out of keeping with his customary earnestness. He danced out the number until the Polish commercial—"Ochyne-pynch-ochyne, Pynch Avenue, Flushing." He mimicked the announcer in the ivory yellow gloom of the tile bathroom—the water closet, as he anachronistically called it. He was ready to go for another polka when he discovered, breathing hard, that the sweat was rolling down his sides, and that another dance would make a shower necessary. He didn't have the time or patience for that. He couldn't bear the thought of drying himself—one of those killing chores he had always hated.

He put on clean drawers, socks. In stocking feet he trod the toes of his shoes to bring out a dull shine. Ramona did not like his taste in shoes. Before the window of the Bally shop on Madison Avenue she pointed at a pair of ankle-high Spanish boots and said, "That's what you need—those vicious-looking black things." Smiling, she looked upward so that he was confronted by the brightness of her eyes. She had marvelous, slightly curved white teeth. Her lips would part and close over these significant teeth, and she had a short, curved, French nose, small and fine; hazel eyes; thick vivid black hair. The weight of her face was mainly in the lower part. A slight defect, in Herzog's view. Nothing serious.

"You want me to dress up like a flamenco dancer?" said Herzog.

"You ought to use a little imagination about clothes—encourage certain aspects of your character."

You would think—Herzog smiled broadly—he was a piece of human capital badly invested. To her surprise, perhaps, he agreed with her. Almost cheerfully, he agreed. Strength, intelligence, feeling, opportunity had been wasted on him. What he could not see, however, was that such Spanish shoes—which, by the way, greatly appealed to his childish taste—would improve his character. And we must improve. Must!

He put on trousers. Not the Italian pants: they'd be uncomfortable after dinner. One of the new poplin shirts was next. He removed all the pins. Then he put on the madras jacket. He bent down to see what he could see of the harbor through the small opening of the bathroom window. Nothing in particular. Only a sense of water bounding the overbuilt island. It was a movement of orientation that he was making, like the glance at his watch which did not tell him the time. And next came his specific self, an apparition in the square mirror. How did he look? Oh, terrific—you look exquisite, Moses! Smashing! The primitive self-attachment of the human creature, that sweet instinct for the self, so deep, so old it may have a cellular origin. As he breathed, he was aware of it, quiet but far-reaching, all through his system, a pleasing hunger in his remotest nerves. *Dear Professor Haldane* . . . No, that was not Herzog's man at this moment. *Dear Father Teilhard de Chardin, I have tried to understand your notion of the inward aspect of the elements. That sense organs, even rudimentary sense organs, could not evolve from molecules described by mechanists as inert. Thus matter itself should perhaps be studied as evolving consciousness . . is the carbon molecule lined with thought?*

His shaven face, muttering in the mirror—great shadows under the eyes. That's okay, he thought; if the light's not too bright, you're still a grand-looking man. For a while yet, you can get women. All but that bitch, Madeleine, whose face looks either beautiful or haggy. Go, then—Ramona will feed you, give you wine, remove your shoes, flatter you, smooth down your hackles, kiss you, pinch your lip with her teeth. Then uncover the bed, turn down the lights, and go into the essentials. . . .

He was half elegant, half slovenly. That had always been his style. If he knotted his tie with care, his shoelaces dragged. His brother Shura, immaculate in his tailored clothes, manicured and barbered at the Palmer House, said this was done on purpose. Once it had perhaps been his boyish defiance, but by now it was an established part of the daily comedy of Moses E. Herzog. Ramona often said, "You're not a true, puritanical American. You have a talent for sensuality. Your mouth gives you away." Herzog could not help putting his fingers to his lip when it was mentioned. But then he laughed the whole thing off. What remained to bother him was that she did not recognize him as an American. That hurt! What else was he? In the Service his mates had also considered him a foreigner. The Chicagoans questioned him suspiciously. "What's on State and Lake? How far west is Austin Avenue?" Most of them seemed to come from the suburbs. Moses knew the city much better than they, but even this was turned against him. "Ah, you just memorized everything. You're a spy. That proves. One of them smart Jews. Come clean, Mose—they're gonna drop you by parachute—right?" No, he became a communications officer, discharged for asthma. Choked by fog, in the Gulf of Mexico, on maneuvers, losing contact owing to his hoarseness. Except that the whole fleet heard him groan, "We're lost! Fucked!"

But in Chicago, in 1934, he was class orator at the McKinley High School, his text taken from Emerson. He didn't lose his voice then, telling the Italian mechanics, Bohemian barrel makers, Jewish tailors *The main enterprise of the world, for splendor . . . is the upbuilding of a man. The private life of one man shall be a more illustrious monarchy . . . than any kingdom in history. Let it be granted that our life, as we lead it, is common and mean. . . . Beautiful and perfect men we are not now. . . . The community in which we live will hardly bear to be told that every man should be open to ecstasy or a divine illumination.* If he had lost craft and crew somewhere near Biloxi, that didn't mean he wasn't in earnest about beauty and perfection. He believed his American credentials were in good order. Laughing, but pained, too, he remembered that a Chief Petty Officer from Alabama had asked him, "Wheah did you loin to speak English—at the Boilitz Scho-ool?"

No, what Ramona meant, as a compliment, was that he had not lived the life of an ordinary American. No, his peculiarities had governed him from the start. Did he see any great value or social distinction in this? Well, he had to endure these peculiarities, so there was no reason why he shouldn't make use of them, a little.

But, speaking of ordinary Americans, what sort of mother would Ramona make? Would she be able to take a little girl to Macy's parade? Moses tried to imagine Ramona, a priestess of Isis, in a tweed suit, watching the procession of floats.

Dear McSiggins. I read your monograph, "The Ethical Ideas of the American Business Community." *A field day for McSiggins. Interesting. Would have appreciated closer investigation of hypocrisy, public and private, in the American accounting system. Nothing to prevent the individual American from claiming as much merit as he likes. By degrees, in Populistic philosophy, goodness has become a free commodity like air, or nearly free, like a subway ride. Best of everything for everybody—help yourself. No one much cares. The honest look, recommended by Ben Franklin as a business asset, has a predestinarian, Calvinistic background. You don't cast doubts on another man's election. You may damage his credit rating. As belief in damnation vanishes, it leaves behind solid formations of Reliable Appearances.*

Dear General Eisenhower. In private life perhaps you have the leisure and inclination to reflect on matters for which, as Chief Executive, you obviously had no time. The pressure of the Cold War . . . which now so many people agree was a phase of political hysteria, and the journeys and speeches of Mr. Dulles rapidly changing in this age of shifting perspectives from their earlier appearance of statesmanship to one of American wastefulness. I happened to be in the press gallery at the UN the day you spoke of the risk of error in precipitating nuclear war. That day I put down a deposit on a chandelier, an old gas fixture, really, on Second Avenue. Another ten bucks squandered on Ludeyville. *I was present also when Premier Khrushchev pounded the desk with his shoe. Amid such crises, in such an atmosphere, there was obviously no time for the more general questions of the sort I have been concerned with.* Indeed, put my life into. But what do you want him to do about that? *I gather from the book by Mr. Hughes, however, and from your letter to him expressing concern about "spiritual values" that I may not be wasting your time in calling your attention to the report of your own Committee on National*

Aims, published at the end of your administration. I wonder
whether the people you appointed to it were the best for the job—
corporation lawyers, big executives, the group now called the In-
dustrial Statesmen. Mr. Hughes has noted how you were shielded
from distressing opinions, insulated, as it were. Perhaps you will
be asking yourself who your present correspondent is, whether a
liberal, an egghead, a bleeding heart, or a nut of some kind. So
let us say he is a thoughtful person who believes in civil usefulness.
Intelligent people without influence feel a certain self-contempt,
reflecting the contempt of those who hold real political or social
power, or think they do. Can you make it all clear, in few words?
It's well known he hates long, complicated documents. *A col-*
lection of loyal, helpful statements to inspire us in the struggle
against the Communist enemy is not what we needed. The old pro-
position of Pascal (1623–1662) that man is a reed, but a thinking
reed, might be taken with a different emphasis by the modern cit-
izen of a democracy. He thinks, but he feels like a reed bending
before centrally generated winds. Ike would certainly pay no attention to this. Herzog tried another approach. *Tolstoi (1828–*
1910) said, "Kings are history's slaves." The higher one stands in
the scale of power, the more his actions are determined. To Tolstoi,
freedom is entirely personal. That man is free whose condition is
simple, truthful—real. To be free is to be released from historical
limitation. On the other hand, GWF Hegel (1770–1831) under-
stood the essence of human life to be derived from history. History,
memory—that is what makes us human, that, and our knowl-
edge of death: "by man came death." For knowledge of death
makes us wish to extend our lives at the expense of others. And this
is the root of the struggle for power. But that's all wrong! thought
Herzog, not without humor in his despair. I'm bugging all
these people—Nehru, Churchill, and now Ike, whom I apparently want to give a Great Books course. Nevertheless, there
was much earnest feeling in this, too. *No civil order, no higher*
development of mankind. The goal, however, is freedom. And
what does a man owe to the State? It was with such considera-
tions, reading your Committee's report on National Aims, that I
seem to have been stirred fiercely by a desire to communicate,
or by the curious project of attempted communication. Or bent
by a disguised passion, offering these ideas about Death and
History to the commander of SHAEF, like mocking flowers

grown in the soil of fever and unacted violence. Suppose, after all, we are simply a kind of beast, peculiar to this mineral lump that runs around in orbit to the sun, then why such loftiness, such great standards? *that I thought of the variation on Gresham's famous Law: Public life drives out private life. The more political our society becomes (in the broadest sense of "political"— the obsessions, the compulsions of collectivity) the more individuality seems lost. Seems, I say, because it has millions of secret resources. More plainly, national purpose is now involved with the manufacture of commodities in no way essential to human life, but vital to the political survival of the country. Because we are now all sucked into these phenomena of Gross National Product, we are forced to accept the sacred character of certain absurdities or falsehoods whose high priests not so long ago were mere pitchmen, and figures of derision—sellers of snake-oil. On the other hand there is more "private life" than a century ago, when the working day lasted fourteen hours. The whole matter is of the highest importance since it has to do with invasion of the private sphere (including the sexual) by techniques of exploitation and domination.*

His tragic successor would have been interested, but not Ike. Nor Lyndon. Their governments could not function without intellectuals—physicists, statisticians—but these are whirling lost in the arms of industrial chiefs and billionaire brass. Kennedy was not about to change this situation, either. Only he seemed to have acknowledged, privately, that it existed.

A new idea possessed Moses. He would offer an outline to Pulver, Harris Pulver, who had been his tutor in 1939 and was now the editor of *Atlantic Civilization*. Yes, tiny, nervous Pulver with his timid, whole-souled blue eyes, his crumbled teeth, the profile of Gizeh's mummy as pictured in Robinson's *Ancient History*, the taut skin hectically spotted with high color. Herzog loved this man in his own immoderate, heart-flooded way. *Listen, Pulver,* he wrote, *a marvelous idea for a much-needed essay on the "inspired condition"! Do you believe in transcendence downward as well as upward? (The terms originate with Jean Wahl.) Shall we concede the impossibility of transcendence? It all involves historical analysis. I would argue that we have fashioned a new utopian history, an idyll, comparing the present to an imaginary past, because we hate the world as it is.*

This hatred of the present has not been well understood. Perhaps the first demand of emerging consciousness in this mass civilization is expressive. The spirit, released from servile dumbness, spits dung and howls with anguish stored during long ages. Perhaps the fish, the newt, the horrid scampering ancestral mammal find their voice and add their long experience to this cry. Taking up the suggestion, Pulver, that evolution is nature becoming self-aware—in man, self-awareness has been accompanied at this stage with a sense of the loss of more general natural powers, of a price paid by instinct, by sacrifices of freedom, impulse (alienating labor, et cetera). The drama of this stage of human development seems to be the drama of disease, of self-revenge. An age of special comedy. What we see is not simply the leveling de Tocqueville predicted, but the plebeian stage of evolutionary self-awareness. Perhaps the revenge taken by numbers, by the species, on our impulses of narcissism (but also on the demand for freedom) is inevitable. In this new reign of multitudes, self-awareness tends to reveal us to ourselves as monsters. This is undoubtedly a political phenomenon, an action taken against personal impulse or against the personal demand for adequate space and scope. The individual is obliged, or put under pressure, to define "power" as it is defined in politics, and to work out the personal consequences of this for himself. Thus he is provoked to take revenge upon himself, a revenge of derision, contempt, denial of transcendence. This last, his denial, is based upon former conceptions of human life or on images of man at present impossible to maintain. But the problem as I see it is not one of definition but of the total reconsideration of human qualities. Or perhaps even the discovery of qualities. I am certain that there are human qualities still to be discovered. Such discovery or recovery is only hampered by definitions which hold mankind down at the level of pride (or masochism), asserting too much and then suffering from self-hatred as a consequence.

But you will be wondering what happened to "the inspired condition." This is thought to be attainable only in the negative and is so pursued in philosophy and literature as well as in sexual experience, or with the aid of narcotics, or in "philosophical," "gratuitous" crime and similar paths of horror. (It never seems to occur to such "criminals" that to behave with decency to another human being might also be "gratuitous.") Intelligent observers

have pointed out that "spiritual" honor or respect formerly re-
served for justice, courage, temperance, mercy, may now be
earned in the negative by the grotesque. I often think that this de-
velopment is possibly related to the fact that so much of "value"
has been absorbed by technology itself. It is "good" to electrify a
primitive area. Civilization and even morality are implicit in
technological transformation. Isn't it good to give bread to the
hungry, to clothe the naked? Don't we obey Jesus in shipping ma-
chinery to Peru or Sumatra? Good is easily done by machines of
production and transportation. Can virtue compete? New tech-
niques are in themselves bien pensant *and represent not only ra-*
tionality but benevolence. Thus a crowd, a herd of bien pensants
has been driven into nihilism, which, as is now well known, has
Christian and moral roots and for its wildest frenzies offers a
"constructive" rationale. (See Polyani, Herzog, et al.)

Romantic individuals (a mass of them by now) accuse this mass
civilization of obstructing their attainment of beauty, nobility,
integrity, intensity. I do not want to sneer at the term Romantic.
Romanticism guarded the "inspired condition," preserved the
poetic, philosophical, and religious teachings, the teachings and
records of transcendence and the most generous ideas of man-
kind, during the greatest and most rapid of transformations, the
most accelerated phase of the modern scientific and technical
transformation.

Finally, Pulver, to live in an inspired condition, to know truth,
to be free, to love another, to consummate existence, to abide with
death in clarity of consciousness—without which, racing and
conniving to evade death, the spirit holds its breath and hopes to
be immortal because it does not live—is no longer a rarefied proj-
ect. Just as machinery has embodied ideas of good, so the technol-
ogy of destruction has also acquired a metaphysical character. The
practical questions have thus become the ultimate questions as
well. Annihilation is no longer a metaphor. Good and Evil are
real. The inspired condition is therefore no visionary matter. It is
not reserved for gods, kings, poets, priests, shrines, but belongs to
mankind and to all of existence. And therefore—

Therefore, Herzog's thoughts, like those machines in the
lofts he had heard yesterday in the taxi, stopped by traffic in
the garment district, plunged and thundered with endless—
infinite!—hungry, electrical power, stitching fabric with inex-

haustible energy. Having seated himself again in his striped jacket he was gripping the legs of his desk between his knees, his teeth set, the straw hat cutting his forehead. He wrote, *Reason exists! Reason* . . . he then heard the soft dense rumbling of falling masonry, the splintering of wood and glass. *And belief based on reason. Without which the disorder of the world will never be controlled by mere organization. Eisenhower's report on National Aims, if I had had anything to do with it, would have pondered the private and inward existence of Americans first of all.* . . . *Have I explained that my article would be a review of this report?* He thought intensely, deeply, and wrote, *Each to change his life. To change!*

Thus I want you to see how I, Moses E. Herzog, am changing. I ask you to witness the miracle of his altered heart —how, hearing the sounds of slum clearance in the next block and watching the white dust of plaster in the serene air of metamorphic New York, he communicates with the mighty of this world, or speaks words of understanding and prophecy, having arranged at the same time a comfortable and entertaining evening—food, music, wine, conversation, and sexual intercourse. Transcendence or no transcendence. All work and no games is bad medicine. Ike went trout fishing and played golf; my needs are different. (More in Herzog's vein of wide-eyed malice.) The erotic must be admitted to its rightful place, at last, in an emancipated society which understands the relation of sexual repression to sickness, war, property, money, totalitarianism. Why, to get laid is actually socially constructive and useful, an act of citizenship. So here I am in the gathering dusk, the striped jacket on my back, sweating again after my wash, shaved, powdered, taking my underlip in my teeth nervously, as if anticipating what Ramona will do to it. Powerless to reject the hedonistic joke of a mammoth industrial civilization on the spiritual desires, the high cravings of a Herzog, on his moral suffering, his longing for the good, the true. All the while his heart is *contemptibly* aching. He would like to give this heart a shaking, or put it out of his breast. Evict it. Moses hated the humiliating comedy of heartache. But can thought wake you from the dream of existence? Not if it becomes a second realm of confusion, another more complicated dream, the dream of intellect, the delusion of total *explanations.*

He had gotten a significant warning once from Daisy's mother, Polina, when he had fallen in love for a while with his Japanese friend Sono, and Polina, the old Russian Jewish suffragette—fifty years a modern woman in Zanesville, Ohio (from 1905 to 1935 Daisy's father drove a soda-pop-and-seltzer truck there)—descended on him. Neither Polina nor Daisy actually knew anything about Sono Oguki then. (What a lot of romances! thought Herzog. One after another. Were those my real career?) But . . . Polina flew in, gray-haired and wide-hipped, with her bag of knitting, an elegant, determined person. She arrived with a Quaker Oats box filled with apple strudel for Herzog—he still felt a pang at the loss of her strudel; it was truly great. But he was aware that his greed for it was childlike, and that there were adult questions to be decided. Polina had the peculiar stiffness and severity of the emancipated woman of her generation. Once a beauty, she was now very dry in appearance, with gold octagonal glasses and the sparse white hairs of an old woman at the corners of her mouth.

They spoke in Yiddish. "What are you going to become?" said Polina, "*ein ausvurf—ausgelassen?*" Outcast—dissolute? The old lady was Tolstoian, puritanical. She did eat meat, however, and she was a tyrant. She was frugal, arid, clean, respectable and domineering. But there was nothing so tart, sweet, soft, and fragrant as her strudel made with brown sugar and green apples. It was extraordinary how much sensuality went into her baking. And she never gave Daisy the recipe. "Well, what about it?" said Polina. "First one woman and then another, then another. Where will it end? You can't abandon a wife, a son for these women—whores."

I should never have had these "explanations" with her, thought Moses. Was it a point of honor to explain myself to everyone? But how could I explain? I myself didn't understand, didn't have a clue.

He stirred. He'd better be on his way. It was growing late. He was expected uptown. But he was not yet ready to leave. He took a new sheet of paper and wrote *Dear Sono*.

She had gone back to Japan long ago. When was it? He

turned his eyes upward as he tried to calculate the length of time, and he saw the white clouds rolling above Wall Street and the harbor. *I don't blame you for going home.* She was a person of means. She owned a house in the country, too. Herzog had seen the colored photographs—an Oriental countryside with rabbits, hens, piglets, her own hot spring in which she bathed. She had a picture of the village blind man who came to massage her. She loved massages, believed in them. She had often massaged Moses, and he had massaged her.

You were right about Madeleine, Sono. I shouldn't have married her. I should have married you.

But Sono had never really learned to speak English. For two years, she and Moses had conversed in French—*petit nègre.* He wrote, *Ma chère, Ma vie est devenue un cauchemar affreux. Si tu savais!* At McKinley High School, from a forbidding spinster, Miss Miloradovitch, he had learned his French. The most useful course I took.

Sono had seen Madeleine only once, but once was enough. She warned me as I sat in her broken Morris chair. "Moso, méfie toi. Prend garde, Moso."

She had a tender heart, and Herzog knew that if he wrote her of the sadness of his life, she would certainly cry. Instantaneous tears. They had a way of appearing without the usual Western preliminaries. Her black eyes rose from the surface of her cheeks in the same way that her breasts rose from the surface of her body. No, he would not write her sad news of any sort, he decided. Instead, he allowed himself to picture her as she might be now (it was morning in Japan), bathing in her steaming spring, her small mouth open, singing. She bathed often, and sang as she washed, her eyes upcast and her lips dainty and tremulous. The songs were sweet and odd, narrow, steep, at times with catlike sounds.

During the troubled time when he was being divorced from Daisy and he came to visit Sono in her West Side apartment, she would immediately run the little tub and fill it with Macy's bath salts. She unbuttoned Moses' shirt, took off his clothes, and when she had him settled ("Easy now, it's hot") in the swirling, foaming, perfumed water she let drop her petticoat and got in behind him, singing that vertical music of hers.

> "Chin-chin
> Je te lave le dos
> Mon Mo-so."

As a young girl she had gone to live in Paris, and she was caught there by the War. She was down with pneumonia when the American troops entered and was still sick when she was repatriated via the Trans-Siberian Railroad. She no longer cared for Japan, she said; the West had spoiled her for life in Tokyo, and her rich father allowed her to study design in New York.

She told Herzog that she was not sure she believed in God, but that if he did she would also try to have faith. If on the other hand he was a Communist she was prepared to become one, too. Because "Les Japonaises sont très fidèles. Elles ne sont pas comme les Américaines. Bah!" Still, American women also amused her. She often entertained the Baptist ladies who were her sponsors with the Immigration Department. She prepared shrimp or raw fish for them or treated them to the tea ceremony. Moses sometimes sat waiting on the stoop of the brownstone opposite when the ladies were slow to leave. Sono with great enjoyment—she was greedy for intrigue (the abysses of female secrecy!)—would come to the window and give him the high sign, pretending to water her plants. She grew little ginkgo trees and cactuses in yoghurt containers.

On the West Side, she occupied three rooms with high ceilings; at the back there grew an ailanthus tree, and one of the front windows contained a giant air-conditioner; it must have weighed a ton. Fourteenth Street bargains filled the apartment—an overstuffed chesterfield, bronze screens, lamps, nylon drapes, masses of wax flowers, articles of wrought iron and twisted wire and glass. Here Sono went back and forth busily on bare feet, coming down on her heels sturdily. Her lovely body was covered unbecomingly in knee-length bargain negligees bought on the stands near Seventh Avenue. Every purchase involved her in a battle with the other bargain hunters. Excitedly holding her soft throat she would tell Herzog with sharp cries what had happened. "Chéri! J'avais déjà choisi mon tablier. Cette femme s'est foncée sur moi. Woo! Elle était noire! Moooan dieu! Et grande! Derrière immense.

Immense poitrine. Et sans soutien-gorge. Tout à fait comme Niagara Fall. En chair noire." Sono puffed out her cheeks and crooked her arms as though suffocating with fat, thrusting out her belly, then displaying her rump. "Je disais, 'No, no, leddy. I here first.' Elle avait les bras comme ça—enflés. Et quelle gorge! Il y avait du monde au balcon. 'No!' je disais. 'No, no, leddy.'" Proudly Sono showed her nostrils, made her eyes heavy and dangerous. She set a hand on her hip. Herzog in the broken Morris chair from the Catholic Salvage said, "That's the stuff, Sono. They can't push the Samurai around on Fourteenth Street."

Abed, he had touched Sono's eyelids experimentally, as she lay smiling. Those strange, complex, soft, pale lids would keep the imprint of a touch for quite a while. *To tell the truth, I never had it so good,* he wrote. *But I lacked the strength of character to bear such joy.* That was hardly a joke. When a man's breast feels like a cage from which all the dark birds have flown—he is free, he is light. And he longs to have his vultures back again. He wants his customary struggles, his nameless, empty works, his anger, his afflictions and his sins. In this parlor of Oriental luxury, making a principled quest—*principled*, mind you—for life-giving pleasure, solving for Moses E. Herzog the puzzle of the body (curing himself of the fatal disorder of worldliness which rejects worldly happiness, this Western plague, this mental leprosy), he seemed to have found his object. But often he sat morose, depressed, in the Morris chair. Well, curse such sadness! But she liked even that. She saw me with the eyes of love, and she said, "Ah! T'es mélancolique—c'est très beau!" It may be that guilt and sadness made me look Oriental. A morose, angry eye, a long upper lip—what people used to call the Chinese Gleep. It was *beau* to her. And no wonder she thought I might be a Communist. The world should love lovers; but not theoreticians. Never theoreticians! Show them the door. Ladies, throw out these gloomy bastards! Hence, loathéd melancholy! In dark Cimmerian desart ever dwell.

Sono's three tall rooms in the brownstone apartment were hung with transparent bargain curtains, like the Far East in the movies. There were many interiors. The inmost was the bed, with sheets of spearmint green, or washed-out chlorophyll,

unmade, everything in disorder. After the bath, Herzog's body
was red. When she had dried and powdered him, she dressed
him in a kimono, her pleased but still slightly unwilling Cau-
casian doll. The stiff cloth cramped him under the arms as he
sat on the pillows. She brought him tea in her best cups. He
listened to her talk. She would tell him the latest scandals of
the Tokyo press. A woman had mutilated her unfaithful lover
and was found with the missing parts in her obi. A locomotive
engineer slept through a signal and killed a hundred and fifty-
four people. Her father's concubine was now driving a Volkswagen. She parked at the gate of the house, for she was not
allowed into the yard. And Herzog thought . . . is this really
possible? Have all the traditions, passions, renunciations,
virtues, gems, and masterpieces of Hebrew discipline and all
the rest of it—rhetoric, a lot of it, but containing true facts—
brought me to these untidy green sheets, and this rippled
mattress? As if anyone cared what he was doing here. As if it affected the fate of the world in any way. It was his own business.
"I got a right," Herzog whispered, though his face neither
changed nor moved. Very good. The Jews were strange to the
world for a great length of time, and now the world is being
strange to them in return. Sono brought out a bottle and
spiked his tea with cognac or Chivas Regal. When she had
taken a few nips herself she gave a playful growl. Herzog could
not help laughing. Sono then brought out her scrolls. Fat merchants made love to slender girls who looked away comically as
they submitted. Moses and Sono sat cross-legged on the bed.
She pointed to things, winking and exclaiming and pressing
her round face to his.

Something was always frying or brewing in her kitchen, a
dark closet rank with fish and soy sauce, seaweed vermicelli,
old tea leaves. The plumbing was often out of order. She wanted
Herzog to have a talk with the Negro janitor, who would only
laugh at her when she demanded service. Sono kept two cats;
their pan was never clean. When Herzog was in the subway,
coming to see her, he already began to smell those odors of
her apartment. Their darkness passed through his heart. He
violently desired Sono, and just as violently did not want to
go. Even now he felt the fever, remembered the smells, experienced the difficulty. He shivered when he rang her bell. The

chain rattled, she pulled open the large door and threw her arms about his neck. Her face was elaborately made up, and she smelled of musk. The cats tried to make an escape. She captured them, and then she cried out—always the same cry—

"Moso! Je viens de rentrer!"

She was breathless. She had run to meet him and beat him home by seconds. Why? Why did she always have to be just under the wire? Perhaps to show that she had an independent and active life; she did not sit waiting. The tall door with the curved top admitted him. Sono secured it again with bolt and chain (precautions of a woman living alone; but she said the super tried to let himself in without knocking). Herzog with a beating heart but composed face entered, looked around with pale-faced dignity at the hangings (sienna, crimson, green) and the fireplace stuffed with the wrappings of her latest purchases, the draftsman's table where she did her homework and where the cats perched. He smiled at eager Sono, and sat down in the Morris chair. "Mauvais temps, eh chéri?" she said, and she began at once to cheer him. She took off his miserable shoes, telling him where she had been. Some lovely Christian Science ladies had invited her to a concert at the Cloisters. She had seen a double feature at the Thalia—Danielle Darrieux, Simone Signoret, Jean Gabin, et Harry Bow-wow. The Nippon-America Society invited her to the United Nations building, where she presented flowers to the Nizam of Hyderabad. Through a Japanese trade mission she also met Mr. Nasser and Mr. Sukarno and the Secretary of State and the President. Tonight she had to go to a night club with the foreign minister of Venezuela. Moses had learned not to doubt her. She always produced a night-club photograph in which she sat beautiful and laughing in a low-cut gown. She had Mendès-France's autograph on a menu. She would never ask Herzog to take her to the Copacabana. This was a mark of her respect for his deep gravity. "T'es philosophe. O mon philosophe, mon professeur d'amour. T'es très important. Je le sais." She rated him higher than kings and presidents.

As she put the kettle on for Herzog's tea, she never failed to describe the events of her day from the kitchen at the top of her voice. She saw a three-legged dog which made a truck swerve into a pushcart. A cabdriver wanted to give her his parrot, but the cats would kill it. She could not accept such a responsibility. A panhandling old woman—*vieille mendiante*—got her to buy a copy of the *Times* for her. That was all the old creature wanted, this morning's *Times*. A policeman said he would give Sono a ticket for jaywalking. A man had exposed himself behind a subway pillar. "Ooooh, c'était honteux—quelle chose!" She measured with her hands from her own body. "One foots, Moso. Très laide."

"Ça t'a plu," Moses said smiling.

"Oh no! Moso, no! Elle était vilain." She was, however, delightfully excited. Moses looked at her gently, suspiciously as well, perhaps, lying back elegantly in the broken reclining chair. The fever he had felt as he was coming had now begun to subside. Even the smells were never quite so bad as he had anticipated. The cats were less jealous of him. They came to be petted. He grew used to their Siamese mewing, more passionate and hungry than that of American cats.

Then she said, "Et cette blouse—combien j'ai payé? Dis-moi."

"You paid—let me see—you paid three bucks for it."

"No, no," she cried, "sixty sen'. Solde!"

"Impossible. Why, that thing is worth five bucks. You must be the greatest shopper in New York."

Gratified, she gave him a brilliant wink and took off his socks, chafing his feet. She brought him tea and poured a double shot of Chivas Regal into it. For him she kept the best of everything. "Veux-tu scrombled eggs, chéri-koko. As-tu faim?" A cold rain was killing desolate New York with its green icy spikes. *When I pass Northwest Orient Airlines, I always mean to price a ticket to Tokyo.* She put soy sauce on the eggs. Herzog ate and drank. All the food was salty. He swallowed a great deal of tea. "We take bath," said Sono, and began to unbutton his shirt. "Tu veux?"

Teas and baths—the steam of boiling water loosened the wallpaper from the green plaster behind. The great console radio through a cloth-of-gold speaker played the music of Brahms. The cats were cuffing shrimp shells under the chairs.

"Oui—je veux bien," he said.

She went to run the water. He heard her singing as she sprinkled the lilac salts and bubble-bath powder.

I wonder who's scrubbing her now.

Sono asked for no great sacrifices. She did not want me to work for her, to furnish her house, support her children, to be regular at meals or to open charge accounts in luxury shops; she asked only that I should be with her from time to time. But some people are at war with the best things of life and pervert them into fantasies and dreams. The Yiddish French we spoke was funny but innocent. She told me no such broken truths and dirty lies as I heard in my own language, and my simple declarative sentences couldn't do her much harm. Other men have forsaken the West, looking for just this. It was delivered to me in New York City.

The bath was not without its occasional trials. At times, Sono examined Herzog's body for signs that he was unfaithful. Lovemaking, she was strongly convinced, turned men lean. "Ah!" she would say. "Tu as maigri. Tu fais amour?" He denied it but she shook her head, continuing to smile, though her face became puffy and bitter. She refused to believe him. But she would forgive him, at last. Her good humor returning, she put him in the tub, climbing in behind him. Singing, or growling mock orders at him in military Japanese. But peace had come. They bathed. She put her feet forward for him to soap. She dipped water in a plastic dish and poured it over his head. Draining the tub at last, she turned on the shower to rinse away the suds, and they stood together smiling under the spray. "Tu seras bien propre, chéri-koko."

Yes, she kept me very clean. With amusement and with sorrow, Herzog recalled it all.

They dried themselves with Turkish towels from 14th Street. She dressed him in the kimono, kissing his chest. He kissed the palms of her hands. Her eyes were tender, shrewd, they showed a thrifty light at times; she knew where to invest her sensuality and how to increase it. She sat him on the bed, and there she served him tea. Her concubine. They sat crosslegged, sipping from the small cups, looking at the scrolls. The door was bolted, the telephone off the hook. Tremulous, Sono's face came near, and she touched his cheek with her chub lips. They helped each other out of the Oriental garments. "Doucement, chéri. Oh, lentement. Oh!" Turning up her eyes so that he saw only the whites.

She tried to explain to me once that earth and the planets were sucked from the sun by a passing star. As if a dog should trot by a bush and set free worlds. And in those worlds life appeared, and within that life such as we—souls. And even stranger creatures than we, she said. I liked to hear this, but I didn't understand her well. I know I kept her from returning to Japan. For my sake, she disobeyed her father. Her mother died, and Sono did not mention it for weeks. And once she said, "Je ne crains pas la mort. Mais tu me fais souffrir, Moso." I hadn't called her in a month. She had had pneumonia again. No one had come to see her. She was weak and pale, and she cried and said, "Je souffre trop." But she did not let him comfort her; she had heard that he was seeing Madeleine Pontritter.

She did, however, say, "Elle est méchante, Moso. Je suis pas jalouse. Je ferai amour avec un autre. Tu m'as laissée. Mais elle a les yeux très, très froids."

He wrote, *Sono, you were right. I thought you might like to know. Her eyes are very cold*. Still, they are her eyes, and what is she to do about them? It would not be practical for her to hate herself. Luckily, God sends a substitute, a husband.

Ah, in the midst of such realizations, a man needs some comfort. Herzog once more set off on his visit to Ramona. As he stood at the door with the long metal shank of the police lock in his hand, his memory sought a certain song title. Was it "Just One More Kiss"? Not that. Nor "The Curse of an Aching Heart." "Kiss Me Again." That was it. It struck him very funny, and laughter made him clumsy as he set up the complicated lock to protect his worldly goods. Three thousand million human beings exist, each with *some* possessions, each a microcosmos, each infinitely precious, each with a peculiar treasure. There is a distant garden where curious objects grow, and there, in a lovely dusk of green, the heart of Moses E. Herzog hangs like a peach.

I need this outing like a hole in the head, he thought as he turned the key. Still, he was going, wasn't he. He was pocketing the key. And now ringing for the elevator. He listened to the sound of the power, the cables threshing. He went down alone, humming "Kiss Me," and trying to capture, as if it were an elusive fragile thread, the reason why these old songs were running through his head. Not the obvious reason. (He had an aching heart, was going forth to be kissed.) The recondite reason (if that was worth finding). He was glad to reach the open air, to breathe. He dried the sweatband of the straw hat with his handkerchief—it was hot in the shaft. And who wore such a hat, such a blazer? Why, Lou Holtz, of course, the old vaudeville comic. He sang, "I picked a lemon in the garden of love, where they say only *peaches* grow." Herzog's face again quickened with a smile. The old Oriental Theatre in Chicago. Three hours of entertainment for two bits.

At the corner he paused to watch the work of the wrecking crew. The great metal ball swung at the walls, passed easily through brick, and entered the rooms, the lazy weight browsing on kitchens and parlors. Everything it touched wavered and burst, spilled down. There rose a white tranquil cloud of plaster dust. The afternoon was ending, and in the widening area of demolition was a fire, fed by the wreckage. Moses heard the air, softly pulled toward the flames, felt the heat. The workmen, heaping the bonfire with wood, threw strips of molding like javelins. Paint and varnish smoked like incense. The old flooring burned gratefully—the funeral of exhausted objects. Scaffolds walled with pink, white, green doors quivered as the six-wheeled trucks carried off fallen brick. The sun, now leaving for New Jersey and the west, was surrounded by a dazzling broth of atmospheric gases. Herzog observed that people were spattered with red stains, and that he himself was flecked on the arms and chest. He crossed Seventh Avenue and entered the subway.

Out of the burning, the dust, down the stairs he hurried underground, listening for a train, fingers examining the coins in his pocket, seeking a subway token. He inhaled the odors of stone, of urine, bitterly tonic, the smells of rust and of lubricants, felt the presence of a current of urgency, speed, of infinite desire, possibly related to the drive within himself, his own streaming nervous vitality. (Passion? Perhaps hysteria? Ramona might relieve him by sexual means.) He took a long breath, inhaling the musty damp air endlessly, on and on, stabbed in both shoulders as his chest expanded, but continuing. Then he let the air out slowly, very slowly, down, down, into his belly.

He did it again, again, and felt better for it. He dropped his fare in the slot where he saw a whole series of tokens lighted from within and magnified by the glass. Innumerable millions of passengers had polished the wood of the turnstile with their hips. From this arose a feeling of communion—brotherhood in one of its cheapest forms. This was serious, thought Herzog as he passed through. The more individuals are destroyed (by processes such as I know) the worse their yearning for collectivity. Worse, because they return to the mass agitated, made fervent by their failure. Not as brethren, but as degenerates. Experiencing a raging consumption of potato love. Thus occurs a second distortion of the divine image, already so blurred, wavering, struggling. The real question! He stood looking down at the tracks. The most real question!

Rush hour was just ended. Almost empty local cars were scenes of rest and peace, conductors reading the papers. Waiting for his uptown express, Herzog made a tour of the platform, looking at the mutilated posters—blacked-out teeth and scribbled whiskers, comical genitals like rockets, ridiculous copulations, slogans and exhortations. *Moslems, the enemy is White. Hell with Goldwater, Jews! Spicks eat* SHIT. *Phone, I will go down on you if I like the sound of your voice.* And by a clever cynic, *If they smite you, turn the other face.* Filth, quarrelsome madness, the prayers and wit of the crowd. Minor works of Death. Trans-descendence—that was the new fashionable term for it. Herzog carefully examined all such writings, taking his own public-opinion poll. He assumed the unknown artists were adolescents. Taunting authority. Immaturity, a new political category. Problems connected with the increasing mental emancipation of untrained unemployables. Better the Beatles. Further occupying the idle moment, Herzog looked at the penny scale. The mirror was wired—could not be smashed except by an ingenious maniac. The benches were bolted down, the candy-vending machines padlocked.

A note to Willie the Actor, the famous bank robber now serving a life sentence. *Dear Mr. Sutton, The study of locks.* Mechanical devices and Yankee genius . . . He began again, *Second only to Houdini*, Willie never carried a gun. In Queens, once, he used a toy pistol. Disguised as a Western Union messenger, he entered the bank and took it over with his cap gun. The challenge was irresistible. Not the money, really, but the problem of getting in, and the companion problem of escape. Narrow-shouldered, with sunk cheeks and the mothy, dapper mustache, blue baggy eyes above, Willie lay thinking of banks. On his inadoor bed in Brooklyn, sucking a cigarette, wearing his hat and a pair of pointed shoes, he had visions of roofs leading to roofs, of power lines, sewer connections, vaults. All locks opened at his touch. Genius cannot let the world be. He had buried his loot in Flushing Meadows, in tin cans. He might have retired. But he took a walk, he saw a bank, a creative opportunity. This time he was caught and went to prison. But he planned a great getaway, made an elaborate mental survey and drew a master plan, crawled through pipes, dug under walls. He almost had it made. The stars were in view. But the screws were waiting when he broke through the earth. They carried him back—this insignificant person, the escape artist; one of the greatest, *and not very far behind Houdini, either. Motive: The power and completeness of all human systems must be continually tested, outwitted, at the risk of freedom, of life.* Now he is a lifer. They say he owns a set of the Great Books, corresponds with Bishop Sheen. . . .

Dear Dr. Schrodinger, In What Is Life? *you say that in all of nature only man hesitates to cause pain. As destruction is the master-method by which evolution produces new types, the reluctance to cause pain may express a human will to obstruct natural law. Christianity and its parent religion, a few short millennia, with frightful reverses* . . . The train had stopped, the door was already shutting when Herzog roused himself and squeezed through. He caught a strap. The express flew uptown. It emptied and refilled at Times Square, but he did not sit down. It was too hard to fight your way out again from a seat. Now, where were we? *In your remarks on entropy* . . . *How the organism maintains itself against death—in your words, against thermodynamic equilibrium* . . . *Being an unstable organization of matter, the body threatens to rush away from us. It leaves. It is real. It! Not we! Not I! This organism, while it has the power to hold its own form and suck what it needs from its environment, attracting a negative stream of entropy, the being of other things which it uses, returning the residue to the world in simpler form. Dung. Nitrogenous wastes. Ammonia.*

But reluctance to cause pain coupled with the necessity to devour . . . a peculiar human trick is the result, which consists in admitting and denying evils at the same time. To have a human life, and also an inhuman life. In fact, to have everything, to combine all elements with immense ingenuity and greed. To bite, to swallow. At the same time to pity your food. To have sentiment. At the same time to behave brutally. It has been suggested (and why not!) that reluctance to cause pain is actually an extreme form, a delicious form of sensuality, and that we increase the luxuries of pain by the injection of a moral pathos. Thus working both sides of the street. Nevertheless, there are moral realities, Herzog assured the entire world as he held his strap in the speeding car, *as surely as there are molecular and atomic ones. However, it is necessary today to entertain the very worst possibilities openly. In fact we have no choice as to that. . . .*

This was his station, and he ran up the stairs. The revolving gates rattled their multiple bars and ratchets behind him. He hastened by the change booth where a man sat in a light the color of strong tea, and up the two flights of stairs. In the mouth of the exit he stopped to catch his breath. Above him the flowering glass, wired and gray, and Broadway heavy and blue in the dusk, almost tropical; at the foot of the downhill eighties lay the Hudson, as dense as mercury. On the points of radio towers in New Jersey red lights like small hearts beat or tingled. In midstreet, on the benches, old people: on faces, on heads, the strong marks of decay: the big legs of women and blotted eyes of men, sunken mouths and inky nostrils. It was the normal hour for bats swooping raggedly (Ludeyville), or pieces of paper (New York) to remind Herzog of bats. An escaped balloon was fleeing like a sperm, black and quick into the orange dust of the west. He crossed the street, making a detour to avoid a fog of grilled chicken and sausage. The crowd was traipsing over the broad sidewalk. Moses took a keen interest in the uptown public, its theatrical spirit, its performers—the transvestite homosexuals painted with great originality, the wigged women, the lesbians looking so male you had to wait for them to pass and see them from behind to determine their true sex, hair dyes of every shade. Signs in almost every passing face of a deeper comment or interpretation of destiny—eyes that held metaphysical statements. And even pious old women who trod the path of ancient duty, still, buying kosher meat.

Herzog had several times seen George Hoberly, Ramona's friend before him, following him with his eyes from one or another of these doorways. He was thin, tall, younger than Herzog, correctly dressed in Ivy League Madison Avenue clothes, dark glasses on his lean, sad face. Ramona, with the accent on "nothing," said she felt nothing but pity for him. His two attempted suicides probably made her realize how indifferent she was to him. Moses had learned from Madeleine that when a woman was done with a man she was done with him utterly. But tonight it occurred to him that, since Ramona was keen on men's styles and often tried to guide his choices, Hoberly might be wearing the clothes she had picked for him. He is vainly appealing, in the trappings of his former happiness and love, like the trained mouse in the frustration experiment. Even being phoned by the police and running to Bellevue in the middle of the night to be by his side now bores Ramona. The whole feeling-and-sensation market has shot up—shock, scandal priced out of range for the average man. You have to do more than take a little gas, or slash the wrists. Pot? Zero! Daisy chains? Nothing! Debauchery? A museum word from prelibidinous times! The day is fast approaching—Herzog in his editorial state—when only proof that you are despairing will entitle you to the vote, instead of the means test, the poll tax, the literacy exam. You must be forlorn. Former vices now health measures. Everything changing. Public confession of each deep wound which at one time was borne as if nothing were amiss. A good subject: the history of composure in Calvinistic societies. When each man, feeling fearful damnation, had to behave as one of the elect. All such historic terrors —every agony of spirit—must at last be released. Herzog began to be almost eager to see Hoberly, to have another look at that face wasted by suffering, insomnia, nights of pills and drink, of prayer—his dark glasses, his almost brimless fedora. Unrequited love. Nowadays called hysterical dependency. There were times when Ramona spoke of Hoberly with great sympathy. She said she had been crying over one of his letters or gifts. He kept sending her purses and perfumes, and long extracts from his journal. He had even sent her a large sum in cash. This she turned over to Aunt Tamara. The old lady opened a savings account for him. Let the money gather a little interest, at least. Hoberly was attached to the old woman. Moses, too, was fond of her.

He rang Ramona's bell and the buzzer opened the lobby door at once. She was considerate that way. One more delicate attention. The arrival of her lover was never routine. The elevator let people out—a fellow with a heavy front, one eye shut, smoking a strong cigar; a woman with two chihuahuas, red nail polish matching the harness of the dogs. And perhaps in the whirling fumes of the street, through two glass doors, his rival watched him. Moses rode up. On the fifteenth floor Ramona had the door ajar, on the chain. She didn't want to be surprised by the wrong man. When she saw Moses, she unbolted and took his hand, drawing him to her side. She offered her face to him. Herzog found it full, and very hot. Her perfume sprang out at him. She wore a white satin blouse, cut to suggest the wrapping of a shawl and showing her bust. Her face was flushed; she did not need the added color of rouge. "I'm glad to see you, Ramona. I'm very glad," he said. He hugged her, discovering in himself a sudden eagerness, a hunger for contact. He kissed her.

"So—you're glad to see me?"

"I am! I am!"

She smiled and shut the door, bolting it again. She led Herzog by the hand along the uncarpeted hall where her heels made a military clatter. It excited him. "Now," she said, "let's have a look at Moses in his finery." They stopped before the gilt, ornate mirror. "You have a great straw hat. And what a coat—Joseph's coat of stripes."

"You approve?"

"I certainly do. It's a beautiful jacket. You look Indian in it, with your dark coloring."

"I may join the Bhave group."

"Which is that?"

"Sharing large estates among the poor. I'll give away Ludeyville."

"You'd better consult me before you start another giveaway program. Shall we have a drink? Perhaps you'd like to wash up while I get the drinks."

"I shaved before leaving the house."

"You look hot, as if you've been running, and you've got soot on your face."

He must have leaned against a subway pillar. Or perhaps it was a smudge from the wreckage bonfire. "Yes, I see."

"I'll get you a towel, dear," said Ramona.

In the bathroom, Herzog turned his tie to the back of his neck to keep it from drooping into the basin. This was a luxurious little room, with indirect lighting (kindness to haggard faces). The long tap glittered, the water rushed forth. He sniffed the soap. *Muguet.* The water felt very cold on his nails. He recalled the old Jewish ritual of nail water, and the word in the Haggadah, *Rachatz!* "Thou shalt wash." It was obligatory also to wash when you returned from the cemetery (*Beth Olam*—the Dwelling of the Multitude). But why think of cemeteries, of funerals, now? Unless . . . the old joke about the Shakespearean actor in the brothel. When he took off his pants, the whore in bed gave a whistle. He said, "Madam, we come to bury Caesar, not to praise him." How schoolboy jokes clung to you!

He opened his mouth under the tap and let the current run also into his shut eyes, gasping with satisfaction. Broad disks of iridescent brightness swam under his lids. He wrote to Spinoza, *Thoughts not causally connected were said by you to cause pain. I find that is indeed the case. Random association, when the intellect is passive, is a form of bondage. Or rather, every form of bondage is possible then. It may interest you to know that in the twentieth century random association is believed to yield up the deepest secrets of the psyche.* He realized he was writing to the dead. To bring the shades of great philosophers up to date. But then why shouldn't he write the dead? He lived with them as much as with the living—perhaps more; and besides, his letters to the living were increasingly mental, and anyway, to the Unconscious, what was death? Dreams did not recognize it. *Believing that reason can make steady progress from disorder to harmony and that the conquest of chaos need not be begun anew every day.* How I wish it! How I wish it were so! How Moses prayed for this!

As for his relation to the dead, it was very bad indeed. He really believed in letting the dead bury their own dead. And that life was life only when it was understood clearly as dying. He opened the large medicine chest. They used to build on the grand scale, in old New York. Fascinated, he studied Ramona's bottles—skin freshener, estrogenic deep-tissue lotion, Bonnie Belle antiperspirant. Then this crimson prescription— twice daily for upset stomach. He smelled it and thought it must contain belladonna—calming for the stomach, mydriatic in the eyes. Made of deadly nightshade. There were also pills for menstrual cramp. Somehow, he didn't think Ramona was the type. Madeleine used to scream. He had to take her in a taxi to St. Vincent's where she cried for a Demerol injection. These forceps-looking things he thought must be for curling the eyelashes. They looked like the snail tongs in a French restaurant. He sniffed the scouring mitten. Especially for the elbows and heels, he thought, to rub away the bumps. He pressed the toilet lever with his foot; it flushed with silent power; the toilets of the poor always made noise. He applied a little brilliantine to the dry ends of his hair. His shirt was damp, of course, but she was wearing perfume enough for them both. And how was he otherwise? All things considered, not too bad. Ruin comes to beauty, inevitably. The space-time continuum reclaims its elements, taking you away bit by bit, and then again comes the void. But better the void than the torment and boredom of an incorrigible character, doing always the same stunts, repeating the same disgraces. But these instants of disgrace and pain could seem eternal, so that if a man could capture the eternity of these painful moments and give them a different content, he would achieve a revolution. How about that!

Wrapping the palm of his hand tightly in the towel, like a barber, Herzog wiped the drops of moisture at his hairline. Next he thought he would weigh himself. He used the toilet first, to make himself a little lighter, and stripped off his shoes without bending, climbing on the scale with an elderly sigh. Between his toes, the pointer swept past the 170 mark. He was regaining the weight he had lost in Europe. He forced his feet into the shoes again, treading down the backs, and returned to Ramona's sitting room—her sitting and sleeping room. She was waiting with two glasses of Campari. Its taste was bitter-sweet and its odor a little gassy—from the gas main. But all the

world was drinking it, and Herzog drank it too. Ramona had
chilled the glasses in the freezer.

"*Salud.*"

"*Sdrutch!*" he said.

"Your necktie is hanging down your back."

"Is it?" He pulled it to the front again. "Forgetful. I once
tucked my jacket into the back of my trousers, coming from
the gentlemen's room, and walked in to teach a class."

Ramona seemed astonished that he would tell such a story
on himself. "Wasn't that dreadful?"

"Not too good. But it should have been very liberating for
the students. Teacher is mortal. Besides, the humiliation didn't
destroy him. This should have been more valuable than the
course itself. In fact, one of the young ladies told me later I
was very human—such a relief to us all. . . ."

"What is funny is how completely you answer any question.
You are a funny man." Engagingly affectionate; her fine large
teeth, tender dark eyes, enriched by black lines, smiled upon
him. "It's the way you try to sound rough or reckless,
though—like a guy from Chicago—that's even more amusing."

"Why amusing?"

"It's an act. Swagger. It's not really you." She refilled his
glass and stood up to go to the kitchen. "I've got to look after
the rice. I'll put on some Egyptian music to keep you cheerful." A wide patent-leather belt set off her waist. She bent over
the phonograph.

"The food smells delicious."

Mohammad al Bakkar and his band began with drums and
tambourines, and then a clatter of wires and braying wind instruments. A guttural pimping voice began to sing, "Mi Port
Said . . ." Herzog, alone, looked at the books and theater
programs, magazines and pictures. A photograph of Ramona
as a little girl stood in a Tiffany frame—seven years old, a wise
child leaning on a bank of plush, her finger pressing on her
temple. He remembered the pose. A generation ago it used to
get them. Little Einsteins. Prodigious wisdom in children.
Pierced ears, a locket, a kiss-me curl, and the kind of early sensuality in tiny girls which he recalled very well.

Aunt Tamara's clock began to chime. He went into her parlor to look at its old-fashioned porcelain face with long gilt

lines, like cat whiskers, and listened to the bright quick notes. Beneath it was the key. To own a clock like this you had to have regular habits—a permanent residence. Raising the window shade of this little European parlor with its framed scenes of Venice and friendly Dutch porcelain inanities, you saw the Empire State Building, the Hudson, the green, silver evening, half of New York lighting up. Thoughtful, he pulled the shade down again. This—this asylum was his for the asking, he believed. Then why didn't he ask? Because today's asylum might be the dungeon of tomorrow. To listen to Ramona, it was all very simple. She said she understood his needs better than he, and she might well be right. Ramona never hesitated to express herself fully, and there was something unreserved, positively operatic about some of her speeches. Opera. Heraldry. She said her feelings for him had depth and maturity and that she had an enormous desire to help him. She told Herzog that he was a better man than he knew—a deep man, beautiful (he could not help wincing when she said this), but sad, unable to take what his heart really desired, a man tempted by God, longing for grace, but escaping headlong from his salvation, often close at hand. This Herzog, this man of many blessings, for some reason had endured a frigid, middlebrow, castrating female in his bed, given her his name and made her the instrument of creation, and Madeleine had treated him with contempt and cruelty as if to punish him for lowering and cheapening himself, for lying himself into love with her and betraying the promise of his soul. What he really must do, she went on, in this same operatic style—unashamed to be so fluent; he marveled at this—was to pay his debt for the great gifts he had received, his intelligence, his charm, his education, and free himself to pursue the meaning of life, not by disintegration, where he would never find it, but humbly and yet proudly continuing his learned studies. She, Ramona, wanted to add riches to his life and give him what he pursued in the wrong places. This she could do by the art of love, she said—the art of love which was one of the sublime achievements of the spirit. It was love she meant by riches. What he had to learn from her—while there was time; while he was still virile, his powers substantially intact—was how to renew the spirit through the flesh (a precious vessel in which the spirit rested). Ramona—bless her!—was as florid in these sermons as in her looks. Oh, what a sweet orator she was! But where were we? Ah, yes, he was to continue his studies, aiming at the meaning of life. He, Herzog, overtake life's meaning! He laughed into his hands, covering his face.

But (sobering) he knew that he elicited these speeches by his airs. Why did little Sono cry, "O mon philosophe—mon professeur d'amour!"? Because Herzog behaved like a philosophe who cared only about the very highest things—creative reason, how to render good for evil, and all the wisdom of old books. Because he thought and cared about belief. (Without which, human life is simply the raw material of technological transformation, of fashion, salesmanship, industry, politics, finance, experiment, automatism, et cetera, et cetera. The whole inventory of disgraces which one is glad to terminate in death.) Yes, he looked like, behaved like, Sono's philosophe.

And after all, why was he here? He was here because Ramona also took him seriously. She thought she could restore order and sanity to his life, and if she did that it would be logical to marry her. Or, in her style, he would desire to be united with her. And it would be a union that really unified. Tables, beds, parlors, money, laundry and automobile, culture and sex knit into one web. Everything would at last make sense, was what she meant. Happiness was an absurd and even harmful idea, unless it was really comprehensive; but in this exceptional and lucky case where each had experienced the worst sorts of morbidity and come through by a miracle, by an instinct for survival and delight which was positively religious—there was simply no other way to talk about her life, said Ramona, except in terms of Magdalene Christianity—comprehensive happiness was possible. In that case, it was a duty; to refuse to answer the accusations against happiness (that it was a monstrous and selfish delusion, an absurdity) was cowardly, a surrender to malignancy, capitulating to the death instinct. Here was a man, Herzog, who knew what it was to rise from the dead. And she, Ramona, she knew the bitterness of death and nullity, too. Yes, she too! But with him she experienced a real Easter. She knew what Resurrection was. He might look down his conscious nose at sensual delight, but with her, when their clothes were off, he knew what it was. No amount of sublimation could replace that erotic happiness, that knowledge.

Not even tempted to smile, Moses listened earnestly, bowing his head. Some of it was current university or paperback chatter and some was propaganda for marriage, but, after such debits were entered against her, she was genuine. He sympathized with her, respected her. It was all real enough. She had something genuine at heart.

When he jeered in private at the Dionysiac revival it was himself he made fun of. Herzog! A prince of the erotic Renaissance, in his *macho* garments! And what about the kids? How would they like a new stepmother? And Ramona, would she take Junie to see Santa Claus?

"Ah, this is where you are," said Ramona. "Aunt Tamara would be flattered if she knew you were interested in her Czarist museum."

"These old-time interiors," said Herzog.

"Isn't it touching?"

"They drugged you with schmaltz."

"The old woman is so fond of you."

"I like her, too."

"She says you brighten up the house."

"That *I* . . ." He smiled.

"Why not? You have a tender trusting face. You can't bear to hear that, can you. Why not?"

"I put the old woman out when I come," he said.

"You're wrong. She loves these trips. She puts on a hat, and gets dressed up. It's such a thing for her to go to the railroad station. Anyway . . ." Ramona's tone changed. "She needs to get away from George Hoberly. He's become her problem now." For a brief instant she was downcast.

". . . Sorry," said Herzog. "Has it been bad lately?"

"Poor man . . . I feel so sorry for him. But come, Moses, dinner is all ready and I want you to open the wine." In the dining room she handed him the bottle—Pouilly Fuissé, well chilled—and the French corkscrew. With competent hands and strong purpose, his neck reddening as he exerted himself, he pulled the cork. Ramona had lighted the candles. The table was decorated with spiky red gladiolas in a long dish. On the windowsill the pigeons stirred and grumbled; they fluttered and went to sleep again. "Let me help you to this rice," said Ramona. She took the plate, good bone china with a cobalt rim (the steady spread of luxury into all ranks of society since the fifteenth century, noted by the famous Sombart, inter alia). But Herzog was hungry, and the dinner was delicious. (He would become austere hereafter.) Tears of curious, mixed origin came into his eyes as he tasted the shrimp remoulade. "Awfully good—my God, how good!" he said.

"Haven't you eaten all day?" said Ramona.

"I haven't seen food like this for some time. Prosciutto and Persian melon. What's this? Watercress salad. Good Christ!"

She was pleased. "Well, eat," she said.

After the shrimp Arnaud and salad, she offered cheese and cold-water biscuits, rum-flavored ice cream, plums from Georgia, and early green grapes. Then brandy and coffee. In the next room, Mohammad al Bakkar kept singing his winding, nasal, insinuating songs to the sounds of wire coathangers moved back and forth, and drums, tambourines and mandolins and bagpipes.

"What have you been doing?" said Ramona.

"Me? Oh, all kinds of things. . . ."

"Where did you go on the train? Were you running away from me?"

"Not from you. But I suppose I was running."

"You're still a little afraid of me, aren't you."

"I wouldn't say that. . . . Confused. Trying to be careful."

"You're used to difficult women. To struggle. Perhaps you like it when they give you a bad time."

"Every treasure is guarded by dragons. That's how you can tell it's valuable. . . . Do you mind if I unbutton my collar? It seems to be pressing on an artery."

"But you came right back. Perhaps that was because of me."

Moses was strongly tempted to lie to her, to say, "Yes, Ramona, it was you." Strict and literal truthfulness was a trivial game and might even be a disagreeable neurotic affliction. Ramona had Moses' complete sympathy—a woman in her thirties, successful in business, independent, but still giving such suppers to gentlemen friends. But in times like these, how should a woman steer her heart to fulfillment? In emancipated

New York, man and woman, gaudily disguised, like two savages belonging to hostile tribes, confront each other. The man wants to deceive, and then to disengage himself; the woman's strategy is to disarm and detain him. And this is Ramona, a woman who knows how to look after herself. Think how it is with some young thing, raising mascara-ringed eyes to heaven, praying, "Oh, Lord, let no bad man come unto my chubbiness."

Besides which, Herzog realized that to eat Ramona's shrimp and drink her wine, and then sit in her parlor listening to the straggling lustfulness of Mohammad al Bakkar and his Port Said specialists, thinking such thoughts, was not exactly commendable. *And Monsignor Hilton, what is priestly celibacy? A more terrible discipline is to go about and visit women, to see what the modern world has made of carnality. How little relevance certain ancient ideas have. . . .*

But at least one thing became clear. To look for fulfillment in another, in interpersonal relationships, was a feminine game. And the man who shops from woman to woman, though his heart aches with idealism, with the desire for pure love, has entered the female realm. After Napoleon fell, the ambitious young man carried his power drive into the boudoir. And there the women took command. As Madeleine had done, as Wanda might as easily have done. And what about Ramona? And Herzog, formerly a silly young thing, now becoming a silly old thing, by accepting the design of a *private life* (approved by those in authority) turned himself into something resembling a concubine. Sono made this entirely clear, with her Oriental ways. He had even joked about it with her, trying to explain how unprofitable his visits to her appeared to him at last. "*Je bêche, je sème, mais je ne récolte point.*" He joked—but no, he was no concubine, not at all. He was a difficult, aggressive man. As for Sono, she was trying to instruct him, to show how a man should treat a woman. The pride of the peacock, the lust of the goat, and the wrath of the lion are the glory and wisdom of God.

"Wherever you were going, with your valise, your fundamentally healthy instincts brought you back. They're wiser than you," said Ramona.

"Maybe . . ." said Herzog. "I am going through a change of outlook."

"Thank goodness you haven't destroyed your birthright yet."

"I haven't been really independent. I find I've been working for others, for a number of ladies."

"If you can conquer your Hebrew puritanism . . ."

"Developing the psychology of a runaway slave."

"It's your own fault. You look for domineering women. I'm trying to tell you that you've met a different type in me."

"I know I have," he said. "And I think the world of you."

"I wonder. I don't think you understand." Here she showed some resentment. "About a month ago you told me I ran a sexual circus. As if I were an acrobat of some kind."

"Why, Ramona, that meant nothing."

"It implied that I had known too many men."

"Too many? No, Ramona. I don't look at it that way. If anything, it does a lot for my self-esteem to be able to keep up."

"Why, the very idea of keeping up betrays you. It makes me angry to hear you say that."

"I know. You want to put me on a higher level and bring out the Orphic element in me. But I've tried to be a pretty mediocre person, if the truth be told. I've done my job, kept up my end, performed my duty, and waited for the old quid pro quo. What I had coming, naturally, was a sock on the head. I thought I had entered into a secret understanding with life to spare me the worst. A perfectly bourgeois idea. On the side, I was just flirting a little with the transcendent."

"There's nothing so ordinary about marrying a woman like Madeleine or having a friend like Valentine Gersbach."

His indignation rose, and he tried to check it. Ramona was being considerate, giving him a chance to sound off to release spleen. This was not what he had come for. And anyway he was growing tired of his obsession. Besides, she had troubles of her own. And the poet said that indignation was a kind of joy, but was he right? There is a time to speak and a time to shut up. The only truly interesting side of the matter was the intimate design of the injury, the fact that it was so penetrating, custom-made exactly to your measure. It's fascinating that hatred should be so personal as to be almost loving. The knife and the wound aching for each other. Much of course depends upon the vulnerability of the intended. Some cry out, and some swallow the thrust in silence. About the latter you could write the inner history of mankind. How did Papa feel when he found that Voplonsky was in cahoots with the hijackers? He never said.

Herzog wondered whether he would succeed in holding all this in, tonight. He hoped he would. But Ramona often encouraged him to give in to it. She not only spread a supper but invited him to sing.

"I don't think of them as exactly a mediocre pair," she said.

"I sometimes see all three of us as a comedy team," said Herzog, "with me playing straight man. People say that Gersbach imitates me—my walk, my expressions. He's a second Herzog."

"Anyway, he convinced Madeleine that he was superior to the original," said Ramona. She lowered her eyes. They moved and then came to rest beneath the lids. By candlelight, he observed this momentary disquiet of her face. Perhaps she thought she had spoken tactlessly.

"Madeleine's greatest ambition, I think, is to fall in love. This is the deepest part of the joke about her. Then there's her grand style. Her tics. To give the bitch her due, she is beautiful. She adores being the center of attention. In one of those fur-trimmed suits she struts in, with her deep color and blue eyes. And when she has an audience and begins spellbinding, there's a kind of flat pass she makes with the palm of her hand, and her nose twitches like a little rudder, and by and by one brow joins in and begins to rise, rise."

"You make her sound adorable," said Ramona.

"We lived together on a high level, all of us. Except Phoebe. She merely went along."

"What is she like?"

"She has attractive features but she looks severe. She comes on like the head nurse."

"She didn't care for you?"

". . . Her husband was a cripple. He knows how to make the most of it, emotionally, with his lurid sob stuff. She had bought him cheap because he was factory damaged. New and perfect, she could never have afforded such a luxury. He knew and she knew and we knew. Because this is an age of insight. The laws of psychology are known to all educated people. Anyway, he was only a one-legged radio announcer but she had him to herself. Then Madeleine and I arrived, and a glamorous life began in Ludeyville."

"It must have upset her when he began to imitate you."

"Yes. But if I was going to be swindled the best way was to do the job in my own style. Poetic justice. Philosophical piety describes the style."

"When did you first notice?"

"When Mady began to stay away from Ludeyville. A few times she holed up in Boston. She said she simply had to be alone and think things over. So she took the kid—just an infant. And I asked Valentine to go and reason with her."

"And this was when he began to give you those lectures?"

Herzog tried to smile away the quick-welling rancor whose source had been touched. He might not be able to control it. "They all lectured. Everyone lectured. People legislate continually by means of talk. I have Madeleine's letters from Boston. I have letters from Gersbach, too. All kinds of documents. I even have a bundle of letters written by Madeleine to her mother. They came in the mail."

"But what did Madeleine say?"

"She's quite a writer. She writes like Lady Hester Stanhope. First of all, she said I resembled her father in too many ways. That when we were in a room together *I* seemed to swallow and gulp up all the air and left nothing for her to breathe. I was overbearing, infantile, demanding, sardonic, and a psychosomatic bully."

"Psychosomatic?"

"I had pains in my belly in order to dominate her, and got my way by being sick. They all said that, all three of them. Madeleine had another lecture about the only basis for a marriage. A marriage was a tender relationship resulting from the overflow of feeling, and all the rest of that. She even had a lecture about the right way to perform the conjugal act."

"Incredible."

"She must have been describing what she had learned from Gersbach."

"You don't need to go into it," said Ramona. "I'm sure she made it as painful as possible."

"In the meantime, I was supposed to wind up this study of mine, and become the Lovejoy of my generation—that's the silly talk of scholarly people, Ramona, I didn't think of it that way. The more Madeleine and Gersbach lectured me, the more I thought that my only purpose was to lead a quiet, regular life. She said this quietness was more of my scheming. She accused me of being on 'a meek kick,' and said that I was now trying to keep her in line by a new tactic."

"How curious! What were you supposed to be doing?"

"She thought I had married her in order to be 'saved,' and now I wanted to kill her because she wasn't doing the job. She said she loved me, but couldn't do what I demanded, because this was so fantastic, and so she was going to Boston one more time to think it all through and find a way to save this marriage."

"I see."

"About a week later, Gersbach came to the house to pick up some of her things. She had phoned him from Boston. She needed her clothes. And money. He and I took a long walk in the woods. It was early autumn—sunny, dusty, marvelous . . . melancholy. I helped him over the rough ground. He poles his way along, with that leg. . . ."

"As you told me. Like a gondolier. And what did he say?"

"He said he didn't know how the fuck he would survive this terrible trouble between the two people he loved most in the world. He repeated that—the two people who meant more to him than wife and child. It was tearing him to pieces. His faith in things was going to be smashed."

Ramona laughed, and Herzog joined her.

"And then?"

"Then?" said Herzog. He remembered the tremor in Gersbach's dark-red powerful face which seemed at first brutal, the face of a butcher, until you came to understand the depth and subtlety of his feelings. "Then we went back to the house and Gersbach packed her things. And what he had mainly come for—her diaphragm."

"You don't mean it!"

"Of course I mean it."

"But you seem to accept it. . . ."

"What I accept is that my idiocy inspired them, and sent them to greater heights of perversity."

"Didn't you ask her what this meant?"

"I did. She said I had lost my right to an answer. It was more of the same from me—pettiness. Then I asked her whether Valentine had become her lover."

"And what kind of answer did you get?" Ramona's curiosity was greatly excited.

"That I didn't understand what Gersbach had given me—the kind of love, the kind of feeling. I said, 'But he took the thing from the medicine chest.' And she said, 'Yes, and he stays overnight with June and me when he comes to Boston, but he's the brother I never had, and that's all.' I hesitated to accept this, so she added, 'Now don't be a fool, Moses. You know how coarse he is. He's not my type at all. Our intimacy is a different kind altogether. Why, when he uses the toilet in our little Boston apartment it fills up with his stink. I know the smell of his shit. Do you think I could give myself to a man whose shit smells like that!' That was her answer."

"How frightful, Moses! Is that what she said? What a strange woman. She's a strange, strange creature."

"Well, it shows how much we know about one another, Ramona. Madeleine wasn't just a wife, but an education. A good, steady, hopeful, rational, diligent, dignified, childish person like Herzog who thinks human life is a subject, like any other subject, has to be taught a lesson. And certainly anyone who takes dignity seriously, old-fashioned individual dignity, is bound to get the business. Maybe dignity was imported from France. Louis Quatorze. Theater. Command. Authority. Anger. Forgiveness. *Majesté*. The plebeian, bourgeois ambition was to inherit this. It all belongs in the museum now."

"But I thought Madeleine herself was always so dignified."

"Not always. She could turn against her own pretensions. And don't forget, Valentine is a great personality, too. Modern consciousness has this great need to explode its own postures. It teaches the truth of the creature. It throws shit on all pretensions and fictions. A man like Gersbach can be gay. Innocent. Sadistic. Dancing around. Instinctive. Heartless. Hugging his friends. Feeble-minded. Laughing at jokes. Deep, too. Exclaiming 'I *love* you!' or 'This I *believe*.' And while moved by these 'beliefs' he steals you blind. He makes realities nobody can understand. A radio-astronomer will sooner understand what's happening in space ten billion light years away than what Gersbach is fabricating in his brain."

"You're far too excited about it," said Ramona. "My advice is to forget them both. How long did this stupidity go on?"

"Years. Several years, anyway. Madeleine and I got together again, a while after this. And then she and Valentine ran my life for me. I didn't know a thing about it. All the decisions were made by them—where I lived, where I worked, how much rent I paid. Even my mental problems were set by them. They gave me my homework. And when they decided that I had to go, they worked out all the details—property settlement, alimony, child support. I'm sure Valentine thought he acted in my best interests. He must have held Madeleine back. He knows he's a good man. He understands, and when you understand you suffer more. You have higher responsibilities, responsibilities that come with suffering. I couldn't take care of my wife, poor fish. He took care of her. I wasn't fit to bring up my own daughter. He has to do it for me, out of friendship, out of pity and sheer greatness of soul. He even agrees that Madeleine is a psychopath."

"No, you can't mean it!"

"I do. 'The poor crazy bitch,' he'd say. 'My heart goes out to that cracked broad!'"

"So he's mysterious, too. What a strange pair!" she said.

"Of course he is," said Herzog.

"Moses," said Ramona. "Let's stop talking about this, please. I feel there's something wrong in it. . . . Wrong for us. Now come . . ."

"You haven't heard it all. There's Geraldine's letter, telling how they mistreat the kid."

"I know. I've read it. Moses, no more."

"But . . . Yes, you're right," said Herzog. "Okay, I'll stop it right now. I'll help you clear the table."

"There's no need to."

"I'll wash the dishes."

"No, you certainly will not wash dishes. You're a guest here. I intend to put them all in the sink, for tomorrow."

He thought, I prefer to accept as a motive not the thing I fully understand but the thing I partly understand. Utter clarity of explanation to me is false. However, I must take care of June.

"No, no, Ramona, there's something about washing dishes that calms me. Now and then, anyway." He fixed the drain, put in soap powder, ran the water, hung his coat on the knob of a cupboard, tucked up his sleeves. He refused the apron Ramona offered. "I'm an old hand. I won't splash."

As even Ramona's fingers were sexual, Herzog wanted to see how she would do ordinary tasks. But the kitchen towel in her hands as she dried the glasses and silver looked natural. So she was not simply pretending to be a homebody. Herzog had at times wondered whether it wasn't Aunt Tamara who prepared the shrimp remoulade before she slipped out. The answer was no. Ramona did her own cooking.

"You should be thinking about your future," said Ramona. "What are you planning to do next year?"

"I can pick up a job of some sort."

"Where?"

"I can't decide whether to be near my son Marco, in the east, or go back to Chicago to keep an eye on June."

"Listen, Moses, it's no disgrace to be practical. Is it a point of honor or something, not to think clearly? You want to win by sacrificing yourself? It doesn't work, as you ought to know by now. Chicago would be a mistake. You'd only suffer."

"Perhaps, and suffering is another bad habit."

"Are you joking?"

"Not at all," he said.

"It's hard to imagine a more masochistic situation. Everybody in Chicago knows your story by now. You'd be in the middle of it. Fighting, arguing, getting hurt. That's too humiliating for a man like you. You don't respect yourself enough. Do you want to be torn to pieces? Is that what you're offering to do for little June?"

"No, no. What good is that? But can I turn the child over to those two? You read what Geraldine said." He knew that letter by heart, and was prepared to recite it.

"Still, you can't take the child from her mother."

"She's my kind. She has my genes. She's a Herzog. They're mentally alien types."

He grew tense again. Ramona tried to draw him away from this subject.

"Didn't you tell me that your friend Gersbach has become a kind of figure in Chicago?"

"Yes, yes. He started out in educational radio, and now he's all over the place. On committees, in the papers. He gives lectures to the Hadassah . . . readings of his poems. In the Temples. He's joining the Standard Club. He's on television! Fantastic! He was such a provincial character, he thought there was only one railroad station in Chicago. And now he's turned out to be a terrific operator—covers the city in his Lincoln Continental, wearing a tweed coat of a sort of salmon-puke color."

"You're getting into a state just thinking about it," said Ramona. "Your eyes get feverish."

"Gersbach hired a hall, did I tell you?"

"No."

"He sold tickets to a reading of his poems. My friend Asphalter told me about it. Five dollars for the front seats, three bucks at the back of the hall. Reading a poem about his grandfather who was a street sweeper, he broke down and cried. Nobody could get out. The hall was locked."

Ramona could not help laughing.

"Ha-ha!" Herzog let out the water, wringing the rag, sprinkling scouring power. He scrubbed and rinsed the sink. Ramona brought him a slice of lemon for the fishy smell. He squeezed it over his hands. "Gersbach!"

"Still," said Ramona earnestly. "You ought to get back to your scholarly work."

"I don't know. I feel I'm stuck with it. But what else is there for me to do?"

"You only say that because you're agitated. You'll think differently when you're calm."

"Maybe."

She led the way to her room. "Shall I play more of that Egyptian music? It has a good effect." She went to the machine. "And why don't you take your shoes off, Moses. I know you like to remove them in this weather."

"It does relieve my feet. I think I will. They're already unlaced."

The moon was high over the Hudson. Distorted by window glass, distorted by summer air, appearing bent by its own white power, it floated also in the currents of the river. The narrow rooftops below were pale, long figures of constriction beneath the moon. Ramona turned the record over, and now a woman was singing to the music of al Bakkar's band "*Viens, viens dans mes bras—je te donne du chocolat.*"

Sitting on the hassock beside him, Ramona took his hand. "But what they tried to make you believe," she said. "It just isn't true."

This was what he was aching to hear from her. "What do you mean?"

"I know something about men. As soon as I saw you I realized how much of you was unused. Erotically. Untouched, even."

"I've been a terrible flop at times. A total flop."

"There are some men who should be protected . . . by law, if necessary."

"Like fish and game?"

"I am not really joking," she said. He saw plainly, clearly, how kind she was. She felt for him. She knew he was in pain, and what the pain was, and she offered the consolation he had evidently come for. "They tried to make you feel that you were old and finished. But let me explain one fact. An old man smells old. Any woman can tell you. When an old man takes a woman in his arms she can smell a stale, dusty kind of thing, like old clothes that need an airing. If the woman has let things go as far as that, and doesn't want to humiliate him when she finds that he really is quite old (people do disguise themselves and it's hard to guess), she will probably go on with it. And that is so awful! But Moses, you are chemically youthful." She put her bare arms about his neck. "Your skin has a delicious odor. . . . What does Madeleine know. She's nothing but a packaged beauty."

He thought what a fine achievement he had made of his life that—aging, vain, terribly narcissistic, suffering without proper dignity—he was taking comfort from someone who really didn't have too much of it to spare him. He had seen her when she was tired, upset and weak, when the shadows came over her eyes, when the fit of her skirt was wrong and she had cold hands, cold lips parted on her teeth, when she was lying on her sofa, a woman of short frame, very full, but after all, a tired, short woman whose breath had the ashen flavor of fatigue. The story then told itself—struggles and disappointments; an elaborate system of theory and eloquence at the bottom of which lay the simple facts of need, a woman's need. She senses that I am for the family. For I am a family type, and she wants me for her family. Her idea of family behavior appeals to me. She was brushing his lips back and forth with hers. She was leading him (somewhat aggressively) away from hatred and fanatical infighting. Her head thrown back, she breathed quickly with excitement, skill, purpose. She began to bite his lip and he drew back, but only from surprise. She held fast to his lip, taking in more of it, and the result was a leap of sexual excitement in Herzog. She was unbuttoning his shirt. Her hand was on his skin. She also reached behind, turning on the hassock, to undo the back of her blouse with the other hand. They held each other. He began to stroke her hair. The scent of lipstick and the odor of flesh came from her mouth. But suddenly they interrupted their kissing. The phone was ringing.

"Oh, lord!" said Ramona. "Lord, lord!"

"Are you going to answer?"

"No, it's George Hoberly. He must have seen you arrive, and he wants to spoil things for us. We mustn't allow him to. . . ."

"I'm not in favor of it," said Herzog.

She turned over the phone and silenced it with the switch at the base. "He had me in tears again, yesterday."

"He wanted to give you a sports car, last I heard."

"Now he's urging me to take him to Europe. I mean, he wants me to show him Europe."

"I didn't know he had that sort of money."

"He doesn't. He'd have to borrow. It would cost ten thousand dollars, staying at the Grand Hotels."

"I wonder what he's trying to get across?"

"What do you mean?" Ramona found something suspect in Herzog's tone.

"Nothing . . . nothing. Only that he thinks you have the sort of money a tour like that would take."

"Money has nothing to do with it. There's simply nothing more in the relationship."

"What was there to begin with?"

"I thought there was something. . . ." Her hazel eyes gave him an odd look; they reproved him; or, more in sadness, asked him why he wanted to say such queer things. "Do you want to make an issue of this?"

"What's he doing in the street?"

"It's not my fault."

"He made his great pitch for you, and failed, so now he thinks he's under a curse and wants to kill himself. He'd be better off at home, on his sofa, drinking a can of beer, watching Perry Mason."

"You're too severe," said Ramona. "Maybe you think I'm giving him up for you and it makes you uneasy. You feel you're pushing him out and will have to be his replacement."

Herzog paused, reflecting, and leaned back in his chair. "Perhaps," he said. "But I think it's that while in New York I am the man inside, in Chicago the man in the street is me."

"But you're not in the least like George Hoberly," said Ramona with that musical lift he very much liked to hear. Her voice, when it was drawn up from her breast, and changed its tone in her throat—that gave Moses great pleasure. Another man might not react to its intended sensuality, but he did. "I took pity on George. For that reason it could never be anything but a temporary relationship. But you—you aren't the kind of man a woman feels sorry for. You aren't weak, whatever else. You have strength. . . ."

Herzog nodded. Once more he was being lectured. And he didn't really mind it. That he needed straightening out was only too obvious. And who had more right than a woman who gave him asylum, shrimp, wine, music, flowers, sympathy, gave him room, so to speak, in her soul, and finally the embrace of her body? We must help one another. In this irrational world, where mercy, compassion, heart (even if a *little* fringed with self-interest), all rare things—hard-won in many human battles fought by rare minorities, victories whose results should never be taken for granted, for they were seldom reliable in anyone— rare things, were often debunked, renounced, repudiated by every generation of skeptics. Reason itself, logic, urged you to kneel and give thanks for every small sign of true kindness. The music played. Surrounded by summer flowers and articles of beauty, even luxury, under the soft green lamp, Ramona spoke to him earnestly—he looked affectionately at her warm face, its ripe color. Beyond, hot New York; an illuminated night which did not need the power of the moon. The Oriental rug and its flowing designs held out the hope that great perplexities might be resolved. He held Ramona's soft cool arm in his fingers. His shirt was open on his chest. He was smiling, nodding a little as he listened to her. Much of what she said was perfectly right. She was a clever woman and, even better, a dear woman. She had a good heart. And she had on black lace underpants. He knew she did.

"You have great capacity for life," she was saying. "And you're a very loving man. But you must try to break away from grudges. They'll eat you up."

"I think that's true."

"I know you think I theorize too much. But I've taken more than one beating myself—a terrible marriage, and a whole series of bad relationships. Look—you have the strength to recover, and it's sinful not to use it. Use it now."

"I see what you mean."

"Maybe it's biology," said Ramona. "You have a powerful system. You know what? The woman in the bakery told me yesterday I was looking so changed—my complexion, my eyes, she said. 'Miss Donsell, you must be in love.' And I realized it was because of you."

"You do look changed," said Moses.

"Prettier?"

"Lovely," he said.

Her color deepened still more. She took his hand and placed it inside her blouse, looking steadily at him, eyes growing fluid. Bless the girl! What pleasure she gave him. All her ways satisfied him—her French-Russian-Argentine-Jewish ways "Let's take off your shoes, too," he said.

Ramona turned out all the lights except the green lamp by the bed. She whispered, "I'll be right back."

"Would you switch off that whining Egyptian, please? He needs his tongue wiped with a dishrag."

She stopped the phonograph with a touch, and said, "Just a few minutes," softly closing the door.

"A few minutes" was a figure of speech. She was long at her preparations. He had gotten used to waiting, saw the point of it, and was no longer impatient. Her reappearance was always dramatic and worth waiting for. In substance, however, he understood that she was trying to teach him something and he was trying (the habit of obedience to teaching being so strong in him) to learn from her. But how was he to describe this lesson? The description might begin with his wild internal disorder, or even with the fact that he was quivering. And why? Because he let the entire world press upon him. For instance? Well, for instance, what it means to be a man. In a city. In a century. In transition. In a mass. Transformed by science. Under organized power. Subject to tremendous controls. In a condition caused by mechanization. After the late failure of radical hopes. In a society that was no community and devalued the person. Owing to the multiplied power of numbers which made the self negligible. Which spent military billions against foreign enemies but would not pay for order at home. Which permitted savagery and barbarism in its own great cities. At the same time, the pressure of human millions who have discovered what concerted efforts and thoughts can do. As megatons of water shape organisms on the ocean floor. As tides polish stones. As winds hollow cliffs. The beautiful supermachinery opening a new life for innumerable mankind. Would you deny them the right to exist? Would you ask them to labor and go hungry while you enjoyed delicious old-fashioned Values? You—you yourself are a child of this mass and a brother to all the rest. Or else an ingrate, dilettante, idiot. There, Herzog, thought Herzog, since you ask for the instance, is the way it runs. On top of that, an injured heart, and raw gasoline poured on the nerves. And to this, what does Ramona answer? She says, get your health back. *Mens sana in corpore sano.* Constitutional tension of whatever origin needed sexual relief. Whatever the man's age, history, condition, knowledge, culture, development, he had an erection. Good currency anywhere. Recognized by the Bank of England. Why should his memories injure him now? Strong natures, said F. Nietzsche, could forget what they could not master. Of course he also said that the semen reabsorbed was the great fuel of creativity. Be thankful when syphilitics preach chastity.

Oh, for a change of heart, a change of heart—a true change of heart!

Into that there was no way to con yourself. Ramona wanted him to go the whole hog (*pecca fortiter!*). Why was he such a Quaker in love-making? He said that after his disappointments of recent date he was glad enough to perform at all, simple missionary style. She said that made him a rarity in New York. A woman had her problems here. Men who seemed decent often had very special tastes. She wanted to give him his pleasure in any way he might choose. He said she would never turn an old herring into a dolphin. It was odd that Ramona should sometimes carry on like one of those broads in a girlie magazine. For which she advanced the most high-minded reasons. An educated woman, she quoted him Catullus and the great love poets of all times. And the classics of psychology. And finally the Mystical Body. And so she was in the next room, joyously preparing, stripping, perfuming. She wanted to please. He had only to be pleased and to let her know it, and then she would grow simpler. How glad she would be to change! How it would relieve her if he said, "Ramona, what's all this for?" But then, would I have to marry her?

The idea of marriage made him nervous, but he thought it through. Her instincts were good, she was practical, capable, and wouldn't injure him. A woman who squandered her husband's money, all psychiatric opinion agreed, was determined to castrate him. On the practical side—and he found it very exciting to have practical thoughts—he couldn't stand the disorder and loneliness of bachelorhood. He liked clean shirts, ironed handkerchiefs, heels on his shoes, all the things Madeleine despised. Aunt Tamara wanted Ramona to have a husband. There must be a few Yiddish words left in the old girl's memory—*shiddach*, *tachliss*. He could be a patriarch, as every Herzog was meant to be. The family man, father, transmitter of life, intermediary between past and future, instrument of mysterious creation, was out of fashion. Fathers obsolete? Only to masculine women—wretched, pitiful bluestockings. (How bracing it was to think shrewdly!) He knew that Ramona was keen about scholarship, his books and encyclopedia articles, Ph.D., University of Chicago, and would want to be Frau Professor Herzog. Amused, he saw how they would arrive at white-tie parties at the Hotel Pierre, Ramona in long gloves and introducing Moses with her charming, lifted voice: "This is my husband, Professor Herzog." And he himself, Moses, a different man, radiating well-being, swimming in dignity, affable to one and all. Giving his back hair a touch. What a precious pair they'd make, she with her tics and he with his! What a vaudeville show! Ramona would get revenge on people who had once given her a hard time. And he? He too would get back at his enemies. *Yemach sh'mo!* Let their names be blotted out! They prepared a net for my steps. They digged a pit before me. Break their teeth, O God, in their mouth!

His face, his eyes especially, dark, intent, he took off his pants, further loosened his shirt. He wondered what Ramona would say if he offered to go into the flower business. Why not? More contact with life, meeting customers. The privations of scholarly isolation had been too much for a man of his temperament. He had read lately that lonely people in New York, shut up in their rooms, had taken to calling the police for relief. "Send a squad car, for the love of God! Send someone! Put me in the lockup with somebody! Save me. Touch me. Come. Someone—please come!"

Herzog couldn't say definitely that he would not finish his study. The chapter on "Romantic Moralism" had gone pretty well, but the one called "Rousseau, Kant, and Hegel" had him stopped cold. What if he should actually become a florist? It was an outrageously over-priced business, but that didn't need to be his problem. He saw himself in striped trousers, suede shoes. He'd have to get used to odors of soil and flowers. Thirty-some years ago, when he was dying of pneumonia and peritonitis, his breath was poisoned by the sweetness of red roses. They were sent, probably stolen, by his brother Shura who worked, then, for the florist on Peel Street. Herzog thought he might be able to stand the roses now. That pernicious thing, fragrant beauty, shapely red. You had to have strength to endure such things or by intensity they might pierce you inside and you might bleed to death.

At this moment Ramona appeared. She thrust the door open

and stood, letting him see her in the lighted frame of bath-room tile. She was perfumed and, to the hips, she was naked. On her hips she wore the black lace underthing, that single garment low on her belly. She stood on spike-heeled shoes, three inches high. Only those, and the perfume and lipstick. Her black hair.

"Do I please you, Moses?"

"Oh, Ramona! Of course! How can you ask! I'm de-lighted!"

Looking downward, she laughed in a low voice. "Oh, yes. I see I please you." She held back the hair from her forehead as she bent a little to examine the effect of her nudity on him—how he reacted to the sight of her breasts and female hips. Open wide, her eyes were intensely black. She held him by the wrist, where his veins were large, and drew him toward the bed. He began to kiss her. He thought, It never makes sense. It is a mystery.

"Why don't you take off your shirt. You won't really need it, Moses."

They both laughed, she at his shirt, he at her costume. It was a stunner! No wonder clothes were so important to Ra-mona, they were the setting of that luxurious jewel, her naked-ness. His laughter as it became silent, internal, was all the deeper. Her black lace pants might be utter foolishness, but they had the desired result. Her methods might be crude, but her calculations were correct. He was laughing, but it got him. His wit was tickled but his body burned.

"Touch me, Moses. Should I touch, too?"

"Oh, please, yes."

"Aren't you glad you didn't run away from me?"

"Yes, yes."

"How does this feel."

"Sweet. Very, very sweet."

"If only you would learn to trust your instincts . . . The lamp, too? Would you rather in the dark?"

"No, never mind the lamp now, Ramona."

"Moses, dear Moses. Tell me you belong to me. Tell me!"

"I belong to you, Ramona!"

"To me only."

"Only!"

"Thank God a person like you exists. Kiss my breasts. Darling Moses. Oh! Thank God."

Both slept deeply, Ramona without stirring. Herzog was awakened once, by a jet plane—something screaming with great power at a terrible height. Not fully roused, he got out of bed and sat heavily in the striped chair, prepared at once to write another message—perhaps to George Hoberly. But when the noise of the plane passed the thought went, too. His eyes were filled by the still, hot, flutterless night—the city, its lights.

Ramona's face, relaxed by love-making and sleep, had a rich color. In one hand she held the frilled binding of the summer blanket, and her head was raised on the pillows in a thinking posture—it reminded him of that photograph of the pensive child in the next room. One leg was free from the covers—the inside of the thigh with its wealth of soft skin and faint ripples —sexually fragrant. Her instep had a lovely fleshy curve. Her nose was curved too. And then there were her plump, pressed toes, in descending size. Herzog, smiling at the sight of her, went back to bed with sleepy clumsiness. He stroked her thick hair and fell asleep.

H E TOOK Ramona to her shop after breakfast. She was wearing a tight red dress, and they were hugging and kissing in the taxi. Moses was stirred and laughed a great deal, saying to himself more than once, "How lovely she is! And I'm making it." On Lexington Avenue he got out with her and they embraced on the sidewalk (since when did middle-aged men behave so passionately in public places?). Ramona's rouge was superfluous, her face was glowing, even burning, and she pressed him with her breasts as she kissed him; the waiting cabbie and Miss Schwartz, Ramona's assistant, both were watching.

Was this perhaps the way to live? he wondered. Had he had trouble enough, and paid his debt to suffering and earned the right to ignore what anyone might think? He clasped Ramona closer, felt that she was swelling, bursting, heart in the body, body in the tight-fitting red dress. She gave him still another perfumed kiss. On the sidewalk before the window of her shop were daisies, lilacs, small roses, flats with tomato and pepper seedlings for transplanting, all freshly watered. There stood the green pot with its perforated brass spout. Drops of water assumed blurred shapes on the cement. In spite of the buses which glazed the air with stinking gases, he could smell the fresh odor of soil, and he heard the women passing by, the rapid knocking of their heels on the crusty pavement. So between the amusement of the cabbie and the barely controlled censure of Miss Schwartz's eyes behind the leaves, he went on kissing Ramona's painted, fragrant face. Within the great open trench of Lexington Avenue, the buses pouring poison but the flowers surviving, garnet roses, pale lilacs, the cleanliness of the white, the luxury of the red, and everything covered by the gold overcast of New York. Here, on the street, as far as character and disposition permitted, he had a taste of the life he might have led if he had been simply a loving creature.

But as soon as he was alone in the rattling cab, he was again the inescapable Moses Elkanah Herzog. Oh, what a thing I am—what a *thing*! His driver raced the lights on Park Avenue, and Herzog considered what matters were like: I fall upon the thorns of life, I bleed. And then? I fall upon the thorns of life, I bleed. And what next? I get laid, I take a short holiday, but very soon after I fall upon those same thorns with gratification in pain, or suffering in joy—who knows what the mixture is! What good, what lasting good is there in me? Is there nothing else between birth and death but what I can get out of this perversity—only a favorable balance of disorderly emotions? No freedom? Only impulses? And what about all the good I have in my heart—doesn't it mean anything? Is it simply a joke? A false hope that makes a man feel the illusion of worth? And so he goes on with his struggles. But this good is no phony. I know it isn't. I swear it.

Again, he was greatly excited. His hands shook as he opened the door of his apartment. He felt he must do something, something practical and useful, and must do it at once. His night with Ramona had given him new strength, and this strength itself revived his fears, and, with the rest, the fear that he might break down, that these strong feelings might disorganize him utterly.

He took off his shoes, his jacket, loosened his collar, opened his front-room windows. Warm currents of air with the slightly contaminated odor of the harbor lifted his shabby curtains and the window shade. This flow of air calmed him slightly. No, the good in his heart evidently didn't count for much, for here, at the age of forty-seven, he was coming home after a night out with a lip made sore by biting and kissing, his problems as unsolved as ever, and what else did he have to show for himself at the bar of judgment? He had had two wives; there were two children; he had once been a scholar, and in the closet his old valise was swelled like a scaly crocodile with his uncompleted manuscript. While he delayed, others came up with the same ideas. Two years ago a Berkeley professor named Mermelstein had scooped him, confounding, overwhelming, stunning everyone in the field, as Herzog had meant to do. Mermelstein was a clever man, and an excellent scholar. At least he must be free from personal drama and able to give the world an example of order, thus deserving a place in the human community. But he, Herzog, had committed a sin of some kind against his own heart, while in pursuit of a grand synthesis.

What this country needs is a good five-cent synthesis.

What a catalogue of errors! Take his sexual struggles, for instance. Completely wrong. Herzog, going to brew himself some coffee, blushed as he measured the water in the graduated cup. It's the hysterical individual who allows his life to be polarized by simple extreme antitheses like strength–weakness, potency–impotence, health–sickness. He feels challenged but unable to struggle with social injustice, too weak, so he struggles with women, with children, with his "unhappiness." Take a case like that of poor George Hoberly—Hoberly, that sobbing prick! Herzog washed off the ring inside his coffee cup. Why did Hoberly rush in a fever to the luxury shops of New York for intimate gifts, for tributes to Ramona? Because he was crushed by failure. See how a man will submit his whole life to some extreme endeavor, often crippling, even killing himself in his chosen sphere. Now that it can't be political, it's sexual. Maybe Hoberly felt he had not satisfied her in bed. But that didn't seem likely, either. Trouble with the member, even a case of ejaculatio praecox, would not throw a woman like Ramona. If anything, such humiliations would challenge or intrigue her, bring out her generosity. No, Ramona was humane. She simply didn't want this desperate character to cast *all* his burdens on her. It's possible that a man like Hoberly by falling apart intends to bear witness to the failure of individual existence. He proves it *can't work*. He pushes love to the point of absurdity to discredit it forever. And in that way prepares to serve the Leviathan of organization even more devotedly. But another possibility was that a man bursting with unrecognized needs, imperatives, desires for activity, for brotherhood, desperate with longing for reality, for God, could not wait but threw himself wildly upon anything resembling a hope. And Ramona did look like a hope; she *chose* to. Herzog knew how that was, since he himself had sometimes given people hope. Emitting a secret message: "*Rely on me.*" This was probably a matter simply of instinct, of health or vitality. It was his vitality that led a man from lie to lie, or induced him to hold out hopes to others. (Destructiveness created lies of its own, but that was another matter.) What I seem to do, thought Herzog, is to inflame myself with my drama, with ridicule, failure, denunciation, distortion, to inflame myself voluptuously, esthetically, until I reach a sexual climax. And that climax looks like a resolution and an answer to many "higher" problems. In so far as I can trust Ramona in the role of prophetess, it is that. She has read Marcuse, N. O. Brown, all those neo-Freudians. She wants me to believe the body is a spiritual fact, the sinstrument of the soul. Ramona is a dear woman, and very touching, but this theorizing is a dangerous temptation. It can only lead to more high-minded mistakes.

He watched the coffee beating in the cracked dome of the percolator (comparable to the thoughts in his skull). When the brew looked dark enough, he filled his cup and breathed in the fumes. He decided to write Daisy saying that he would visit Marco on Parents' Day, not plead weakness. Enough malingering! He decided also that he must have a talk with lawyer Simkin. Immediately.

He ought to have phoned Simkin earlier, knowing his habits. The ruddy, stout Machiavellian old bachelor lived with his mother and a widowed sister and several nephews and nieces on Central Park West. The apartment itself was luxurious, but he slept on an army cot in the smallest of the rooms. His night table was a pile of legal volumes and here he worked and read, far into the night. The walls were covered from top to bottom by abstract-expressionist paintings, unframed. At six Simkin rose from his cot and drove his Thunderbird to a small East Side restaurant—he found out the most authentic places, Chinese, Greek, Burmese, the darkest cellars in New York; Herzog had often eaten with him. After a breakfast of onion rolls and Nova Scotia, Simkin liked to lie down on the black Naugahyde sofa in his office, cover himself with an afghan knitted by his mother, listening to Palestrina, Monteverdi, as he elaborated his legal and business strategies. At eight or so he shaved his large cheeks with Norelco, and by nine, having left instructions for his staff, he was out, visiting galleries, attending auctions.

Herzog dialed, and found Simkin in. At once—it was a ritual—Simkin began complaining. It was June, the month for weddings, two junior members of the firm were absent—honeymooning. What idiots! "Well, Professor," he said, "I haven't seen you in a while. What's on your mind?"

"First, Harvey, I ought to ask whether you can advise me. You are a friend of Madeleine's family, after all."

"Let's say, instead, that I have a relationship with them. For you I have sympathy. No Pontritter needs my sympathy, least of all Madeleine, that bitch."

"Recommend another lawyer if you want to keep out of it."

"Lawyers can be expensive. You aren't rolling in money, I take it."

Of course, Herzog reflected, Harvey is curious. He'd like to know as much as possible about my situation. Am I being sensible? Ramona wants me to consult her lawyer. But that might commit me to something else again. Besides, her lawyer would want to protect Ramona from me. "When are you free, Harvey?" said Herzog.

"Listen—I picked up two paintings by a Yugoslavian primitive—Pachich. He's just in from Brazil."

"Can we meet for lunch?"

"Not today. Lately the Angel of Death has taken charge. . . ." Herzog recognized the peculiar notes of Jewish comedy that Simkin loved, his elaborate shows of dread, his cosmic mock dismay. "Getting and spending I lay waste my powers. . . ." Simkin went on.

"Half an hour."

"Let's have dinner at Macario's. I'll bet you never even heard of it. . . . I thought not. You *are* a hick." He shouted harshly to his secretary, "Bring me that column Earl Wilson wrote about Macario. You hear me, Tilly?"

"Are you busy all day long?"

"I have to go to court. Those schmucks are in Bermuda with their brides while I fight the *Moloch-ha-movos* alone. Do you know what you pay for one serving of spaghetti al burro at Macario's? Guess."

I must go along, Herzog reflected. He rubbed his brows with thumb and forefinger. "Three-fifty?"

"Is that your idea of expensive? Five dollars and fifty cents!"

"My God, what do they put in it?"

"Sprinkled with gold dust, not cheese. No, seriously, I have to try a case today. I—myself. And I loathe courtrooms."

"Let me pick you up in a cab and drive you downtown. I'll be right over."

"But I'm waiting for the client here. I'll tell you what, if I have a few minutes to spare later . . . You sound very nervous. My cousin Wachsel is in the District Attorney's office. I'll leave word with him. . . . Well, as long as my guy isn't here yet, why don't you tell me what it's all about."

"It's about my daughter."

"You want to sue for custody?"

"Not necessarily. I'm concerned about her. I don't know how the child is."

"Besides which, you'd like to get revenge, I imagine."

"I send the support money regularly and always ask after June, but never a word in reply. Himmelstein, the layer in Chicago, said I wouldn't stand a chance in a custody suit. But I don't know how the girl is being brought up. I do know they shut her up in the car when she bothers them. How far do they go?"

"Do you think Madeleine is an unfit mother?"

"Of course I think so, but I hesitate to rush between the kid and her mother."

"Is she living with this guy, your buddy? Remember when you were running away to Poland last year and made your will? You named him executor and guardian."

"I did? Yes . . . I remember now. I guess I did."

He could hear the lawyer coughing, and knew it was a feigned cough; Simkin was laughing. You could hardly blame him. Herzog himself was somewhat amused by his sentimental faith in "best friends," and could not help thinking how much he must have added to Gersbach's pleasure by his gullibility. Obviously, thought Moses, I wasn't fit to look after my own interests, and proved my incompetence every day. A stupid prick!

"I was kind of surprised when you named him," said Simkin.

"Why, did you know anything?"

"No, but there was something about his looks, his clothes, his loud voice, and his phony Yiddish. And such an exhibitionist! I didn't like the way he hugged you. Even kissed you, if I recall. . . ."

"That's his exuberant Russian personality."

"Oh, I'm not saying he's queer, exactly," Simkin said. "Well, is Madeleine shacked up with this gorgeous guardian? You could at least investigate. Why don't you hire a private investigator?"

"A detective! Of course!"

"The idea grabs you?"

"It certainly does! Why didn't I think of it myself?"

"Do you have the kind of money that takes? Now that's *real* money!"

"I go back to work in a few months."

"Even so, what can you earn?" Simkin always spoke of Moses' earnings with a ring of sadness. Poor intellectuals, so badly treated. He seemed to wonder why Herzog did not resent this. But Herzog still accepted Depression standards.

"I can borrow."

"Private investigation costs a tremendous amount. I'll explain it to you." He paused. "The big corporations have created a new aristocracy under the present tax structure. Cars, planes, hotel suits—fringe benefits. Also restaurants, theaters, et cetera, good private schools have been priced out of range for the low-salaried man. Even the cost of prostitution. The deductible medical expense has enriched psychiatrists, so even suffering costs more now. As for the various dodges in insurance, real estate, et cetera, I could tell you about them, too. Everything is subtler. Large organizations have their own C.I.A. Scientific spies who steal secrets from other corporations. Anyhow, detectives get big fees from the carriage trade, so that when you low-income fellows come along you have to deal with the worst element in this racket. Many a plain blackmailer calls himself a private investigator. Now I could give you a piece of useful advice. Do you want it?"

"Yes—yes, I do. But . . ." Herzog hesitated.

"But what's my angle?" Simkin, as Herzog had intended, put the question for him. "I suppose you're the only person in New York who doesn't know how Madeleine turned on me—such slanders! And I was like an uncle to her. Living in lofts, among those theater types, the child was like a frightened puppy. I took pity on Mady. I gave her dolls, I took her to the circus. When she was old enough to enter Radcliffe, I paid for her wardrobe. But then when she was converted by that dude monsignor I tried to talk to her; and she called me a hypocrite and crook. She said I was a social climber, using her father's connections, and nothing but an ignorant Jew. Ignorant! I took the Latin medal at Boys' High in 1917. All right. But then she injured a little cousin of mine, an epileptic girl, a sickly, immature, innocent frail mouse of a woman who couldn't take care of herself—never mind the awful details."

"What did she do?"

"That's another long story."

"So you're not protecting Madeleine any more. I didn't hear what she said against you."

"Maybe you don't remember it. She gave me some pretty sharp wounds, believe me. Never mind that. I'm a greedy old money-grubber—I don't claim I'm a candidate for sainthood, but . . . Well, that's just the frenzy of the world. Maybe you don't always take cognizance, Professor, being absorbed in the true the good and the beautiful like Herr Goethe."

"Okay, Harvey. I know I'm not a realist. I haven't got the strength to make all the judgments a man must make to be realistic. What advice were you going to give me?"

"Here's something to think about, as long as my stinking client hasn't arrived. If you really want to bring suit . . ."

"Himmelstein said a jury would take one look at my gray hairs and give a verdict against me. Perhaps I could dye my hair."

"Get a clean-cut gentile lawyer from one of the big firms. Don't have a lot of Jews yelling in the court. Give your case dignity. Then you subpoena all the principals, Madeleine, Gersbach, Mrs. Gersbach, and put them on the stand under oath. Warn them of perjury. If the questions are asked in the right way, and I'm willing to coach your clean-cut lawyer, and mastermind the whole trial, you'll never have to touch a hair of your head."

With his sleeve, Herzog wiped the sweat that broke out on his forehead. He was suddenly very hot. The heat, which pricked his skin, also released the scent of Ramona's body which he had absorbed. It was mixed with his own odors.

"Are you with me?"

"I'm listening, go on," said Herzog.

"They'll have to come clean, and they themselves will make

your whole case for you. We can ask Gersbach when this affair with Madeleine started, how he got you to bring him to the Midwest—you did, didn't you?"

"I got him the job. I rented the house for them. I arranged to have the garbage-disposal unit installed in the sink. I measured the windows so that Phoebe could decide whether to bring her drapes from Massachusetts."

Simkin made one of his token exclamations of astonishment. "Well, which woman is he living with?"

"That I don't really know. I'd like to confront him myself—could I conduct the examination in court?"

"That's not feasible. But the lawyer can ask your questions for you. You could crucify that cripple. And Madeleine—she's had it all her own way so far. It never enters her mind that you have any rights. Wouldn't she come down to earth with a bang!"

"I often think, if she died I'd get my daughter back. There are times when I know I could look at Madeleine's corpse without pity."

"They tried to murder *you*," Simkin said. "In a manner of speaking, they meant to." Herzog sensed that his words about Madeleine's death had excited Simkin and made him eager to hear more. He wants me to say that I actually feel capable of murdering them both. Well, it's true. I've tested it in my mind with a gun, a knife, and felt no horror, no guilt. None. And I could never imagine such a crime before. So perhaps I might kill them. But I'll say no such thing to Harvey.

Simkin went on: "In court, you must prove they have an adulterous relationship to which the child is exposed. In itself, sexual intimacy doesn't count. An Illinois court gave custody to a call girl, the mother, because whatever tricks she performed she saved them for hotel rooms. The courts don't expect to stop the whole sexual revolution of our time. But if the fucking is at home and the child exposed to it, the judicial attitude is different. Damage to the little psyche."

Herzog listened, looking through the window with a hard gaze, and tried to master the spasms of his stomach and the twisted, knotted sensations of his heart. The telephone seemed to pick up the sound of his blood, rhythmic, thin, and quick, washing within his skull. Perhaps it was only a nervous reflex of his eardrums. The membranes appeared to shiver.

"Understand," said Simkin, "it would hit all the Chicago papers."

"I've got nothing to lose, I'm practically forgotten in Chicago. The scandal would hit Gersbach, not me," said Herzog.

"How do you figure?"

"He's on the make everywhere and cultivates all the Chicago hot-shots—clergymen, newspapermen, professors, television guys, federal judges, Hadassah ladies. Jesus Christ, he never lets up. He organizes new combinations on television. Like Paul Tillich and Malcolm X and Hedda Hopper on one program."

"I thought the fellow was a poet and a radio announcer. Now he sounds like a TV impresario."

"He's a poet in mass communications."

"He really has got you, hasn't he. By golly, if this isn't something in your bloodstream."

"Well, how would you like it if you woke up to see that all your best tries were nothing but sleepwalking?"

"But I don't understand this Gersbach's game."

"I'll tell you. He's a ringmaster, popularizer, liaison for the elites. He grabs up celebrities and brings them before the public. And he makes all sorts of people feel that he has exactly what they've been looking for. Subtlety for the subtle. Warmth for the warm. For the crude, crudity. For the crooks, hypocrisy. Atrocity for the atrocious. Whatever your heart desires. Emotional plasma which can circulate in any system."

Simkin was perfectly delighted with such an outburst, Herzog knew. He even understood that the lawyer was winding him up, putting him on. But that did not stop him. "I've tried to see him as a type. Is he an Ivan the Terrible? Is he a would-be Rasputin? Or the poor man's Cagliostro? Or a politician, orator, demagogue, rhapsode? Or some kind of Siberian shaman? Those are often transvestites or androgynes. . . ."

"Do you mean to say that those philosophers you've studied for so many years are all frustrated by one Valentine Gersbach?" said Simkin. "All those years of Spinoza—Hegel?"

"You're ribbing me, Simkin."

"Sorry. That wasn't a good joke."

"I don't mind. It seems true. Like taking swimming lessons on the kitchen table. Well, I can't answer for the philosophers. Maybe power philosophy, Thomas Hobbes, could analyze him. But when I think of Valentine I don't think of philosophy, I think of the books I devoured as a boy, on the French and Russian revolutions. And silent movies, like *Mme. Sans Gêne*—Gloria Swanson. Or Emil Jannings as a Czarist general. Anyway, I see the mobs breaking into the palaces and churches and sacking Versailles, wallowing in cream desserts or pouring wine over their dicks and dressing in purple velvet, snatching crowns and miters and crosses. . . ."

Herzog knew very well when he talked like this that he was again in the grip of that eccentric, dangerous force that had been capturing him. It was at work now, and he felt himself bending. At any moment he might hear a crack. He must stop this. He heard Simkin laughing softly and steadily to himself with, probably, one small hand placed in restraint on his fat chest, and wrinkles of cheerful satire in play about his bushy eyes and hairy ears. "Emancipation resulting in madness. Unlimited freedom to choose and play a tremendous variety of roles with a lot of coarse energy."

"I never saw a man pour wine over his dick in any movie—when did you ever see that?" said Simkin. "At the Museum of Modern Art? Besides, in your mind, you don't identify yourself with Versailles or the Kremlin or the old regime, or anything like that, do you?"

"No, no, of course not. It's nothing but a metaphor, and probably not a good one. I only meant to say that Gersbach won't let anything go, he tries everything on. For instance, if he took away my wife, did he have to suffer my agony for me, too? Because he could do even that better? And if he's such a tragic-love figure, practically a demigod in his own eyes, does he have to be also the greatest of fathers and family men? His wife says he's an ideal husband. Her only complaint was that he was so horny. She said he was on top of her every night. She couldn't keep up the pace."

"Who did she complain to?"

"Why, to her best friend, Madeleine, of course. Who else? And the truth is that Valentine is a family man, along with everything else. He alone knew how I felt about my kid and wrote me weekly reports about her, faithfully, with real kindliness. Until I found out he gave me the grief he was consoling me for."

"What did you do then?"

"I looked all over Chicago for him. Finally, I sent him a telegram from the airport as I was leaving. I wanted to say that I'd kill him on sight. But Western Union doesn't accept such messages. So I wired five words—Dirt Enters At The Heart. The first letters spell death."

"I'm sure he was bowled over by the threat."

Herzog did not smile. "I don't know. He is superstitious. But as I said, he is a family man. He fixes the appliances at home. When the kid needs a snowsuit he shops for it. He goes to Hillman's basement and brings back rolls and pickled herring in his shopping bag. In addition, he's a sportsman—college boxing champ at Oneonta, despite his wooden leg, he says. With pinochle players he plays pinochle, with rabbis it's Martin Buber, with the Hyde Park Madrigal Society he sings madrigals."

"Well," said Simkin, "he's nothing but a psychopath on the make, boastful and exhibitionistic. A bit clinical, maybe, except that he's a recognizable Jewish type. One of those noisy crooks with a booming voice. What kind of car does this promoter poet drive?"

"A Lincoln Continental."

"Heh, heh."

"But as soon as he slams the door of his Continental he begins to talk like Karl Marx. I heard him at the Auditorium with an audience of two thousand people. It was a symposium on desegregation, and he let loose a blast against the affluent society. That's how it is. If you've got a good job, about fifteen grand a year, and health insurance, and a retirement fund, and maybe some stock as well, why shouldn't you be a radical too? Literate people appropriate all the best things they can find in books, and dress themselves in them just as certain crabs are supposed to beautify themselves with seaweed. And then there was the audience, a comfortable audience of conventional business people and professionals who look after their businesses and specialties well enough, but seem confused about everything else and come to hear a speaker express himself confidently, with emphasis and fire, direction and force. With a head like a flaming furnace, a voice like a bowling alley, and the wooden leg drumming the stage. To me he's a curiosity, like a Mongolian idiot singing *Aïda*. But to *them* . . ."

"By golly, you are worked up," said Simkin. "Why are you suddenly talking about the opera? As you describe him, it's perfectly plain to me the fellow is an actor, and I know damn well Madeleine is an actress. That I've always realized. But take it easy. This exaggeration is bad for you. You eat yourself alive."

Moses was silent, shutting his eyes for a moment. Then he said, "Well, maybe so . . ."

"Wait up, Moses, I think my client is here."

"Oh, all right, I won't keep you. Let's have your cousin's number and I'll meet you downtown later."

"This can't wait."

"No, I have to reach a decision today."

"Well, I'll try to find a little time. Now taper off."

"I need fifteen minutes," said Herzog. "I'll prepare all my questions."

Moses as he took Wachsel's number was thinking that perhaps the best thing he could do was to stop asking people for advice and help. That in itself might change the entire picture. He printed Wachsel's number more legibly on the pad. In the background he heard Simkin shouting rudely at his client. Something about an ant-eater . . . ?

He unbuttoned his shirt and let it fall behind him to the bathroom floor. Then he ran the water in the sink. The crude oval of the basin was smooth and beautiful in the gray light. He touched the almost homogeneous whiteness with his fingertips and breathed in the water odors and the subtle stink rising from the throat of the waste pipe. Unexpected intrusions of beauty. This is what life is. He bent his head under the flowing tap and sighed with shock and then with pleasure. *Dear M. de Jouvenel, If the aims of political philosophy be as you say to civilize power, to impress the brute, to improve his manners and harness his energy to constructive tasks, I would like to say,* he was no longer addressing de Jouvenel, *that the sight of James Hoffa on your television show the other night made me realize how terrible a force angry single-mindedness can be. I was sorry*

*for the poor professors on your panel whom he was chewing up. I'll
tell you what I would have said to Hoffa. "What makes you think
realism must be brutal?"* Herzog's hands were on the taps; the
left now shut off the warm water, the right increased the pressure of the cold. It poured over his scalp and his neck. He was
shivering with the extreme violence of thought and feeling.

At last he straightened his dripping head and wrapped it in
the towel, rubbing and shaking his head in an effort to recover
some degree of calm. As he was doing this, it occurred to him
that this going into the bathroom to pull himself together was
one of his habits. He seemed to feel that here he was more effective, more master of himself. In fact, he remembered, for a
few weeks in Ludeyville he required Madeleine to make love
on the bathroom floor. She complied, but he could see when
she lay down on the old tiles that she was in a rage. Much good
could come of that. This is how the all-powerful human intellect employs itself when it has no real occupation. And now he
pictured the November rain dropping from the sky on his half-
painted house in Ludeyville. The sumacs spilled the red Chinese paper of their leaves, and in the shivering woods the
hunters were banging away at the deer—bang, bang, bang—
driving home with dead animals. The gunsmoke was slow to
rise from the woods' edge. Moses knew that in her heart his
recumbent wife was cursing him. He tried to make his lust comical, to show how absurd it all was, easily the most wretched
form of human struggle, the very essence of slavery.

Then suddenly Moses recalled something quite different
that had happened at Gersbach's house just outside Barrington
about a month later. Gersbach was lighting the Chanukah candles for his little son, Ephraim, garbling the Hebrew blessing,
then dancing with the boy. Ephraim was buttoned into his
clumsy sleepers, and Valentine, powerful and gimpy, undaunted
by mutilation—that was his great charm; sulk because he was a
cripple? Screw that! He was dancing, pounding, clapping his
hands, his flamboyant hair, always brutally barbered at the
neck, moving up and down, and he looked at the boy with fanatical tenderness, eyes dark and hot. Whenever that look
came over him the ruddy color of his face seemed to be drawn
entirely into his brown eyes and it made his cheeks seem
almost porous. I might have guessed already, from Mady's look,

that spurt of breath that came from her when she laughed spontaneously. That look was deep. Strange. A look like a steel binder bent open. She loves that actor.

Oneself is simply grotesque! Herzog stated it impulsively, though with pain, and his mind immediately looking for formal stability, catching (as he was lathering, clipping the blade into his injector razor) at ideas, of Professor Hocking's latest book *whether justice on this earth can or cannot be general, social, but must originate within each heart. Subjective monstrosity must be overcome, must be corrected by community, by useful duty. And, as you indicate, private suffering transformed from masochism. But we know this. We know, we know, know it! Creative suffering, as you think . . . at the core of Christian belief.* Now what is it? Herzog urged himself to be clearer. What really is on my mind? Probably this: shall I put those two on the stand under oath, torture them, hold a blowtorch to their feet? Why? They have a right to each other; they seem even to belong together. Why, let them alone. But what about justice?—Justice! Look who wants justice! Most of mankind has lived and died without—totally without it. People by the billions and for ages sweated, gypped, enslaved, suffocated, bled to death, buried with no more justice than cattle. But Moses E. Herzog, at the top of his lungs, bellowing with pain and anger, has to have justice. It's his *quid pro quo,* in return for all he has suppressed, his right as an Innocent Party. *I love little pussy her coat is so warm, and I'll sit by the fire and give her some food, and pussy will love me because I am good.* So now his rage is so great and deep, so murderous, bloody, positively rapturous, that his arms and fingers ache to strangle them. So much for his boyish purity of heart. Social organization, for all its clumsiness and evil, has accomplished far more and embodies more good than I do, for at least it sometimes gives justice. I am a mess, and talk about justice. I owe the powers that created me a human life. And where is it! Where is that human life which is my only excuse for surviving! What have I to show for myself? Only this! His face was before him in the blotchy mirror. It was bearded with lather. He saw his perplexed, furious eyes and he gave an audible cry. *My God! Who is this creature? It considers itself human. But what is it? Not human of itself. But has the longing to be human. And like a troubling dream, a per-*

sistent vapor. A desire. Where does it all come from? And what is it? And what can it be! Not immortal longing. No, entirely mortal, but human.

As he was putting on his shirt he made plans to visit his son on Parents' Day. The Trailways Bus for Catskill left the West Side Terminal at seven A.M. and made the trip on the Thruway in less than three hours. He remembered two years ago milling on the dusty playing field with kids and parents, the coarse boards of the barracks, the tired goats and hamsters, leafless bushes, and the spaghetti served on paper plates. By one o'clock he would be utterly beat, and the hours before bus time would be difficult and sad, but he must do everything possible for Marco. As for Daisy, it would spare her a trip. She had been having troubles of her own, her old mother having grown senile. Herzog knew of this from many sources, and it affected him strangely to hear that his former mother-in-law, handsome, autocratic, every inch the suffragist and "modern woman" with her pince-nez and abundant gray hair, had lost her self-control. She had got it into her head that Moses had divorced Daisy because she was a streetwalker, carried the yellow ticket—Polina in her delusions became a Russian again. Fifty years in Zanesville, Ohio, melted away when she pleaded with Daisy to stop "going with men." Poor Daisy had to listen to this every morning after she had sent the boy off to school and was herself leaving for work. An utterly steady, reliable woman, responsible to the point of grimness. Daisy was a statistician for the Gallup Poll. For Marco's sake she tried to make the house cheerful, but she had no talent for this, and the parakeets and the plants and goldfish and gay reproductions of Braque and Klee from the Museum of Modern Art seemed to increase its sadness. Similarly, in her neatness, the straight seams of her stockings, her face with its powder and the brows realigned with pencil to give a more spirited expression, Daisy never overcame her heavy-heartedness. After cleaning the bird cage and feeding all her little creatures and watering the plants, she still had to face her senile mother in the entryway. And Polina commanded her to give up this life of shame. Then she began, "Daisy, I beg you." And at last she pleaded on her knees, getting down with difficulty, a broad-hipped old woman, the white braids hanging, her gray head long and slender—much feminine delicacy still in the shape of that head—and the pince-nez swinging on the silk cord. "You can't go on like this, my child."

Daisy tried to raise her from the ground. "All right, Mama. I'll change. I promise."

"Men are waiting for you, in the street."

"No, no, Mama."

"Yes, men. This is a social evil. You'll catch a disease. You'll die a terrible death. You must stop. Moses will come back if you do."

"All right. Please stand up, Mama. I'll stop."

"There are other ways to make a living. Please, Daisy, I beg you."

"No more, Mama. Come, sit down."

Shaky and clumsy, with awkward haunches and feeble knees, old Polina rose from the floor and Daisy guided her to her chair. "I'll send them all away. Come, Mama. I'll turn on the television. You want to watch the cooking school? Dione Lucas, or the Breakfast Club?" The sun came through the venetian blinds. The sputtering, flickering images on the screen looked yellow. And gray, genteel Polina, this high-principled old woman, iron at the core, knitted all day before the TV. The neighbors looked in on her. Cousin Asya came from the Bronx now and then. On Thursdays the cleaning woman was there. But Polina, now in her eighties, at last had to be placed in a home for the aged somewhere on Long Island. So this is how the strongest characters end!

Oh, Daisy, I am very sorry about this. I pity . . .

One sad thing after another, Herzog thought. His shaved cheeks stinging, he rubbed them with witch hazel, drying his fingers on his shirttails. He took up hat, coat, and necktie and hurried down the gloomy stairway to the street—the elevator was far too slow. At the hack stand he found a Puerto Rican driver who was touching up his sleek black hair with a pocket comb.

Moses knotted his tie in the back seat. The cabbie turned around to look. He studied him.

"Where to, Sport?"

"Downtown."

"You know, I think I got a coincident to tell you." They ran eastward toward Broadway. The driver was observing him in the mirror as he drove. Herzog also bent forward and deciphered the name beside the meter: Teodoro Valdepenas. "Early in the morning," said Valdepenas, "I seen a guy on Lexington Avenue dressed like you, with the exact same model coat. The hat."

"Did you see his face?"

"No . . . the face I didn't see." The taxi rattled into Broadway, and sped toward Wall Street.

"Where, on Lexington?"

"Like the sixties."

"What was the fellow doing?"

"Kissing a broad in a red dress. That's why I didn't see the face. And what I mean *kissing*! Was it you?"

"It must have been me."

"How do you like that!" Valdepenas slapped the wheel. "Boy! Out of millions. I took a guy from La Guardia, over the Triboro and the East River Drive and left him off at Seventy-second and Lexington. I seen you kissing a broad and then I get you two hours afterwards."

"Like catching the fish that swallowed the queen's ring," said Herzog.

Valdepenas turned slightly to look at Herzog over his shoulder. "That was a real nice-looking broad. Stacked! Terrific! Your wife?"

"No. I'm not married. She's not married."

"Well, boy, you're all right. When I get old I'm going to be doing just like you. Why stop! And believe you me, I stay away from young chicks already. You waste your time with a broad under twenty-five. I quit on that type. A woman over thirty-five is just beginning to be serious. That's the kind that puts down the best stuff. . . . Where are you going?"

"The City Courthouse."

"You a lawyer? A cop?"

"How could I be a detective in this coat?"

"Hombre, detectives even go in drag now. What do I care! Listen to me. I got real burned up at a young chick last mont'. She just lies on the bed chewing gum and reading a magazine. Like she's saying 'Do me something!' I said, 'Listen, Teddy's here. What's this gum? Magazines?' She said, 'All right, let's get it over.' How's that for an attitude! I said, 'In my hack, that's where I hurry. You ought to get a punch in the teeth for talkin' like that.' And I'll tell you something. She was a no-good lay. A broad eighteen don't know even how to shit!"

Herzog laughed, largely from astonishment.

"That's right, ain't it?" said Valdepenas. "You ain't no kid."

"No, I'm not."

"A woman over forty really appreciates . . ." They were at Broadway and Houston. A boozer, stubble-faced, jaws strong and arrogant, waited with a filthy rag to wipe the windshields of passing cars, holding out his hand for tips. "Look how that bum operates here," said Valdepenas. "He smears the glass. The fat guys pay out. They shiver in their pupick. They're scared not to. I seen these Bowery slobs spit on cars. They better not lay a hand on my hack. I keep a tire tool right here, boy. I'd bust the sonofabitch on the head!"

On slanting Broadway lay the heavy shadow of summer. Second-hand desks and swivel chairs, old green filing cases were exposed on the sidewalk—aquarium green, dill-pickle green. And now financial New York closed in, ponderous and sunless. Just below was Trinity Church. Herzog remembered that he had promised to show Marco the grave of Alexander Hamilton. He had described to him the duel with Burr, the bloody body of Hamilton brought back on a summer morning in the bottom of a boat. Marco listened, pale and steady, his freckled Herzog face revealing little. Marco never seemed to wonder at the immense (the appalling!) collection of facts in his father's head. At the aquarium Herzog supplied the classi-fication of fish scales—"the cotenoid, the placoid . . ." He knew where the coelacanth had been caught, the anatomy of a lobster's stomach. He offered all this to his son—we must stop this, Herzog decided—guilty conduct, an overemotional father, a bad example. I try too hard with him.

Valdepenas was still talking when Moses paid him. He an-swered cheerfully, but by rote. He had stopped listening. Ora-torical lechery, momentarily amusing. "Keep sockin' away, Doc."

"See you again, Valdepenas."

He turned to face the vast gray court building. Dust swirled on the broad stairway, the stone was worn. Going up, Herzog found a bouquet of violets, dropped from the hand of a woman. Perhaps a bride. Little perfume remained in them, but they made him remember Massachusetts—Ludeyville. By now the peonies were wide open, the mock-orange bushes fragrant. Madeleine sprayed the lavatory with syringa deodorant. These violets smelled to him like female tears. He gave them burial in a trashcan, hoping they had not dropped from a disappointed hand. He went through the four-bladed revolving door into the lobby, fishing in his shirt pocket for the folded slip of paper with Wachsel's phone number. It was still too early to call. Simkin and his client hadn't had time enough to get downtown.

With time on his hands Herzog wandered in the huge dark corridors upstairs where swinging padded doors with small oval windows led into courtrooms. He peered into one of these; the broad mahogany seats looked restful. He entered, respectfully removing his hat and nodding at the magistrate, who took no notice of him. Broad and bald, all face, deep voiced, resting his fist on documents—Mr. Judge. The chamber, with ornate ceiling, was immense, the walls buff but somber. When one of the police attendants opened the door behind the bench you saw the bars of the detention cells. Herzog crossed his legs (with a certain style: his elegance never deserted him even when he scratched himself), and, dark-eyed, attentive, averted his face slightly as he prepared to listen, a tendency inherited from his mother.

Very little seemed at first to be happening. A small group of lawyers and clients almost casually talked things over, arranged details. Raising his voice, the magistrate interrupted.

"But just a minute, here. Do you say . . . ?"

"He says . . ."

"Let me hear the man himself. Do you say . . . ?"

"No, sir, I don't."

The magistrate demanded, "Well what do you mean, then? Counsel, what is this supposed to mean?"

"My client's plea is still the same—not guilty."

"I did not . . ."

"Mistuh judge, he did," a Negro voice said, without insistence.

". . . Dragged this man, drunk, off St. Nicholas Avenue, into the cellar of premises at—what is the exact address? With intention to rob." This was the magistrate's overriding basso; he had a broad New York accent.

From behind, Herzog was now able to make out the defendant in this case. He was the Negro in filthy brown pants. His legs appeared to be trembling with nervous strength. He might have been about to run a race; he even crouched slightly, in the big cocoa-brown pants, as if at the starting line. But about ten feet before him were the shining prison bars. The plaintiff wore a bandage on his head.

"How much money did you have in your pocket?"

"Sixty-eight cents, your honor," the bandaged man said.

"And did he force you to enter the basement?"

The defendant said, "No, suh."

"I didn't ask you. Now keep your mouth shut." The magistrate was vexed.

The injured man now turned his bandaged head. Herzog saw a black, dry, elderly face, eyes red-rimmed. "No suh. He said he given me a drink."

"Did you know him?"

"No, suh, but he was given me a drink."

"And you went with this stranger to the cellar at—address? Bailiff, where are those papers?" Moses now became aware how the magistrate diverted himself and the courtroom loafers with a show of temperament. These were dull routines otherwise. "What happened down in the cellar?" He studied the forms the bailiff had passed him.

"He hit me."

"Without warning? Where was he standing, behind you?"

"I couldn't see. The blood started to comin' down. In my eyes. I couldn't see."

Those tense legs desired their freedom. They were ready for flight.

"And he took the sixty-eight cents?"

"I grabbed him and started in to holler. Then he give me another lick."

"What did you hit this man with?"

"Your honor, my client denies that he struck him," the

lawyer said. "They are acquaintances. They were out drinking together."

The black face, framed in bandages, heavy-lipped, dry, eyes red, stared at the lawyer. "I don't know him."

"Any of those blows might have killed this fellow."

"Assault with intent to rob," Herzog heard. The magistrate added, "I assume plaintiff was drunk to begin with."

That is—his blood was well thinned with whisky as it dropped into the coal dust. Whisky-blood was bound to be shed in some such way. The criminal began to go, the same wolfish tension within his voluminous, ridiculous pants. The cop, with pads of police fat on his cheeks, looked almost kindly as he led him to the cells. Lard-faced, he held the door open and sent him on his way with a pat on the shoulder.

A new group stood before the magistrate, a plainclothesman testifying. "At seven-thirty-eight P.M. at a urinal in the lower level men's lavatory, Grand Central Station . . . this man (name given) standing in the adjacent space reached over and placed his hand upon my organ of sex at the same time saying . . ." The detective, a specialist in men's toilets, Herzog thought, loitering there, a bait. By the speed and expertness of the testimony you knew it was routine. "I therefore arrested him for violations. . . ." Before the plainclothesman had finished listing the ordinances by number, the magistrate was saying, "Guilty—not guilty?"

The offender was a tall young foreigner; a German. His passport was shown. He wore a long brown leather coat tightly belted, and his small head was covered with curls; his brow was red. He turned out to be an intern in a Brooklyn hospital. Here the magistrate surprised Herzog, who had taken him for the ordinary gross, grunting, ignorant political magistrate, putting on an act for the idlers on the benches (including Herzog). But, both hands tugging at the neck of his black robe, demonstrating by this gesture, thought Herzog, that he wanted the accused man's lawyer to stop, he said, "Better advise your client if he pleads guilty he'll never practice medicine in the U.S.A."

That mass of flesh rising from the opening of the magistrate's black cloth, nearly eyeless, or whale-eyed, was, after all, a human head. The hollow, ignorant voice, a human voice. You don't destroy a man's career because he yielded to an impulse in that ponderous stinking cavern below Grand Central, in the cloaca of the city, where no mind can be sure of stability, where policemen (perhaps themselves that way given) tempt and trap poor souls. Valdepenas had reminded him that cops now went in drag to lure muggers, or mashers, and if they could become transvestites in the name of the law, what else would they think of! The deeper creativity of police imagination . . . He opposed this perverse development in law enforcement. Sexual practices of any sort, provided they didn't disturb the peace, provided they didn't injure minor children, were a private matter. Except for the children. Never children. There one must be strict.

Meanwhile he watched keenly. The case of the intern was continued, and the principals in an attempted robbery appeared at the bar. The prisoner was a boy; though his face was curiously lined, some of its grooves feminine, others masculine enough. He wore a soiled green shirt. His dyed hair was long, stiff, dirty. He had pale round eyes and he smiled with empty—no, worse than empty—cheerfulness. His voice, when he answered questions, was high-pitched, ice-cold, thoroughly drilled in its affectations.

"Name?"

"Which name, your honor?"

"Your own name."

"My boy's-name or my girl's-name?"

"Oh, I see. . . ." The magistrate, alerted by this, swept the courtroom, rounding up his audience with his glance. *Now hear this.* Moses leaned forward. "Well, which are you, a boy or a girl?"

The cold voice said, "It depends what people want me for. Some want a boy, and others a girl."

"Want what?"

"Want sex, your honor."

"Well, what's your boy's-name?"

"Aleck, your honor. Otherwise I'm Alice."

"Where do you work?"

"Along Third Avenue, in the bars. I just sit there."

"Is that how you make your living?"

"Your honor, I'm a prostitute."

Idlers, lawyers, policemen grinning, and the magistrate himself relishing the scene deeply—only one stout woman standing by with bare, heavy arms did not participate in this. "Wouldn't it be better for your business if you washed?" the magistrate said. Oh, these actors! thought Moses. Actors all!

"Filth makes it better, judge." The icy soprano voice was unexpectedly sharp and prompt. The magistrate showed intense satisfaction. He brought his large hands together, asking, "Well, what's the charge?"

"Attempted holdup with toy pistol Fourteenth Street Notions and Drygoods. He told the cashier to hand over the money and she struck him and disarmed him."

"A toy! Where's the cashier?"

She was the stout woman with the thick arms. Her head was dense with graying quills. Her shoulders were thick. Earnestness seemed to madden her pug-nosed face.

"That's me, your honor. Marie Poont."

"Marie? You're a brave woman, Marie, and a quick thinker. Tell us how it happened."

"He only made in his pocket like a gun, and gave me a bag to fill with money." A heavy and simple spirit, Herzog saw; a mesomorph, in the catchword; the immortal soul encased in this somatic vault. "I knew it was a trick."

"What did you do?"

"I have a baseball bat, your honor. The store sells them. I gave a slam on the arm."

"Good for you! Is this what happened, Aleck?"

"Yes sir," he answered in his clear, chill voice. Herzog tried to guess the secret of this alert cheerfulness. What view of things was this Aleck advancing? He seemed to be giving the world comedy for comedy, joke for joke. With his dyed hair, like the winter-beaten wool of a sheep, and his round eyes, traces of mascara still on them, the tight provocative pants, and something sheeplike, too, even about his vengeful merriment, he was a dream actor. With his bad fantasy he defied a bad reality, subliminally asserting to the magistrate, "Your authority and my degeneracy are one and the same." Yes, it must be something like that, Herzog decided. Sandor Himmelstein declared with rage that every living soul was a whore. Of course

the magistrate had not spread his legs literally; but he must
have done all that was necessary within the power structure to
get appointed. Still, nothing about him denied such charges,
either. His face was illusionless, without need of hypocrisy.
Aleck was the one who claimed glamour, even a certain amount
of "spiritual" credit. Someone must have told him that fellatio
was the path to truth and honor. So this bruised, dyed Aleck
also had an idea. He was purer, loftier than any square, did not
lie. It wasn't only Sandor who had such ideas—strange, minimal ideas of truth, honor. Realism. Nastiness in the transcendent position.

There was a narcotics record. That was to be expected. He
need the money for the dope, was that it?

"That was it, your honor," said Aleck. "I almost didn't try
because this lady looked so butch. I knew she might be tough.
But I took a chance anyway."

Unless spoken to, Marie Poont said nothing. Her head
hung forward.

The magistrate said, "Aleck, if you keep this up you'll be in
Potter's Field. . . . I give you four-five years."

In the grave! Eyes really empty, and this strained sweetness
rotted from the lips. Well, Aleck, how about that? Will you
think—be serious? But where would it get Aleck to be serious?
What could he hope from it? Now he was going back to the
cell, and he called out, "G'by all. Good-by." Sugary and lingering. "By-ee." An icy voice. They pushed him out.

The magistrate shook his head. These fairies, what a bunch!
He fetched up a handkerchief from the black gown and wiped
his neck, raising his chin and catching the gold of many lights
on his face. He was smiling. Marie Poont still waited, and he
said, "Thank you, Miss. And you may go now."

Herzog discovered that he had been sitting, legs elegantly
crossed, the jagged oval rim of his hat pressed on his thigh, his
striped jacket still buttoned and strained by his eager posture,
that he had been watching all that happened with his look of
intelligent composure, of charm and sympathy—like the old
song, he thought, the one that goes, "There's flies on me,
there's flies on you, but there ain't no flies on Jesus." A man
who looked so fine and humane would be outside police juris-
diction, immune to lower forms of suffering and punishment.

Herzog shifted his weight on the bench, forcing his hand into his pocket. Did he have a dime for the phone? He must call Wachsel. But he couldn't reach his coins (was he getting fat?) and he stood up. As soon as he was on his feet, he realized that there was something the matter with him. He felt as though something terrible, inflammatory, bitter, had been grated into his bloodstream and stung and burned his veins, his face, his heart. He knew he was turning white, although the pulses beat violently in his head. He saw that the magistrate was staring at him, as though Herzog owed him the courtesy of a nod in leaving his courtroom. . . . But he turned his back, and hurried into the corridor, thrusting aside the swinging doors. He opened his collar, struggling with the stiff buttonhole of the new shirt. The sweat broke out on his face. He began to breathe more normally as he stood beside the broad high window. It had a metal grille at its base. Through this a draft of cooler air passed, and the dust silently circulated under the folds of the green-black window blind. Some of Herzog's dearest friends, not to mention his Uncle Arye—his own father, come to think of it—had died of heart failure, and there were times when Herzog thought he might be having an attack too. But no, he was really very strong and healthy, and no . . . What was he saying? He finished his sentence, however: no such luck. He must live. Complete his assignment, whatever that was.

The burning within his chest subsided. It had felt like swallowing a mouthful of poison. But he now grasped the floating suspicion that this poison rose from within. He knew in fact that it did. What produced it? Must he suppose that something once good in him had spoiled, gone bad? Or was it originally bad? His own evil? To see people in the hands of the law agitated him. The red forehead of the medical student, the trembling legs of the Negro he found horrible. But he was suspicious of his own reaction, too. There were people, Simkin, for instance, or Himmelstein, or Dr. Edvig, who believed that in a way Herzog was rather simple, that his humane feelings were childish. That he had been spared the destruction of certain sentiments as the pet goose is spared the ax. Yes, a pet goose! Simkin seemed to see him as he saw that sickly innocent girl, the epileptic cousin whom Madeleine supposedly injured.

Young Jews, brought up on moral principles as Victorian ladies were on pianoforte and needlepoint, thought Herzog. And I have come here today for a look at something different. That evidently is my purpose.

I willfully misread my contract. I never was the principal, but only on loan to myself. Evidently I continue to believe in God. Though never admitting it. But what else explains my conduct and my life? So I may as well acknowledge how things are, if only because otherwise I can't even be described. My behavior implies that there is a barrier against which I have been pressing from the first, pressing all my life, with the conviction that it is necessary to press, and that something must come of it. Perhaps that I can eventually pass through. I must always have had such an idea. Is it faith? Or is it simply childishness, expecting to be loved for doing your bidden task? It is, if you're looking for the psychological explanation, childish and classically depressive. But Herzog didn't believe that the harshest or most niggardly explanation, following the law of parsimony, was necessarily the truest. Eager impulses, love, intensity, passionate dizziness that make a man sick. How long can I stand such inner beating? The front wall of this body will go down. My whole life beating against its boundaries, and the force of balked longings coming back as stinging poison. Evil, evil, evil . . . ! Excited, characteristic, ecstatic love turning to evil.

He was in pain. He should be. Quite right. If only because he had required so many people to lie to him, many, many, beginning, naturally, with his mother. Mothers lie to their children from demand. But perhaps his mother had been struck, too, by the amount of melancholy, her own melancholy, she saw in Moses. The family look, the eyes, those eye-lights. And though he recalled his mother's sad face with love, he couldn't say, in his soul, that he wanted to see such sadness perpetuated. Yes, it reflected the deep experience of a race, its attitude toward happiness and toward mortality. This somber human case, this dark husk, these indurated lines of submission to the fate of being human, this splendid face showed the responses of his mother's finest nerves to the greatness of life, rich in sorrow, in death. All right, she was beautiful. But he hoped that things would change. When we have come to better terms with death, we'll wear a different expression, we human beings. Our looks will change. *When* we come to terms!

Nor had she always lied to spare his feelings. He remembered that late one afternoon she led him to the front-room window because he asked a question about the Bible: how Adam was created from the dust of the ground. I was six or seven. And she was about to give me the proof. Her dress was brown and gray—thrush-colored. Her hair was thick and black, the gray already streaming through it. She had something to show me at the window. The light came up from the snow in the street, otherwise the day was dark. Each of the windows had colored borders—yellow, amber, red—and flaws and whorls in the cold panes. At the curbs were the thick brown poles of that time, many-barred at the top, with green glass insulators, and brown sparrows clustered on the crossbars that held up the iced, bowed wires. Sarah Herzog opened her hand and said, "Look carefully, now, and you'll see what Adam was made of." She rubbed the palm of her hand with a finger, rubbed until something dark appeared on the deep-lined skin, a particle of what certainly looked to him like earth. "You see? It's true." A grown man, in the present, beside the big colorless window, like a static sail outside Magistrate's Court, Herzog did as she had done. He rubbed, smiling; and it worked; a bit of the same darkness began to form in his palm. Now he stood staring into the black openwork of the brass grille. Maybe she offered me this proof partly in a spirit of comedy. The wit you can have only when you consider death very plainly, when you consider what a human being really is.

The week of her death, also in winter. This happened in Chicago, and Herzog was sixteen years old, nearly a young man. It occurred on the West Side. She was dying. Evidently Moses wanted no part of that. He was already a free-thinker. Darwin and Haeckel and Spencer were old stuff to him. He and Zelig Koninski (what had happened to that gilded youth?) disdained the branch library. They bought thick books of all sorts out of the thirty-nine-cent barrel at Walgreen's—*The World as Will and Idea* and *The Decline of the West*. And what was going on! Herzog knitted his brows to force his memory to work. Papa had the night job, and slept days. You had to tiptoe through the house. If you woke him he was furious. His overalls, reeking of linseed oil, were hung behind the bathroom door. At three in the afternoon, half dressed, he came out for his tea, silent, his face filled with stern anger. But by and by he became an entrepreneur again, doing business out of his hat on Cherry Street, opposite the Negro whorehouse, among the freight trains. He had a roll-top desk. He shaved his mustache. And then Mama started to die. And I was in the kitchen winter nights, studying *The Decline of the West*. The round table was covered with an oilcloth.

That was a frightful January, streets coated with steely ice. The moon lay on the glazed snow of the back yards where clumsy lumber porches threw their shadows. Under the kitchen was the furnace room. The janitor stoked the fire, his apron a burlap sack, his Negro beard gritty with the soft coal. The shovel scraped on the cement, and then clanged in the mouth of the furnace. He would slam the metal door shut with his shovel. And then he carried ashes out in bushels—old peach baskets. As often as I could, I hugged the laundry girls, down in the tub room. But I was poring over Spengler now, struggling and drowning in the oceanic visions of that sinister kraut. First there was antiquity, for which all men sigh—beautiful Greece! Then the Magian era, and the Faustian. I learned that I, a Jew, was a born Magian and that we Magians had already had our great age, forever past. No matter how hard I tried, I would never grasp the Christian and Faustian world idea, forever alien to me. Disraeli *thought* he could understand and lead the British, but he was totally mistaken. I had better resign myself to Destiny. A Jew, a relic as lizards are relics of the great age of reptiles, I might prosper in a false way by swindling the *goy*, the laboring cattle of a civilization dwindled and done for. Anyway, it was an age of spiritual exhaustion—all the old dreams were dreamed out. I was angry; I burned like that furnace; reading more, sick with rage.

When I looked away from the dense print and its insidious pedantry, my heart infected with ambition, and the bacteria of vengeance, Mama was entering the kitchen. Seeing light under the door, she came the whole length of the house, from the sickroom. Her hair had to be cut during her illness, and this made those eyes hard to recognize. Or no, the shortness of her hair merely made their message simpler: *My son, this is death.*

I chose not to read this text.

"I saw the light," she said. "What are you doing up so late?" But the dying, for themselves, have given up hours. She only pitied me, her orphan, understood I was a gesture-maker, ambitious, a fool; thought I would need my eyesight and my strength on a certain day of reckoning.

A few days afterward, when she had lost the power to speak, she was still trying to comfort Moses. Just as when he knew she was breathless from trudging with his sled in Montreal but would not get up. He came into her room when she was dying, holding his school books, and began to say something to her. But she lifted up her hands and showed him her fingernails. They were blue. As he stared, she slowly began to nod her head up and down as if to say, "That's right, Moses, I am dying now." He sat by the bed. Presently she began to stroke his hand. She did this as well as she could; her fingers had lost their flexibility. Under the nails they seemed to him to be turning already into the blue loam of graves. She had begun to change into earth! He did not dare to look but listened to the runners of children's sleds in the street, and the grating of peddlers' wheels on the knotted ice, the hoarse call of the apple peddler and the rattle of his steel scale. The steam whispered in the vent. The curtain was drawn.

In the corridor outside Magistrate's Court, he thrust both hands into his trousers pockets and drew up his shoulders. His teeth were on edge. A bookish, callow boy. And then, he thought, there was the funeral. How Willie cried in the chapel! It was his brother Willie, after all, who had the tender heart. But . . . Moses shook his head to be rid of such thoughts. The more he thought, the worse his vision of the past.

He waited his turn at the phone booth. The instrument, when he got it, was humid from the many mouths and ears that used it. Herzog rang the number Simkin had given him. Wachsel said no, he had no messages from Simkin, but Mr. Herzog was welcome to come up and wait. "No, thanks, I'll phone again," Herzog said. He had absolutely no ability to wait in offices. He never had been able to wait for anything. "You don't happen to know—is he in the building somewhere?"

"I know he's here, all right," said Wachsel. "I have an idea it's a criminal case. And that would be . . ." He rattled off a list of room numbers.

Herzog fixed on a few of these. He said, "I'll go and have a look around and call you again in half an hour, if you don't mind."

"No, I don't mind. We're open for business all day! Whyn't you try the eighth floor. Little Napoleon—with that voice you should be able to hear him through the walls."

In the first courtroom Herzog entered after getting this suggestion there was a jury trial. He was one of a small number of people in the polished wooden rows. Within a few minutes he had forgotten Simkin entirely.

A young couple, a woman and the man she had been living with in a slum hotel, uptown, were being tried for the murder of her son, a child of three. She had had the boy by another man who deserted her, said the lawyer in his presentation. Herzog observed how gray and elderly all these lawyers were, people of another generation and a different circle of life—tolerant, comfortable people. The defendants could be identified by their looks and clothing. The man wore a stained and frayed zipper jacket and she, a redheaded woman, with a wide ruddy face, had on a brown print house dress. Both sat stolid, to all appearances unmoved by the testimony, he with his low sideburns and blond mustache, she with blunt freckled cheekbones and long, hidden eyes.

She came from Trenton, born lame. Her father was a garage mechanic. She had a fourth-grade education, I.Q. 94. An older brother was the favorite; she was neglected. Unattractive, sullen, clumsy, wearing an orthopedic boot, she became delinquent at an early age. Her record was before the court, the lawyer went on, even, mild and pleasant. An angry uncontrollable girl, from first grade. There were affidavits from teachers. There were also medical and psychiatric records, and a neurological report to which the lawyer particularly wished to call the court's attention. This showed his client had been diagnosed by encephalogram as having a brain lesion capable of altering her behavior radically. She was known to have violent epileptoid fits of rage; her tolerance for emotions controlled from the affected lobe was known to be very low. Because she was a poor crippled creature, she had often been molested, later sexually abused by adolescent boys. Indeed, her file in children's court was very thick. Her mother loathed her, had refused to attend the trial, was quoted as saying, "This is no kid of mine. We wash our hands of her." The defendant was made pregnant at nineteen by a married man who lived with her several months, then went back to his wife and family. She refused to give the child for adoption, lived for a while in Trenton with it, and then moved to Flushing, where she cooked and cleaned for a family. On one of her weekends she met the other defendant, at the time employed as porter in a lunchroom on Columbus Avenue, and decided to live with him at the Montcalme Hotel on 103rd Street—Herzog had often passed the place. You could smell the misery of it from the street; its black stink flowed out through open windows— bedding, garbage, disinfectant, roach killer. His mouth was dry and he sat forward, straining to hear.

The medical examiner was on the stand. Had he seen the dead child? Yes. Did he have a report to make? He did. He gave the date and circumstances of the examination. A hefty, bald, solemn man with fleshy and deliberate lips, he held his notes in both hands like a singer—the experienced, professional witness. The child, he said, was normally formed but seemed to have suffered from malnutrition. There were signs of incipient rickets, the teeth were already quite carious, but this was sometimes a symptom that the mother had had toxemia in pregnancy. Were any unusual marks visible on the child's body? Yes, the little boy had apparently been beaten. Once, or repeatedly? In his opinion, often beaten. The scalp was torn. There were unusually heavy bruises on the back and legs. The shins were discolored. Where were the bruises heaviest? On the belly, and especially in the region of the genitals, where the boy seemed to have been beaten with something capable of breaking the skin, perhaps a metal buckle or the heel of a woman's shoe. "And what internal findings did you make?" the prosecutor went on. There were two broken ribs, one an older break. The more recent one had done some damage to the lung. The boy's liver had been ruptured. The hemorrhage caused by this may have been the immediate cause of death. There was also a brain injury. "In your opinion, then, the child died violently?" "That is my opinion. The liver injury would have been enough."

All this seemed to Herzog exceptionally low-pitched. All— the lawyers, the jury, the mother, her tough friend, the judge—behaved with much restraint, extremely well controlled and quiet-spoken. Such calm—inversely proportionate to the murder? he was thinking. Judge, jury, lawyers and the accused, all looked utterly unemotional. And he himself? He sat in his new madras coat and held his hard straw hat. He gripped his hat strongly and felt sick at heart. The ragged edge of the straw made marks on his fingers.

A witness was sworn, a solid-looking man of thirty-five or so, in a stylish oxford gray summer suit, of Madison Avenue cut. His face was round, full, jowly, but his head had little height above the ears and was further flattened by his butch haircut. He made very good gestures, pulling up his trouser legs as he sat, freeing his shirt cuffs and leaning forward to answer questions with measured, earnest, masculine politeness. His eyes were dark. You could see his scalp furrow as he frowned, weighing his answers. He identified himself as a salesman in the storm-window business, screens and storm windows. Herzog knew what he meant—aluminum sashes with triple tracks: he had read the ads. The witness lived in Flushing. Did he know the accused woman? She was asked to stand, and she did, a short hobbling figure, dark-red hair frizzy, the long eyes recessed, skin freckled, lips thick and dun-colored. Yes, he knew her, she had lived in his house eight months ago, not exactly employed by him, no, she was a distant cousin of his wife, who felt sorry for her and gave her a room—he had built a small apartment in the attic; separate bathroom, air-conditioner. She was asked to help with housework, naturally, but she also took off and left the boy for days at a time. Did he ever know her to mistreat the child? The kid was never clean. You never wanted to hold him on your lap. He had a cold sore, and his wife at last put salve on it, as the mother would not. The child was quiet, undemanding, clung to its mother, a frightened little boy, and he had a bad smell. Could the witness further describe the mother's attitude? Well, on the road, they were driving to visit the grandmother and stopped at Howard Johnson's. Everyone ordered. She had a barbecued beef sandwich and when it came began to eat and fed the child nothing. Then he himself (indignant) gave the boy some of his meat and gravy.

I fail to understand! thought Herzog, as this good man, jowls silently moving, got off the stand. I fail to . . . but this is the difficulty with people who spend their lives in humane studies and therefore imagine once cruelty has been described in books it is ended. Of course he really knew better— understood that human beings *would* not live so as to be understood by the Herzogs. Why should they?

But he had no time to think of this. The next witness was already sworn, the clerk at the Montcalme; a bachelor in his fifties; slack lips, large creases, damaged cheeks, hair that looked touched up, voice deep and melancholy, with a sinking rhythm to every sentence. The sentences sank down, down, until the last words were lost in rumbling syllables. An alcoholic once, judged Herzog from the look of his skin, and there was a certain faggotty prissiness in his speech, too. He said he had kept an eye on this "unfortunate pair." They rented a housekeeping room. The woman drew Relief money. The man had no occupation. The police came a few times to ask about him. And the boy, could he tell the court anything about him? Mostly that the child cried a lot. Tenants complained, and when he investigated he found the kid was kept shut in a closet. For discipline, was what the defendant told him. But toward the end the boy cried less. On the day of his death, however, there was a lot of noise. He heard something falling, and shrieks from the third floor. Both the mother and the boy were screaming. Someone was fooling with the elevator, so he ran upstairs. Knocked at the door, but she was screaming too loud to hear. So he opened and stepped in. Would he tell the court what he saw? He saw the woman with the boy in her arms. He thought she was hugging him, but to his astonishment she threw him from her with both arms. He was hurled against the wall. This made the noise he had been hearing below. Was anyone else present? Yes, the other defendant was lying on the bed, smoking. And was the child now screaming? No, at this time he was lying silent on the floor. Did the clerk then speak? He said he was frightened by the look of the woman, her swollen face. She turned red, crimson, and screamed with all her might, and she stamped her foot, the one with the built-up heel, he noticed, and he was afraid she would go for his eyes with her nails. He then went to call the police. Soon the man came downstairs. He explained that her boy was a problem child. She could not toilet-train him. He drove her wild sometimes the way he dirtied himself. And the crying all night! So they were talking when the squad car came. And found the child dead? Yes, he was dead when they arrived.

"Cross-examination?" said the bench. The defense lawyer waived examination with a movement of long white fingers, and the judge said, "You may step down. That will be all."

When the witness stood, Herzog stood up, too. He had to move, had to go. Again he wondered whether he was going to come down with sickness. Or was it the terror of the child that had gotten into him? Anyway, he felt stifled, as if the valves of his heart were not closing and the blood were going back into his lungs. He walked heavily and quickly. Turning once in the aisle, he saw only the lean gray head of the judge, whose lips silently moved as he read one of his documents.

Reaching the corridor, he said to himself, "Oh my God!" and in trying to speak discovered an acrid fluid in his mouth that had to be swallowed. Then stepping away from the door he stumbled into a woman with a cane. Black-browed, her hair very black though she was middle-aged, she pointed down-ward with the cane, instead of speaking. He saw that she wore a cast with metal clogs on the foot and that her toenails were painted. Then getting down the loathesome taste, he said, "I'm sorry." He had a sick repulsive headache, piercing and ugly. He felt as if he had gotten too close to a fire and scalded his lungs. She did not speak at all but was not ready to let him off. Her eyes, prominent, severe, still kept him standing, identi-fying him thoroughly, fully, deeply, as a fool. Again—silently—*Thou fool!* In the red-striped jacket, the hat tucked under his arm, hair uncombed, eyes swollen, he waited for her to go. When she left at last, going, cane, cast, clogs, down the speck-led corridor, he concentrated. With all his might—mind and heart—he tried to obtain something for the murdered child. But what? How? He pressed himself with intensity, but "all his might" could get nothing for the buried boy. Herzog experienced nothing but his own *human feelings*, in which he found nothing of use. What if he felt moved to cry? Or pray? He pressed hand to hand. And what did he feel? Why he felt himself—his own trembling hands, and eyes that stung. And what was there in modern, post . . . post-Christian America to pray for? Justice—justice and mercy? And pray away the monstrousness of life, the wicked dream it was? He opened his mouth to relieve the pressure he felt. He was wrung, and wrung again, and wrung again, again.

The child screamed, clung, but with both arms the girl hurled it against the wall. On her legs was ruddy hair. And her lover, too, with long jaws and zooty sideburns, watching on the bed. Lying down to copulate, and standing up to kill. Some kill, then cry. Others, not even that.

NEW YORK could not hold him now. He had to go to Chicago to see his daughter, confront Madeleine and Gersbach. The decision was not reached; it simply arrived. He went home and changed from the new clothes in which he had been diverting himself, into an old seersucker suit. Luckily, he had not unpacked when he came back from the Vineyard. He checked the valise quickly and left the apartment. Characteristically, he was determined to act without clearly knowing what to do, and even recognizing that he had no power over his impulses. He hoped that on the plane, in the clearer atmosphere, he would understand why he was flying.

The superjet carried him to Chicago in ninety minutes, due west, flying against the rotation of the planet and giving him an extension of afternoon and sunlight. Beneath, the white clouds were foaming. And the sun, like the spot that inoculated us against the whole of disintegrating space. He looked into the blue vacancy and at the sharp glitter of wingborne engines. When the plane bucked, he held his lip with his teeth. Not that he feared flying, but it occurred to him that if the ship were to crash, or simply explode (as had happened over Maryland recently, when human figures were seen to spill and fall like shelled peas), Gersbach would become June's guardian. Unless Simkin tore up the will. *Dear Simkin, shrewd Simkin, tear up that will!* There would also be two insurance policies, one bought by Father Herzog for his son Moshe. Only see how this child, young Herzog, had turned out—wrinkled, perplexed, pain at heart. I'm telling myself the truth. As heaven is my witness. The stewardess offered him a drink, which he refused with a shake of the head. He felt incapable of looking into the girl's pretty, healthful face.

As the jet landed, Herzog turned back his watch. He hurried from gate 38 and down the long corridor to the auto rental office. To identify himself, he had an American Express card, his Massachusetts driver's license, his university credentials. He himself would have been suspicious of such diverse addresses, to say nothing of the soiled, wrinkled seersucker suit worn by this applicant, Moses Elkanah Herzog; but the official who took his application, a sweet-mannered, bosomy, curly, fat-nosed little woman (even in his present state Herzog felt moved to smile faintly) only asked whether he wanted a convertible or a hard-top. He chose the hard-top, teal blue, and drove off, trying to find his way under the greenish glare of the lamps and dusty sunlight amid unfamiliar signs. He followed the winding cloverleaf into the Expressway and then joined the speeding traffic—in this zone, 60 m.p.h. He did not know these new sections of Chicago. Clumsy, stinking, tender Chicago, dumped on its ancient lake bottom; and this murky orange west, and the hoarseness of factories and trains, spilling gases and soot on the newborn summer. Traffic was heavy coming from the city, not on Herzog's side of the road, and he held the right lane looking for familiar street names. After Howard Street he was in the city proper and knew his way. Leaving the Expressway at Montrose, he turned east and drove to his late father's house, a small two-story brick building, one of a row built from a single blueprint—the pitched roof, the cement staircase inset on the right side, the window boxes the length of the front-room windows, the lawn a fat mound of grass between the sidewalk and the foundation; along the curb, elms and those shabby cottonwoods with blackened, dusty, wrinkled bark, and leaves that turned very tough by midsummer. There were also certain flowers, peculiar to Chicago, crude, waxy things like red and purple crayon bits, in a special class of false-looking natural objects. These foolish plants touched Herzog because they were so graceless, so corny. He was reminded of his father's devotion to his garden, when old Herzog became a property owner toward the end of his life—how he squirted his flowers at evening with the hose and how rapt he looked, his lips quietly pleased and his straight nose relishing the odor of the soil. To right and left, as Herzog emerged from the rented hard-top, the sprinklers turned and danced, scattering bright drops, fizzing out iridescent veils. And this was the house in which Father Herzog had died a few years ago, on a summer night, sitting up in bed suddenly, saying, "*Ich shtarb!*" And then he died, and that vivid blood of his turned to soil, in all the shrunken passages of his body. And then the body, too—ah, God!—wastes away; and leaves its bones, and even the bones at last wear away and crumble to dust in that shallow place of deposit. And thus humanized, this planet in its galaxy of stars and worlds goes from void to void, infinitesimal, aching with its unrelated significance. *Unrelated?* Herzog, with one of his Jewish shrugs, whispered, " *Nu, maile.* . . ." Be that as it may.

In any case, here was his late father's house in which the widow lived, Moses' very ancient stepmother, quite alone in this small museum of the Herzogs. The bungalow belonged to the family. No one wanted it now. Shura was a multimillionaire, he made that obvious enough. Willie had gone far in his father's construction-materials business—owned a fleet of those trucks with tremendous cylinder bodies that mixed cement en route to the job where it was funneled, pumped (Moses was vague about it) into the rising skyscrapers. Helen, if her husband was not in Willie's class, was at least well off. She rarely spoke of money any more. And he himself? He had about six hundred dollars in the bank. Still, for his purposes, he had what he needed. Poverty was not his portion; unemployment, slums, the perverts, thieves, victims in court, the horror of the Montcalme Hotel and its housekeeping rooms, smelling of decay and deadly bug juice—these were not for him. He could still take the superjet to Chicago when he had the impulse, could rent a teal-blue Falcon, drive to the old house. Thus he realized with peculiar clarity his position in the scale of prerogatives—of affluence, of insolence, of untruth, if you like. And not only his position, but when lovers quarreled they had a Lincoln Continental to shut a weeping child up in.

Face white, mouth grim, he mounted the stairs in the shadow of approaching sunset, and pressed the button. It had a crescent moon in the middle which lighted up at night.

The chimes rang inside, those chromium tubes above the door, xylophone metal, that played "Merrily We Roll Along," all but the last two notes. He had long to wait. The old woman, Taube, always had been slow, even in her fifties, thorough, deliberate, totally unlike the dexterous Herzogs—they had all inherited their father's preposterous quickness and elegance, something of the assertiveness of that one-man march with which old Herzog had defiantly paraded through the world. Moses was rather fond of Taube, he told himself; perhaps to feel differently toward her would have been too troubling. The unsteady gaze of her round prominent eyes was possibly caused by a radical resolve to be slow, a life-long program of delay and stasis. Creepingly, she accomplished every last goal she set herself. She ate, or sipped, slowly. She did not bring the cup to her mouth but moved her lips out toward it. And she spoke very slowly, to give her shrewdness scope. She cooked with fingers that did not grip firmly but was an excellent cook. She won at cards, poking along, but won. All questions she asked two or three times, and repeated the answers half to herself. With the same slowness she braided her hair, she brushed her exposed teeth, or chopped figs, dates, and senna leaves for her digestion. Her lip grew pendulous as she aged and her neck gradually thickened at the shoulders so that she had to hold her head forward somewhat. Oh, she was very old now, in her eighties and far from well. She was arthritic; one eye had a cataract. But unlike Polina she had a clear mind. No doubt her troubles with Father Herzog, stormier and more hot-headed and fractious as he aged, had strengthened her brain.

The house was dark, and anyone but Moses would have gone away, assuming there was no one at home. He, however, waited, knowing she would presently open. In his youth he had watched her take five minutes to open a bottle of soda—an hour to spread the dough over the table when she baked. Her strudel was like jeweler's work, and filled with red and green gems of preserves. At last he heard her at the door. Links of brass chain rose in the narrow opening. He saw old Taube's dark eyes, more somber now, and more extruded. The glass winter door still separated her from Moses. He knew it would also be locked. The old people had been guarded and suspicious in their own house. Moreover, Moses knew the light was behind him; he might not be recognized. And he was not the same Moses, anyway. But, although she studied him like a stranger, she had already identified him. Her intellect was not slow, whatever else.

"Who is it?"

"It's Moses. . . ."

"I don't know you. I'm alone. Moses?"

"Tante Taube—Moses Herzog. Moshe."

"Ah—Moshe."

Slow lame fingers released the catch. The door was shut to free the links from strain, and then opened, and—merciful God!—what a face he saw, how grooved with woe and age, lined downward at the mouth! As he came in she raised feeble hands to embrace him. "Moshe . . . Come in I'll make a light. Shut the door, Moshe."

He found the switch and turned on the very dim bulb of the entry hall. It shed a pinkish color; the old-fashioned glass of the fixture reminded him of the *ner tamid*, the vigil light in the synagogue. He shut the door on the watered fragrance of lawns as he entered. The house was close and faintly sour with furniture polish. The remembered luster was there in the faint twilit parlor—cabinets and tables, with inlaid tops, the brocaded sofa in its gleaming protective plastic, the Oriental rug, the drapes perfect and rigid on the windows with laterally rigid venetian blinds. A lamp went on behind him. He discovered on the console phonograph a smiling picture of Marco as a little boy, bare-kneed, on a bench, a fresh face, and charming, dark hair combed forward. And next to it was he himself in a photo taken when he got his M.A., handsome but somewhat jowly. His younger face expressed the demands of ingenuous conceit. A man in years he then was, but in years only, and in his father's eyes stubbornly un-European, that is, innocent by deliberate choice. Moses refused to know evil. But he could not refuse to experience it. And therefore others were appointed to do it to him, and then to be accused (by him) of wickedness. Among the rest was a picture of Father Herzog in his last incarnation—an American citizen—handsome, smooth-shaven, with none of his troubled masculine defiance, his one-time impetuousness or passionate protest. Still, to see Father Herzog's face in his own house melted Moses. Tante Taube was coming up with slow steps. She kept no photograph of herself here. Moses knew that she had been a stunning girl, despite her Habsburg lip; and even in her fifties when he first knew her as the Widow Kaplitzky she had had thick handsome strong brows and a heavy braid of animal brown; a soft if somewhat slack figure held rigid by her "gorselette." She didn't want to be reminded of her beauty or her former vigor.

"Let me look at you," she said, coming before him. Her eyes were puffy, but steady enough. He stared at her, and tried to prevent the horror from coming into his face. He guessed that it was putting in her plates that had delayed her. She had new ones, poorly made—no arch but a straight line of teeth. Like a woodchuck, he thought. Her fingers were disfigured, with loose skin that had worked forward over the nails. But those fingertips were painted. And what changes did she see in him? "Ach, Moshe, you changed."

He limited his answer to a nod. "And how are you?"

"You see. The living dead."

"You live alone?"

"I had a woman—Bella Ockinoff from the fish store. You knowed her. But she was not clean."

"Come, Tante, sit down."

"Oh, Moshe," she said, "I can't sit, I can't stand, can't lay. Better, already, next to Pa. Pa is better off than me."

"Is it so bad?" Herzog must have betrayed more emotion than he knew, for he now found her eyes examining him rather sharply, as if she did not believe that his feeling was for her and tried to find the real source of it. Or was it the cataract that gave her that expression? He guided her to a chair, holding her arm, and sat on the plastic-covered sofa. Under the tapestry. Pierrot. Clair de Lune. Venetian moonlight. All that phooey banality that oppressed him in his student days. It had no special power over him now. He was another man and had different purposes. The old woman, he saw, was trying to find what he had come for. She sensed that he was strongly agitated, missed his habitual vagueness, the proud air of abstraction in which M. E. Herzog, Ph.D., had once been clothed. *Them days is gone forever.*

"You working hard, Moshe?"

"Yes."

"Making a living?"

"Oh, yes."

The old woman bowed her head a moment. He saw the scalp, her thin gray hair. Exiguous. The organism had done all it could.

He clearly understood that she was communicating her right to live in this Herzog property, even though by staying alive she was depriving him of this remaining part of the estate.

"It's okay, I don't grudge you, Tante Taube," he said.

"What?"

"Just go on living, and don't worry about the property."

"You're not dressed well, Moshe. What's the matter, is it a hard time?"

"No. I wore an old suit for the plane."

"You got business in Chicago?"

"Yes, Tante."

"The children all right? Marco?"

"He's at camp."

"Daisy didn't married yet?"

"No."

"You have to pay her alimony?"

"Not very much."

"I was not a bad stepmother? Tell the truth."

"You were a good stepmother. You were very good."

"I did mine best," she said, and in this meekness he glimpsed her old disguises—the elaborate and powerful role she had played with Father Herzog as the patient Widow Kaplitzky, once wife of Kaplitzky the prominent wholesaler, childless, his only darling, wearing a locket set with little rubies and traveling in Pullman drawing rooms—the Portland Rose, the 20th Century—or on the *Berengaria*, first class. As the second Mrs. Herzog she did not have an easy life. She had good reason to mourn Kaplitzky. "*Gottseliger* Kaplitzky," she always called him. And she once had told Moses, "*Gottseliger* Kaplitzky didn't want I should have children. The doctor thought it would be bad for mine heart. And every time . . . Kaplitzky-*alehoshalom* took care on everything. I didn't even looked."

Recalling this, Herzog very briefly laughed. Ramona would like "I didn't even looked." She always looked, bent close, held back a falling lock of hair, cheeks flushing, greatly amused by his shyness. As last night, lying down, opening her arms to him . . . He must wire her. She would not understand his disappearance. And then the blood began to beat in his head. He remembered why he was here.

He sat near the very spot where Father Herzog, the year before his death, had threatened to shoot him. The cause of his rage was money. Herzog was broke, and asked his father to underwrite a loan. The old man questioned him narrowly, about his job, his expenses, his child. He had no patience with

Moses. At that time I was living in Philadelphia, alone, making my choice (it was no choice!) between Sono and Madeleine. Perhaps he had even heard I was about to be converted to Catholicism. Someone started such a rumor; it may have been Daisy. I was in Chicago then because Papa had sent for me. He wanted to tell me about the changes in his will. Day and night, he thought how he would divide his estate, and thought accordingly of each of us, what we deserved, how we would use it. At odd times, he'd telephone and tell me I had to come right away. I'd sit up all night on the train. And he'd take me into a corner and say, "I want you to hear, once and for all. Your brother Willie is an honest man. When I die, he'll do as we agreed." "I believe it, Papa."

But he lost his temper every time, and when he wanted to shoot me it was because he could no longer bear the sight of me, that look of mine, the look of conceit or proud trouble. The elite look. I don't blame him, thought Moses as Taube slowly and lengthily described her ailments. Papa couldn't bear such an expression on the face of his youngest son. I aged. I wasted myself in stupid schemes, *liberating* my spirit. His heart ached angrily because of me. And Papa was not like some old men who become blunted toward their own death. No, his despair was keen and continual. And Herzog again was pierced with pain for his father.

He listened awhile to Taube's account of her cortisone treatments. Her large, luminous, tame eyes, the eyes that had domesticated Father Herzog, were not watching Moses now. They gazed at a point beyond him and left him free to recall those last days of Father Herzog. We walked to Montrose together to buy cigarettes. It was June, warm like this, the weather bright. Papa wasn't exactly making sense. He said he should have divorced the Widow Kaplitzky ten years ago, that he had hoped to enjoy the last years of his life—his Yiddish became more crabbed and quaint in these conversations—but he had brought his iron to a cold forge. *A kalte kuzhnya, Moshe. Kein fire.* Divorce was impossible because he owed her too much money. "But you have money now, don't you?" said Herzog, blunt with him. His father stopped, staring into his face. Herzog was stunned to see in full summer light how much disintegration had already taken place. But the remaining elements, incredibly vivid, had all their old power over Moses—the straight nose, the furrow between the eyes, the brown and green colors in those eyes. "I need my money. Who'll provide for me—you? I may bribe the Angel of Death a long time yet." Then he bent his knees a little—Moses read that old signal; he had a lifetime of skill in interpreting his father's gestures: those bent knees meant that something of great subtlety was about to be revealed. "I don't know when I'll be delivered," Father Herzog whispered. He used the old Yiddish term for a woman's confinement—*kimpet*. Moses did not know what to say, and his answering voice was not much above a whisper. "Don't torment yourself, Papa." The horror of this second birth, into the hands of death, made his eyes shine, and his lips silently pressed together. Then Father Herzog said, "I have to sit down, Moshe. The sun is too hot for me." He did, suddenly, appear very flushed, and Moses supported him, eased him down on the cement embankment of a lawn. The old man's look was now one of injured male pride. "Even I feel the heat today," said Moses. He placed himself between his father and the sun.

"I may go next month to St. Joe for the baths," Taube was saying. "To the Whitcomb. It's a nice place."

"Not alone?"

"Ethel and Mordecai want to go."

"Oh . . . ?" He nodded, to keep her going. "How is Mordecai?"

"How can he be in his age?" Moses was attentive until she was well started and then he returned to his father. They had had lunch on the back porch that day, and that was where the quarrel began. It had seemed to Moses, perhaps, that he was here as a prodigal son, admitting the worst and asking the old man's mercy, and so Father Herzog saw nothing except a stupid appeal in his son's face—incomprehensible. "Idiot!" was what the old man had shouted. "Calf!" Then he saw the angry demand underlying Moses' look of patience. "Get out! I leave you nothing! Everything to Willie and Helen! You . . . ? Croak in a flophouse." Moses rising, Father Herzog shouted, "Go. And don't come to my funeral."

"All right, maybe I won't."

Too late, Tante Taube had warned him to keep silent, raising her brows—she had still had brows then. Father Herzog rose stumbling from the table, his face distorted, and ran to get his pistol.

"Go, go! Come back later. I'll call you," Taube had whispered to Moses, and he, confused, reluctant, burning, stung because his misery was not recognized in his father's house (his monstrous egotism making its peculiar demands)—he reluctantly got up from the table. "Quick, quick!" Taube tried to get him to the front door, but old Herzog overtook them with the pistol.

He cried out, "I'll kill you!" And Herzog was startled not so much by this threat, which he did not believe, as by the return of his father's strength. In his rage he recovered it briefly, though it might cost him his life. The strained neck, the grinding of his teeth, his frightening color, even the military Russian strut with which he lifted the gun—these were better, thought Herzog, than his sinking down during a walk to the store. Father Herzog was not made to be pitiful.

"Go, go," said Tante Taube. Moses was weeping then.

"Maybe you'll die first," Father Herzog shouted.

"Papa!"

Half hearing Tante Taube's slow description of Cousin Mordecai's approaching retirement, Herzog grimly recovered the note of that cry. *Papa—Papa.* You lout! The old man in his near-demented way was trying to act out the manhood you should have had. Coming to his house with that Christianized smirk of the long-suffering son. Might as well have been an outright convert, like Mady. He should have pulled the trigger. Those looks were agony to him. He deserved to be spared, in his old age.

And then there was Moses with puffy weeping eyes, in the street, waiting for his cab, while Father Herzog hastily walked up and back before these windows, staring at him in agony of spirit—yes, you got that out of him. Walking quickly there, back and forth in his hasty style, dropping his weight on the one heel. The pistol thrown down. Who knows whether Moses shortened his life by the grief he gave him. Perhaps the stimulus of anger lengthened it. He could not die and leave this half-made Moses yet.

They were reconciled the following year. And then more of the same. And then . . . death.

"Should I make a cup of tea?" said Tante Taube.

"Yes, please, I'd like that if you feel up to it. And I also want to look in Papa's desk."

"Pa's desk? It's locked. You want to look in the desk? Everything belongs to you children. You could take the desk when I die."

"No, no!" he said, "I don't need the desk itself, but I was passing from the airport and thought I'd see how you were. And now that I'm here, I'd like to have a look in the desk. I know you don't mind."

"You want something, Moshe? You took your Mama's silver coin case the last time."

He had given it to Madeleine.

"Is Papa's watch chain still in there?"

"I think Willie took it."

He frowned with concentration. "Then what about the rubles?" he asked. "I'd like them for Marco."

"Rubles?"

"My grandfather Isaac bought Czarist rubles during the Revolution, and they've always been in the desk."

"In the desk? I surely never seen them."

"I'd like to look, while you make a cup of tea, Tante Taube. Give me the key."

"The key . . . ?" Questioning him before, she had spoken more quickly, but now she receded again into slowness, raising a mountain of dilatory will in his way.

"Where do you keep it?"

"Where? Where did I put it? Is it in Pa's dresser? Or somewheres else? Let me remember. That's how I am now, it's hard to remember. . . ."

"I know where it is," he said, suddenly rising.

"You know where it is? So where is it?"

"In the music box, where you always used to keep it."

"In the music . . . ? Pa took it from there. He locked up my social-security checks when they came. He said all the money *he* should have. . . ."

Moses knew he had guessed right. "Don't bother, I'll get it," he said. "If you'll put the kettle on. I'm very thirsty. It's been a hot, long day."

He helped her to rise, holding her flaccid arm. He was

having his way—a poor sort of victory and filled with dangerous consequences. Going forward without her, he entered the
bedroom. His father's bed had been removed. Hers stood
alone with its ugly bedspread—some material that reminded
him of a coated tongue. He breathed the old spice, the dark,
heavy air, and lifted the lid of the music box. In this house he
had only to consult his memory to find what he wanted. The
mechanism released its little notes as the cylinder turned
within, the small spines picking out the notes from *Figaro*.
Moses was able to supply the word:

> *Nel momento*
> *Della mia cerimonia*
> *Io rideva di me*
> *Senza saperlo.*

His fingers recognized the key.

Old Taube in the dark outside the bedroom said, "Did you
found it?"

He answered, "It's here," and spoke in a low, mild voice,
not to make matters worse. The house was hers, after all. It
was rude to invade it. He was not ashamed of this, he only recognized with full objectivity that it was not right. But it had to
be done.

"Do you want me to put the kettle on?"

"No, a cup of tea I can still make."

He heard her slow steps in the passage. She was going to the
kitchen. Herzog quickly made for the small sitting room. The
drapes were drawn. He turned on the lamp beside the desk.
In seeking the switch he tore the ancient silk of the shade, releasing a fine dust. The name of this color was old rose—he
felt certain of it. He opened the cherry-wood secretary, braced
the wide leaf on its runners, drawing them out from either side.
Then he went back and shut the door, first making sure Taube
had reached the kitchen. In the drawers he recognized each
article—leather, paper, gold. Swift and tense, veins standing
out on his head, and tendons on the hands, he groped and
found what he was looking for—Father Herzog's pistol. An
old pistol, the barrel nickel-plated. Papa had bought it to keep
on Cherry Street, in the railroad yards. Moses flipped the gun
open. There were two bullets. This was it, then. He rapidly

clicked it shut and put it in his pocket. There it made too large a bulge. He took out his wallet and replaced it with the gun. The wallet he buttoned in his hip pocket.

Now he began to search for those rubles. Those he found in a small compartment with old passports, ribbons sealed in wax, like gobs of dried blood. *La bourgeoise Sarah Herzog avec ses enfants, Alexandre huit ans, Hélène neuf ans et Guillaume troisans,* signed by Count Adlerberg *Gouverneur de St. Petersbourg.* The rubles were in a large billfold—his playthings of forty years ago. Peter the Great in a rich coat of armor, and a splendid imperial Catherine. Lamplight revealed the watermarks. Recalling how he and Willie used to play casino for these stakes, Herzog uttered one of his short laughs, then made a nest of these large bills in his pocket for the pistol. He thought it must be less conspicuous now.

"You got what you want?" Taube asked him in the kitchen.

"Yes." He put the key on the enameled metal table.

He knew it was not proper that he should think her expression sheeplike. This figurative habit of his mind crippled his judgment, and was likely to ruin him some day. Perhaps the day was near; perhaps this night his soul would be required of him. The gun weighed on his chest. But the protuberant lips, great eyes, and pleated mouth *were* sheeplike, and they warned him he was taking too many chances with destruction. Taube, a veteran survivor, to be heeded, had fought the grave to a standstill, balking death itself by her slowness. All had decayed but her shrewdness and her incredible patience; and in Moses she saw Father Herzog again, nervy and hasty, impulsive, suffering. His eye twitched as he bent toward her in the kitchen. She muttered, "You got a lot of trouble? Don't make it worser, Moshe."

"There's no trouble, Tante. I have business to take care of. . . . I don't think I can wait for tea, after all."

"I put out Pa's cup for you."

Moses drank tap water from his father's teacup.

"Good-by, Tante Taube, keep well." He kissed her forehead.

"Remember I helped you?" she said. "You shouldn't forget. Take care, Moshe."

He left by the back door; it made departure simpler. Honeysuckle grew along the rainspout, as in his father's time, and fragrant in the evening—almost too rich. Could any heart become quite petrified?

He gunned his motor at the stoplight, trying to decide which was the faster route to Harper Avenue. The new Ryan Expressway was very quick but it would land him in the thick of the Negro traffic on West 51st Street, where people promenaded, or cruised in their cars. There was Garfield Boulevard, much better; however, he was not sure he could find his way through Washington Park after dark. He decided to follow Eden's to Congress Street and Congress to the Outer Drive. Yes, that would be fastest. What he would do when he got to Harper Avenue he hadn't yet decided. Madeleine had threatened him with arrest if he so much as showed his face near the house. The police had his picture, but that was sheer bunk, bunk and paranoia, the imperiousness of imaginary powers that had once impressed him. But there was now a real matter between him and Madeleine, a child, a reality—June. Out of cowardice, sickness, fraud, by a bungling father out of a plotting bitch, something genuine! This little daughter of his! He cried out to himself as he raced up the ramp of the Expressway that nobody would harm *her*. He accelerated, moving in his lane with the rest of the traffic. The thread of life was stretched tight in him. It quivered crazily. He did not fear its breaking so much as his failing to do what he should. The little Falcon was storming. He thought his speed was terrible until a huge trailer truck passed him on the right, when he realized that this was not the time to risk a traffic ticket—not with a pistol in his pocket—and lifted his foot from the pedal. Peering left and right, he recognized that the new Expressway had been cut through old streets, streets he knew. He saw the vast gas tanks, crowned with lights, from a new perspective, and the rear of a Polish church with a Christ in brocades exhibited in a lighted window, like a showcase. The long curve eastbound passed over the freight yards, burning with sunset dust, rails streaking westward; next, the tunnel under the mammoth post office; next, the State Street honky-tonks. From the last slope of Congress Street the distortions of dusk raised up the lake like a mild wall crossed by bands, amethyst, murky blue, irregular silver, and a slate color at the horizon, boats hanging rocking inside the breakwater, and helicopters and small aircraft whose lights teetered overhead. The familiar odor of the fresh water, bland but also raw, reached him as he sped south. It did not seem illogical that he should claim the privilege of insanity, violence, having been made to carry the rest of it—name-calling and gossip, railroading, pain, even exile in Ludeyville. That property was to have been his madhouse. Finally, his mausoleum. But they had done something else to Herzog—unpredictable. It's not everyone who gets the opportunity to kill with a clear conscience. They had opened the way to justifiable murder. They deserved to die. He had a right to kill them. They would even know why they were dying; no explanation necessary. When he stood before them they would have to submit. Gersbach would only hang his head, with tears for himself. Like Nero—*Qualis artifex pereo.* Madeleine would shriek and curse. Out of hatred, the most powerful element in her life, stronger by far than any other power or motive. In spirit she was his murderess, and therefore he was turned loose, could shoot or choke without remorse. He felt in his arms and in his fingers, and to the core of his heart, the sweet exertion of strangling—horrible and sweet, an orgastic rapture of inflicting death. He was sweating violently, his shirt wet and cold under his arms. Into his mouth came a taste of copper, a metabolic poison, a flat but deadly flavor.

When he reached Harper Avenue he parked around the corner, and entered the alley that passed behind the house. Grit spilled on the concrete; broken glass and gravelly ashes made his steps loud. He went carefully. The back fences were old here. Garden soil spilled under the slats, and shrubs and vines came over their tops. Once more he saw open honeysuckle. Even rambler roses, dark red in the dusk. He had to cover his face when he passed the garage because of the loops of briar that swung over the path from the sloping roof. When he stole into the yard he stood still until he could see his way. He must not stumble over a toy, or a tool. A fluid had come into his eyes—very clear, only somewhat distorting. He wiped it away with fingertips, and blotted, too, with the lapel of his coat. Stars had come out, violet points framed in roof shapes, leaves, strut wires. The yard was visible to him now. He saw the clothesline—Madeleine's underpants and his daughter's little

shirts and dresses, tiny stockings. By the light of the kitchen
window he made out a sandbox in the grass, a new red sandbox with broad ledges to sit on. Stepping nearer, he looked
into the kitchen. Madeleine was there! He stopped breathing
as he watched her. She was wearing slacks and a blouse fastened with a broad red leather and brass belt he had given her.
Her smooth hair hung loose as she moved between the table
and the sink, cleaning up after dinner, scraping dishes in her
own style of abrupt efficiency. He studied her straight profile
as she stood at the sink, the flesh under her chin as she concentrated on the foam in the sink, tempering the water. He
could see the color in her cheeks, and almost the blue of her
eyes. Watching, he fed his rage, to keep it steady, up to full
strength. She was not likely to hear him in the yard because
the storm windows had not been taken down—not, at least,
those he had put up last fall at the back of the house.

He moved into the passageway. Luckily the neighbors were
not at home, and he did not have to worry about their lights.
He had had his look at Madeleine. It was his daughter he wanted
to see now. The dining room was unoccupied—after-dinner
emptiness, Coke bottles, paper napkins. Next was the bathroom window, set higher than the rest. He remembered, however, that he had used a cement block to stand on, trying to
take out the bathroom screen until he had discovered there was
no storm window to replace it. The screen was still in, therefore. And the block? It was exactly where he had left it, among
the lilies of the valley on the left side of the path. He moved it
into place, the scraping covered by the sound of water in the
tub, and stood on it, his side pressed to the building. He tried
to muffle the sound of his breathing, opening his mouth. In
the rushing water with floating toys his daughter's little body
shone. His child! Madeleine had let her black hair grow
longer, and now it was tied up for the bath with a rubber band.
He melted with tenderness for her, putting his hand over his
mouth to cover any sound emotion might cause him to make.
She raised her face to speak to someone he could not see. Above
the flow of water he heard her say something but could not
understand the words. Her face was the Herzog face, the large
dark eyes *his* eyes, the nose his father's, Tante Zipporah's, his
brother Willie's nose, and the mouth his own. Even the bit of

melancholy in her beauty—that was his mother. It was Sarah
Herzog, pensive, slightly averting her face as she considered
the life about her. Moved, he watched her, breathing with
open mouth, his face half covered by his hand. Flying beetles
passed him. Their heavy bodies struck the screen but did not
attract her notice.

Then a hand reached forward and shut off the water—a
man's hand. It was Gersbach. He was going to bathe Herzog's
daughter! Gersbach! His waist was now in sight. He came into
view stalking beside the old-fashioned round tub, bowing,
straightening, bowing—his Venetian hobble, and then, with
great trouble, he began to kneel, and Herzog saw his chest, his
head, as he arranged himself. Flattened to the wall, his chin on
his shoulder, Herzog saw Gersbach roll up the sleeves of his
paisley sports shirt, put back his thick glowing hair, take the
soap, heard him say, not unkindly, "Okay, cut out the monkeyshines," for Junie was giggling, twisting, splashing, dimpling,
showing her tiny white teeth, wrinkling her nose, teasing.
"Now hold still," said Gersbach. He got into her ears with the
washrag as she screamed, cleaned off her face, the nostrils,
wiped her mouth. He spoke with authority, but affectionately
and with grumbling smiles and occasionally with laughter he
bathed her—soaped, rinsed, dipping water in her toy boats to
rinse her back as she squealed and twisted. The man washed
her tenderly. His look, perhaps, was false. But he had no *true*
expressions, Herzog thought. His face was all heaviness, sexual
meat. Looking down his open shirt front, Herzog saw the
hair-covered heavy soft flesh of Gersbach's breast. His chin was
thick, and like a stone ax, a brutal weapon. And then there
were his sentimental eyes, the thick crest of hair, and that hearty
voice with its peculiar fraudulence and grossness. The hated
traits were all there. But see how he was with June, scooping
the water on her playfully, kindly. He let her wear her mother's
flowered shower cap, the rubber petals spreading on the
child's head. Then Gersbach ordered her to stand, and she
stooped slightly to allow him to wash her little cleft. Her father
stared at this. A pang went through him, but it was quickly
done. She sat again. Gersbach ran fresh water on her, cumber-
somely rose and opened the bath towel. Steady and thorough,
he dried her, and then with a large puff he powdered her. The

child jumped up and down with delight. "Enough of this wild stuff," said Gersbach. "Put on those p-j's now."

She ran out. Herzog still saw faint wisps of powder, that floated over Gersbach's stooping head. His red hair worked up and down. He was scouring the tub. Moses might have killed him now. His left hand touched the gun, enclosed in the roll of rubles. He might have shot Gersbach as he methodically salted the yellow sponge rectangle with cleansing powder. There were two bullets in the chamber. . . . But they would stay there. Herzog clearly recognized that. Very softly he stepped down from his perch, and passed without sound through the yard again. He saw his child in the kitchen, looking up at Mady, asking for something, and he edged through the gate into the alley. Firing this pistol was nothing but a thought.

The human soul is an amphibian, and I have touched its sides. Amphibian! It lives in more elements than I will ever know; and I assume that in those remote stars matter is in the making which will create stranger beings yet. I seem to think because June looks like a Herzog, she is nearer to me than to them. But how is she near to me if I have no share in her life? Those two grotesque love-actors have it all. And I apparently believe that if the child does not have a life resembling mine, educated according to the Herzog standards of "heart," and all the rest of it, she will fail to become a human being. This is sheer irrationality, and yet some part of my mind takes it as self-evident. But what in fact can she learn from them? From Gersbach, when he looks so sugary, repulsive, poisonous, not an individual but a fragment, a piece broken off from the mob. To shoot him!—an absurd thought. As soon as Herzog saw the actual person giving an actual bath, the reality of it, the tenderness of such a buffoon to a little child, his intended violence turned into *theater*, into something ludicrous. He was not ready to make such a complete fool of himself. Only self-hatred could lead him to ruin himself because his heart was "broken." How could it be broken by such a pair? Lingering in the alley awhile, he congratulated himself on his luck. His breath came back to him; and how good it felt to breathe! It was worth the trip.

Think! he noted to himself in the Falcon, on a pad under the map light. *Demographers estimate that at least half of all the*

*human beings ever born are alive now, in this century. What a
moment for the human soul! Characteristics drawn from the genetic pool have, in statistical probability, reconstituted all the best
and all the worst of human life. It's all around us. Buddha and
Lao-tse must be walking the earth somewhere. And Tiberius and
Nero. Everything horrible, everything sublime, and things not
imagined yet. And you, part-time visionary, cheerful, tragical
mammal. You and your children and children's children . . .
In ancient days, the genius of man went largely into metaphors.
But now into facts . . . Francis Bacon. Instruments.* Then
with inexpressible relish he added, *Tante Zipporah told Papa he
could never use a gun on anyone, never keep up with teamsters,
butchers, sluggers, hooligans, razboiniks. "A gilded little gentleman." Could he hit anyone on the head? Could he shoot?*

Moses could confidently swear that Father Herzog had
never—not once in his life—pulled the trigger of this gun.
Only threatened. As he threatened me with it. Taube defended
me then. She "saved" me. Dear Aunt Taube! A cold forge!
Poor Father Herzog!

But he was not yet willing to call it a day. He had to have a
talk with Phoebe Gersbach. It was essential. And he decided
not to phone her and give her an opportunity to prepare herself, or even refuse to see him. He drove directly to Woodlawn
Avenue—a dreary part of Hyde Park, but characteristic, *his*
Chicago: massive, clumsy, amorphous, smelling of mud and decay, dog turds; sooty façades, slabs of structural *nothing*, sense-
lessly ornamented triple porches with huge cement urns for
flowers that contained only rotting cigarette butts and other
stained filth; sun parlors under tiled gables, rank areaways, gray
backstairs, seamed and ruptured concrete from which sprang
grass; ponderous four-by-four fences that sheltered growing
weeds. And among these spacious, comfortable, dowdy apartments where liberal, benevolent people lived (this was the university neighborhood) Herzog did in fact feel at home. He was
perhaps as midwestern and unfocused as these same streets.
(Not so much determinism, he thought, as a lack of deter-
mining elements—the absence of a formative power.) But it
was all typical, and nothing was lacking, not even the sound of

roller skates awkwardly gritting on the pavement beneath new summer leaves. Two poky little girls under the green transparency of street lamps, skating in short skirts, and with ribbons in their hair.

A nervous qualm went through him now that he was at Gersbach's gate, but he mastered it and went up the walk, rang the bell. Phoebe approached quickly. She called, "Who is it?" and seeing Herzog through the glass was silent. Was she scared?

"It's an old friend," said Herzog. A moment passed, Phoebe, despite the firmness of her mouth, hesitating, eyes large-lidded beneath her bangs. "Won't you let me in?" Moses asked. His tone made refusal unthinkable. "I won't take much of your time," he said as he was entering. "We do have a few matters to discuss, though."

"Come in the kitchen, will you."

"Sure . . ." She didn't want to be surprised talking to him in the front room or overheard by little Ephraim, who was in his bedroom. In the kitchen she shut the door and asked Herzog to sit. The chair her eyes were looking at was beside the refrigerator. There he would not be seen from the kitchen window. With a faint smile he sat down. From the extreme composure of her slender face he knew how her heart must be pounding, working perhaps even more violently than his. An orderly person, self-controlled in high degree, clean—the head nurse—she tried to maintain a businesslike look. She was wearing the amber beads he had brought her from Poland. Herzog buttoned up his jacket to make sure the butt of his gun did not show. The sight of a weapon would certainly frighten her to death.

"Well, how are you, Phoebe?"

"We're all right."

"Comfortably settled? Liking Chicago? Little Ephraim still in the Lab School?"

"Yes."

"And the Temple? I see that Val taped a program with Rabbi Itzkowitz—what did he call it? 'Hasidic Judaism, Martin Buber, *I and Thou.*' Still the Buber kick! He's very thick with these rabbis. Maybe he wants to swap wives with a rabbi. He'll work

his way round from 'I and Thou' to 'Me and You'—'You and
Me, Kid!' But I suppose you'd draw the line there. You
wouldn't go along with everything."

Phoebe made no answer and remained standing.

"Maybe you think I'll leave sooner if you don't sit. Come,
Phoebe, sit down. I promise you I haven't come to make
scenes. I have only one purpose here, in addition to wanting to
see an old friend. . . ."

"We're not really old friends."

"Not by calendar years. But we were so close out in Ludeyville. That is true. You have to think of duration—Bergsonian
duration. We have known each other in duration. Some people
are *sentenced* to certain relationships. Maybe every relationship
is either a joy or a sentence."

"You earned your own sentence, if that's how you want to
think about it. We had a quiet life till you and Madeleine descended on Ludeyville and forced yourself on me." Phoebe,
her face thin but hot, eyelids unmoving, sat down on the edge
of the chair Herzog had drawn forward for her.

"Good. Say what you think, Phoebe. That's what I want. Sit
back. Don't be afraid. I'm not looking for trouble. We've got
a problem in common."

Phoebe denied this. She shook her head, with a stubborn
look, all too vigorously. "I'm a plain woman. Valentine is from
upstate New York."

"Just a rube. Yes. Knows nothing about fancy vices from the
big city. Didn't even know how to dial a number. Had to be
led step by step into degeneracy by me—Moses E. Herzog."

Stiff and hesitant, she turned her body aside in her abrupt
way. Then she came to a decision and turned to him again with
the same abruptness. She was a pretty woman, but stiff, very
stiff, bony, without self-confidence. "You never understood a
thing about him. He fell for you. Adored you. Tried to become an intellectual because he wanted to help you—saw what
a terrible thing you had done in giving up your respectable
university position and how reckless you were, rushing out to
the country with Madeleine. He thought she was ruining you
and tried to set you on the right track again. He read all those
books so you'd have somebody to talk to, out in the sticks,
Moses. Because you needed help, praise, flattery, support, af-

fection. It never was enough. You wore him out. It nearly killed him trying to back you up."

"Yes . . . ? What else? Go on," said Herzog.

"It's still not enough. What do you want from him now? What are you here for? More excitement? Are you still greedy for excitement?"

Herzog no longer smiled. "Some of what you say is right enough, Phoebe. I was certainly floundering in Ludeyville. But you take the wind out of me when you say you were leading a perfectly ordinary life up there in Barrington. Until Mady and I came along with the books and the theatrical glamour, high-level mental life, scattering big-shot ideas and blowing whole ages of history. You were scared by us because we—Mady especially—gave him confidence. As long as he was only a small-time gimpy radio announcer, he might bluff at being a big shot, but you had him where you wanted him. Because he is a bluffer and a screwball, a kind of freak, but *yours*. Then he got bolder. He gave his exhibitionism scope. Quite right, I'm an idiot. You were even right to dislike me, if only because I wouldn't see what was happening and in that way put another burden on you. But why didn't you say something? You watched the whole thing going on. It went on for years, and you said nothing. I wouldn't have been so indifferent if I saw the same thing happening to *you*."

Phoebe hesitated to speak of this and turned even paler. She said, at last, "It's not my fault that you refuse to understand the system other people live by. Your ideas get in the way. Maybe a weak person like me has no choice. I couldn't do anything for you. Especially last year. I was seeing a psychiatrist, and he advised me to keep away. To keep away from you, most of all from you and all your trouble. He said I wasn't strong enough, and you know it's true—I'm not strong enough."

Herzog considered this—Phoebe was weak, that was certainly the truth. He decided to get to the point. "Why don't you divorce Valentine?" he said.

"I see no reason why I should." Her voice immediately recovered strength.

"He's deserted you, hasn't he?"

"Val? I don't know why you say that! I'm not deserted."

"Where is he now—this evening? This minute?"

"Downtown. On business."

"Oh, come on, don't pull that stuff on me, Phoebe. He's living with Madeleine. Do you deny it?"

"I most certainly do. I can't imagine how you ever got such a fantastic idea."

Moses leaned with one arm against the refrigerator as he shifted in his chair and took out a handkerchief—the scrap of kitchen towel from his New York apartment. He wiped his face.

"If you would sue for divorce," he explained, "as you have every right to do, you could name Madeleine for adultery. I'd help raise the money. I'd underwrite the whole cost. I want Junie. Don't you see? Together we could nail them. You've let Madeleine drive you here and there. As if you were a nanny goat."

"That's the old devil in you talking again, Moses."

Nanny goat was a mistake; he was making her more obstinate. But, anyway, she was going to follow her own line. She'd never share any plan of his.

"Don't you want me to have custody of June?"

"I'm indifferent to that."

"You have your own war with Madeleine, I suppose," he said. "Fighting over the man. A cat fight—a female sex fight. But she'll beat you. Because she's a psychopath. I know you've got reserve strength. But she's a nut, and nuts win. Besides, Valentine doesn't want you to get him."

"I really don't understand what you're saying."

"He'll lose his value to Madeleine as soon as you withdraw. After the victory, she'll have to throw him out."

"Valentine comes home every night. He's never out late. He should be here soon. . . . When I'm even a little delayed somewhere, why, he gets frantic with worry. He phones all over the city."

"Perhaps that's just hope," said Moses. "Hope disguised as concern. Don't you know how that is? If you get killed in an accident, he cries and packs up and moves in with Madeleine for good."

"That's your devil speaking again. My child is going to keep *his* father. You still want Madeleine, don't you!"

"Me? Never! All that hysterical stuff is finished. No, I'm glad to be rid of her. I don't even loathe her much any more.

And she's welcome to all she chiseled from me. She must have been banking my money all along. Okay! Let her keep it with my blessing. Bless the bitch! Good luck and good-by. I bless her. I wish her a busy, useful, pleasant, dramatic life. Including *love*. The best people fall in love, and she's one of the best, therefore she loves this fellow. They both *love*. She's not good enough to bring up the kid, though. . . ."

If he were a wild pig, and those bangs of hers a protective hedge—Phoebe's brown eyes were as vigilant as that. And yet Moses was sorry for her. They bullied her—Gersbach; Madeleine through Gersbach. But Phoebe herself meant to win this contest. It must be inconceivable to her that one should set such modest, such minimal goals—table, market, laundry, child—and still lose the struggle. Life couldn't be as indecent as that. Could it? Another hypothesis: sexlessness was her strength; she wielded the authority of the superego. Still another: she acknowledged the creative depth of modern degeneracy, all the luxuriant vices of emancipated swingers, and thus accepted her situation as a poor, neurotic, dry unfortunate, mud-stuck, middle-class woman. To her, Gersbach was no ordinary man, and because of his richness of character, his spiritual-erotic drive, or God knows what foot-smelling metaphysics, he required two wives or more. Maybe these two women lent this piece of orange-tufted flesh to each other for widely different needs. For three-legged copulation. For domestic peace.

"Phoebe," he said. "Admitting you're weak—but how weak are you? Excuse me. . . . I find this pretty funny. You have to deny *everything*, and keep up a perfect appearance. Can't you admit even a tiny bit?"

"What good would that do you?" she asked sharply. "And also, what are you prepared to do for me?"

"I? I'd help . . ." he began. But he checked himself. It was true, he couldn't offer much. He really was useless to her. With Gersbach she could still be a wife. He came home. She cooked, ironed, shopped, signed checks. Without him, she could not exist, cook, make beds. The trance would break. Then what?

"Why do you come to me, if you want custody of your daughter? Either do something by yourself or forget it. Let me alone, now, Moses."

This, too, was perfectly just. Silent, he stared hard at her. The early and native tendency of his mind, lately acting without inhibitions, found significance in small bloodless marks on her face. As if death had tried her with his teeth and found her still unripe.

"Well, thank you for this talk, Phoebe. I'm going." He stood up. There was a softer kindliness in Herzog's expression, not often seen. Rather awkwardly he took Phoebe's hand, and she could not move fast enough to avoid his lips. He drew her closer and kissed her on the head. "You're right. This was an unnecessary visit." She freed her fingers.

"Good-by, Moses." She spoke without looking at him. He would not get more from her than she was able to spare. ". . . You've been treated like dirt. That's true. But it's all over. You should get away. Just get away from this now."

The door was shut.

Crumbs of decency—all that we paupers can spare one another. No wonder "personal" life is a humiliation, and to be an individual contemptible. The historical process, putting clothes on our backs, shoes on the feet, meat in the mouth, does infinitely more for us by the indifferent method than anyone does by intention, Herzog wrote in the rented Falcon. *And since these good commodities are the gifts of anonymous planning and labor, what intentional goodness can achieve (when the good are amateurs) becomes the question. Especially if, in the interests of health, our benevolence and love demand exercise, the creature being emotional, passionate, expressive, a relating animal. A creature of deep peculiarities, a web of feeling intricacies and ideas now approaching a level of organization and automatism where he can hope to be free from human dependency. People are practicing their future condition already. My emotional type is archaic. Belongs to the agricultural or pastoral stages . . .*

Herzog could not say what the significance of such generalities might be. He was only vastly excited—in a streaming state—and intended mostly to restore order by turning to his habit of thoughtfulness. Blood had burst into his psyche, and for the time being he was either free or crazy. But then he realized that he did not need to perform elaborate abstract intellectual work—work he had always thrown himself into as if it were the struggle for survival. But not thinking is not necessarily fatal. Did I really believe that I would die when thinking stopped? Now to fear such a thing—that's really crazy.

He went to spend the night with Lucas Asphalter, telephoning from a sidewalk booth to invite himself over. "I won't be in the way, will I? Have you got anybody there with you? No? I want you to do me a special favor. I can't phone Madeleine to ask to see the child. She hangs up on me as soon as she recognizes my voice Will you call and arrange for me to pick up June tomorrow?"

"Why, of course," said Asphalter. "I'll do it now and have the answer for you when you get here. Did you just blow in, on impulse? Unplanned?"

"Thank you, Luke. Please do it now."

He left the booth reflecting that he really must rest tonight, try to get some sleep. At the same time, he hesitated somewhat to lie down and shut his eyes; tomorrow he might not be able to recover his state of simple, free, intense realization. He therefore drove slowly, stopping at Walgreen's, where he bought a bottle of Cutty Sark for Luke and playthings for June—a toy periscope through which she could look over the sofa, around corners, a beach ball you inflated with your breath. He even found time to send a wire to Ramona from the yellow Western Union office at Blackstone and 53rd. *Chicago business two days* was his message. *Much love.* Trust her, she'd find comfort while he was away, not be despondent in "desertion" as he would have been—his childish disorder, that infantile terror of death that had bent and buckled his life into these curious shapes. Having discovered that everyone must be indulgent with bungling child-men, pure hearts in the burlap of innocence, and willingly accepting the necessary quota of consequent lies, he had set himself up with his emotional goodies—truth, friendship, devotion to children (the regular American worship of kids), and potato love. So much we know now. But this— even this—is not the whole story, either. It only begins to approach the start of true consciousness. The necessary premise is that a man is somehow more than his "characteristics," all the emotions, strivings, tastes, and constructions which it pleases him to call "My Life." We have ground to hope that a

Life is something more than such a cloud of particles, mere facticity. Go through what is comprehensible and you conclude that only the incomprehensible gives any light. This was by no means a "general idea" with him now. It was far more substantial than anything he saw in this intensely lighted telegraph office. It all seemed to him exceptionally clear. What made it clear? Something at the very end of the line. Was that thing Death? But death was not the incomprehensible accepted by his heart. No, far from it.

He stopped to gaze at the fine hand beating its way over the face of the clock, the yellow furniture of another era—no wonder large corporations raked in such profits; high charges, old equipment, no competitors, now that Postal Telegraph was knocked out. They certainly got more mileage out of these yellow desks than Father Herzog did out of the same kind of furniture on Cherry Street. That was across from the cathouse. When the madame didn't pay them off the cops threw the whores' beds out of the second-story windows. The women shrieked Negro curses as they were pushed into the wagon. Father Herzog, the businessman, musing at these aliens of vice and brutality, police and barbarous obese women, stood among such tables—standard second-hand equipment acquired in warehouse sales. Here my ancestral fortune was founded.

In front of Asphalter's house he locked the Falcon for the night, leaving Junie's gifts in the trunk. He felt certain she would love the periscope. There was much to be seen in that house on Harper Avenue. Let the child find life. The plainer the better, perhaps.

He was met on the staircase by Asphalter.

"I've been waiting for you."

"Is something wrong?" said Herzog.

"No, no, don't worry. I'm picking June up at noon tomorrow. She goes to a play school, half-days."

"Wonderful," Herzog said. "No trouble?"

"With Madeleine? None at all. She doesn't want to see you. Otherwise, you can visit with your little girl to your heart's content."

"She doesn't want me to come with a court order. Legally, she's in a dubious position, with that crook in the house. Well, let's have a look at you." They entered the apartment where the light was better. "You've grown a bit of a beard, Luke."

Nervously and shyly Asphalter touched his chin, looking away. He said, "I'm brazening it out."

"Compensation for the sudden unfortunate baldness?" said Herzog.

"Fighting a depression," said Asphalter. "Thought a change of image might be good . . . Excuse my pad."

Asphalter had always lived in such graduate-student filth. Herzog looked about. "If I ever have another windfall I'll buy you some bookshelves, Luke. About time you got rid of these old crates. This scientific literature is heavy stuff. But look, you've got clean sheets on the studio couch for me. This is very kind of you, Luke."

"You're an old friend."

"Thanks," said Herzog. To his surprise he found difficulty in speaking. A swift rush of feeling, out of nowhere, caught his throat. His eyes filled up. The potato love, he announced to himself. It's here. To advert to his temperament, call things by the correct name, restored his control. Self-correction refreshed him. "Luke, did you get my letter."

"Letter? Did you send me one? I sent you a letter."

"Never saw it. What was it about?"

"About a job. Remember Elias Tuberman?"

"The sociologist who married that gym teacher?"

"Don't joke. He's general editor of Stone's Encyclopedia, and has a million to spend on revision. I'm in charge of the biology. He's looking for you to take over in history."

"Me?"

"He said he read your book on Romanticism and Christianity over again. Didn't think too highly of it in the fifties when it came out, but must have been blind. It's a monument, he says."

Herzog looked grave. He began to make up several answers but abandoned them all. "I don't know whether I'm still a scholar. When I left Daisy, apparently I quit that, too."

"And Madeleine snatched it right up."

"Yes. They divvied me up. Valentine took my elegant ways and Mady's going to be the professor. Isn't she coming up for her orals?"

"Right away."

Remembering now the death of Asphalter's monkey, Herzog said, "What got into you, Luke? You didn't catch T.B. from your pet, did you?"

"No, no. I've taken the tuberculin test regularly. No."

"You must have been out of your mind, giving Rocco mouth-to-mouth respiration. That's letting eccentricity go too far."

"Did they report that too?"

"Of course. How else would I know? How did it get into the papers?"

"One of the little bastards in Physiology picks up a few bucks by spying for the *American*."

"Didn't you know the monkey was tubercular?"

"I knew he was ailing, but had no idea. And I certainly wasn't expecting to be so hard hit by his death." Herzog was not prepared for the solemnity of Asphalter's look. His new beard was vari-colored but his eyes were even blacker than the hair he had lost. "It really threw me into a spin. I thought that palling around with Rocco was a gag. I didn't realize how much he meant to me. But the truth is, I realized that no other death in the world could have affected me so much. I had to ask myself whether the death of my brother would have shook me up half as much. I think not. We're all some kind of nut or other, I realize. But . . ."

"You don't mind if I smile," Herzog apologized. "I can't help it."

"What else can you do?"

"A man could do worse than to love his monkey," said Herzog. "*Le cœur a ses raisons.* You've seen Gersbach. He was a dear friend of mine. And Madeleine *loves* him. What have you got to be ashamed of? It's one of those painful emotional comedies. Did you ever read Collier's story about the man who married a chimpanzee? *His Monkey Wife.* An excellent story."

"I've been horribly depressed," said Asphalter. "It's better now; but for about two months I did no work, and I was glad I had no wife or kids to hide these crying jags from."

"All because of that monkey?"

"I stopped going to the lab. I doctored myself with tranquilizers, but that couldn't continue. I had to face the music, finally."

"And you went to Doctor Edvig?" Herzog was laughing.

"Edvig? No, no. Another headshrinker. He calmed me down. But that was only two hours a week. The rest of the time, I was shaking. So I got some books out of the library. . . . Have you read the book by that Hungarian woman Tina Zokóly about what to do in these crises?"

"No. What does she say?"

"She prescribes certain exercises."

Moses was interested. "What are they?"

"The main one is facing your own death."

"How do you do that?"

Asphalter tried to maintain an ordinary, conversational, descriptive tone. Obviously it was a very difficult thing for him to talk about. Irresistible, though.

"You pretend you have already died," Asphalter began.

"The worst has happened. . . . Yes?" Herzog turned his head as if to hear better, listen more intently. His hands were folded in his lap, his shoulders had dropped with fatigue, his feet were turned inward. The musty bookish room with a clamp-light affixed to one of the crates and the stirring of leaves in the summer street brought Herzog some peace. *True things in grotesque form,* he was thinking. He knew how that was. He felt for Asphalter.

"The blow has fallen. The agony is over," said Asphalter. "You're dead, and you have to lie as if dead. What's it like in the casket? Padded silk."

"Ah? So you construct it all. Must be pretty hard. I see. . . ." Moses sighed.

"It takes practice. You have to feel and not feel, be and not be. You're present and absent both. And one by one the people in your life come and look. Father. Mother. Whoever you loved, or hated."

"And what then." Herzog, wholly absorbed, looked at him more obliquely than ever.

"And then you ask yourself, 'What have you got to say to them now? What do you feel for them?' Now there's nothing to say but what you really thought. And you don't say it to them because you're dead, but only to yourself. Reality, not illusions. Truth, not lies. It's over."

"Face death. That's Heidegger. What comes out of this?"

"As I gaze up from my coffin, at first I can keep my attention on my death, and on my relations with the living, and then other things come in—every time."

"You begin to get tired?"

"No, no. Time after time, I see the same things." Lucas laughed nervously, painfully. "Did we know each other when my father owned the flophouse on West Madison Street?"

"Yes, I used to see you at school."

"When the Depression hit, we had to move into the old hotel ourselves. My father made an apartment on the top story. The Haymarket Theatre was a few doors away, do you remember?"

"The burlesque house? Oh yes, Luke. I used to cut school to watch the bumps and grinds."

"Well, first of all, what I begin to see is the fire that broke out in that building. We were trapped in the loft. My brother and I wrapped up the younger kids in blankets and stood by the windows. Then the hook-and-ladder company came and rescued us. I had my little sister. The firemen took us down, one by one. Last of all was my Aunt Rae. She weighed nearly two hundred pounds. Her dress flew up as the fireman carried her. He was very red in the face from the weight and strain. A great Irish face. And I was standing below and watched her buttocks coming slowly nearer—that tremendous rear part, and the huge cheeks, so pale and helpless."

"And is this what you see when you play dead? A fat-assed old auntie saved from death."

"Don't laugh," said Asphalter, himself grimly laughing. "That's one of the things I see. Another is the burlesque broads from next door. Between turns, they didn't have anything to do. The picture was running—Tom Mix. They got bored in their dressing rooms. So they'd come out in the street and play baseball. They loved it. They were all big hearty cornfed girls, they needed exercise. I'd sit on the curb and watch them play."

"They were in their burlesque costumes?"

"All powdered and rouged. Their hair done up. And their tits heaving as they pitched and batted and ran the bases. They played piggy-move-up—softball. Moses, I swear to you . . ."

Asphalter pressed his hands to his bearded cheeks, and his voice shook. His fluid black eyes were bewildered, painfully smiling. Then he drew his chair back, out of the light. Perhaps he was about to cry. I hope he won't, thought Herzog. His heart went out to him.

"Don't feel so bad, Luke. Now listen to me. Maybe I can tell you something about this. At least I can tell you how I see it. A man may say, 'From now on I'm going to speak the truth.' But the truth hears him and runs away and hides before he's even done speaking. There is something funny about the human condition, and civilized intelligence makes fun of its own ideas. This Tina Zokóly has got to be kidding, too."

"I don't think so."

"Then it's the old *memento mori*, the monk's skull on the table, brought up to date. And what good is that? It all goes back to those German existentialists who tell you how good dread is for you, how it saves you from distraction and gives you your freedom and makes you authentic. God is no more. But Death is. That's their story. And we live in a hedonistic world in which happiness is set up on a mechanical model. All you have to do is open your fly and grasp happiness. And so these other theorists introduce the tension of guilt and dread as a corrective. But human life is far subtler than any of its models, even these ingenious German models. Do we need to study *theories* of fear and anguish? This Tina Zokóly is a nonsensical woman. She tells you to practice overkill on yourself, and your intelligence answers her with wit. But you're pushing matters. This is self-ridicule to the degree of anguish. Bitterer and bitterer. Monkeys and buttocks and chorus girls playing piggy-move-up."

"I was hoping we could have a talk about this," said Asphalter.

"Don't abuse yourself too much, Luke, and cook up these fantastic plots against your feelings. I know you're a good soul, with real heartaches. And you believe the world. And the world tells you to look for truth in grotesque combinations. It warns you also to stay away from consolation if you value your intellectual honor. On this theory truth is punishment, and you must take it like a man. It says truth will harrow your soul because your inclination as a poor human thing is to lie and to live by lies. So if you have anything else waiting in your soul to be revealed you'll never learn about it from these people. Do you have to think yourself into a coffin and perform these exercises with death? As soon as thought begins to deepen it reaches death, first thing. Modern philosophers would like to recover the old-fashioned dread of death. The new attitude which makes life a trifle not worth anyone's anguish threatens the heart of civilization. But it isn't a question of dread, or any such words at all. . . . Still, what can thoughtful people and humanists do but struggle toward suitable words? Take me, for instance. I've been writing letters helter-skelter in all directions. More words. I go after reality with language. Perhaps I'd like to change it all into language, to force Madeleine and Gersbach to have a *Conscience*. There's a word for you. I must be trying to keep tight the tensions without which human beings can no longer be called human. If they don't suffer, they've gotten away from me. And I've filled the world with letters to prevent their escape. I want them in human form, and so I conjure up a whole environment and catch them in the middle. I put my whole heart into these constructions. But they are constructions."

"Yes, but you deal with human beings. What have I got to show? Rocco?"

"But let's stick to what matters. I really believe that brotherhood is what makes a man human. If I owe God a human life, this is where I fall down. 'Man liveth not by Self alone but in his brother's face. . . . Each shall behold the Eternal Father and love and joy abound.' When the preachers of dread tell you that others only distract you from metaphysical freedom then you must turn away from them. The real and essential question is one of our employment by other human beings and their employment by us. Without this true employment you never dread death, you cultivate it. And consciousness when it doesn't clearly understand what to live for, what to die for, can only abuse and ridicule itself. As you do with the help of Rocco and Tina Zokóly, as I do by writing impertinent letters. . . . I feel dizzy. Where's that bottle of Cutty Sark? I need a shot."

"You need to go to sleep. You look ready to cave in."

"I don't feel bad at all," said Herzog.

"I've got some things to do, anyway. Go to sleep. I haven't finished grading all my exams."

"I guess I am folding," Moses said. "The bed looks good."

"I'll let you sleep late. Plenty of time," said Asphalter. "Good night, Moses." They shook hands.

AT LAST he embraced his daughter, and she pressed his cheeks with her small hands and kissed him. Hungry to feel her, to breathe in her childish fragrance, to look in her face, her black eyes, touch her hair, the skin under her dress, he pressed her little bones, stammering, "Junie, sweetie. I've missed you." His happiness was painful. And she with all her innocence and childishness and with the pure, or amorous, instinct of tiny girls, kissed him on the lips, her careworn, busted, germ-carrying father.

Asphalter stood by, smiling but feeling somewhat awkward, his bald scalp perspiring, his new parti-colored beard looking hot. They were on the long gray staircase of the Museum of Science in Jackson Park. Busloads of children were entering, black and white flocks, herded by teachers and parents. The bronze-trimmed glass doors flashed in and out, and all these little bodies, redolent of milk and pee, blessed heads of all hues, shapes, the promise of the world to come, in the eyes of benevolent Herzog, its future good and evil, hurried in and out.

"My sweet June. Papa missed you."

"Poppy!"

"You know, Luke," Herzog spoke out with a burst, his face both happy and twisted. "Sandor Himmelstein told me this kid would forget me. He was thinking of his own Himmelstein breed—guinea pigs, hamsters."

"Herzogs are made of finer clay?" Asphalter put it in the interrogative form. But it was courteous, he meant it kindly. ". . . I can meet you right at this spot at four p.m.," he said.

"Only three and a half hours? Where does she get off! Well, all right, I won't quarrel. I don't want any conflict. There's another day tomorrow."

One of his units of mental extension swelling and passing, a lengthy aside (Much heartbreak to relinquish this daughter. To become another lustful she-ass? Or a melancholy beauty like Sarah Herzog, destined to bear children ignorant of her soul and her soul's God? Or would humankind find a new path, making his type—he would be glad of that!—obsolete? In New York, after giving a lecture, he had been told by a young executive who came up rapidly, "Professor, Art is for Jews!" Seeing this slender, blond, and violent figure before him, Herzog had only nodded and said, "It used to be usury"), departed with another of those twinges. That's the new realism, he thought. "Luke? Thank you. I'll be here at four. Now don't you spend the day brooding."

Moses carried his daughter into the museum to see the chickens hatching. "Did Marco send you a postcard, baby?"

"Yes. From the camp."

"You know who Marco is?"

"My big brother."

So Madeleine was not trying to estrange her from the Herzogs, whatever course of madness she was running.

"Have you gone down in the coal mine, here in the museum?"

"It scared me."

"Do you want to see the chickies?"

"I seen them."

"Don't you want to see them more?"

"Oh, yes. I like them. Uncle Val took me last week."

"Do I know Uncle Val?"

"Oh, Papa! You fooler." She hugged his neck, snickering. "Who is he?"

"He's my stepfather, Papa. You *know* it."

"Is that what Mama tells you?"

"He's my stepfather."

"Was he the one who locked you up in the car?"

"Yes."

"And what did you do?"

"I was crying. But not long."

"And do you like Uncle Val?"

"Oh, yes, he's fun. He makes faces. Can you make good faces?"

"Some," he said. "I have too much dignity to make good faces."

"You tell better stories."

"I expect I do, sweetheart."

"About the boy with the stars."

So she remembered his best inventions. Herzog nodded his head, wondering at her, proud of her, thankful. "The boy with all the freckles?"

"They were like the sky."

"Each freckle was just like a star, and he had them all. The Big Dipper, Little Dipper, Orion, the Bear, the Twins, Betelgeuse, the Milky Way. His face had each and every star on it, in the right position."

"Only one star nobody knew."

"They took him to all the astronomers."

"I saw astronomers on television."

"And the astronomers said, 'Pooh, pooh, an interesting coincidence. A little freak.'"

"More. More."

"At last he went to see Hiram Shpitalnik, who was an old old old man, very tiny, with a long beard down to his feet. He lived in a hatbox. And he said, 'You must be examined by *my* grandfather.'"

"He lived in a walnut shell."

"Exactly. And all his friends were bees. The busy bee has no time for sorrow. Great-grandfather Shpitalnik came out of the shell with a telescope, and looked at Rupert's face."

"The boy's name was Rupert."

"Old Shpitalnik had the bees lift him into position, and he looked and said it *was* a real star, a new discovery. He had been watching for that star. . . . Now, here are the chicks." He held the child on the railing, to his left, so that she would not press against the pistol, wrapped in her great-grandfather's rubles. These were in his right breast pocket still.

"They're yellow," she said.

"They keep it hot and bright in there. See that egg wobble? The chick is trying to get out. Soon his bill will go through the shell. Watch."

"Papa, you don't shave at our house any more, why not?"

He must stiffen his resistance to heartache now. A kind of necessary hardness was demanded. Otherwise it was as the savage described the piano, "You fight 'im 'e cry." And this Jewish art of tears must be suppressed. In measured words he answered, "I have my razor in another place. What does Madeleine say?"

"She says you didn't want to live with us any more."

He kept his anger from the child. "Did she? Well, I always want to be with you. I just can't."

"Why?"

"Because I'm a man, and men have to work, and be in the world."

"Uncle Val works. He writes poems and reads them to Mama."

Herzog's sober face brightened. "Splendid." She had to listen to his trash. Bad art and vice hand in hand. "I'm glad to hear it."

"He looks ooky when he says them."

"And does he cry?"

"Oh, yes."

Sentiment and brutality—never one without the other, like fossils and oil. This news is priceless. It's sheer happiness to hear it.

June had bent her head, and held her wrists to her eyes.

"What's the matter darling?"

"Mama said I shouldn't talk about Uncle Val."

"Why?"

"She said you'd be very very angry."

"But I'm not. I'm laughing my head off. All right. We won't talk about him. I promise. Not one word."

An experienced father, he prudently waited until they reached the Falcon before he said, "I have presents for you in the trunk!"

"Oh, Papa—what did you bring!"

Against the clumsy, gray, gaping Museum of Science she looked so fresh, so new (her milk teeth and sparse freckles and big expectant eyes, her fragile neck). And he thought how she would inherit this world of great instruments, principles of physics and applied science. She had the brains for it. He was already intoxicated with pride, seeing another Madame Curie in her. She loved the periscope. They spied on each other from the sides of the car, hiding behind tree trunks and in the arches of the comfort station. Crossing the bridge on the Outer Drive they walked by the lake. He let her take off her shoes and wade, drying her feet afterward in his shirttail, carefully brushing out the sand between her toes. He bought her a box of

Cracker Jack which she nibbled on the grass. The dandelions had blown their fuses and were all loose silk; the turf was springy, neither damp as in May nor dry and hard as in August, when the sun would scorch it. The mechanical mower was riding in circles, barbering the slopes, raising a spray of clippings. Lighted from the south the water was a marvelous, fresh heavy daylight blue; the sky rested on the mild burning horizon, clear except toward Gary, where the dark thin pillars of the steel hearths puffed out russet and sulphur streams of smoke. By now the lawns at Ludeyville, uncut for two years, must be simply hayfields, and local hunters and lovers were breaking in again, most likely, shattering windows, lighting fires.

"I want to go to the aquarium, Papa," said June. "Mama said you should take me."

"Oh, did she? Well, come on then."

The Falcon had grown hot in the sun. He opened the windows to cool it. He had an extraordinary number of keys, by now, and must organize them better in his pockets. There were his New York house keys, the key Ramona had given him, the Faculty Men's Lounge key from the university, and the key to Asphalter's apartment, as well as several Ludeyville keys. "You must sit in the back seat, honey. Creep in, now, and pull down your dress because the plastic is very hot." The air from the west was drier than the east air. Herzog's sharp senses detected the difference. In these days of near-delirium and wide-ranging disordered thought, deeper currents of feeling had heightened his perceptions, or made him instill something of his own into his surroundings. As though he painted them with moisture and color taken from his own mouth, his blood, liver, bowels, genitals. In this mingled way, therefore, he was aware of Chicago, familiar ground to him for more than thirty years. And out of its elements, by this peculiar art of his own organs, he created his version of it. Where the thick walls and buckled slabs of pavement in the Negro slums exhaled their bad smells. Farther West, the industries; the sluggish South Branch dense with sewage and glittering with a crust of golden slime; the Stockyards, deserted; the tall red slaughterhouses in lonely decay; and then a faintly buzzing dullness of bungalows and scrawny parks; and vast shopping centers; and the cemeteries after these—Waldheim, with its graves for Herzogs past and present; the Forest Preserves for riding parties, Croatian picnics, lovers' lanes, horrible murders; airports; quarries; and, last of all, cornfields. And with this, infinite forms of activity—Reality. Moses had to see reality. Perhaps he was somewhat spared from it so that he might see it better, not fall asleep in its thick embrace. Awareness was his work; extended consciousness was his line, his business. Vigilance. If he borrowed time to take his tiny daughter to see the fishes he would find a way to make it up to the vigilance-fund. This day was just like—he braced himself and faced it—like the day of Father Herzog's funeral. Then, too, it was flowering weather—roses, magnolias. Moses, the night before, had cried, slept, the air was wickedly perfumed; he had had luxuriant dreams, painful, evil, and rich, interrupted by the rare ecstasy of nocturnal emission—how death dangles freedom before the enslaved instincts: the pitiful sons of Adam whose minds and bodies must answer strange signals. Much of my life has been spent in the effort to live by more coherent ideas. I even know which ones.

"Papa, you must turn here. This is where Uncle Val always turns."

"Okay." He observed in the mirror that the slip had distressed her. She had mentioned Gersbach again. "Hey, Pussycat," he said. "If you say anything about Uncle Val to me, I'll never tell. I'll never ask you any questions about him. Now don't you ever worry about it. It's all silliness."

He had been no older than June when Mother Herzog instructed him to say nothing about that still in Verdun. He remembered the contraption well. Those pipes were beautiful. And the reeking mash. If he was not mistaken, Father Herzog emptied sacks of stale rye bread into the vat. In any case, secrets were not too bad.

"There's nothing wrong with a few secrets," he said.

"I know lots of them." She stood directly behind him in the back seat and stroked his head. "Uncle Val is very nice."

"Why of course he is."

"But I don't like him. He doesn't smell good."

"Ha, ha! Well, we'll get him a bottle of perfume and make him smell terrific."

He held her hand as they mounted the aquarium staircase, feeling himself to be the father whose strength and calm judgment she could trust. The center court of the building, whitened by the skylight, was very warm. The splashing pool and luxuriant plants and soft tropical fishy air forced Moses to take a grip on himself, to keep up his energy.

"What do you want to see first?"

"The big turtles."

They went up and down the obscure gold and green alleys.

"This fast little fish is called the humuhumuu-elee-elee, from Hawaii. This slithering beast is the sting ray and has teeth and venom in its tail. And these are lampreys, related to hag-fish, they fasten their sucker mouths on other fish and drink until they kill them. Over there you see the rainbow fish. No turtles in this aisle, but look at those great things at the end. Sharks?"

"I saw the dolphins at Brookfield," said June. "They wear sailor hats, ring a bell. They can dance on their tails and play basketball."

Herzog picked her up and carried her. These children's outings, perhaps because they were pervaded with so much emotion, were always exhausting. Often, after a day with Marco, Moses had to put a cold compress on his eyes and lie down. It seemed his fate to be the visiting father, an apparition who faded in and out of the children's lives. But this peculiar sensitivity about meeting and parting had to be tamed. Such trembling sorrow—he tried to think what term Freud had for it: partial return of repressed traumatic material, ultimately traceable to the death instinct?—should not be imparted to children, not that tremulous lifelong swoon of death. This same emotion, as Herzog the student was aware, was held to be the womb of cities, heavenly as well as earthly, mankind being unable to part with its beloved or its dead in this world or the next. But to Moses E. Herzog as he held his daughter in his arms, looking through aqueous green at the hagfish and smooth sharks with their fanged bellies, this emotion was nothing but tyranny. For the first time he took a different view of the way in which Alexander V. Herzog had run Father Herzog's funeral. No solemnity in the chapel. Shura's portly, golf-tanned friends, bankers and corporation presidents, forming an imposing wall of meat as heavy in the shoulders, hands, and cheeks as they were thin in the hair. Then there was the cortege. City

Hall had sent a motorcycle escort in recognition of Shura Herzog's civic importance. The cops ran ahead with screaming sirens, booting cars and trucks aside so that the hearse could speed through lights. No one ever got to Waldheim so fast. Moses said to Shura, "While he lived, Papa had the cops at his back. Now . . ." Helen, Willie, all four children in the limousine, laughed softly at this remark. Then as the coffin was lowered and Moses and the others wept, Shura said to him, "Don't carry on like a goddamn immigrant." I embarrassed him with his golfing friends, the corporation presidents. Maybe I was not entirely in the right. Here he was the good American. I still carry European pollution, am infected by the Old World with feelings like Love—Filial Emotion. Old stuporous dreams.

"*There* is the turtle!" June shouted. The thing rose from the depths of the tank in its horny breastplate, the beaked head lazy, the eyes with aeons of indifference, the flippers slowly striving, pushing at the glass, the great scales pinkish yellow or, on the back, bearing beautiful lines, black curved plates mimicking the surface tension of water. It trailed a fuzz of parasitic green.

For comparison they went back to the Mississippi River turtles in the pool at the center; their sides were red-straked; they dozed on their logs and paddled in company with catfish over a bottom shaded by ferns, strewn with pennies.

The child had now had enough, and so had her father. "I think we'll go and get you a sandwich. It's lunchtime," he said.

They left the parking lot carefully enough, Herzog later thought. He was a circumspect driver. But getting his Falcon into the main stream of traffic he should perhaps have reckoned with the long curve from the north on which the cars picked up speed. A little Volkswagen truck was on his tail. He touched the brakes, meaning to slow up and let the other driver pass. But the brakes were all too new and responsive. The Falcon stopped short and the small truck struck it from behind and rammed it into a utility pole. June screamed and clutched at his shoulders as he was thrown forward, against the steering wheel. The kid! he thought; but it was not the kid he had to worry about. He knew from her scream that she was not hurt, only frightened. He lay over the wheel, feeling weak, radically weak; his eyes grew dark; he felt that he was losing ground to nausea and numbness. He listened to June's screams but could not turn to her. He notified himself that he was passing out, and he fainted away.

They spread him out on the grass. He heard a locomotive very close—the Illinois Central. And then it seemed somewhat farther off, blundering in the weeds across the Drive. His vision at first was bothered by large blots, but these dwindled presently to iridescent specks. His pants had worked themselves up. He felt a chill in his legs.

"Where's June? Where's my daughter?" He raised himself and saw her between two Negro policemen, looking at him. They had his wallet, the Czarist rubles, and the pistol, of course. There it was. He closed his eyes again. He felt the nausea return as he considered what he had gotten himself into. "Is she all right?"

"She's okay."

"Come here, Junie." He leaned forward and she walked into his arms. As he felt her, kissed her scared face, he had a sharp pain in his ribs. "Papa lay down for a minute. It's nothing." But she had seen him lying on this grass. Just past the new building beyond the Museum. Stretched limp, looking dead, probably, while the cops went through his pockets. His face felt bloodless, hollow, stiff, its sensations intensely reduced, and this frightened him. From the pricking of his hair at the roots he thought it must be turning white all at once. The police were giving him a few minutes to come to himself. The blue light of the squad car flashed, revolving. The driver of the small truck was staring at him, angry. A little beyond, the grackles were walking, feeding, the usual circle of lights working flexibly back and forth about their black necks. Over his shoulder Herzog was aware of the Field Museum. If only I were a mummy in that cellar! he thought.

The cops had him. Their silent looks gave him this information. Because he was holding Junie they waited; they might not be too rough with him just yet. Already stalling for time, he acted more dazed than he really felt. The cops could be very bad, he had seen them at work. But that was in the old days. Perhaps times had changed. There was a new Commissioner. He had sat close to Orlando Wilson at a Narcotics Conference last year. They had shaken hands. Of course it wasn't worth mentioning; anyway, nothing would antagonize these two big Negro cops more than hints of influence. For them, he was part of today's haul, and with his rubles, the gun, he couldn't hope that they would simply let him go. And there was the teal-blue Falcon crumpled against the utilities pole. The traffic rushing by, the road with its blazing cars.

"You Moses?" the older of the two Negroes asked. There it was—that note of deadly familiarity that you heard only when immunity was lost.

"Yes, I'm Moses."

"This your chile?"

"Yes—my little girl."

"You better put your handkercher to your head. You got a little cut, Moses."

"Is that so?" This explained the pricking under his hair. Unable to locate his handkerchief—the scrap of towel—he unknotted his silk tie and folded it, pressed the broad end to his scalp. "Nothing to it," he said. The child had hidden her head in his shoulder. "Sit down by Papa, sweetheart. Sit on the grass right next to me. Papa's head hurts a little." She obeyed. Her docility, her feeling for him, what seemed to him the wise, tender sense of the child, her sympathy, moved him, pressed his guts. He put a protective, wide, eager hand on her back. Sitting forward, he held the tie to his scalp.

"You got the permit for this gun, Moses?" The cop pursed his large lips as he waited for the answer, brushing the small bristles of his mustache upward with his fingernail. The other policeman spoke with the driver of the Volkswagen truck, who was wildly angry. Sharp-faced, his nose sharp and red, he was glaring at Moses, saying, "You're going to take that guy's license away, aren't you?" Moses thought, I'm in bad because of the pistol, and this fellow wants to pour it on. Warned by this indignation, Herzog held his own feelings in.

"I asked you once, I ask you again, Moses, you got a permit?"

"No sir, I haven't."

"Two bullets in here. Loaded weapon, Moses."

"Officer, it was my father's gun. He died, and I was taking it back to Massachusetts." His answers were as brief and patient as he could make them. He knew he would have to repeat his story, over and over.

"What's this money here?"

"Worthless, officer. Like Russian Confederate money. Stage money. Another souvenir."

Not devoid of sympathy, the policeman's face also expressed a fatigued skepticism. He was heavy-lidded, and on his silent, thick mouth there was a sort of smile. Sono's lips had looked a little like this when she questioned him about the other women in his life. Well—the variety of oddities, alibis, inventions, fantasies the police ran into every day . . . Herzog, making his reckonings as intelligently as he could, though he had a heavy weight of responsibility and dread inside him, believed it might not be so easy for this cop to type him. There were labels to fit him, naturally, but a harness cop like this would not be familiar with them. Even now there was possibly some tinge of pride in this reflection, so tenacious was human foolishness. "Lord, let the angels praise thy name. Man is a foolish thing, a foolish thing. Folly and sin play all his game. . . ." Herzog's head ached and he could remember no more verses. He lifted the tie from his scalp. No sense in letting it stick; it would pull away the clot. June had put her head in his lap. He covered her eyes from the sun.

"We have to diagram this accident." The copper in his shiny pants squatted beside Herzog. From his fat, bulging hips his own gun hung low. Its brown butt of cross-hatched metal and the cartridge belt looked very different from Father Herzog's big, clumsy Cherry Street revolver. "I don't see the title of this Falcon, here."

The small car was staved in at both ends, the hood gaping like a mussel shell. The engine itself could not be damaged much; no fluids had trickled out. "It's rented. I picked it up at O'Hare. The papers are in the glove compartment," said Herzog.

"We got to get these facts, here." The policeman opened a folder and began to mark the thick paper of a printed form with his yellow pencil. "You come out of this parking lot—what speed?"

"I was creeping. Five, eight miles an hour—I just nosed out."

"You didn't see this fellow coming?"

"No. The curve was hiding him, I suppose. I don't know. But he was right on my bumper when I got into the lane." He bent forward, trying to change his position and ease the pain in his side. He had already arranged with his mind to disregard it. He stroked June's cheek. "At least she wasn't hurt," he said.

"I just lifted her out the back window. The door got jammed. I looked her over. She's okay." The mustached Negro frowned, as if to make plain that he did not owe Herzog—a man with a loaded gun—any explanations whatever. For it was the possession of this clumsy horse pistol with two cartridges, not the accident, that would be the main charge against him.

"I'd have blown my brains out if anything happened to her."

The squatting cop, to judge by his silence, had no concern with what Moses might have done. To speak of any use of the revolver, even against himself, was not very smart. But he was still somewhat stunned and dizzy, brought down, as he pictured it, from his strange, spiraling flight of the last few days; and the shock, not to say desperation, of this sudden drop. His head still swam. He decided that this foolishness must stop, or things would go even worse. Running to Chicago to protect his daughter, he almost killed her. Coming to offset the influence of Gersbach, and to give her the benefit of his own self— man and father, et cetera—what did he do but bang into a pole. And then the child saw him dragged out fainting, cut on the head, the revolver and the rubles sliding from his pocket. No, weakness, or sickness, with which he had copped a plea all his life (alternating with arrogance), his method of preserving equilibrium—the Herzog gyroscope—had no further utility. He seemed to have come to the end of *that*.

The driver of the Volkswagen utilities truck, in a green jumper, was giving his account of the accident. Moses tried to make out the letters stitched in yellow thread over his pocket. Was he from the gas company? No telling. He was laying the whole guilt on him, of course. It was very inventive—creative. The story deepened every moment. Oh, the grandeur of self-justification, thought Herzog. What genius it brought out in these mortals, even the most rednosed. The ripples in this fellow's scalp followed a different pattern from the furrows in his forehead. You could make out his former hairline by this means. A certain number of skimpy hairs remained.

"He just cut out in front of me. No signal, nothing. Whyn't you give him the drunk test? That's drunken driving."

"Well, now, Harold," the older Negro said. "What was your speed?"

"Why, Jesus! I was way below the limit."

"A lot of these company drivers like to give private cars the business," said Herzog.

"First he cut in front, then he slammed his brake."

"You mashed him pretty hard. That means you were crowdin' him."

"That's right. Looks like to me . . ." The senior policeman pointed two, three, five times with the rubber tip of his pencil before he spoke another word; he made you consider the road (there Herzog seemed to see the rushing of the Gadarene swine, multi-colored and glittering, not yet come to their cliff). "Looks to me, you were pushin' him, Harold. He couldn't get in the next lane so he thought he'd slow and give you a chance to pass. Hit the brake too hard, and you clobbered him. I see from the staple marks on your license you already got two moving violations."

"That's right, and that's why I've been extra careful."

God keep this anger from burning up your scalp, Harold. A very unbecoming red color, and all ridges, like a dog's palate.

"Looks like to me, if you hadn't been on top of him, you wouldn't have hit him so flush. You'd 'a tried to turn, and got him on the right. Got to write you a ticket, Harold."

Then, to Moses, he said, "I got to take you in. You gonna be booked for misdemeanor."

"This old gun?"

"Loaded . . ."

"Why, it's nothing. I have no record—never been booked."

They waited for him to get to his feet. Sharp-nosed, the Volkswagen-truck driver knitted his ginger brows at him and, under his red, angry stare, Herzog stood and then picked up his daughter. She lost her barrette as he lifted her. Her hair came free beside her cheeks, quite long. He could not bend again to hunt for the tortoise-shell clip. The door of the squad car, parked on a slope, opened wide for him. He could now feel for himself what it was like to be in custody. No one was robbed, no one had died. Still he felt the heavy, deadly shadow lying on him. "And this is just like you, Herzog," he said to himself. He could not escape self-accusation. For this big,

nickel-plated pistol, whatever he had vaguely intended yesterday to do with it, he should have left today in the flight bag
under Asphalter's sofa. When he had put on his jacket in the
morning and felt the awkward weight on his chest, then and
there he might have stopped being quixotic. For he was not a
quixote, was he? A quixote imitated great models. What models did he imitate? A quixote was a Christian, and Moses E.
Herzog was no Christian. This was the post-quixotic, post-
Copernican U.S.A., where a mind freely poised in space might
discover relationships utterly unsuspected by a seventeenth-
century man sealed in his smaller universe. There lay his
twentieth-century advantage. Only—they walked over the
grass toward the wheeling blue light—in nine-tenths of his existence he was exactly what others were before him. He took
the revolver (his purpose as intense as it was diffuse) because
he was his father's son. He was almost certain Jonah Herzog,
afraid of the police, of revenue inspectors, or of hoodlums,
could not stay away from these enemies. He pursued his terrors and challenged them to blast him (Fear: could he take it?
Shock: would he survive?). Ancient Herzogs with their psalms
and their shawls and beards would never have touched a revolver. Violence was for the goy. But they were gone, vanished,
archaic men. Jonah, for a buck, had bought a gun, and Moses,
this morning, had thought, "Oh, hell—why not," and, buttoning the jacket, went down to his car.

"What are we going to do about this Falcon?" he asked the
police. He stopped. But they pushed him on, saying, "Don't
you worry about that. We'll take care of it."

He saw the tow truck coming up with its crane and hook. It
too had the blue light spinning above its cab.

"Listen," he said, "I have to get this kid home."

"She'll get home. She ain't in no danger."

"But I'm supposed to turn her over at four."

"You got almost two hours."

"But isn't this going to take longer than an hour? I'd certainly appreciate it if you'd let me look after her first."

"Get goin', Moses. . . ." Grimly kind, the senior patrolman
moved him along.

"She hasn't eaten lunch."

"You in worse shape than she is."

"Come on, now."

He shrugged and crumpled the stained necktie, letting it drop at the roadside. The cut was not serious; it had stopped bleeding. He handed June in, and when he was seated in the fiery heat of the blue plastic rear, he took her on his lap. Is this, by chance, the reality you have been looking for, Herzog, in your earnest Herzog way? Down in the ranks with other people—ordinary life? By yourself you can't determine which reality is real? Any philosopher can tell you it's based, like all rational judgment, on common proof. Only this particular way of doing it was perverse. But it was only human. You burn the house to roast the pig. It was the way humankind always roasted pigs.

He explained to June, "We're going for a ride, darling." She nodded and was silent. Her face was tearless, clouded, and this was far worse. It hurt him. It tore his heart. As if Madeleine and Gersbach weren't enough, *he* had to come running with his eager love and excitement, hugging, kissing, periscopes, anxious emotions. She had to see him bleeding from the head. His eyes smarted, and he shut them with thumb and forefinger. The doors slammed. The motor gave a raw snort and raced smoothly, and the dry rich summer air began to flow in, flavored with exhaust gas. It aggravated his nausea like a forced draft. When the car left the lake front he opened his eyes on the yellow ugliness of 22nd Street. He recognized the familiar look of summer damnation. Chicago! He smelled the hot reek of chemicals and inks coming from the Donnelly plant.

She had watched the cops going through his pockets. At her age he had seen everything vividly. And everything was beautiful or frightful. He was spattered forever with things that bled or stank. He wondered if she must remember just as keenly. As he remembered chicken slaughtering, as he remembered those fiery squawks when the hens were dragged from the lath coops, the shit and sawdust and heat and fowl-musk, and the birds tossed when their throats were cut to bleed to death head down in tin racks, their claws going, going, working, working on the metal shield. Yes, that was on Roy Street next to the Chinese laundry where the vermilion tickets fluttered, lettered with black symbols. And this was near the lane—Herzog's heart began to pound; he felt feverish—where he was overtaken by a man one dirty summer evening. The man clapped his hand over his mouth from the back. He hissed something to him as he drew down his pants. His teeth were rotten and his face stubbled. And between the boy's thighs this red skinless horrible thing passed back and forth, back and forth, until it burst out foaming. The dogs in the back yards jumped against the fences, they barked and snarled, choking on their saliva—the shrieking dogs, while Moses was held at the throat by the crook of the man's arm. He knew he might be killed. The man might strangle him. How did he know! He guessed. So he simply stood there. Then the man buttoned his army coat and said, "I'm going to give you a nickel. But I have to change this dollar." He showed him the bill and told him to wait where he was. Moses watched him recede in the mud of the lane, stooping and gaunt in the long coat, walking swiftly, with bad feet; bad feet, evil feet, Moses remembered; almost running. The dogs stopped barking, and he waited, afraid to stir. At last he fetched up his wet pants and went home. He sat on the stoop awhile and then turned up at supper as if nothing had happened. Nothing! He washed his hands at the sink with Willie and came to the table. He ate his soup.

And later when he was in the hospital and the good Christian lady came, the one with the button shoes and the hatpin like a trolley-rod, the soft voice and grim looks, she asked him to read for her from the New Testament, and he opened and read, "Suffer the little children to come unto me." Then she turned to another place, and it said, "Give and it shall be given unto you. Good measure . . . shall men give into your bosom."

Well, there is a piece of famous advice, grand advice even if it is German, to forget what you can't bear. The strong can forget, can shut out history. Very good! Even if it is self-flattery to speak of strength—these aesthetic philosophers, they take a posture, but power sweeps postures away. Still, it's true you can't go on transposing one nightmare into another, Nietzsche was certainly right about that. The tender-minded must harden themselves. Is this world nothing but a barren lump of coke? No, no, but what sometimes seems a system of prevention, a denial of what every human being knows. I love my children, but I am the world to them, and bring them nightmares. I had this child by my enemy. And I love her. The sight of her, the odor of her hair, this minute, makes me tremble with love. Isn't it mysterious how I love the child of my enemy? But a man doesn't need happiness for *himself*. No, he can put up with any amount of torment—with recollections, with his own familiar evils, despair. And this is the unwritten history of man, his unseen, negative accomplishment, his power to do without gratification for himself provided there is something great, something into which his being, and all beings, can go. He does not need meaning as long as such intensity has scope. Because then it is self-evident; it *is* meaning.

But all this has got to stop. By *this* he meant such things as this ride in the squad car. His filial idea (practically Chinese) of carrying an ugly, useless revolver. To hate, to be in a position to do something about it. Hatred is self-respect. If you want to hold your head up among people . . .

Here was South State Street; here movie distributors used to hang their garish posters: Tom Mix plunging over a cliff; now it's only a smooth empty street where they sell glassware to bars. But what is the philosophy of this generation? Not God is dead, that point was passed long ago. Perhaps it should be stated Death is God. This generation thinks—and this is its thought of thoughts—that nothing faithful, vulnerable, fragile can be durable or have any true power. Death waits for these things as a cement floor waits for a dropping light bulb. The brittle shell of glass loses its tiny vacuum with a burst, and that is that. And this is how we teach metaphysics on each other. "You think history is the history of loving hearts? You fool! Look at these millions of dead. Can you pity them, feel for them? You can nothing! There were too many. We burned them to ashes, we buried them with bulldozers. History is the history of cruelty, not love, as soft men think. We have experimented with every human capacity to see which is strong and admirable and have shown that none is. There is only practicality. If the old God exists he must be a murderer. But the one true god is Death. This is how it is—without cowardly illusions." Herzog heard this as if it were being spoken slowly inside his head. His hand was wet and he released June's arm. Perhaps what had made him faint was not the accident but the premonition of such thoughts. The nausea was only apprehension, excitement, the unbearable intensity of these ideas.

The car stopped. As if he had come to police headquarters in a rocking boat, over the water, he wavered when he got out on the sidewalk. Proudhon says, "God is *the* evil." But after we search in the entrails of world revolution for *la foi nouvelle*, what happens? The victory of death, not of rationality, not of rational faith. Our own murdering imagination turns out to be the great power, our human imagination which starts by accusing God of murder. At the bottom of the whole disaster lies the human being's sense of a grievance, and with this I want nothing more to do. It's easier not to exist altogether than accuse God. Far more simple. Cleaner. But no more of that!

They handed his daughter out to him and escorted them to the elevator, which seemed roomy enough for a squadron. Two men who had been pinched—two other men in custody—went up with him. This was 11th and State. He remembered it. Dreadful here. Armed men came in, got out. As he was ordered, he followed the stout Negro policeman with the huge hands and wide hips down the corridor. Others walked behind him. He would need a lawyer and he thought, naturally, of Sandor Himmelstein. He laughed to think what Sandor would say. Sandor himself used police methods, clever psychology, the same as in the Lubianka, the same the world over. First he emphasized the brutal, then when he got the desired results he relaxed, could afford to be nicer. His words were memorable. He had screamed that he would drop from the case and let the shysters take Moses over, lock him up back and front, close his mouth, shut his bowels, put a meter on his nose and charge him by the breath. Yes, yes, those were unforgettable words, the words of the teacher of Reality. They were indeed. "You'll be glad to think of your death, then. You'll step into your coffin as if it were a new sports car." And then, "I'll leave my wife a rich widow, not too old to screw around, either." This he often repeated. It amused Herzog, now. Flushed, grimy, his shirt bloodspotted, he thought of it, grinning. I shouldn't look down on old Sandor for being so tough. This is his personal, brutal version of the popular outlook, the American way of life. And what has my way been? I love little pussy, her coat is so warm, and if I don't hurt her she'll do me no harm, which represents the childish side of the same creed, from which men are wickedly awakened, and then become snarling realists. Get smart, sucker! Or Tante Taube's version of innocent realism: "*Gottseliger* Kaplitzky took care on everything. I never even looked." But Tante Taube was canny as well as sweet. Between oblivion and oblivion, the things we do and the things we say . . . But now he and June had been brought into a big but close room, and he was being booked by another Negro policeman, a sergeant. He was well along in years, smoothly wrinkled. His creases were extruded, not internal. His color was dark yellow, Negro gold. He conferred with the arresting policeman and then looked at the gun, took out the two bullets, whispered more questions to the cop in shiny pants who bent down to whisper secretly.

"Okay, you," he then said to Moses. He put on his Ben Franklin spectacles, two colonial tablets in thin gold frames. He took up his pen.

"Name?"

"Herzog—Moses."

"Middle initial?"

"E. Elkanah."

"Address?"

"Not living in Chicago."

The sergeant, fairly patient, said again, "Address?"

"Ludeyville, Mass., and New York City. Well, all right, Ludeyville, Massachusetts. No street number."

"This your child?"

"Yes, sir. My little daughter June."

"Where does she live?"

"Here in the city, with her mother, on Harper Avenue."

"You divorced?"

"Yes, sir. I came to see the child."

"I see. You want to put her down?"

"No, officer—sergeant," he corrected himself, smiling agreeably.

"You're bein' booked, Moses. You weren't drunk were you? Did you have a drink today?"

"I had one last night, before I went to sleep. Nothing today. Do you want me to take an alcohol test?"

"It won't be necessary. There's no traffic charge against you. We're booking you on account of this gun."

Herzog pulled down his daughter's dress.

"It's just a souvenir. Like the money."

"What kind of dough is this?"

"It's Russian, from World War I."

"Just empty your pockets, Moses. Put your stuff down so's I can check it over."

Without protest, he laid down his money, his notebooks, pens, the scrap of handkerchief, his pocket comb, and his keys.

"Seems to me you've got a mess of keys, Moses."

"Yes, sir, but I can identify them all."

"That's okay. There's no law against keys, exceptin' if you're a burglar."

"The only Chicago key is this one with the red mark on it. It's the key to my friend Asphalter's apartment. He's supposed to meet me at four o'clock, by the Rosenwald Museum. I've got to get her to him."

"Well, it ain't four, and you ain't goin' anywhere yet."

"I'd like to phone and head him off. Otherwise, he'll stand waiting."

"Well, now, Moses, why ain't you bringin' the kid straight back to her mother?"

"You see . . . we're not on speaking terms. We've had too many scraps."

"Appears to me you might be scared of her."

Herzog was briefly resentful. The remark was calculated to provoke him. But he couldn't afford to be angry now. "No, sir, not exactly."

"Then maybe she's scared of you."

"This is how we arranged it, with a friend to go between. I haven't seen the woman since last autumn."

"Okay, we'll call your buddy and the kid's mama, too."

Herzog exclaimed, "Oh, don't call her!"

"No?" The sergeant gave him an odd smile, and rested for a moment in his chair as if he had gotten from him what he wanted. "Sure, we'll bring her down here and see what she's got to say. If she's got a complaint in against you, why, it's worse than just illegal possession of firearms. We'll have you on a bad charge, then."

"There isn't any complaint, sergeant. You can check that in the files without making her come all this way. I'm the support of this child, and never miss a check. That's all Mrs. Herzog can tell you."

"Who'd you buy this revolver from?"

There it was again, the natural insolence of the cops. He was being goaded. But he kept himself steady.

"I didn't buy it. It belonged to my father. That and the Russian rubles."

"You're just sentimental?"

"That's right. I'm a sentimental s.o.b. Call it that."

"You sentimental about these here, too?" He tapped each of the bullets, one, two. "All right, we'll make those phone calls. Here, Jim, write the names and numbers."

He spoke to the copper who had brought Herzog in. He had been standing by, fat-cheeked, teasing the bristles of his mustache with his nail, pursing his lips.

"You may as well take my address book, the red one there. Bring it back, please. My friend's name is Asphalter."

"And the other name's Herzog," said the sergeant. "On Harper Avenue, ain't it?"

Moses nodded. He watched the heavy fingers turning the pages of his Parisian leather address book with its scribbles and blots. "It'll put me in bad if you notify the child's mother," he said, making a last attempt to persuade the sergeant. "Why wouldn't it be the same to you if my friend Asphalter came here?"

"Go on, Jim."

The Negro marked the places with red pencil, and went. Moses made a special effort to keep a neutral look—no defiance, no special pleading, nothing of the slightest personal color. He remembered that he once believed in the appeal of a direct glance, driving aside differences of position, accident, one human being silently opening his heart to another. The recognition of essence by essence. He smiled inwardly at this. Sweet dreams, those! If he tried looking into his eyes, the sergeant would throw the book at him. So Madeleine was coming. Well, let her come. Perhaps that was what he wanted after all, a chance to confront her. Straight-nosed and pale, he looked intently at the floor. June changed her position in his arms, stirring the pain in his ribs. "Papa's sorry, sweetheart," he said. "Next time we'll go see the dolphins. Maybe the sharks were bad luck."

"You can sit down if you want," said the sergeant. "You look a little weak in the legs, Moses."

"I'd like to phone my brother to send his lawyer. Unless I don't need a lawyer. If I have to post a bond . . ."

"You'll have to post one, but I can't say how big, yet. Plenty of bondsmen settin' here." He motioned with the back of the hand, or with a wag of his wrist, and Moses turned and saw all sorts of people ranged behind him, along the walls. In fact, there were two men, he now noticed, loitering near, bondsmen by their natty appearance. He neutrally recognized that they were sizing him up as a risk. They had already seen his plane ticket, his keys, pens, rubles, and his wallet. His own car, wrecked on the Drive, would have secured a small bond. But a rented car? A man from out of state, in a dirty seersucker, no necktie? He didn't look good for a few hundred bucks. If it's no more than that, he reflected, I can probably swing it without bothering Will, or Shura. Some fellows always make a nice impression. I never had that ability. Due to my feelings. A passionate heart, a bad credit risk. Asked to make this practical judgment on myself, I wouldn't make it any differently.

It came back to him how he used to be banished to left field when sides were chosen in the sand lot, and when the ball came and he missed it because he was musing about something everyone would cry out, "*Hey! Ikey-Moe. Butterfingers! Fucky-knuckles! You lookin' at the butterflies? Ikey-Fishbones. Fishbones!*" Although silent, he participated in the derision.

His hands were clasped about his daughter's heart, which was beating quickly and lightly.

"Now, Moses, why you been carryin' a loaded gun. To shoot somebody?"

"Of course not. And, please, sergeant, I don't like the kid to hear such things."

"You the one that brought it along, not me. Maybe you just wanted to scare somebody. You sore at somebody?"

"No, sergeant, I was only going to make a paperweight of it.

I forgot to take out the bullets, but that's because I don't know much about guns so it didn't occur to me. Will you let me make a phone call?"

"By and by. I ain't ready to. Sit down while I take care of other business. You sit and wait for the kid's mama to come."

"Could I get a container of milk for her?"

"Give Jim, here, two bits. He'll fetch it."

"With a straw, eh, June? You'd like to drink it with a straw." She nodded and Herzog said, "Please, a straw with it, if you don't mind."

"Papa?"

"Yes, June."

"You didn't tell me about the most-most."

For an instant he did not remember. "Ah," he said, "you mean that club in New York where people are the most of everything."

"That's the story."

She sat between his knees on the chair. He tried to make more room for her. "There's this association that people belong to. They're the most of every type. There's the hairiest bald man, and the baldest hairy man."

"The fattest thin lady."

"And the thinnest fat woman. The tallest dwarf and the smallest giant. They're all in it. The weakest strong man, and the strongest weak man. The stupidest wise man and the smartest blockhead. Then they have things like crippled acrobats, and ugly beauties."

"And what do they do, Papa?"

"On Saturday night they have a dinner-dance. They have a contest."

"To tell each other apart."

"Yes, sweetheart. And if you can tell the hairiest bald man from the baldest hairy man, you get a prize."

Bless her, she enjoyed her father's nonsense, and he must amuse her. She leaned her head on his shoulder and smiled, drowsy, with small teeth.

The room was hot and close. Herzog, sitting off to one side, took in the case of the two men who had come up in the elevator with him. A pair of plainclothesmen giving testimony—

the Vice Squad, he soon realized. They had brought a woman too. He hadn't noticed her before. A prostitute? Yes, obviously, for all her respectable middle-class airs. In spite of his own troubles, Herzog looked on and found himself listening keenly. The plainclothesman was saying, "They were having a hassle in this woman's room."

"Sip your milk, June dear," said Herzog. "Is it cold? Drink it nice and easy, darling."

"You heard them from the corridor?" said the sergeant. "What's it about?"

"This fellow was yelling about a pair of earrings."

"What about earrings? The ones she's wearing? Where'd you get them?"

"I bought them. From him. It was just business."

"On payments, which you didn't make."

"You were gettin' paid."

"He was takin' it out in trade. I see," the sergeant said.

"The way it figures," said the plainclothesman, explaining with a heavy, dull face, "he brought this other fellow along and after she did the trick he tried to get the ten bucks for himself because she owed him on the earrings. She wouldn't give up the money."

"Sergeant!" the second man pleaded. "What do I know! I'm from out of town."

From the town of Nineveh, with those twisting swarthy brows. Moses watched with interest, whispering occasionally to the child to divert her attention. The woman looked oddly familiar, despite her smeary makeup, emerald eye shadow, dyed hair, the thickening pride of her nose. He wanted very much to ask her a question. Had she attended McKinley High School? Did she sing in the Glee Club? Me too! Don't you remember? Herzog? Herzog who gave the class oration—who spoke on Emerson?

"Papa, the milk won't come."

"Because you've chewed the straw. Let's get the kinks out of it."

"We got to get out of here, sergeant," said the jewel salesman. "We got people waiting for us."

The wives! thought Herzog. The wives were waiting!

"You two fellows related?"

The jewel salesman said, "He's my brother-in-law, just visiting from Louisville."

The wives, one of them a sister, were waiting. And he, too, Herzog, was waiting, light-headed with anticipation. Could this really be Carlotta from the Glee Club who sang the contralto solo in "Once More with Joy" (from Wagner)? It was not impossible. Look at her now. Why would anyone want to give a broad like this a bang? Why! He knew well enough why. Look at the heavy veins in her legs, and look at those breasts, huddled together. They looked as if they had been washed but not ironed. And that slightly herring-eyed look, and her fat mouth. But he knew why. Because she had dirty ways, that was why. Lewd knowledge.

At this moment Madeleine arrived. She came in, saying, "Where is my child . . . !" Then she saw June on Herzog's lap and crossed the room quickly. "Come here to me, baby!" She lifted the milk container and put it aside, and took up the girl in her arms. Herzog felt the blood beating in his eardrums, and a great pressure at the back of the head. It was necessary that Madeleine should see him, but her look was devoid of intimate recognition. Coldly she turned from him, her brow twitching. "Is the child all right?" she said.

The sergeant motioned to the Vice Squad to make way. "She's fine. If she had even a scratch on her we'd have taken her to Michael Reese." Madeleine examined June's arms, her legs, felt her with nervous hands. The sergeant beckoned to Moses. He came forward, and he and Mady faced each other across the desk.

She wore a light blue linen suit and her hair fell loose behind her. The word to describe her conduct was *masterful*. Her heels had made a commanding noise clearly audible in this buzzing room. Herzog took a long look at her blue-eyed, straight, Byzantine profile, the small lips, the chin that pressed on the flesh beneath. Her color was deep, a sign with her that consciousness was running high. He thought he could make out a certain thickening in her face—incipient coarseness. He hoped so. It was only right that some of Gersbach's grossness should rub off on her. Why shouldn't it? He observed that she was definitely broader behind. He imagined what clutching and rubbing was the cause of that. Uxorious business—but that was not the right word . . . Amorous.

"Is this the girl's daddy, lady?"

Madeleine still refused to grant him a look of recognition. "Yes," she said, "I divorced him. Not long ago."

"Does he live in Massachussetts?"

"I don't know where he lives. It's none of my business."

Herzog marveled at her. He could not help admiring the perfection of her self-control. She never hesitated. When she took the milk from Junie she knew precisely where to drop the container, though she had been only an instant in the room. By now she had certainly made an inventory of all the objects on the desk, including the rubles, and the gun, of course. She had never seen it, but she could identify the Ludeyville keys by the round magnetic clasp of the ring, and she would realize the pistol belonged to him. He knew her ways so well, all her airs, the patrician style, the tic of her nose, the crazy clear hauteur of the eyes. As the sergeant questioned her, Moses, in his slightly dazed but intense way, unable to restrain associations, wondered whether she still gave off those odors of feminine secretions—the dirty way she had with her. That personal sweet and sour fragrance of hers, and her fire-blue eyes, her spiky glances and her small mouth ready with any wickedness would never again have the same power over him. Still, it gave him a headache merely to look at her. The pulses in his skull were quick and regular, like the tappets of an engine beating in their film of dark oil. He saw her with great vividness—the smoothness of her breast, bared by the square-cut dress, the smoothness of her legs, Indian brown. Her face, especially the forehead, was altogether too smooth, too glabrous for his taste. The whole burden of her severity was carried there. She had what the French called *le front bombé*; in other terms, a pedomorphic forehead. Ultimately unknowable, the processes behind it. See, Moses? We don't know one another. Even that Gersbach, call him any name you like, charlatan, psychopath, with his hot phony eyes and his clumsy cheeks, with the folds. He was unknowable. And I myself, the same. But hard ruthless action taken against a man is the assertion by evildoers that he is fully knowable. They put me down, ergo they claimed final knowledge of Herzog. They *knew* me! And I hold with Spinoza (I hope he won't mind) that to demand what is impossible for any human being, to exercise power where it can't be exercised, is tyranny. Excuse me, therefore, sir and madam, but I reject your definitions of me. Ah, this Madeleine is a strange person, to be so proud but not well wiped—so beautiful but distorted by rage—such a mixed mind of pure diamond and Woolworth glass. And Gersbach who sucked up to me. For the symbiosis of it. Symbiosis and trash. And she, as sweet as cheap candy, and just as reminiscent of poison as chemical sweet acids. But I make no last judgment. That's for them, not me. I came to do harm, I admit. But the first bloodshed was mine, and so I'm out of this now. Count me out. Except in what concerns June. But for the rest, I withdraw from the whole scene as soon as I can. Good-by to all.

"Well, he give you a hard time?" Herzog who had been listening subliminally heard the sergeant put this question.

He said tersely to Madeleine, "Watch it, if you please. Let's not have unnecessary trouble."

She ignored this. "He bothered me, yes."

"He make any threats?"

Herzog waited, tense, for her reply. She would consider the support money—the rent. She was canny, a superbly cunning, very canny woman. But there was also the violence of her hatred, and that hatred had a fringe of insanity.

"No, not directly to me. I haven't seen him since last October."

"To who, then?" The sergeant pressed her.

Madeleine evidently would do what she could to weaken his position. She was aware that her relations with Gersbach offered grounds for a custody suit and she would therefore make the most of his present weakness—his idiocy. "His psychiatrist," she said, "saw fit to warn me."

"Saw fit! Of what!" said Herzog.

Still she spoke only to the sergeant. "He said he was concerned. Doctor Edvig is his name if you want to talk to him. He felt it necessary to advise me . . ."

"Edvig is a sucker—he's a fool," said Herzog.

Madeleine's color was very high, her throat flushed, like pink—like rose quartz, and the curious tinge had come into her eyes. He knew what this moment was to her—happiness! Ah, yes, he said to himself, Ikey-Fishbones has dropped another pop fly in left field. The other team is scoring—clearing all bases. She was making brilliant use of error.

"Do you recognize this gun?" The sergeant held it in his yellow palm, turning it over with delicate fingers like a fish—a perch.

The radiance of her look as it rested on the gun was deeper than any sexual expression he had ever seen on her face. "It's his, isn't it?" she said. "The bullets, too?" He recognized the hard clear look of joy in her eyes. Her lips were pressed shut.

"He had it on him. Do you know it?"

"No, but I'm not surprised."

Moses was watching June now. Her face was clouded again; she seemed to frown.

"Did you ever file a complaint against Moses, here?"

"No," said Mady. "I didn't actually do that." She took a sharp breath. She was about to plunge into something.

"Sergeant," said Herzog. "I told you there was no complaint. Ask her if I've ever missed a single support check."

Madeleine said, "I did give his photograph to the Hyde Park police."

He warned her that she was going too far. "Madeleine!" he said.

"Shut it up, Moses," said the sergeant. "What was that for, lady?"

"In case he prowled around the house. To alert them."

Herzog shook his head, partly at himself. He had made the kind of mistake today that belonged to an earlier period. As of today it was no longer characteristic. But he had to pay an earlier reckoning. When will you catch up with yourself! he asked himself. When will that day come!

"Did he ever prowl?"

"He was never seen, but I know damn well he did. He's jealous and a troublemaker. He has a terrible temper."

"You never signed a complaint, though?"

"No. But I expect to be protected from any sort of violence."

Her voice went up sharply, and as she spoke, Herzog saw the sergeant take a new look at her, as if he were beginning to make out her haughty peculiarities at last. He picked up the

Ben Franklin glasses with the tablet-shaped lenses. "There ain't going to be any violence, lady."

Yes, Moses thought, he's beginning to see how it is. "I never intended to use that gun except to hold papers down," he said.

Madeleine now spoke to Herzog for the first time, pointing with a rigid finger to the two bullets and looking him in the eyes. "One of those was for me, wasn't it!"

"You think so? I wonder where you get such ideas? And who was the other one for?" He was quite cool as he said this, his tone was level. He was doing all he could to bring out the hidden Madeleine, the Madeleine he knew. As she stared at him her color receded and her nose began to move very slightly. She seemed to realize that she must control her tic and the violence of her stare. But by noticeable degrees her face became very white, her eyes smaller, stony. He believed he could interpret them. They expressed a total will that he should die. This was infinitely more than ordinary hatred. It was a vote for his nonexistence, he thought. He wondered whether the sergeant was able to see this. "Well, who do you think that second imaginary shot was for?"

She said no more to him, only continued to stare in the same way.

"That'll be all now, lady. You can take your child and go."

"Good-by, June," said Moses. "You go home now. Papa'll see you soon. Give us a kiss, now, on the cheek." He felt the child's lips. Over her mother's shoulder, June reached out and touched him. "God bless you." He added, as Madeleine strode away, "I'll be back."

"I'll finish bookin' you now, Moses."

"I've got to post bond? How much?"

"Three hundred. American, not this stuff."

"I wish you'd let me make a call."

As the sergeant silently directed him to take one of his own dimes, Moses still had the time to note what a powerful police-face he had. He must have Indian blood—Cherokee, perhaps, or Osage; an Irish ancestor or two. His sallow gold skin with heavy seams descending, the austere nose and prominent lips for impassivity, and the many separate, infinitesimal gray curls on his scalp for dignity. His rugged fingers pointed to the phone booth.

Herzog was tired, dragged out, as he dialed his brother, but far from downcast. For some reason he believed he had done well. He was running true to form, yes; more mischief; and Will would have to bail him out. Still, he was not at all heavy-hearted but, on the contrary, felt rather free. Perhaps he was too tired to be glum. That may have been it, after all—the metabolic wastes of fatigue (he was fond of these physiological explanations; this one came from Freud's essay on Mourning and Melancholia) made him temporarily light-hearted, even gay.

"Yes."

"Will Herzog in?"

Each recognized the other's voice.

"Mose!" said Will.

Herzog could do nothing about the feelings stirred by hearing Will. They came to life suddenly at hearing the old tone, the old name. He loved Will, Helen, even Shura, though his millions had made him remote. In the confinement of the metal booth the sweat burst out instantly on his neck.

"Where've you been, Mose? The old woman called last night. I couldn't sleep afterwards. Where are you?"

"Elya," said Herzog, using his brother's family name, "don't worry. I haven't done anything serious, but I'm down at Eleventh and State."

"At Police Headquarters?"

"Just a minor traffic accident. No one hurt. But they're holding me for three hundred bucks bond, and I haven't got the money on me."

"For heaven's sake, Mose. Nobody's seen you since last summer. We've been worried sick. I'll be right down."

He waited in the cell with two other men. One was drunk and sleeping in his soiled skivvies. The other was a Negro boy, not old enough to shave. He wore a fawn-colored expensive suit and brown alligator shoes. Herzog said hello, but the boy chose not to answer. He stuck to his own misery, and looked away. Moses was sorry for him. He leaned against the bars, waiting. The wrong side of the bars—he felt it with his cheek.

And here were the toilet bowl, the bare metal bunk, and the flies on the ceiling. This, Herzog realized, was not the sphere of *his* sins. He was merely passing through. Out in the streets, in American society, that was where he did his time. He sat down calmly on the bunk. Of course, he thought, he'd leave Chicago immediately, and he'd come back only when he was ready to do June good, genuine good. No more of this hectic, heart-rent, theatrical window-peering; no more collision, fainting, you-fight-'im-'e-cry encounters, confrontations. The drone of trouble coming from the cells and corridors, the bad smell of headquarters, the wretchedness of faces, the hand that turned the key of no better hope than the hand of this stuporous sleeper in his urine-stained underpants—the man who has eyes, nostrils, ears, let him hear, smell, see. The man who has intellect, heart, let him consider.

Sitting as comfortably as the pain in his ribs would permit, Herzog even jotted a few memoranda to himself. They were not very coherent or even logical, but they came quite naturally to him. This was how Moses E. Herzog worked, and he wrote on his knee with cheerful eagerness, *Clumsy, inexact machinery of civil peace. Paleotechnic, as the man would say. If a common primal crime is the origin of social order, as Freud, Róheim et cetera believe, the band of brothers attacking and murdering the primal father, eating his body, gaining their freedom by a murder and united by a blood wrong, then there is some reason why jail should have these dark, archaic tones. Ah, yes, the wild energy of the band of brothers, soldiers, rapists, etc. But all that is nothing but metaphor. I can't truly feel I can attribute my blundering to this thick unconscious cloud. This primitive blood-daze.*

The dream of man's heart, however much we may distrust and resent it, is that life may complete itself in significant pattern. Some incomprehensible way. Before death. Not irrationally but incomprehensibly fulfilled. Spared by these clumsy police guardians, you get one last chance to know justice. Truth.

Dear Edvig, he noted quickly. *You gave me good value for my money when you explained that neuroses might be graded by the inability to tolerate ambiguous situations. I have just read a certain verdict in Madeleine's eyes, "For cowards, Not-being!" Her disorder is super-clarity. Allow me modestly to claim that I am*

much better now at ambiguities. I think I can say, however, that
I have been spared the chief ambiguity that afflicts intellectuals,
and this is that civilized individuals hate and resent the civiliza-
tion that makes their lives possible. What they love is an imagi-
nary human situation invented by their own genius and which
they believe is the only true and the only human reality. How odd!
But the best-treated, most favored and intelligent part of any so-
ciety is often the most ungrateful. Ingratitude, however, is its so-
cial function. Now there's an ambiguity for you! . . . Dear
Ramona, I owe you a lot. I am fully aware of it. Though I may
not be coming back to New York right away, I intend to keep in
touch. Dear God! Mercy! My God! Rachaim olenu . . . melekh
maimis . . . *Thou King of Death and Life . . . !*

His brother observed, as they were leaving police headquarters, "You don't seem too upset."

"No, Will."

Above the sidewalk and the warm evening gloom the sky
carried the long gilt trails of jets, and the jumbled lights of
honky-tonks, just north of 12th Street, were already heaving
up and down, a pale mass in which the street seemed to end.

"How do you feel?"

"I feel fine," said Herzog. "How do I look?"

His brother said discreetly, "You could do with a little rest.
Why don't we stop and have you looked at by my doctor."

"I don't think that's necessary. This small cut on my head
stopped bleeding almost immediately."

"But you've been holding your side. Don't be a fool, Mose."

Will was an undemonstrative man, substantial, shrewd,
quiet, shorter than his brother but with thicker, darker hair. In
a family of passionately expressive people like Father Herzog
and Aunt Zipporah Will had developed a quieter, observant,
reticent style.

"How's the family, Will—the kids?"

"Fine . . . What have you been doing, Moses?"

"Don't go by appearances. There's less to worry about than
meets the eye. I'm really in very good shape. Do you remember when we got lost at Lake Wandawega? Floundering in the
slime, cutting our feet on those reeds? That was really dangerous. But this is nothing."

"What were you doing with that gun?"

"You know I'm no more capable of firing it at someone than Papa was. You took his watch chain, didn't you? I remembered those old rubles in his drawer and then I took the revolver too. I shouldn't have. At least I ought to have emptied it. It was just one of those dumb impulses. Let's forget it."

"All right," said Will. "I don't mean to embarrass you. That's not the point."

"I know what it is," Herzog said. "You're worried." He had to lower his voice to control it. "I love you too, Will."

"Yes, I know that."

"But I haven't behaved very sensibly. From your standpoint . . . Well, from any reasonable standpoint. I brought Madeleine to your office so you could see her before I married her. I could tell you didn't approve. I didn't approve of her myself. And she didn't approve of me."

"Why did you marry her?"

"God ties all kinds of loose ends together. Who knows why! He couldn't care less about my welfare, or my ego, that thing of value. All you can say is, 'There's a red thread spliced with a green, or blue, and I wonder why.' And then I put all that money into the house in Ludeyville. That was simply crazy."

"Perhaps not," said Will. "It is real estate, after all. Have you tried to sell it?" Will had great faith in real estate.

"To whom? How?"

"List it with an agent. Maybe I'll come and look it over."

"I'd be grateful," said Herzog. "I don't think any buyer in his right mind would touch it."

"But let me call Doctor Ramsberg, Mose, and have him examine you. Then come home and have some dinner with us. It would be a treat for the family."

"When could you come to Ludeyville?"

"I've got to go to Boston next week. Then Muriel and I were going out to the Cape."

"Come by way of Ludeyville. It's close to the Turnpike. I'd consider it a tremendous favor. I have to sell that house."

"Have dinner with us, and we can talk about it."

"Will—no. I'm not up to it. Just look at me. I'm stinking dirty, and I'd upset everyone. Like a lousy lost sheep." He laughed. "No, some other time when I'm feeling a little more normal. I look as if I'd just arrived in this country. A D.P. Just as we arrived from Canada at the old Baltimore and Ohio Station. On the Michigan Central. God, we were filthy with the soot."

William did not share his brother's passion for reminiscence. He was an engineer and technologist, a contractor and builder; a balanced, reasonable person, he was pained to see Moses in such a state. His lined face was hot, uneasy; he took a handkerchief from the inner pocket of his well-tailored suit and pressed it to his forehead, his cheeks, under the large Herzog eyes.

"I'm sorry, Elya," said Moses, more quietly.

"Well—"

"Let me straighten myself up a bit. I know you're concerned about me. But that's just it. I'm sorry to worry you. I really am all right."

"Are you?" Will sadly looked at him.

"Yes, I'm at an awful disadvantage here—dirty, foolish, just bailed out. It's just ridiculous. Everything will look a lot different in the East, next week. I'll meet you in Boston, if you like. When I've got myself in better order. There's nothing you can do now but treat me like a jerk—a child. And that's not right."

"I'm not making any judgments on you. You don't have to come home with me, if that embarrasses you. Although we're your own family . . . But there's my car, across the street." He gestured toward his dark-blue Cadillac. "Just come along to the doctor so I can be sure you weren't hurt in the accident. Then you can do what you think best."

"All right. Fair enough. There's nothing wrong. I'm sure of it."

He was not entirely surprised, however, to learn that he had a broken rib. "No lung puncture," the doctor said. "Six weeks or so in tape. And you'll need two or three stitches in your head. That's the whole story. No heavy lifting, straining, chopping, or other violent exercise. Will tells me you're a country gentleman. You've got a farm in the Berkshires? An estate?"

The doctor with grizzled backswept hair and small keen eyes looked at him with thin-lipped amusement.

"It's in bad repair. Miles from a synagogue," said Herzog.

"Ha, your brother likes to kid," Dr. Ramsberg said. Will faintly smiled. Standing with folded arms he favored one heel, somewhat like Father Herzog, and had a bit of the old man's elegance but not his eccentricities. He had no time for such stuff, thought Herzog, running a big business. No great interest in it. Other things absorb. He's a good man, a very good man. But there's a strange division of functions that I sense, in which I am the specialist in . . . in spiritual self-awareness; or emotionalism; or ideas; or nonsense. Perhaps of no real use or relevance except to keep alive primordial feelings of a certain sort. He mixes grout to pump into these new high-risers all over town. He has to be political, and deal, and wangle and pay off and figure tax angles. All that Papa was inept in but dreamed he was born to do. Will is a quiet man of duty and routine, has his money, position, influence, and is just as glad to be rid of his private or "personal" side. Sees me spluttering fire in the wilderness of this world, and pities me no doubt for my temperament. Under the old dispensation, as the stumbling, ingenuous, burlap Moses, a heart without guile, in need of protection, a morbid phenomenon, a modern remnant of other-worldliness—under that former dispensation I would need protection. And it would be gladly offered by him—by the person who "knows-the-world-for-what-it-is." Whereas a man like me has shown the arbitrary withdrawal of proud subjectivity from the collective and historical progress of mankind. And that is true of lowerclass emotional boys and girls who adopt the aesthetic mode, the mode of rich sensibility. Seeking to sustain their own version of existence under the crushing weight of *mass*. What Marx described as that "material weight." Turning this thing, "my personal life," into a circus, into gladiatorial combat. Or tamer forms of entertainment. To make a joke of your "shame," your ephemeral dimness, and show why you deserve your pain. The white modern lights of the small room were going round, wheeling. Herzog himself felt that he was rotating with them as the doctor wound the medicinal-smelling tapes tightly about his chest. Now, to get rid of all such falsehoods . . .

"I have an idea my brother could do with some rest," said Will. "What's your opinion, doctor?"

"He looks as if he's been going pretty hard, that's true."

"I'm going to spend a week at Ludeyville," Moses said.

"What I mean is complete rest—bed rest."

"Yes, I know I seem to be in a state. But it's not a bad state."

"Still," said Herzog's brother, "you worry me."

A loving brute—a subtle, spoiled, loving man. Who can make use of him? He craves use. Where is he needed? Show him the way to make his sacrifice to truth, to order, peace. Oh, that mysterious creature, that Herzog! awkwardly taped, helped into his wrinkled shirt by brother Will.

H E REACHED his country place the following afternoon, after taking a plane to Albany, from there the bus to Pittsfield, and then a cab to Ludeyville. Asphalter had given him some Tuinal the night before. He slept deeply and was feeling perfectly fine, despite his taped sides.

The house was two miles beyond the village, in the hills. Beautiful, sparkling summer weather in the Berkshires, the air light, the streams quick, the woods dense, the green new. As for birds, Herzog's acres seemed to have become a sanctuary. Wrens nested under the ornamental scrolls of the porch. The giant elm was not quite dead, and the orioles lived in it still. Herzog had the driver stop in the mossy roadway, boulder-lined. He couldn't be sure the house was approachable. But no fallen trees blocked the path, and although much of the gravel had washed down in thaws and storms the cab might easily have gotten through. Moses, however, didn't mind the short climb. His chest was securely armored in tape and his legs were light. He had bought some groceries in Ludeyville. If hunters and prowlers had not eaten it, there was a supply of canned goods in the cellar. Two years ago he had put up tomatoes and beans and raspberry preserves, and before leaving for Chicago he had hidden his wine and whisky. The electricity of course was turned off but perhaps the old hand pump could be made to work. There was always cistern water to fall back on. He could cook in the fireplace; there were old hooks and trivets— and here (his heart trembled) the house rose out of weeds, vines, trees, and blossoms. Herzog's folly! Monument to his sincere and loving idiocy, to the unrecognized evils of his char-acter, symbol of his Jewish struggle for a solid footing in White Anglo-Saxon Protestant America ("The land was ours before we were the land's," as that sententious old man declared at the Inauguration). I too have done my share of social climbing, he thought, with hauteur to spare, defying the Wasps, who, because the government gave much of this continent away to the railroads, stopped boiling their own soap circa 1880, took European tours, and began to complain of the Micks and the

Spicks and the Sheenies. What a struggle I waged!—left-handed but fierce. But enough of that—here I am. *Hineni!* How marvelously beautiful it is today. He stopped in the overgrown yard, shut his eyes in the sun, against flashes of crimson, and drew in the odors of catalpa-bells, soil, honeysuckle, wild onions, and herbs. Either deer or lovers had lain in this grass near the elm, for it was flattened. He circled the house to see whether it was much damaged. There were no broken windows. All the shutters, hooked from within, were undisturbed. Only a few of the posters he had put up warning that this property was under police protection had been torn down. The garden was a thick mass of thorny canes, roses and berries twisted together. It looked too hopeless—past regretting. He would never have the strength to throw himself into such tasks again, to hammer, paint, patch, splice, prune, spray. He was here only to look things over.

The house was as musty as he had expected. He opened a few windows and shutters in the kitchen. The debris of leaves and pine needles, webs, cocoons, and insect corpses he brushed away. What was needed, immediately, was a fire. He had brought matches. One of the benefits of a riper age was that you became clever about such things—foresightful. Of course he had a bicycle—he could ride to the village to buy what he had forgotten. He had even been smart enough to set the bike on its saddle, to spare the tires. There was not much air in them, but they'd get him down to the Esso station. He carried in a few pine logs, kindling, and started a small blaze first, to make sure of the draft. Birds or squirrels might have nested in the flues. But then he remembered that he had climbed out on the roof to fasten wire mesh over the chimneys—part of his frenzy of efficient toil. He laid on more wood. The old bark dropped away and disclosed the work of insects underneath—grubs, ants, long-legged spiders ran away. He gave them every opportunity to escape. The black, dry branches began to burn with yellow flames. He heaped on more logs, secured them with the andirons, and continued his examination of the house.

The canned food had not been touched. There was fancy-goods bought by Madeleine (always the best of everything), S. S. Pierce terrapin soup, Indian pudding, truffles, olives, and then grimmer-looking victuals bought by Moses himself at

Army surplus sales—beans, canned bread, and the like. He made his inventory with a sort of dreamy curiosity about his onetime plan for solitary self-sufficiency—the washer, dryer, the hot-water unit, pure white and gleaming forms into which he had put his dead father's dollars, ugly green, laboriously made, tediously counted, divided in agony among the heirs. Well, well, thought Herzog, he shouldn't have sent me to school to learn about dead emperors. "My name is Ozymandias, king of kings:, /Look on my works, ye Mighty, and despair!" But self-sufficiency and solitude, gentleness, it all was so tempting, and had sounded so innocent, it became smiling Herzog so well in the description. It's only later you discover how much viciousness is in these hidden heavens. *Unemployed consciousness,* he wrote in the pantry. *I grew up in a time of widespread unemployment, and never believed there might be work for me. Finally, jobs appeared, but somehow my consciousness remained unemployed. And after all,* he continued beside the fire, *the human intellect is one of the great forces of the universe. It can't safely remain unused. You might almost conclude that the boredom of so many human arrangements (middle-class family life, for instance) has the historical aim of freeing the intellect of newer generations, sending them into science. But a terrible loneliness throughout life is simply the plankton on which Leviathan feeds. . . . Must reconsider. The soul requires intensity. At the same time virtue bores mankind. Read Confucius again. With vast populations, the world must prepare to turn Chinese.*

Herzog's present loneliness did not seem to count because it was so consciously cheerful. He peered through the chink in the lavatory where he used to hide away with his ten-cent volume of Dryden and Pope, reading "I am His Highness' dog at Kew" or "Great wits to madness sure are near allied." There, in the same position as in former years, was the rose that used to give him comfort—as shapely, as red (as nearly "genital" to his imagination) as ever. Some good things do recur. He was a long time peering at it through the meeting of masonry and lumber. The same damp-loving grasshoppers (giant orthoptera) still lived in this closet of masonry and plywood. A struck match revealed them. Among the pipes.

It was odd, the tour he made through his property. In his

own room he found the ruins of his scholarly enterprise strewn over the desk and the shelves. The windows were so discolored as to seem stained with iodine, and the honeysuckles outside had almost pulled the screens down. On the sofa he found proof that the place was indeed visited by lovers. Too blind with passion to hunt in darkness for the bedrooms. But they'll get curvature of the spine using Madeleine's horsehair antiques. For some reason it particularly pleased Herzog that his room should be the one chosen by the youth of the village—here among bales of learned notes. He found girls' hairs on the curving armrests, and tried to imagine bodies, faces, odors. Thanks to Ramona he had no need to be greatly envious, but a little envy of the young was quite natural too. On the floor was one of his large cards with a note in which he had written *To do justice to Condorcet* . . . He hadn't the heart to read further and turned it face down on the table. For the present, anyway, Condorcet would have to find another defender. In the dining room were the precious dishes that Tennie wanted, crimson-rimmed bone china, very handsome. He wouldn't need that. The books, muslin-covered, were undisturbed. He lifted the cloth and glanced at them with no special interest. Visiting the little bathroom, he was entertained to see the lavish fittings Madeleine had bought at Sloane's, scalloped silver soap dishes and flashing towel racks too heavy for the plaster, even after they were fastened with toggle bolts. They were drooping now. The shower stall, for Gersbach's convenience—the Gersbachs had had no shower in Barrington—was thoughtfully equipped with a handrail. "If we're going to put it in, let's make it so Valentine can use it," Mady had said. Ah, well—Moses shrugged. A strange odor in the toilet bowl attracted his notice next, and raising the wooden lid he found the small beaked skulls and other remains of birds who had nested there after the water was drained, and then had been entombed by the falling lid. He looked grimly in, his heart aching somewhat at this accident. There must be a broken window in the attic, he inferred from this, and other birds nesting in the house. Indeed, he found owls in his bedroom, perched on the red valances, which they had streaked with droppings. He gave them every opportunity to escape, and, when they were gone, looked for a nest. He found the young owls in the large light fixture over the bed where he and Madeleine had known so much misery and hatred. (Some delight as well.) On the mattress much nest litter had fallen— straws, wool threads, down, bits of flesh (mouse ends) and streaks of excrement. Unwilling to disturb these flat-faced little creatures, Herzog pulled the mattress of his marriage bed into June's room. He opened more windows, and the sun and country air at once entered. He was surprised to feel such contentment . . . contentment? Whom was he kidding, this was joy! For perhaps the first time he felt what it was to be free from Madeleine. Joy! His servitude was ended, and his heart released from its grisly heaviness and encrustation. Her absence, no more than her absence itself, was simply sweetness and lightness of spirit. To her, at 11th and State, it had been happiness to see him in trouble, and to him in Ludeyville it was a delicious joy to have her removed from his flesh, like something that had stabbed his shoulders, his groin, made his arms and his neck lame and cumbersome. *My dear sage and imbecilic Edvig. It may be that the remission of pain is no small part of human happiness. In its primordial and stupider levels, where now and then a closed valve opens again.* . . . Those strange lights, Herzog's brown eyes, so often overlaid with the film or protective chitin of melancholy, the by-product of his laboring brain, shone again.

It cost him some effort to turn over the mattress on the floor of June's old room. He had to move aside some of her cast-off toys and kiddie furniture, a great stuffed blue-eyed tiger, the potty chair, a red snowsuit, perfectly good. He recognized also the grandmother's bikini, shorts, and halters, and, among other oddities, a washrag which Phoebe had stitched with his initials, a birthday present, a possible hint that his ears were not clean. Beaming, he pushed it aside with his foot. A beetle escaped from beneath. Herzog, lying under the open window with the sun in his face, rested on the mattress. Over him the great trees, the spruces in the front yard, showed their beautiful jaggedness and sent down the odor of heated needles and gum.

It was here, until the sun passed from the room, that he began in earnest, from tranquil fullness of heart, to consider another series of letters.

Dear Ramona. Only "Dear"? Come, Moses, open up a little. *Darling Ramona. What an excellent woman you are.* Here he paused to consider whether he should say he was in Ludeyville. In her Mercedes she could drive from New York in three hours, and it was probable that she would. God's blessing on her short but perfect legs, her solid, well-tinted breasts, and her dashing curved teeth and gypsy brows and curls. *La devoradora de hombres.* He decided, however, to date his letter Chicago and ask Lucas to remail it. What he wanted now was peace—peace and clarity. *I hope I didn't upset you by copping out. But I know you're not one of those conventional women it takes a month to appease because of a broken date. I had to see my daughter, and my son. He's at Camp Ayumah, near Catskill. It's turning into a busy summer. Several interesting developments. I hesitate to make too many assertions yet, but at least I can admit what I never stopped asserting anyway, or feeling. The light of truth is never far away, and no human being is too negligible or corrupt to come into it.* I don't see why I shouldn't say that. *But to accept ineffectuality, banishment to personal life, confusion* . . . Why don't you try this out, Herzog, on the owls next door, those naked owlets pimpled with blue. *Since the last question, also the first one, the question of death, offers us the interesting alternatives of disintegrating ourselves by our own wills in proof of our "freedom," or the acknowledging that we owe a human life to this waking spell of existence, regardless of the void. (After all, we have no positive knowledge of that void.)*

Should I say all this to Ramona? Some women think that earnestness is wooing. She'll want a child. She'll want to breed with a man who talks to her like this. *Work. Work. Real, relevant work.* . . . He paused. But Ramona was a willing worker. According to her lights. And she loved her work. He smiled affectionately on his sunlit mattress.

Dear Marco. I've come up to the old homestead to look things over and relax a bit. The place is in pretty good shape, considering. Perhaps you'd like to spend some time here with me, only the two of us—roughing it—after camp. We'll talk about it Parents' Day. I'm looking forward to that, eagerly. Your little sister whom I saw in Chicago yesterday is very lively and as pretty as ever. She received your postcard.

Do you remember the talks we had about Scott's Antarctic

Expedition, and how poor Scott was beaten to the Pole by Amundsen? You seemed interested. This is a thing that always gets me. There was a man in Scott's party who went out and lost himself to give the others a chance to survive. He was ailing, footsore, couldn't keep up any longer. And do you remember how by chance they found a mound of frozen blood, the blood of one of their slaughtered ponies, and how thankful they were to thaw and drink it? The success of Amundsen was due to his use of dogs instead of ponies. The weaker were butchered and fed to the stronger. Otherwise the expedition would have failed. I have often wondered at one thing. Hungry as they were, the dogs would sniff at the flesh of their own and back away. The skin had to be removed before they would eat it.

Maybe you and I could take a trip at Xmas to Canada just to get the feel of genuine cold. I am a Canadian, too, you know. We could visit Ste. Agathe, in the Laurentians. Expect me on the 16th, bright and early.

Dear Luke—Be so kind as to post these enclosures. I hope to hear your depression is over. I think your visions of the aunt being rescued by the fireman and of the broads playing piggy-move-up are signs of psychological resiliency. I predict your recovery. As for me. . . . As for you, thought Herzog, you will not tell him how you feel now, all this overflow! It wouldn't make him happier. Keep it to yourself if you feel exalted. Anyway, he may think you've simply gone off your nut.

But if I am out of my mind, it's all right with me.

My dear Professor Mermelstein. I want to congratulate you on a splendid book. In some matters you scooped me, you know, and I felt like hell about it—hated you one whole day for making a good deal of my work superfluous (Wallace and Darwin?). However, I well know what labor and patience went into such a work—so much digging, learning, synthesizing, and I'm all admiration. When you are ready to print a revised edition—or perhaps another book—it would be a great pleasure to talk over some of these questions. There are parts of my projected book I'll never return to. You may do what you like with those materials. In my earlier book (to which you were kind enough to refer) I devoted one section to Heaven and Hell in apocalyptic Romanticism. I may not have done it to your taste, but you ought not to have overlooked it completely. You ought to have a look at the mono-

graph by that fat natty brute Egbert Shapiro, "From Luther to Lenin, A History of Revolutionary Psychology." His fat cheeks give him a great resemblance to Gibbon. *It is a valuable piece of work. I was greatly impressed by the section called Millenarianism and Paranoia. It should not be ignored that modern power-systems do offer a resemblance to this psychosis. A gruesome and crazy book on this has been written by a man named Banowitch. Fairly inhuman, and filled with vile paranoid hypotheses such as that crowds are fundamentally cannibalistic, that people standing secretly terrify the sitting, that smiling teeth are the weapons of hunger, that the tyrant is mad for the sight of (possibly edible?) corpses about him. It seems quite true that the making of corpses has been the most dramatic achievement of modern dictators and their followers (Hitler, Stalin, etc.).* Just to see—Herzog tried this on, experimenting—whether Mermelstein didn't have a vestige of old Stalinism about him. *But this fellow Shapiro is something of an eccentric, and I mention him as an extreme case. How we all love extreme cases and apocalypses, fires, drownings, stranglings, and the rest of it. The bigger our mild, basically ethical, safe middle classes grow the more radical excitement is in demand. Mild or moderate truthfulness or accuracy seems to have no pull at all. Just what we need now!* ("When a dog is drowning, you offer him a cup of water," Papa used to say, bitterly.) *In any case, if you had read that chapter of mine on apocalypse and Romanticism you might have looked a little straighter at that Russian you admire so much—Isvolsky? The man who sees the souls of monads as the legions of the damned, simply atomized and pulverized, a dust storm in Hell; and warns that Lucifer must take charge of collectivized mankind, devoid of spiritual character and true personality. I don't deny this makes some sense, here and there, though I do worry that such ideas, because of the bit of suggestive truth in them, may land us in the same old suffocating churches and synagogues. I was somewhat bothered by borrowings and references which I considered "hit and run," or the use of other writers' serious beliefs as mere metaphors. For instance, I liked the section called "Interpretations of Suffering" and also the one called "Toward a Theory of Boredom." This was an excellent piece of research. But then I thought the treatment you gave Kierkegaard was fairly frivolous. I venture to say Kierkegaard meant that truth has lost its force*

with us and horrible pain and evil must teach it to us again, the
eternal punishments of Hell will have to regain their reality
before mankind turns serious once more. I do not see this. Let us
set aside the fact that such convictions in the mouths of safe, comfortable people playing at crisis, alienation, apocalypse and desperation, make me sick. We must get it out of our heads that this
is a doomed time, that we are waiting for the end, and the rest
of it, mere junk from fashionable magazines. Things are grim
enough without these shivery games. People frightening one another—a poor sort of moral exercise. But, to get to the main point,
the advocacy and praise of suffering take us in the wrong direction and those of us who remain loyal to civilization must not go
for it. You have to have the power to employ pain, to repent, to be
illuminated, you must have the opportunity and even the time.
With the religious, the love of suffering is a form of gratitude to
experience or an opportunity to experience evil and change it
into good. They believe the spiritual cycle can and will be completed in a man's existence and he will somehow make use of his
suffering, if only in the last moments of his life, when the mercy of
God will reward him with a vision of the truth, and he will die
transfigured. But this is a special exercise. More commonly suffering breaks people, crushes them, and is simply unilluminating.
You see how gruesomely human beings are destroyed by pain,
when they have the added torment of losing their humanity first,
so that their death is a total defeat, and then you write about
"modern forms of Orphism" and about "people who are not
afraid of suffering" and throw in other such cocktail-party expressions. Why not say rather that people of powerful imagination, given to dreaming deeply and to raising up marvelous and
self-sufficient fictions, turn to suffering sometimes to cut into
their bliss, as people pinch themselves to feel awake. I know that
my suffering, if I may speak of it, has often been like that, a more
extended form of life, a striving for true wakefulness and an an-
tidote to illusion, and therefore I can take no moral credit for it.
I am willing without further exercise in pain to open my heart.
And this needs no doctrine or theology of suffering. We love apocalypses too much, and crisis ethics and florid extremism with its
thrilling language. Excuse me, no. I've had all the monstrosity I
want. We've reached an age in the history of mankind when we
can ask about certain persons, "What is this Thing?" No more of

that for me—no, no! I am simply a human being, more or less. I am even willing to leave the more or less in your hands. You may decide about me. You have a taste for metaphors. Your otherwise admirable work is marred by them. I'm sure you can come up with a grand metaphor for me. But don't forget to say that I will never expound suffering for anyone or call for Hell to make us serious and truthful. I even think man's perception of pain may have grown too refined. But that is another subject for lengthy treatment.

Very good, Mermelstein. Go, and sin no more. And Herzog, perhaps somewhat sheepish over this strange diatribe, rose from the mattress (the sun was moving away) and went downstairs again. He ate several slices of bread, and baked beans—a cold bean sandwich, and afterward carried outside his hammock and two lawn chairs.

Thus began his final week of letters. He wandered over his twenty acres of hillside and woodlot, composing his messages, none of which he mailed. He was not ready to pedal to the post office and answer questions in the village about Mrs. Herzog and little June. As he knew well, the grotesque facts of the entire Herzog scandal had been overheard on the party line and become the meat and drink of Ludeyville's fantasy life. He had never restrained himself on the telephone; he was too agitated. And Madeleine was far too patrician to care what the hicks were overhearing. Anyway, she had been throwing him out. It reflected no discredit on her.

Dear Madeleine—You are a terrific one, you are! Bless you! What a creature! To put on lipstick, after dinner in a restaurant, she would look at her reflection in a knife blade. He recalled this with delight. *And you, Gersbach, you're welcome to Madeleine. Enjoy her—rejoice in her. You will not reach me through her, however. I know you sought me in her flesh. But I am no longer there.*

Dear Sirs, The size and number of the rats in Panama City, when I passed through, truly astonished me. I saw one of them sunning himself beside a swimming pool. And another was looking at me from the wainscoting of a restaurant as I was eating fruit salad. Also, on an electric wire which slanted upward into a banana tree, I saw a whole rat-troupe go back and forth, harvesting. They ran the wire twenty times or more without a single collision. My suggestion is that you put birth-control chemicals in the baits. Poisons will never work (for Malthusian reasons; reduce the population somewhat and it only increases more vigorously). But several years of contraception may eliminate your rat problem.

Dear Herr Nietzsche—My dear sir, May I ask a question from the floor? You speak of the power of the Dionysian spirit to endure the sight of the Terrible, the Questionable, to allow itself the luxury of Destruction, to witness Decomposition, Hideousness, Evil. All this the Dionysian spirit can do because it has the same power of recovery as Nature itself. Some of these expressions, I must tell you, have a very Germanic ring. A phrase like the "luxury of Destruction" is positively Wagnerian, and I know how you came to despise all that sickly Wagnerian idiocy and bombast. Now we've seen enough destruction to test the power of the Dionysian spirit amply, and where are the heroes who have recovered from it? Nature (itself) and I are alone together, in the Berkshires, and this is my chance to understand. I am lying in a hammock, chin on breast, hands clasped, mind jammed with thoughts, agitated, yes, but also cheerful, and I know you value cheerfulness—true cheerfulness, not the seeming sanguinity of Epicureans, nor the strategic buoyancy of the heartbroken. I also know you think that deep pain is ennobling, pain which burns slow, like green wood, and there you have me with you, somewhat. But for this higher education survival is necessary. You must outlive the pain. Herzog! you must stop this quarrelsomeness and baiting of great men. *No, really, Herr Nietzsche, I have great admiration for you. Sympathy. You want to make us able to live with the void. Not lie ourselves into good-naturedness, trust, ordinary middling human considerations, but to question as has never been questioned before, relentlessly, with iron determination, into evil, through evil, past evil, accepting no abject comfort. The most absolute, the most piercing questions. Rejecting mankind as it is, that ordinary, practical, thieving, stinking, unilluminated, sodden rabble, not only the laboring rabble, but even worse the "educated" rabble with its books and concerts and lectures, its liberalism and its romantic theatrical "loves" and "passions"—it all deserves to die, it will die. Okay. Still, your extremists must survive. No survival, no* Amor Fati. *Your immoralists also eat meat. They ride the bus. They are only the most bus-sick travelers. Humankind lives mainly upon perverted ideas. Perverted, your ideas are no better than those of the Christianity you condemn. Any philosopher who wants to keep his contact with mankind should pervert his own system in advance to see how it will really look a few decades after adoption. I send you greetings from this mere border of grassy temporal light, and wish you happiness, wherever you are. Yours, under the veil of Maya, M.E.H.*

Dear Dr. Morgenfruh. Dead for some time now. *This is Herzog, Moses E.* Discover yourself. *We played billiards in Madison, Wisconsin.* Tell him more. *Until Willie Hoppe arrived to demonstrate, and put us to shame.* The great billiard artist got absolute obedience from those three balls; as if he whispered to them, stroked them a little with his cue, and they would part and kiss again. And old Morgenfruh with his bald head and fine, humorous, curved nose and foreign charm, applauding, getting up all his breath to exclaim "Bravo." Morgenfruh played the piano and made himself weep. Helen played Schumann better but she had less at stake. She frowned at the music as if to show that it was dangerous, but that she could tame it. Morgenfruh, however, groaned, sitting at the keys in his fur coat. Next he sang along, and lastly he cried—it overcame him. He was a splendid old man, only partly fraudulent, and what more can you ask of anyone? *Dear Dr. Morgenfruh, Latest intelligence from the Olduvai Gorge in East Africa gives grounds to suppose that man did not descend from a peaceful arboreal ape, but from a carnivorous, terrestrial type, a beast that hunted in packs and crushed the skulls of prey with a club or femoral bone. It sounds bad, Morgenfruh, for the optimists, for the lenient hopeful view of human nature. The work of Sir Solly Zuckerman on the apes in the London Zoo, of which you spoke so often, has been superseded. Apes in their own habitat are less sexually driven than those in captivity. It must be that captivity, boredom, breeds lustfulness. And it may also be that the territorial instinct is stronger than the sexual. Abide in light, Morgenfruh. I will keep you posted from time to time.*

Despite the hours he spent in the open he believed he still looked pale. Perhaps this was because the mirror of the bathroom door into which he stared in the morning reflected the massed green of the trees. No, he did not look well. His excitement must be a great drain on his strength, he thought.

And then there was the persistently medicinal smell of the tapes on his chest to remind him that he was not quite well. After the second or third day he stopped sleeping on the second floor. He didn't want to drive the owls out of the house and leave a brood to die in the old fixture with the triple brass chain. It was bad enough to have those tiny skeletons in the toilet bowl. He moved downstairs, taking with him a few useful articles, an old trench coat and rain hat, his boots ordered from Gokey's in St. Paul—marvelous, flexible, handsome snakeproof boots; he had forgotten that he had them. In the storeroom he made other interesting discoveries, photographs of the "happy days," boxes of clothing, Madeleine's letters, bundles of canceled checks, elaborately engraved wedding announcements, and a recipe book belonging to Phoebe Gersbach. The photographs were all of him. Madeleine had left those behind, taking the others. Interesting—her attitude. Among the abandoned dresses were her expensive maternity outfits. The checks were for large sums, and many of these were paid to Cash. Had she secretly been saving? He wouldn't put it past her. The announcements made him laugh; Mr and Mrs Pontritter were giving their daughter in marriage to Mr Moses B Herzog Ph D.

In one of the closets he found a dozen or so Russian books under a stiff painter's drop cloth. Shestov, Rozanov—he rather liked Rozanov, who was, luckily, in English. He read a few pages of *Solitaria*. Then he looked over the paint situation— old brushes, thinners, evaporated, crusted buckets. There were several cans of enamel, and Herzog thought, What if I should paint up the little piano? I could send it out to Chicago, to Junie. The kid is really highly musical. As for Madeleine, she'll have to take it in, the bitch, when it's delivered, paid for. She can't send it back. The green enamel seemed to him exactly right, and he wasted no time but found the most usable brushes and set himself to work, full of eagerness, in the parlor. *Dear Rozanov.* He painted the lid of the piano with absorption; the green was light, beautiful, like summer apples. *A stupendous truth you say, heard from none of the prophets, is that private life is above everything. More universal than religion. Truth is higher than the sun. The soul is passion. "I am the fire that consumeth." It is joy to be choked with thought. A good man*

can bear to listen to another talk about himself. You can't trust
the people who are bored by such talk. God has gilded me all over.
I like that, God has gilded me all over. Very touching, this man,
though extremely coarse at times, and stuffed with violent
prejudices. The enamel covered well but it would probably
need a second coat, and he might not have enough paint for
that. Putting down the brush he gave the piano lid time to
dry, considering how to get the instrument out of here. He
couldn't expect one of the giant interstate vans to climb this
hill. He would have to hire Tuttle from the village to come in
his pick-up truck. The cost would amount to something like a
hundred dollars, but he must do everything possible for the
child, and he had no serious problems about money. Will had
offered him as much as he needed to get through the summer.
*A curious result of the increase of historical consciousness is that
people think explanation is a necessity of survival. They have to
explain their condition. And if the unexplained life is not worth
living, the explained life is unbearable, too. "Synthesize or perish!" Is that the new law? But when you see what strange notions,
hallucinations, projections, issue from the human mind you begin to believe in Providence again. To survive these idiocies . . .
Anyway the intellectual has been a Separatist. And what kind of
synthesis is a Separatist likely to come up with?* Luckily for me, I
didn't have the means to get too far away from our common
life. I am glad of that. I mean to share with other human beings
as far as possible and not destroy my remaining years in the
same way. Herzog felt a deep, dizzy eagerness to *begin.*

He had to get water from the cistern; the pump was too
rusty; he had primed it and worked the handle but only tired
himself. The cistern was full. He raised the iron lid with a pry
bar and put down a bucket. It made a good sound, dropping,
and you couldn't get softer water anywhere, but it had to be
boiled. There was always a chipmunk or two, a rat, dead at the
bottom though it looked pure enough when you drew it up,
pure, green water.

He went to sit under the trees. *His* trees. He was amused,
resting here on his American estate, twenty thousand dollars'
worth of country solitude and privacy. He did not feel an owner.
As for the twenty grand, the place was certainly not worth
more than three or four. Nobody wanted these old-fashioned

houses on the fringes of the Berkshires, not the fashionable
section where there were music festivals and modern dancing,
riding to hounds or other kinds of snobbery. You couldn't
even ski on these slopes. No one came here. He had only gentle, dotty old neighbors, Jukes and Kallikaks, rocking themselves to death on their porches, watching television, the
nineteenth century quietly dying in this remote green hole.
Well, this was his own, his hearth; these were *his* birches, catal-
pas, horse chestnuts. His rotten dreams of peace. The patri-
mony of his children—a sunken corner of Massachusetts for
Marco, the little piano for June painted a loving green by her
solicitous father. That, too, like most other things he would
probably botch. But at least he would not die here, as he had
once feared. In former summers, when cutting the grass, he
would sometimes lean on the mower, overheated, and think,
What if I were to die suddenly, of a heart attack? Where will
they put me? Maybe I should pick my own spot. Under the
spruce? That's too close to the house. Now he reflected that
Madeleine would have had him cremated. *And these explanations are unbearable, but they have to be made. In the seventeenth
century the passionate search for absolute truth stopped so that
mankind might transform the world. Something practical was
done with thought. The mental became also the real. Relief from
the pursuit of absolutes made life pleasant. Only a small class of
fanatical intellectuals, professionals, still chased after these absolutes. But our revolutions, including nuclear terror, return the
metaphysical dimension to us. All practical activity has reached
this culmination: everything may go now, civilization, history,
meaning, nature. Everything! Now to recall Mr. Kierkegaard's
question* . . .

*To Dr. Waldemar Zozo: You, Sir, were the Navy psychiatrist
who examined me in Norfolk, Va., about 1942, and told me I was
unusually immature. I knew that, but professional confirmation
caused me deep anguish. In anguish I was not immature. I could
call upon ages of experience. I took it all very seriously then. Anyway, I was subsequently discharged for asthma, not childishness. I
fell in love with the Atlantic.* O the great reticulated, mountain-
bottomed sea! *But the sea fog paralyzed my voice, and for a
communications officer it was the end. However, in your cubicle,
as I sat naked, pale, listened to the sailors at drill in the dust,*

*heard what you told me about my character, felt the Southern
heat, it was unsuitable that I should wring my hands. I kept them
lying on my thighs.*

*From hatred at first, but later because I became objectively in-
terested, I followed your career in the journals. Your article "Ex-
istential Unrest in the Unconscious" recently beguiled me. It was
really quite a classy piece of work. You don't mind if I speak to
you in this way, I hope. I am really in an unusually free condition of mind. "In paths untrodden," as Walt Whitman marvelously put it. "Escaped from the life that exhibits itself . . ." Oh,
that's a plague, the life that exhibits itself, a real plague! There
comes a time when every ridiculous son of Adam wishes to arise
before the rest, with all his quirks and twitches and tics, all
the glory of his self-adored ugliness, his grinning teeth, his sharp
nose, his madly twisted reason, saying to the rest—in an overflow
of narcissism which he interprets as benevolence—"I am here to
witness. I am come to be your exemplar." Poor dizzy spook! . . .
Escaped, anyway, as Whitman says, from the life that exhibits itself and "talked to by tongues aromatic." . . . But here is a further interesting fact. I recognized you last spring in the Primitive
Art Museum on 54th Street.* How my feet ached! I had to ask
Ramona to sit down. *I said to the lady I had come with, "Isn't
that Dr. Waldemar Zozo?" She happened also to know you, and
brought me up to date: You were quite rich, a collector of African
antiquities, your daughter a folk singer, and much else. I realized sharply how I still loathed you. I thought I had forgiven you,
too. Isn't that interesting? Seeing you, your white turtle-necked
shirt and dinner jacket, your Edwardian mustache, your damp
lips, the back hair trained over your bald spot, your barren
paunch, apish buttocks* (chemically old!) *I recognized with joy
how I abhorred you. It sprang fresh from my heart after 22 years!*

His mind took one of its odd jumps. He opened a clean
page in his grimy notebook, and in the twig-divided shade of a
wild cherry, infested with tent caterpillars, he began to make
notes for a poem. He was going to try an Insect Iliad for Junie.
She couldn't read, but maybe Madeleine would allow Luke
Asphalter to take the child to Jackson Park and read the installments to her as he received them. Luke knew a lot of natural history. It would do him good, too. Moses, pale with this
heartfelt nonsense, stared at the ground with brown eyes,

standing round-shouldered, the notebook held behind him as he thought it over. He could make the Trojans ants. The Argives might be water-skaters. Luke might find them for her along the edge of the lagoon, where those stupid caryatides were posted. The water-skaters, therefore, with long velvet hairs beaded with glittering oxygen. Helen, a beautiful wasp. Old Priam a cicada, sucking sap from the roots and with his trowel-shaped belly plastering the tunnels. And Achilles a stag-beetle with sharp spikes and terrible strength, but doomed to a brief life though half a god. At the edge of the water he cried out to his mother

> *Thus spoke Achilles*
> *And Thetis heard him in the ooze,*
> *Sitting beside her ancient father*
> *In glorious debris, enough for all.*

But this project was quickly abandoned. It wasn't a good idea, really not. For one thing, he wasn't stable enough, he could never keep his mind at it. His state was too strange, this mixture of clairvoyance and spleen, *esprit de l'escalier*, noble inspirations, poetry and nonsense, ideas, hyperesthesia—wandering about like this, hearing forceful but indefinite music within, seeing things, violet fringes about the clearest objects. His mind was like that cistern, soft pure water sealed under the iron lid but not entirely safe to drink. No, he was better occupied painting the piano for the child. Go! let the fiery claw of imagination take up the green brush. Go! But the first coat was not dry yet, and he wandered out to the woods, eating a piece of bread from the package he carried in his trench-coat pocket. He was aware that his brother might now show up at any time. Will had been disturbed by his appearance. It was unmistakable. And I had better look out, thought Herzog, people do get put away, and seem even to intend it. I have wanted to be cared for. I devoutly hoped Emmerich would find me sick. But I have no intention of doing that—I am responsible, responsible to reason. This is simply temporary excitement. Responsible to the children. He walked quietly into the woods, the many leaves, living and fallen, green and tan, going between rotted stumps, moss, fungus disks; he found a hunters' path, also a deer trail. He felt quite well here, and calmer. The silence sustained him, and the brilliant weather, the feeling that he was easily contained by everything about him *Within the hollowness of God*, as he noted, *and deaf to the final multiplicity of facts,* as well as, *blind to ultimate distances. Two billion light-years out. Supernovae.*

> *Daily radiance, trodden here*
> *Within the hollowness of God*

To God he jotted several lines.

How my mind has struggled to make coherent sense. I have not been too good at it. But have desired to do your unknowable will, taking it, and you, without symbols. Everything of intensest significance. Especially if divested of me.

Returning once more to practical considerations, he must be very careful with Will and talk to him only in the most concrete terms about concrete matters, like this property, and look as ordinary as possible. If you wear a wise look, he warned himself, you'll be in trouble, and fast. No one can bear such looks any longer, not even your brother. Therefore, watch your face! Certain expressions burn people up, and especially the expression of wisdom, which can lead you straight to the loony bin. You will have earned it!

He lay down near the locust trees. They bloomed with a light, tiny but delicious flower—he was sorry to have missed that. He recognized that with his arms behind him and his legs extended any way, he was lying as he had lain less than a week ago on his dirty little sofa in New York. But was it only a week—five days? Unbelievable! How different he felt! Confident, even happy in his excitement, stable. The bitter cup would come round again, by and by. This rest and well-being were only a momentary difference in the strange lining or variable silk between life and void. *The life you gave me has been curious,* he wanted to say to his mother, *and perhaps the death I must inherit will turn out to be even more profoundly curious. I have sometimes wished it would hurry up, longed for it to come soon. But I am still on the same side of eternity as ever. It's just as well, for I have certain things still to do. And without noise, I hope. Some of my oldest aims seem to have slid away.* But I have others. *Life on this earth can't be simply a picture.* And terrible forces in me, including the force of admiration or praise, powers, including loving powers, very damaging, making me almost an idiot because I lacked the capacity to manage them. *I may turn out to be not such a terrible hopeless fool as everyone, as you, as I myself suspected.* Meantime, to lay off certain persistent torments. To surrender the hyperactivity of this hyperactive face. But just to put it out instead to the radiance of the sun. *I want to send you, and others, the most loving wish I have in my heart. This is the only way I have to reach out—out where it is incomprehensible. I can only pray toward it. So . . . Peace!*

For the next two days—or were there three?—Herzog did nothing but send such messages, and write down songs, psalms, and utterances, putting into words what he had often thought but, for the sake of form, or something of the sort, had always suppressed. Once in a while he found himself painting the little piano again, or eating bread and beans in the kitchen, or sleeping in the hammock, and he was always slightly surprised to discover how he had been occupied. He looked at the calendar one morning, and tried to guess the date, counting in silence, or rather groping over nights and days. His beard informed him better than his brain. His bristles felt like four days' growth, and he thought it best to be clean-shaven when Will arrived.

He built a fire and heated a pan of water, lathered his cheeks with brown laundry soap. Clean-shaven, he was extremely pale. His face had become much thinner, too. He had just put down his razor when he heard the smooth noise of an engine at the foot of the drive. He ran into the garden to meet his brother.

Will was alone in his Cadillac. The great car got up the hill slowly, scraping its underbelly on rocks and bending the tall growth of weeds and canes. Will was a masterful driver. He might be short but there was nothing timid about him, and as for the beautiful Italian Plum finish of the Cadillac he was not the sort of man to fret about a few scratches. On level ground, under the elm, the car stood idling. Two Chinese fangs of vapor came from the rear, and William got out, his face lined in the sun. He took in the house, Moses approaching eagerly. What must Will feel? Moses wondered. He must be appalled. What else could he be?

"Will! How are you?" He embraced his brother.

"How are you, Moses. Are you feeling all right?" Will might act as conservative as he pleased. He could never conceal his real emotions from his brother.

"I just shaved. I always look white after shaving, but I feel well. Honest, I do."

"You've lost weight. Maybe ten pounds, since you left Chicago. It's too much," said Will. "How's your rib?"

"Doesn't bother me a bit."

"And the head?"

"Fine. I've been resting. Where's Muriel? I thought she was coming, too."

"She took the plane. I'm going to meet her in Boston."

Will had learned to conduct himself with restraint. A Herzog, he had a good deal to hold down. Moses could remember a time when Willie, too, had been demonstrative, passionate, explosive, given to bursts of rage, flinging objects on the ground. Just a moment—what was it, now, that he had thrown down? A brush! That was it! The broad old Russian shoe brush. Will slammed it to the floor so hard the veneer backing fell off, and beneath were the stitches, ancient waxed thread, maybe even sinew. But that was long ago. Thirty-five years ago, easily. And where had it gone, the wrath of Willie Herzog? my dear brother? Into a certain poise and quiet humor, part decorousness, part (possibly) slavery. The explosions had become implosions, and where light once was darkness came, bit by bit. It didn't matter. The sight of Will stirred Moses' love for him. Will looked tired and wrinkled; he had been on the road a long time, he needed something to eat, and a rest. He had taken this long trip because he was concerned about him, Moses. And how considerate of him not to bring Muriel.

"How was the drive, Will? Are you hungry? Shall I open a can of tuna?"

"You're the one that doesn't seem to have eaten. I had something on the road."

"Well, come, sit down a while." He led him toward the lawn chairs. "It was lovely here when I took care of the grounds."

"So this is the house? No, I don't want to sit, thanks. I'd rather move around. Let's see it."

"Yes, this is the famous house, the house of happiness," said Moses, but he added, "As a matter of fact, I *have* been happy here. None of this ingratitude."

"It seems well built."

"From a builder's viewpoint it's terrific. Imagine what it would cost today. The foundations would hold the Empire State Building. And I'll show you the hand-hewn chestnut beams. Old mortice and tenon. No metal at all."

"It must be hard to heat."

"Not so hard. Electric baseboards."

"I wish I were selling you the current. Make a fortune . . . But it is a beautiful spot, I'll give you that. These trees are fine. How many acres have you got?"

"Forty. But surrounded by abandoned farms. Not a neighbor in two miles."

"Oh . . . Is that good?"

"Very private, I mean."

"What are your taxes?"

"One-eighty-six or so. Never over one-ninety."

"And the mortgage?"

"There's only a small principal. Payments and interest are two hundred and fifty a year."

"Very good," said Will approvingly. "But now tell me, how much money have you put into this place, Mose?"

"I've never totaled it up. Twenty grand, I guess. More than half of it in improvements."

Will nodded. His arms crossed, he gazed upward at the structure with his partly averted face—he too had this hereditary peculiarity. Only his eyes were quietly and firmly shrewd, not dreaming. Moses, however, saw without the slightest difficulty what Will was thinking.

He expressed it to himself in Yiddish. *In drerd aufn deck. The edge of nowhere. Out on the lid of Hell.*

"In itself, it's a fine-looking piece of property. It may turn out to be a pretty reasonable investment at that. Of course, the location *is* a bit peculiar. Ludeyville isn't on the map."

"No, not on the Esso map," Moses conceded. "The state of Massachusetts knows where it is, naturally."

Both brothers smiled slightly, without looking at each other.

"Let's look over the interior," said Will.

Moses gave him a tour of the house, beginning in the kitchen. "It needs an airing."

"It is a bit musty. But handsome. The plaster is in excellent condition."

"You need a cat to police the fieldmice. They winter in here. I'm fond of them but they chew everything. Even book bindings. They seem to love glue. And wax. Paraffin. Candles. Anything like that."

Will showed him great politeness. He did not confront him harshly with fundamentals, as Shura would have done. There was a certain sweet decency in Will. Helen had it, too. Shura would have said, "What a jerk you were to sink so much dough into this old barn." Well, that was simply Shura's way. Moses loved them all, notwithstanding.

"And the water supply?" said Will.

"Gravity-fed, from the spring. We have two old wells, too. One of them was ruined by kerosene. Someone let a whole tankful of kerosene leak out and soak down. But it doesn't matter. The water supply is excellent. The cesspool is well built. Could accommodate twenty people. You wouldn't need orange trees."

"Meaning what?"

"It means that at Versailles Louis Quatorze planted oranges because the excrement of the court made the air foul."

"How nice to have an education," said Will.

"To be pedantic, you mean," said Herzog. He spoke with a great deal of caution, taking special pains to give an impression of completest normalcy. That Will was studying him—Will who had become the most discreet and observant of the Herzogs—was transparently plain. Moses thought he could bear his scrutiny fairly well. His haggard, just-shaven cheeks were against him; as was the whole house (the skeletons in the toilet bowl, the owls in the fixtures, the half-painted piano, the remains of meals, the wife-deserted atmosphere); his "inspired" visit to Chicago was bad, too. Very bad. It must be noticeable, also, that he was in an extraordinary state, eyes dilated with excitement, the very speed of his pulses possibly visible in his large irises. *Why must I be such a throb-hearted character . . .*

But I am. I am, and you can't teach old dogs. Myself is thus and
so, and will continue thus and so. And why fight it? My balance
comes from instability. Not organization, or courage, as with
other people. It's tough, but that's how it is. On these terms I, too—
even I!—apprehend certain things. Perhaps the only way I'm
able to do it. Must play the instrument I've got.

"You've been painting this piano, I see."

"For June," said Herzog. "A present. A surprise."

"What?" Will laughed. "Are you planning to send it from
here? Why it'll cost two hundred bucks in freight. And it
would have to be fixed up, tuned. Is it such a great piano?"

"Madeleine bought it at auction for twenty-five bucks."

"Take my word for it, Moses, you can buy a nice old piano
right in Chicago, at a warehouse sale. Lots of old instruments
like this, kicking around."

"Yes . . . ? Only I like this color." This apple, parrot green,
the special Ludeyville color. Moses' eyes were fixed upon his
work with a certain inspired persistency. He was near a point of
open impulsiveness, and some peculiarity might now dart forth.
He couldn't allow that to happen. Under no circumstances
must he utter a single word that might be interpreted as irrational. Things already looked bad enough. He glanced away
from the piano into the clear shade of the garden, and tried to
become as clear as *that*. He deferred to his brother's opinion.
"Okay. Next trip, I'll get her a piano."

"What you've got here is an excellent summer house," said
Will. "A little lonely, but nice. If you can clean it up."

"It can be lovely here. But you know, we might make it a
Herzog summer resort. For the family. Everyone put in a little
money. Cut the brush. Build a swimming pool."

"Oh, sure. Helen hates travel, you know that. And Shura is
just the man to come up here where there are no race horses,
or card games, or other tycoons, or broads."

"There are trotter races at the Barrington Fair. . . . No, I
guess that's not such a good idea, either. Well, perhaps we
could make it into a nursing home. Or move it to another
location."

"Not worth it. I've seen mansions wrecked for slum clearance or for new superhighways. This isn't worth dismantling.
Can't you rent it out?"

Herzog silently grinned, staring with piercing humor at Will.

"All right, Mose, the only other suggestion is that you put it up for sale. You won't get your money out of it."

"I could go to work and become rich. Make a ton of money, just to keep this house."

"Yes," said Will. "You might." He spoke gently to his brother.

"Odd situation I've gotten into, Will—isn't it?" said Moses. "For me. For us—the Herzogs, I mean. It seems a strange point to arrive at after all the other points. In this lovely green hole . . . You're worried about me, I see."

Will, troubled but controlled, one of the most deeply familiar and longest-loved of human faces, looked at him in a way that could not be mistaken. "Of course I'm worried. Helen too."

"Well, you mustn't be distressed about me. I'm in a peculiar state, but not in a bad one. I'd open my heart to you, Will, if I could find the knob. There's no reason to be upset about me. By God, Will, I'm about to cry! How did that happen? I won't do it. It's only love. Or something that bears down like love. It probably is love. I'm in no shape to buck it. I don't want you to think anything wrong."

"Mose—why should I?" Will spoke in a low voice. "I have something deep-in for you, too. I feel about the way you do. Just because I'm a contractor doesn't mean I can't understand what you mean. I didn't come to do you harm, you know. That's right, Mose, take a chair. You look out on your feet."

Moses sat on the old sofa, which gave off dust as soon as you touched it.

"I'd like to see you less agitated. You must get some food and sleep. Probably a little medical care. A few days in the hospital, taking it easy."

"Will, I'm excited, not sick. I don't want to be treated as though I were sick in the head. I'm grateful that you came." Silently and stubbornly he sat, persisting, putting down his violent, choking craving for tears. His voice was dim.

"Take your time," said Will.

"I . . ." Herzog found his voice again and said distinctly, "I want to be straight about one thing. I'm not turning myself over to you out of weakness, or because I can't make my own way. I don't mind taking it easy in some hospital for a few days. If you and Helen decided that that was what I should do, I see no objection. Clean sheets and a bath and some hot food. Sleep. That's all pleasant. But only a few days. I have to visit Marco at camp on the sixteenth. That's Parents' Day and he's expecting me."

"Fair enough," said Will. "That's no more than right."

"Only a while back, in New York, I had fantasies about being put in the hospital."

"You were only being sensible," said his brother. "What you need is supervised rest. I've thought about it, too, for myself. Once in a while, we all get that way. Now"—he looked at his watch—"I asked my physician to phone a local hospital. In Pittsfield."

As soon as Will had spoken, Moses sat forward on the sofa. He could not find words. He only made a negative sign with his head. At this, Will's face changed, too. He seemed to think he had pronounced the word hospital too abruptly, that he ought to have been more gradual, circumspect.

"No," said Moses, still shaking his head. "No. Definitely."

Now Will was silent, still with the pained air of a man who had made a tactical error. Moses could easily imagine what Will had said to Helen, after he had bailed him out, and what a worried consultation they had had about him. ("What shall we do? Poor Mose—maybe it's all driven him mad. Let's at least get a professional opinion about him.") Helen was great on professional opinions. The veneration with which she said "professional opinion" had always amused Moses. And so they had approached Will's internist to ask if he would, discreetly, arrange something in the Berkshire area. "But I thought we already agreed," said Will.

"No, Will. No hospitals. I know you and Helen are doing what brother and sister should. And I'm tempted to go along. To a man like me, it's a seductive idea. 'Supervised rest.'"

"And why not? If I'd found some improvement in you I might not have brought it up," said Will. "But look at you."

"I know," said Moses. "But just as I begin to be a little rational you want to hand me over to a psychiatrist. It *was* a psychiatrist you and Helen had in mind, wasn't it?"

Will was silent, taking counsel with himself. Then he sighed and said, "What harm could there be in it?"

"Was it any more fantastic for me to have these wives, children, to move to a place like this than for Papa to have been a bootlegger? We never thought he was mad." Moses began to smile. ". . . Do you remember, Will—he had those phony labels printed up: White Horse, Johnnie Walker, Haig and Haig, and we'd sit at the table with the paste-pot, and he'd flash those labels and say, 'Well, children, what should we make today?', and we'd start to cry out and squeak 'White Horse,' 'Teacher's.' And the coal stove was hot. It dropped embers like red teeth in the ash. He had those dark green lovely bottles. They don't make glass like that, in those shapes, any more. My favorite was White Horse."

Will laughed softly.

"Going to the hospital would be fine," said Herzog. "But it would be just the wrong thing to do. It's about time I stopped laboring with this curse—I think, I figure things out. I see exactly what I should avoid. Then, all of a sudden, I'm in bed with that very thing, and making love to it. As with Madeleine. She seems to have filled a special need."

"How do you figure that, Moses?" Will joined him on the sofa, and sat beside him.

"A very special need. I don't know what. She brought ideology into my life. Something to do with catastrophe. After all, it's an ideological age. Maybe she wouldn't make a father of anyone she liked."

Will smiled at Moses' way of putting it. "But what do you intend to do here now?"

"I may as well stay on. I'm not far from Marco's camp. Yes, that's it. If Daisy'll let me, I'll bring him here next month. What I'll do is this, if you'll drive me and my bike into Ludeyville, I'll have the lights and the phone turned on. Tuttle'll come up and mow the place. Maybe Mrs. Tuttle will clean up for me. That's what I'll do." He stood up. "I'll get the water running again, and buy some solid food. Come, Will, give me a lift down to Tuttle's."

"Who is this Tuttle?"

"He runs everything. He's the master spirit of Ludeyville. A tall fellow. He's shy, to look at, but that's only more of his shrewdness. He's the demon of these woods. He can have the lights burning here within an hour. He knows all. He overcharges, but very, very shyly."

Tuttle was standing beside his high, lean, antiquated gas pumps when Will drove up. Thin, wrinkled, the hairs on his corded forearms bleached meal-white, he wore a cotton paint cap and between his false teeth (to help him kick the smoking habit, as he had once explained to Herzog) he kept a plastic toothpick. "I knew you was up in the place, Mr. Herzog," he said. "Welcome back."

"How did you know?"

"I saw the smoke onto your chimney, that's the first of all."

"Yes? And what's the second?"

"Why, a lady's been tryin' to get you on the telephone."

"Who?" said Will.

"A party in Barrington. She left the number."

"Only her number?" said Herzog. "No name?"

"Miss Harmona, or Armona."

"Ramona," said Herzog. "Is she in Barrington?"

"Were you expecting someone?" Will turned to him in the seat.

"No one but you."

Will insisted on knowing more. "Who is she?"

Somewhat unwillingly, and with an evasive look, Moses answered, "A lady—a woman." Then, putting off his reticence—why, after all, should he be nervous about it?—he added, "A woman, a florist, a friend from New York."

"Are you going to return her call?"

"Yes, of course." He observed the white listening face of Mrs. Tuttle in the dark store. "I wonder," he said to Tuttle. ". . . I want to open the house. I have to get the current on. Maybe Mrs. Tuttle will help me clean the place a bit."

"Oh, I think she might."

Mrs. Tuttle wore tennis shoes and, under her dress, the edge of her nightgown showed. Her polished fingernails were tobacco-stained. She had gained much weight in Herzog's absence, and he noted the distortion of her pretty face, the heaviness of her neglected dark hair and the odd distant look in her gray eyes, as if the fat of her body had an opiate effect on her.

He knew that she had monitored his conversations with Madeleine on the party line. Probably she had heard all the shameful, terrible things that had been said, listened to the rant and the sobbing. Now he was about to invite her to come to work, to sweep the floors, make his bed. She reached for a filter cigarette, lit it like a man, stared through smoke with tranced gray eyes and said, "Why, I think so, yes. It's my day off from the mortel. I been working as a chambermaid over in the new mortel on the highway."

"Moses!" said Ramona, on the telephone. "You got my message. How lovely you're in your place. Everybody in Barrington says if you want things done in Ludeyville, call Tuttle."

"Hello, Ramona. Didn't my wire from Chicago reach you?"

"Yes, Moses. It was very considerate. But I didn't think you'd stay away long, and I had a feeling about your house in the country. Anyway, I had to visit old friends in Barrington, so I drove up."

"Really?" said Herzog. "What day of the week is this?"

Ramona laughed. "How typical. No wonder women lose their heads over you. It's Saturday. I'm staying with Myra and Eduardo Misseli."

"Oh, the fiddler. I only know him to nod to at the supermarket."

"He's a charming man. Do you know he's studying the art of violin-making? I've been in his shop all morning. And I thought I must have a look at the Herzog estate."

"My brother is with me—Will."

"Oh, splendid," said Ramona, in her lifted voice. "Is he staying with you?"

"No, he's passing through."

"I'd love to meet him. The Misselis are giving a little party for me. After dinner."

Will stood beside the booth, listening. Earnest, worried, his dark eyes discreetly appealed to Moses to make no more mistakes. I can't promise that, thought Moses. I can only tell him that I don't contemplate putting myself in the hands of Ramona or any woman, at this time. Will's gaze held a family look, a brown light as clear as any word.

"No, thank you," said Herzog. "No parties. I'm not up to them. But look, Ramona . . ."

"Should I run up?" said Ramona. "It's silly, being on the phone like this. You're only eight minutes away."

"Well, perhaps," said Herzog. "It occurs to me I have to come down to Barrington anyway, to shop, and to have my phone reconnected."

"Oh, you're planning to stay awhile in Ludeyville?"

"Yes. Marco'll be joining me. Just a moment, Ramona." Herzog put a hand over the instrument and said to Will, "Can you take me into Barrington?" Will of course said yes.

Ramona was waiting, smiling, a few minutes later. She stood beside her black Mercedes in shorts and sandals. She wore a Mexican blouse with coin buttons. Her hair glittered, and she looked flushed. The anxiety of the moment threatened her self-control. "Ramona," said Moses, "this is Will."

"Oh, Mr. Herzog, what a pleasure to meet Moses' brother."

Will, though wary of her, was courteous nevertheless. He had a quiet, tidy social manner. Herzog was grateful to him for the charming reserve of his courtesy to Ramona. Will's glance was sympathetic. He smiled, but not too much. Obviously he found Ramona impressively attractive. "He must have been expecting a dog," thought Herzog.

"Why, Moses," said Ramona, "you've cut yourself shaving. And badly. Your whole jaw is scraped."

"Ah?" He touched himself with vague concern.

"You look so much like your brother, Mr. Herzog. The same fine head, and those soft hazel eyes. You're not staying?"

"I'm on my way to Boston."

"And I simply had to get out of New York. Aren't the Berkshires marvelous? Such green!"

Love-bandit, the tabloids used to print over such dark heads. In the twenties. Indeed, Ramona did look like those figures of sex and swagger. But there was something intensely touching about her, too. She struggled, she fought. She needed extraordinary courage to hold this poise. In this world, to be a woman who took matters into her own hands! And this courage of hers was unsteady. At times it trembled. She pretended to look for something in her purse because her cheek quivered. The perfume of her shoulders reached his nostrils. And, as almost always, he heard the deep, the cosmic, the idiotic masculine response—*quack*. The progenitive, the lustful quacking in the depths. *Quack. Quack.*

"You won't come to the party then?" said Ramona. "And when am I going to see your house?"

"Why, I'm having it cleaned up a little," said Herzog.

"Then can't we . . . Why don't we have dinner together?" she said. "You, too, Mr. Herzog. Moses can tell you that my shrimp remoulade is rather good."

"It's better than that. I never ate better. But Will has to go on, and you're on a holiday, Ramona, we can't have you cooking for three. Why don't you come out and have dinner with me?"

"Oh," said Ramona with a new rise of gaiety. "You want to entertain me?"

"Well, why not? I'll get a couple of swordfish steaks."

Will looked at him with his uncertain smile.

"Wonderful. I'll bring a bottle of wine," said Ramona.

"You'll do nothing of the sort. Come up at six. We'll eat at seven and you can still get back to your party in plenty of time."

Musically (was it a deliberate effect? Moses could not decide), Ramona said to Will, "Then good-by, Mr. Herzog. I hope we shall meet again." Turning to get into her Mercedes, she put her hand momentarily on Moses' shoulder. "I expect a good dinner. . . ."

She wanted Will to be aware of their intimacy, and Moses saw no reason to deny her this. He pressed his face to hers.

"Shall we say good-by here, too?" said Moses as she drove off. "I can take a cab back. I don't want to make you late."

"No, no, I'll run you up to Ludeyville."

"I'll go in here and get my swordfish. Some lemon, too. Butter. Coffee."

They were on the last slope before Ludeyville when Will said, "Am I leaving you in good hands, Mose?"

"Is it safe to go, you mean? I think you can, with confidence. Ramona's not so bad."

"Bad? What do you mean? She's stunning. But so was Madeleine."

"I'm not being left in anyone's hands."

With a mild, soft look of irony, sad and affectionate, Will

said, "Amen. But what about this ideology. Doesn't she have some?"

"This will do, here, in front of Tuttle's. They'll take me in the pickup, bike and all. Yes, I think she has some. About sex. She's pretty fanatical about it. But I don't mind that."

"I'll get out and make certain of the directions," said Will.

Tuttle, as they walked slowly past him, told Moses, "I think we'll have that current onto your house in a few minutes."

"Thanks . . . Here, Will, take a little of this arborvitae to chew. It's a very pleasant taste."

"Don't decide anything now. You can't afford any more mistakes."

"I've asked her to dinner. Only that. She goes back to the party at Misseli's—I'm not going with her. Tomorrow is Sunday. She's got a business in New York, and she can't stay. I won't elope with her. Or she with me, as you see it."

"You have a strange influence on people," said Will. "Well, good-by, Mose. Maybe Muriel and I will stop by on our way west."

"You'll find me unmarried."

"If you didn't give a goddamn, it wouldn't matter. You could marry five more wives. But with your intense way of doing everything . . . and your talent for making a fatal choice."

"Will, you can go with an easy mind. I tell you . . . I promise. Nothing like that will happen. Not a chance. Good-by, and thanks. And as for the house . . ."

"I'll be thinking about that. Do you need money?"

"No."

"You're sure? You're telling the truth? Remember, you're talking to your brother."

"I know whom I'm talking to." He took Will by the shoulders and kissed him on the cheek. "Good-by, Will. Take the first right as you leave town. You'll see the turnpike sign."

When Will had gone, Moses waited for Mrs. Tuttle in the seat by the arborvitae, having his first leisurely look at the village. *Everywhere on earth, the model of natural creation seems to be the ocean. The mountains certainly look that way, glossy, plunging, and that haughty blue color. And even these scrappy lawns. What keeps these red brick houses from collapse on these billows is their inner staleness. I smell it yawning through the screens. The odor of souls is a brace to the walls. Otherwise the wrinkling of the hills would make them crumble.*

"You got a gorgeous old place here, Mr. Herzog," said Mrs. Tuttle as they drove in her old car up the hill. "It must've cost you a penny to improve it. It's a shame you don't use it more."

"We've got to get the kitchen cleaned up so I can cook a meal. I'll find you the brooms and pails and such."

He was groping in the dark pantry when the lights went on. Tuttle is a miracle man, he thought. I asked him at about two. It must be four-thirty, five.

Mrs. Tuttle, a cigarette in her mouth, tied her head up in a bandanna. Beneath the hem of her dress the peach nylon of her nightgown nearly touched the floor. In the stone cellar Herzog found the pump switch. At once he heard the water rising, washing into the empty pressure tank. He connected the range. He turned on the refrigerator; it would take a while to get cold. Then it occurred to him to chill the wine in the spring. After that, he took up the scythe to clear the yard, so that Ramona would have a better view of the house. But after he had cut a few swathes his ribs began to ache. He didn't feel well enough for this sort of work. He lay stretched in the lawn chair, facing south. As soon as the sun lost its main strength the hermit thrushes began, and while they sang their sweet fierce music threatening trespassers, the blackbirds would begin to gather in flocks for the night, and just toward sunset they would break from these trees in waves, wave after wave, three or four miles in one flight to their waterside nests.

To have Ramona coming troubled him slightly, it was true. But they would eat. She would help him with the dishes, and then he'd see her to her car.

I will do no more to enact the peculiarities of life. This is done well enough without my special assistance.

Now on one side the hills lost the sun and began to put on a more intense blue color; on the other they were still white and green. The birds were very loud.

Anyway, can I pretend I have much choice? I look at myself and see chest, thighs, feet—a head. This strange organization, I know it will die. And inside—something, something, happiness . . . "Thou movest me." That leaves no choice. Something produces intensity, a holy feeling, as oranges produce orange, as grass green, as birds heat. Some hearts put out more love and some less of it, presumably. Does it signify anything? There are those who say this product of hearts is knowledge. "Je sens mon cœur et je connais les hommes." But his mind now detached itself also from its French. *I couldn't say that, for sure. My face too blind, my mind too limited, my instincts too narrow. But this intensity, doesn't it mean anything? Is it an idiot joy that makes this animal, the most peculiar animal of all, exclaim something? And he thinks this reaction a sign, a proof, of eternity? And he has it in his breast? But I have no arguments to make about it. "Thou movest me." "But what do you want, Herzog?" "But that's just it—not a solitary thing. I am pretty well satisfied to be, to be just as it is willed, and for as long as I may remain in occupancy."*

Then he thought he'd light candles at dinner, because Ramona was fond of them. There might be a candle or two in the fuse box. But now it was time to get those bottles from the spring. The labels had washed off, but the glass was well chilled. He took pleasure in the vivid cold of the water.

Coming back from the woods, he picked some flowers for the table. He wondered whether there was a corkscrew in the drawer. Had Madeleine taken it to Chicago? Well, maybe Ramona had a corkscrew in her Mercedes. An unreasonable thought. A nail could be used, if it came to that. Or you could break the neck of the bottle as they did in old movies. Meanwhile, he filled his hat from the rambler vine, the one that clutched the rainpipe. The spines were still too green to hurt much. By the cistern there were yellow day lilies. He took some of these, too, but they wilted instantly. And, back in the darker garden, he looked for peonies; perhaps some had survived. But then it struck him that he might be making a mistake, and he stopped, listening to Mrs. Tuttle's sweeping, the rhythm of bristles. Picking flowers? He was being thoughtful, being lovable. How would it be interpreted? (He smiled slightly.) Still, he need only know his own mind, and the flowers couldn't be used; no, they couldn't be turned against him. So he did not throw them away. He turned his dark face toward the house again. He went around and entered from the front, wondering what further evidence of his sanity, besides refusing to go to the hospital, he could show. Perhaps he'd stop writing letters. Yes, that was what was coming, in fact. The knowledge that he was done with these letters. Whatever had come over him during these last months, the spell, really seemed to be passing, really going. He set down his hat, with the roses and day lilies, on the half-painted piano, and went into his study, carrying the wine bottles in one hand like a pair of Indian clubs. Walking over notes and papers, he lay down on his Recamier couch. As he stretched out, he took a long breath, and then he lay, looking at the mesh of the screen, pulled loose by vines, and listening to the steady scratching of Mrs. Tuttle's broom. He wanted to tell her to sprinkle the floor. She was raising too much dust. In a few minutes he would call down to her, "Damp it down, Mrs. Tuttle. There's water in the sink." But not just yet. At this time he had no messages for anyone. Nothing. Not a single word.

CHRONOLOGY

NOTE ON THE TEXTS

NOTES

Chronology

1915   Born Solomon Bellows in Lachine, Quebec, on June 10, fourth child of Abram Bellows and Lescha Gordin, Russian–Jewish immigrants from St. Petersburg. (The family name was changed from "Belo" on arriving in Canada in 1913. Abram Bellows was an importer of dry goods, baker, and junk-dealer. One sister, Zelda, nine years older than Bellow, and two brothers Movscha, seven years older, and Samuel, four years older, were born in Russia.)

1918   Family moves to Saint Dominique Street, in a poor area of Montreal. (Bellow will later write: "The Jewish slums of Montreal during my childhood, just after the First World War, were not too far removed from the ghettos of Poland and Russia. Life in such places was anything but ordinary.") Parents speak Russian and Yiddish; their children speak English and Yiddish at home; French is spoken on the street. Bellow later claims the Armistice parade as one of his earliest memories.

1923   Falls ill with peritonitis and pneumonia, and spends six months in Royal Victoria Hospital, Montreal, where he reads, and is deeply affected by, the New Testament Gospels. Father becomes a bootlegger helping to smuggle liquor into the United States.

1924   Father goes to Chicago to work for cousin's bakery. In July, the rest of family is smuggled across the border to join him. They live on the east side of Humboldt Park. Bellow takes up violin. Attends Lafayette School and Columbus Elementary School. His main source for books is the Budlong branch of Chicago Public Library on North Avenue.

1930   Graduates from Sabin Junior High School. Enters Tuley High School, where he befriends Isaac Rosenfeld, Oscar Tarcov, and Sam Freifeld, all aspiring writers.

1931   Family moves to a more prosperous area of Chicago on the west side of Humboldt Park.

1933   Graduates from Tuley in January. Mother dies of breast
        cancer in February. Moves out of home in fall, and takes
        room in a boarding house near the University of Chicago,
        where he is now enrolled along with his classmate Isaac
        Rosenfeld.

1934   Father remarries; he is now the successful owner of the
        Carroll Coal Company.

1935   During the winter the driver of one of the Carroll Com-
        pany's trucks is killed. Without insurance, father is forced
        to pay costs, and can no longer afford $100-per-quarter
        fees of University of Chicago. Bellow is forced to leave
        university and returns home; in fall transfers to North-
        western University, where he takes dual major in English
        and anthropology, the latter under Melville J. Herskovits.

1936   First published piece, "Pets of the North Shore," a whim-
        sical sketch about dogs and their owners, appears in *The
        Daily Northwestern*. Literary editor of university paper re-
        jects one of his short stories. Wins third prize in "Campus
        in Print" story competition; story appears under a newly
        adopted name, Saul Bellow: "I wanted to break with
        everybody, even my own family, so I chose the other
        name, which was a legitimate name, and belonged to me."

1937   Becomes associate editor of *The Beacon,* a monthly jour-
        nal, to which he contributes many pieces. Receives B.A.
        from Northwestern with honors in anthropology and
        sociology; goes on to graduate fellowship in Department
        of Sociology and Anthropology at University of Wiscon-
        sin, Madison, where Isaac Rosenfeld is a Ph.D. candidate.
        Works on a thesis on culture of French Canadians, but is
        soon discouraged ("Every time I worked on my thesis, it
        turned out to be a story"). Leaves before the end of the
        year.

1938   Returns to Chicago, where he marries Anita Goshkin.
        Works in his brother Maurice's coalyard, but is fired for
        absenteeism. Takes a part-time job in the fall teaching
        anthropology and English composition at Pestalozzi-
        Freobel Teachers College on South Michigan Avenue.
        His assigned reading list (which he will substantially re-
        tain through decades of teaching) includes Lawrence,
        Dostoevsky, Dreiser, and Flaubert. Works on the Federal
        Writers' Project, part of the New Deal Works Progress

Administration; his job is to compile sketches of contemporary American authors.

1940   Travels to Mexico in summer; reads Lawrence's *Mornings in Mexico* and Stendhal. Arrives in Mexico City on August 21, to find that Trotsky had been assassinated the day before; views body at morgue. Stories rejected by *The Saturday Evening Post* and *The Kenyon Review.*

1941   *Partisan Review* (May–June) publishes short story "Two Morning Monologues." Works on a novel entitled "The Very Dark Trees"; after being rejected by several publishers, it is accepted by William Roth of the Colt Press for $150.

1942   Visits New York, where Isaac Rosenfeld is studying at NYU. Meets Alfred Kazin; spends time with poet Delmore Schwartz. Draft board defers him until end of term at Pestalozzi Teachers College; in June defers him again until mid-July. William Roth, now enlisted, cancels publication of "The Very Dark Trees," sending Bellow consolatory $50. Bellow burns manuscript.

1943   Applies unsuccessfully for a Guggenheim fellowship. During summer, rejected for job at *Time* by Whittaker Chambers, editor of the magazine's books and arts pages. Works as editor on *Encyclopedia Britannica's* "Syntopicon," a two-volume supplement to the "Great Books of the Western World" project. "Notes of a Dangling Man" appears in *Partisan Review* (September–October).

1944   Novel *Dangling Man* published in March by Vanguard Press. Edmund Wilson describes it in *The New Yorker* as "one of the most honest pieces of testimony on the psychology of a whole generation who have grown up during the depression and the war." The book sells a total of 1,506 copies. Son Gregory born in April. Draft board again defers Bellow, who has been diagnosed with inguinal hernia. Studio executive at MGM, seeing author photograph in newspaper, offers to make him a Hollywood star, playing "the guy who loses the girl to the George Raft type or the Errol Flynn type."

1945   Volunteers in April for the Merchant Marine, and is assigned to the Atlantic district headquarters in Sheepshead Bay, Brooklyn. Moves to New York in September. Lives on Pineapple Street, Brooklyn Heights, writing book reviews and reading for publishers; works on novel *The Victim*.

1946 A second Guggenheim application is rejected. In the fall, becomes assistant professor at the University of Minnesota, Minneapolis; meets Robert Penn Warren, who is at work on *All the King's Men*.

1947 Travels to Europe in July, visiting Paris, Madrid, and Granada. Writes "Spanish Letter" for *Partisan Review*. Returns to Minneapolis in September. *The Victim* is published in November by Vanguard Press and sells 2,257 copies.

1948–49 Receives Guggenheim fellowship after third application. With the foundation's $2,500 and a $3,000 advance for his next novel from his new publisher, Viking, travels in the fall to Paris, where he will live for the next two years. Meets Georges Bataille, Maurice Merleau-Ponty, and Albert Camus at the home of his Chicago friend Harold Kaplan. Other Paris friends include Herbert Gold, Mary McCarthy, Lionel Abel, and William Phillips. Works on a third novel, "The Crab and the Butterfly," about two invalids in a Chicago hospital. Abandons novel in progress in October 1949 and begins *The Adventures of Augie March*. (Writes later: "The book just came to me. All I had to do was be there with buckets to catch it.") "From the Life of Augie March" appears in November *Partisan Review*. Visits London in December; meets Cyril Connolly, Henry Green, and Stephen Spender.

1950 In summer, gives lectures at Salzburg Seminar in American Studies. Visits Venice, Florence, and Rome, where he works for six weeks on *Augie March* in the Borghese Gardens. Meets Alberto Moravia and Ignazio Silone. Returns to New York in October; takes a modest apartment in Forest Hills, Queens.

1951 Becomes interested in sexual and emotional therapy of Wilhelm Reich. Begins Reichian therapy with Dr. Chester Raphael; spends hours sitting in "orgone box," supposed to concentrate "orgone energy." Hired as part-time assistant professor at NYU. Applies unsuccessfully for a renewal of Guggenheim fellowship; borrows $500 from Viking. *Commentary* publishes his story "Looking for Mr. Green." Departs for Salzburg Seminar in December, stopping en route in Paris. Reads passages of *Augie March* to his Salzburg students.

1952   Returns to New York in mid-February. Travels west to lecture at universities of Washington and Oregon. Spends time with Theodore Roethke and Dylan Thomas in Seattle. A dramatization of *The Victim* opens off-Broadway in May. Receives a $1,000 grant from the American Academy of Arts and Letters. Spends summer at Yaddo writers' colony in Saratoga Springs, New York. Translates Isaac Bashevis Singer's story "Gimpel the Fool" from the Yiddish (Singer's first appearance in English). In fall, takes creative-writing job at Princeton as Delmore Schwartz's assistant, where he meets John Berryman and wife, Eileen Simpson. Meets Sondra Tschacbasov. Suffers severe case of pneumonia in December. An excerpt from *Augie March* appears in *The New Yorker*.

1953   In September, takes one-year job at Bard College, in Annandale-on-Hudson, New York. At Bard, befriends Keith Botsford and Jack Ludwig. His temporary landlord is Chanler Chapman, later a model for the hero of *Henderson the Rain King*. *The Adventures of Augie March* is published in September. Gives interview to *New York Times*. In December, receives royalty check for $2,000. Takes temporary apartment on Riverside Drive in New York, where he spends weekends.

1954   Wins National Book Award for *Adventures of Augie March*. Writes "How I Wrote Augie March's Story" in *New York Times* in January: "The book was writing itself very rapidly. I was coming to be strangely independent of place. Chicago itself had grown exotic to me." Separates from Anita Goshkin. Leaves Bard in June; spends summer in Wellfleet, Massachusetts, where friends include Mary McCarthy, Harry Levin, and Alfred Kazin. Applies for another grant from the Guggenheim Foundation. Works on "Memoirs of a Bootlegger's Son," a fictional portrait of Bellows family in Montreal, portions of which will later be incorporated into *Herzog*.

1955   Father dies of an aneurysm in May. The Guggenheim Foundation grants him a second fellowship. In August visits small towns in Illinois for *Holiday* travel piece. Spends next eight months in Reno, Nevada, while waiting for divorce.

1956   Marries Sondra Tschacbasov in Reno in February. Works
            on novel *Henderson the Rain King*. Visited in April by
            Arthur Miller and Marilyn Monroe. Finishes novella *Seize
            the Day*, which appears in the summer issue of *Partisan
            Review*. In July, childhood friend Isaac Rosenfeld dies of
            heart attack in Chicago, aged 38. Buys house in Tivoli,
            New York, with the help of $8,000 legacy from father.
            Spends the fall at Yaddo, where he becomes friends with
            John Cheever. *Seize the Day* is published in November.

1957   Second son, Adam, is born in January. Takes temporary
            appointment for the spring semester at the University of
            Minnesota, where he spends time with John Berryman; in
            Bellow's absence, Ralph Ellison moves into Tivoli house.
            Meets 23-year-old Philip Roth in Chicago. Spends the fall
            in Chicago, teaching at Northwestern. In "The Univer-
            sity as Villain," published in *The Nation* in November, ac-
            cuses English departments of being full of "discouraged
            people who stand dully upon a brilliant plane, in charge
            of masterpieces but not themselves inspired."

1958   Finishes early draft of *Henderson the Rain King* in March.
            Dictates the novel's revisions for six weeks to secretary in
            Tivoli house. In fall, returns to teach at University of
            Minnesota. Enters therapy with a clinical psychologist.

1959   *Henderson the Rain King* is published in February. Re-
            ceives $16,000 grant from the Ford Foundation. Returns
            to Tivoli for summer. Works on play *The Last Analysis*.
            Separates from Sondra Tschacbasov in November. Stays
            briefly at Yaddo and then in Herbert Gold's New York
            apartment before going to Europe for a lecture tour of
            Poland and Yugoslavia at the invitation of the State
            Department.

1960   *The Noble Savage,* a journal co-edited by Bellow, Jack
            Ludwig, and Keith Botsford, appears in February (five
            numbers will be published); contributors include Harold
            Rosenberg, Ralph Ellison, and John Berryman. In March,
            visits Italy, Israel, and England. Returns from Europe in
            March; enters therapy with sexologist Dr. Albert Ellis.
            Spends summer at Tivoli. Divorce becomes final in June.
            In "The Sealed Treasure," essay published in the July
            TLS, argues against modern Flaubertian aestheticism, and
            its "disappointment with its human material," in favor of

an American novel that might more optimistically search for the "sealed treasure" of ordinary inner life.

1961   Teaches spring term at the University of Puerto Rico. Marries Susan Glassman in November. Spends fall at the University of Chicago, where he has temporary teaching appointment.

1962   Works steadily on novel *Herzog*. Made honorary Doctor of Letters, Northwestern University. Attends White House dinner for André Malraux in May. An excerpt from *The Last Analysis* appears in the summer issue of *Partisan Review*. Accepts five-year appointment as professor at the Committee on Social Thought of the University of Chicago, and moves into Hyde Park apartment. (Will stay at University of Chicago for thirty years.) John Steinbeck, who has just been awarded the Nobel Prize in Literature, inscribes copy of Nobel lecture to Bellow: "You're next."

1963   Old school friend Oscar Tarcov dies, aged 48. Made honorary Doctor of Letters, Bard College. "Some Notes on Recent American Fiction" is published in *Encounter* in November.

1964   Third son, Daniel, born in March. Spends July and August on Martha's Vineyard, finishing *Herzog* and *The Last Analysis*. *Herzog* is published in September, and reaches top of the best-seller list in October. *The Last Analysis* opens on Broadway the same month; closes within a month. Donates manuscripts of *Augie March* and *Henderson the Rain King* to University of Chicago. Pat Covici, Viking editor and dedicatee of *Herzog,* dies of heart attack in October.

1965   Now increasingly wealthy from *Herzog* sales, gives the Tivoli house to Bard. *Herzog* wins the National Book Award in March. Attends festival of the arts at White House in June, at which he reads from *Herzog*. (Festival is controversial because of Vietnam War, and Edmund Wilson and Robert Lowell return their invitations.) Is interviewed at length for *Paris Review*. Spends summer on Martha's Vineyard.

1966   Receives the Prix Internationale de Litterature (Formentor Prize). Delivers keynote address at PEN Congress in New York in June, declaring: "We have at present a large literary community and something we can call, *faute de mieux,* a literary culture, in my opinion a very bad one." *Under the Weather,* a trilogy of one-act plays, opens at the Fortune Theatre in London in the summer; opens in October in New York, where it closes in less than two weeks. Lectures in the fall at the American Embassy in London; travels to Holland and Poland. By the end of the year, marriage has ended. Moves out of Chicago apartment. Begins work on novel *Mr. Sammler's Planet.*

1967   Travels to Israel to cover Six-Day War for *Newsday* in June, writing a series of four articles. Spends summer in rented house in East Hampton, where he sees Saul Steinberg and Harold Rosenberg. Essay "Skepticism and the Depth of Life" published in anthology *The Arts & the Public.*

1968   Becomes Chevalier des Arts et Lettres in January. B'nai Brith confers Jewish Heritage Award for Excellence in Literature. Gives talk in the spring at San Francisco State College, where he is heckled by novelist Floyd Salas, a faculty member; incorporates detailed description of the incident into his new novel. Spends September at Villa Serbelloni, Rockefeller Foundation villa on Lake Como. A collection of stories, *Mosby's Memoirs,* is published in October. Travels to London in December to see his publisher George Weidenfeld.

1969   Continues to work on *Mr. Sammler's Planet,* describing it as "a dramatic essay of some sort, wrung from me by the crazy Sixties." In March, enters analysis with Heinz Kohut.

1970   *Mr. Sammler's Planet* is published. On his first trip to Africa in February, visits Nairobi and Addis Ababa. In April delivers lecture at Purdue University entitled "Culture Now: Some Animadversions, Some Laughs," in which he attacks 1960s avant-gardism in the arts. Receives honorary degree in May from New York University. Spends June in Israel, attending symposium at Tel Aviv U.S. Cultural Center and a banquet in Jerusalem where Elie Wiesel and Golda Meir speak. Becomes chairman of Committee on Social Thought (will retain position until 1975). In December, *Anon,* a new journal, again co-edited with Keith Botsford, appears for only one issue.

1971   Wins third National Book Award for *Mr. Sammler's Planet*. A revival of *The Last Analysis* opens off-Broadway in June; closes August 1. Travels to London in fall to serve as judge for Booker Prize for Fiction; visits Lisbon, Turin, and Dublin. John Berryman writes to him: "Let's join forces, large and small, as in the winter beginning of 1953 in Princeton, with the Bradstreet blazing and Augie fleecing away. We're promising."

1972   John Berryman commits suicide in January. Visits Japan in April and Europe in August. Delivers lecture "Literature in the Age of Technology" at the Smithsonian in November.

1973   In April, stays for several weeks at Monks House, Rodmell (former home of Virginia and Leonard Woolf), where he works on novel *Humboldt's Gift*. Receives honorary degrees from Harvard and Yale. Begins attending meetings of the Chicago Anthroposophical Society.

1974   Marries Alexandra Ionescu Tulcea, a professor of mathematics at Northwestern, in November.

1975   Attends White House dinner in January for British Prime Minister Harold Wilson. Delivers proofs of *Humboldt's Gift* in June, and travels to London, where he meets Owen Barfield, English scholar of Rudolf Steiner's anthroposophical thought, with whom he will carry on a long correspondence. Spends time at Costa del Sol home of his British publisher Barley Alison. *Humboldt's Gift* is published in August. In October, begins three-month sabbatical in Israel, where, for a projected nonfiction book, he interviews A. B. Yehoshna, Amos Oz, Abba Eban, Jerusalem mayor Teddy Kollek, and Prime Minister Yitzhak Rabin. Louis Simpson attacks *Humboldt's Gift* in *The New York Times* in December, claiming that the novel's fictionalized portrait of Delmore Schwartz denigrates American poets.

1976   Visits Stanford, where he renews friendship with John Cheever. Receives Pulitzer Prize in May for *Humboldt's Gift* (prize is mocked in the novel as "the pullet surprise, a dummy newspaper publicity award given by crooks and illiterates—for the birds"). Excerpt from *To Jerusalem and Back* appears in *The New Yorker* in July. First District

Court of Chicago rules that Bellow has misled Susan
Glassman about his stated income, and orders him to pay
her legal costs of $200,000. *To Jerusalem and Back* is
published in October. In the same month Bellow wins the
Nobel Prize, following a unanimous decision of the committee. In his Stockholm speech in December, argues
against the anti-humanism of the *nouveau roman*, and re-
asserts his belief that fiction must not "give up the connection of literature with the main human enterprise."

1977   Gives Jefferson Lecture in the Humanities in March.
        Works on the "Chicago Book," a work of reportage that
        will later become novel *The Dean's December.* In Septem-
        ber, is held in contempt of court by Cook County judge
        and sentenced to ten days in jail for failing to pay in-
        creased alimony to Susan Glassman; sentence is appealed
        and later voided, and Bellow is never jailed. Spends aca-
        demic year in Boston, where both he and Alexandra
        Tulcea teach at Brandeis.

1978   Attends memorial service in July for Harold Rosenberg,
        along with Dwight Macdonald, Saul Steinberg, and Mary
        McCarthy. Leaves Viking, his publisher of thirty years, for
        Harper & Row, with large advance for "nonfiction book
        about Chicago." Travels to Romania in December, where
        he attends funeral of his mother-in-law, a former minister
        of health.

1979   Work in progress shifts from nonfiction "Chicago Book"
        to *The Dean's December,* which will include Romanian
        scenes. Rents summer house in West Halifax, Vermont.

1981   Visits London in spring, and in October attends Tuley
        High School's fiftieth reunion for classes of 1931 and 1932.
        Continues to work on *The Dean's December.*

1982   Spends spring semester as guest lecturer at the University
        of Victoria, British Columbia. *The Dean's December* is
        published in February to mixed reviews. In June, attends
        John Cheever's funeral; tells mourners, "Our friendship, a
        sort of hydroponic plant, flourished in the air." In Sep-
        tember, visits London and Paris, where he appears on
        Bernard Pivot's literary television show *Apostrophes.*

1984   At work on short stories; "What Kind of Day Did You
        Have?" (a fictionalized portrait of Harold Rosenberg) ap-
        pears in *Vanity Fair* in February. Collection of stories,

Him with His Foot in His Mouth, is published in May. Lachine Public Library is renamed after Bellow; he attends building's commemoration on June 10, his birthday, and gives a speech in both French and English: "The human soul has its own way to declare its own freedom and to develop itself in its own way, and it is not true to say: 'Show me where you came from and I'll tell you what you are.'" Visits his birthplace at 130 Eighth Avenue.

1985   Anita Goshkin, first wife, dies in March, followed by his two brothers, Maurice, in May, and Sam, in June. His marriage to Alexandra Tulcea begins to break up. Delivers lecture at the Ethical Culture Society in New York, in which he quips that he meant *Herzog* "as an attack on higher education in America."

1986   In January attends rancorous PEN Congress in New York, where he falls into heated argument with Günter Grass about poverty and the spiritual life in America. Leaves Harper & Row in November for William Morrow.

1987   *The Closing of the American Mind,* by Chicago colleague and friend Allan Bloom, is published in March, with an introduction by Bellow, and becomes a best seller. Has an emotional reunion with Isaac Rosenfeld's son in New York. In April, travels to Israel for a conference on his work at University of Haifa, at which Allan Bloom, Martin Amis, A. B. Yehoshua, and Amos Oz give lectures. Interviewed by *New York Times* about Allan Bloom and controversies over multiculturalism, remarks: "Who is the Tolstoy of the Zulus, the Proust of the Papuans? I'd be glad to read him." Novel *More Die of Heartbreak* appears in June. Spends summer in Vermont.

1989   Returns to Viking with *A Theft,* a novella published in March as a paperback original. In May, sells manuscript of *Mr. Sammler's Planet* to New York Public Library for $66,000. Marries Janis Freedman in August. Takes teaching job at Boston University for fall semester. Has house built near Brattleboro, Vermont, which subsequently becomes summer home. Novella *The Bellarosa Connection* is published in December.

1990   Friends and relatives, including his three sons, Philip Roth, and Saul Steinberg, gather for 75th birthday party in West Dover, Vermont. In October, Mayor Richard M.

Daley gives belated birthday party at the Art Institute in Chicago. Receives medal in November from the National Book Foundation for "distinguished contribution to American letters." Allan Bloom falls ill.

1991   *Something to Remember Me By*, a collection of three long stories also including *A Theft* and *The Bellarosa Connection*, is published in fall. Reads title story at Harvard in October to celebrate inauguration of new university president Neil Rudenstine. Travels to Florence in November to give a talk about Mozart at the Teatro Comunale.

1992   Allan Bloom, visited every day by Bellow in his last months, dies in October, probably from complications from HIV; Bellow delivers eulogy at memorial service. Visits Paris, where he sees old Chicago friend H. J. Kaplan.

1993   Becomes University Professor at Boston University in the fall.

1994   Collected essays published as *It All Adds Up*. Ralph Ellison dies. Writes op-ed piece for *New York Times* in March entitled "Papuans and Zulus," an attempt to revise his earlier controversial comments, and praises *Chaka* by Thomas Mofolo, a Zulu novel which he had read as a student, as "a profoundly, unbearably tragic book." Contracts ciguatera poisoning in April from eating contaminated shellfish in St. Martin; suffers heart failure and double pneumonia, and spends three weeks in coma, close to death. Recovers very slowly.

1995   Short story "By the St. Lawrence" appears in *Esquire* (July). At end of year, returns to Chicago, and speaks to a crowd of a thousand in Mandel Hall on "Literature in a Democracy." Begins *News from the Republic of Letters,* a literary journal, with Keith Botsford as co-editor.

1996   In February, ends twenty-five-year relationship with literary agent Harriet Wasserman, and engages Andrew Wylie as his new agent. Susan Glassman dies in December, aged 63.

1997   *The Actual,* a novella, published in April. Attends ceremony in July at National Portrait Gallery, Washington, D.C., for unveiling of portrait. Harriet Wasserman publishes *Handsome Is,* a memoir of her relationship with Bellow.

1999   Works on novel *Ravelstein,* a fictionalized account of his friendship with Allan Bloom. Daughter, Naomi Rose, born in December.

2000   *Ravelstein* is published to warm reviews and controversy stemming from its treatment of Bloom's homosexuality and Bellow's statement in an interview that Bloom's death was AIDS-related (claim is challenged by some, and Bellow revises novel's galleys to omit references to HIV and AIDS in published version).

2001   *Collected Stories* published in March, with a preface by Janis Bellow.

2005   Dies on April 5 at his home in Brookline, Mass., and is buried in Morningside Cemetery, Brattleboro, Vermont.

Note on the Texts

This volume contains Saul Bellow's novella *Seize the Day* (1956), along with his novels *Henderson the Rain King* (1959) and *Herzog* (1964).

Bellow finished *Seize the Day*, a novella with working titles such as "Here and Now," "Hail and Farewell," "One of Those Days," and "Carpe Diem," early in 1956. It was included in its entirety in the Summer 1956 issue of *Partisan Review*, then published in book form in November 1956 by Viking Press. An English edition followed in 1957, published by Weidenfeld and Nicholson. This volume prints the text of the 1956 Viking Press edition of *Seize the Day*.

After working steadily on *Henderson the Rain King* throughout 1956 and 1957, Bellow completed a draft of the novel in March 1958 and submitted it to Pascal Covici, his editor at Viking Press. He continued to make changes to the novel in the months that followed, revising and adding chapters, and as the book neared its final form he dictated passages to a secretary provided by Viking. *Henderson the Rain King* was published in February 1959 by Viking; the English edition, published by Weidenfeld and Nicholson, was brought out the same year. The text of the 1959 Viking Press edition of *Henderson the Rain King* is the text printed here.

Begun in 1961, with excerpts appearing in *Esquire* not long afterward, *Herzog* was submitted in draft form to Viking Press early in 1964. Characteristically for Bellow, the novel was substantially revised after this draft was completed. As he wrote his former student Ruth Miller in June 1964: "Since November, things have gone something like this: Finished *Herzog*, rewrote my silly play [*The Last Analysis*]. Taught school; re-wrote *Herzog*, did another version of the play; prepared the novel for the printer, went to NYC to see [his son] Adam and cast the play; came home and found galleys, rewrote the book again on the galleys." *Herzog* was published by Viking Press in September 1964; the English edition, brought out by Weidenfeld and Nicholson, was published the same year. The present volume prints the text of the 1964 Viking Press edition of *Herzog*, seventh printing (November 1964), which contains several emendations to the text of the novel as first published. For example, at 462.11, "can't" is corrected to "can"; at 502.5, "Fritzl's" is corrected to "Fritzel's"; at 593.9, "the *peaches* are supposed to grow." is emended to "they say only *peaches* grow."; at 600.11, "Demarol" is corrected to "Demerol"; and at 615.1, "The moon had risen" is emended to "The moon was high".

This volume presents the texts of the original printings chosen for inclusion here, but it does not attempt to reproduce nontextual features of their typographic design. The texts are presented without change, except for the correction of typographical errors. Spelling, punctuation, and capitalization are not altered, even when inconsistent or irregular. The following is a list of typographical errors corrected, cited by page and line number: 27.28–29, luminal; 39.10, it's; 47.23, blessing."; 59.39, purgiatory; 181.16, therefore; 296.24, primeeval; 301.20, go to; 321.27, perpiring; 353.16, Of; 397.33, Romilaya; 404.37, hassel; 620.6, *fortiter!*); 697.36, hinding.

Notes

In the notes below, the reference numbers denote page and line of this volume (the line count includes headings). No note is made for material included in standard desk-reference books. Biblical quotations are keyed to the King James Version. Quotations from Shakespeare are keyed to *The Riverside Shakespeare*, ed. G. Blakemore Evans (Boston: Houghton Mifflin, 1974). For references to other studies, and further biographical background than is contained in the Chronology, see: Gloria L. Cronin and Blaine H. Hall, *Saul Bellow: An Annotated Bibliography, Second Edition* (New York: Garland Publishing, 1987); James Atlas, *Bellow: A Biography* (New York: Random House, 2000).

SEIZE THE DAY

8.5   the Fulbright investigation?] As chairman of the Senate Banking and Currency Committee, Arkansas senator William J. Fulbright led an investigation into the stock market in 1954–55 because of concerns about improprieties during the bull market of the mid-1950s. The commission found no "major abuses" in the market.

10.31   love . . . long.] Final line of Shakespeare's Sonnet 73 (beginning "That time of year thou may'st in me behold"); the penultimate line is quoted four sentences later.

11.7   "Yet . . . laurels."] First line of John Milton's elegy "Lycidas" (1637).

11.9   Sunk . . . floor] "Lycidas," line 167.

17.29   Milton Sills?] Silent movie star (1882–1930).

17.30–31   Conway . . . Bancroft?] Conway Tearle (1878–1939), actor who starred mostly in silent movies, opposite actresses such as Mary Pickford and Clara Bow; Jack Mulhall (1887–1979), actor whose career peaked in the silent era and first years of sound films; George Bancroft (1882–1956), actor whose films included *Underworld* (1927), *Docks of New York* (1928), *Thunderbolt* (1929), and *Mr. Deeds Goes to Town* (1936).

17.32   George Raft type] Actor George Raft (1895–1980) played gangsters and other tough-guy roles in movies such as *Scarface* (1932) and *The Glass Key* (1935).

17.37   Edward G. Robinson] Romanian-born actor (1893–1973) known for his gangster roles in *Little Caesar* (1931), *Key Largo* (1948), and other films.

18.1   William Powell,] Actor (1892–1894) who played Dashiell Hammett's detective Nick Charles in *The Thin Man* (1934) and four sequels; he also starred in films such as *The Great Ziegfeld* (1936) and *My Man Godfrey* (1936).

18.2   Buddy Rogers . . . sax?] Actor Charles "Buddy" Rogers (1904–1999) was also a trombonist and bandleader.

56.19   Purple Gang] Group of mostly Jewish gangsters and bootleggers active in Detroit in the 1920s and 30s.

60.11   Korzybski,] Scientist Alfred H. Korzybski (1879–1950), founder of the field of general semantics, outlined in *Science and Society* (1933).

60.12   W. H. Sheldon,] William H. Sheldon (1898–1977), psychologist and researcher of the relation between physical types and personality; he was the author, with S. S. Stevens and W. B. Tucker, of *The Varieties of Human Physique* (1940).

60.24   Velvel?] Yiddish name meaning "wolf."

72.11   *Yiskor*] Prayer service remembering the dead on Yom Kippur and other important holidays.

75.5–7   Come . . . breast!] Keats, *Endymion* (1818), Book IV, lines 279–81.

75.32–34   I thought . . . best.] *Endymion*, Book IV, lines 282–84.

78.28–29   old Pigtown and Charlie Ebbets] Pigtown was a neighborhood in the Flatbush section of Brooklyn where Dodgers owner Charles Ebbets built Ebbets Field, the team's ballpark, on the site of a garbage dump.

89.10–11   *Science and Sanity*] See note 60.11.

HENDERSON THE RAIN KING

104.38   like Shelley's . . . companionless.] See Shelley, "To the Moon": "Art thou pale for weariness / Of climbing heaven, and gazing on the earth, / Wandering companionless / Among the stars that have a different birth,— / And ever-changing, like a joyless eye / That finds no object worth its constancy?"

113.22   De Vogüé] French diplomat, travel writer, and literary critic Eugène-Melchior de Vogüé (1848–1910).

119.6   Monte Cassino . . . bombed;] Allied bombers destroyed the Benedictine monastery on Monte Cassino, which commanded the main highway to Rome, on February 15, 1944, following an unsuccessful American attempt to capture the abbey, January 24–February 11. Subsequent attacks by

British, Indian, and New Zealand troops failed to drive the Germans from Monte Cassino, which was finally captured by Polish forces on May 18, 1944.

119.7–8   murder . . . Texans] The 36th Infantry Division, formed from the Texas National Guard, made two unsuccessful attacks across the Rapido, a deep and fast-flowing river near Monte Cassino, between January 20 and 22, 1944, during which the division lost 1,681 men killed, wounded, or captured.

120.11–12   "They shall . . . field."] Daniel 4:25.

122.5–6   Sir Wilfred Grenfell] English physician (1865–1940) who established medical missions in Labrador and Newfoundland.

122.6   Albert Schweitzer.] Physician, theologian, and musician Albert Schweitzer (1875–1965) founded a hospital in Lambaréné (in present-day Gabon, Africa) and spent most of his life working there.

127.6–7   "Goe happy rose] Opening of Robert Herrick's poem "To the Rose."

128.29   *Thaïs.*"] Opera (1894) by Jules Massenet, based on a novel by Anatole France.

128.32   "Rispondi! . . . (Mozart).] From Mozart's opera *Così fan tutti* (1790).

128.32–34   "He was despised . . . (Handel).] From Handel's oratorio *Messiah* (1741).

131.39–132.2   "For who . . . appeareth?"] From Handel's *Messiah*, based on Malachi 3:2.

158.32   "The Village Blacksmith"] Poem (1842) by Henry Wadsworth Longfellow.

158.32–33   "sweet . . . Allegra"] First line of Henry Wadsworth Longfellow's poem "The Children's Hour" (1860), slightly misquoted (it begins "Grave Alice and laughing Allegra").

161.1–2   Montcalm . . . Abraham.] French commander Louis-Joseph Montcalm (1712–1759) was wounded in battle on the Plains of Abraham in Quebec on September 13, 1759, and died the next day.

163.3–4   "I do . . . sleep."] Shelley, "To Mary —," section III, from "The Revolt of Islam" (1818).

179.1   God . . . souls,] Cf. Albert Einstein as quoted by his biographer Philipp Frank: "I shall never believe that God plays dice with the world."

182.29–30   Agnus Dei . . . Mozart.] Lines beginning the "Lamb of God" litany of the Mass: "Lamb of God, who takes away the sins of the world, have mercy on us." Mozart's musical setting is from his *Requiem Mass* (1791).

194.23–24   bomb-scare man . . . company] Known as the "Mad Bomber," George Metesky (1903–1994), a mentally unstable former employee of the Consolidated Edison electric company, planted about 30 bombs in New York City in the 1940s and 50s.

196.33–34   poem . . . reality.] See T. S. Eliot, "Burnt Norton" (1935), from *Four Quartets*: "Go, go, go, said the bird: human kind / Cannot bear very much reality."

206.23–25   man whom Joseph . . . Dothan.] See Genesis 37:15–17.

208.10–11   General Gordon at Khartoum] English general George Gordon (1833–1885) was killed during the capture of Khartoum by troops of the Mahdi (Muhammad Ahmad, 1844–1885).

211.37–38   Grincez les dents! Fâchez-vous."] Grind your teeth! Get angry.

212.39   "wo bist du, soldat?"] Where are you, soldier?

213.15–16   man Slocum . . . dams.] Harvey Slocum (1887–1961) was a consultant on dam construction projects including the Hoover Dam, the Grand Coulee Dam, and the Bhakra Dam in India.

219.4   fort comme la mort.] Strong like death.

222.6–7   the question . . . wall.] See Tennyson's "Flower in the Crannied Wall" (1869): "Flower in the crannied wall, / I pluck you out of the crannies;— / Hold you here, root and all, in my hand, / Little flower—but *if* I could understand / What you are, root and all, and all in all, / I should know what God and man is."

246.40–247.1   "Enough . . . joy!"] Concluding lines of Whitman's "The Mystic Trumpeter."

248.26–27   "Father . . . do."] Cf. Jesus' words on the cross at Luke 23:34.

251.28   Atalantas] In Ovid's *Metamorphosis*, a woman who challenged her suitors to a race in which the loser was put to death; she was finally defeated by Hippomones when she stopped to pick up three golden apples given to him by Venus that he had dropped during the race.

275.16–17   'Written in Prison.'] By English poet John Clare (1793–1864).

286.12–13   Dutch flood . . . opened.] On November 2, 1570, a tidal wave broke through sea walls in Holland, then occupied by troops of Charles V of Spain led by the Duke of Alva (Fernando Alvarez de Toledo, 1508–1582).

288.32–34   Sir Richard . . . Livingstone] Richard Burton (1821–1890), explorer, writer, and translator; John Hanning Speke (1827–1864), explorer of East Africa who traveled with Burton in search of the source of the Nile; Mungo Park (1771–1806), Scottish explorer of West Africa; David Livingstone (1813–1873), Scottish explorer.

293.34–35   *luth suspendu . . . résonne.*] Cf. "Le Refus" by French poet
Pierre Jean de Béranger (1780–1857): "Mon cœur est un luth suspendu; /
Sitôt qu'on le touche il résonne" ("My heart is a suspended lute; / As soon
as it is touched, it resounds"). A slight variant of these lines is the epigraph
to Edgar Allan Poe's story "The Fall of the House of Usher."

324.7   *The Triumph over Pain*,] René Fülöp-Miller's biography of anes-
thesia pioneer William Morton (1819–1868).

324.7–8   medical biographies . . . Metchnikoff.] Canadian physician
William Osler (1849–1919); American neurosurgeon Harvey Cushing (1869–
1939); Hungarian physician Ignaz Semmelweis (1818–1865); Russian microbi-
ologist Eli Metchnikoff (1845–1916).

325.2   Freuchen and Gontran de Poncins] Danish explorer Peter
Freuchen (1886–1957) lived for several years in Greenland with the Inuit;
French traveler Gontran de Poncins spent more than a year in the Canadian
Arctic in 1938–39, the basis for his book *Kabloona: Among the Inuit* (written
with Lewis Galantière).

338.31–32   'The tigers . . . instruction.'] One of the proverbs of hell in
Blake's "Marriage of Heaven and Hell" (1790–93).

362.2   Axel Munthe] Swedish physician Axel Munthe (1857–1949), author of the popular autobiography *The Story of San Michele* (1929).

HERZOG

419.15   *Walter Winchell*] Gossip columnist (1897–1972) for the New York
Daily Mirror.

420.36   *Tutto fa brodo.*] Every little bit helps.

441.6–7   *Je me . . . brouillard.*] I remember often enough . . . I think
of the Marszalkowska in the fog. (The Marszalkowska is central Warsaw's pri-
mary thoroughfare.)

441.31–32   *Ici . . . longtemps.*] Today everything is wasted. / Ten days in
Warsaw—not a long time.

442.16   *Guéri de cette petite maladie.*] Cured of this little illness.

442.17–18   *Pas grave du tout*,] Not serious at all.

442.19–20   *J'embrasse . . . amie.*] I kiss your little hands, friend.

445.22–23   Simmel on religion] Among the many works of German sociologist Georg Simmel (1858–1918) is *Religion* (1912).

445.23   Teilhard de Chardin] French Jesuit theologian Pierre Teilhard de
Chardin (1881–1955), author of *The Divine Milieu* and *The Phenomenon of
Man*, published posthumously in 1957 and 1959, respectively.

445.23   Whitehead]   English philosopher Alfred North Whitehead (1861–1947).

462.27   *Trybuna Ludu*]   People's Tribune.

463.1   Mr. McCloy]   John J. McCloy (1895–1989) was the U.S. High Commissioner for Germany from 1949 to 1952.

463.17   *Lazarus and Dives*]   See Luke 16:19–31.

463.34   *Professor Hoyle*]   English astronomer Fred Hoyle (1915–2001), whose many books include *Frontiers of Astronomy* (1955), *Men and Materialism* (1956), and *Star Formation* (1963).

464.19   *Dr. Bhave*]   Vinoba Bhave (1895–1982), disciple of Gandhi whose Bhudan Yajna movement advocated land reform in India.

464.29   Pather Panchali]   Film (1955) directed by Satyajit Ray.

466.12   *Rachel Carson*]   Biologist, environmental activist, and writer (1907–1964), author of *Silent Spring* (1962).

466.12   *Dr. Teller*]   Nuclear physicist Edward Teller (1908–2003).

469.29   *Barth, Tillich, Brunner,*]   Karl Barth (1886–1986), influential Swiss theologian and author of the multi-volume study *The Church Dogmatics*; Paul Tillich (1886–1965), German-born theologian and author of *The Courage To Be* (1952) and *Dynamics of Faith* (1957); Swiss theologian Emil Brunner (1889–1966).

475.14   Hadassah]   Zionist women's organization.

475.14   Martin Buber]   Martin Buber (1878–1965) popularized Hasidism in *Tales of Rabbi Nachman of Breslov* (1906) and *Legends of the Bal Shem Tov* (1908). In 1923, the philosophical work *I and Thou* established his international reputation.

475.32   Vladimir of Kiev]   Also called Vladimir the Great (c. 956–1015), grand prince of Kiev and the first Christian ruler of Kievan Rus.

475.32   Tikhon Zadonsky]   Russian Orthodox monk and bishop (1724–1783), canonized in 1860.

482.1   *Governor Stevenson*]   Adlai Stevenson (1900–1965), the Democratic Party's nominee for president in 1952 and 1956, served as governor of Illinois from 1949 to 1953.

483.34–35   *the Powells*]   I.e., African-American leaders like Adam Clayton Powell (1908–1972), congressman and civil-rights activist.

483.37   *Commissioner Wilson*]   Chicago Police Commissioner Orlando Wilson.

484.28   *Mr. Udall*]   Stewart Udall (b. 1920), congressman and Secretary of the Interior from 1961 to 1969.

485.1   Ricardo Cortez]   Stage name of Vienna-born movie actor Jacob
Krantz (1899–1977), cast as a Latin-lover type in films such as *Argentine Love*
(1924).

485.8   *Joachim da Floris*]   Italian mystic and monk (c. 1132–1202).

487.1   Tikhon Zadonsky]   See note 475.33.

487.1   Herzen]   Russian political philosopher and editor Alexander
Herzen (1812–1870), advocate for the peasantry.

487.7–8   "Like . . . fools."]   Cf. Ecclesiastes 7.6: "For as the crackling
of thorns under a pot, so is the laughter of the fool; this also is vanity."

487.37   Comfort's work]   English physician, novelist, and anarchist Alex
Comfort (1920–2000) was the author of *Authority and Delinquency in the
Modern State* (1950) and *Sexual Behaviour in Society* (1950).

487.37–39 Poggioli? . . . Rozanov,]   Among the works of the Italian
literary critic Renato Poggioli (1907–1963) was the monograph *Rozanov* (1957),
about the Russian essayist, philosopher, and aphorist Vasily Rozanov (1856–
1919).

488.29–30 Soloviëv . . . Museum,]   Russian poet and mystic Vladimir
Solovyov (1853–1900) claimed to have had a mystical vision in the British Museum of an embodiment of the truth he called the Divine Sophia.

489.13   Berdyaev]   Russian political philosopher and religious thinker
Nikolai Berdyaev (1874–1948).

489.14   *Sobornost*]   Roughly translated, "community-ness" or universal
consensus.

492.12–13 *industrial defilement . . . Tempe*"]   See John Ruskin, *Fors
Clavigera* (1871–84): "There was a rocky valley between Buxton and Bake-
well, once upon a time, divine as the Vale of Tempe; you might have seen the
Gods there morning and evening. . . . You cared neither for Gods nor
grass, but for cash. . . . You enterprised a Railroad through the valley—you
blasted its rocks away, heaped thousands of tons of shale into its lovely
stream."

492.33–34 *Graf Pototsky*]   The Potocki family was one of Poland's oldest
and most influential aristocratic families.

493.6–7   the delirious professions, *as Valéry calls them*]   In *Monsieur Teste*
(1929).

493.21–24 *Bulgarian, Banowitch, . . .* crowds]   Banowitch is based on
the Bulgarian novelist Elias Canetti (1905–1994), author of the study of crowd
psychology *Crowds and Power* (1960).

493.38   "DOM, SFARDEYA, KINNIM" in the Haggadah]   Three of the
plagues afflicting Egypt as described in the book of Exodus: the rivers of

blood (*dom*), the plague of frogs (*sfardeya*), and the transformation of dust into lice (*kinnim*, sometimes translated "mosquitoes").

497.3   *macher*,]   Big shot.

502.27   *Yiches*]   Lineage.

503.3   *mein zisse n'shamele.*]   My sweet little soul.

507.29   *chazan*]   Cantor.

507.31–32   "*Mi* . . . land.]   Sentence from the *siddur*, Hebrew prayer book.

519.39–40   Beauregard]   Brigadier General P.G.T. Beauregard (1818–1893) led the attack on Fort Sumter, South Carolina, on April 12, 1861, which initiated the Civil War.

520.2   Island Number 10]   Island in the Mississippi River in Missouri, captured by Union forces in April 1862.

520.2   Andersonville]   Confederate military prison in Andersonville, Georgia.

521.20–21   *For dying . . . death*,]   Cf. Kierkegaard, *The Sickness Unto Death* (1849): "For dying means that it is all over; but dying the death means to live to experience death."

524.36   Arbeiter-Ring,]   Arbeter Ring, fraternal organization for American Jews.

528.21–22   "The wind bloweth . . . thereof. . . ."]   John 3:8.

532.7–9   Tyrone Power . . . Church.]   The second of Power's three marriages was performed by Monsignor William Hemmick in Rome in January 1949. Although Power had divorced his first wife the year before, the couple received a papal blessing.

532.9–10   in Leonard Lyons]   Syndicated gossip column of New York *Post* journalist Leonard Lyons.

537.31–32   QUOS VULT PERDERE DEMENTAT,]   Those whom [the gods] wish to destroy are driven mad.

541.28–29   from a favorite source]   William Blake, "The Marriage of Heaven and Hell" (1790–93).

542.39–40   Park . . . Nimkoff]   University of Chicago sociologists Robert E. Park (1864–1944) and Ernest W. Burgess (1886–1966), authors of the textbook *Introduction to the Science of Sociology* (1921) and *The City* (1925); sociologists William F. Ogburn (1886–1959) and Meyer F. Nimkoff (1904–1965), authors of *Sociology* (1940) and *A Handbook of Sociology* (1947).

545.26–27   *Hulme . . . "split religion."*]   In Hulme's *Speculations: Essays on Humanism and the Philosophy of Art*, edited by Herbert Read (1958).

545.33–34   "Je sens . . . les hommes."]   I know my own heart and understand my fellow men: Rousseau, *Confessions*, Book One, second paragraph.

548.12   *Mamzer!*]   Bastard.

548.13   *Kaddish*]   Mourning prayer.

551.8   *Yiskor . . . Imi*]   The beginning of the *Yizkor* mourning prayer.

551.22   *landtsman*]   A fellow Jew coming from the same town or municipality in Europe.

551.38   *shicker*]   Drunkard.

552.28   *freilich*]   Gay, carefree.

553.7   *Genug schon.*]   Enough already.

553.24   *dreckische*]   Dirty.

554.4   Pobedonostsev]   Konstantin Petrovich Pobedonostsev (1827–1907), conservative Russian statesman and advisor to czars Alexander III and Nicholas II.

555.36   *misnagid,*]   Rationalist Jew opposed to the Hasidim of Eastern Europe.

559.23   *mit strauss federn*]   With ostrich feathers.

559.33   *Gemara*]   One of two parts of the Talmud, a commentary on the Mishna, the other part.

560.14   *in der heim*]   In the homeland.

560.21   *lichtigen Gan-Eden*]   Beautiful paradise.

561.1   Kavkaz]   The Caucasus.

561.24   *finsternish*]   Darkness.

561.26   *alle sieben glicken*]   All seven lucky things.

561.27   *edel-mensch*]   Man of honor.

562.1   *schmid*]   Blacksmith.

562.9   an *amhoretz*]   An ignorant man.

562.26   *razboiniks*]   Bandits.

562.33   *gazlan*]   Robber.

562.39   *leite*]   People.

563.2   *klug bist du*]   You're smart.

563.13   *yingele*]   Little one.

565.3   *Landtsleit*]   Plural of *landtsman* (see note 551.22).

566.12   *El malai rachamim.*]   Prayer for the dead.

567.36–568.2   For when . . . through.]   Paraphrase of Kierkegaard's remark: "Not famine, not pestilence, not war will bring back seriousness. It is not till the eternal punishments of hell regain their reality that man will turn serious."

570.34   Salle Gaveau]   Recital hall in Paris for vocal and chamber music concerts.

573.7   Mohammad al Bakkar]   Lebanese-born singer and orchestra leader Mohammed el-Bakkar (d. 1959).

576.24   *Professor Haldane*]   English geneticist, biochemist, and evolutionary biologist J.B.S. Haldane (1892–1964), author of popular works on science that included *The Causes of Evolution* (1932) and *Science and Everyday Life* (1939).

577.26–29   *The main . . . history.*]   From Emerson's essay "The American Scholar" (1837).

577.29–33   *Let it . . . illumination.*]   From Emerson's essay "Man the Reformer" (1841).

578.37   *book by Mr. Hughes*]   *The Ordeal of Power: A Political Memoir of the Eisenhower Years* by Emmet John Hughes, journalist and speechwriter for Eisenhower.

579.27   "*by man came death.*"]   1 Corinthians 15:21.

579.40   SHAEF]   Supreme Headquarters Allied Expeditionary Force, headquarters of Allied forces in Europe from late 1943 to the end of World War II.

580.4–5   *Gresham's famous Law*]   "Bad money drives out good money."

580.37   *Jean Wahl*]   French philosopher and poet (1888–1974).

585.14–15   *Ma chère . . . savais!*]   My dear, my life has become a frightful nightmare. If you knew!

586.2   Je te lave le dos]   I wash your back.

586.14–15   "Les Japonaises . . . Américaines.]   Japanese are very faithful. They aren't like the Americans.

586.37–587.2   "Chéri! . . . En chair noire."]   Dear! I had already chosen my apron. This woman rushed at me. Woo! She was black. Myyyyyy God! And big! Big butt. Big chest. And without a bra. Completely like Niagara Fall. In black flesh.

587.5–6   Elle avait . . . balcon.]   She had arms like this—swollen. And what a bust! She had huge boobs.

587.35–36   Hence . . . dwell.]   Lines 1 and 10 from Milton's poem *L'Allegro* (1631).

589.5   Je viens de rentrer!]   I just got back.

589.18   "Mauvais temps,]   Bad times.

590.6–7   c'était honteux—quelle chose!]   That was shameful—such a thing!

590.8–9   Très laide." / "Ça t'a plu,"]   Very ugly. / You liked it.

591.16   "Tu as maigri. Tu fais amour?]   You've got skinny. You make love?

591.26   Tu seras bien propre,]   You will be very clean.

591.39   Doucement, chéri. Oh, lentement.]   Gently, dear. Oh, slowly.

592.9   "Je . . . souffrir,]   I do not fear death. But you make me suffer.

592.12   "Je souffre trop."]   I suffer enough.

592.15–17   "Elle . . . froids."]   She is wicked, Moso. I am not jealous. I will make love with another. You've left me. But she has very, very cold eyes.

595.21   Bishop Sheen]   Catholic Bishop Fulton J. Sheen (1895–1979), host of the television shows *Life Is Worth Living* and *The Fulton Sheen Program*.

595.22   *Dr. Schrodinger*]   Nobel Prize–winning Austrian physicist Erwin Schrödinger (1887–1961).

605.4–5   spread of luxury . . . Sombart]   In *Luxury and Capitalism* (1921), by the German sociologist and economist Werner Sombart (1863–1941).

606.31   "*Je bêche, je sème, mais je ne récolte point.*"]   I dig, I sow, but I do not harvest.

607.35   the poet said]   W. B. Yeats, in a 1936 letter.

609.25   Lady Hester Stanhope.]   English traveler (1776–1839) whose memoirs were published posthumously.

610.4   Lovejoy]   Historian Arthur Oncken Lovejoy (1873–1962), author of *The Great Chain of Being* (1936) and founder of the *Journal of the History of Ideas*.

615.6–7   "*Viens . . . chocolat.*"]   Come, come into my arms—I give you chocolate.

619.34   *Mens sana in corpore sano.*]   Sound mind in a sound body.

620.6   *pecca fortiter!*]   Sin boldly.

620.34   *shiddach*]   Match arranged by a matchmaker.

620.34   *tachliss*]   Practical result.

625.2–3   I fall . . . bleed.] Shelley, "Ode to the West Wind" (1819), line 45.

627.4   Marcuse, N. O. Brown] German-born political philosopher Herbert Marcuse (1898–1979), author of *Eros and Civilization* (1955) and *One-Dimensional Man* (1964); American writer Norman O. Brown (1913–2002), author of *Life Against Death: The Psychoanalytic Meaning of History* (1959)

628.21–22   "Getting . . . powers] Cf. Wordsworth, "The World Is Too Much With Us" (1807), line 2.

628.30   *Moloch-ha-movos*] The angel of death.

633.12–13   Paul Tillich] See note 469.29.

633.13   Hedda Hopper] Gossip columnist (1885–1966), actress, and host of a radio program.

633.33   Cagliostro] Sicilian adventurer and charlatan (1743–1795).

634.8   Emil Jannings as a Czarist general.] In *The Last Command* (1928).

636.35   *M. de Jouvenel*,] Bertrand de Jouvenel (1903–1987), French political philosopher, social scientist, and novelist, author of *On Power* (1945) and *The Art of Conjecture* (1964).

638.7   Prof. Hocking's] Philosopher William Ernest Hocking (1873–1966), author of *The Coming World Civilization* (1956) and *Strength of Men and Nations* (1959).

651.34   Haeckel and Spencer] German biologist, zoologist, and illustrator Ernst Haeckel (1834–1919); English philosopher Herbert Spencer (1820–1903). Both men vigorously championed Darwin's ideas.

661.38   "*Ich shtarb!*"] I'm dying!

666.24   "*Gottseliger*] Holy man.

671.11–14   *Nel . . . saperlo.*] From the libretto to Mozart's *The Marriage of Figaro*, in which Figaro sings: "Nel momento della mia cerimonia ei godeva leggendo: e nel verderlo io ridevo di me senza saperlo." ("At the moment of my wedding ceremony he enjoyed reading her letter, and seeing him I laughed at myself without knowing it.")

674.15   *Qualis artifex pereo.*] What an artist the world is losing: Nero's last words.

679.37–38   'Hasidic Judaism . . . *I and Thou.*'] See note 475.14.

688.30   "*Le cœur a ses raisons.*] The heart has its reasons. From Pascal, *Pensées* (1670), 277: "The heart has its reasons, which reason does not know."

692.26–28   'Man . . . abound.'] William Blake, *Vala, or The Four Zoas* (1797–1807), "Night the Ninth."

706.12–14   Gadarene . . . cliff)]   See Matthew 8:28–34, Mark 5:1–20, and Luke 8:26–39.

711.6   *la foi nouvelle*,]   The new faith.

711.24   Lubianka,]   KGB headquarters and prison in Lubyanka Square in Moscow.

724.23   *Róheim*]   Hungarian-born psychoanalyst Géza Róheim (1891–1953).

730.30–32   "The land was ours . . . Inauguration]   From Robert Frost's 1941 poem "The Gift Outright," read at the presidential inauguration of John F. Kennedy.

731.2   *Hineni!*]   Here I am!: Abraham's declaration to God as he prepares to sacrifice Isaac in the book of Genesis.

732.8–10   "My name . . . despair!"]   From Shelley's 1817 sonnet "Ozymandias."

735.7–8   *La devoradora de hombres.*]   The devourer of men.

742.35   *Rozanov.*]   See note 487.37–39.

745.9–10   "*In paths untrodden,*" . . . *itself*]   Whitman, "In Paths Untrodden," lines 1 and 3.

745.19   "*talked to . . . aromatic.*"]   "In Paths Untrodden," line 9.

746.19   *esprit d'escalier*]   Staircase wit, or missing the chance for a perfect comeback.

762.4–5   "*Je sens . . . hommes.*"]   See note 545.33–34.

Library of Congress Cataloging-in-Publication Data

Bellow, Saul.
  [Novels. Selections]
  Novels, 1956–1964 / Saul Bellow.
      p. cm. — (The Library of America ; 169)
   Contents: Seize the day—Henderson the Rain King—Herzog.
  ISBN 978–1–59853–002–5 (alk. paper)
   I. Title. II. Seize the Day. III. Henderson the Rain King. IV.
Herzog.

PS3503.E4488A6 2007
813'.52—dc22   2006046687

THE LIBRARY OF AMERICA SERIES

The Library of America fosters appreciation and pride in America's literary heritage by publishing, and keeping permanently in print, authoritative editions of America's best and most significant writing. An independent nonprofit organization, it was founded in 1979 with seed money from the National Endowment for the Humanities and the Ford Foundation.

This book is set in 10 point Linotron Galliard,
a face designed for photocomposition by Matthew Carter
and based on the sixteenth-century face Granjon. The paper
is acid-free lightweight opaque and meets the requirements
for permanence of the American National Standards Institute.
The binding material is Brillianta, a woven rayon cloth made
by Van Heek-Scholco Textielfabrieken, Holland. Compo-
sition by Dedicated Business Services. Printing by
Malloy Incorporated. Binding by Dekker Book-
binding. Designed by Bruce Campbell.